Give Us Bad Boys & Billionaires
L.M. Mountford

Edited by Readabit: Copy Editing and Proofreading Services Est 2018 L.M. Mountford–1st Ed.
ISBN: 978-1-83502-022-7
Cover Art by 'The Book Brander'

Give Us BAD BOYS & BILLIONAIRES

THE LORD OF LUST

L.M. MOUNTFORD

Falling For My Son's Best Friend

Prologue

Watching her son drive down the road, Elizabeth Clarke sighed heavily.

Today should have been one of the happiest days of her life. He'd done it. After five years - five long years of waiting, procrastination and disappointment, he'd finally done it. Victor, her sweet baby boy, was finally moving out and going to university.

It hadn't been easy. He'd done abysmally in his GCSEs, barely scraping a passing grade, so he'd taken a break to work and save some money before going out and blowing it under the guise of travelling. He'd wanted to find himself, he'd told her, see the world. And he had, from what she could gather. He'd seen the world, one club at a time.

She doubted she'd ever know what he'd got up to out there, and she didn't want to. He hadn't written or called, just turned up on the doorstep, then a few days later enrolled in the city college for various courses. He'd worked hard, got his head down, studied, and finally, he had done it.

She should have been ecstatic, proud, and practically bouncing off the walls. What mother wouldn't be?

Yet all Elizabeth felt was a sense of abandonment. He was going, leaving her all alone with… *Him.*

The thought sent a shiver down her spine that had nothing to do with the autumn breeze whispering through her long raven hair.

When the car turned around the street's bend, time seemed to hold its breath and Elizabeth wanted so badly to bend the laws of space and time around that moment, that last glimpse of her son, and stretch it on for an eternity. Then he was gone and who knew when she would see him again.

Of course, deep, deep down, she knew she was being silly. Oxford wasn't exactly Beirut. Victor was just a few hours' drive away. Close enough that he could come home for every Sunday roast.

And go back after.

That bitter pill drove her back indoors.

Desperate to keep busy, she set about doing the one job that had always proved as a source of comfort to her - cleaning. There was usually so much she needed to do, so many jobs that had to be done. A household of a young adult male was one that never stayed clean and required constant attention. Unfortunately, there was now a very vital part of that equation, which was no longer prevalent in her life. Without which it no longer felt like home. Without Victor, it was just another immaculate showroom, a haunted residence for a lingering spirit, the ghost of a neat and impeccable mother, and the base-camp of her travelling salesman husband.

Elizabeth furrowed her brow with disgust as she looked upon the neat pile of stacked plates and dishes in her cupboard, laundry ironed and folded away, and practically sparkling worktops. Then she felt her stomach tighten.

How could it be? Was there something she had forgotten, no that couldn't be it. She had followed the same routine she had always done and yet, somehow; she had finished five hours' worth of work in less than half an hour.

With a dispirited sigh, she walked across her now impeccably clean kitchen and fell into one of her dining table chairs. Resting her head in her hands, she tried to think of something, anything, to do.

God, how had her life come to this?

Patrick, he was why. That bastard had always been the source of her misery.

In school she'd always been outgoing, adventurous, the popular girl, always doing something. Be it tennis training or dance classes, going out with friends or babysitting the neighbourhood's kids - anything that would get her out of the house.

Then Patrick had entered her life and less than five months after her eighteenth birthday, they were married.

He'd been so handsome then. They'd made a lovely photo couple. The strapping rugby captain, all muscle and easy smiles, with the leggy athletic beauty on his arm in flowing white lace. The gown had been a work of art. It took a lot of looking in the photos to see the bump, the memento of a night she could only remember as an alcoholic haze, but that would completely reshape her life.

It had been a small ceremony for family and friends. Then he'd promptly whisked her across to the small house his parents had bought them on the other side of the county, near where Somerset met Devonshire in one of the areas of many sleepy little villages. Ideally located for his new role in the family business, but far away from her friends and family.

So, she'd become a mother and a housewife. The iconic role reversal from party girl and athlete to domestic goddess. And she'd revelled in it, the challenge of being a new mother, the thrill of bringing life into the world.

For Patrick, however, the switch had come as a nasty shock.

The walking, talking definition of a good time Charlie, his family had set him up in a role he'd been born to, salesman for their peat factory. And if the idea of going from garden centre to garden centre, sweet talking them into buying his family's products, hadn't quite lived up to the fast-talking rugby star's dreams of adult life, then he certainly hadn't bargained on all his hard work going to support his wife and child.

Or that he'd have to keep it in his pants.

She gave a dry laugh at the notion, before her eyes suddenly lit up.

Jennifer!

Chapter One

Years ago, the road had been a quiet snaking stretch of tarmac, but back in 1993, work had begun on a site that would become one of the UK's largest shopping outlet villages. In less than a year, Clarke's Village had transformed the A-39 into a bustling thoroughfare that during rush hour could be lined with bumper-to-bumper congestion. At ten in the morning, however, when all the rest of the world was being swept up in the ebb and flow of everyday life, there was very little in the way of traffic.

Sleek and polished to a high shine, the electric blue Audi TT convertible sped along the snaking stretch of singlelane tarmac. Heedless of the rain pelting the windscreen, Elizabeth kept her foot to the floor, relishing in the sweet rush of adrenaline as she sped through the numerous villages dotting the A-39.

She loved driving.

Fast driving was like great sex. It was freedom, a complete surrender to the moment. Behind the wheel, she forgot the disappointments, forgot the broken dreams, her sham of a marriage. She forgot all the downward slopes her life had taken. There was only the road, the rush, and the sexy throb of the engine purring through her. It was her escape.

There was no warning for the turning, just a sudden gaping maw in the surrounding woodland as the tarmac branched off. Used to the turn, Elizabeth dropped a gear and dragged the wheel around, adding just a dab of brake as the TT swung gracefully round the hairpin, then corrected for the straight and sped on. It was a reckless manoeuvre, stupid even in the rain along such a treacherous blind turn, but the momentary, stomach flipping rush made the risks seem rather insignificant.

Of course, she never had much to worry about in her Audi. The TT responded to her every command like the fine German engineered automobile it was.

Which was good, because off of the A-39, the way became a snaking lane of old tarmac and blind turns behind any number of which could await the hulk of an oncoming tractor or bus.

She floored it, and the Audi turned from a purring kitten to a raging tiger. It roared and kept roaring until she pulled into the familiar L-shaped driveway of *Forbidden Fruit* Cottage.

Despite its name, *Forbidden Fruit* Cottage was, in fact, a bungalow. A stately bungalow, though, with numerous extensions and surrounded by three acres of private land. It also happened to be the only property within two miles.

Heedless of the rain, Elizabeth got out of the sports car and sauntered up to the front door. Overhead, the sky was dark and subdued; the sun blotted out by the canopy of thick grey clouds. The rain, that had been a mere trickle when she set off, fell in a continuous sheet that drenched her from head to toe in the few strides to the front step.

All too aware of the icy rivulets running down the back of her neck, she raised a hand to knock, only for the door of heavy English oak, painted a deep blue with a plaque stamped *Forbidden Fruit*, to suddenly swing inward.

Elizabeth felt her breath catch.

Oh my…

Chapter Two

"Well, this is certainly a pleasant surprise. Hello there, Mrs Clarke." Hugh Becket could barely keep his grin at bay as he opened the door. *Damn, she's still so fucking gorgeous.*

"Oh…" Elizabeth had the deer in headlights look as she took him in. "Ugh, hi Hugh, is your mum in?"

"I'm afraid you just missed her. She and the old man have flown south for the winter and left me here to mind the fort." As he spoke, he eyed her hungrily, giving her a slow once over, then another for good measure. "You look good." *She always had.*

"Thanks… err, you mind letting me in? It's pissing it down out here. I'm getting soaked." *Good to know.*

"Sure, I'll get you a towel." He stepped aside to let her pass, his eyes dropping down to admire her backside as she passed. It took a feat of Herculean endurance for him not to whistle. Drenched as they were, her already skinny jeans moulded to her deliciously curved backside like a second skin. And that spaghetti top didn't exactly leave much to the imagination, either.

Suddenly very aware of the erection straining against the front of his own jeans, he pulled the door shut and wheeled around to the airing cupboard. There, he busied himself with rummaging through the ample assortment of towels on the shelves, careful to take just long enough for the very prominent bulge to diminish, for the most part, anyway. However, the task was made all the more difficult by the fact he could practically feel her eyes now travelling over him.

It was only when he was certain she would grow suspicious by his prolonged search that he reluctantly turned back and handed her a fluffy pink towel. At the time, though, her eyes were already a little further south, and they seemed to grow two sizes too big when they fixed on his groin. Which, in turn, responded to the attention.

Oh… shit.

"Can I get you anything? Tea? Coffee?" Hugh quickly asked, careful to keep his voice level even as she openly ogled him for a moment before dragging her eyes away.

"Err, tea, please. I could murder a brew." With that, she snatched the towel and fled into the living room.

Oh God, was that monster his cock or did he just stick a bloody cucumber down his trousers?

Furiously scrubbing her hair with the towel, Elizabeth felt her cheeks burning at the memory of the appendage straining against Hugh's trousers.

Oh fuck, he's huge… Did I do that to him?

The thought came out of nowhere and sent a pulse of heat straight down to her clit. Shocked, she immediately tried to brush it aside, but then couldn't help remembering the way he'd been watching her, the hot predatory gleam in his eyes as he'd looked her over.

She knew that look. It was a hot look, dark and hungry and very, very dangerous in the eyes of a young stud.

She'd seen it a lot when she was younger. On Saturday nights out when she went out to hit the town with her girlfriends. The clubs and bars would be thronged with packs of men who'd watched them with that same look. Like packs of wild dogs, eyeing up a fresh juicy bit of meat. Some of Patrick's mates had given her that same look over the years too, when they'd had a few too many and were likely to get handsy…

But to see Hugh giving her that same look. No, it couldn't be.

She'd known him and his mother for years, since he and Victor were kids in playschool. He was young enough to be her son. He was her friend's son, and her own son's best friend. And she was too old for him, much too old.

I'm old enough to be his mother.

"Tea's up!"

Her heart leapt at the husky voice.

Aimlessly scrubbing her hair, she swung around to find Hugh standing in the doorway, holding two steaming mugs. The vision was as breath-taking as it had been when he had been standing in the doorway. The image of him, in those casual *distressed* jeans and tight shirt, radiating such raw masculinity, an alpha male at ease in his territory, made her long to be twenty years younger.

He placed them on the coffee table.

"Still lots of milk and three sugars, right?"

Placing the towel over the headrest of one of the two matching armchairs that encircled one side of the table, she sat in one corner of the sofa that sat opposite. Able to practically feel the heat of his eyes on her skin through her clothes, she picked up the mug and sipped. Sweet and just that little bit shy of hot. Perfect. "Cheers."

Elizabeth sipped and sipped until she knew she couldn't avoid talking to Hugh any longer without seeming rude. Then she mentally kicked herself. She was being ridiculous.

This was Hugh, just Hugh. It didn't matter that he had grown into a smouldering and sexy-as-hell Adonis. It was still Hugh. She focused on that, trying to think of the little boy she'd used to watch play in the park.

"So, Jen and Mike took off to the sun and gave you run of the house, huh? Where'd they go?"

"Gran Canaria," he answered, sitting beside her. As it was a two-seater, there was just enough room on the sofa for them both, just. "Dad scored a big commission, so they rented a condo out there for the month to celebrate."

"Lucky for some…" Elizabeth could feel herself shaking from his closeness. His tone was offhand and casual, but the way the smokiness of his voice curled around the words, he might as well have been whispering dirty fuck-metalk right in her ear. "So, does this mean you've finished your pupillage?"

He picked his own mug up off the glass tabletop. "Yep, I'm now a fully certified and experienced lawyer."

"That's great." Her breath caught as he drank, her eyes immediately fixing on the subtle movements of his throat as he swallowed. Then she noticed his eyes, those intense, baleful blue eyes, burning bright against the inky dark of his pupils, watching her over the rim. She quickly looked away. "What are you going to do now? Take a break here while your parents are away, then head off back to the city? Get snapped up by some big firm and become a hotshot city lawyer? I could just see you in the Old Bailey, parading around in your robe and wig. Then hitting the streets with your expensive tailored suits and flash super car to turn all the girls heads. You were always a flash git, even when you and Victor were kids."

"Ouch," he mocked a hurt look. Then, putting the mug down, he rounded on her, the force of his presence enough to have her edging back into the sofa. "No, actually I'm here to stay. I took a job with a small firm down in Taunton. And I'm not involved in criminal law. I handle insurance."

"Insurance?"

"Yeah, insurance, and a bit of property law. It's less glamorous but steadier." As he spoke, Elizabeth couldn't help noticing he was edging closer. "And my clients aren't likely to throw acid in my face if I can't get them off."

Their growing proximity had awareness tingling through her arms, and heat gathering in the pit of her belly. "Fair point. So, you've just moved back into your old room? Aren't you a bit… err, *big* for that now?"

"A little." He teased and actually winked at her. "That's why I'm kipping in the spare room while I look for a place of my own."

"To rent?"

"Afraid so."

He was getting closer, too close.

"Well, it shouldn't take long to find somewhere, if you know where to look. You know, there are some delightful places over my way." Fuck, why had she said that?

"I remember." His voice lowered, growing hotter like the space between them. "You'll have to show me around. Give me the grand tour."

In spite of herself, Elizabeth's heart leapt at the idea.

"Sure, pop round anytime you're free and I'd be happy to show you the neighbourhood." God, what was she saying? She really needed to stop talking now. But she couldn't stop herself. It had just come out as her mind swam with the thought of him and her, alone, that body pushing up against her, all hard and male, his wicked mouth doing unspeakable things.

No, this wasn't good. She needed to get things onto a safer ground. "I know Victor would love it. You haven't seen him in ages. And it's such a great place to start a family. I'm sure your girlfriend will love it."

He smirked, as if he could see how close she was to snapping. And revelled in it. "Well, that sounds great. All I need to do now is to find a wife."

"Oh, so there's no one…"

"Oh, there's someone," he said. "There has been for a long time. She just doesn't know it *yet*."

Elizabeth felt a lump developing in her throat, her heart racing like a bird in a cage. "Well, I'm sure she's a very special girl."

"She is, but I'm not really interested in girls." He closed the gap, his big hand moving to gently rest on her denim encased thigh. "I prefer more mature women. Women who know what they want and how to get it." She

wanted him.

Wanted to touch him, taste him, bite him.

Wanted to lick her way down those delicious abs, tear those damn jeans off with her teeth, and suck his big fucking cock until-

He kissed her hungrily, all heat and instinct.

Chapter Three

She gasped, a soft whimper of protest, as the feeling of his lips crushing against hers set every nerve in her alive, but she didn't pull away. She didn't resist as his tongue danced across the roof of her mouth, ravishing her with lush licks that made her toes curl before entangling with hers. Nor did she try to escape when his powerful hands enveloped her, cupping her buttocks with exquisite force and dragging her across, so his resurrected cock pushed against the throbbing heat at her centre.

Then she was straddling his lap, the softness of his hair tickling the skin between her fingers as she fisted it and kissed him back, and nothing seemed to matter.

She didn't know what she was doing, but suddenly she didn't care.

She didn't care that it was wrong. Didn't care that he was her son's best friend. Didn't care that he was half her age.

She didn't care that she was a married woman.

He was just too much, too much for her to resist, to deny.

Hugh groaned, a low throaty sound when she sucked his tongue, the throbbing purr tingling down her spine to spike in her clit as his fingers squeezed her bum, crushing her to him. The sting and his roughness turned her on all the more. Fuck, she'd forgotten how good this could feel.

How good it should feel.

It had been so long since a man had made her feel like this, she couldn't help her little squeak of protest when he pulled away. Even so, a part of her screamed that it was for the best. They couldn't do this. It was wrong; it was so very bad…

"Hugh!" His name left her in a hot breathy moan as his lips covered that sensitive spot behind her ear and sucked.

She couldn't believe what was happening. What she was doing.

It was so surreal, like she was waking from a dream but not quite all the way, and was now trapped in that void where dreams met reality.

She didn't do this. She'd never done anything like this.

But she'd wanted to. Fantasised about it. Dreamt about it, but never…

Heat, want, and greed surged through her as tingling sensations zapped through her from her head to the tips of her fingers and toes. Moans poured from her, hot and wanton. Somewhere in the back of her subconscious, she just registered the weight of his desire pushing against the heat throbbing in the cradle of her hips. The idea that she was affecting this young stud as potently as he was her was so exciting, she couldn't resist. She needed to touch him, feel him.

Her hands moved slowly, cautiously, almost ridiculously so, given their predicament. However, she couldn't help it. Half afraid the lightest touch, too bold, might shatter the spell and repulse him.

So, Elizabeth clung to him, her body crushed to his, hands pawing at his back through his shirt. He felt so hard. Not bulky the way bodybuilders strived for, but solid, corded and toned. A slab of marble, chiselled layer by layer into a work of art, like Michael Angelo's *David* given life.

At any other moment, she might have wondered how the devil he had managed it, while at the same time juggling the hectic life of a lawyer in training. However, now, all she wanted was to see him, feel his skin, and worship him. If only his bloody shirt wasn't tucked so neatly into his jeans, barring her from immediate access. It just wasn't fair. It would take too long for her to pull it loose, and the act itself presented the considerable problem of having to take her hands off him.

Worse still, Hugh was faster and bolder, much bolder.

While his mouth worked her into a frenzy, ravishing her sensible tendons with licks and nips, one of his hands worked its way up beneath her top. It was cold against her heated skin, but the chill only added to the sensuousness of his touch. His fingers brushed over her naked flesh, up her midriff, over her ribs, gathering up the hem of her top as it went. He was careful to avoid her breasts, however, and neglect made her nipples ache as he pushed the garment up and over her bountiful cleavage.

He left the spaghetti-string top there, bunched and rolled up under her arms. With a final nip of her earlobe, he pulled back to admire his handiwork. In a dark, far-flung corner of her mind that was still capable of rational thought, a voice urged her to come to her senses and slap that smug look off his gorgeous face and cover herself.

She quickly pushed aside, however, when she saw the look in his eyes as he took her in. How long had it been since Patrick had looked at her like that? Had he ever?

He rumbled an approving purr. Deep and low, it thrummed through his body into hers wherever their skin touched, making her sex clench. Clearly, he liked what he saw, and the thought made her glad she'd worn the red lace bra adorned with black filigree.

It was a tad too expensive and ornate to be considered practical, but the way it pushed her tits up and lifted the years, made the expense a thing of little account.

Her ass also happened to look great in the matching thong, if she said so herself.

"Mmm… your tits are amazing."

His words thrummed through her, straight down to her pulsing clit, as the pad of his thumb brushed brazenly over her breasts, teasing around her bra. Just inches from where she needed it.

"You know, I used to dream about fucking them when I was younger. I'd jerk off thinking about burying my cock in them while that mouth sucked me off, but what really made me blow was thinking about them bouncing while I fucked you. Especially when I went balls deep, and you begged me to give it to you, to take your creamy cunt…"

Her breath came in short gasps that were only slightly due to the way he was plumping her cleavage, that huge palm rubbing over her nipple through the lace in the most exquisite torture. His dirty words were a seduction in their own right. The thought of him stroking that monster while he dreamed of having his way with her. It was more than she could stand.

No man had ever treated her like this. He was rough and knew what he wanted, knew what she wanted, even if she didn't know it. He made her feel. Made her lose herself in the moment. She couldn't think. She couldn't remember why she was there, or where she was, or even what had brought her to this sofa with this stranger.

This wasn't the boy she'd known.

That boy had grown up. Become a man. A man who took what he wanted.

And he wanted her.

Wanted her so lustily, he ripped the bra away like it was dental floss. With a flick of his wrist, he discarded the expensive piece of lingerie, banished it to a place out of sight. Then the damp, delicious heat of his mouth replaced it, sucking in her nipple, making her gasp ragged breaths.

"Oh god, what… what are you doing to me…" she panted, her back arching as he brought his other hand up to cup and knead her neglected tit. Sparks and starbursts sizzled through her as he worshipped her breasts. Then abruptly, he switched, and his fingers rolled her slick right bud into a heightened state of arousal while his tongue swirled around and around her left in ever shrinking circles, until she just wanted to scream.

Somehow, Hugh knew just how to play her body like a fiddle.

Grabbing and squeezing, biting and sucking, rolling and pinching her nipples, he made her feel things…

He made her feel like a woman again. Made her feel all the things she'd forgotten in her years of captivity. Her years of bondage, in matrimony, bound to a weak, whimpering sham of a man.

Made her feel that feeling again. That slick heat throbbing so insistently down in her centre and the delicious friction that accompanied it every time she moved.

He made her feel things, and she wanted more.

"Mmm… Yeah… that's it… fuck… you bad boy!"

The words were out before she really knew what she was saying. Almost by their own volition, her hands had threaded through his hair, both pulling him to her and steadying her as she ground her body into his.

And suddenly Elizabeth's entire world was focusing on that feeling of him sliding along her folds, through all the layers of lace and denim, to grind against her clit.

God! He feels even bigger than he looks…

The feeling brought the universe crashing down around her.

This wasn't right.

She couldn't do this.

She didn't do… this.

She was a respectable woman, a married woman. She didn't have random quickies with men half her age. She didn't shag strange men, even if they were the embodiment of a fucking sex god!

No! She couldn't do this… she mustn't … she … she … No … No…

"No!"

In other circumstances, the look of stunned disbelief on Hugh's face as he jumped back would have looked rather comical. However, Elizabeth was in too much of a rush to appreciate it.

"I'm… sorry… that… that was a mistake. I should… I shouldn't have done that." Scrambling back off of the sofa and to her feet, she pushed her top down, being careful to walk around the coffee table and put as much space between her and her ravisher as possible as she did.

Then, without waiting for his reply, she was out of the room, down the hall, through the door, in her car and gone.

Chapter Four

Back home, in the safety of her kitchen, Elizabeth could barely keep her hands from shaking as she sipped her tea. The residual arousal clawed at her, thrumming her nerves like taut guitar strings.

The tea took the edge off a little.

"God! What was that?"

She couldn't believe what she'd done, and with Hugh, of all people.

It was like something out of a bloody porno. Throwing herself at a hot stud after seeing he had a gigantic cock. All that was missing was the delivery man with a funny accent and the big sausage pizza.

Oddly, though, she didn't feel the least bit guilty. Frustrated, sure. Disappointed, maybe. Horny, fuck yeah! But no guilt.

Why would she? Patrick had his indiscretions, his little playthings, his… *whores!*

So what if she had a little slip with a dark and dashing toy-boy? She was a woman. She had needs.

But to do it, or nearly do it, with Hugh!

Her friend's son. Hell, he was her own son's friend, and not just any friend, his best friend. He was as off limits as it got. And all the hotter for it.

She quickly chugged her drink, desperate to quell the memory of his hands on her, the searing heat of his touch sizzling across her skin, working its way too – *No!*

Damn it all to hell, she needed to get laid. That would get it all out of her system. How long had it been anyway? Two months, maybe even three? Yes, that was it. She needed to get fucked, that was all. She needed…

She paused, an idea lurching to mind, and she looked to the kitchen window. The sky overhead was still grey and overcast, growing darker by the second as dusk crept in, but the rain was stopping.

Her lips broke into a sly smile when her gaze landed on the large and luxurious hot tub on the back porch.

Keeping his foot down hard on the accelerator, Hugh turned off the Bridgwater Road and sped down the residential street towards the Clarke family's household on the outskirts of the Bampton area. A glance at his Omega told him it was a little after eight. *Not much further now…*

He didn't know what he was going to say, but he just couldn't leave things standing with Elizabeth the way they were. It felt like he'd been waiting his whole life to have a chance with Elizabeth Clarke, and now that he'd tasted her, he wasn't about to let her get away.

Not now, not after he'd waited for so long.

Heedless of the rain pounding his windscreen, he sped his BMW M5 down the residential streets, taking the swerving bends lined by detached red brick and grey stone homes like turns on the Nürburgring.

The years of going to and from Mrs Clarke's house with his mum had drilled the route into his memory, but it had been a while. He almost thought he'd gone too far until he spotted Elizabeth's Audi and pulled in behind it on the drive.

Most of the ground floor lights in the house were on, but, much to his delight, there was no sign of Mr Clarke's Alfa Romeo 4C. The old git might have complicated things, but if he was away on one of his infamous *business* trips, then his wife would be all alone.

And if her performance in his parent's living room was any indication, she desperately needed a little TLC. Well, maybe a little less T and a whole lot of L.

Shutting the quietly purring BMW down, he slid out of the driver's seat, pocketed the fob, and walked up the drive to the front door. His mouth suddenly drier than the desert, he tapped his knuckles against the painted timbers of the front door.

Against the soft patter of the rain, the knocks echoed like the blasts of a cannon. Suddenly nervous, Hugh couldn't help brushing himself down, trying to smooth his clothes as he awaited an answer.

None came.

He knocked again, a little harder this time. Still no answer.

Okay, time for Plan B.

There was a time when he and Victor knew all the secret ways in and out of each other's homes. Now the memories came swimming back. Dropping down into a crouch, he slinked round the edge of the building, beneath the overhanging ledge of the family room's window seat, and through the flower beds. The fake rock was exactly where he remembered, nestled into the roots of a stump that had once been a towering apple tree.

Retrieving the key, he rose up and moved around to the side of the house and unlocked the padlock securing the ornate iron side gate between the house and the garage.

A quick open-palmed push had the gate swinging open with a low creak that practically screamed his presence to the world. Someone obviously hadn't been keeping on top of the building maintenance.

The alleyway between the two buildings leading to the back garden was inky black all the way to the steps of the back porch, but he could hear commotion up ahead. A sound like water bubbling on the hob.

There was something else too, something softer, almost indistinguishable from the background, but that made his dick instinctively stir to life. He couldn't believe his luck. Heart hammering excitedly in his chest, he followed the sounds and, edging forward, slowly peered around the edge.

Elizabeth was in her hot tub, her head propped on a rolled towel beside an almost empty wine glass. It was a very deep model, more than half sunken into the porch, yet the steaming, bubbling water came all the way up to her shoulders. Nonetheless, the tops of her breasts were clearly visible as, eyes closed and biting her lip, she arched her back; her left hand fondling her cleavage.

In the soft golden hue of the back-porch light, it was obvious she had forgone a swimsuit.

Hugh greedily drank in the view. He'd been dreaming of this moment, picturing it ever since he first started noticing girls, no, since he'd started to notice women. He'd never been really interested in girls. They were always so prissy and uptight, or always playing games. They didn't know what they wanted or how to satisfy a man. And while their bodies were fun to play with, they could never compare to the lush, full curves of a mature woman.

Mrs Clarke was the very epitome of a mature, beautiful woman.

His fantasy.

His goddess.

Patrick, that son of a bitch, didn't deserve her. He'd neglected and abandoned her, so tonight, Hugh would make her his.

He could just hear her panting, soft, wanton moans. They were music to his ears and almost without realising what he was doing, his free hand began fumbling with the button of his far too tight trousers. He could scarcely breathe from the tightness. He had to be set free, to relieve the tension building in his groin…

"Mmm…" she purred, hot and breathy. "Fuck… Yes… give me that cock… oh-my-god… I need it, yes…"

Nearly tearing his trousers open, he grabbed his cock. He couldn't see her other hand, but he didn't need to. He could picture her fingering her slick wet pussy, working herself up, first one, then two fingers, her hips rolling and growing more urgent as she got closer. He matched her pace, pumping his cock, the shaft slick with precum, and greedily devoured the sight of her playing with her dusky pink nipple. Twisting and tugging, imitating the very treatment he'd given it just hours earlier.

He answered her low moans by thrusting himself into the tight coil of his fist. Still pent up from their earlier encounter, Hugh knew he wouldn't last long, and though he'd seen his share of pornography, this was the first time he'd ever watched a woman masturbate in real life. It was the most erotic thing he'd ever seen.

Porn was cheap titillation. Sex manufactured with all the passion and intensity stripped away, like Ikea flat pack furniture.

Once you'd seen one, you'd seen them all.

This was anything but cheap titillation. This was seduction. Hugh would never tire of watching her.

She was a living woman, repressed and denied, A font of pent up sexual tension just starting to bubble to the surface and in desperate need of a good, hard-

"Oh, God… that's it baby… pound that pussy… oh god… I'm gonna- fuck, I'm cumming, I'm cumming… Hugh!"

Oh shit!

He froze, his fist tight just under the head. The sound of her calling out his name in that ragged breathy voice, triggered a chain reaction that pushed him over the edge.

He came hard, shooting a thick stream of cum that arced into the darkness. Yet his eyes never strayed from the view of Elizabeth as her own climax ripped through her.

The orgasm she'd reached while thinking of him…

Chapter Five

Elizabeth had never expected to be doing this. She'd only wanted a soak in the hot tub, but then everything had spiralled out of control.

Her idea had worked.

As she lay soaking in the hot water, all her tension had just seemed to melt away and she was content to do nothing more than let the jets work their magic, carrying her away, back to that sofa in Jennifer's living room.

Hugh was with her, above her, topless, with his jeans hanging low on his hips.

He was kissing her again, hot and hungry kisses. She could feel his desire for her burning strong and pressing demandingly between her thighs as he rolled his hips.

Sinking deeper into her fantasy, heat that had nothing to do with the hot tub spiralled around her belly. A long sigh passed her lips as her hands mirrored her fantasy. Already stiff, her nipples tingled as her fingers teased around them and sensation rippled down her spine in a rush that had her cupping and squeezing her heavy bosom while her other palm moved down her belly.

"Mmm… Oh yes, you're such a bad boy…"

Hugh laid her down across the sofa, his hands ripping the clothes from their bodies. Then he was covering her, and she could barely keep from drooling as he took himself in hand, stroking from base to tip so that a milky drop appeared.

She wanted to lick it, taste it. No, taste him, and more. So much more. Only he was faster…

She moaned, biting her lip in pleasure as the feeling of a finger sliding through her sent a white-hot shiver of delight coursing through her centre. It was a poor substitute for a real cock, but she'd missed the feeling of having something inside her for so long that she hardly cared and began rocking against the invading digit.

"Fuck… Yes… give me that cock… oh-my-god… I need it, yes…"

Oh god, what was wrong with her?

It had never been like this, even in those years after Victor was born and Patrick had spent more and more time away on business trips. She had kept her composure and forewent the sexual urges. Life had been simpler back then. Her days had been full, the nights lonely, but she had been too preoccupied with her role of being a young mother to give much thought to her neglected libido.

Now, however, things were different. Victor was away at university. She was alone, and what she had once thought insignificant was resurfacing with a vengeance.

She was shaking, every nerve in her body tingling with sensations as she used her thumb to play with her clit while working two fingers in and out. Almost mindless with the clawing need to cum, her body tensed under the duress of hot waves and she moaned again, only louder, not caring who heard as she came for the first time in longer than she could remember.

God, how had she gone without a man for so long?

Then, as the waves receded and afterglow settled, she felt it.

It was only a momentary distraction. A prickling sensation of awareness that tickled the back of her neck and tingled through her skin, but it was enough.

Someone was watching her.

The thought had her on instant alert, the vulnerability of her position, and the repercussions of what she had been doing, suddenly glaringly oblivious. Nervously, she looked up and around at the upper windows of the homes that encircled her back garden. They were all dark behind the drawn curtains and blinds, however, that did not distract her from the certainty that someone was out there.

She could feel their eyes on her and strangely, rather than feeling violated by the intrusion, it was turning her on all over again. The idea that someone she couldn't see was watching her through the gloom thrilled her, made her belly flutter and core pulse excitedly. It was such an exciting feeling, it almost tempted her to give her audience an encore.

God, when had she become such an exhibitionist?

From his hideaway, Hugh had a near perfect view of Elizabeth rising up out of the hot tub and towelling herself dry. She seemed to take her time and spent much more time than necessary patting away every lingering drop of water before wrapping the towel around herself and hurrying back into the house.

All right, genius, what now?

Tucking his still-stiff erection back into his trousers, he glanced back down the pathway. He could go back the way he'd come and try the front door again. She would hear him this time and answer, but then what would he say? He hadn't given the matter any thought on the drive over, and after what he'd just witnessed, he'd probably be as tongue tied as a virgin on a date with Madison Ivy.

Or he could go home, think on the matter a little bit, then come back in the morning, after she'd…

After she'd what? Calmed down? He dismissed the notion immediately. He wouldn't go back, not now. He'd waited too long for this chance. He couldn't, he wouldn't, he…

He wheeled around, crossed the garden, and stormed up the porch to the back door. Knowing it was unlocked, he twisted the knob and pushed the door open.

Elizabeth stood with her back to him, her towel replaced by a black silk dressing gown that barely covered her lush derriere. He could hear her humming a low melody as she busied herself with fastening the belt around her waist. Unable to resist the opportunity, he crossed the kitchen in quick strides and reached out a hand to cup her arse.

Totally oblivious to his presence, Elizabeth shrieked and whirled around, her eyes widening at the sight of him.

"Hugh! What are you-"

Her reprimand quickly died as he seized her lips with his, silencing her with a deep kiss. For one harrowing moment, she tried to break free, wriggling and squirming and pushing against the solid mass enveloping her. However, his powerful hands held her close, crushing her to him. Then his tongue swept past her lips, and the fight left her completely. He felt her relax, and he urged her back, his big hands squeezing her butt, then hoisting her up onto the counter.

There were no words or gestures. No explanations given or required.

His need for her was like an all-consuming fire in his blood, a raging inferno that would not be sated until he had devoured every bit of her. With a mind to do just that, he took advantage of his new leverage to deepen the kiss, their tongues becoming locked in an intimate dance that had them both panting with passion as he moved in between her splayed thighs.

She braced her hands against his torso, urgently pushing his jacket down his arms before moving up to bury themselves in his hair. Their hips were rolling together in synchronised motions and they wantonly devoured one another until the need for oxygen forced Elizabeth to pull away. However, Hugh was not so easily deterred and trailed kisses along her jaw before bending down to nip along her neck, making her gasp and moan in undisguised delight. "Oh God … No … We can't … we shou-oh!"

Her protestations were weak and lacked any conviction when spoken amidst such needy tones. Paying them no heed, he crouched down between her thighs and hitched her long legs over his shoulders. She didn't fight him, and he turned his eyes up to hold her gaze as he dipped his head.

Elizabeth couldn't believe what was happening.

Everything was going so fast. One minute she was just wondering what she should do for dinner. The next she was being hoisted atop her kitchen cabinets, watching Hugh's gorgeous, chiselled face going down between her legs.

It was a scene taken straight out of her fantasies and when his tongue flicked over her still oversensitive clit, she completely forgot all of her earlier objections. Arching with a low moan, she shoved a hand into his hair, pulling his mouth against her. Her suddenly overheated sex rippled as his tongue plunged in and began feasting on her with deep, swirling licks.

"Mmm… you're so tasty Mrs Clarke…" Hugh growled, his tongue never ceasing in its exploration as he ate her hungrily. "I could eat your cunt all night."

He buried his face in her tender flesh, completely immersing him in her core as her cream flowed readily into his greedy mouth. She had a unique flavour, one he couldn't get enough of, and sucked her folds before working his tongue in and out, orally fucking her into delirium.

"Hugh… Oh fuck!" Elizabeth was on the verge of losing all control. Her whole body was aquiver from the things his mouth was doing to her. Still sensitive from her selfinduced climax, she knew it wouldn't be long before she reached her peak. Her thighs tightened instinctively, trying to hold him in place while she greedily bucked and ground her pelvis against him in a desperate attempt to make his tongue go as deep as possible.

This was something Patrick had never done for her. Though he expected it often, her loving husband never felt the need to return the favour. Hugh, however, was more than happy to attend to her, and oh God was he was so good at it. Already she could feel herself returning to the edge of that sweet precipice. Her hand clutched desperately at clumps of his hair as his tongue mercilessly pillaged her core, stretching to its limit and caressing her deeper than she'd ever thought possible. It felt like he was licking her everywhere at once.

Eager to give her what she craved, Hugh altered tactics and, with both arms coiled around her thighs, pivoted her up ever so slightly. This new position afforded him greater access to her body, and he didn't wait before switching to suckle her clit.

"Oh, sweet Jesus… Hugh, please, please… I… I… oh my god, you're going to make me cum again… yes, yes, yes, oh fuck I'm gonna cum, I'm gonna…"

She thought she was going to die.

When he sucked her little bundle of nerves, a thousand different explosions went off in her head at once. Oh yes, she was going to die. She was going to burn up in the fires of her own ecstasy.

"Yeah, cum for me, Mrs Clarke," Hugh growled, staring up at her, his gaze dark and hot with lust. "You're so fucking sexy. Feed me your wet cunt and cum on my face as I eat your pussy."

She looked so amazing like this, so dishevelled and uninhibited, so unlike the woman he had known while growing up.

Caught in his stare, Elizabeth couldn't look away. Even as the orgasm exploded through her, called up by his very command, she was possessed, rooted by the desire burning in his eyes, the sheer sensuality of watching him go down on her as waves rushed over her. They crested higher and higher until the storm passed, and it had reduced her to a panting mess.

Licking his lips clean, Hugh lowered her legs off of his shoulders and rose up to his full height between her drooping limbs. At some point, he must have unfastened his trousers. They were open and his cock stood rampant between muscular thighs, the wide crest poised at her cleft. With a roll of his hips, he dragged the weeping tip along her folds to nudge her oversensitive clit.

The contact sent a thrill through Elizabeth that made her back arch. She wanted this. No, she needed this, but not here, not in her kitchen.

"Take me to bed."

Chapter Six

Hugh Didn't question her decision. With a nod, he heaved her up and crushed her to him. Instinctively, she crossed her legs over his buttocks and swept her hands over his shoulders, scoring him lightly with her nails and marvelling at the wall of muscle beneath his shirt. He carried her effortlessly out of the kitchen, down the hall, and up the stairs to the master bedroom.

He didn't bother turning on the light. Elizabeth was glad of that. The darkness helped her nervousness, made her feel like she was somewhere other than her family home, and it hid the photos. They were many- and everywhere, photos of birthdays and events, of her family and friends, of Victor. She didn't think she could do this with him watching.

However, there was enough light for Hugh to discern the outline of the grand canopied king-size bed. He made straight for it, but he didn't notice the rug at its foot. He slipped, and they tumbled together onto the neatly made covers, with Elizabeth on top.

She felt a thrill shiver down her spine as she took in the sight of the young man lying beneath her, unable to keep the devious smirk from her lips.

Strong, intelligent, and handsome, there wasn't a redblooded woman alive that wouldn't give her right arm just to have him look at them the way he was at her. And yet, at this moment, he only had eyes for her, the mother of his best friend. A middle-aged housewife who had given the best years of her life to a neglectful, drunkard and adulterer. What had she ever done to get so lucky?

Smirking wickedly, Elizabeth winked, then shuffled her butt back down his legs.

Hugh gave her a quizzical look. "Mrs Clarke?"

"I love it when you call me that," she purred, keeping her eyes locked on his until she found what she was looking for and gave a surprised gasp. "Wow, you've grown into such a *big boy*."

Then, with her eyes still burning into his, she dipped her head and dragged the flat of her tongue up the underside of his cock from root to tip before going to work on him.

Hugh groaned and fisted the sheets, unable to look away as she bowed her head. Those full pink lips stretched tight and gliding down his cock, sucking him in.

"Oh fuck, Mrs Clarke…"

Whenever he called her that, it just sounded so dirty. Elizabeth couldn't help moaning around her mouthful. And he was a mouthful. She'd wanted to take him all in, but he was much too big for that. Only a third of the way down and she was already at her limit. Yet that only made her feel naughtier. He just smelled so good, and his taste- she'd never known a man could taste so good. Pulling back, her cheeks hollowed as she sucked and mouthed his thick crown.

"Is this what you want, Hugh, your best friend's mum, sucking your cock?"

Releasing the head, she swirled her tongue around and around the wide crest, before pulling back to tease the tip with flicking licks. Then she was dragging the flat of her tongue up and down his length, like she was licking an ice lolly, and all the while still looking up into his eyes.

"Mmm… such a yummy cock. I bet you make all the girls choke with this big dick…"

It was too much. Hugh couldn't take it.

"Oh, shit!" he groaned, eyes rolling up and his head falling back into the bed's soft embrace.

Elizabeth grinned inwardly, relishing the feeling of his cock pulsing under her tongue. "I want it, you bad boy. Wanna feel this big dick splitting me open. I need it!"

Quick as a snake, Hugh lurched up, seized her around the waist and hurled her to the bed. Then, looming above her, he pulled his shirt over his head. With a flick of his wrist, he cast it aside. His shoes and trousers were gone just as quickly, leaving him standing before her in all his naked glory, the weak light glittering over his sculpted muscles and casting him in a godly radiance.

She didn't have time to enjoy the view, however. In the blink of an eye, he was on top of her. With a quick tug, he had her robe undone and over her head. She gasped at his sudden ferocity, his new dominance a complete turn on that had her all but panting as the weight of his erection settled against her throbbing clit.

"Ready?"

"Yes!" Elizabeth wanted to scream. What was he waiting for? Couldn't he see that she'd never been more ready for anything in all her life? "Yes, damn it, just fuck me, you bast-oh!"

Her back arched as her every sense was consumed by the delicious burn of his cock driving home. He filled her so completely, she could feel his every ridge and thick ropy vein coiled about his trunk. It was such a delicious sensation. She couldn't help fisting the sheets as her long legs closed around the sexy V-line of his waist and dug her heels into his flanks, urging him on.

Yet Hugh held firm. He had to.

Fuck, she felt so good, all hot, slick and so fucking snug. It was almost unbearable. It was only through force of sheer will that he was able to tear himself down from the edge before it was too late. Then her lush inner walls wrapped around him, squeezing his dick like a fist in a warm velvet glove. And it was too much.

He had to move.

"Oh god, oh shit… oh fuck!" Elizabeth felt ready to burst as Hugh started rolling his hips, drawing back, then driving home, going deliciously deep as the flair of his hips spread her legs back. His pace was intolerably slow, but with each fervent drive she could feel herself opening to him, her delicate tissues stretching around every delicious inch of him. It was so raw, so intense.

Sex with her husband was nothing compared to this. Even the way he was looking at her. Patrick had never looked at her that way. He didn't want to possess her, to own and use her as though she were property. He wanted simply to love her, to be with her in every way that two people could be. The way nobody had ever been with her before.

This wasn't just lust or longing, this was something more, something deeper, something both sacred and beautiful.

Elizabeth couldn't stand it. "Oh god, I'm cumming"

"That's it, cum for me, *Mrs Clarke*." His command was a low growl in her ear before he kissed her, smashing his mouth to hers, his tongue stroking hers as she came.

Shaking, riding the waves, Elizabeth clung to him, hands grabbing and clawing every bit of him she could reach, barely able to hang on. Desperate for more, she moved with him, grinding against each lunge of his big dick even as they sent her spiralling higher and higher.

Feeling her writhe under him, Hugh was certain he was orbiting madness.

It took all of his will not to give into his dark side, his primitive side. The debased animal that lurked in the heart of every man. The beast that yearned to take this woman, to make her beg and scream his name. It clawed at his resolve, whispering a sweet song of dominance and mastery. Yet he wanted this to be more than just fucking.

Now was his chance to show her, to prove to her, that there was more for her than just the mundane existence of a lonely housewife for her. That he was a better man than her good-for-nothing husband. His time had come and hooking an arm round her waist, he pulled her close, driving her hot little cunt all the way down to his root, as he reared back and pushed up onto his knees.

"Oh God!" Elizabeth gasped, ripping her lips from his in a long moan as his new angle of penetration scraped her sweet spot just right.

The way he held her had her hips pinned to his, and as he rocked back and forth, dragging her clit deliciously over his abdomen. The sensation was so intense it made her head spin. Completely absorbed in her own pleasure, her lips had formed an 'O' shape and with each jolting thrust, her whole body jumped delightedly to meet him, causing her enchantingly full breasts to bounce. "Yes, yes, yes! Harder baby! Please… fuck me harder!"

"Yeah, ride my dick Mrs Clarke, ride it!"

"Oh my god… so much… so deep… oh fuck… it's amazing!" She was shaking again, her whole body humming as waves of sensation washed through her and goose bumps rose up all over her skin.

"You love my cock, don't you?"

"Yes! I love it, fuck my pussy more, I want it, I love it"

"Is it better than your husband's?"

To emphasise his question, he buried himself in her warmth again and saw the dam inside her crack beneath a sudden mini climax that caused her eyes to roll. Her body trembled as liquid ecstasy rushed through her and Hugh watched with unabashed delight, fucking her through the pleasure with quick stabs of his cock.

"So … so much better, oh fuck. I had no idea what I've been missing… I… I never knew sex could be so… so good! Fuck me more! Make me take it! Use me like he never cou-oh!" The cry left her lips before her mind could register what she had said, yet it was too late. Her body was melting in a sea of liquid pleasure and all sense of words and thought had left her. Moaning hotly as she tossed her head from side to side, her sweat dampened mane of raven hair fanning out around her, she caught only the briefest glimpse of him smirking down at her. It was a very hot look on him. It made the throbbing knot in her centre pulse dangerously, pushing her towards her pleasure's violent pinnacle.

"And who is the best fuck of your life?" Perspiration glistened across his bronzed skin and a few salty drops rolled down his neck as he felt himself nearing his limit.

"You! Oh Fuck… you Hugh… it… oh god, yes… it was always you… so good… I can't take it… I'm… I'm cumming!"

Even as she spoke, she could feel her arms coiling around his neck as her arse gyrated in his lap. They were so close now, it perfumed her every gasping breath with his musky scent and she was suddenly aware of how hot his skin felt against her body. The sensations were so intense, her world had dissolved into a brilliant rush of colour and she couldn't tell where one tide of pleasure ceased and the next began as they merged into one continuous flood of glorious ecstasy.

Was she going mad?

Or perhaps this was what it felt like to die?

Maybe death by sex wasn't just some delightful male fantasy, and this terrific young stud had indeed fucked her into an early grave.

"Yeah, that's it, cum for me Mrs Clarke, cum all over my… my- oh fuck! I'm cumming too!"

The visual stimuli of her gorgeous naked body writhing and wriggling atop his pillaging shaft, combined with the feel of her juices coating him as her walls closed tight, sent him over the edge. After being restrained for so long, the force of his release was like nothing he had ever experienced, and a thunderous groan bellowed from his lips as his seed surged into her womb.

Still joined in the most intimate of fashions, they collapsed together in a tangled mass of limbs on the bed, their chests heaving with laboured breaths. Sweat made their bodies glisten in the low light, yet neither made any effort to move. Feeling safe and content in the others' presence, they fell into a blissful sleep.

Epilogue

Elizabeth didn't want to wake.

Usually, she was an early riser and would be up with the sun. There were chores to do, breakfasts to make, and an evermounting list of jobs. Her jobs.

However, today she just couldn't bring herself to do it. It felt safe here, safe and warm. Here she felt at peace, content.

Light, so dazzling with all the magnificence of the dawn, blanketed her naked body. Winter was coming. Its frosty breath wafted through the window, caressing her skin with soft and tantalising fingers fragrant with all the flavours of Autumn.

Half asleep, she trembled as the air teased down her back and arms, stirring goose flesh, and it was only when arms, strong as oak and corded with muscle, coiled around her waist, pulling her back against the wall of a hard male body lying beside her that she settled. Satisfied to just lie back and enjoy the moment, Elizabeth made no effort to resist as he crushed her to him, a soft moan escaping her as her breasts were pressed into his chiselled torso and the weight of his cock rose up to nestle in the cradle of her thighs. It was such a delectable sensation, the feeling of his hands around her, his breath hot on her neck, the heat radiating off his body, enveloping her, dragging her back down into sweet serenity as she listed to the deep rhythmic drumming of his heart.

And she couldn't remember ever feeling so sated.

Despite it all, she fought against the urge to curl into him, to sleep and prolong the moment across the boundless seas of eternity. Taken instead by the sudden need to see him, and an irrational fear that it might have all been a dream. A hot, wonderful, sweaty dream.

The greatest fucking dream of my life.

Just the memory of it stoked the embers in her core to new life. Suddenly more awake than asleep, she peeled her eyes back slowly to meet the stormy grey-blue eyes watching her from beneath sandy sleep-tousled hair.

"Mmm… good morning," he purred in that smoky voice that made her whole body tighten. Or maybe it was the way his mouth moved over the words, slow and seductive, pronouncing each syllable with delicious purpose. He had a very nice mouth. Thin peach coloured lips perfectly shaped with a sexy indent in the corner from where he had frequently bitten them when he was concentrating. A mouth made for kissing, licking, and doing the most wicked things. And that jaw, like an anvil with the perfect amount of rough to tease her inner thighs when he was tonguing her clit.

She couldn't help blushing at the memory, the heat in her core spreading out in a scarlet flush as she averted her gaze.

No one had ever looked at her the way he had just then. It was so intense, so intimate. Much too intimate. Like he was seeing her, truly seeing her. Seeing more than the neglected married woman in desperate need of a good shag. More than just Victor's mother. More than…

She couldn't bear it. "No."

"What?" he smirked, pulling her closer, practically skin to skin. He was hard, like chiselled stone, but they fit together perfectly. A carved marble Adonis shaped just for her.

"Don't look at me like that… it's embarrassing."

"I can't help it. Mmm… that blush is just so sexy." He dipped his head to nip the curve of her neck, his tongue quick to sooth the delicious hurt.

"No… please… you can't, I'm still sore- oh!" She gasped when he scraped that sweet spot behind her ear, her eyes rolling. His hand came up to knead her breast, thumb and forefinger, rolling her nipple so roughly she couldn't help arching into his palm.

"Mmm… you have amazing tits."

Tonguing the shell of her ear, Hugh seized upon Elizabeth's momentary distraction to push her back down onto the bed, caging her glorious naked body with his before taking a nipple into his mouth. He sucked greedily, and the delicious cocktail of heat and suction around her sensitive nub had her back arching, her fingers fisting his sandy strands.

"Oh god… mmm…" she moaned, clutching his head to her breast as the fog of pleasure descended.

Damn him!

Why did he have to be so good? How was she supposed to resist this young stud when just the feel of his mouth on her breast was enough to make her loins throb with liquid passion? "I … can't … oh god! Stick it in… fuck me! Fuck me with that big dick!" Hugh, however, was in no hurry.

Licking the tip of her nipple, he slowly reached between her quivering thighs and slid a finger along her wet sex while gently circling her clit with his thumb. Low sounds flowed from her in heated breaths as her hips rolled wantonly against his touch. And taking that as his cue, he suddenly snapped her legs open. Hearing her surprised squeak, he grinned wolfishly around her breast before moving into position, the rounded crest of his cock sliding up and down her folds…

The sound rang out as loud and shrill as a banshee's wail.

Lost in the depths of her fantasy, it hit Elizabeth like a bucket of ice water.

Atop the bedside table, the digital clock was flashing, illuminating the time in bright red numerals. Its alarm sang its ear-splitting song.

Besides her, Patrick lurched awake.

"Oh shit, I'm late!" he barked, jumping up from the bed and gathering up his clothes from the floor.

Tangled in the bed's voluminous sheets, Elizabeth watched as her husband pulled his trousers up his legs and shoved his shirt down a waistband that visibly strained to contain his suety bulk before waddling out their bedroom.

Downstairs, the front door slammed shut behind him. His Alfa's V12 engine roared to life, its tires squealed, and there was a blast of a protesting neighbour's horn as he sped off down the street.

With a sigh, Elizabeth rolled over and silenced the cursed clock before falling back into the mound of pillows.

He didn't spare her so much as a backwards glance.

So, what else is new.

It was the same every time he had to go away on a sales trip. She'd like to say she was used to it, but the idea that he could just up and leave her without even saying goodbye left a very bitter taste in the back of her throat.

Had he ever even loved her? Had there ever been a chance for them?

Hot tears began to well at the corners of her eyes.

No, I won't cry! She told herself. *I won't cry for him. He's not worth it.*

For what felt like hours, Elizabeth toyed with the idea of going back to sleep. However, her body was trembling with unspent passion and before long the burning in her loins, that constant reminder of how close she'd come, drove her from her bed. Letting the sheets fall to the floor, she quickly donned her fluffy pink dressing gown before walking down the steps that led up to and from the master bedroom. Going through the hall and into the kitchen, she busied herself for a moment with the task of making a strong cup of tea before walking out into the back garden and breathing in the cool morning air.

It was hard to believe it was already October. Her garden was as beautifully vibrant as it had been in spring. The trees were still green. Everywhere flowers bloomed and birds sang.

Nothing was right, and yet it was all so perfect. So much like her own life.

And now, for another week, she was free.

It had been a month since that night. The night that had changed her life. A month since she had given into temptation, broken her marriage vows, and surrendered her body and soul to another man.

A month since she had taken Hugh Becket as her lover. Hugh, the boy she'd watched growing up, the young lawyer just coming home after years of living in the city.
Hugh, her son's best Friend.

And the greatest fuck of my life.

Something had happened to her that night. Something that went beyond mere sex. He'd opened her eyes to a whole new world, given her a glimpse of something new and exciting. Something she'd never dreamed she was capable of. She wanted to experience it.

Her son, her precious baby boy, was all grown up and away at university. Her husband was never at home. This was a new day, a new start, and a new chapter of her life. She was free to find herself, to discover who she was. She would recreate herself, and she knew just where to start.

Going back into the house, she retrieved her brandnew laptop from its hideaway under the kitchen table and started it up. Entering the password that was guaranteed to be uncrackable, at least to her dear loving husband who hadn't remembered their anniversary once in all their years of marriage, she selected the pre-installed Word processor. The screen went white with the infamous white page.

What better way to reinvent herself than by creating her character in a book?

Sipping her tea, she considered the screen for a moment, then typed.

Confessions of a Trophy Wife.

By Liz Becket

The End…

Submitting To My Billionaire Bosshole

Chapter One

I stand before them, bare and unadorned, a sacrificial lamb for their lusts.

My world is black, the blindfold ensuring I can't see a thing, but I can feel them. Feel them arrayed around me, their eyes raking over me, devouring me from head to toe. Making my skin shiver with gooseflesh as the heat of their eyes burns across my breasts before licking down the flat of my belly to my…

I can hear them too. Their murmurs and bawdy jokes. I know I should feel insulted. They're acting like I'm some prize stud mare they're preparing to bid on. But the game is just too exhilarating.

I'm standing before them, naked and blindfolded, waiting for their command, and I love it.

I feel **him** coming up behind me.

He doesn't say a word, doesn't make a sound, but the sensation he always sends through me when he's near ripples up my spine, sending the pit of my belly into cartwheels. Then he's right behind me. So close, I can feel **it** nestling between my buttocks. I have to force myself to stay still, my heart fluttering like a robin redbreast in a cage.

"Don't move," he orders, his voice low so only I can hear, his breath curling over the skin of my neck, making my whole-body *tingle. It is a very sexy voice, as deep and cultured as a lush red wine, and authoritative. The voice of a man who gives orders all day and expects them to be obeyed.*

It sends tiny shocks of ecstasy rushing straight down to the hot slickness at my centre and makes my clit greedily throb for more.

I nod my understanding, then hiss a soft gasp, more from surprise than pain, as he slaps my ass.

"Don't move," he repeats, louder this time, emphasising every word so our audience can hear. The stinging handprint he leaves on my poor butt seems to burn deliciously in answer. A part of me wants to nod again, to push him and see how far he will go, but I don't. I remain still and obedient, compliant. Submissive.

His hands come up slowly, enveloping me from behind, the tips of his fingers sliding up my belly and over my ribs to cup my breasts. I whimper at the contact. Robbed of sight, my other senses seem heightened, making my already sensitive tits deliciously tender as he rolls and tweaks my stiff nipples.

I heard him chuckle as my back curls, offering up more of my not inconsiderable cleavage. Secretly, that mischievous part of me hopes he might punish me again. Perhaps bend me over and spank me in front of all these men.

He is subtler than that. Instead, he takes his time, plumping and kneading with just the right amount of attention and neglect to work my body into a heated frenzy that has me all but chewing my lower lip.

"Such a horny girl."

His tone is hot and hungry, much like the way his cock is pushing against my butt and smearing slickness along my thighs, and I know he is enjoying this as much as I am. He enjoys teasing, being in control while pushing his paramour to the brink and watching her writhe in delirious ecstasy.

So I writhe. Mewing soft kittenish sounds, I push back with a roll of my hips, grinding my butt along his length, the thick mushroom head sliding closer and closer to my burning cun-

"Kora… Kora! Are you listening?"

Chapter Two

Startled out of my thoughts, I looked up to see my supervisor standing over me, hands on her hips and watching me pointedly from behind her pearl mask.

Oh crap…

My belly did a triple somersault under that look. Though by no means unkind, in the few weeks I'd been working under her, Demeter had quickly set about ensuring I knew she was a woman not to be pissed about. Who would enjoy *punishing* any girl that forgot it.

And had, frequently.

Heat blossomed across my cheeks. I quickly nodded before looking down at my feet. "Yes, Ma'am."

I always had difficulty meeting her eyes. She was just one of those women who could totally disarm you with a look and carried herself with the confidence of a woman who owned her sexuality. I was completely overwhelmed by her and couldn't help feeling totally inadequate whenever she was close. Against her cascade of lush chestnut-red curls, sharp angular features, intense blue-grey eyes and gorgeous 4'11 build that seemed made for her leather corset styled bustier, I was a plain Jane.

"Sure."

I could feel her gaze scorching my skin as she eyed me, clearly not believing my less-than convincing lie, and I could just imagine her long and immaculate eyebrow arching beneath the mother-of-pearl likeness of her namesake. God only knows how long she might have been watching me just standing here, lost in my own little world.

My stomach flipped again, winding itself into a tight little knot. This wasn't the first time she'd caught me daydreaming. I'd been warned before, but I couldn't help myself. It was this place. It practically oozed sex appeal- as did the clientele.

God, please don't let me get the sack…

I needed this job. Student loans, along with my parents' debts, had left me broke. I couldn't afford to get my ass thrown back onto the job market after only a couple of weeks.

To my surprise, she just sighed and shrugged, like I was a naughty child that just wouldn't learn a simple lesson. "Go attend to the gentleman at table 12."

I couldn't believe my ears. "Ta-table… *12?*" Just saying that had the heat licking out from my centre, making my knees shake and my already slick pussy purr.

Oh God, no! Not 12, I'm not ready for that.

"12," she reiterated, in a tone that could cow the God of thunder. "He's waiting."

It was the epic clash of ice and fire. The cool edge to her tone crashed over the warmth in my centre.

Nodding again, I darted around her, so desperate to be out of my alcove and her sight, before she changed her mind, that I only just caught myself as I stepped out into the main smoking room. The close call earned me a hissed *tisk* from Demeter. *Graceful,* I hastily remind myself.

A maiden of the Olympus club is always graceful, and ready to serve.

Set amongst the heights of Midtown's numerous highrise buildings, the Olympus Club was New York City's best kept secret. The exclusive *Gentleman's* club of the city's elite. The den of vice and skulduggery. A house that catered to any and every pleasure. There was just one rule. Discretion.

The patrons valued their privacy and the *secrecy* the Olympus Club assured. Any member or maiden, regardless of wealth or position, status or connections, discovered discussing Olympus, would immediately be branded *'excommunicado'*.

The smoking room rang to the song of chinking of crystal and soft girlish giggles.

It was a masculine place. The furnishings were all deep, rich, hardwood and leather. Leather so supple and deeply padded that the management liked to joke they should arrange a contest to test it against a baby's bottom and a Labrador pup's fur, just to see which was softer. Original Picasso's and Monet's, Van Gogh's, and one that looked suspiciously like a 'liberated' Da Vinci, adorned the timber panelling. However, the greatest hidden treasure was the 'trillion dollar' view overlooking the cityscape, commanding views across Times Square and all the way downtown.

It took every last ounce of my self restraint not to succumb to the lure of the floor to ceiling window that made up the smoking room's outer wall as I slid around the frolicking patrons. One little look and it was as if all of New York knelt at my feet. I dare say that was the idea. Nothing stroked the egos of the mighty more than being made to feel like gods.

If nothing else, it was a long way up from my parent's place in Washington Heights.

Dionysus, the barman, looked up at me as I approached the bar and presented me with a serving tray decorated with sterling silver filigree.

"N-number 12," I said, my voice still a little shaky at the prospect.

God, get a grip girl, he's just a man.

By the way he moved so expertly towards a specific bottle, I had no doubt he knew exactly what to serve each patron. Though a most impressive number of decanters and bottles stood at the ready, they were just a fraction of what the Olympus's cellar had to offer, and he filled a tumbler with scotch, adding just a single cube of ice.

If I didn't know better, I would have sworn there was just a hint of a smirk to his lips as he placed the glass on my tray. Then he returned to his station, so I put it out of my mind.

There was no point dwelling on such things. Dionysus was practically an institution at the Club. He knew all the stories, all the skeletons hidden away, and not just those figurative ones. He wouldn't say a thing, even if I called him out and asked what was so funny.

As if I didn't already know.

All around the smoking room, patrons of all ages and shapes sat in the high-backed armchairs like they had been poured into them. Outside these walls, these were the cream of the crop, the living embodiment of Mrs Caroline Astor's four hundred. Businessmen and actors, politicians and bankers, lawyers, financiers, landowners… old money and new. Within the Olympus Club, however, and away from the prying eagled-eyed paparazzi, they could be true to themselves and embrace their more dark and primitive impulses.

Some drank Diamond Jubilee whiskey and smoked Gurka Cigars. Some gambled, either with cards, or the lives of their employees, moving them as they would pawns on a chessboard. And some enjoyed the benefits of their personal attendants.

I only half saw them as I pass by, the clash of white on black amongst the crowd, a tangle of limbs, bodies writhing upon a bulging chair. Hair ruffled and cheeks flushed. The tailored garments they'd ensured were immaculate in front of the cameras, like peacocks presenting their tail-feathers, and that no doubt cost more than anything I could earn in a decade, carelessly dishevelled, with buttons undone, ties loosened, and other articles cast away while the culprit wiggled her fine derrière in his lap.

None of it was full-on sex. Even here, few members would be so brazen out in the open. Regardless, they made no effort to hide their activities as I passed by; the tray raised over my head and the silks of my *uniform* fluttering with every step. Then again, why should they? I was only a maiden.

As the ancient gods would disguise themselves as men and women to walk among their subjects, to see but be unseen, so the maidens of the Olympus Club would dress as such. We hid our faces at all times, behind half-masks of our namesakes. Our bodies dressed in a uniform of half transparent silks that showed off as much skin as possible while keeping the necessary parts covered. On the premises, we left our names behind. Here we were servants, the gods of old, who made the world and now live upon it solely to serve.

I am just a servant of the house. I fetch and serve drinks, but at least the money's good. And there are the fringe benefits…

Table 12 was called a table only out of courtesy. In fact, it was nothing more than a little square side table to one of the better armchairs. The occupant sat half-cloaked in shadow, eased back and reading a small leather-bound book with one hand. Unlike all the other members, he was dressed smartly casual, forgoing his usual contemporary suits for a pair of khaki chinos and a crisp pale blue polo-shirt. The buttons were undone, just hinting at the chiselled muscles beneath in a way that made me long to explore that rugged physique.

Amongst this den of predators and alpha dogs, he was at ease and in his element. The top male, the only one with no need to prove himself.

Chapter Three

"S-Senator…" My voice trembled around the word. Just being in his presence affected me, put me on edge.

My breath caught in my throat as his eyes darted up to fix on me, scrutinising me.

The look immediately sent a hot shiver through my centre. At the same time, I quelled under his gaze, shrinking until I felt only an inch tall.

His penitent stare.

I'd seen that look before, dozens of times, in fact.

His instakill. The devastating look he reserved for journalists that asked him ridiculous questions. It always made for damn good television, but I never thought I'd find *that* look directed at me. It was ridiculously hot.

Forcing a dry swallow that rasped my throat all the way down, I presented my tray to him. "Y-your drink, Sir… Scotch on the ro-"

"You're new." It wasn't a question, merely a statement of an obvious fact.

I nearly jumped out of my skin as his low growl thrummed through me. "Yes! I mean… Yes, sir." I looked away, heat burning my cheeks- and other places further south.

Jeez, his voice couldn't sound any more made for fuckin' if it came with a side of strawberries and cream for dippin'.

He had the sexiest voice. Low and gravely but with a flowing command that had been forged on the playing fields of Eton or Oxford. The sort of voice that could inspire fear, demand respect, or reduce a poor, sex-starved girl to a puddle of wanton horniness with just a word. It was the voice in all my fantasies, the one I heard ordering me to cum for him.

Yet here he was silent.

Fighting to control the hot pulsing turning my knees to jelly, I slowly raised my eyes back up. He was still watching me, his eyes a hard icy blue, baleful and intense against the surrounding shadow. He was watching me, raking me from head to toe, studying me the way the wolf studied its prey, judging whether the meal would be worth the effort, before exploding into a run after the bunny.

He held my gaze for a moment, and I felt like he was looking into me, through me. Then he shifted, leaning forward so slowly I felt my breath catch as the shadow was peeled back.

Oh… My… God…

It wasn't a kind face. Nothing about Senator Richard Sharpe could ever be called kind. No, it was as hard and jagged as obsidian, a broad chunk of rock that a master mason had chiselled into a work of art. With that square jaw rough with stubble, sharp nose, wicked twist of a mouth, and raven black hair just that bit too long, he looked more like a soldier of fortune than a paper-pushing bureaucrat. And all the sexier for it.

I struggled to keep my nerve as his eyes raked over me with more interest than could ever be considered appropriate in the outside world.

But here, anything goes.

"Has anyone claimed you yet?" He asked it as calmly as he would enquire about the weather.

"What, no!" I exclaimed quickly, too quickly. "I mean, no Sir they haven't." Feeling the heat returning to my face, I placed the Senator's whisky on his table. "I'm not-"

"Such a waste." The Senator rose to his feet like a cobra rearing from the grass to loom over me.

So big... he never looked this impressive on TV.

Ignoring the drink I'd just laid down for him, he stepped around me, his eyes scorching lines of fire that seemed to burn through my already skimpy uniform as they took me in from head to toe again. Then he did the unthinkable and gently touched his hand to the base of my back.

"Beautiful."

"Senator... I... I..." I stammered, not sure what to say, barely even able to form words. Fire and electricity crackled at his touch, raising a rush of gooseflesh where our skins touched. Lush heat ignited and pooled in my centre.

No, this wasn't right. I couldn't let this go on. I mustn't. Club rules may be lax as far as the members were concerned, but for the staff, and in particular the maidens, they were very strict.

"You take good care of yourself." Another statement. His fingers brushed gently up my spine, then slid just under my ribs as he continued walking around me. My legs quickly turned to jelly under his scrutiny. I knew I needed to put some distance between me and this man, but my body refused to move as he stroked that place just below my left breast.

"I-I try, Sir," I forced out, my throat thick and uncooperative as I tried to restrain the moan that wanted to burst free as he drew closer and closer. "Please... Senator... I..."

To my surprise, and considerable disappointment, his hand suddenly dropped away, and he slid back into his chair with all the panther-like grace with which he had arisen from it, before taking up his drink and holding it out to me. "Here. Drink with me."

"Oh! Err, no Sir, I'm not supposed to-"

"I wasn't asking." He dismissed my refusal by pressing the glass up to my lips. "Drink."

Fingers shaking, I accept the drink, sipping it cautiously. I wasn't much of a drinker, even on nights out I'd only stuck to the fruity, colourful, girly cocktails, and it was all I could do not to gag. The whiskey burned like fire all the way down, the taste strong but smoky and not at all unpleasant.

He watched me as I drank, the way a wolf watched a deer, observing, waiting for that one perfect moment to pounce. The look sent a throb of desire straight through my centre and I couldn't resist a second swallow before he pulled the glass away.

Raising it up to his mouth, he downed the hard alcohol and placed the tumbler back on the table.

This was my chance, my one and only chance to slink away with my tail between my legs. I knew it was time to go, but I was captivated. Hypnotised by the sight of a single drop of amber rolling down his chin and my body wouldn't obey my commands anymore. The sight of him brushing that drop of whiskey away with his thumb, then sucking the pad clean, was the sexiest damn thing I've ever seen.

Forcing a dry swallow, I scrambled to regain my composure. "C-c-can I… I mean, will there be anything else, Sir?"

The Senator reached down and fingered the fastenings of his chinos. His eyes flashed like sunlight dancing on blue ice. "Mmm… Yes. There is just one more thing."

Chapter *Four*

I averted my eyes, the sound of the zip cascading over me like ice water as I looked for something, anything, that might otherwise require my attention. "I'll fetch you a girl."

"No."

My mouth felt drier than the desert. "Bu-but what am I-"

"I want you, Kora."

"Please, *Senator*." My heart was beating so hard I could barely speak. "I'm only a maiden. I'm not allowed to-"

"Are you talking back to me? Look at me!" His voice did not raise with the command, but the sudden delicious harshness was as dangerous as it was irresistible. My eyes swivelled obediently, the view that greeted me sending a spike through my centre to my clit. "I said, I want you. You did this to me, so it's only right you should attend to my *little* problem." Except there was nothing little about his problem.

I did that?

There was at least six inches of stiff cock rising out of the fist curled around its root and midsection, ending in a cut crown that was shiny with pre-cum and flushed a vivid purple.

I'm no virgin. I've seen my share of dicks, and learned to enjoy the bodies attached, but they had been mere boys.

Senator Sharpe was a man with a man's cock. All ten inches of it!

The sight of it made me forget we were right in the middle of the most exclusive club in New York, surrounded by some of the richest and most influential people in the world.

Sweeping my tongue across my dry lips, I reached out. Heat radiated off him, and I could practically feel his pulse pounding as I touched a finger to the place just beneath his broad crest. Jesus, he was hard, but also soft, like steel wrapped in warm silk. And hot, so fucking hot.

A good maiden should always attend to the members' needs.

"That's it, *Kora*..." That wasn't my name, not my legal name anyway, but the pained ecstasy in his tone, the sheer wanton restraint, had goosebumps rising all across my body and drew my gaze up to his. The heat in his eyes told me all. He wanted me. Wanted all of me to possess and dominate. And he could take me. He knew I was his, whether I would admit it or not.

Holding his gaze, I bowed my head, his heady flavour spilling over my taste buds as I curled my tongue around that thick crown and took him into my mouth. However, the senator's only response was to arch his brow, that granite jaw locked in a silent challenge.

I gladly accepted. Heart pounding, I mouthed the plush head, sucking and drinking up the heady salty goodness of his pre-cum.

Still, he gave no outward sign, but I could feel the tension amassing within him, the pressure building as his cock grew thicker, harder within my mouth, so I kicked things up a notch. I sank to my knees between his. Placing both my hands on his trouser clad thighs, the muscles beneath bunching at my touch, I pivoted so he could see himself bulging against the inside of my cheek and dragged my mouth down the right side of his shaft, down to where his hand still grasped it, offering himself to me. I teased my tongue around the whitening knuckles, then came slowly back up his left flank before taking him into my mouth.

There was movement on the very edge of my vision, and it gave me a perverse thrill to know that the people around were starting to take notice. I glimpsed them nudging and gesturing, shifting to get a better view. They were attempting to be subtle about it, but made little real effort to hide their interest.

I was beyond caring. I have always loved giving head. Loved the thrill of having so much power over people so much stronger than me and making them come undone. It was a potent mix, intoxicating. Swept along by the heat of the moment and drawn in the eroticism that the senator seemed to radiate, my only thought was on the task. I didn't care who saw, who watched. I wanted to beat this man, this titan. I wanted to shatter his control, break his willpower, and make him cum in my mouth.

I'd wanted to take him all in, but there was just too much of him. He was too big to deep throat- just the head seemed to fill my mouth to the brim- so I teased between going fast and slow, sucking him in as deep as I dared before pulling back.

"Oh, *fuck…*" His low, almost edgy groan was music to my ears and my neglected pussy pulsed and burned in wanton need as his fingers threaded through my hair, fisting and forcing me back down.

He held me there, his hips churning up, fucking my mouth with the savage intensity I had only ever fantasised about. Hot, salty tears burned my eyes. I couldn't breathe, he was going too deep, had me forced down so far my nose was nestled in the nest of dark curls, but I couldn't have cared less.

Then I felt the rush of victory as, with a ragged groan and a penetrating thrust that took him all the way into my throat, he came.

He came hard.

Unable to pull away with the Senator's white knuckled grip forcing me down, I sucked him greedily, drinking every hot creamy shot. I kept on sucking even after he had spilled everything he had to give, milking him for all he was worth.

"Mmm…" He purred, the hand falling from my hair to collar my throat. He forced me to abandon my new toy and pulled me up to look him in the eye. "That was very good." He was still hard but tucked himself back inside his chinos, his eyes dark and burning into mine with barely restrained lust. "But now it's time, Kora."

Chapter Five

The senator didn't offer any explanations as he led me, and I didn't ask.

Shame and embarrassment burned my cheeks. I could feel every eye in the lounge on me as we passed, but I didn't dare meet them. Not even when I glimpsed Demeter glowering at me, her eyes scorching trails across my back, down to where the large hand was moulding my buttocks. I was so getting fired for this.

Then he took me through the back door, into a small square foyer that housed a single elevator, the entrance to the underworld. It was a dark, unfurnished place with naked stone walls. Four life size sculptures etched from polished black marble stood sentry in each corner. They were impressive figures, taken straight out of the pages of Frank Miller's *300* and poised with swords raised and Hoplite shields bared. Behind their plumed Corinthian helmets, garnets had been set in the place of eyes and blazed in defiance. At the base of each, a plaque was set upon a plinth, stamped with one of four legends in gold print–Penthos, Curae, Nosoi and Geras.

The elevator door slid open as we approached, the bright interior throwing long shadows across the floor. I blinked, the light blinding. The Senator held me close and guided me through. Yet the closeness was almost as disabling as the brightness. Awareness shivered up my skin and just the sound of his breathing had me coming out in goosebumps.

If the foyer was small, then the elevator was practically claustrophobic. A tiny space barely large enough for one, with walls lined by plush red velvet. The only distinguishing feature was a brass control plate etched with the name *Charon* etched across the top and a row of buttons to reach the five floors above.

Under these was a scanner plate.

This was my first time going into the Underworld. It was the private area of the Olympus Club that only members and their personal attendants were permitted to enter. Unlike its namesake, which had been believed to be on the edge and beneath the world of ancient Greece, Olympus's Underworld took up the floors directly above the club.

Senator Sharp removed a gold coin from his pocket and pressed it to the scanner.

"Where are you taking me?" I asked when the car began to rise, my heart pounding in my breast.

"Somewhere private. I have a proposition for you, Kora." He didn't look at me, but I could feel him watching me all the same. It made me feel hot, made my sex slick and tits heavy.

"Yes? What's that? Sir." I licked my lips, my mouth dry.

"Patience," He dismissed, the hand on my back brushing up and down the curve of my spine through my silks. "*All good things to those who wait.*"

Up and down, up and down, getting lower and lower until his hand brushed under the folds of my uniform. I felt my legs start to tremble. Tingles shivered out from where skin touched skin, spiralling straight up to my poor, neglected clit.

I clamp my legs together, trapping his hand between them even as I rubbed my thighs together, desperate for some friction to quell the need raging down there.

"Open,"

I had never enjoyed being bossed around, but the quiet authority in his tone made it feel so right, even as my body screamed in protest. I obeyed, splaying my thighs as far as they would comfortably go. Then his fingers took over, his hand cupping my greedy sex.

"Already so wet?" His tongue slid around the shell of my ear as one of his digits slid through my creamy folds to circle my clit. "Want more?"

"Please…" My tone was breathy, desperate and pleading. I couldn't stop myself from fisting his top and clinging to him for dear life as my legs almost gave way, the spike of pleasure from the contact going from my core to my fingertips.

"Please?" the senator parroted, pressing down on my little bundle of nerves before drawing the finger back.

I bit back my protest, along with half a dozen sarcastic retorts. "Please… Sir-ohh!" As he pushed his thick finger into me, my mouth fell open in a low moan and his mouth crushed against mine.

It was not a soft kiss. It was hungry and violent. His mouth claimed mine, the silky softness of his tongue mirroring the strokes of his finger, delving inside me with an expertise that had my core tightening. It was too much. I couldn't stand it. Despite myself, my hips rolled, my blood pumping fast and hot as the world spun around us and–

He pulled away as the elevator chimed, his finger slipping out of my heat and leaving me feeling woefully empty. Breathing hard, I leaned up on my tiptoes to follow, but the Senator just stepped around me, through the opening doors into…

Oh my god! It's Hades's Palace…

I'd thought it was just a joke. A gag to play on the F.N.G.s, (The *Fucking New Gods)*, but there it was.

The word was, it was a premium extra exclusive add on that was available to only one member of the Olympus Club. None of the staff; maidens or even the attendants, knew which member it was, so most of them thought it was a myth, like most of the other stories they'd heard about The Underworld.

I couldn't believe it. Hade's Palace, the secret, exclusive penthouse/ fuck pad was real!

Stepping out of the elevator, I seemed to move from the light into the nightscape of New York City. Though no lights were on inside, the radiance of the city, and the full moon above, glowed through the tall windows and balcony's French doors, giving it an almost starlit twilight.

It was too dark for me to make out much furniture, but I could tell what there was, was carved from polished black stone, as were the floor tiles and architecture. Everything was stone, except for the four-poster bed. A king-size, of course, fitted with raven silk sheets and piled high with what could only have been the biggest, softest pillows I have ever seen.

I wasn't sure where to look, so instead I focused on the one familiar fixture of the room.

Senator Sharpe stood staring out across the city with his arms behind his back, like an emperor looking out across his domain. Or a god.

I approached him cautiously, suddenly so very aware of how large he was as his impressive build was framed alongside the spear of the Empire State Building.

"Do you ever take the time to just look at it?" he asked, still not looking at me.

"Umm… No,"

"You should. It is a beautiful city by moonlight," he sighed. "I love this view. It almost makes the mercenary rates the management charge for this little place worth it."

"Well, I never have time to just stop and look."

"Shame."

"I have commitments, loans- student loans!" I quickly clarify, for some reason overcome by a need to explain, to make him understand. "And my mother's medical treatments-
"

"I know. Second stage lung and throat cancer. Two different strains of cancer forming simultaneously is a very unfortunate coincidence." He pivoted to face me, and I felt my breath catch at the raw intensity in his eyes. "And costly."

I didn't say anything. I didn't even ask how he knew about my mom. Given the secretive nature of the Olympus Club, my contract included not just numerous nondisclosure agreements, but a legal agreement, stating my consent to an unspecified number of background checks a year. Of course, the details of such checks were supposed to be confidential, but it wasn't hard for me to imagine some of the more influential members being given brief peeks.

"What would you say if I told you your mother could be receiving a consultation from the best oncologist in the country? All expenses and treatment fully covered and free of charge."

"I'd tell you to stay on your meds. Goodnight." I wheel away, tears burning in the corner of my eyes as the world spun. How dare he. No one uses my mother like that, no one!

"I can make it happen." He says after me. "This time tomorrow, she can be on a private jet. A consultation with Dr Leo Getts scheduled for first thing the day after tomorrow."

I didn't look back, not until I was in front of the elevator, my finger poised over the call button.

I wanted to, but I just couldn't bring myself to push.

He was shitting me. He had to be. It was just too good to be true. That sort of treatment, hell, just an hour's consultation would cost an arm and a leg, never mind the expense of crossing the country, and lodging, private nursing staff…

But what if he was on the level?

A single tear slid down my check as I turned back to face the senator, only to find him towering over me. I hadn't even heard him coming after me.

I bite back my surprised gasp. "Wh-what would I have to do?"

"Be my attendant." His arms cage me as he flattens both hands on the elevator, bracing himself as he bends forward, closing the gap so we were nose to nose, his eyes dark and hot.

"You're joking?"

He had to be. While attendants continued to receive the basic salary, the additional costs of their exclusivity and *services* were covered by their '*Masters*'. The price, and terms, were negotiated between the two parties, and could sometimes even go so far as positions in real world jobs. But what he was offering went beyond generous.

"Never."

He more growled than said the word, and our closeness was so intoxicating I could practically feel it vibrating through me. "You're the only maiden I can trust. *They* haven't had their claws in you yet, and they never will, if I claim you tonight. I need you, *Kora*."

His proximity and the raw intensity in his tone made it impossible for me to look him in the eye. "But you can't... I mean, maidens need a minimum of two years' service before they can be considered for an attendant. I've only been here a month..."

I was shaking. Need and desperation had my blood running hot and thick through my veins.

He chuckled. "Yes, I know. Recommended by the Honourable Justice Lovejoy, the father of a university friend who you dormed with for a few months until you moved in with a local boyfriend. You remained friends with her but broke up with him after you found him in bed with his boyfriend."

The remark grounded me slightly, giving me a muchneeded surge of anger that helped get a momentary grip of myself and wheel away from him to face the comforting cool steel front of the elevator. "You've done your homework. Do *they* have my bra size in their background checks, too?"

"Anything's obtainable, Kora, even you." He whispered in my ear, before curving over me to sweep his tongue around the shell, his hands enfolding my waist. "And you never wear a bra."

Wound up tight in a knot of tension, I practically jumped out of my skin when, as if to prove his point, he cupped my right breast through my robe.

I won't lie, I've always had very nice tits, well rounded and perhaps a bit more generously proportioned than most woman with my build, but with absolutely no sag, and topped by dusky nipples that my lovers seemed to just love sucking.

For all my bountiful offering however, his hand completely covered my cleavage and I couldn't help my whimper when he plumped my breast.

"W-what if I refuse?" Almost beyond speech, I was panting with the words. *Touching… He's touching my… he shouldn't… I must – oh God…*

"You won't." He purred, rolling one of my tender nipples between his thumb and finger, their roughness exciting my skin through my robe.

"N-n-noo-oh!"

His musky scent was everywhere, all around me, fogging my brain and invading my thoughts. Damn, he smelt so good.

"No, you want what I'm offering." He took my left hand in his and guided it down to the crotch of his trousers. My core tightened and throbbed at the feeling of his renewed hard-on straining against the fabric. "It's all yours for the taking. All you have to do is say *yes…*"

Then he spun me around to face him and took my mouth before I could form a word.

It was all aggression and heat. Not so much a kiss as a claiming. I whimpered as his tongue found mine, stroking me with lush coaxing licks that had me melting against him as my damn needy pussy purred with delight. In the next instant, his arms were around me, his hands curling around my waist, grabbing my butt and crushing me against the wall of hard virile male, making me feel how *hard* he was.

I needed to be strong. This was my chance. I had to stop, had to pull away or slap him or knee him, or, or just, something…

Anything…

Anything but grab his hair and return the kiss, my spine curling up so he could feel my cleavage push against him, one leg sliding up his, coiling round his-

Oh God. No, no! I had to push him away. Push him away now before it was too late.

But I couldn't. It was all too much for me. He was too much for me.

My pussy was hot, my breasts heavy and tender with nipples that just ached for attention, and all I could think about was that this was Senator Richard Sharp. The Senator Richard Sharp. The man I had been crushing on since I saw his first ever televised political debate, and he was kissing me.

No, he wasn't kissing me. His mouth was basically fucking mine, and I loved it.

Somewhere in a distant, still coherent corner of my mind, I could feel him guiding me backward. I didn't resist. Rather, I practically climbed up on him, my legs coiling around his waist, hips gyrating against the bulge of his dick as he took me deeper into the room, until he had me pinned against one of the massive fourposter beams.

My whole body shivered deliciously at the feeling of being cornered by this big alpha male, overwhelmed by the feeling of his massive cock sliding along my slit through our mesh of clothes. It was the most divine torture. The barrier teased me by preventing any real depth, while the mix of textures rubbing over my tender tissues drove me wild. God, he felt so good. So big. So-it wasn't enough.

I needed more of him.

"Mmm… say it, Kora." The senator growled, pulling back just enough to break the kiss, before he buried his face in the crook of my neck.

"I shouldn't." He sucked hard on my pulse spot, making me gasp as desire shot through me. "I mustn't… please!"

"Please what?" he growled again, setting me down on legs that shook like jelly as he nipped trails of fire.

I whimpered, shaking my head, my body hot and thrumming like a taught violin string.

Oh, God… Oh God! This can't be happening. This can't be-

"Say it!" His hands encircled my wrists, raising them up above my head before pressing them to the timber post.

"Yes!" I couldn't stop the flood. His words, the way he held me, pinned me to his bed and devoured my very being. It was too much. "Yes. I want more. You can have me however you want. I'm all yours. Just give me more."

Chapter Six

"Good girl," he praised, and gave my ear lobe a long suck, before drawing back. "Now, don't move."

The command sent a shiver through me, its gruff, nononsense tone echoing the voice from my fantasises. I obeyed.

His face impassive, the Senator collared both of my wrists in one of his hands, before reaching for something out of my line of sight. Heat rushed through me when he raised what it was up for me to see.

Dangling between his thumb and forefinger was a red silk scarf.

Oh God, where did that come from?

"Don't move," he repeated, and the thrill it gave me to hear that lush commanding tone had me biting my lip in anticipation.

It wasn't just a command. This was a test. He was daring me, baiting me to test the boundaries of this new role.

I was his attendant now. I must obey his every command immediately and without hesitation, or I'll be punished.

And in return, he'll take care of all of mom's medical bills.

He swept the scarf around my wrists once, tied off, then repeated the tie around the bed post. It wasn't anything as secure as handcuffs, but the silk was much kinder to my skin and a testing tug from the senator proved I wouldn't be getting away any time soon.

He took a moment to admire his handiwork.

"Mmm… Very good, Kora," he purred. Awareness rippled up my spine, and I felt my skin rise with goosebumps as he trailed a finger down the underside of my right arm. "You're mine now. You're going to have to do everything I say."

I nodded, my heart racing as his finger trailed down my silks to the swell of my breasts, my nipples standing unashamedly against the fabric.

"I do mean *everything*, Kora."

"Yes, Master-oh!" I couldn't help my kittenish gasp when he cupped the swell of my left breast and thumbed the tip. "Mmm… Give it to me, please… do anything you want to me. I'm yours."

"Yes, you are." he breathed, squeezing my cleavage through my garment, the warmth of his touch bleeding through the silk to lick my skin. "But you have to earn your place as my attendant."

"Yes, make me earn it." It was the sweetest torture. My body hummed with tension and the need to move, to arch and offer myself to him, to force his hand to where I needed it, was almost overwhelming. Damnit, I had to resist.

Don't move. Just don't move, you can do this, you can…

"You'll beg for it." His eyes flashed at the promise.

Despite my resolve to obey, when his thumb and finger closed around my nipple and twisted it, it was all too much.

"Yes!" My head rolled, the moan flowing from me in painful ecstasy as my spine curled.

Even his softest touch sent fire and electricity through my core.

"Kora." His tone was clipped, disapproving. "I told you, don't move. I see I'm going to have to teach you obedience."

"I-I'm sorry Master. It won't happen again."

"I know." The Senator gave my nipple another twist, this time a little harder. Not enough to hurt, but enough for me to know. Then his hand was moving again, fingers brushing over the swells of my bosom, beneath the folds of silk to the bounty of naked skin, and down. Down the valley of my breasts. Down the flat-plain of my belly. And down to the string of well-sodden fabric that was all that covered my throbbing sex.

"I've been a bad girl. Very, very bad, teach me to be good. I'll do any… anythi- oh God!"

He cupped my pussy through my panties, his middle finger sliding through the outline of my swollen folds to press down on my clit. I was so sensitive that just that brief contact set off supernovas behind my eyes.

I couldn't take it. I had to touch him. I needed to grab him, feel the muscles rippling under his skin and lust pounding in his chest. I couldn't bear it, except the scarf held me fast and wouldn't loosen, no matter how much I twisted and tugged against it. All I could do was claw desperately at the timber as he traced the line of my sex through my panties with a maddening softness that made my skin tingle and feel too tight.

"You're soaked. What am I going to do with you, Kora? You must really be gagging for it.".

"Yes, I—I need it Master. Give it to me, I want it, I want it." My hips rocked into his touch, desperate to steer his attentions back towards my little bundle of nerves. Fuck, I didn't care if I sounded like a wanton slut. I didn't care at all.

He took me and made me forget my inhibitions.

With a look, he'd made me forget all my determination not to fall into such a role. A word from him had reduced me to a steaming mess of sexual frustration. And just a touch had me on the verge of losing my mind. Fuck, I was so close, just a little more. That's all I needed. Just a little more and I would cum all over his fingers.

"Good girl, you're being much more honest now. But still so disobedient," he chuckled, lowering his head until we were almost nose to nose. "It wouldn't be a punishment if I just gave you what you wanted now, would it?" Hooking his finger under my underwear, he quickly pulled it aside.

I moaned, shaking my head even as I strained to reach him, offering my lips to him in open invitation. "N-no…"

It's hard to say whether I was agreeing with him or protesting.

Either way, I watched wide-eyed as the senator made a show of bringing his wet and shiny finger up to his lips and sucked it clean. "Mmm… you're delicious."

I lost all control at that. My core clamped down in wanton spasms while my hips bucked and my body started to tremble. I was so tight with sexual tension, one good pluck would have me twanging like a guitar string. "Oh God, you're such a tease."

"Yes, and you love it."

"I love it." I could practically feel his lips brushing over mine, so close, just one more inch.

His hand cupped the nape of my neck, then his mouth was back on mine, swallowing my moan as his finger pushed inside me.

He started slowly, with just that one *thick* finger hooked forward to stroke the place behind my clit, the broad pad deliciously rough against my delicate tissues. It stirred me into a frenzy as he pushed the digit back and forth, somehow managing to keep perfect rhythm with his tongue so the dual stimulation worked to maximum effect.

Whoever said men couldn't multitask had obviously never been finger banged by Senator Richard Sharpe. "Remember. Don't. Move," he growled against my mouth in that hot authoritative tone, emphasising each word as a second finger pushed into me and sent me spiralling.

"I... I can't! I- oh fuck- I'm cumming!" I couldn't resist it. My orgasm washed over me like a wave on the rocks and had me arching in his arms, straining against my bonds in violent, bucking tremors of ecstasy.

"Oh? You bad girl," he chided, dragging kisses along my jaw and down my neck. "You know you're going to have to be punished for this?"

I couldn't think. My world was shattering as I rode his fingers, the waves rushing over me, growing more powerful. Then his thumb pressed into my clit and I went wild. "Oh fuck! Yes! I'm such a bad girl... mmm... punish me... Master!"

"Oh... I will, later, but for now..." The hand on my neck moved down to the base of my spine, half supporting me and half pulling me against him as he bent down, his lips catching my right nipple and sucking.

His thumb rolled over my clit while he pushed his fingers in and out, in and out, working me into a frenzy. Helpless to resist, all I could do was writhe, throwing my head from side to side, clawing the post as heat and ecstasy radiated through from my core, out to my fingers and toes.

He pulled his mouth away, his eyes dark and burning up at me as he tongued my nipple through my silks and bore down on my clit with his thumb. "You just keep cumming, and so easily, you really have been gagging for it, haven't you, Kora?"

I was melting in his arms, the very fibre of my being turning to liquid and running down my thighs as my hips pumped greedily onto his fingers and thumb, sensation amassing in my core. "It's not... not my fau-oh fuck! I can't help it, you just..."

He licked his way back up my neck, his breathing quick and hungry with lust. "What do I do to you? Go on, say it Kora."

"You just keep making me cum!"

"Mmm… Good girl, now look into my eyes…" I obeyed.

I would always obey. No matter what he wanted, I was his. He could have anything. For him, I would do anything.

"Cum for me, Kora, cum all over my fingers!" His words were hot against my lips and the intensity in his kiss as he took my lips made my mind go blank.

"Please… no more… I can't take it anymore…" I panted when my brain started working again, and the blood stopped roaring in my ears.

He'd made me cum so hard, every muscle in my body felt like jelly and I didn't have the strength to stand. If it wasn't for his arm around me, I think I might very well have collapsed.

"Oh, my dear, sweet, innocent little Kora, I'll never stop." The dark promise in his tone sent renewed shivers through me, but then his fingers slipped from my heat and I was left feeling empty, and somehow even hornier as he brought the fingers to his mouth and licked them clean. "God, you just keep cumming, but you're still so tight. This is going to be better than I thought."

Somewhere very, very deep down and far away, a mousy voice in my head asked what he meant, but I was too far gone to care.

He lowered me to the floor, so I sat propped against the bed, the silk tie sliding down the polished beam with me. When he straightened, I found myself staring at his covered cock. Somehow, even confined by his chinos, it looked larger than before, and was clearly visible as a massive bulge straining against the length of his right thigh.

I licked my lips hungrily and, leaning forward, mouthed him through his trouser leg. When I traced the curve of his crown with my tongue, he made a strangled sound in the back of his throat. "That's it. Such a dirty girl…"

I nodded, much too eagerly. "Yes, I'm a dirty girl, Master. Your attendant. Let me serve you. I need it… I can't wait any longer…"

"But you will," he ordered, his lips pressed firmly together as he looked down at me, like a teacher preparing to punish a disobedient student. "You're mine now, Kora, my attendant, my little toy."

I swallowed, the very thought of it making me bite my lower lip in anticipation. "And I have to do everything you say."

"Yes."

The chinos were undone with a quick movement of his hands and his renewed erection surged upward to stand tall before my eyes, its length thickly veined, the head slick and flushed with colour. With one hand, he angled his dick down to point at my mouth. "So, attend to me." I didn't need to be told twice.

I sucked him in greedily, taking him in as deep as I could, moaning as his salty goodness spilled over my tongue. His cock felt even more amazing in my mouth the second time around, and the way he watched me going down on him, with those eyes dark with lust, only made it that much hotter. I returned the gaze hotly as I pulled back to his crest, then pushed forward again, watching with rapt attention as he pulled his top over his head to reveal a glorious bounty of male perfection.

I drank him in and wanted nothing more than to reach out and run my nails down that broad chest of defined muscle, his light dusting of black hair seeming only to add to his appeal. Strange, I'd never really found chest hair to be attractive, but on him, it only added to his allure. It made him look wild and untamed, and contrasted so vividly with the image of control he portrayed on the pages of GQ.

He was everything I'd ever imagined and so much more.

Spurred on by his little strip tease, I sucked harder, my cheeks hollowing as I drew him in. There were no fancy tricks this time. I just went all out and worshiped his dick with my mouth.

Then his hand slid through my hair, fisting and twisting, holding me still as his hips started rolling.

"Yeah… let your master fuck your mouth," the Senator groaned in a guttural rasp that sent a shiver straight down to the still heat between my legs. "Get me nice and wet for your tight little cunt."

His hips churned, the circles growing larger, forcing me to take him deep, deeper than I'd ever taken a man before.

This was new territory for me. Whenever I'd given head before, I'd always been the one in charge. It was all part of the thrill, but the senator somehow took that control away. Now he had the power, and I gave in to his commands like a good attendant.

And I loved it.

He fucked my mouth hard, but with perfect control, his pace unwavering. I could feel him passing through the gate of my throat, the crown pulsing and swelling, and it made me crazy with need, desperate to feel him between my legs, filling me up-

He pulled back, withdrawing completely from my mouth. Then his arms were around me and he'd pulled me back to my feet, into a deep lush kiss that had me melting all over again. This was the first time anyone had ever kissed me straight after I'd sucked them, and the idea that he must be able to taste himself was so kinky, I almost came.

And while his mouth took mine, his hands brushed up my arms to where I was manacled to the bedpost. Much to my embarrassment, the tie came undone with a quick tug. However, I had no time to enjoy my freedom, as no sooner had the silk come away than he was spinning me around, pushing me up against the post.

I clung to it gratefully, my legs still a bit too shaky. Smooth and polished to a high shine, the timber felt deliciously cool against my overheated skin. "M-Master, please!"

"Patience, Kora. You really need to learn patience if you want to be my attendant." His low promise had me tingling all over, as did the way his hands slid down my back and under my silks to the string of my panties.

The delicate fabric snapped like dental floss under his huge hands. Then he hiked my silks up and over my butt and nudged my legs open further with his knees.

I obeyed and leant forward more, raising my ass in the air. I should have been embarrassed, knowing he could see *me,* all of me, my most private and personal places, but I wanted him to see.

"Ahh!" I gasped as he gave my backside a swat.

It hurt a little, but then the sting dissolved into hot pleasure and I couldn't resist giving a quick, inviting wiggle. Fuck, what was wrong with me? I'd never been into spanking before. Hell, I was acting like a complete slut, and I didn't care. The Senator was everything my dreams and fantasies had promised, and I just knew he was going to be so much more before he was finished with me.

"Like that, Kora?" the Senator asked, slowly rubbing the hot spot his hand had left across my right cheek, massaging the heat into my skin. "Want more?"

Somewhere, there was the soft sound of a drawer opening and closing. Then a packet tearing. But I was too consumed by the wantonness rippling through me to give it much thought. It just felt so good, I just couldn't stand it. "Yes!"

He withdrew his hand, letting the warmth bleed away. "Yes?"

I could feel him. Feel it. Feel its heat licking up my folds before its blunt tip pressed into my little bundle of nerves and fireworks sparked behind my eyes. I edged back, raising my hips to try to slide onto him, only for him to pull back.

For a long moment, there was nothing. It was as if time held its breath for us and the sudden solitude of the moment made my heart thunder in my ears. And I was too scared to move, to breathe, in case all this shattered around me and revealed itself as nothing but just another incredible dream.

Then his mouth was by my ear, his voice a rumble that had my pussy clenching.

"Yes what?"

"Master!" I wailed, pleading. He'd driven me mad, and I was just too horny to care. In all my life, nothing had ever gotten me this worked up. I needed him inside me. Needed to feel his hardness filling me up. "Please, Master… my cunt's so wet for you… give it to me… please, give it to me-oh oh God, oh fuck-"

There was pleasure, a sudden rush of sensation that spiralled out to my fingers and toes, but there was also pain. First there was a potent and very fiery bite, then a deep satisfying burn that made me ache for more as he slid into me, the wide crest parting my folds, stretching my delicate tissues and spreading me open, then pushing inexorably into my heat.

"Look at me, Kora."

I threw a desperate look back at him, my mouth dropping open in a long, voiceless cry as he filled me, that first thrust splitting me open and driving into my core. Fuck, I could barely breathe through the feeling. None of my previous lovers had prepared me for this. He was just too much.

"Mmm… you pull that sexy face when you're getting fucked and your pussy's so snug," he purred, grinning down at me as he continued pressing forward, with just the perfect amount of force, until he seemed to have gone as deep as he could go. "Just like fucking a virgin."

Heat flushed through my body, and I wanted to beg him not to say such dirty things, but I couldn't get the words out. Then one of his hands was cupping my nape and urged me down until I was bent at the waist, opening me up as he withdrew.

He drew back slowly, leaving me with a growing feeling of emptiness as he pulled out, until just the head remained inside me. Then he pressed in again, his hips snapping forward, and my head rolled back in agonising bliss. "So-so big… I can't… too-too much…" I panted, my nails scouring the timber of the frame. This new angle had him stimulating a whole load of new nerves I had never felt before and he was so deep inside me, I could feel him throbbing through the rubber.

"You can, Kora. And you will," he promised, his dark and cultured voice growing ragged with passion. He repeated the move again, sliding out, then thrusting back into me, then again, and again, building to a rhythm as his other hand on my hip began pulling me back to meet him.

Each time, he went a little deeper. Working inch after inch inside me, until I felt like I was going to burst and was on the verge of going out of my mind.

My body, however, only craved more and pressed back to meet him, my greedy sex convulsing and throbbing, wrapping around him and sucking him in. "M-Master!"

The Senator chuckled at my plea, the sound so very gruff and primal, his hips slapping wetly against my butt as he made me take him even deeper. "Mmm… you feel so good, Kora, your pussy was made for my dick," he declared, like a captain claiming a newly discovered land.

"Y-y-yes, that's your pussy… oh my god, yes! My little pussy is all yours, Master. Oh fuck, it's yours… use me… make me take my master's cock… make me take it… take it… take itoh!"

The mini orgasm swept through me hard and fast when he finally made me take him all and his wide crest struck *that* place deep inside me. He didn't let me rest or come down from the high, but fucked me through my release, circling his hips in tight little rolls as my walls clamped down around him and refused to let go.

I absorbed everything he had to give me, savouring every thick and gloriously hard inch of him, and craved more. Then his arms were around me, cradling me, drawing me back against him and driving me down onto his cock.

He was in complete control, my master in name and body, and I'd never dreamed someone, anyone, could dominate me so completely. I let him take me, my hands falling to my sides, fisting and balling against the pleasure while my head rolled back onto his shoulder as each curl of his hips drove me up onto my tiptoes.

"Oh, God… oh God, you-you're going to make me cum again…"

I could feel *it* building, a hot throbbing knot in my centre and I pushed down, grinding against his cock, suddenly just needing to reach that peak. "Master, I'm gonna cum all over your dick… please… plea-!"

"You're gorgeous, Kora," he husked in my ear, his hands moving over me, touching and feeling, fanning the flames of my desire. Gathering up my silks, he dragged the garment from me and cast it aside before one of his hands came up to cup my left breast, plumping it while his thumb teased over my hard nipple. "Now… touch yourself."

"Master?" I gasped, breathless and close, so close that my legs were shaking with it. I was on the edge. I just needed a little more.

"I want you to make yourself cum, Kora."

"Master, please, I don't… I can't… it's embarrassing…" I pleaded, shaking my head even as his free hand took mine, and put it over the throbbing heat at my centre.

"Cum," he ordered, and I couldn't resist. There was something so illicit and sexy about the feeling of being skin to skin with the senator. It made me feel wild and desperate and I rubbed my clit, fast and hard, three fingers thrumming over the little bud as he continued driving in me from behind.

"That's it, cum for me, Kora, cum for your master."

The dual cocktail of pleasures ignited a firework in my brain, and I stilled as the pleasure-shock of it washed over me, shaking me to my core in a delicious whiteout of sensation. And when I came down from the heights, I found myself stretched out across the bed with Senator Richard standing over me.

Breathing hard, my whole being a mass of tingling aftershocks, I could only watch in awe as he loomed over me. He looked so huge and great, so much more than flesh and bone. Like a god.

He was my Hades.

I'd played the role of a goddess, bound and chained for the service of mortals. He'd freed me. He'd freed me, unchained me and taken me to the underworld, his dark realm where he'd brought out all my forbidden and secret desires. Now I was his.

His attendant. His servant.

His Kora.

He didn't say a word. Just pushed his trousers down his long legs. I didn't know when he'd removed his shoes and socks, and I didn't care. I just knew what he wanted and obediently opened myself to him, my eyes riveted to his cruelly handsome face as he came for me, crawling up the bed until he was between my legs

"Mmm… such a sweet little cunt," he purred, bowing his head down to inhale the scent of my sex. "I've wanted to eat this pussy since I first set eyes on you, Kora."

The feeling of his breath wafting over my sex sent a hot shiver of desire straight through me. "Master, I-"

He dragged his tongue up my folds, making my hips jump and I moaned a long sweet sound, before his mouth descended on my swollen and tender clit. He sucked with an intensity that had me clawing at the sheets, my body instinctively twisting away, desperate to escape the too-fierce pleasure of his mouth.

"Stay still," he growled, the low thrum of his words vibrating through the place our bodies joined and straight to my core.

"Oh, God!" My head rolled as his hands wound around my legs, cupped my ass, and pulled me against his mouth. "Master… please… put your dick back in… I need it… plea-oh! Oh, my god!"

He thrust his tongue inside me, deep inside me, and lashed my inner walls with twirling swirls that quickly sent me spiralling.

I was going to cum again.

I couldn't stop it. The multiple orgasms he'd already lavished upon me had left me raw and sensitive, too sensitive. And the image of his eyes, dark and smouldering, watching me from between my legs was just too much. I couldn't stand it. I couldn't-

I couldn't fucking believe it.

I wanted to scream and beat the bed as he reared back, leaving me hanging on the edge. "N-no! Don't… stop…"

Instead, he caged me with his body, that sinful mouth pressing to mine as the full weight of his desire settled against me. He kissed me for a long moment, his wily tongue resuming its sinful dance, working me into a breathless frenzy before he pulled back just enough to drink in the sight of me stretched out beneath him.

What a sight I must have looked.

When he touched my mask, I didn't resist. Nor did I try to stop him when he pulled it from me, but nor could I meet his eyes. I'd seen the pictures on social media and google. I knew the sort of woman Senator Richard Sharp liked. I didn't match up.

He liked blonde super models with delicate features and plenty of ass. Not raven-haired, doe eyed bookworms that made Hermione Granger look like Lara Croft.

I was a realist. I knew the score, but even so, I couldn't bear to see his look of disappointment.

"Look at me, Kora." Cupping my chin, he angled my head to look up at him. My mouth was dry by the time I met his eyes, their depths almost black with lust. There was no disappointment there. No rejection. Just want. "You're so beautiful. Let no one tell you any different."

Still looking deep into my eyes, he thrust forward.

I gasped a voiceless cry, my back arching at the feeling of him surging inside me, filling me and pushing me back into the sudden rush of a mini-orgasm. It swept through me hard and fast and I was still shaking as he began rolling his hips, pulling back, then thrusting home. It wasn't fast, but nor was it slow. It was firm and steady, and pushed the sensations coursing through me on and on.

I was enslaved by the vision of him above me, his arms braced on either side of me, his muscles moving beneath his skin, bunching and tensing and powering the relentless draw and thrust of his hips. I watched him in awe, unable to tear my eyes from the sight of his dick sliding in and out of my sex, the condom stretched tight and shiny with my creamy desire.

He was a work of art. A machine built with the sole function of fucking me into oblivion.

"Mmm… no one's ever fucked you like I do, have they, Kora?"

"No… not like you… no one… oh my god…" My hips churned as I tried to match him, my feet slipping and sliding on the silken sheets as I fucked him back, until he seized both my legs and raised them up onto his shoulders, opening me up completely I could feel him reaching my stomach. "Oh my god… feels so good… so fucking good and deep… I'm all yours Master, your little slut… I'm your good, little, slutty attendant!"

"Yes, you are Kora. Mine. All mine." He reinforced his ownership with each deep thrust, the delicious friction of it igniting a fire in my head that was melting my mind.

"I just want to be yours. Your good little toy… use my body to make your dick cum… I'm just here to please you… take me however you want… I'm yours-oh fuck-I'm all yours!"

And I was. I was his toy, ready and willing to do whatever he wanted, whenever he wanted me.

"Oh, fuck-oh fuck- Master," Orgasm after orgasm began pouring through me, coming on so fast and hard, I could barely tell where one ended and the next began. "It's too-too much… I can't, can't stop cumming!"

"Yeah! That's it, Kora," the senator groaned, his head dipping down to nip and suck at my tingling nipples. "Keep cumming for me, baby, milk my dick with your greedy little cunt."

The Senator was getting close too. I could feel it in the way his once measured thrusts quickened, as if he was racing to get me off just one more time.

So I bared down on him, fighting the terminus of my ceaseless orgasms to wrap my inner walls around him, wanting nothing so much as I did at that moment to make him blow. I wanted to see the pleasure twist him. I wanted to feel all his passion and desire flow through me. I wanted to know that I'd done that to him, reduced the most powerful man in New York City to a sweaty, sated mess. I wanted-

"Oh fuck, here I come!" he rasped, gritting his teeth, momentarily trying to fight the stirring in his balls as he pulled out of me. Without my Master inside me, I felt cold and empty, but then he was on top of me and I forgot all of that. The Senator tore the condom off before fisting himself as he angled the red throbbing crown to me. "Open."

I did as I was ordered. And like the Persephone of ancient times, who ate the apple seeds offered by Hades and was so bound to the underworld for all eternity, I leaned up, took him in and drank down everything he had to give me.

He came hard, the hot salty build up filling up my mouth and running down my chin as I sucked him through it, his low rasping grunts and moans music to my ears. I swallowed it all greedily, then licked him clean, swirling my tongue around his throbbing crest, then up and down his shaft. I didn't miss a drop, like the good little attendant I was.

Only when I was certain he was clean did I pull off and promptly collapsed back into the warm embrace of the wonderfully cool silk sheets.

I couldn't remember the last time I'd felt so tired.

My eyes felt so heavy, and the world grew hazy as the aftermath of the most amazing sex of my life settled over me. I needed to sleep, just for a few hours.

"Kora."

My eyes snapped open, suddenly wide awake. "Master?"

He grinned down at me, one of his massive hands coming down to stroke my hair as his dick stood to attention an inch from my nose. "Patience, Kora, the night's still young, and I have a lot to teach you about serving the Senator…"

One *Night*

Chapter One

It was maddening. Infuriating. How could someone so drop dead sexy be so oblivious?

Exasperated, Faye forced herself to look away, searching for something, anything, to distract her from the oh-so-delectable source of her frustrations. Seated at her desk as they were, the adjacent window would serve her needs perfectly, but she had to drag her eyes up to it under the guise of dropping her pen and running a hand through her hair.

It was only seven, but the sky was dark, and the moon was full, shining high above, its radiance illuminating the long skeletal fingers of the only tree in her student shared accommodation's back garden. She could remember planting a very similar tree in her parent's garden on a bright summer's day when she was just a little kid in playschool. Every year, on the anniversary of that planting, *he* would come round to her parent's house and they'd play around it until they got so tired, they couldn't move and would stretch out and lie in the shade.

The memory made her heart hurt with longing.

Damn it. Why did she ever agree to this? It was New Year's Eve and such a beautiful evening. She could have been doing anything. Washing her hair. Shopping online. Browsing the Amazon indie selection for some new, struggling, and overlooked author's tall, dark, and surly Book Boyfriend to go with the B.O.B hiding away in her bedside drawer. Instead, she was stuck in her bedroom, all alone, with…him.

With all the subtlety her frazzled neurons could muster, she pivoted ever so slightly, drawn inexplicably, and fixed her gaze on Terry.

The image of him reclining in his chair, fingering through the pages of a textbook, his tight-fitting white shirt and tan chinos teasing at the broad, chiselled physique hiding just beneath the surface, set the butterflies in her stomach to flight. His face, those cheekbones and marble jaw, rough with a neatly trimmed goatee that was in such contrast to his shoulder-length mane of near-black hair that was always ruffled and just that bit too long; and begged for her to run her fingers through. And those eyes. Those dark chocolate eyes, piercing and *knowing*, as if he could see through her with a look and know all her secrets and make her feel like a little girl all over again.

He was a feast to behold, the very symbol of power and masculinity. Her saviour. Her protector. Her knight in shining armour. And still as completely and utterly clueless as the day they'd first met, back when they were just little kids, standing alone on the outskirts of the playground on the first day of school.

They'd been the very poster children for the boy and girl next door; if a couple of streets apart. Friends for longer than forever. They'd walked to school together. He'd protected her from the bullies when they teased her about her glasses. She'd tended to his cuts and bruises when he fell. He pushed her to try new things. She snuck looks at him when he wasn't looking.

Wherever he led, she'd follow. And she'd cried like a baby for three days after he began to notice girls. Or rather, other girls. Blondes. Brunettes. Redheads. Actresses. Models. Pornstars. Cheerleaders. Girls with big tits, small tits, long legs, big butts. Just about every type of girl but her.

She'd done everything she could think of to try and get him to notice her. Cut her hair. Changed her fashion choices. Showed some skin. Even swapped her glasses for contacts. That at least had provoked something in him, as a few weeks later he'd commented that he preferred her with glasses. Not exactly the reaction she'd been hoping for, and she'd never felt more self-conscious than when she was fishing in her bag for her emergency spectacles five minutes later.

Finally, she'd done the unthinkable. To try and make Terry jealous, she'd started dating Harry Toogood. Never was anyone so aptly named.

Just the thought of him sent a shudder down her spine.

Faye had not been overly attracted to Harry. Though good-looking, he was also a rich toff whose sizeable ego made it a wonder there was room for anyone else in his immediate vicinity. But he was one of *those* boys. So, when he asked her out one Friday as they were coming out of class, with Terry just three steps behind, she saw her chance. She accepted, just loud enough for

Terry to overhear while he was chatting animatedly with Neve Gibson.

From the start, the date had been a disaster, but it had ended in a nightmare. She couldn't remember it clearly. It was more than just a group of hazy thoughts, jumbled and chaotic, with no sense of time.

She'd woken up in A&E the next afternoon. The duty nurse had been very kind and assured her she'd be fine with time. No lasting damage. What the fuck did she know?

The same, however, couldn't be said for Harry after Terry had learned what happened.

He'd been the first to come to visit her, he'd walked her home, and after that he'd always been by her side, even waiting until she'd got her university acceptance letter before making his applications. That is, until *she* came along.

"Hey, Faye, hello? You okay over there?"

She nearly jumped out of her skin at his question and looked up to find him watching her from behind his book, his brow furrowed with concern. Embarrassed at having been caught daydreaming, she felt her face burn scarlet and hurriedly replied in a manner that she could only pray sounded nonchalant. "Y-yeah I'm fi-fine! I'm fine. Just… thinking. Yeah, I'm thinking." She gave him a broad smile.

Terry laid his book down on the desk, clearly not believing a word of it. "Faye..." he warned, trying to look stern, but the edge to his voice just sent a rush of heat straight down to the pit of her belly.

Resigned to her fate, she sighed and dropped her gaze back down to her own textbook. He was right, of course. Her scholarship depended on her keeping her grades up. Her last report, however, had shown her GPA on a steady decline. She needed to spend this bit of downtime between terms to get her head down and study. But how was she ever supposed to concentrate with such an edible distraction?

Ever since he'd first come into her life, from the very moment she first laid eyes on him, he'd been a distraction. Her distraction.

She'd tried telling herself it was just a crush, that she'd grow out of it, but it did no good. Terry was her addiction, and the more he came into her world, the more she longed for him. By the time she learned the true depth of her feelings for him, however, it was too late.

Terry had fallen in love.

Fallen in love with Elsa, a business management student who, like them, was also minoring in English Lit and had happened to of chose the seat next to Terry's. A random act of chance that had turned Faye's world upside down and inside out. Now he belonged to her. Now, he was forbidden fruit, and that was always the sweetest.

It just wasn't fair. *That bitch doesn't deserve him!*

These were dangerous thoughts, but she couldn't help it. It wasn't that she didn't like Elsa. In fact, if they'd met under any other circumstances, she was sure they could have been the very best of friends. It was just-

"Faye? Are you sure you're alright?" Terry was openly watching her, his eyes furrowed with concern, making her realise she'd been caught staring again. "Do you want me to get you a glass of water or something?" *Or something, definitely.* "No… I'm fine." Yet opportunity had knocked and in what she hoped was a casual manner, she swept a hand across her forehead, brushing her fringe from her eyes before blowing an overly exaggerated breath and saying "but could we please stop for a few minutes and take a break? This room's just way too small for the both of us to be cooped inside all night."

For a moment, she feared Terry might protest further, but then he seemed to have second thoughts and gave in.

"Alright Faye, you win." He gave a defeated shrug, causing her to all but squeal with delight as she jumped out of her chair. However, Terry moved with a measured slowness and though he too was secretly glad for the reprieve, he did his best not to appear too eager before joining her at the door.

Like a good host, Faye escorted Terry down the winding stairs that led into the modest communal living room. A stark but comfortable room. It was loosely furnished with a coffee table, bookcase, sofas and a T.V..

"Just make yourself at home," she said, gesturing lazily towards one sofa before reclining back on its sister on the opposite side of the table. Grabbing the remote off the coffee table, she turned on the television and began to avidly flick through the channels. She might as well enjoy the moment. It was a rare thing for her to have control of the telly. Her housemates all had their own specific shows they just couldn't miss, but they were all out, celebrating the dawn of a new year and wouldn't be back until morning…

Not sure of what else to do, Terry followed her instructions and sat down stiffly on the edge of the seat. Faye had a point. That room was too bloody small.

However, there was nothing on T.V. that interested him.

Despite all of his convictions, he couldn't help watching the vision of loveliness across from him.

Still flicking through the channels, Faye had adopted a less than ladylike pose, with one of her exquisitely long legs dangling over the sofa's arm while the other stretched across the table. It was entirely innocent of course yet dressed as she was in that all too short white skirt, he couldn't help letting his eyes glide over her perfect milky skin, greedily admiring her smooth waist and voluptuous curves before noticing the way her head was tilted back to expose her long neck. *Why does she always have to be so beautiful?*

And he couldn't help himself. In his mind's eye, he watched that long neck arching, those full lips panting out hot moans as he climbed onto the sofa and ravaged her, her enticing form squirming and writhing beneath him. The idea was as delicious as it was inappropriate, and he knew he would have taken her right there if he only had the balls to risk ruining their friendship.

Ruining their friendship and having his said bollocks clipped.

Fuck, what's wrong with me? He loved Elsa, didn't he? He certainly thought he did. She was kind, intelligent and when they were together, it was like every day couldn't be more perfect. So why was he still thinking about Faye that way?

It was wrong, immoral even. She was his best friend, but he just couldn't help himself.

Suddenly, he felt very warm and was all too aware of how tight his trousers were becoming. Yet, before he could stop himself, his eyes moved up to Faye's breasts. Her white cotton cardigan stretched across her bosom and left nothing to the imagination. Captivated, he never noticed Faye watching him out of the corner of her eyes.

She gave an exaggerated cough that had Terry quickly coming back to his senses and looking away as Faye slid those long legs off the furniture before pushing up and walking slowly around his sofa. Being as quiet as a mouse, she leant over the back and stared down at the man beneath her, causing his dark eyes to snap upward.

Almost nose to nose with her, Terry swallowed. He was acutely aware of her closeness and when she shifted, eyes twinkling with mischief, he was presented with a close-up view of her plunging neckline.

Mouth dry and cock harder than steel, he had to fight the sudden urge to reach up and touch her before forcing himself to meet her eyes.

"Break over? That was fast…"

Scarcely able to keep her smirk at bay, Faye nodded before turning to walk up the stairs, fully aware that his eyes were on her.

Terry couldn't tear his eyes away. He watched her like a hawk, noticing every curve and shake of her delectable rump while his feet carried him up the stairs of their own accord. He wanted to touch her, to feel the heat of her skin and the curve of her arse, to taste the sweetness of her flavour as he devoured her before he bent her over and buried himself in that inviting rump. It took all his fortitude to look away before they entered her room.

Silently, he begged all the world's deities for every book ever printed to spontaneously burst into flames.

It didn't matter that the thought bordered National Socialism, just so long as he could get the hell out of there before he jumped on Faye, ravaged her, shagged her, or just made a complete and utter arse of himself. His pleas fell on deaf ears.

Chapter Two

She was trying to kill him. It was the only explanation. Faye was trying to kill him, slowly and painfully.

Despite his best efforts to the contrary, he noticed everything. Every little move she made. How she would occasionally lick her lips then tilt her head, exposing the long slope of her neck, or bite her lips whenever she was concentrating. His heart all but burst when she needed to stretch and would cross her hands behind her head and arch, slowly, oh so slowly, so that her breasts were all but bursting from her sweater and the hem rose up to show off her flat milky navel. But his favourite was when she started to make notes and would every now and then pause, her tongue curling around her pencil as she considered the text. He would have given his right nut just to be that pencil for a few moments.

It happened so slowly, he never saw it coming…

Faye hadn't known what else to do.

For all her less than considerable wiles, Terry was proving about as corruptible as Jesus Christ and she was all out of ideas.

Leaning across the desk, she presented him with her finished notes. She almost shivered with ecstasy as she felt the heat of his gaze roaming across her skin. He wanted her, she knew it; but he did nothing.

So, instead, she made the first move.

Chapter Three

It was only chaste, yet Terry was too surprised to do anything but go with the flow. In one move, he wrapped his arm around her waist and pulled her across the desk and into his lap as her tongue found his in a carnal dance that sent electricity racing down his spine. Turning in his hold, Faye straddled his waist and wantonly ground her hips onto his lap, the heat of her desire burning through the fabric of their clothes to wash over his cock.

Desperate, almost mad with lust, he bucked against her, sliding the weight of his cock along her folds through her panties as he crushed her to him, hard. Hard enough to make her moan, a sound that was music to his ears.

She tastes so… good.

She did. She had the softest, sweetest lips he had ever tasted, and her mouth- it was divine. It had been made to be kissed, but he wanted more. He wanted her, all of her. He wanted… *Faye!*

Reality hit.

Realising what he was doing, he stood up so abruptly it made Faye squeal and tumble back onto the desk.

She looked up at him with glassy eyes.

"Terry…?"

"I'm sorry Faye, this… we... we need to stop," he said, breathless and unable to meet her gaze. "T-This is... we shouldn't... I, I mean, I shouldn't have done that. I'm sorry."

Faye managed to suppress her sobs. "B-but... but why? You want me, *Terr*. I know you do. So why, just once?"

The pleading in her tone tore at his heart. "Because I… You're my friend, and I just don't want to ruin things..." His voice softened as he tried desperately to make her understand. "What about Elsa?" "I'm not going to tell her. All I want is one night. Just one night, nothing else… just once. It's not going to change anything, Terry, I promise…" A stray tear rolled down her cheek and Faye didn't have the heart to brush it aside. She'd come so close, he couldn't turn her down, not now.

So, instead, Faye threw herself at him. Literally.

Too surprised to get out of the way, Terry could only gawk dumbly as she barrelled into his legs. She sent him reeling back onto the bed that took up one whole corner of the room. Then she was on him. With one move, she ripped open his trousers, then pulled his boxers down.

Oh…my…God! In spite of the fear winding her belly into a thick rope of knots, Faye licked her lips as his cock stood rampant before her eyes.

Fingers shaking, she reached out and tried to wrap her hand around him. He was so thick she couldn't even get her thumb and finger to meet. Marvelling at the way it pulsed and throbbed, she started to pump her hand. She took her time, running her hand down from the swollen head to the thick base and then back again with the slow, almost hypnotic motions she'd heard could work guys into a frenzy.

Scarcely able to breathe, Terry could only seize the sheets with white-knuckled fists as his whole body seemed to writhe beneath the siren's hand job. With that first touch, Faye had stolen all his strength away. He was powerless and completely unable to stop himself from bucking into her hand with every stroke of her palm. He knew he shouldn't be enjoying this, that it wasn't right, but just felt so good. He couldn't resist.

"F-Faye wh... what... what are you doing? No... oh fuck… Stoooohhhh!"

His whole body spasmed at the lush heat that suddenly whispered over his flesh. Breath and pulse quickening, he looked down in time to watch his friend lean in and wrap those full, kissable lips around the head of his cock.

"You want me, don't you, Terry?" she asked, running her tongue along the edge of his crown. "Mmm…I know you do. Your cock's so big and delicious."

Though she had virtually no first-hand experience giving head, Faye made up for that with determination and continued to slowly run her hand up and down his thick column, while her mouth, tongue, and teeth played with the swollen head.

"Oh God, Faye… Please… Stop." His voice was choked and thick with pleasure.

Faye couldn't resist giving him a sly, playful smile. God, his flavour, that musky scent, the very…feeling. She'd had no idea sex could feel like this.

It was incredible to have such power over him. It both thrilled her and turned her on, got her heart pumping and made her panties soaked. She wanted to make it last forever, but knew she needed to move things along before her nerve broke. So Faye dipped lower, her lips flowing over the slick, velvety flesh, stretching to their limit as she began to bob her head.

Terry thought he was going to go mad. The head of his cock was tingling with sensations. It was so sensitive that he could feel everything as she took him into that hot cavern of wonders. He could feel the way her teeth scraped across the edges. The swift creases of her tongue on the tip, even the delicious rush of warmth that washed over him every time she inhaled. He knew he shouldn't be enjoying this so much. That it was wrong. She was his best friend, and he had a girlfriend. Everything told him he should make her stop before this went too far, but it just felt so good.

She was barely halfway down when his hips began to churn. Despite her resolve to take him all in, when the thick crest breached her throat, she gagged. The reflex was as violent as anything she'd ever felt. Instinctively knowing she was at her limit, she pulled back until she could breathe again. Lingering there only long enough to catch her breath, however, she reached down and grabbed the bottom of her top. With one quick tug, she pulled the snug garment up and over her breasts.

Mesmerised by her beauty, Terry didn't dare look away as Faye's bountiful cleavage bounced and jiggled with every dip of her head as she resumed working on him. They were larger than Elsa's, but not so overly large that they appeared comical or artificial, and tipped by rosy nipples that he so badly wanted to lick. Just to see if they tasted as good as they looked.

Glancing up in time to catch him openly ogling her, Faye would have smiled if her mouth wasn't so full.

His eyes grew wider than saucers as he watched her drop both her hands to her sides, gather up the objects of his attention, and lean in to envelop the remainder of his cock between her tits. Continuing to suckle the weeping head, she began slowly sliding her chest up and down, massaging the thick base with her breasts, timing her motions to match her mouth's slow up and down rhythm.

Unable to breathe or think, Terry felt as though his life's thread was hanging on the edge of a knife. On one side was his self-control, on the other, his release from this torturous pleasure Faye was conjuring up. He hungered for both but knew that giving into one would extinguish the other...

In theory, it should have been an easy choice. Elsa was his girlfriend. He loved her, he thought, and was determined not to do anything that might jeopardise the relationship. Unfortunately, his body seemed to have its own ideas.

"Oh shit!" he gasped as he felt his orgasm coming. One last stroke was all it took. In a rush, rope after rope of his thick, creamy seed flooded her waiting mouth. Faye swallowed greedily. Only when she had got every last drop did she pull off.

"Mmm… you're delicious," she cooed, raising her eyes to meet his. "Please sir, can I have some more…" Her voice failed her when she saw the primal hunger gleaming back at her like quick-silver. Suddenly afraid, she tried to back away, but one of his large hands came down to seize her bunched up top and yank it over her head and arms. Unprepared for his sudden aggression, her body folded to his will as, with one move, he rose, lifted her and threw her across the bed. Surprised by the abrupt change in him, she didn't dare move from there as he dragged her skirt and soaked panties down her legs.

Stepping in behind her, Terry seized her waist and pulled her back, so his crown brushed over her folds and lodged against her exposed clit.

"Oh…" Faye squealed, stars bursting behind her eyes.

"Just once," he breathed again in that low, sexy tone. His breath hot on the back of her neck, that tongue teasing her ear. "Hold on to something."   With another roll, he entered her.

"Fuck!"

The burn of her vagina stretching around him as he filled her was utterly overwhelming and seemed to go on and on. No, *he* seemed to go on and on. Fisting the sheets against the delicious ache, she was immediately grateful for all those quiet evenings alone with her kindle, and her B.O.B. In the beginning, it had seemed like a woefully inadequate way to lose her virginity, but without them, there'd be no way she would ever have accommodated him. Victory loves preparation, indeed.

The odd position was making her feel somewhat disorientated. Her whole body felt like it was on fire, but beneath that, there was an exquisite feeling of fullness, the likes of which she could never have imagined.

She was just starting to get used to the feeling when he suddenly switched and began to withdraw, pulling back from her desperate sucking grip, until just the head remained inside her. Then he pushed back in.

"This what you want, baby?" Terry growled, dragging her back to meet him as he did, opening her up a bit more and sliding deeper.

"Y-yes…"

"You love it, don't you?"

He repeated the slow draw, then thrust again, and then again, working up a smooth, steady rhythm that quickly had the heavy weight of his balls slapping her clit.

"It's so good... feels so fucking good... I... I can't..."

"Can't what Faye?"

She gasped and babbled in an answer.

Utterly overwhelmed, Faye's mouth gaped as she felt him forcing himself a little deeper inside her every time. She felt so full, almost ready to burst. With every stroke, his thick member was hitting that spot deep inside her. God, she had never known sex could be this good. She wanted more, and of its own accord, her body responded by moving to meet his thrusts, rocking and grinding her bottom against his pelvis.

Swept up in the rising tide that signalled an approaching orgasm, she had to squeeze her eyes shut against the pleasure as hot tears of ecstasy crept down her cheeks like the cream rolling down her legs. Burning like liquid desire through her veins, her orgasm promised to be a big one, and she was sure she'd be walking funny for days.

On second thought, nothing, not her B.O.B or any other toy, living or rubber, could ever hope to have prepared her for the storm Terry was stirring inside her.

"Oh, it's so fucking good! Fuck me, Terry! Fuck my little pussy so good!"

Terry was happy to oblige. "Mmm... I never guessed you were such a little slut. Begging to get fucked like my own dirty little whore, while I use your hot little cunt like my fuck toy."

This was madness, but he didn't care. With a white-knuckled grip on her, he snapped his hips back and forth in a violent rhythm that filled the space between them with wet slaps and made the bed rock and bang against the wall. In layman's terms, he was fucking Faye, and it was clear she loved every moment of it. With each thrust, he poured all his years of pent up lust and desire for this girl into her body and she would rock and grind her succulent bottom back against his pelvis in a wanton frenzy. Only it wasn't enough, it would never be enough. He wanted her, all of her, and not just this once…

"Oh… oh my God… oh my God… oh-oh-oh fuck you're going to make me cum! You're gonna make me- I'm cumming! I'm cumming!"

Consumed by the wild passion of their forbidden tryst, time seemed to hold its breath as bursts of brilliant colour ignited behind her eyes and the knot in her centre erupted in wild convulsions that rippled with white-hot fire through her nerves, from her core to the tips of her fingers.

"Yeah! Cum for me, Faye," Terry ordered, supporting her, continuing his furious pace without missing a beat. "Cum all over my cock."

"Yes!" Faye babbled senselessly, her long legs trembling violently as wave after wave crashed over her, the orgasm extending into two. Then three.

She was only vaguely aware that she was growing light-headed. Fog encroached on the edge of her vision. God, he was too much. "Use me however you want! Make me your little toy… That's your pussy, it's yours! I... I love you, Terry! I love you, fuck me whenever you want to… I... I..."

"Oh fuck! Faye!" Caught off guard by her words, his release came upon him so suddenly, it was all Terry could do not to succumb right then and there. He knew he should pull out, but something deep down, dark and very primal, wanted to mark her. To take that final step and claim her as his own. It was that side that won out and with a low grunt, he came inside her, his balls tightening until black spots danced before his eye as he flooded her core with his thick creamy seed.

They collapsed together onto the bed. Exhausted, they rolled and twisted until they found themselves beneath the sheets and curled together, spooning in the bliss that carried them both to sleep. There were no words said. No feelings that needed to be said. They both just knew...

When Faye awoke in the morning, to the bright new dawn, the first of a new year filled with possibilities, Terry was gone.

Claiming My Best Friend

Chapter One

Alex didn't know how much more he could stand.

This feeling of connection was so intense, it was driving him mad. No, she was driving him mad.

This wasn't how he'd planned for the evening to go. Deep down, a part of him was screaming that they should stop, that this was wrong, and everything would change between them, but he just couldn't. Not now. She was just too intoxicating. The feel of her writhing around him; luxurious heat enveloping him, squeezing and rippling around his cock, dragging him in. He was drowning in her and he loved every second of it.

They had started slow, but all that was gone now and her normally sweet voice was now low and throaty with lust as he thrust harder and deeper. Her hands were everywhere. Fisting in the sheets. Grabbing the headboard. Drawing lines of fire down his back before finally coming to settle on his buttocks, nails biting deep. He knew he shouldn't look, that he was too close, but he just couldn't tear his eyes away. She was so beautiful. Stretched out beneath him, her head was rolling back into those long raven tresses, back arched and bountiful, ivory bosom bouncing as her lips curled up, grinding her clit into his root, demanding more.

How long had he wanted to see her this way? Needed to meet, to claim the freaky little sex kitten she had kept chained inside for so long?

Unabashed and unrestrained. Shaking with need and eyes dark with ecstasy. This was a part of herself she was sharing only with him. The thought sent a tremor of primitive possessiveness coursing through him. She was his.

"Sarah…"

"Sir, we will be beginning our landing approach soon," a female voice said, stirring Alex from his dreams and dragging him back to the world. Dazzling rays of sunlight shone through his half-closed shutter and his eyes blinked against the sudden brightness before he reached out and shut the barrier. His legs ached, and he tried to stretch. Only the taut nylon belt across his waist forced him to remain seated and so he settled for reaching beneath his glasses and rubbing the sleep from his eyes. Only after he'd reclined back into the padded leather seat did he notice the stewardess standing over him.

She was a pretty thing, in her early twenties with naturally blonde hair, catlike, jade-green eyes and a sweet heart-shaped face and a pale complexion that complimented the Airline's uniform she filled out so nicely. Though Alex couldn't help noticing that she had perhaps one too many buttons of the shirt undone, giving him a glimpse of a bright pink bra as she leaned forward to offer him the drink tray.

"Would you care for any refreshments before we land, sir?"

All too aware of the erection bunched uncomfortably down his trouser leg, the memory of the dream still burning his loins, he nervously accepted a cup of sweet, milky tea. As she moved to the next aisle, he couldn't help admiring the way the knee-length navy skirt emphasised the sway of her buttocks as she walked. First class certainly had its perks.

He drained the airline mug in one swig, the liquid warmth easing the parched feeling in his throat while the sudden rush of caffeine gave him a much-needed jolt of life. He had had difficulty sleeping on the plane due to sudden bouts of turbulence, and when sleep came, it was infested by dreams.

The intercom buzzed to life just as the pretty stewardess was making a return trip to collect the passengers' rubbish and used receptacles. Though the flight was based out of London Gatwick, the captain's accent was difficult to place. So thick and leathery, Alex had trouble narrowing it down further than Australian, New Zealand or perhaps one of the southern white African States.

"All right, Ladies and gentlemen, we have just been cleared to land at Sydney airport. Please make sure your seat backs and tray tables are in their full upright position, that your seatbelt is securely fastened, and all carry-on luggage is stowed underneath the seat in front of you or in the overhead bins. Please turn off all electronic devices until we are safely parked at the gate. The flight attendants are currently walking around the cabin to make a final compliance check and pick up any remaining cups and glasses. Thank you."

Alex grimaced at the thought of landing, then as his cup was taken, an idea occurred to him and he reached over to flip the blind covering his window. Light flooded his vision, and he quickly turned away to let his eyes adjust before turning back to look outside. The full beauty of Sydney was spread out beneath him. He felt his heart leap with excitement at seeing the Australian city for the first time before the Airbus began to bank and he sunk back into his seat.

His centre of gravity shifted with the plane and he felt a sudden sickly feeling in the pit of his stomach as the roar of the aircraft's descent filled his ears and shocked his brain. Feeling the inevitable dip as the plane's nose descended, Alex tried to imagine himself somewhere else.

Anywhere else.

Walking the pier at Weston-Super-Mare. Seeing a show at the Bristol Hippodrome. Eating fish and chips in his parents' living room on Friday's after school.

He tried to focus on that, but then he saw Sarah sitting across from him, sneaking chips from his plate and giggling playfully when he tried to grab them back. Then they were right back in that room at the Holiday Inn on prom night, their naked bodies entwined and…

"Ladies and gentlemen, welcome to Sydney Airport. The Local time is 01:00 pm, and the temperature is a balmy twenty-six Celsius. For your safety and comfort, we ask that you please remain seated with your seatbelt fastened until the Captain turns off the Fasten Seatbelt sign. This will indicate that we have parked at the gate and that it is safe for you to move about the cabin. We remind you to please wait until inside the terminal to use any electronic devices. I'd like to thank you for joining us on this trip and we are looking forward to seeing you on board again in the future. Have a nice day."

'Goddamnit!' Alex silently cursed as his heart raced with a potent cocktail of arousal and frustration.

Despite the captain's instructions, many of the passengers had already begun to rise from their seats. Glancing at the elderly woman sitting in the seat next to his and then down to the bulge in his trousers, he decided to wait until the flow had subsided and only then did he unfasten his seatbelt. He rose from his seat and gratefully stretching his legs as the old woman he'd been sitting next to disappeared into the thinning crowd. He reached up into the overhead compartment and quickly retrieved his holdall from the back.

Slinging it over his shoulder and joining the rapidly thinning line of departing passengers, Alex felt his heart flutter and couldn't help the blush that crept over his cheeks as the pretty stewardess who'd woken him and served him tea stepped out of the first-class kitchen. Seeing him there, she smiled and handed him a small card before wishing him an enjoyable holiday. Stepping through the airlock and into the air-conditioned tunnel that led to the arrival's terminal, he let himself be led by the press of bodies before raising the card to eye level. One side was blank except for the airline's logo, but turning it over he felt his blush deepen at seeing two sets of phone numbers written in red ink and Alexis – Call me X scribbled beneath them.

He quickly stored the card in the inside pocket of his jacket.

Following the signs for arrivals at every intersection, he let out an impressed whistle as the tunnel suddenly opened out onto passport control, a huge chamber lit by rows of skylights and which was split across the middle by a row of counters and hulking machines. Joining the closest queue, he fished out his new passport and boarding pass from the bag before handing them to an elderly lady at the counter while two men fed the holdall into the x-ray machine. He tried not to appear too nervous as he glimpsed the bag as it appeared on the monitor, but no alarms went off and it took him a moment to realise the lady was speaking to him.

"I'm sorry?"

"Are you carrying any fruits or vegetables?" she asked again, her voice throaty and with an obvious note of annoyance at having to repeat herself.

"No."

"Reason for travel, business or pleasure?"

"I'm visiting an old friend," he said truthfully, but then she flashed him a look over her round glasses and he added, "Pleasure."

"Anything to declare?"

"No."

She stamped his passport hard enough it produced an audible thump, then handed it back without another glance. Pocketing the booklet, Alex turned away, then paused and glanced back at the woman at the desk.

"Did you sue them?"

"Who?" She didn't even spare him a second look up from her work as another of the passengers stepped forward.

"The charm school." He didn't wait for her response before grabbing his holdall and walking out of immigration, muttering "Aussie Battleship."

Despite his one-way ticket, he'd only brought the one bag and so moved past baggage claim and out into a wideopen atrium filled with shops and cafés. A single service desk with four busy operators stood in its centre. Three separate arrival boards hung from the ceiling and on the distant wall, above the three sets of automatic doors leading out onto the street, a large sign proclaimed WELCOME in the bold blue font on a white field.

Spotting the huge crowd of people gathered to meet their respective arrivals, Alex quickly cast his eyes over the throng of faces and name cards, but there was no sign of her. It was unlike her to be tardy but reasoning that she had probably just been caught in traffic. He began walking towards the nearest café when he heard a familiar voice suddenly cry his name. His heart leaping at the sound, he wheeled around and was almost knocked off his feet when a body slammed into his chest.

Chapter Two

"Sarah?"

"Alex! Oh God Alex… it's so good to see you!" Sarah cried, wrapping her arms around his neck, drawing him into a tight embrace as her eyes began to sparkle.

"I've… I've missed you so much, Alex. You have no idea what it means to me that you're here."

"Hey… Sarah… stop… I can't… too tight…"

"Oh! Sorry," she apologised, loosening her hold on him but staying close for another few moments before stepping back. "It's good to see you."

"Yeah, you too Sarah," Alex gasped whilst rubbing his throat, more for effect than to soothe the numbing ache she'd left.

Embarrassed, Sarah refused to meet his gaze, and no sooner had she stepped back from the hug she gestured for him to follow.

"My car's this way. I was so worried I'd miss you that I left it on a double yellow line. Oh God, I hope I haven't got a ticket, the fines here are really expensive and my…"

Alex was only half listening as he followed her through the crowd, trying to pretend not to notice the amused looks that trailed after them. It wasn't hard, in truth, he could barely take his eyes off Sarah and his heart leapt with panic every time she vanished behind a body, even if it was just for a moment.

She'd changed.

Gone were the baggy boy clothes. She'd swapped her old shapeless t-shirts for a long-sleeved cut-off top that showed off all of her perfectly flat middle. A pair of skinny jeans hugged her gloriously long legs and made the old adage of going on forever woefully and utterly inadequate when combined with those cowgirl boots. Her hair was different too. Longer, with more body. She'd taken it out of her customary ponytail, so it framed her face and tumbled down around her shoulders to the small of her back. Bouncing with her movements, the wash of glorious raven locks directed his eyes down to the swells of her buttocks and he had to force himself to look away.

Stepping from the cool air-conditioned atrium and out into the heat of the Australian summer felt like stepping into an oven at full burn and he was immediately grateful for his jacket's cooling charms. There was a breeze blowing, but it was hot and dusty and offered little relief from the merciless heat as he raced to keep up with her. Despite Sarah's concerns, a long line of vehicles was parked in front of the terminal with an ever-constant queue waiting for a space to clear. She led him past more than half a dozen vehicles before coming to a stop beside a gleaming black XK Jaguar convertible. Reaching into a handbag she had hanging off her shoulder, she produced a set of keys that, with one click of the fob, had the roof folding down and the boot popping open.

Whistling his admiration as Sarah got into the driver's seat, he flung his holdall into the rear of the car before shutting it with a smooth push and then let himself into the passenger side. Turning the ignition, Sarah let the engine roar impressively to life before shifting into gear and, with half a turn of the wheel, pulled into the first opening.

Buckling his seatbelt, Alex was immediately thrown all the way back into his seat as Sarah pulled out onto the motorway and put her foot to the ground, speeding from twenty to one hundred kilometres per hour.

In school, she had kept to her books. He never would have guessed she would be a closet speed freak.

It was nonetheless a pleasant surprise. It was good to know that she was, at last, letting her hair down. He just hoped the cost of the discovery wasn't him becoming a red smear across some stretch of Australian motorway.

"How are Rich and Janet?" Sarah finally asked, keeping her attention on the road ahead and not noticing Alex suddenly stiffen in his seat. "After I sent you that email, I considered contacting them too, but I just couldn't think of anything to say."

"What? Sarah Snow lost for words. Now I've heard everything!" Alex shot her a sideways smirk and said, "last I heard, Rich was working for his dad. I don't know about Janet."

"Really?" she asked, unable to keep her surprise hidden as she quickly glanced at him. "But you two were so close, she was even saying you guys were talking about working things out and getting back together."

"We did, and things were going pretty well for a while, but we broke up nearly a year ago. There were *complications.*"

He hoped that explanation would satisfy her, but Sarah was ever curious and, though she nodded, he could tell she wanted to know more. Despite himself, he found the words coming out before he could stop them.

"It's a long story, but I guess we just had different ideas of what life would be like after graduation. She wanted the life she'd gotten used to at university. Nightly girls' nights and weekends away. I wanted something steady, a family, career, the whole nine yards, you know. Janet could never understand that." Alex paused. He needed to consider his next words carefully and gave a moment's serious thought as to the best way to put it before continuing slowly. "In the end, I think we both knew it wouldn't work. It was just a matter of who would admit it first."

Sarah, much to his relief, didn't press the matter further, and they spent the next few moments in silence as Alex considered his failed relationship with Janet. What he'd told Sarah had been true, from a certain point of view. They'd both realised the inevitable end. Only Janet had realised it much sooner than he had. For Alex, the truth had become apparent whilst they were attending one of his firm's cocktail parties, celebrating the start of a tour for their newest, and most successful, signing artists. Alex had discovered the singer, Augustus Flemingworth, singing karaoke in a club and offered him a break. His presence was expected and, as she was a fan of most indie rock, he'd brought Janet for their weekly date night.

Janet had never been one to drink, but that night she had consumed an ample sum while he'd been forced to talk shop. He had been politely trying to brush off a job offer from a representative from a competing agency when he suddenly noticed Janet had vanished. Concerned, he discarded subtlety and bluntly refused the offer before searching. It didn't take long. The party was being hosted at the singer's new flat in one of Chelsea's more choice buildings, and he'd visited the place enough times for him to navigate a path through the press of bodies without getting lost. When he found her, she had been the centrepiece of a foursome on Augustus Flemingworth's bed. Sandwiched between them were two of the catering staff whose names he'd never asked after, and she was busily performing fellatio upon Flemingworth.

It is an interesting feeling to have your world fall apart around you. For Alex, it was like being plunged headfirst into an icy lake. He had stood there completely numb for a moment before retreating away from the open door and leaving the party without saying a word to any of the revellers. Not sure of what to do, he had gone home, packed up all his things before writing her a hasty note to say that it was over. He hadn't seen Janet since.

"I'm so sorry Alex…" Sarah whispered, her voice shaky as she glanced at him nervously. "I can't imagine how that must have felt-"

"Forget it, I have," Alex snapped, his voice hitching with a note of pent-up anger. "Goddamnit, what happened to you, Sarah? You just disappeared. I thought… we could - I woke up, and you were gone."

"Alex…" She looked like she was about to say more, but then a high-quality recording of Beethoven's Fifth Symphony filled the car. Giving him an apologetic glance, she took one hand off the wheel and reached into the side of her door to withdraw a small earpiece with flashing bright green LEDs. Fixing it to her ear, she pressed the answer button before returning both hands to the wheel. "Hello." Her voice remained even and friendly as she greeted whoever was calling her.

Almost seething, Alex sunk back into his chair and watched the world outside the car fly by. A tall blue road sign announced that they were driving down the M5 and Alex tried to compare the city's triple carriageway with its rural English equivalent. The exercise helped calm the storm raging inside of him, and he felt a sudden surge of self-loathing. He'd never meant to get angry with her. She deserved better from him than that.

Realising they were approaching an intersection, he breathed a quick sigh of relief as the traffic light suspended above the junction changed from bright green to yellow. Instead of slowing, however, Sarah suddenly slammed her foot down on the accelerator, challenging the light while angrily speaking into the earpiece. "What do you mean, they need me to come in? I told Ramon I couldn't do any shots this week. No, I have a friend staying with me. He's come all the way from England and has only just arrived. I can't just leave him to… well, why can't we just…. but what about… oh fine! I'll be there in half an hour."

She pressed the button to end the call before angrily hurling it behind the seat just as they zoomed under the lights, an instant before the amber hue turned a bloody red.

"Oh Alex, I'm so sorry but I have to pop into work."

"This really shouldn't take any longer than an hour, Alex, I promise," Sarah assured him as they walked along a cobblestone path that traversed the edge of a stretch of beach along Sydney's eastern coast.

Panting heavily as the sun beat down on them, Alex could do little more than a grunt in acknowledgement as he struggled to keep up with her.

Sun-kissed and dazzling, the beach reminded Alex of something from the old David Hasselhoff show 'Baywatch' he'd watched as a kid. The only thing missing was a scantily clad Pamela Anderson running into the water in slow motion.

Everywhere he looked, beneath clear blue skies, there were dunes of sugar fine sand leading down to turbulent white-capped waters of turquoise and deep cerulean. Despite the picturesque conditions, the sandbanks were sparse for all but the occasional dog walker or, of course, lifeguard.

"So, what exactly is it you do again?" Alex asked, before using the back of his hand to wipe away the sweat trickling down his brow. Never in his life had he felt more overdressed. His heavy denim trousers felt stifling and his shirt was sticking to his back like a second skin. Thank god Sarah had insisted he leave his leather jacket in the car.

Still a good four or five strides ahead, Sarah glanced back over her shoulder and flashed him a mischievous smile in way of an answer before adding hastily as she walked on, "You'll see soon enough."

She was completely at ease in the sizzling temperatures. Cursing himself for not checking the Australian weather before he'd left for the airport, Alex couldn't help letting his eyes linger on her buttocks for a moment before hurriedly glancing up to see if she'd noticed.

His throat was parched but to his relief, a light breeze began to blow, ruffling his hair and cooling his skin. Grateful for the reprieve, Alex turned his head up to the horizon and caught his first glimpse of what could only have been their destination.

Against the glare of the sun, the scene was at first hard to discern, but as they approached, he began to make out the shapes of a dozen men and woman milling around two caravans. Further down the bank, down by the rolling surf, a cluster of chairs was overshadowed by a huge parasol and faced three tall light stands fixed with umbrella covered strobe lights

A makeshift photography studio? he thought. It certainly wasn't what he'd expected. Although Sarah had forever been a fountain of information and opinions, he had never heard her express an interest in photography.

They were just approaching the closest caravan when a young woman with styled and dyed dark red hair dressed in a pale blue shirt and snug fitting grey jeans, and holding a clipboard, stepped out of the open doorway in its side. She looked to be deep in thought, but that evaporated the moment she caught sight of them.

"Sarah!" she called, raising the hand with the clipboard over her head in greeting as she broke into a run towards the pair. "Oh, thank God! You have to hurry. Rodarick is going ape. He's even threatening to sue if we miss the light for this shoot. I tried to tell him there's always tomorrow, but he just starts screaming shit at me in Fren-oh. Hi," she said, noticing Alex for the first time before leaning in close to Sarah and saying, "say, girl, who's your cute friend?" Blushing, Sarah avoided the girl's gaze. "Jules, this is Alex, Alex, this is my assistant Julia."

"Alex-wait, you mean *the* Alex."

Plainly growing uncomfortable with the conversation, Sarah made an extra effort to look offhand as she said, "yes, Alex Rike, we went to school together back in England. Look, I'll deal with Rodarick. Can you please escort Alex over to the viewing area while I get ready?"

"Sure, oh, I can't wait to hear what juicy stories he has."

Then, before Sarah, or Alex for that matter, could object, Julia had run up to him, seized his hand, and began dragging him towards the roaring surf. Not sure what to say, Alex could only look back, but Sarah was already making her way towards the open caravan.

"So, you're the famous Alex Rike. You can't imagine how long I've waited to meet you," she said after a moment, her voice silky.

"What... I mean... um oh, why's that?"

"Sarah often speaks of you. She said you were the most amazing man she has ever met, and that she has never had a truer friend. When she told me that, I knew I just had to meet you. Good men are a rare commodity and Sarah's just too smart to be so wrong about you."

"I've never known Sarah to be wrong," he murmured, suddenly feeling especially warm under the blazing sun. "Has she ever mentioned anyone else? From England, I mean."

"No one in particular. She spoke of some bloke...Robert...something Wallaby a few times, but it was mostly just in passing, though once she said that he was the most insufferable ignoramus she had ever encountered." Alex couldn't help but snigger.

Richard might be many things, but ignorant wasn't one of them. He'd known the truth well enough, but that didn't stop Sarah's ex being a cunt whenever he deemed it appropriate. *And it certainly didn't stop me from introducing his perfect nose to my fist.*

"So, what was Sarah like back home? She doesn't talk about the old days much."

"Sarah doesn't talk about anything much." His Kris Kristofferson impression was as rusty as the actor's Texan growl, but it made Jules chuckle nonetheless.

"No, she was…" Alex paused. How often had he pondered that question? Though the answers rarely eluded him, the prospect of picking just one to sum her up entirely made his pulse quicken and his mouth dry. Or perhaps it was merely the heat. "Brilliant," he continued. "There was no challenge she couldn't master. Anything she set her mind to, she could do, but she could also be a real ball breaker. She always followed the rules to the letter. Though she'd always denied it, I think a part of her secretly liked my frequent attempts to get us into trouble."

She giggled again. "So, you were a *corrupting* influence?"

"Absolutely." Alex grinned and this time, they both laughed. They were almost at the surf after skirting the edges of the milling mass, and Alex could smell the rich saltiness of the sea air. For a moment, he thought she was about to lead him into the turbulent waters when Jules suddenly veered right and led him up the bank to the shade of the parasol. The viewing area, as Sarah had called it, turned out to be just a group of seven or so unfolded camping chairs with a cooler.

Bending down, she withdrew a chilled bottle of coke and handed it to Alex before helping herself to one. Unscrewing the lid, she took a long swig of the soft drink before moaning happily. She screwed on the lid and dropped it back into the blue box, closing it with a kick of her heel. "Okay, make yourself comfortable and Sarah will be down in just a few moments." Without waiting for a response, she turned on her heel and began walking back towards the caravan, pausing a moment before she left the shade to throw one last glance back at him and say "Hmm… I guess it's true what they say about tall thin men."

Alex almost choked on his mouthful of coke. Feeling his cheeks flush with embarrassment, he turned away quickly before Jules could see the blush and instead looked down at the sea. *What the hell has Sarah been telling people?*

Remembering the drink in his hand and his parched throat, he half drained the bottle in a single long swallow. It was warmer than he would have liked, but the fizzy liquid was sweeter than ambrosia, and he finished it off with just two more swigs. He was about to look for a rubbish bin when a portly middle-aged man with heavily tanned skin, greying military cut hair, and a curled goatee strode between the set of light stands. Dressed in a long white robe and leather Jesuscreeper sandals, he would have reminded Alex of a born-again prophet had he not also had a pair of Ray-Ban sunglasses around his neck and been holding an expensive camera.

Caught up in his own private tempest, he was shouting and ranting at anyone who dared to step too close in what Alex thought to be French.

The man's presence caused a tremor to run through the throng of people around the site and they began to fall back behind the light stands, just in time for Alex to glimpse a figure swathed entirely in a hooded robe of billowing white silk, strolling through the surf. Realising the show was about to start, Alex looked back at the caravans in the hope of catching a glimpse of Sarah walking down the beach. However, there was no sign of her on the dunes or amongst the crowd of onlookers, all of whom he noticed happened to be staring in the same direction.

Following their gaze back to the robed figure, he watched the individual step out of the surf and walk up the bank towards them. The silk masked them completely, but the damp sea air caused the silk to cling to their skin and he was treated to a thrilling peak of golden flesh as the figure passed. For the briefest moment, he was certain he had glimpsed rosy lips smiling at him from beneath the hood. Suddenly anxious, he had to fight the urge to leap over the folding chairs and pull the figure's hood down as the urge to see who lay beneath nearly drove him mad. His world began to slow as the figure, long-legged and graceful, took the last few steps towards the onlookers before reaching up and pushing the garment clear and letting it fall to the sand.

The sight stole his breath away.

Sun-kissed and gorgeous, Sarah Snow stood upon the sand in nought but the pooling silk at her feet and a seashell two-piece bikini. The top only just hid the swells of her bosom. Her skin aglow with the midday radiance. She followed the photographer's direction as he shouted at her to lay on her side with her back to the surf. Alex could feel his breath catching as he watched her throw an arm carelessly high and arch her back, pressing her breasts in his direction. She lay still for a moment, then her eyes shifted in his direction and she winked…

Rodarick's camera began to click, the flash blinding.

Chapter Three

Hot and sweaty, with sand sticking to the most unimaginable of places, Alex felt as if he had never enjoyed a shower more than he did at that moment.

Despite Sarah's assurances that the shoot wouldn't take very long, he had sat in that 'viewing area' for about three hours before she had come to collect him. It would have been nice to think he had been cool about it, or at least to have handled the situation well, but that would have been a lie and Sarah had only giggled at his shocked expression before dragging him off to a late lunch at her favourite Chinese restaurant. He would never have thought of it, but he had enjoyed listening to her explain the differences between true oriental cooking and the western comparison. It had reminded him of their more peaceful days in school and of the girl he had known so very long ago.

Upon arrival at her home, a modest two-bedroom flat in the Balmain suburbs, Sarah had given him a tour before excusing herself to freshen up and Alex had been glad of the chance to have a much-needed shower. The scalding water pelted his body in a ceaseless torrent, easing the stiffness in his muscles and scouring the sand from his skin. Unfortunately, the water could not cleanse him of all his troubles and as his hands swept his flesh with soapy suds, he brooded over the enigma that was Sarah Snow.

She had changed so much since those days in school, flourishing while everything else in Alex's life had withered and died. The girl he'd once known had become a woman unlike any he'd known, but despite it all, she was still Sarah Snow, the odd little orphan girl, the dearest of any friend, the first woman he had ever loved…

A stiffening sensation in his loins quickly reminded him of the dangers of such thoughts. Feeling strangely embarrassed, and more than a little dirty for getting an erection in Sarah's shower, he reluctantly turned the hot water to cold. The sudden icy blast made him almost leap out of the stall, and his engorged shaft quickly wilted as the soapy lather ran off his body onto the porcelain before draining away.

Shivering, Alex quickly turned the water off and pushed the fogged glass of the cubicle door aside. The bathroom was thick with a warm cloud of steam and he was forced to reach out blindly for the towel he'd placed close by before towelling himself down and wrapping it around his waist. Stepping from the shower into the cloud of steam, he traced a path from memory to the door leading to the adjoining bedroom.

The room was lit only by the dim glow of the bedside table lamp. Alex shut the door before any steam could leak into the bedroom.

Though he couldn't exactly call the room spartan, it would be a long stretch by any imagination to consider it homely. Sarah had, of course, furnished it with all the basics, a double bed, bedside tables, a chest of draws. However, the walls were painted pale, the carpeting basic, and there were no decorations or photos to speak of, nothing to give the room the feel of a home. It was almost as if he were staying in a hotel.

He'd left the room's one window open and could feel a cool evening breeze blowing in from the not so distant bay. Its touch was like ice against his flesh and he shivered when a cold drop fell from his still damp hair to roll down his spine. Feeling it pool against the towel, he undid the fluffy white cloth and let the damp material fall around his feet to leave him standing naked in the glow of the lamp.

His holdall sat open in the centre of the bed, and as he looked inside, he suddenly realised how little he'd packed. Everything about this trip had been rushed. He'd scarcely given any thought to what he might wear and had simply grabbed anything that looked suitable, or else clean, for the tropical island climate. With only three tops and a pair of black jeans for his selection, he'd have to have Sarah take him shopping sometime in the next few days.

Grabbing a pair of black boxers, he quickly pulled on the undergarment before dressing in his only pair of clean trousers and pulling on a dark red shirt. Doing up all but the top two buttons, he towelled his hair one more time before glancing sideways to the mirror fixed to the back of the room's door. Satisfied with his appearance, he switched the bedside lamp off and, guided by the warm orange twilight shining in through the window, left via the door opposite the foot of the bed and into the hallway beyond.

The door to Sarah's bedroom was directly opposite the guest room and it was shut tight. He was about to head towards the living room when he thought he heard a series of muffled gasps from beneath the door. Worried, he paused before the pine barrier, raised a hand to knock, and then suddenly thought better of it. Dismissing the sounds as woman's stuff, he turned on his heel and followed the carpeted corridor to the flat's living area.

Sarah seemed to have made greater effort to decorate the living room than she had with the guest room. Though undeniably utilitarian, its design was just what he would have expected of her. There was only one sofa, a two-cushioned piece of supple black leather set against the main inner wall and within easy reach of the two-tiered coffee table in the centre of the room. A corner of the room was dominated by a desk upon which sat a laptop, printer, and Sony CD player, as well as a mass of papers and pens. Three four-shelf bookcases had been arranged around the desk, all heavily laden with an assortment of books and ornaments, two of which were mostly hard backed reference books while the third was creased and dog-eared paper volumes. Curious, he took one of the more *used* softbacks off the case's top shelf, only to feel his cheeks burn scarlet as he read the title.

The Intimate Adventures of a London Call Girl… Christ, Sarah reads sex books! Embarrassed, He hurriedly put the book back in its place and almost tripped over the cat bed that had been subtly stowed in the corner as he backed away.

Sara's ginger tomcat was curled up fast asleep, too lost in his own dreams to notice he'd almost been flattened. Alex quietly stepped over the sleeping beast before performing a quick sweep of the rest of the living room, but there was nothing remarkable however except for a virtually brand-new Sony thirtysomething inch LCD T.V. and DVD player set up on a modern metal and glass stand in the opposite corner. Neither machine looked to have been used recently and had thin coatings of dust, but there was a pile of DVD cases beside the player. Unable to resist investigating, he bent forward for a closer look. *Serendipity, Fatal Attraction, Basic Instinct, Titani-*

"Find anything you like?" a voice whispered in his ear, making Alex jump and wheel around to find Sarah standing there, a sly smile tilting her full rosy lips. Her hair was still damp from the shower and she'd changed into a silky black robe that she'd tied around her waist. Feeling ominous, like a child caught with his hand in the biscuit tin, he could only look down in shame as his face burned a bright red until he heard

Sarah giggle and say, "Oh, don't look so guilty, Alex. I said to make yourself at home, didn't I?"

With a surprisingly firm grip, she took his hand and guided him to the sofa before playfully pushing him into the leather cushion. She walked through the archway in the wall that led to her kitchen. "I'll get us something to drink."

His eyes followed her until she was gone from sight, his heart beating like a drum in his chest. What was wrong with him? This was Sarah, his Sarah. Why was he so nervous? He knew her as well as he knew himself, and she considerably more so. So, what had changed? Why could he not take his eyes off her? Why was her voice suddenly like music to his ears?

Of course, in his heart, Alex already knew the answer. He'd thought about it a lot over the past few weeks, and he feared it as much as he longed for it. Her rejection would kill him more assuredly than anything else on earth.

His thoughts fell silent when Sarah stepped back into the room, holding two shot glasses in one hand and a bottle of pale blue alcohol bearing the insignia of a serpent in the other.

"You still like Vodka, right?" she asked, placing both glasses on the table and unscrewing the top.

"Thanks." Eyeing the pale blue vodka cautiously, he raised the shot glass. "*Nostrovia,*" Tossing his head back, he swallowed it quickly, the familiar taste of straight Vodka rolling over his taste buds, flooding his senses. No sooner had he placed the shot glass down, he felt the first kickback rising in his throat, his fingers tingling. It was over quickly, but then the second was upon with startling swiftness, and he could feel a heat burning through his chest, spreading over his lungs, turning his breath smoky. That should have been the end of it, but he could feel the third growing and glanced at Sarah, who was smiling down at him as she held the glass to her lips. He opened his mouth to speak and coughed violently.

"Wow."

"*Na Zdorovie*, Alex," she replied, her perfect lips pronouncing the Russian toast fluently. Alex tried to stop her, his hand rising as his lips mouthed the words, but Sarah gently tipped the glass back and drained the contents. She swallowed it all without caution, then after a moment pursed her lips and whistled.

Alex's chest heaved with the effort of breathing, but he could not tear his gaze from the vision of Sarah standing before him, her rosy lips pursed, half-veiled eyes watching him with playful amusement. She was toying with him, but what was her game?

"Mmm…" she moaned as she sat next to him on the sofa. "It takes a bit of getting used to, but it gives one hell of a buzz."

A buzz. Is that what she calls this? Alex wasn't an innocent. Since his break-up with Janet, he'd learned to indulge himself and enjoy a glass or two in the evenings, dulling the memories that plagued his moments of solitude. He knew the feeling that came with having one too many, but that was a mere shadow of the sensations rushing through him now. Every cell in his body felt energised. A fire was raging in his chest, and a thick canopy of smoke fogged his thoughts. His movements felt foreign, both sluggish and, at the same time, accelerated. He tried to think of something to say, but as his eyes watched her, his mouth opened and words came spilling out before he realised what he had said. "You know, you never did answer my question. What happened after prom? Why'd you wait five years to get back in touch?"

Sarah didn't answer. Seemingly stunned by his sudden outburst, she went as still as marble and turned her gaze away from him to watch her cat sleeping in his bed. Her eyes were glassy and, when she blinked, a tear rolled down her cheek.

Dammit, Rike, you just couldn't keep your big mouth shut, could you? Inwardly cursing his own stupidity, Alex shifted round and reached out to touch her shoulder, but again thought better of it at the last moment and retracted his hand.

"Oh God, Sarah, I'm sor…"

"I found them, Alex." Sarah's voice lacked all emotion. She raised a hand to brush the tear aside. "My parents, I found them. They're dentists, can you believe it? My folks, dentists with their own surgery on Harley Street. I went to see them that morning, after… I never told you because I knew you wouldn't approve, but they're my parents. I wanted to meet them, know who they are, why they didn't want me.

"Sarah-" Alex's mouth was dry.

"They didn't even notice me. I went in and there they were, standing there talking to patients. I knew it was them. I tried to speak, but then my mother told me to take a seat. She looked straight at me and didn't even see me. I've waited all my life to meet them and they've no idea I exist. I-I was just aanother pa-pat-patient."

The tears were coming strong. Alex wanted to say something, but what? He placed a hand on her shoulder. It wasn't much, but it seemed to help as she didn't push him away and after a moment, he could feel the shaking that wracked her beginning to subside. Brushing the tears away, she lifted her gaze away from the sleeping feline.

"He tried to kiss me, you know."

"What!" The sound was higher than Alex had intended, but suddenly it felt like there was a tennis ball lodged in his throat that he just couldn't swallow. "… Who?"

"Rodarick."

"So, what did you do?"

"I hit him."

"Seriously?" Despite himself, Alex couldn't help a small chuckle.

"Yep, knocked the *crapaud* flat on his arse, then stormed out. He's such a pig." The tension easing, she relaxed back into his embrace. "I'm sorry Alex, I just couldn't deal with it. I wanted to get away, so I just grabbed the first flight out of London and worked what jobs I could find. That was until Jules *discovered* me working in a bookshop last year and recommended me to the agency's talent scout. I've been with them ever since."

Alex knew he should have let sleeping dogs lie. All he had to do was hold his tongue and let the moment pass, but the vodka spoke for him. "You could have called, I was worried."

Sarah turned to face him, her eyes lowered and a guilty smile turning her lips. "I know, I'm sorry Alex, I just didn't want to ruin things."

"You couldn't ruin anything, Sarah," he assured her, trying to sound comforting before a notion suddenly struck him. "So, why did you send me that email?"

Sarah began to blush. "I was drunk."

This time, he made no effort to disguise the laughter. "Drunk?"

She looked away, her face burning a bright red. "Jules, she took me out for a girls' night out. I had a few too many rum and cherry cokes and started telling her all about you. She tracked you down the next day and while I was still a bit tipsy, she got me to send you an email."

This time, they both laughed.

"Then everything happened so fast and when you said you were coming to visit; I was so happy." She turned back to him, a warm, genuine smile lighting up her face. "I really have missed you Alex."

Alex could only smile as their eyes met, a hot shiver running down his spine. "I've missed you too."

All notion of time slipped away, and Alex found himself wishing that that moment would never end as he looked into Sarah's bright hazel orbs and felt his heart swell. He wanted nothing more than to take her in his arms and crush her against him, to seize her lips in a passionate embrace. With the drink in him, he might actually have done so if Sarah had not suddenly jumped to her feet.

"Ooh, come on, let's dance," declared Sarah, sauntering over to the desk and fiddling with the CD player until jazz music began echoing from the speaker. Alex's heart jumped as he recognised Michael Bublé's *Sway* and he had a sudden feeling of déjà vu as Sarah began to dance, her hips swaying seductively to the beat as she took his hand and dragged him from the sofa.

It must have been the drink that did it. One moment he was skirting around her like a timid rabbit, the next their bodies were locked together in a rhythmic tempest as he surrendered to the music and her wishes. A hair's breadth divided them. With every breath, her scent filled him, and he could recall the taste of her lips on his. He could feel breasts pressing against him, her hardened nipples clearly visible against the silken fabric. His hands were on her, running lightly over the sultry curve of her spine, down to the swells of her buttocks. He felt his hand moving on its own accord, squeezing the firm orbs, crushing her to him hard enough to make her gasp. The sound stirred his shaft to life, but when she began to pull back, he was afraid he might have gone too far, until she twisted and began to rock her backside against him, massaging his engorged arousal as her arms wound around his neck. Her head tilted back. Their lips were nearing, opening bit by bit in readied acceptance as his arms curled around her front, rising slowly over her ribs to clasp her breasts. He could feel her breath on his cheek, her lips so close, her eyes falling shut, his own darkening-

Meoowwwwww!

The sound startled them, bringing them back to reality, and Alex's head wheeled around, only to see the tomcat stretching out. The commotion, it seemed, had awoken the feline, who, in turn, had returned the favour. Turning back, he saw Sarah blink as reality, and the realisation of what they had almost done, surge through her. Unable to meet his gaze, she stepped back, turned and ran back through the hallway.

He heard her bedroom door slamming shut.

"Shit…"

Chapter *Four*

Unable to sleep, Alex stared blankly up at the ceiling. It was well past midnight, but his thoughts were plagued by what had happened in Sarah's living room.

What had he been thinking? Sarah was his oldest friend. Now he would be lucky if she would ever talk to him again. If she didn't, what should he do then? Grovel, perhaps? Janet had given him plenty of practice at that toward the end. Would Sarah enjoy seeing him on his hands and knees, or perhaps she would demand that he leave her home and never come back. Maybe it would be better if he wasn't there to see it. He could easily leave a note, grab a cab to Sydney Airport and buy a ticket for the next flight back to England. Maybe that would be best, maybe…

"No." Shaking his head dismissively, he rolled onto his side and watched a shadow shift across the wall, the reflection of himself staring back at him from the mirror on his bathroom door.

He would not leave, the morning would be uncomfortable, there might be some awkward moments and heated words but, in the end, they would come through it. He had already lost Sarah once. It wouldn't happen again.

Click.

The sound was so subtle, for a moment Alex thought it was just a whisper on the wind and he dismissed it from his thoughts. Then a shadow stretched across the floor and he realised he was not alone. He could hear bare feet padding across the floor, every second bringing them closer. Faking sleep, he counted them off in his head, estimating how many more before they were at the foot of the bed, and then he opened his eyes.

Sarah stood before him, a look of complete nervous determination set on her soft, delicate features.

"Sarah."

"Shh… don't talk."

Though her words were gently spoken, the command brokered no argument, and he could only watch in stunned hypnosis as she stepped over the frame and knelt upon the bed, the mattress sinking slightly under their combined weights as she crouched over him. She was still wearing her robe.

Without saying a word, she began undoing the tie of her robe so that the garment hung open before reaching up and pushing it back off her shoulders. It pooled on the bedsheets and left her naked to his gaze, except for a single pair of lacy black panties. Alex tried to say something, but at the sight of her near naked body bathed in moonlight and the silver rays cascading over her beauty, the words fled from him and he could only stare in wondrous amazement as she leaned down to place a gentle kiss on his lips. Losing all conscious thought, he immediately tried to deepen the embrace and encircled her thin waist, only to have her suddenly break the embrace and forcefully push him back onto the bed. Stunned by her sudden forcefulness, he could do nothing more than stare up at her as she began going lower.

Unable to stand the heat of the covers, Alex had planned to sleep upon them in only his boxers. Suddenly realising his own nakedness, Alex shifted embarrassedly until Sarah stilled him with a stern look as she lightly trailed her fingers down his lean, athletically chiselled torso. Though it had been some time since he had played for the school Rugby team, Alex had been making regular visits to a local gym to stay in shape and it was plain to see that Sarah was pleased with what she saw. Her touch was like fire against his skin and he could feel his flesh quivering as she bent down to ravage his torso. His eyes closed, and a gasp escaped him as her greedy lips wrapped around his flat nipples, her tongue teasing the buds before she drew back to kiss a delicious path down his torso. He shuddered as her lithe fingers seized the hem of his boxers and pulled them down over the swelling bulge of his arousal. His erection sprang free to stand tall before her gaze. "Mmm…I'd forgotten just how big you are, Alex." Sarah purred, her eyes smouldering with desire as she took in the sight of his cock. Suddenly feeling like a piece of meat, Alex felt his breath catch in his throat as her cool fingers began to ever so softly trace the bulging veins along his shaft, slowly moving down from the tip to the thick base, and then back up to the tip.

The feeling was almost too much for Alex and his breath seethed through gritted teeth as he struggled to hold off the release that suddenly threatened to overwhelm him as her thumb massaged across his glands.

"Sa-Sarah…ah…" He gasped, his hips lifting off the bed as her fingers closed around his shaft. She held him for a moment, her grip tightening just enough to make the head swell, his column pulsating in her grasp before she began to rhythmically stroke. Alex shuddered, a sudden tremor rising out of his loins so quickly that he was afraid it was all over, only to watch a clear drop of fluid form on the tip of his shaft and coat the crown in a milky liquid. Sarah didn't wait for permission before leaning down, strands of raven hair tickling his thighs and closing her perfect lips around the tip.

Fisting the sheets, Alex's eyes widened to the size of saucers as he watched her take him into the wet warmth of her mouth. He could feel her tongue upon his cock, its silky wetness flicking rapidly over the sensitive tip before twirling around the velvety flesh, massaging him as she drew him in, and an excited hiss escaped him as he felt her teeth scrape over the pulsating organ. Unable to stand it, his eyes squeezed shut and his head lolled back into the pillows, his death-grip on the sheets turning his knuckles white as she used both her hands and mouth to such divine effect.

"Oh… God Sarah… don-don't stop… don't stop…" he gasped, making no effort to hide the pleading tone as the sensations she was stirring within him almost drove him into a frenzy. For Alex, the idea that it was Sarah, his wonderful, talented, brilliant Sarah, doing this to him was more erotic than he dared imagine. He had to fight the overwhelming urge to cum as he felt her slowly working her way down past the engorged head, sucking it adoringly even as his hips jerked up off the mattress of their own accord and she struggled to accommodate the girth of his rigid shaft.

Keeping her movements slow and her wondrous tongue pressed tight against his cock's underside, Sarah began drawing more of him into her warmth. It was a divine torture. Alex had no thoughts but for those of her hand stroking the lower length of his arousal, her plush rosy lips stretched tight around his pulsating flesh, her tongue's subtle teasing, the gentle scraping of her teeth, and the awful slowness of it all. *So… so slow, how can she be so slow?*

Sinking her mouth down the length of his arousal, she took almost a third of him in, the tip just touching the entrance to her throat, before slowly drawing back until just the bulbous head remained inside her warm mouth. She sucked it wantonly, swirling her tongue around the sensitive ridge before repeating the process.

She developed her rhythm quickly, stroking and squeezing his cock with her fingers while her lips devoured him. Slow and sensual, Sarah was all but purring with delight as her lips, tongue, and hand moved in perfect sync and it took only a moment of her sweet torture to drive him wild. He fought to remain in control, but he was overwhelmed by the sensations she was stirring inside of him, and her name escaped him in a ragged gasp. Encouraged by his display of pleasure, she doubled her efforts, sucking on him hungrily as her head began to bob along the upper half of his arousal.

Feeling his head starting to spin as her pace quickened, Alex had no idea how he had managed to hold on for so long as he absorbed every hot, wicked sensation she sent shooting through his nervous system. Unable to resist the overwhelming urge, his hips started to rock and gyrate in time to her tempo, churning in whatever way rewarded him with even more of the blissful magic the saucy witch was conjuring. Janet had never done anything like this.

Almost delirious with pleasure, he knew he had to see her, to see the look in her eyes and know that this wasn't just a wondrous fantasy brought about by pent-up lust. Pushing himself upward with his hands, he forced his eyes open and stared down in utter rapture at the vision laid out before him. Just the sight of Sarah on her knees, her gorgeous body clad only in those lacy panties, inky hair cascading over her shoulders and back as she twisted her torso, tits jiggling with every subtle movement, was enough to send a hot shiver up his spine that left him dangling over the precipice of release.

He watched transfixed, unable to move for fear of what sweet oblivion might befall him, as her luscious lips slid along the length of his cock, his hips jerking every time he felt her tongue flick over the pulsating tip. It took a moment for him to realise that she was watching him closely, studying his every reaction to the scrutiny only Sarah Snow could muster, learning what he preferred and committing it to memory.

"Does it feel good, baby?" she asked, her big hazel eyes staring up at him innocently while her plush lips stretched around the bulbous tip, the vibration of her words trembling deliciously down his engorged flesh. Such visual stimulation was too much, and Alex's mouth fell open in several ragged moans as the pressure in his loins exploded. Panting, he tried desperately to push Sarah away, but she merely batted the hand aside as thick ropes of his creamy seed erupted inside her mouth. She drank it all down without complaint, drawing every last drop of his climax down her heavenly throat before finally releasing him with the last swirl of her tongue.

His chest heaving and vision shifting in and out of focus, Alex collapsed back into the bed's embrace. Too dazed to speak, he watched through half-lidded eyes as Sarah rose to her feet, surprisingly surefooted on the bouncy mattress. Without saying a word, she seized the hem of her panties and pushed them down her long legs. Totally naked, she stepped out of her underwear and kicked the garment aside before straddling his hips and lowering herself down to his still erect arousal. Planting both hands on his abdomen to steady herself, she brought their bodies close enough for him to feel the warmth radiating from her slick folds. She held herself there and as their eyes met, Alex glimpsed her confidence falter for the first time since she'd entered the bedroom.

"Alex…please…be gentle. This is my first time since…since..."

"Really?" Alex couldn't believe it after what she had just done. Surely it couldn't be true.

"You mean you haven't…haven't been with anyone else?"

"No." Sarah's features hardened. "I'm not a slut Alex. I don't shag people, I don't…well I mean..." Suddenly blushing, she brought her left hand up to touch his cheek. "You're the only man I've ever wanted, Alex Rike."

His heart leaping for joy, Alex pushed himself up from the bed into a seated position, putting them almost nose to nose as his hands snaked their way around her legs and up to her taut buttocks. She shot him a questioning look, but he only grinned before seizing her perfectly rounded arse and hoisted her up on his shoulders.

"Well, in that case…"

Feeling his erection grow almost painful as he drank in the sight of her nakedness, the musky scent of her arousal infesting his every breath, Alex flattened his hands against her buttocks to steady her before burying his face into her heat.

"Mmm…*beautiful.*"

"What do you think you are- oh!" Sarah moaned, throwing her head back in utter rapture as he plunged his tongue into her carnal depths. Fuelled by an unquenchable thirst, he showed her no mercy and lashed at her slick inner walls while kneading her buttocks, relishing the feel of her perfectly sculpted rump in his grasp.

Obviously unprepared for the sudden wash of pleasure, Sarah could only pant in sheer wide-eyed delight as he skilfully ravished her depths, his tongue plunging deeper than she'd thought possible. Then suddenly her fingers were seizing his hair and he could feel her legs closing around his neck as she made to draw him closer, trying to get more of the sensations he was stirring within her.

"Does it feel good, Sarah?" he teased, echoing the very same words she'd used to send him over the edge.

"Yes...oh yes! Yes!" she cried, her body trembling as her hips began to roll in tiny eager circles. "It…it feels so good…You're incredible…ohhh…God…more…more…"

Realising she was close, he withdrew his tongue from her depths, but before she could protest, he slid the muscle greedily along her folds and up to the pert bud of her clitoris. Eager to bestow the bliss of release upon her, he took the small bundle of nerves between his teeth and tugged it gently before pressing his tongue against it. Sarah shrieked at the contact, her entire lower body writhing in his grasp as he began keenly lashing the swollen bud.

"Ooh God! I can't take this…yes…yes…right there…" she begged, her thighs closing so tight around his throat he was in danger of being choked. She was writhing so fiercely, it was difficult for Alex to maintain his tongue's contact with her clit and he might have dropped her altogether had he not been keeping an ironclad grip.

"So…so good… oh God don't stop…don't stop, oh yes…!" Suddenly her eyes squeezed shut and her entire body began to shake as the pleasure erupted inside her, flooding his lips with her nectar's exotic spice. Quickly becoming addicted to the taste of her, Alex drank down every drop while continuing to lick her through her release, the hand in his hair still holding him fast against her convulsing core.

When at last she went limp in his arms, Alex didn't waste a moment and gently lowered her down from his shoulders. Supporting her somewhat inconsiderable weight as she came down from her orgasmic high, he lowered her into position over his straining erection, barely able to contain his self-satisfied smirk at her half-lidded look of bliss. Yet for his part, Alex was in agony as his anticipation of what was about to come caused the tightness in his erection to grow all the more prominent with each passing moment and it was only a sheer force of will that kept him from surging on ahead. He'd waited too long for this moment to ruin it now.

Rousing slowly from her pleasure induced delirium, Sarah could only blink in wonderment as their eyes met before she suddenly realised she was straddling his waist. Unflinching, she gave him a confirming nod, before wrapping her arms around his neck, pressing their bodies together as she leaned forward.

"I love you, Alex," she whispered, her voice hitching with breathless excitement, before devouring his lips in a fierce kiss as she rolled her hips and plunged down onto his engorged arousal.

"Oh God!" she gasped, breaking the kiss as she felt herself take centimetre after centimetre into her channel, torn between the pain of her body trying to accommodate his intrusion and the wondrous sensation of being once again joined to the man she loved.

"So-so tight…" Alex moaned, overwhelmed by the feeling of her stretching around him, moulding to him like molten velvet as she took his shaft in all the way to the base. He could feel her insides writhing around him, sending hot rushes along his spine, and he had to fight the urge to buck against her as she wiggled in his lap before rolling her hips. Though slow at first, the friction of her motions was delicious, and he collapsed back into the bed's embrace as she started moving up and down, working more of him into her body.

Flattening her hands against his chest to steady herself as she rose over him, Sarah didn't miss a beat and started a slow up and down motion, her pace quickening with each descent as her natural wetness coated his arousal. Relishing the feel of her tightness gliding along his length, her walls clinging to him and massaging his engorged flesh, Alex made no move to interfere. Dreading that he may cause her more discomfort than pleasure, he pushed his every reserve of selfcontrol to its limit, forcing himself to remain still as she rose until just the tip remained inside her before dropping onto him again. No words or moans escaped her. She was entirely focused on the task at hand, but he could hear her quietly gasp with each intrusion and he had to bite his lower lip to keep from moaning every time she took him inside. Yet when she flexed her muscles around him, he couldn't hold back and instinctively bucked against her, thrusting deeper into her warmth.

"Oh…!" Sarah moaned, throwing her head back in complete bliss. Suddenly afraid, Alex made to hold her still, but she would have none of it and continued rolling her hips, her motions growing bolder and bolder until she was all but bouncing on his cock.

"So-so good…oh God…do it again Alex…I want it…I want it…"

Never one to defy her, he used his hold on her hips to guide her motions, suddenly thrusting up into her every downward glide, matching her stroke for stroke as she gave into her pleasure and rode him with a wild abandon. Gone was the reasoned and logical Sarah Snow he had known. Now there was only the wild, sexual beast she kept chained and hidden behind so many piles of books. He had glimpsed it that night they'd spent together after prom, but only now, as she surrendered entirely to the pleasure coursing through her, did he truly witness the beauty of her transformation.

"Mmm…right there…yes…right there…right-oh God…fuck me!" she cried, her mouth agape and features locked in a state of rapturous delight as she arched her back and vigorously rode his bucking shaft to untold heights of ecstasy. "Oh, God…it's so good…I can't take it…fuck me harder…harder!"

It was the first time Alex had heard her curse and the profanity almost pushed him over the brink as he relished the feeling of her snug channel massaging his cock, the heat of her core drawing him in with every stroke, sucking in every fibre of his being as if to consume him whole.

The bed began to rock and squeak as her strides evolved into a rhythm of upward glides, then crashing downward slams while he thrust up to meet her, driving himself deeper into her channel and causing her firm, round breasts to bounce with every impact. On one deep thrust, her back arched and she threw her head from side to side in delirium, a curtain of her hair whirling around her eyes, whilst a wild cry of delight was ripped from her lips. Realising he'd hit her sweet spot, he focused on hitting that same spot again and felt a pained hiss seething past his lips as the sudden jolt had her clawing his torso.

"Oh my god…you bad boy…. mmm, ooh-yeah fuck me harder… I want it…holy fuck you're going to make me climax!"

Almost on the brink, Sarah uttered a final wild cry before her legs gave way and she plummeted back down upon his cock, taking him all the way inside. Not ready to stop, however, she started rocking upon him. Glistening drops of sweat ran down her skin, her hair hanging lank past her shoulders as she flung herself against him, fucking him as hard as her exhausted limbs would allow. The tempo was fast and hard. Edging closer to his own release, Alex matched her motions, rocking upward, using short, hard thrusts to bury his cock inside her. The beauty writhed and moaned and gasped with each exquisitely thrilling penetration, her hands leaving their perch on his taut abdomen to glide up her waist to cup her breasts.

Rapidly approaching his breaking point, Alex watched entranced as her right hand kneaded her bouncing cleavage, rolling her pebbled nipple between her thumb and forefinger, the pliant flesh moulding to her palm whilst her left ran up her neck, over her cheek, and into her sweat-dampened hair. She was so close and, feeling her hanging over that abyss, caught between the sweetest oblivion and agonising wanton longing, he couldn't bear to prolong her torment any further. Tightening his hold on her hips, he ground her upon his shaft and lurched upward, crushing their bodies together as he began attacking her neck. Kissing, licking, and nipping every bit of exposed skin within reach, he found his every sense flooded with the very essence of Sarah Snow, the taste of her, the scent of her, the very sound of her soul singing within her as she gasped and moaned. It was all too much, and yet not enough, never enough. He wanted to experience everything about this angelic creature, to know her entirely, and then relearn everything over and over.

Her hand fisted in his hair as he nibbled her collarbone, directing him where she wanted his attention the most while pressing her soft bosom against his hard chest and rolling her hips to ride his upward thrusts. Trailing fiery kisses up along the curve of her chin, he bit her earlobe before whispering in her ear, "I love you, Sarah."

Her climax struck like a bolt of lightning at his words. Throwing her head back and uttering a voiceless scream as her body began to violently quake, Sarah clung to him for dear life, her entire existence shattering in his arms. Feeling her spasm around him as each wave of her climax crashed over her, each stronger than the last, Alex knew he was done and gave a coarse, guttural cry before thrusting into her one last time, spilling himself inside her warmth as he crushed her to him.

Spent and exhausted, they collapsed onto the bed in a naked heap of tangled limbs. Sarah had passed out from the intensity of the pleasure coursing through her still and, buried to the hilt within her, Alex could do little more than hold her close as he swept the covers aside before burying them both beneath the sweat soaked fabric. Sleep finally made his eyelids heavy, yet he couldn't help smiling as he gazed upon her, watching as she snuggled against him.

When he was sure she was asleep, he wrapped his arms around her and drew her tightly against him. In ancient times, the birds sang *all journeys end in lovers meeting*, yet he couldn't help thinking his greatest journey had only just begun. He didn't care, what did it matter, either way, they were together again. And in Sydney, of all places.

Unfinished

CHAPTER ONE

Damn him! How can he be so good at this? Panting hot lustful breaths as her slender fingers buried themselves in the lush softness of his hair, Vickey tried to fight back her moans as her lover's tongue parted her folds. Swivelling deep, its silky smoothness teased her senses into delirium. Desperate for more, she opened her legs wider, surrendering herself and opening up to him in the most intimate of ways. "Mmm- Ah! Jake! Ahhh! Oh fuck... Please!"

He always knew just where to touch, where to lick, to suck. She couldn't explain it. He just seemed to know how to get her hot, how to have her crying out as the fiery serpent spread from his villainous tongue to coil within her belly, heat seeping through her being in a flood of white-hot pleasure. "Oh! There, right there!"

It was so incredibly delicious. He might just drive her insane.

"That's it, love, don't be shy. You love this, don't you? Me eating you. Licking your clit," *he whispered, his voice reverberating through her most sensitive spot, feeding her desire.* "Want some more?" *He blew across her clit, as though to emphasise the question, and the feeling of his warm breath rushing over the pearl, seeming to brush over every nerve in her body, had her bucking and writhing against him, eyes squeezed shut against waves of delirious pleasure.* "Yes. Yes! Don't stop. Don't stop. Don- oh my fucking God! I'm gonna cum!" *she gasped, her voice trembling as he buried his head between her thighs, eating her with a starving hunger, tongue drinking in her flowing nectar before swirling around her clit. Then he was sucking, cheeks hollowing, drawing her little bud from the safety of its hood and into a sensory overload that had her head spinning.*

*"Open your eyes, angel. Watch me eat your delicious cunt."
His words were hot and dirty. She shook her head, the hot knot of
tension spiking deliciously at his words and the feeling of his tongue
fluttering over her centre. It was too much. Any more and she would
shatter. She couldn't take it. She couldn't-*

*"Open your eyes." He didn't raise his voice. He didn't have
to. The command was in his tone, and her body obeyed. His eyes
gleamed up at her from between her thighs. His hot, predatory gaze
burning into hers as that merciless tongue slid over and under. It
was so erotic. So...*

"Vickey? Hello! You still with us over there?"

Vickey blinked through the haze to find Erika sitting
across the table, waving a dainty but expertly manicured hand
tipped with silver and white nails. Angela sat beside her, not
saying anything, but that sly little grin pulling at the corner of
the fiery redhead's mouth spoke volumes. At the very least, it
was enough to assure Vickey that her flatmate knew exactly
what was going on.

Heat blooming across her face, she dropped her gaze
to their table, refusing to meet their eyes. *Dammit, I did it again.
What's wrong with me? Why can't I get him out of my head?*

"Geez, Vi, you could make a cherry look pale," Erika
observed, dropping her hand to take a long sip of her colourful
cocktail, draining the glass. "Mmm… that's good. My usual
now, Mike," she called to the burly chap behind the bar.
Though not exactly their local, they were there just often
enough to be called regulars and have a slate for their drinks.
They paid off just enough that Mike, the publican, and his staff
would let them slide when they wanted a drink but were
having a bad week. Or if they showed off a bit of thigh and
asked *nicely*. "So, who brought that blush to your cheeks?"

Vickey shuddered and kept her eyes down, resisting
the impulse to touch the heat still burning her skin. The Crown
was the quaint, old-fashioned sort of establishment one would
expect to find lost in the pages of an Agatha Christie or Jane
Austen novel, with a piano in one corner, oak beams running

across the ceiling, and a huge old oak bar framed by every sort of bottle and glass. It was a quiet pub where friends could meet and chat after work, but hardly a place to discuss the man haunting her dreams whenever she closed her eyes.

"Oh, I know," Angela cut in. "It's him. Right? The guy you were seeing." The small grin spread into a smile that was surely evil incarnate. "The one you've been pining for."

"Piss off!" Vickey rounded, forcing a smile, but she was unable to resist rising to the bait.

The redhead shot a sideways look at Erika and winked. "He's all she thinks about."

"Goddammit Angie!" The heat was practically radiating off her now. "I told you to stop eavesdropping on me when I go to bed!"

"I ain't been droppin' no eaves miss, honest." Angie grinned like the Cheshire Cat. "Wish I could, Vick, but you're a screamer, and I live vicariously." The redhead laughed again as her roommate flipped her the bird.

"Isn't it bad enough you steal my clothes when I'm out? Don't think I don't recognise that top you're flaunting."

Angela's smile dropped. "Aww… come on. You know this looks way cuter on me."

"Is that your idea of an excuse? I know the only reason you want it is so you can show off your tits to every guy who walks by our booth."

"Exactly." She gave an exaggerated wiggle that had her already emphasised breasts jiggling within the confines of the plunging halter that had rhinestones along the hem of the bust. "They get a show, and in return, I get a free drink. Isn't that trade worth your sacrifice?"

"No. I want my top back," Vickey countered dryly, refusing to back down. She needed to stay on the attack and keep the conversation moving.

"What, you want me to strip off right here? In front of everyone?" She grinned and gestured over her shoulder to where a group of lads were clustered around a tallboy. "I know it's Christmas, Vick, but shouldn't I wait to let one of those lucky guys open his present?"

"Don't act like you wouldn't," Vickey countered. "Anyway, I bet it's not something half the guys here haven't opened before."

"You bitch." Angela laughed, only to be checked by the sudden appearance of a fresh tray of drinks.

"Hey girls," a waitress by the name of Autumn greeted. She was a natural head-turner with sun-kissed curls and rosy cheeks, and she was made all the more noticeable by the little two-piece Santa uniform that showed off plenty of thigh and midriff. "These are from the guy over at table thirteen." She shuddered, though made sure to keep it as nonchalant as possible so that only the three other women around the table would notice before tilting her head. Vickey followed the movement.

At first, it looked like she was indicating to the lads around the tall boy, but the black number nine stamped to the edge of the brass plate suggested otherwise. So instead she looked past the lads to the far end of the pub where a fortysomething guy with a greasy top-knot was drooping in a chair.
The table's brass plate was marked thirteen.

Following Vickey's gaze, Angela visibly deflated, and it was all Erika could do not to burst into hysterics. Seeming to sense he had an audience, the guy then turned towards them, smiled and raised his half-a-lager. His broad smile made him look remarkably like Jabba the Hutt, and all three girls quickly looked away.

"Thanks," Angela mumbled to Autumn's retreating back, then pushed the drink over to Vickey. "Okay, bad example. But I-"

"Wait a minute!" Erika's eyes were suddenly bright. "You mean that guy, right? The one you said was a marathon man? Looks kinda like a young-ish Sean Bean, only with a goatee. Oh... he was hot, but..." She looked from Angela to

Vickey. "Didn't you give him the elbow last month?" *Geez, thanks Erika.*

Immediately aware of both sets of eyes fixing on her, Vickey dropped her gaze down to the drink Angela had passed her. Eyes pricking with tears, she refused to let either woman see her cry and instead focused on the bubbles rising to pop on the murky top of the Rum and Coke. Had it really only been a month? And to think, they had been so happy.

She had been so happy.

It was such a strange idea, her, happy.

But she had been at the time. That's how it had been with the others. A few dates, that was all. Then she'd end things. No attachments. No teary farewells or goodbyes. No commitment. No emotion. It was the best way. Best for her, and most certainly best for them.

And she'd been fine with it every time. They were just men, after all. If necessary, the best parts of them could be replaced by a pair of Triple-A batteries and a trip to the toy aisle in Ann Summers. But with Jake…

It was madness, pure madness, but in the space of a few weeks, he had completely consumed her in a way no other man had. Made her feel complete and safe. Happy.

Now he was gone, and it was her fault.

Sipping the rum, she wiped away the tear burning her cheek with the side of her hand.

Angela didn't buy the act for a second. "God, what's with you?"

"What?" Vickey asked, avoiding the redhead's scrutinising stare.

"*What?*" she parroted, then arched a long elegant brow. "Come off it, Vick. Don't give us that load of old pony. You never go out with a guy for more than a handful of dates before cutting him out of your life. Then this guy comes along, and you're suddenly attached to him at the hip. You sicken us with a routine that would make Shakespeare tom and dick. Then you break up with him out of the blue. Now I have to drag you out by your hair just to get you to come out for a drink on Christmas Eve." Her smirk dropped. "Seriously, what is it about this guy?"

"It's nothing."

Angela rolled her eyes. "Really? Because I could have sworn that was *The Only Way is Essex* you were watching when I came home."

"I like-"

"You can't stand soaps," Erika countered, cutting her off before she could even finish the lie.

"It's entertaining."

"It's shit."

Vickey shot her another glare but made no effort to defend the program further. A veteran of all things soap, reality, and celebrity T.V.. If Erika said it was crap, then there was no argument.

She sighed and put her glass down, defeated. "It's nothing. He's... different."

"Different?" Angela asked. "Different how?"

Vickey shrugged. She couldn't explain it. Jake wasn't like other men. Not the kind her friends understood. He was dark and dangerous. Full of that confidence which bordered on arrogance but with that sexy, irresistible bite. Dominating, but not overbearing. Scary without terror. He was a complete enigma. Even to her. "Just... different."

Erika and Angela shared a look that made Vickey's belly somersault. She knew that look.

"So, what does he do?" Erika finally asked, taking a long draw on her cider, watching her across the glass.

Vickey blinked. "I... I don't know."

"He didn't tell you?" Angela leant forward, scrutinising.

"I never asked."

"But how come?"

And there it was, the question that she dreaded. How could she tell them she was afraid to ask? Afraid of what his answer might be?

Vickey wasn't a liar. She'd grown up with liars. She'd learnt to lie before she could walk. She was possibly one of the greatest liars who'd ever lived. She'd seen the hurt they caused. She hated lying. She certainly didn't want to lie to two of the only true friends she'd ever had, but she'd seen the truth.

Jake never made a big deal about her finding it that time, but it was there.

Stashed away in his drawer, between a packet of paracetamol and a box of condoms.

A SIG Sauer P226.

Only certain men carried those. And none of them worked jobs that made good gossip. Good, healthy gossip anyway.

"It just never came up," Vickey shrugged, trying to appear nonchalant. "But he works a lot of strange hours and keeps himself in shape. Not very toned, but healthy, like he does a lot of running. And his stamina is amazing, so maybe he's a personal trainer." That at least was a half-truth. She'd never liked those muscle-bound guys. They were so heavy and slow, all show and no bite. Jake had been just her type, tall and lean but with muscle in all the right places.

Erika shot Angela a knowing sideways look. "Maybe he's married."

The words were like an icy shiver down Vickey's spine. "What?"

Angela didn't miss a beat. "Yeah, he's married and seeing you on the side."

"No."

"Well, where does he live?" asked Erika, now beaming.

"I don't... I think in one of those new towers they built on the East End a couple of years ago. But he only took me there a couple of times and I never paid much attention."

Where did he live? The cabby had always been waiting for them and she'd always been too *preoccupied* to pay much attention to where he was taking her. "He's married."

Vickey grit her teeth, growing angry with that smug smile playing across her roommate's peach coloured lips. "No, he's not."

Angela gave her a withering look. "Oh, have a day off, Vick. He doesn't tell you anything about himself, works weird hours, takes you back to a flat that could be anywhere in the city for all you know-"

"What about his phone?" Erika asked.

Vickey rounded on her. "What about it?"

"W-was he on it a lot?" Her friend seemed to shrink under her glare. "Did he ever try and hide it from you, refuse to let you use it or-"

"No, Erika. I never asked to use his phone, and he never made a big deal out of it. He's not married, so just drop it." Knowing she needed to calm dawn, Vickey grabbed the Rum and Coke and took a drink. It didn't help. "And what does it matter now? It's over, remember? I broke it off. Not him. Me!"

"It's nothing to be ashamed of," Erika pressed on regardless, though changing tact, as if worried the accusations had somehow insulted her. "You certainly wouldn't be the first. My mum once met this guy who had a girlfriend and a wife, he... he told them all he drove juggernauts so they wouldn't-"

"He's not married!" Vickey snapped, with more certainty than she had any right to have. The hot ice of her tone cutting off any remaining argument Erika might have had and made her friend's eyes drop to stare at the now empty cider glass.

Vickey immediately regretted being so sharp with her. She hadn't meant to be, but she couldn't help it. He wasn't married, she just knew it. Men lying about their marriage didn't turn up with the sorts of bruises Jake would sprout overnight. Or look at her the way he had; as if he were looking into her, to the centre of her being. No one had ever looked at her that way before. *He can't be married. He just can't!*

Angela nervously cleared her throat. "What did he think about your dad's breakout?"

"He didn't know."

"But… how?" Erika looked up, surprise written across her face. "Your dad's escape from Belmarsh was all over the news."

"I told him my surname's Romano. It was my mother's maiden name."

"So, you never…" Erika paused.

"What?"

Angela leaned forward, voice hushed. "Told him about your family?"

Vickey snorted, "Of course not. God, what do you suggest? Shag him senseless, then go, *Hey, babe, that was wild. Oh, by the way, you know that escaped murderer who's been all over the news? That's my dad.* I've heard some crazy pillow talk, but that about takes the biscuit. Then just for kicks, I could add, *'And if the wrong person sees us together, Terrance Daley is likely to cut your cock off and feed you your balls'.*" She gave another dry laugh, then threw back the remains of the Rum and Coke, ignoring the way her friends exchanged worried looks at the mention of Daley.

Forty years ago, Terrance Daley - or just Terry to his friends, the River Police, Flying Squad, and Daily Mail readers- had been an infamous enforcer of Freddie Foreman. Five years ago, The Mail had called him The People's King of London, but Vickey had only ever known him as *Uncle Terry.*

Suddenly, she was there again. In that room. The night cold and crawling over her skin, fingers grasping her chin, sour breath reeking of whisky hissing in her ear. "*Good girl, now lie down on the bed and let Uncle Terry see…*"

"Jesus! Vickey… Vickey!" Angela and Erika stood around her. "You're as white as a sheet."

"What's wrong? You feelin' alright?"

"Y… yeah. I'm fine." *Christ, where did that come from?*

She shook her head, trying to clear the fog, and suddenly was all too aware of the sweat clinging to her brow. Then, she realised just about every head in the bar was watching their table. "Listen… I've got to go."

"What?"

"Where are you going-"

"Are you sure you're-"

"Want us to come-"

"Maybe we should get you checked out-"

She shook them off. "No. No, I'm fine." Grabbing her jacket from the back of the chair, she slung her handbag over a shoulder. "I just need some air. To think. Yeah. I'll see you later." Then, eyes glassy and heart pounding, she was moving past a shaken Autumn, round the bar, and through the door into the winter night.

Chapter Two

Christmas was only a couple of hours away and, to mark the holiday, *Seven* had been decked in blue and white. Projectors in the ceiling made it look as if snowflakes were falling around the dancers, who were writhing together through the clouds of dry ice fog enveloping the floor.

The floor-to-ceiling windows of the manager's office made up the wall overlooking the dancefloor. However, the view was lost on Jake. *Are you down there?*

The throngs were pressed so tight together, it was virtually impossible to tell one person from the next, but he could imagine her down there, writhing and gyrating to the beat against a faceless male, hot and eager…

His fingers twitched at the thought and he had to force down the impulse to reach for the sidearm hidden beneath his leather ¾ jacket. Though the P226 was his weapon of choice, the lighter, smaller, standard-issue Glock 17 was the more practical choice when it came to these messenger-boy jobs. Not only was it lighter and more easily concealed under a jacket, it's all-polymer design meant it was less likely to set off the basic security systems and metal detectors found in civilian recreational areas.

Get a grip, man. It was ridiculous. He was being ridiculous. A slip of a girl, barely in her twenties. What had he expected? Marriage and happily ever after? Those were nothing but fantasies when you joined the Squad. Hell, if she hadn't broken it off, he soon would have. For her sake, if not for his. She deserved better.

"Well, well, well…"

Shit! Jake had his hand in his jacket, thumb flipping the catch of the shoulder holster strap and his palm fastening round the textured grip of the Glock in the moment it took his head to whip back.

He relaxed slightly when he saw who was standing in the office's door.

"When Mr Margrave said he was sending someone, I certainly wasn't expecting it to be you, of all people, Jake Talbert."

"I wasn't his first choice," Jake agreed, letting his hand fall to his side. At five feet six and shaped like a propped-up bag of suet in a black, handmade, three-piece suit, with a receding mop of hair more grey than black that curled at the sides and a pudgy face, Henry Yate was not what anyone would consider threatening. "But your message said it was urgent, and it's Christmas Eve. The rest of the Flying Squad have plans, so here I am."

Yate moved around the desk to sit back in the padded swivel chair with legs crossed and hands steepled in his lap. The pose was supposed to appear relaxed but only made his hands look like a bustle of fat little sausages. "I heard you weren't about much these days. Word is, it's been a busy couple of weeks for you."

"They've had their moments."

"I'll say. Intimidating witnesses. Assaulting suspects. Not to mention beating that poor bugger half to death in a billiards hall. And in front of witnesses." Pearly whites glinted as he fixed Jake with a smile that would likely curdle milk. "I heard you're out of control. Something about a bird blowing you out, giving you the Dear John routine. So now you're under investigation, chained to a desk. You know, in these times of civil unrest, it's a real comfort to know those brave boys in blue take the time to remember their duty and professional integrity. If only all law enforcement took such time to protect us law-abiding citizens from the filth that walks our streets."

"And here I thought you drove everywhere nowadays?"

Yate's smile dropped. "Touché."

"Well, I wouldn't let my unpredictability and violent tendencies bother you," Jake said with forced nonchalance as he walked around the desk to sit in the chair opposite the older man. These games were all part of the routine. "I had a bad break. I needed to vent, and that wanker in the hall decided to be a smart arse. So, we played a game of doctor." He shrugged, leaning back and folding his arms. "He lost."

"Yes, those clips on YouTube made that obvious. Shame they didn't also show the firearm he allegedly had concealed on his person."

"You know, the enquiry's psychologist remarked on that too, but it's hard to argue with evidence found on the scene."

"Unless it's a plant."

There was an adequate response to that, but Jake had to force himself not to bite. Yate was little more than a two-bit snitch, a common rogue with several dodgy businesses who made it his business to have all twenty little sausage digits in every dirty, bent, and stolen pie in London, and an ear to the ground in all the right and wrong places. He was the owner and manager of *Seven,* but it was a smokescreen, a bit of cloak and dagger, something to look good on the self-assessment. Yate's true business was information, and he didn't discriminate. It was no secret he sold to both the villains and the law of London, but, because he never went too far and always threw both sides a bone, he was untouchable.

And the powers-that-be had decreed Jake must play this stupid fat fucker's little games.

Yate went on. "Of course, your recent recommendation for the Saint George might have had something to do with that."

Jake's eyes narrowed. *Now, just how did you learn about that, you slimy bastard?*

"D-notices aren't what they used to be." Yate grinned, apparently reading his thoughts. "Out of curiosity, you killed how many jihadists? Ten?"

"Six," Jake snarled.

"Six," Yate parroted, his smile broad and knowing. "Quite a bit of luck you had there. And at such an opportune time. Extraordinary. I bet that put those CID boys out of joint. All that effort they went through to conceal the Browning. They finally have your balls in a vice, then you go and pull a stunt like that and the Chief Constable himself tells them to put it-"

"Yate!" Though he did not raise his voice above a whisper, Jake's tone was sharper than a razor. "I have better things to do than listen to you crow all night. Now, are you going to tell me what's so important that I had to come over here on Christmas Eve, or do I have to drag you down to lockup for the night for wasting my time?"

Yate smiled, knowing he'd won this round. "Terry's planning a score."

"*The People's King*? You do surprise me," Jake said in a tone dripping with sarcasm. "You'll have to do better than that. He's legit, remember?"

"Yes, but all jobs still require his seal of approval. This is still his town," Yate pointed out. "There isn't a major heist goin' down in the borough that hasn't received his nod of approval."

"That may be, but that amounts to conspiracy, at best, and it's bloody hard to get a conspiracy conviction without rock-solid evidence." Jake eased back into the chair. "Everyone knows Terry's in it up to his neck. Half the MET is working to drag him down off his podium and the other half is in his pocket. I know that whenever I arrive on the scene, Terry has his fingers in it, then flaunts his immunity by building a new wing to the children's hospital on the proceeds. But so long as every villain I drag in keeps swearing he's the mastermind, I can't touch him. And no one is going to stand up in the Old Bailey, point to Terry Daley, and go 'that's him, your honour. That's the geeza'. Nobody's that stupid. Not after what happened to Stanton's kid."

"After his fall he was drawn to the block, and there his bowels withdrawn, and he was divided into four parts," Yate recited. "Such a terrible way to die. And so young. They say Terrance himself gave Mad Dog the order." Suddenly, Yate's small, watery rat-like eyes were fixed on Jake. Then, his smile suddenly mocking, he went on. "To prove his loyalty, he butchered his own son before the boy could give evidence against Daley. Then murdered his wife for protecting him. Now he's on the run. Tell me, did they ever find his daughter?"

An icy hand settled around Jake's heart at the mention of the Stanton girl.

He'd heard the stories of Terrance Daley's playroom. It was an underworld myth. A fabrication. Probably cooked up by Daley himself to add terror to his infamy. Even so, there were some things it didn't bear thinking about.

"Such a sweet girl," Yate pressed. "The boy I can almost understand, but to think a father might knowingly hand his own innocent child over to tha-"

"*Harry*, I'm beginning to lose my rag with you." Emphasising Yate's Christian name with deadly purpose, Jake had to force himself to stay calm. "The Flying Squad was formed to tackle commercial armed and unarmed robberies. Not chase leads on escaped convicts playing truant. Mad Dog Jack Stanton is a murderer, a thug, and an extortionist. He demands money with menace and makes bodies disappear. He doesn't get tilled to the nines and wave water pistols at cashiers' heads." He pushed up from the chair, braced his hands on the desk's leather top and leant forward to look the other man square in the eye. "If you have information on where he might be hiding, I suggest you dial 999. Otherwise, unless you give me something tangible, you'll be drinking your Christmas dinner through a straw in intensive care."

There were tricks to a good threat. It was all about the perceived capability of violence. A man with his gun out but shaking like a fairy was just as likely to piss his pants as carry it through and the world could see it. But the smallest gesture, the right look, transformed a man into a monster. And from him, a good threat was deadlier than any muscle-bound gorilla with a shooter.

Deflating like a punctured balloon under the younger man's cold blue glare, Yate pulled open a desk drawer and pulled out a pocket voice recorder that he placed on the leather top. Easing back into his seat, Jake eyed the device suspiciously before nodding. "Go on…"

Moving so quickly, he almost fell out of his seat. Yate pawed the device like a monkey trying to open a fiddly banana, his fingers thumbing the recorder until he finally managed to find the Play button. Someone had obviously prepared it in advance because no sooner had he depressed the trigger than Terrance Daley's old, scratchy voice, heavily flavoured by the East End, spoke, caught in the midst of giving some oration that would have given dear old Adolf a turn.

"Shut it off," Jake said after about twenty minutes. "Is this genuine?"

"Oh yes," Yate confirmed, taking a long draw on his cigar before placing it on the ashtray and stopping the recording. He had fully regained his composure. "Terrance booked my back room for a little Christmas function for a few colleagues. So, I arranged for a few of these to be placed here and there shortly after he arrived. Very good at that sort of thing, are my girls."

"Well, that's very interesting, *Harry*. I'm very impressed. In fact, I'm just fucking astounded. You got Terry on tape. Talking with a lot of people who may or may not be villains, discussing a heist any criminal in Greater London will probably be discussing tonight, or his plans to move a bookcase, repaint his bathroom, kitchen, or Saint Paul's bloody fucking cathedral. I mean…" Jake's eyes narrowed. "What the hell is wrong with you? You fucking idiot. How could you be so fuckin' stupid?"

Yate's mouth gaped. "I-I don't understand."

"Oh, you don't? Well, let me enlighten you, you tart. It's shit, Yate. This. Is. Shit!" Jake pronounced the last three words with a deadly emphasis. "There are no names. No times, dates, not even a damn street address. He's meticulous about avoiding saying anything that can link him to any crime, past or currently in the works. I can't get a warrant based on this. I couldn't even get planning permission. Will you wear a wire?"

"Me?" The older man visibly paled, horrified by the suggestion. "Good Lord, no. I'm not… I mean, I couldn't. Daley would kill me. He'd throw me to his dogs."

"You're a lying, cheating pimp, Yate," Jake growled. "Not only have you not given me probable cause, but by recording this and playing it for me, you've made it so that any case I try to start based on it will be thrown out for illegal tapping, invasion of privacy, and God knows what else his high-priced brief can dream up. He might even try to drag you up on charges. You want to take that chance? Because I assure you, Terrance will."

Yate was suddenly so white he looked like he was about to be sick and his lip was practically trembling. "No."

"That's what I thought." Rising out of his chair, Jake walked around the desk to stand in front of Yate and snatched the recorder from his chubby fingers. "You drag me over here again for this bullshit and I'll hand this tape over to The People's King myself." He turned on his heel to leave.

"What? No… you can't!"

"Watch me."

The switch was concealed in the same drawer that Yate had stored the recorder. A panic button that, when triggered, activated the alarm in the office's concealed side room. It only took a moment for Yate to trigger the switch and another for the door, disguised as a bookcase, to swing open.

They were dressed like twins in matching black suits and came sulking out like well-trained dogs. One going right. The other left. Circling.

The first minder was a monster of a man. An immense six-foot-five brute, more than twenty stone of muscle, with blond hair cropped short and a bushy tash under a nose that was squashed and crooked from numerous breaks.

The second was nearly as tall, but where his companion was all raw power, this one was lean and wiry, broad-chested but long-limbed and narrow-hipped, like a chimpanzee that had learned to walk upright. He had the face of a monkey to match with long dark hair, large round eyes, and a big toothy grin that Jake had the immediate urge to slap off his face.

"Well, look who it is, Pinky and Perky. What's the matter boys, CBeebies give you the axe?" Jake asked, stopping in the very centre of the room as both men came to a pause, one at his front and the other at his back. His mind raced, trying to put a name to a face, but he didn't recognise either of them. *Not from this manor. Now, why would the stupid fat bastard be getting out-of-town muscle?*

"Is this fella giving you hassle, Mr Yate?" the monster asked in a deep, near unintelligible drawl that could only have come from the Welsh Valleys.

The other's grin stretched almost ear to ear, making him look all the more like a primate. "Would you like us to escort him out for you sir?" *No doubt there, a fucking Scouser! No wonder he looks like a monkey.*

Yate was out of his chair and pointing frantically at Jake. "That… that recorder. It's mine. I want it. Stop him!"

Yate, you really are a stupid, fat bastard. Jake shot the older man a cold, narrow-eyed look as he twisted, trying to keep both minders in view.

The Welshman stepped forward, hand outstretched.

"I'm gonna have to take that from you."

"This is police business," Jake growled, twisting to face the bigger man. "You boys scuttle back to your cage before someone gets a slap."

The Liverpudlian moved closer, cracking his knuckles. "Ha, would you get a load of this tosser. Old Bill? He's as much Old Bill as me ma's the Duchess of Cambridge. Oh, and didn' that sound like hostility to you, Jones?"

"That it did. And we don't like hostility, do we, Tim?" They both grinned; as if the very thought of a fight made them giddy. "Now, I don't think you heard me. I'm afraid I must insist, mate. Or I'm going to take it."

Jake's gaze darted from Jones to Tim, and then back to the Welshman. *Tim and Jones? More like Bill and bleedin' Ben.*

"Well, looks like you're not giving me much choice…" He held the recorder up for them to see, then out as if about to pass it to Jones, only to pocket it. "Well, come and get it." They came at him as one.

Though Tim was the faster, it was Jones who reached Jake first, a titanic fist curling through the air. The punch should have hit him dead in the side of his head, just behind his ear, a blow almost certain to stun, if not knock out. Except, the smaller man side-stepped, so it passed by harmlessly, before sticking his foot out, tripping the big man, then slipping down and under Tim's attack. That should have left the smaller of the two men open, but he had not devoted himself fully to the attack and his reflexes were good enough to check himself as he went, countering Jake's riposte by twisting away, keeping his delicate flank out of the line of attack.

Jake didn't wait. This was the more dangerous of the two, the faster and more controlled. He had to be put down hard and fast. Or he'd let the Welshman take the lead, using the bigger man as a shield whilst he attacked from all around. So, Jake came on hard, his first punch a winding jab to the throat, sending the Liverpudlian reeling. Jake followed with his second attack, a devastating phoenix fist to the solar-plexus that had the slightly bigger man doubling over, opening him up for a *coup de grâce.*

And then it was over.

The punch slid past the ribs and into the liver with such a force that it had Tim crumpling to the floor like a sack of potatoes as Jake, his only means of support, slid away. The monkey grin was gone, replaced by a twisted grimace of agony as colour bled into his face and he writhed on the floor, desperately trying to draw in the breath to scream.

It took all of three moves to put the Liverpudlian down. Three moves. Three blows. Three moments.

Jones was just clambering back to his feet when Jake turned to him. Red-faced, the big Welshman's eyes moved back and forth between Jake and the writhing heap on the floor. He wanted to attack but had been unnerved by his associate's quick dispatch. Now his mind was working, weighing the odds.

Jake couldn't help his grin. At barely seven metres squared, Yate's office would never have been his first choice to fight such an uncommonly large man. Space and speed were vital when fighting stronger men. Should he trip over a piece of furniture or become entangled with the brute, he was as good as dead. But an unsure or angry foe was far more likely to make mistakes.

"Alright. Come on! Come on sheep shagger! Bah! Bah!" Jake mocked.

That did the trick.

Bellowing with what could have been an instinctive hatred that all Celts retain for their Saxon neighbours, Jones lunged. And Jake let him. Let him come in close. Let him close the gap, then parried the coming blow with a sweep of his arm that deflected Jones's punch as Jake stepped in with one of his own, straight between the bigger man's eyes. Bone knuckled bone as the Welshman's charge drove him onto the blow, crushing the already crumpled cartilage in his nose so that it seemed to explode in crimson, before Jake's follow-up kick sent him stumbling into the back of a leather sofa.

With a colossal hand pressed to the bloodied mess of his face, Jones glared back at Jake before his eyes darted sideways to an end table, upon which stood, well within arm's reach, a foot-tall sculpture of the Venus de Milo. He sidestepped, hand outstretched.

"Don't you bloody dare." The Glock was in Jake's hand, sights trained on the pulped ruin that had been the Welshman's nose.

Jones froze. "Don… Don't shoot."

"Then don't make me. Keep them up, yes, that's it, above the shoulders." Jake advanced forward slowly. "Now, Sunshine, I'm afraid this is either about to get very messy or go very, very…" The Paras could teach a man just about everything there was to know about blood and pain, but nothing ever really beat the classics. So, he settled for kneeing the bigger man in the balls. "Bad for you."

Eyes rolling, Jones's knees buckled, and he slumped to the ground, unconscious

"Not so big now, are you?" Grinning, Jake holstered the pistol and, without sparing a glance back at the Welshman, turned on his heel and stepped over the equally unconscious Tim.

Yate could barely contain himself. "Sergeant! Wait! No… Jimmy Dawson"

Jake paused, hand outstretched, to grasp the door handle. He threw a backward look across his shoulder. "What about him?"

"He was there. He'll talk to you."

"Dawson's no grass." Jake's eyes narrowed.

"No. But he's angry at Terry. Reckons Daley owes him because he kept his mouth shut and did his bird when some geezer from the regional crime squad offered him an early release from Brixton. In exchange for pointing the finger at Terry."

"That's all they offered?"

"Well, that and the arresting officer's head on a plate." Jake barked with laughter. "Ha! I bet they bloody did. I knew it, the sneaky slags. So why would Jimmy talk to me and not them?"

"Why?" Yate looked as if the younger man had grown a second head. "Because if he talks to the regional boys, Terry will know it before the end of the hour. Angry or not, Daley scares the shit out of poor little Jimmy."

"Just about every villain in London is terrified of Terry, and most of the coppers on the manor as well, it's how the bastard stays on top. Get to the point."

"Why you? Well, you're the guy who put him in Brixton in the first place. He spent most of his sentence there in a wheelchair on your account. If you go to him, make him see reason, he'll probably do whatever you want."

"And if he declines?"

Harry shrugged. "Wheelchairs are still covered under the NHS."

Jake laughed again, then reached back into his jacket, pulled out the recorder, and threw it to Yate. With hands clapping like a seal, the fat man just managed to catch the device. "Merry Christmas, Yate. I'll be in touch."

Chapter Three

On any other night, the Docklands would have been a bustling hive of people and cars. But with less than an hour until Christmas, most of the inhabitants of London were already indoors.

Immune to the chilly December night, Vickey let her feet carry her, not really caring where. She just needed to… to what?

She'd told Erica and Angela she wanted to think. But that wasn't true. She couldn't bear to think. Thinking led to memories. And those memories always led her back to *him*.

It had been so long since the last time. She'd almost forgotten how painful the memories could be. *Ten years on, but one wrong thought and I'm right back there again.*

Why did it have to happen now, when she was already so messed up from Jake?

No, she couldn't go there. Couldn't bear to even think about *him*.

So, she walked and walked, until she finally came to one of the many redeveloped warehouses that infested the ancient city. But where others had been reborn as luxury flats, shopping complexes, and heritage sites, this single red brick structure remained much as it had done a hundred years ago but for a bright neon sign above the door that said in bold red letters *Seven*.

Vickey had heard the name before. Erika had mentioned it once or twice. A club?

Suddenly, she knew what she needed to do.

Chapter Four

Jake wasn't a drinker by nature and never touched a drop when he was on the job. He'd seen too many good mates go down bad roads that way. Drink might be a soldier's best friend away from the lines, however it could seriously fuck up a career quicker than a Rupert with a chip on his shoulder if not kept in check.

But he was off the clock, and he seriously needed a drink.

The server behind the bar, an obvious toff with blond hair gelled into what Jake could only describe as a failed bird's nest, only looked at him when he ordered a Black and Tan. It took three tries before he finally got the cocktail right.

"That'll be eleven forty-five, *sir*," he said with an obviously forced smile as he placed the infusion on the bar.

Jake all but gaped as he fished in his jean's pocket for his wallet. "Eleven forty-fucking-five? I asked for a drink, not the time. Where did you get the beer, Japan?" Indignant, he put a twenty-pound note on the bar and scooped up the glass. "You could have at least made it a pint."

The toff ignored the jab and took the note over to the till before bringing him his change. "Can I get you anything else?"

"At twelve quid a beer, not bloody likely." But the server had already gone to another patron, so Jake just shoved the change back into his pocket and twisted round to face the dancefloor. Leaning back, he sipped the B&T, watching, instinctively looking for something he was utterly terrified of finding.

They'd met in a place just like this. She'd been working as a waitress in the club and he'd been out for a celebratory drink with the rest of the squad. She'd taken their drinks, and he'd engaged with a bit of banter. It had been completely innocent, but then they'd crossed paths in his regular cafe where he went for his tea break when working at HQ. Then again, at the end of the week, when he'd been grabbing a ready-meal, and she'd been on the till. It turned out she worked in a temp agency. It had been the end of her shift and seeing his choice of cuisine, she'd offered to make him dinner if he would walk her home. It might have been more banter, but it hadn't stopped him from offering to drive her.

The age gap wasn't an issue. He'd never asked why she never accepted the frequent offers of permanent employment from her numerous temp jobs. She'd never asked about his job or why he kept 'illegal' firearms in his drawer or had to leave suddenly sometimes, or why he always came back with cuts and bruises that would make Mike Tyson think twice. They'd just clicked.

Goddamnit, get a grip man. She's gone. She left. You're done. Get over it- He froze.

There she was. Vickey Romano, gyrating on the dancefloor in tight skinny jeans that drew every eye to her luscious derriere and a long-sleeved, halter-style sweater that stretched across her cleavage while showing off her milky midriff.

Fuck, she was gorgeous. So gorgeous. Just seeing her tore at him, made his heart skip and his cock hard.

Her dancing was a thing to behold. Graceful. Seductive. Neither slow nor fast, but a pace that was entirely her own and utterly bewitching. She gave it her all, moving her hands up her body, through her long raven locks, to join over her head as she rocked her hips and abdomen, inviting someone, anyone, to come hither.

He watched her from his perch at the bar. Drinking in her every move and contour, observing her the way a falcon watches a rabbit in the meadow. But in the back of his mind, he remembered the feeling of those long legs wrapped around him. Those delicate fingers on his skin, in his hair, urging him on as he devoured her luscious pussy. Remembered the softness of her raven locks sliding through his fingers, the heat of her skin on his, the taste of her rosy nipples, the kittenish moans she made whenever he fingered her clit while fucking her from behind…

He wanted her, regardless. Wanted to go over and kiss her, take her, mark her somehow so all the world knew she was his.

He tossed back and drained the Tan & Black. *Utrinque Paratus.*

Ready for Anything

If it weren't for the seasonal décor, one could almost have been forgiven for thinking it was anything other than a national holiday in less than an hour. *Seven* was bustling. The music was loud. The atmosphere sultry. And the patrons were hot and heavy.

Utterly consumed by the beat and flow of the music, Vickey let it sweep her away. She wanted to lose herself in the music, forget the pain, the loneliness.

This was what she'd needed. This freedom. The momentary release of knowing she was lost, just one amongst many. A girl like any other. *They* couldn't touch her here.

There were no hunters in the crowd. No one looking to claim the bounty on her head. No hunters, just watchers.

She could feel eyes on her from somewhere, hot and hungry, raking her from head to toe.

And suddenly, the music blaring out through the speakers changed. The chronic pop Christmas song switched to the sensual throb of a jazz storm, making her very core vibrate to its seductive rhythm.

It's true what they say,
Love is blind, so,
we must find our way.

You know my name
Come into my world,
See through my eyes.
Hear my words,
And know what I say

Remember
We've been dreaming this life
But when you need me,
I'll hold you close
Hold you tight

Love you forever
As we're together this night, I'm
broken without you...

The eyes never left her as she let the music guide her, giving herself over to its sensual beat as the heat raked her from head to toe, sizzling across her skin. It was as thrilling as it was unnerving.

Exaggerating the swing of her hips, Vickey did a slow three-sixty, her eyes glancing left and right. Where was he? Her watcher? She could feel him, close by, and getting closer. Weaving between all these bodies, using the tight press to conceal himself. A predator, but not the kind she was used to. She could see that sort easily enough, leering at her over their date's shoulder or over a glass, like dogs after a bone. Obvious. Pathetic. But this guy?

He was different. Exciting. It felt like she was dancing for him. Just for him.

Maybe she'd even let him pick her up, take her home. It had been weeks since she'd last gotten laid, and she needed it. Needed to bury these feelings. A hot, hard fuck had always been good for that, good for burying the pain and letting her forget, if only for a moment. Jake had been so good at that.

No, forget him. He's a guy, just another guy. A big, hard dick with powerful hands and a wicked tongue. She didn't need him. *Any of the rogues here would do-*

A shiver of awareness rippled up her spine, then hands were on her- large, powerful hands, enveloping her, rough fingers tingling across the skin of her belly, drawing her against a male body.

It's true what they say,
Love is blind, so, we must
find our way.

As we play this game,
A game of lies
You know my name
You know my world
I am yours
So, you are mine

Something inside Vickey yielded under the aroma of raw masculinity, fogging her thoughts. The guy smelled of leather, sweat, and… something else, something so familiar it made her core throb. His hands were everywhere and nowhere. Brushing over her midriff, along the hem of her jeans, and up her ribs, exploring practically every bit of skin he could reach, ferreting out the spots that had her tingling at his touch. Still caught in the song's beat, she arched like a cat into his touch, arms reaching back to encircle his neck, grinding against his groin, the weight of his arousal pressing along the curve of her derriere.

"Mmm… naughty girl," he growled in her ear, close enough that she could hear him over the music but far enough away that she could feel his words on the slope of her neck. The words sent delicious shivers down her spine. *That voice! That voice!* She tried to turn, to face him, but he held her firmly, pressed tight against his body with the subtle dominance that drove her wild. *No, it couldn't be, not here, not him!*

Then her mind went blank.

He was kissing her. Small, hot little kisses up her neck to the spot just beneath her ear, making her knees weak and

pussy throb, yearning for attention. She matched him, pushing
back, rubbing against him, relishing the feel of his hard body,
her hands reaching, exploring the muscular ridge of his back
and shoulders, nails biting whenever he teased *that* spot.

He was working her into a state, and utterly absorbed
in the feelings his mouth was conjuring, she almost didn't
notice him fingering the fastenings of her jeans, popping the
button.

"No!" she half gasped, half moaned, panic rising in her
breast. This was going too far. He wouldn't.

"Relax. Just go with it." He pushed, suckling her pulse
spot.

"Oh, God."

He was insane. There were too many people. Anyone
could see. All it would take was one glance, a curious look, but
the risk only made her hotter. And the thought of it, getting
finger-fucked here, in the middle of this club in Wapping, on
the dancefloor, surrounded by all these people practically
dripping with lust, had her legs spreading, giving his
wandering fingers licence to slip into her jeans, beneath her
panties.

Remember
I'm there for you our love
will always be true

It's true what they say,
Love is blind,
So, we must find our way. Break
through the surface.
See through my eyes.
Know my heart
Say my name

"You're so wet."

She could practically hear his smirk as he ever so gently brushed a finger across her folds. Not hard enough to enter her, but still enough to collect some of the creamy dew seeping down her thighs and tease across her clit in small circles.

Her moan was throaty and desperate, her hips rolled, seeking more contact. "Someone might see."

"Yes, and that makes you hot, doesn't it?" he growled in her ear, so close and low now it was entirely dangerous and exciting, like sex given voice. "The thought of being watched, of getting caught…"

Goosebumps rose all over her body. The music was loud, reverberating around the club, blending into white noise amidst the holler of the bodies enveloping them, but Vickey's attention was fixed on that voice. She didn't miss a word, his every syllable pushing her into sensory overload as those fingers, those damn wicked fingers, rubbed up and down her slit. He applied just that little bit of extra pressure each time he touched her clit and then dragged his finger downward, until she could feel her body opening, his fingertip dragging along her inner tissues.

"Don't!" she whispered in a voice much too husky to pretend she didn't want this, want him.

Whilst one hand was doing such wicked unspeakable things with her pussy, the other was reaching up, coarse fingers sliding up under the hem of her sweater to brush the underside of her breasts, teasing and feather-soft. It turned her nipples to stiff, almost painful peaks, yearning for attention.

She didn't need to look to know her arousal was visible through her sweater.

"No! We can't mmm… Stop… Don't stop. No!" Her body throbbed and clenched around his finger when it pushed inside, penetrating her to the knuckle, and she made no effort to hide her wanton grinding on his palm.

Vickey should have been embarrassed, even ashamed of her responsiveness. She was letting this complete stranger do and say these naughty things to her, but he was right. Just the thought of doing these things here, in such a public place, where anyone could see… It was more than just thrilling. It was pure addiction, a fire in her blood that drove her wild. "That's it, love. Feels good, doesn't it?"

Panting from the feelings he was evoking inside her, she stubbornly shook her head, refusing to answer.

"Oh?" Though he tried to sound abashed, his hold on her never slacked and she could practically hear the grin in his voice. The sexy bastard was enjoying this, enjoying baiting her and making her bend to his whim. "If you want me to stop…" He began to withdraw.

"No!" Her thighs snapped shut around his hand.

"Oh? So, you want *more*?" His finger curled inside her, swirling leisurely, stroking her insides.

"Yes!" It felt like an eternity since anyone had done this to her. Jake had been the last, and she would have given anything in the world for it to be him in this anonymous creature's place, his hands stroking her, fingers inside her. But Jake was gone, off somewhere else, probably fucking some lucky little tart. She'd seen to that. So now she had to make her bed, and shag in it until dawn, until she'd worn herself out on this walking dildo.

And he was quite a dildo indeed. Hard as steel and straining quite vividly against the fabric of his jeans, she could practically feel the heat of him radiating through their clothes. The weight of his desire pushed up against her, grinding in that all so delicious way that had her rocking and grinding, fucking herself on his hand. "Yes! More! I want… more!"

"Naughty girl," he purred, the low throb of his voice coursing through her as she thrust against his single digit, trying to incite him. Then her mind was blank, lost in a whiteout as his mouth fell upon hers, swallowing her moan as he pushed a second digit inside her, thumb pad rubbing circles over and around her clit. And all the while, his tongue mimicked the movement of his fingers, swirling and spinning, flitting in and out of her hot cavern.

It was too much.

Too good.

Then suddenly he was gone.

No! Maddened from her closeness, her eyes snapped open to meet a hauntingly familiar pair of cool blue eyes. "Jake."

He'd let his hair grow out until it almost reached his shoulders and shaved his goatee. But there was no doubt. It was him.

"Hello, angel." He grinned that devastating grin that never failed to make her wet for him and had her thighs rubbing together of their own volition, desperate to rekindle the contact he was denying her. "Does it really turn you on so much? Getting finger-fucked here? Where anyone could see? Maybe some already have…" The dishevelled look suited him. Made him look younger, enhancing the strong lines of his jaw, and, if it was possible, even more dangerous when combined with his black leather jacket, jeans and shirt. "How 'bout we really give them a show?" And to her horror, he brought his hand to his lips, the hand that had just been buried in her jeans, buried inside her, and licked one slick and shiny finger-tasting her in the middle of the crowded dancefloor.

She came.

Remember

I'm broken without you
You want to save me
But together we're stronger Together
What's broken can be fixed
But my love for you Will
never die.

CHAPTER FIVE

This was a very bad idea.

He'd only gone up to talk to her, but then…

The shadowy back corner didn't offer much cover, but it was quieter here and they were far enough out of the way, hidden behind a private booth, that Jake was confident nobody could see. He had pinned her to the wall, hands braced, penning her in with his body as their tongues danced a fiery duet and her fingers clutched at his jacket.

"This… this is… we should stop…" she gasped, tearing her lips from his. Her objections, however, only opened more skin for him to kiss so he dipped down to ravish the slope of her neck with nips and licks while working his way between her legs. Needing her to feel how hard she'd gotten him. And he was hard. Hemmed in by the tight confines of his denim prison, his cock felt like a solid length of steel between his legs. The pressure amassing inside wasn't exactly painful, but by no means was it pleasant, either.

It demanded release, and he fully intended to grant that wish. Later.

"Mmm… but you're so wet," he whispered, gently nipping the spot where her neck and collar met before soothing it with a slow, leisurely lick. "Come on, say you want me. Your needy little pussy must be throbbing for my cock."

Arching into his mouth, Vickey fisted his hair, pulling him closer. "No, no! Jake! Please…"

She was nervous, her voice low and breathless, still worried they'd be caught, but that wanton tone was music to his ears. He collared both her wrists in one hand, pinning them behind her back with enough force to make her gasp.

"Ah. Ah. Ah… No touching." He was sinking to his knees, the fingers of his free hand curling into the waistband of her jeans.

"Jake?" she gasped, louder now, as the denim pooled around her boots, exposing her to his hungry eyes.

"Well, look at these." His grin was toothy as he took in her vibrant crimson and black underwear. Part lace, part filigree, but entirely sexy. It hugged her so tight, the outline of her folds was clearly visible through the fabric. "Such sexy panties. Did you come out looking to get fucked?" He pushed a finger into the centre of the garment, gently rubbing up and down, tracing the line of her furrow. "Mmm… and you're so wet." His mouth watering at the heady aroma of her arousal, he drew in a long, exaggerated breath.

"Ja-Jake-oh!"

He licked her through the lace, the point of his tongue sweeping up the cleft in a slow drag up and over her clit, collecting all the creamy dew that had seeped through. It was the briefest tease of contact, but it was enough to make her knees all but buckle as her hips jumped, pleading for more.

"You're so responsive, you dirty girl. Hasn't someone been getting any lately?"

"No-no-no! Please, Jake, don't…"

"Have you fucked anyone else?" Jake repeated, pushing his finger into her heat, then dragging it up to bear down on her clit. "Answer me."

"No! No, there's been no one else! Just- please Jake, I- oh God! Just you. Just you! Don't-don't tease me, I can't-oh fuck, there right there! I can't take it! Eat me! Fuck me! I don't care, just make me cum."

Jake's mouth enveloped the bud of her clit through the lace, and he sucked. Hard. He had dreamed of this moment. Of having her beneath him again, at his mercy, begging him to finish her. In those moments, he had teased and toyed with her, driven her to the brink of ecstasy, only to pull back and start over. But here, now, he just couldn't deny her.

Instead, he watched the orgasm sweep over her with almost perverse fascination, drinking her in, recommitting every moment to memory. How her skin flushed, the way she arched and thrashed, forcing her eyes shut against the pleasure and worrying her bottom lip to keep from moaning. She was perfect. A deity. The goddess of love, beauty, and debauchery. There was nothing he wouldn't do for her. He was her faithful servant, enslaved to worship at her feet.

Restrained as she was, her release racked her like a storm. Jake sucked her all the way through, her flavour like honeyed wine on his tongue, and as it passed, her legs gave way. Rising to meet her, he released the hold on her wrists to steady her while his other hand hooked around her thigh, raising one long leg.

"Wrap your leg around me."

She obeyed, but the difference in their heights forced her to raise herself onto the tiptoes of the other leg to do so. Jake dipped his head to take her mouth in a long, lush kiss. Swirling his tongue around hers, the hand that had been holding her leg dipped down to the crotch of his jeans, where his cock formed a very obvious bulge. While that hand worked at the buttons, the hand that had been supporting her back teased down the nubs of her spine to cup her bum, two fingers hooking under and drawing back the drenched thong.

When he pulled back, glazed eyes struggled to focus on him. "Ja-Jake?"

He swept his tongue across his bottom lip, collecting the last of her heady cream. "Delicious." Then time held its breath.

Holding her gaze, he rolled his hips, watching as Vickey's eyes widened, and that cute little mouth formed a delicious 'O' as his broad crest passed through her folds into lush, welcoming heat.

And it took all his restraint not to lose himself right there.

Jake lived for this moment. When he pushed inside, when their bodies joined, and two came as close to becoming one as it was humanly possible. When he saw the look in her eyes that told him she could feel him inside her. It filled him with a sense of pure primitive conquest. She was his. This beautiful little sex-kitten was all his, and he was going to make sure she knew it. She was his.

"T-too much… s-so big b-bu-but so good!" Vickey panted, her tone pleading and her hands seizing anything she could cling to.

Jake gritted his teeth against his answering moan as her muscles flexed around him, bearing down on his cock. She needed time to adjust, to get used to the feeling of a man inside her again, but he couldn't wait.

He needed her. Now!

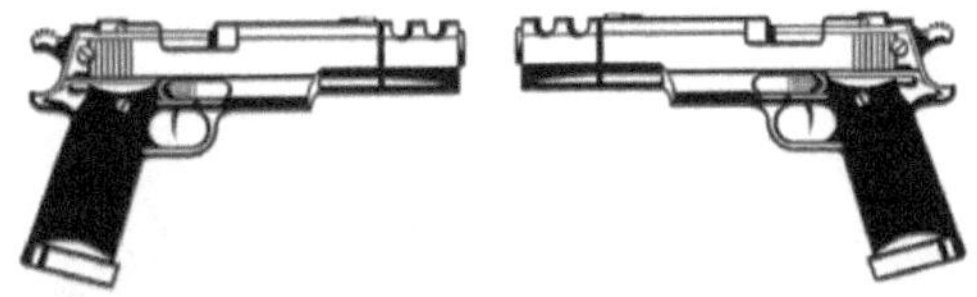

She felt as much as heard Jake's low growl of pleasure. The deep rumble hummed through his skin into hers as he pulled back, withdrawing until more than half his length had left her before driving back home. The sudden delicious shock of deeper penetration had Vickey's head rolling back. "Jake!"

"Yeah, that's it. You missed my cock. Didn't you?" With his hands only half supporting her, he repeated the move.

"Yes!" She couldn't believe this was happening. It was so surreal, like something straight out of a Sylvia Day novel. Jake. Here. Fucking her against the wall in a dark corner of this sleazy Docklands club. And she, utterly helpless to do anything about it, powerless in his arms as he pinned her to the wall. The odd position was making her feel disoriented and her pussy was sucking wantonly on his cock.

God, she had missed this. He was too big for her. Too long. Too thick. It was always a struggle for her to accommodate him, but when he was fully sheathed inside her, he stretched her out and left her feeling completely stuffed. Using what little leverage her one foot could give her to grind herself against him while digging her heel into the base of his spine, she urged him on, craving the raw, primal heat that only Jake could invoke in her.

"Fuck! You feel so good!" he panted. "This has you so hot, knowing anyone could come by and see you getting fucked."

"J-Jake!" She wanted to deny it. But just the vision conjured up by that statement had her ready to burst. Instead, she pushed back and ground her throbbing clit against his pelvis, craving more.

"I'm going to make you scream, love. Make you scream so loud so the whole place will hear you begging me to fuck you, to make you cum." Then he heaved her into the air.

The motion was so quick. So sudden. It made her half squeak in fright and half moan with ecstasy. She was forced to relinquish her hold, to throw her arms around his neck, clinging to him with all her might. He had an incredible body, like marble, not bulky, but etched and defined. She longed to see him, to pull those clothes from him and bask in his magnificence and feel his warmth pressing around her. But then he began to pump her up and down, his cock slamming into her with wild abandon.

"Oh fuck! Jake! No! Not so-fuck! I can't-Oh fuck! Yes! Fuck me! Fuck me!" Her voice was rising, growing louder with the sensations stirring in her centre. Desperate to smother the sounds he was drawing out of her, she buried her face in the hollow of his throat to kiss, bite, and suck all the skin she could reach.

God, his strength was amazing. Even pounding into her like a jackhammer, driving into her harder and deeper than before, he supported her so easily, as though she weighed less than a feather. Manipulating her. Using her. Controlling her with irresistible force as large hands squeezed her arse hard enough to make her gasp, driving her up and down, his thick cock sawing through her wet heat, touching those places she had never known existed before she'd met this man.

It felt like he would split her in two at any moment.

Anything he wanted, he could have. She was his for the taking. She couldn't take it. It was too good, too much. He was right. She was going to scream. Any moment now, he was going to shove his big dick inside her all the way, bump her clit, and she would shatter and scream for the whole club to hear!

"Jake!" she breathed in his ear, taking her lobe between her teeth, her inner walls squeezing him. "Make me ride your big cock, baby- oh fuck! Oh my God, yes, yes, yes!"

Fuck, this was it. She couldn't stop. He was going to make her cum, and she was going to scream. Oh God, she was going to scream, and she didn't care. Let them all hear. Let them see. She didn't care. She only needed…

"Cum for me, angel." Jake's mouth caught her lips in a searing kiss the instant he thrust up to meet her halfway as he brought her down and buried himself inside her all the way to the root, forcing her over the edge.

The orgasm ripped through her in waves of fire, fast and hard, rippling outward from the pit of her stomach to the tips of her fingers and toes. The scream that left her was voiceless, but she could feel herself shaking as if the very fibre of her being was trying to escape the bounds of flesh and soar free to the heavens.

She clung to Jake with everything she had. He was her anchor to the mortal world and seemed content to let her ride the waves of her orgasm until the heat and frenzy ebbed slowly away to leave her floating in the warm comfort she only knew with him. Here, in his arms, she could forget. She could forget about her father and the family he murdered, the old paedophile calling himself *The People's King,* the men hunting her, the bounty.

Whatever he was. However bad he might be for her. Jake made her feel safe and whole. He was the only one who could.

For that, she would love him forever.

Chapter Six

Breathing hard, the black spots still dancing before his eyes from the intensity of his orgasm, Jake held the girl close, savouring the feel of her. It felt so right, her in his arms, holding her. It always did. Even when everything around them was wrong, she felt right.

She was perfect.

"That was… something."

Snuggling closer, Vickey murmured a sleepy "Mmm-" She stiffened, "Oh God."

"Why, thank you, angel, but I'm just a man." The joke came easily to his lips, even as his insides knotted at her tone. Fear? What could she have to be afraid of with him?

"I-I have…" Her voice was weak, but the force with which she pushed away from him was as strong as ever. She looked a state. Sweater crumpled and creased. Skin flushed. Hair dishevelled. Lips bruised and swollen. All the hallmarks of a woman who'd just been thoroughly shagged and was about to take the walk of shame. "I have to go."

Jake watched her go about getting dressed, noting with a small sense of satisfaction the way her legs were shaking as she struggled to pull her jeans on while still wearing those slip-on shoes. She didn't look at him. Rather, she seemed to be making a point of looking anywhere but. Then she was gone, stumbling away from him, away from the dark, around a bend into the light as the dancefloor beyond was suddenly lit up and shouts and cheers trumpeted *Merry Christmas*.

Jake watched her go. He didn't say a word, only watched with a bemused smile playing across his lips, and when she was gone, he slumped back against the wall. The wall he'd just so readily fucked her against.

He fumbled to do his jeans up with only the slightest care. The task made all the more awkward for the fact he was still hard as a rock. Once was never enough with that girl. He couldn't explain it, but there was just something about her that made him able to go all night. When he was satisfactorily covered, he reached into his pocket and pulled out a box of fags and his old regimental lighter. He shook a cigarette free, took it between his lips and, with a practised flick of his wrist and lit the end. Ignoring the *No Smoking* sign hanging barely a metre away, he took a long drag, let out a breath of grey smoke, and began to laugh.

"God, I love you Vickey Romano."

High above, sunken into the ceiling, one of *Seven's* numerous security cameras continued to record.

Daddy's Forbidden Temptations

Chapter One

Richard Martin always hated Holmes & Raine's Christmas parties. The décor reminded him of a cheap Hammer Horror set. The atmosphere was reminiscent of a funeral. And worst of all, they were organised in August and hosted in early November.

Each year, the bosses would present a laundry list of reasons for the premature celebration, but everyone knew those were merely a smokescreen, devised to mask the fact that it cost considerably less to hold a Christmas party before December. Frankly, Richard wondered why they bothered even holding a party, or, for that matter, made attendance mandatory.

Subtly pushing up his left sleeve cuff, he checked his watch for what felt like the hundredth time. To his utter disgust, the digital display indicated that it was just *10:03 pm*. The *party* would go on for at least another hour, maybe even two, God forbid!

The dining hall of the Cheltenham Premier Inn was a hive of colour and light as the *value* disco ball fitted to the ceiling pelted the chamber with light beams and the speakers blared out a stream of Christmas hits from the 90s. The walls were decorated in red and white. Mistletoe hung on strands of crimson silk, and an artificial Christmas tree stood in the centre of the room beside a folding table heavily laden with snacks and refreshments. The guests appeared jubilant and festive as they revelled in small groups evenly spaced around the cavernous chamber, mirroring the groups that clung together around the office's coffee and tea machines. They were garbed elegantly in suits and dresses, a façade of wealth and importance that was as phoney as their smiling faces. God, he needed a drink.

Resisting the urge to check his watch, Richard got up from his assigned seat and moved into the crowd, the wooden soles of his shoes clapping loudly on the tiles as he weaved a path between the mingling bodies, nodding politely at anyone who noticed him, towards the overloaded folding table. There were ample snacks and refreshments, Asda's finest. Diced sausage rolls, cocktail sausages, crisps, biscuits, fruit and cheese on cocktail sticks, mini-pizzas, and even some slices of chocolate sponge, all laid out in white china bowls and saucers around two large bottles of Jacob's Creek and Honeyed Jack Daniel's, as well as a jug of iced orange squash. Two high towers of Styrofoam cups had been erected between the bottles.

Taking the cup on the top of the tower, he contemplated the wine for a moment, tempted to pour a drink, but then thought better of it. Alice would kill him if she found out. Grumbling inwardly, he mournfully poured himself a squash. The wine was probably vinegar anyway, he reasoned, before twisting to take another look around the room while sipping the fruity beverage.

He glimpsed Stacy Stevens, a pretty part-timer, in the firm's mailroom with long raven black hair and milky skin, nervously edging through the crowd in her black lacy dress and flat-bottomed shoes; somehow seeming even more uncomfortable than him amongst the revellers. Nearby, he saw Mark McClaine, his office colleague and friend, and his wife Rachael deep in conversation with another couple he didn't recognise. And deepest amidst the denizens, the firm's MD, Derik Holmes, was conversing with the heads of departments and grinning broadly as he took long swigs from a monogrammed silver and crocodile-leather hip flask. Silverhaired, rosy-faced, and with the frame of a barrel wrapped in Armani, Derik was the very embodiment of opulent living and Richard could only hope the man didn't notice him for he was awfully fond of mocking and belittling anyone whom he considered beneath him. Fortunately, the four department heads seemed to be commanding the full wrath of the Director's humour and he failed to notice the lowly bookkeeper standing beside the refreshments. Alas, there was no sign of Alice amidst the sea of faces, but neither, thankfully, could he see…

"Well, well, well, look who we have here?" an all too familiar voice said silkily.

Fuck. Throwing his head back, Richard drained the cup in a single swig before placing it back on the table and turning, slowly, around to be confronted by the vision of his supervisor, Scarlet Holmes, standing before him. Strikingly beautiful with soft features and sun-kissed skin, her hair was long, wavy tresses of honey blonde that reached down to her shoulders. Clad in a dark blue pencil dress that went well with her almost unnaturally bright baby blue eyes and clung to her slender figure, the low-cut V-neckline offering a tantalising glimpse of her ample cleavage, she would have seemed utterly radiant if he hadn't known the beauty was only skin deep.

"Hi Scarlet," he said nervously before flashing her a smile he was certain Stevie Wonder would have seen through; "enjoying the party?"

"Mmm…" she purred, watching him with a wicked amusement that Richard wasn't sure he liked. Then again, he rarely knew how to feel around Scarlet Holmes. Though she'd only been twenty-three and barely out of University when she joined the firm, she was also the CEO's daughter and had leapt over the heads of a dozen more highly qualified employees to get the Accounting Supervisor's position. What made it all the worse was, unlike the stereotypical cliché of a ditzy boss's daughter, Scarlet actually knew her trade. Despite having an attitude that constantly swung from aggressive to flirtatious, she had a genuine business acumen as well as a knack for people and figures. She was ambitious and worked tirelessly to ensure that she and her people regularly went above and beyond. Thanks largely to her efforts, they were now the top performing team in the firm and rumour had it, she was about to be promoted to the Head of the Accounts Department. However, there were also whispers. Rumour had it that she'd had numerous affairs with more than half the firm's employees, many of whom were happily married. For his part, Richard preferred not to put stock in the storm of office gossip that followed where ever she went, but in one thing, at least, the rumours were true. She was a real tight arse. "Where's your wife? I haven't seen her. Is everything alright between you two?"

"Oh…" His eyes flickered towards the door leading out of the hall to the building's main foyer, hoping against hope to see his wife sashaying towards them. "Alice just stepped out for a minute. She had to take a call but couldn't hear herself over the music." His tongue darted out to moisten his dry lips. "She should be back any minute now." And he hoped that was true. The words sounded hollow to his ears, sounding foreign and unfamiliar and he suddenly had the feeling of being trapped as he realised just how close they were, her curvaceous body all but pinning him against the table. "So-so, how's your father? He looks like he's…enjoying himself."

He gestured with a nod over her shoulder and Scarlet twisted to a look back across the hall to where her father was telling a very animated story. At the sight of a short and portly man with thinning red-grey hair Richard had seen around the office a few times but had never been introduced to, standing a few paces away, she made only a token effort to cover her laugh with a cough. With a face such a deep shade of red it was almost purple and watching the inside of his cup so intently, clearly determined to look anywhere but at his immediate superior, the tomfoolery could only have been at his expense.

"Well, you know Daddy, always happy so long as there is a drink in his glass and minions to torment." It was meant as a joke and Richard tried to match her gleeful chuckle, but his heart just wasn't in it and he could tell she saw through the façade. Suddenly, her playfulness evaporated.

When she turned back, the stern mask that so often watched him like a hawk whenever he handed in his reports suddenly glared up at him with eyes as cold and hard as diamonds. The shift was so abrupt it almost gave him vertigo. "He has his eye on you."

"Me?" Swallowing the knot suddenly rising in his throat, he forced himself to hold her gaze, fighting the impulse to glance towards the Director. The urge was like burning fishing lures hooked into his eyes, tugging insistently, and he fully expected to spy the Managing Director shooting him a glare, the mirror image of his daughter's. But why? What the hell would walrus face want with him?

"The Prometheus Account." Scarlet supplied by way of explanation, arching one perfectly plucked eyebrow. Full pink lips pulled tight into an almost indefinable line.

Prometheus was a London based construction and land developments company that had several branches throughout the continent and, according to their books, also had contracts in parts of Central America, Asia, Africa and the Middle East. Though it was not exactly an uncommon practice for big organisations to outsource their accounts, indeed Holmes & Raine had more than a dozen such contracts, there was no question that the Prometheus Account was a big deal. Rumour had it that Derik Holmes had superseded two department heads to ensure his daughter received the account. With explicit instructions, it was to be given top priority. Whether that was true or not, she, in turn, had called Richard into her office and instructed him to delegate his workload around the rest of the team. She wanted Prometheus to be his sole concern. Everything else was to go on the back burner. So he had.

She'd also told him to have it done ASAP. That had been three weeks ago, and the reports were still stashed on the flash drive he kept locked away in his desk drawer.

"Ahhh..." He swallowed, the knot in his stomach leaping sickeningly into his throat. He should have known. Hell, he should have given her the damn USB last week. Withholding it had been stupid.

For all the weight laid on his shoulders, it hadn't taken him long at all to sort and organise and check Prometheus' accounts. It was such easy work; a trained chimp would have been up to the task. Their records were meticulous and immaculate. The numbers perfect. And, what with the pressure to finish the job, the importance of the contract to the company and the fact his performance review was upcoming; withholding the data was more trouble than his job's worth. Withholding it had been very stupid, but Richard couldn't help himself. In his twelve years in accounting, he had never seen anything like it, and that irked him. He couldn't put his finger on what, the numbers were just…too perfect. Or too perfect to be genuine.

Of course, it wasn't any concern of his. He wasn't an analyst. It wasn't his job to sort out conundrums. He just kept the client's books. When he was done, he sent reports to Scarlet with notes about his concerns and recommendations, if any; but in this, he couldn't help himself.

It almost felt like there was a challenge hidden amidst the sheer mass of paper and data, of piles of receipts, invoices and spreadsheets. Something secret only he could see. Hidden, waiting, daring him to find it. So, he'd begun to dig, looking deeper, trying to solve a mystery that common sense screamed didn't exist, but that the small voice in the back of his mind refused to let go, like some naughty schoolboy playing truant to go on a great adventure in the land of Narnia.

Sooner or later though, the boy needed to go back through the wardrobe, and if the Managing Director had his eye on Richard... So far, every money trail had turned up empty and by itself, mere professional curiosity wasn't worth losing a job over. Or, worse still, becoming the next punchline in one of walrus face's jokes.

Baleful blue eyes glared up at him, chunks of blue ice burning bright against a sea of soft beauty. Richard forced a small, reassuring smile. "I'll have them on your desk Monday.

"Good" That single word was like a storm passing to unveil sunbursts. She beamed with the radiance, her golden skin lighting up with a warmth that chased any hint of chill away as those luscious pink lips curled into a smile. "See that you do, or else I might just have to give you a spanking." She winked.

Richard gawped, not sure whether to believe his own ears. Had she really just said that?

To anyone who might have glanced their way, the gesture would have appeared innocent. Yet her eyes lost none of their intensity as she watched him, and her playful tone sent a warm, involuntary shiver coursing up his spine. What the fuck?

He remembered all the stories he'd heard people at work gossiping about the people who'd told them and the wide range of vague, outlandish details that seemed to grow more and more extraordinary with each retelling. It was all hearsay. Mostly just the petty vindictiveness of someone who'd been put out, or thought her job should have been theirs, or just the usual rambling talk that always seemed to blossom around a famous name. There had never been any proof, and until now, Richard had barely given them much thought. But that look in her eyes made him ready to believe every word. He'd seen it on the cats he sometimes saw stalking city streets on his morning drive to work. There was the same confidence, the same purpose and… hunger.

She watched him the way a stalking cat would observe a bird pecking in the mud, utterly fixed in its own world and ripe for the plucking, and the thought had him instinctively averting his gaze. Whatever this game was, he didn't want a part of it. However, knowing she was waiting for him to say something, he opened his mouth to agree but the words that should have come caught in his throat and all he could do was nod in acknowledgement. Heat blossoming across his cheeks, he swallowed, his mouth so dry it felt like forcing down a lemon. Goddamnit, he needed a drink.

Her eyes flashed, victorious fire dancing over cool blue ice. Then, as if only just realising she was making him uncomfortable, her smile faltered for a moment and turned apologetic. "Awww don't worry, Dick. I was only kidding," she cooed like he was a small child or pet dog. "I think you better have another drink. If your face gets any redder, they might mistake you for Rudolph and hang you on the wall." She giggled, the sound all girlish and mocking. "It's already a rather striking likeness. Maybe with a pair of antlers-"

More relieved than embarrassed by her dismissal, Richard turned back to the refreshments before Scarlet had finished speaking. With the Styrofoam cup still in hand and grateful for some much-needed space between him and the teasing wench, he reached out for the jug of squash. To his horror, the hand was shaking. No! God, get a grip man. Don't let her get to you.

As if she knew his thoughts, Scarlet stepped in close enough for him to inhale her perfume. Something sharp and expensive.

"Here, let me," she offered. Brushing his hand aside, she seized the handle and, despite it being almost full, raised the jug one-handed. With a slight pivot of her hips to face him, she filled his cup almost all the way to the top, her gaze unwavering, boring into his with that look of predatory glee, seeing through him, into him. It was unnervingly similar to the look Alice shot him whenever she suspected he was up to something. "There." She put the jug down before finally breaking the contact to give the drink a quizzical look. "Just orange? You don't want to mix it with something a little stronger?"

"N-no thanks. I'm driving." Barely able to get his tongue around the words, Richard had to fight the urge to immediately knock the drink back. Fuck, where the hell was Alice? What could Samantha have to say that couldn't wait for tomorrow? He looked down at the orange in his cup, wished, though he'd never been much of a drinker, that it could be something fermented, and added under his breath without thinking, "Alice would kick my arse if she found out I'd been drinking." The moment he'd said them, he regretted the words. Beaten, he surrendered and chucked the juice back in almost one big gulp. It was deliciously refreshing and eased the knots in his gut in a single rush of watered citrus.

"Ohhh…" Mirth lit up Scarlet's eyes. "Well, isn't someone a slave driver. Come on, Dick, I promise I won't tell…" she teased, playfully reaching for the Honeyed Jack Daniel's. Richard struggled not to grin at the impish mischief on her face.

"No, it's fine, I don't really like mixing drinks anyway."

She feigned a pout that had no doubt melted her daddy's heart more than once. It had the effect of making her look so serenely demure and girlish. He might have been convinced she was sincere if not for that wild glint in her eyes. It was a sinful look on her, the perfect melding of innocent and wicked. All that was missing was an Anne Summers costume, probably a nurse or cheerleader's uniform.

A shiver coursed up at his spine at the thought of Scarlet in such a skimpy ensemble. Her long legs encased in knee socks and vanishing into a miniskirt that seemed to promise a glimpse of whatever she had on, or not, underneath with every movement. A tight-fitting crop top stretched tight over her full breasts but cut just short enough to show off her flat stomach. Golden hair bouncing in pigtails as she played with a set of pom-poms…

Richard mentally shook himself, trying to clear the image. He wasn't a horny teen anymore. Those sorts of thoughts were trouble. He was married. And she was his boss. Off limits didn't even begin to cover it. However, his body apparently disagreed and, to his horror, the image roused a very vital part of his anatomy into life. Registering the stirring, he instinctively glanced down to see an already visible bulge rising against his left trouser leg. He shifted, trying to cover his visibly straining erection before glancing back up. But Scarlet must have already noticed because the pouting girl was gone. Instead, she was grinning toothily, her eyes bright. Pink tongue darting out to slowly moisten her full kissable lips, she mouthed "busted."

Time held its breath. Somewhere in the hall, a guffaw rang out. The timing was purely coincidental, but even still the humiliation hit him like a bucket of ice water. Dammit, what the fuck was going on? He couldn't believe this was happening. He needed to think, to get some air before this got any worse and his boss decided to whip out her phone to immortalise the moment.

Contrary to being impeded, however, the realisation he'd been caught only had Richard's cock stiffening to full mast against its confinement. To his enormous relief, no one else appeared to notice.

Scarlet's eyes widened, her smile faltering to form a perfect 'O'. "Oh... my!"

Well-aware of what had caught her attention, Richard turned his eyes up to the hall's plain white ceiling and ornamental brass chandelier-style lights draped with tinsel, desperate to look at something, anything, but the woman eyeing his dick. To his enormous relief, no one else appeared to have noticed. He felt like a little Robin red breast that had spotted a cat stalking it in the grass and taken flight, rising high on a wing of elation and the adrenaline of escaping death. Only to be swatted from the sky and brought crashing back down, its last moment consumed by the image of the sleek feline body arching into the sky, hooked claws reaching out and fangs bared. I tawt I taw a puddy tat, indeed.

"Have you heard anything about your promotion?" he asked without thinking, studying the interlaced webs of gold, red and green tinsel that enveloped the nearest light.

"Y-yes…" For all her customary swagger, the silky soft voice sounded breathless and the shaky timbre drew his gaze irresistibly back to her. Scarlet glared back at him. Her eyes narrowed and cheeks tinged a faint shade of pink. She seemed to be musing about whether to say more, searching for a trap behind the question, and the uncertainty reflected in those bright blue irises had him blowing out a slow breath that released all the tension from his body.

Scarlet obviously sensed, or noticed, the change in him, however, because the gleam of predatory amusement returned to her eyes. She'd play whatever game he had in mind, and she'd play to win. "Daddy says the job's mine if I want it, but first I need to get my house in order. He's starting to think we might have a loose cannon on deck." She leant casually back against the refreshments table with her hands gripping the edges to distribute her weight and back, curving just enough to emphasise her breasts. It was a pose that would have put many magazine centrefolds to shame. "But let's not talk shop. This is a party, after all. How is your son, Alex, isn't it? I saw the pictures on your desk. He must be nearly two now?" Richard held her gaze, refusing to take the bait even as his eyes were instinctively drawn to the slopes of her breasts. "Almost sixteen months, yes." He swallowed, a bitter taste rising in the back of his throat, not liking the way this conversation was turning. "And he's fine, hasn't quite got the hang of walking yet. Can't quite find his feet, so he's always losing his balance mid-step. We've had a lot of scuffs and tears, but he keeps getting back up." He couldn't quite keep the pride from his voice. So many kids would burst into a fit of tears whenever they fell over and refuse to move until their parents picked them up, but Alex never stopped. Even in tears, he would push himself up and keep crawling to where he wanted to go.

"And you and Alice are coping well?" she asked, cocking her head to the side. A curl of locks fell out of place, but Scarlet didn't brush it aside, her eyes searching his. "I doubt it could have been easy starting a family so soon after losing your job.

Your career taking such a huge step back and having to pack up your lives to move here. Not many marriages could weather the storm so well. Maybe you two should write one of those self-help books. Money woes and job lows - A couple's survival guide." She chuckled, the sound dry and mocking.

Forcing a small smile, Richard resisted the impulse to give her the finger. I prefer Don't Let the Tarts Get You Down. "We're Fine." Of course, it was a half-truth. They fought, sometimes like cats and dogs, over nothing at all, and other times they fought to avoid the very real issues looming over them. There had been many of those recently, but he wasn't about to discuss that with Scarlet.

"I see." With that, she pushed away from the table and fingered the stray lock of hair back behind her ear. "Tell me, Dick, would you consider it cheating to kiss me under the mistletoe?" She said it casually, as if it was as every day as asking about the weather.

Already on edge and walking on eggshells, the broadside caught Richard completely by surprise and had him almost doubling over in a fit of dry, heaving coughs so violent it was a marvel he didn't choke. "Ex-ex-excuse me?" he stammered, certain he must have misheard her.

Smiling teasingly, she stepped closer so that as she looked up; they were almost nose-to-nose. "It was a perfectly simple question." A hand tipped by baby blue nails reached out, taking the cup from his grasp and placing it on the refreshment table before tracing her finger up along the lapel of his jacket and along the line of his jaw. "Would you consider kissing another woman under the mistletoe as being unfaithful to your wife?"

Her eyes flickered to the ceiling overhead and, pressing firmly on his chin, she tilted his head back. Too stunned to resist, he followed her gaze skyward to where three leaves of mistletoe were hanging off a scrap of crimson silk dangling above their heads.

Richard's chest constricted. "I...I..."

"Cat got your tongue?"

Richard wheeled, the pit falling out of his stomach as the all too familiar voice asked and brought a frosty blast of reality. Alice Serena Martin stood not three steps away with her arms crossed and glaring at her husband. "Am I interrupting something?" she asked icily.

"Darling," Richard tried to make the greeting sound reassuring, but the rush of fear and arousal the sight of her provoked in him at that moment made it hard to do anything. Even after all the years they'd been married, the sight of her could still leave him speechless. Pale as milk and utterly gorgeous, she wore only the smallest amount of makeup and a sultry, backless evening gown of black satin that moulded perfectly to her hourglass figure. A slit from thigh to hem flashed a glimpse of smooth, flawlessly toned legs that seemed to go forever as she walked. Though shorter than most, her tiny stature barely scraping five feet when propped up by the stilettos she'd worn for the party, his wife was a downright knockout with her sharp, pronounced bone structure, hair that ran down her back in a long wash of silken mahogany, and intense grey-blue eyes.

Yet now her beauty had been contorted into a twisted mask that gave her the hard face of a hawk. Eyes that had stared up at him with such love and devotion, now piercing with accusation. That look cut deeper than steel. He wanted to say something to reassure her, but, somehow, a line like 'it's not what it looks like' just didn't seem it.

"Ahh, Alice!" Scarlet stepped around Richard, into the older woman's sights. She beamed, her eyes alight with wicked delight. "There you are. We were just talking about you."

Alice's cool gaze shifted to the blonde, her lips pursing into a fine line "Indeed."

"In fact, *Dick* was just telling me about your son. He's such a handsome little boy, you must be very proud.

"Yes."

Scarlet gave Richard a slow, appraising look, then smiled knowingly. "He's the spitting image of his father. Good luck keeping the girls away. You'll have to beat them off with a big pole." Dread's cold fingers crept down Richard's spine at Scarlet's added emphasis. Dammit, was she going to try and start a fight?

Though the women had only met on a handful of occasions, exchanging barely more than a handful of words each time, for whatever instinctive, irrational reason, the atmosphere had crackled around them. He could feel it building, raising the hairs on the back of his neck, and knew that rather than finding salvation in his wife, he'd jumped straight out of the frying pan, into the fire.

"Well, I'll manage." Missing nothing, Alice's gaze narrowed momentarily on her husband, who couldn't help shifting guiltily on the balls of his feet under the hawk-like stare, before returning to the younger woman. "But I'm sure you can give me a few pointers sometime. *Dick* tells me you've handled lots of woodwork around the firm." She forced a wry smile. Richard, of course, had never said anything of the sort, but he wasn't about to contradict her. "Your father must be very proud that you're treating his staff so well after he gave you a job?"

For all of a moment, Scarlet's eyes widened in surprise. Then she recovered her composure and her smile melted away into a small, derisive twist. "What can I say? I like to keep the men under me satisfied. Dick's never has any complaints." Alice's nostrils flared and the fingers that had been creeping down Richard's spine closed around his gut, but Scarlet appeared not to notice. She shrugged, her eyes trailing over Alice from head to toe, scrutinising her like she would a document that came across her desk. "That's such a lovely dress, Alice. Is it new?"

Oh, fuck! Richard didn't need to look at his wife to know that, if Scarlet was trying to pick a fight, then she'd just hit her mark. He knew he should step in, but Alice shot a look that warned him to stay out of it. The corner of her lip rose just enough to reveal the glint of white teeth, something she only did when she meant business and had him glancing nervously around the room.

Fortunately, no one seemed interested in taking advantage of the buffet or paying the confrontation any notice, yet.

"You deserve to treat yourself." Scarlet pushed on, her voice laced with a sympathetic tone that was all pity and mocking. "Was it hard to find one in your new size? It would be just awful after you worked so hard to shed the last of that pesky baby weight, but I guess some things just can't be helped..."

Alright, he needed to put an end to this. Whatever Scarlet's game was, she had gone over the line.

Like so many women, Alice had always been overly selfconscious of her appearance. While no one could ever accuse his 110-pound wife, who could put away a whole pizza like Richard did a good 18oz steak, of being anorexic, she was borderline obsessive about her weight. One of her main requirements, when they'd been flat hunting, was that there had to be a nearby gym, and she visited it almost daily. After Alex was born, she'd worked hard to rid herself of the pregnancy pounds and even harder now to maintain her figure. She would give back as good as she got and believed in taking the bull by the horns. If a child tried to fob off not doing their homework, she called them on it. When something went wrong at home and he wasn't in, she dealt with it.

So, if Scarlet wanted a fight, Alice would damn well give her one. Even if that was exactly what the little strumpet was counting on.

Richard opened his mouth to intervene, not at all interested in finding out just what his wife might say, or do for that matter, with so many people around them. Only Scarlet rounded on him before he could get a word out. Her eyes were bright with an impish mischief that made him want to run a hand through his hair.

"Anyway." She cocked her head as if remembering an afterthought, her hair tumbling over one shoulder and exposing the long slope of her neck, as well as giving him a glimpse down the valley of her breasts. "I just so happened to notice that piece of mistletoe hanging up there. So, I asked *Dickie* if he considers it being unfaithful to kiss me." She slid forward a step. Heat bristled across the back of Richard's neck, the fury in Alice's stare burning his skin as Scarlet pressed into him and touched a hand to his cheek before he could think to pull away. The closeness as intoxicating as the perfume suddenly fogging his thoughts and her eyes held his. "It's such a small tradition I know, but they say it's bad luck to ignore it."

"Ohhh really?" Alice shouldered past the younger woman. Scarlet reeled, almost sprawling to the floor, before catching her balance at the last moment. "Then allow me." Her hands tangled in husband's hair, fisting and dragging his head down so their lips crashed together in a fierce kiss.

The sudden embrace stole his breath away and he couldn't help uttering a ragged moan as her tongue forced its way past his lips to meet his in a feverish dance. His hands rose on their own accord to circle around her waist before trailing down her back to grasp her full buttocks, roughly pulling her against him and drawing a low moan from his wife. Then, just as quickly as she had begun, Alice broke the kiss and drew away from the embrace. Short of breath, Richard could only grin down at his wife's satisfied smirk.

"Yea! Get in there, Richard, my son!" Mark called, followed by a sudden uproar of applause and catcalls as every face in the hall zeroed in on them. Breathing hard, Richard forced a smile and raised a hand in thanks, only to be elbowed in the ribs by the equally embarrassed Alice.

"Geez, get a room." Scarlet snarled, her smirk replaced by a scowl. "Maybe you should go before they demand an encore. See you on Monday, *Dick*." Then, starting to worry her bottom lip, she turned on her heel. "Nice to see you again Alice."

"Bitch," Alice cursed under her breath, watching the younger woman's retreating figure with a look of utter malice, before taking her husband's hand in hers and dragging him through the mass of clapping hands and out of the two huge glass doors that opened out onto the Premier Inn's rear garden. It was a cold night, even for mid-November, and the cloudless canopy above twinkled with stars that lit the ground just enough for them to make out the cobbled path leading around the structure to the car park. A frigid wind whistled by and Richard hesitated, remembering that Alice hadn't been wearing a jacket, but she dragged him along. Though wearing five-inch heels, she traversed the tricky stones with ease while he was left almost tumbling over his own feet to keep up with her.

Polished and gleaming, their immaculate black Volkswagen Golf would have been almost invisible in the hotel's car park if not for the solitary lamppost standing sentinel, bathing the vehicle in golden light. Unlocking it with a quick press on the key in his pocket, he held the passenger side door open for his wife to enter the vehicle before closing it and moving around to get in the driver's side. However, no sooner had he pushed the key into the ignition did Alice round on him.

"So, what really happened between you and that tart, Scarlet?" she hissed, seething like a cobra in her venom.

"What? Nothing…. nothing at all…" Richard gasped, shooting her an uneasy smile that he prayed she might find convincing. Her stern look promised otherwise, however, and he quickly turned back to the windscreen, a heavy sigh passing his lips as he fastened his seatbelt and activated the dipped headlights. "Really… it was nothing; she was just asking me a question about mistletoe. And that's all." Twisting the key, he let the engine roar to life and then reversed out of the space before shifting into gear and driving from the car park out onto Gloucester Road.

"Ohhh really…*Dick?*" she spat accusingly, the nickname rolling off her tongue as a long serpentine hiss.

"Ugh! Bloody hell, Alice, this is ridiculous!" he growled, tearing his eyes off the road for a moment to shoot her a reproachful glare. Fortunately, there was little traffic, and the Golf purred like a kitten as they sped along the deserted dual carriageway, angrily challenging every traffic light at a steady 60mph. Yet when a metallic blue Vauxhall convertible roared out of the darkness, overtaking them with a sound like a thunderclap, he couldn't resist the challenge and sped after it. Flooring it, he'd caught up to the sleek two-seater in a matter of seconds, but at a glance from Alice, he eased off the throttle. "Look, I swear, nothing is going on between Scarlet and me."

She watched him suspiciously for a moment more before finally relaxing into her seat, yet he knew she wasn't convinced. Alice was anything but a fool; she'd heard the whispers about his supervisor and, like any good loving wife, she was concerned.

They'd first met fifteen years ago at the University of Bristol. She'd been a 'fresher' studying English literature and out with her *BFFs* on a Saturday night. He'd been a struggling second-year Business Studies student working a double shift in the popular student bar, The Burning Book. While he'd been on the taps, she'd ordered a round of Bloody Marys and when she paid, had handed him a £20 note and a napkin with her mobile number scribbled down. She'd been the first girl to show any real interest in him and, utterly bedazzled by the petite stunner, he'd called her immediately after his shift. Five years later, they were both graduates with promising careers. Alice an English teacher in a prestigious secondary school, him a junior banker. They were also newlyweds, young and in love.

For the first few years of their life as husband and wife, they'd rented a comfortable little flat well within walking distance of Bristol's city centre. However, disaster struck in 2004 when his bank was bought out and amidst the fallout,

Richard had lost his job. For the following year they'd lived on a blend of his savings and Alice's salary while he looked for work in the city, but the economic devastation of the recession had left him floundering in a raging river of unemployment and without their prosperous joint income, they'd been forced to move to the smaller, *cheaper*, city of Gloucester.

Feeling the tension hanging between them like a great steelball and collar as they left the lights of Cheltenham in their wake and sped down the black stretch of road, Richard changed the subject. "What did Samantha have to say?" Samantha Swift was Alice's oldest and dearest friend, as well as her maid of honour at their wedding. "Shouldn't she be attending to her latest husband's bank balance? Or has the Internet finally run out of shoes and gold?" Alas, the joke fell on deaf ears.

"She's getting divorced."

"What?" He shot her a disbelieving sideways glance. "The ink on her marriage certificate hasn't even dried yet, and she's getting divorced. What happened? Did she bleed the poor bastard dry already? They've only been married a few months."

Growing angry, Alice glared back at him. "No, this time it's different. She caught him in the hot tub with their dog walker." *Damn.*

Feeling his cheeks burn with embarrassment, Richard kept his gaze rooted to the road ahead. Road signs indicated a roundabout half a mile ahead and beyond that, the horizon burned with golden radiance. *Home sweet home.*

Founded at the dawn of the first century AD, on the order of Roman Emperor Nerva and the pride of the Mercian King Æthelred, Gloucester was built along the banks of the River Severn, close to the Welsh border. Though primarily an industrial mecca, the city was a wealth of history and culture, with Tudor architecture still adorning its central streets and the fabled cathedral at its heart.

They drove in silence for several long moments, street lamps bathing them in warm light as they entered the city area. Cruising down Eastern-Avenue past rows of warehouse stores that lined either side, he glimpsed two sets of traffic lights changing from emerald, to amber, to crimson, and began to brake. Downshifting gears, he quickly floored it as the lights changed back just before they came to a complete stop. There were two more sets of lights, but both stayed green as they approached and passed. Despite it being ten-thirty on a Saturday night, the roads were dead and deserted but for the odd cyclist. Houses sprung like weeds as they drove around a roundabout, past a Tesco's garage and took the last exit of an even larger roundabout, capped by a grass isle in its centre. There the road became thin and narrow, winding round numerous snaking twists and flanked with rows of two-storied brick houses on either side, passing a cemetery and an old primary school encircled by high iron spear fencing.

"She's moving into her parents' house on Friday," Alice announced suddenly as they swerved off the main road after passing an ancient church. "I told her you'd be happy to help." She glared at him venomously, as if daring him to refuse.

Steering the vehicle into their parking space, Richard took the car out of gear and put the handbrake on. Taking the key out of the ignition, he turned to his wife, gave her a genuine smile, and said, "Anything for you."

Leaning forward, he seized her lips in a passionate kiss.

Chapter Two

Though the living room door was shut, Richard could dimly hear a movie playing as he shut the front door behind him and Alice. Recognising the cheesy dialogue, he couldn't help but groan in disappointment. *Oh God, please no, not Twilight again!*

The flat was a huge leap down from the one they'd had in Bristol. On the third floor of a five-storey tower block, it had two small bedrooms, one bathroom, and boasted views overlooking Gloucester Park as well as a security door and parking. The rent was also cheap because the flat was on the less desirable side of town.

Slipping off her shoes, Alice went ahead of him and vanished through the wide archway on their right into the kitchen to make a cup of tea whilst he moved down the darkened foyer towards the living room's closed door. "Hey Rebecca, we're home."

A startled gasp and hurried footfalls sounded in answer, and the door was suddenly swung open to reveal a slender feminine figure, shadowed against the bright glare of the living room.

"Hi Mr Martin, sorry, I didn't hear you come in."

"That's okay Rebecca. I know we're back a bit earlier than we said," he assured her, blinking against the sudden flood of light. Fortunately, his eyes adjusted quickly to the blaze, discerning the girl's soft doe-like eyes staring up at him from beneath the smooth wash of dark brown hair that she'd tied into a side braid over her left shoulder. Just nineteen, she had a long, sweet face and a petite yet shapely form that was clad in tight blue jeans and a pink floral T-shirt that ended just above her flat navel. "Has Alex been behaving himself?"

"Oh, he's been just wonderful. Little tyke hasn't made a peep since I put him down." Smiling up at him, she stepped back to let him pass into the flat's living room.

Neither spartan nor lavish, the furnishings were mainly teak and pine, equally as decorative as they were functional, as well as a wide three-person sofa of supple black leather that had been pressed against the wall and a Sony DVD player and 32′ television that were mounted on the opposite wall. As he'd feared, the film *Twilight* was playing on the flat screen.

"So, how was the party? Did you have a good time?"

"Boring really. In fact, we were kicked out," he said, barely able to keep the wide grin at bay as he recalled Scarlet's venomous, jilted glare. He would probably pay merry hell for it on Monday, however. Scarlet always loved to play games and Alice had thrown a fine challenge her way tonight.

She may have won the battle, but he was sure the war had only just begun.

Plainly befuddled, Rebecca's eyebrow arched at his comment and for a moment he thought she would press him for further details, but the kettle began to whistle, and he heard Alice shout out a greeting to the girl. As she turned to reply, he took the opportunity to slip past and crossed the room in six quick strides before going through the open doorway leading to the bath and bedrooms. Taking care not to make a sound as he moved down the shadowy antechamber, he crept past the connecting bathroom and master bedroom before coming to the infant's room. Pushing the door ajar, just far enough for him to squeeze through, he stepped cautiously into the gloom beyond. A blue nightlight bathed the interior in a low gloom, illuminating the Star Wars cartoon wallpaper and providing just enough light for him to trek a route around the dozens of toys that lay scattered across the floor.

Sleeping peacefully in his cot, the infant Alexander never stirred as his father approached. If it had not been for his stormy grey-blue eyes and thick dark brown hair, the boy would have been the spitting image of his father and the sight of him curled around his favourite stuffed puppy brought a smile to Richard's face. Given their tenuous financial state, many of their friends and relatives had been surprised by his and Alice's decision to go through with the unexpected pregnancy. But Alice had always wanted to be a mother, and as there was simply no way of telling when the economy would heal, be it ten years or even a hundred. Life was just too short to turn down the blessing life handed them, and they had never been happier since little Alex came into their lives.

Bending forward, he placed a gentle kiss on the child's brow before drawing back and retreating from the room, gently pulling the door shut as he went.

Knowing he should go and pay Rebecca for her help but too eager to get out of his suit, he entered the master bedroom and flicked the light switch before casually shrugging off his jacket. Hurling it across the bed, he'd just begun fingering his tie when there was a sudden knock at the door and he turned around to see Rebecca standing in the doorway, with a sheepish look on her face and her *Twilight* DVD case in hand. Concern stabbed his heart with an icy dagger.

"Hey…Mr Martin, I'm sorry to interrupt you but I'm setting off now and well…my dad's gone away for a couple of days and before he left, he managed to screw up our laptop. I hate to ask, but he'll be home tomorrow and if he comes back to find it broken, he'll just blame me and force me to buy a new

one, so…if it's not too much trouble, could you… well um-"
The words were spilling from her in a tide of emotion and she
looked on the verge of tears.

Richard gave her a reassuring smile. "Of course I can. You
go on home and I'll be up to take a look in a minute."

"You will! Oh, thank you Mr Martin; I really appreciate
this." Visibly relaxing, she turned on her heel and headed back
through to the living room, leaving Richard alone with his
thoughts and a quickly mounting temper.

"That rat bastard."

Though they lived on the floor above, he had only met
Rebecca's father on one or two occasions, but each had left a
lasting impression. Unlike his daughter, Derik Blaire was
squat, heavy-shouldered, and prone to violent outbursts. Once
happily married and a carrier squaddie, he'd been cashiered
after getting drunk and striking an NCO whilst off duty, but
still in uniform. A court-martial found him guilty of
insubordination, behaviour unbecoming, and wilfully striking
a non-commissioned officer. He'd lost his pension and been
sentenced to confinement for three years before receiving a
dishonourable discharge. In the months after his release, he
was dismissed from six occupations before apparently
abandoning the search for work. His wife, tired of his bullshit,
left him for a younger man and moved up to Yorkshire to
escape his continued harassment, leaving their daughter with
her growingly aggressive and substance dependent father.

Richard was reluctant to ask about the pair's main source of
income. He knew Rebecca worked part-time in a shop over in
the Quays, as well as babysitting for them and a few other
families in the building. However, that could hardly cover the
costs of living, so he was sure there had to be more there than
just met the eye.

Loosening his necktie enough to pull it over his head, he hurled the cloth across the bed to join his jacket before starting upon his black shirt but then thought better of it. He and Alice would be going to bed soon enough. There was no point dirtying fresh clothes. Even so, a stab of old vanities caused him to pause before his wife's standing mirror. Tall, cleanshaven, and relatively comely, he had deep blue eyes and medium length raven hair that framed a sharp jaw. Though only thirty-seven, his hair had been salted with a streak of silver, but Alice assured him it made him appear distinguished; he just prayed it didn't foretell his going bald.

Deciding he needed a drink, Richard moved on to the kitchen to find Alice already leaning against the fridge and sipping a steaming cup of tea, waiting for him. A half glass of wine sat on the counter beside her.

"How's Alex?" she asked, setting the cup down on the side and crossing her arms over her waist as he reached for the wine.

"Sleeping peacefully, thank God, and if we're lucky, he'll stay that way till morning. I swear that kid has a set of lungs on him that could wake the dead." Watching her carefully, he brought the glass to his lips and drained it in one swig. It tasted bitter, and he openly shuddered in disgust.

Alice, however, paid no mind to his displeasure. A few stray strands came loose from her thick mane to hang over her eyes, but she brushed them back into place without taking her gaze off him. "So, are you going to help her?"

"Of course I am."

She gave an approving nod. "It's shameful the way he treats her. The sooner she moves out of there, the better." They'd often heard Rebecca talk about moving out, going to live with friends or whatever boy teased her heart. Sometimes she even mentioned renting a little place of her own. However, she never seemed to be able to find enough money and after a few weeks, she'd lose her enthusiasm for the idea until the next time her father lost his temper and threw something at her. "Though I think she will miss you, Richard."

The remark caught him by surprise, and he coughed so hard the wine in his belly almost repeated on him. "Me? I have no idea what you mean, Love."

A sly smile lit up Alice's features and her throaty voice developed a noticeably playful tone. "How could you miss it? She's got a crush on you, Richard," she chuckled. "You're clueless. She watches your every move and smiles whenever she sees you. If she knows you're home, the poor girl gets dolled up just so you'll say she's pretty. And you know, I can't say that I'm not a little jealous." Stepping forward, she took the glass from his hand and placed it on the counter before closing the gap between them, her finger tracing invisible symbols over his chest. "She really is quite beautiful, isn't she?"

Richard's throat ran dry. Was she serious? Was she baiting him, or just stating a fact? Alice had always been blunt, and nobody could deny that Rebecca was certainly very pretty, but how could he agree with her without inadvertently risking her wrath? "Alice, I-"

Her lips silenced him as she suddenly went up onto the tips of her toes, their mouths crashing together in a devouring embrace as her hands moved to encircle his neck. Fierce and demanding, she held nothing back and quickly took the kiss deeper, the passion of it setting a fire in his flesh as her slick tongue invaded the moist warmth of his mouth to meet his own in a feverish dance. He felt his trousers growing tight as his cock sprang to life, powerless to resist his wife's errant ministrations as she drew him against her, one long shapely leg rising, curling around him.

His heart hammered in his chest as he wound his arms around her waist, drawing her closer. Her full breasts pressed against his chest, pebbled nipples poking through the satin like diamonds, and he could feel the heat of her desire against his thigh. His hands, so large upon her tiny frame, trailed down her spine to seize her buttocks, causing her to gasp into the kiss as he pulled her against his hard arousal. It had been so long, he needed her. Now, atop the counter, against the fridge, on the floor, he didn't care. He just had to have her...

"She really is quite beautiful, isn't she?" Her words echoed in his ears, sending a hot shiver down his spine as an image of Rebecca appeared before his eyes. She was arching in pleasure, locked in his arms, whimpering softly as he tasted the hollow of her throat. It was only a momentary lapse, but the mental image was enough to make him jump back, breaking the embrace.

Flushed and breathless, Alice almost lost her balance, and she flashed him an insidious look that both chilled and enflamed his ardour. "What's wrong?"

Fighting to catch his breath, Richard couldn't meet her gaze as guilt's cold fist turned his innards to ice. "We ca-can't do this now. I promised to help Rebecca; her father will be home tomorrow. If I don't go now, it'll be too late."

For a moment she looked as if she were about to protest, but she had always been fond of the girl and after a moment her face softened. She gave a short, defeated nod before turning away. "Fine, just don't be too long."

Her frosty tone was as much a dismissal as a slap in the face, yet as he departed the kitchen, he distinctly heard her declare, "I'll be waiting." The words were rich with promise, and he didn't know whether to cheer or weep.

Chapter Three

He knocked three times and then waited as the sound echoed nine times off the tower's inner walls. The air was thick with the sickly-sweet reek of drugs and somewhere a couple were shouting, their thunderous curses echoing through the walls like clangs on a bell. However, he was too distracted by the painful ache in his groin to take much notice. Digging his hand into his pocket, he tried to relocate his still swollen erection, but the trousers were barely large enough for him to thrust himself down the right leg. The inner pent-up agony persisted, nonetheless.

Shifting uncomfortably, he raised his hand to knock again, only to hear the *click* of the lock's inner mechanics unlocking before the door swung inward to reveal a vision of such beauty that Richard's breath caught, his engorged flesh growing ever more painful. Gone were her tight blue jeans and pink floral top. Instead, Rebeca had changed into a lacy, black robe that was tied around her narrow waist and barely covered her pale ivory thighs. She had also taken her hair out of its braid so that it cascaded down her back in a tangle of lustrous dark curls and framed her soft features.

She lit up at the sight of him. "Oh Mr Martin, thank God, I was starting to worry you weren't coming."

Once again, Alice's words echoed in his ears and Richard felt the heat rising in his cheeks as he realised he was staring. Flashing a hollow smile and praying she wouldn't notice the bulge straining against his right trouser leg, he said, "Rebecca, how many times have I asked you to call me Richard? Mr Martin makes me sound like some whining old geezer."

"Well, you are an old man, Mr Martin." Giggling playfully, she stepped aside to let him enter. "Would you like something to drink? Tea? Coffee?"

"Ahh…tea, milk and two sugars please and, *thanks*," he said, his voice dripping with sarcasm at the joke as he moved into the flat. The layout was almost identical to that of his and Alice's and he quickly moved down the hall into the Blaire's living room. With dim, off-cream walls and filled only by a small jumble of cheap mismatched furniture, it looked larger than it actually was.

A grubby old grey and blue denim sofa faced an even more ancient Panasonic television that had been mounted upon a near modern looking glass and steel stand that was certainly more functional than decorative. There was a single, threetiered, mahogany veneer, bookcase, its shelves sagging under a dozen piles of dog-eared military and spy fiction paperbacks, a ceramic bowl atop a walnut look-alike end table under the window, as well as a massive opening night poster from the 80's hit-movie *Predator* that had been framed and hung on a wall. At the back of the room, a tall display case of solid teak stood in stark contrast to the items of veneered plywood scattered around it and held an impressive collection of Rebecca's swimming trophies. From a young age, the girl had been an avid swimmer and had even gone on to represent Gloucester in three county events, but after her parents' divorce, she had lost much of her enthusiasm for the sport. Now she rarely went more than once or twice a month.

The computer desk stood opposite the display case, the laptop already open and booting up. It was an ancient HP that hadn't been updated beyond Window's *Vista*. Sitting on the threadbare ottoman that the Blaire's employed as a chair and grimacing at the uncomfortable sensation in his semi-hard manhood, he logged into Rebecca's account and was immediately confronted by the problem as a virus conjured up an obviously falsified police lockdown. He tapped a few select keys, but to no effect. Next, he tried to open the start menu, but the virus brought up a warning box and cancelled the command. Finally, he logged out and entered Derik's account. The result was the same.

After a moment, Rebecca entered with his tea and placed it on an old *Top Gear* magazine lying beside the laptop. "Any luck?"

"Does this happen every time you log on?"

"Yes. It's been like this now for two days," she replied, her voice trembling as she peered far enough over his shoulder for him to taste her scent, reminding him of the first breath of spring. The scent steeled his length. "Can you fix it?"

Richard didn't answer. Instead, he pressed down on the power button until the screen went blank. Restarting the machine, he quickly switched to safe mode before letting it load up. Again, logging into the girl's profile, he waited a moment to make sure it didn't change again before going into its control panel and initiating a system restore to the pre-set point. It was a pretty routine trick that would work 99 times out of a 100. However, when he logged on for the third time, the scowling face of the law immediately opposed him.

"It might take a while."

Repeating the process of placing it in safe mode, he then filed through the recent system downloads and found that there were more than two hundred from the past thirty-six hours. He deleted them all, sipping his tea and cursing under his breath every time one or a dozen would randomly regenerate. When all of them were finally put down for good, he restarted the laptop and was finally met by Rebecca's normal background of a '*Hello Kitty*' poster.

Exhaling a long breath, he gratefully pushed away from the desk and stretched his legs out to relieve the cramp building in his knees. It felt like he'd been at the desk for hours, but his tea was still lukewarm, so it couldn't have been any more than twenty minutes.

Throwing one leg over and around the ottoman, he twisted to face the sofa where Rebecca was now reclining, watching some cheesy Jennifer Aniston rom-com that was playing on ITV2 whilst eating from a carton of ice cream. The sight of her soft pink lips wrapped around the spoon sent a hot pulse straight down his spine and he heard her moan in delight, her soft brown eyes falling closed as she savoured its sweetness…

"There you go Rebecca, all done."

"Really!" Startled out of her trance, her head whirled to face him and as she shifted, the lace of her gown moved with her, flashing him a momentary glimpse of her soft ivory bosom. "Ohhh…thank you, thank you, Mr Martin!"

"You're welcome, Rebecca." It was time to go; he knew it as well as he knew the desire stirring in his loins. And yet he could not will his legs to move. "But you should really consider updating your security, or perhaps switching to a more secure browser."

"I know we do. I keep telling Dad, but he just ignores me. He thinks it will cost too much money. Ohhh…thank you so much Mr Martin, I don't know what I would have done without you." Then, almost giddy and still clutching her carton of ice cream, she sprang up from her seat and raced across the room to throw her arms around him in a tight hug. The embrace caught Richard off guard, and he could do little more than bask in the feeling of her young body pressed against him. He could feel her breath on his neck, hot as a furnace and tickling his every weak spot as the sweetness of her scent filled his every breath, causing a fog to descend upon his mind.

Time seemed to slip away. He couldn't say for how long she clung to him, yet when she finally broke the embrace, he felt light-headed and she couldn't meet his gaze. A blush touched her cheeks pink, and she quickly stepped back. He should go now. This was his chance, before things got even more complicated; all he had to do was politely say goodbye, leave, and then everything would be fine…

Yet the moment came and went, and the silence hung between them as a heavy iron collar, binding them to each other.

"You're eating ice cream, what flavour?" he finally asked, desperate for anything that might ease the tension.

Rebecca, however, seemed to have forgotten all about the carton and it was only when she looked down and saw it there that she realised icy drops of condensation were running off her fingers. "Ohhh…it is Tesco's Cherrylicious." She had such a sweet voice. Why hadn't he ever noticed it before? "Would you like some?"

Damn, he had always had a weakness for cherries. He knew he shouldn't, yet when she offered him the spoon, its head filled with a blend of fluffy white vanilla and thick gooey cherry, he couldn't resist and obediently opened his mouth to accept the sweet treat. The taste of it flooded his senses, as deliciously bitter as it was sweet, and he swallowed it all greedily. Yet as she pulled the spoon away, a single creamy drop escaped the corner of his mouth and ran wetly down his chin. He moved to brush it aside, but Rebecca's spoon was quicker, and she scooped up the droplet before bringing it to her own lips.

"Mmm…delicious," she moaned, and he realised it wasn't the ice cream's bitter-sweet flavour she had tasted, but his own. Seeming to sense his scrutiny, she suddenly stilled, and when their eyes met, they both knew the truth.

Heart pounding, he reached out and took the utensil from her before hurling it aside with a flick of his wrist. Then they came together, and he could feel his head spinning as their lips met. Rebecca didn't hesitate; the ice cream carton was gone, discarded. He knew not where or when, and she was upon him, straddling his waist. Wrapping her arms around his neck, she kissed him hungrily, her lips parting and her small tongue pressing against his lips, demanding entry.

Richard knew he should stop this before things went too far, but his body was acting on its own and his mouth opened to accept her, passionately returning the kiss as his hands seized her backside and crushed her to him. *She tastes like…cherries.*

Surrendering to the moment, a low growl rumbled through him as he lost himself in the intoxicating sweetness of her lips. He could feel her breasts pressing against him as her tongue ran wild within his mouth, brushing over his teeth and tickling the roof of his orifice. She let out a small moan as his tongue slipped over hers and hotly twirled around the probing muscle, pressing it back into the warmth of her mouth. All too aware of his fully engorged arousal straining for release from its tight confines, he used his hold on her buttocks to draw her closer, letting her feel the effect she was having on him as their tongues danced. Whimpering with pleasure, Rebecca eagerly responded by rocking her hips against his own and a hot shiver ran down his spine as he felt the damp heat of her desire through the mesh of garments.

Only when his breath was exhausted, and the need for air utterly dire, did he break the kiss. Yet drunk on her sweetness, he couldn't stop; grabbing deep ragged breaths, he swooped down and began to nip a trail of fire from the sensitive spot just under her ear, down the soft slope of her neck, and to the exposed crook of her shoulder. Gasping hotly in a mixture of pleasure and pain at every tiny subtle bite, Rebecca tilted her head back, exposing more skin for him to kiss as her fingers tangled in his hair, a ragged moan escaping her as his tongue traced the ridge of her collarbone.

Richard didn't care that he was leaving marks, that the girl's neck was red and glistening; he couldn't stop, couldn't get enough. He was addicted to her taste, her scent, the softness of her skin, and even the very feel of her writhing against him drove him wild; but it wasn't enough.

Tight and firm, her lace covered buttocks filled his hands nicely and he couldn't resist squeezing the luscious mounds, making the beauty moan, before trailing his hands up along her sides, mentally mapping the sensual curves before hooking a finger over the robe's belt. With a quick tug, the tie came undone, and the garment fell open. Keeping one hand locked to her narrow waist, the other slid beneath the folds of the robe to explore the previously hidden delights. Softer than silk but hot to the touch, her skin trembled at his lightest contact and he ran his fingers teasingly over the bumps of her ribs before coming to her bosom.

His hand moulded to her left breast, eager digits kneading the soft, supple flesh whilst his thumb and forefinger rolled the pebbled nipple. Thrilled by his touch, she arched her back, pressing her cleavage further into his palm, and moaned in utter wonder as he trailed his tongue along her collarbone in small gentle kisses, soothing the bite marks, her fingers tugging at his hair each time his thumb playfully squeezed her pert bud.

"Oh Mr Martin…mmm…yessss…*harder!*" she gasped, her breathing ragged with barely suppressed moans, before bowing her head and plunging her tongue into his ear, arousing him further.

His cock jumping at the strange sensation, Richard growled before releasing his hold on her breast and rearing backwards, ceasing his attentions to her neck, drawing an all too audible whimper of protest from Rebecca. Paying no mind to her discontent, he reached up with both hands and pushed the robe off her shoulders and down her arms, leaving her flawless ivory skin naked to his eyes, except for a matching thong of black lace. He wantonly devoured the sight of her near naked beauty. Lithe and willowy, she had a swimmer's body and though he was accustomed to the sight of her flat stomach and long shapely legs, it was as if he were seeing her for the first time. Full and firm, her tear-drop shaped breasts rose and fell with her every breath. Their milky complexion contrasted perfectly with her dusky pink nipples.

"I know they're…not very big," admitted Rebecca, her voice flat and barely above a whisper, drawing his attention up to her face as she disentangled her fingers from his hair to cross her arms over her chest. She couldn't meet his gaze and all the confidence was leeching from her features to leave an unmistakable mask of doubt, perhaps even fear; fear that he might find her unsatisfactory or repulsive.

The very idea filled him with such sour emotion that he was almost overwhelmed by the urge to crush her to him and promise her she was beautiful. Instead, he raised his hand to her wrists and gently lowered her arms. "No Rebecca, they're perfect; you're perfect."

She looked at him in alarm, her eyes misty with tears, yet before she could speak, his lips touched hers in a kiss. It was sweet and tender, and she didn't resist. When he pulled away, she tried to follow, but he swooped down and took her right nipple between his lips, making her gasp in pleasure. She arched into his touch, giving him easier access to her ample cleavage as his tongue playfully circled her nipple, drawing tantalising rings of fire around the stiff bud before sensually grazing it with his teeth.

"Ohhh…Mr Martin!" she moaned; he could feel her rocking earnestly against the bulge of his arousal. Her small hands moved to claw at his head, seizing great clumps of his raven locks before running down his neck and roaming the broad plane of his shoulders and back, his muscles bunching and contracting at the feel of her nails scraping through the thin cotton of his shirt. Shivering in a mix of pleasure and agony at her sharp touch, his hand moved back up to roughly knead her neglected breast while his lips continued their assault. No longer teasing, he began to suckle ravenously, his tongue skilfully flicking across her nipple while the rough pad of his thumb massaged its twin, enjoying the way she responded to his every touch.

No match for such an onslaught, Rebecca's head tipped back. She uttered a torrent of delightful sounds as she basked in the sensations he was stirring within her. Moaning and writhing against the trapped bulge of his arousal, her hands fumbled with the buttons of his shirt, her digits clumsy from her inexperience and desperation to rid him of the garment. When the last popped free, the shirt fell open and her hand moved down between their bodies, cupping the weight of his cock through his trousers.

"So-so big…" she gasped out hotly and he couldn't help uttering a low moan against her breast at the feeling of her fingers closing around him, her palm jerking up and down as she massaged his length. "Ooh God; please…take me to bed, Mr Martin!"

With his mind fogged by lust, Richard couldn't resist her and released her breast before seizing her buttocks with both hands and standing up from the ottoman. Squealing with delight, Rebecca crossed her legs over his waist and wrapped her arms securely around his neck, effectively clinging to him for dear life as he hoisted her up and carried her out of the living room and into the darkened hallway. Though this was the first time he'd been in this part of the Blaire's flat, as its layout was identical to that of his own, it was easy for him to navigate the gloom of the narrow antechamber towards the minor bedroom at its end, which he guessed was Rebecca's.

He was tempted to try for the handle, but the feeling of Rebecca's lips on his neck persuaded him there was no time. One good kick was all he needed to have the door swing open.

Chapter Four

Rebecca's room was bright and vibrant, with pale blue wallpaper and polished pine furnishings. Framed posters of various animals hung on the walls, as well as a wall-mounted *Sony* combi, LCD television and DVD player, and a divan double bed that dominated one corner of the room. Approaching the side of the bed, he dropped her unceremoniously upon the divan, causing the girl to squeal with alarm, before stepping back and shrugging off his shirt. As the garment pooled around his feet, he felt goosebumps erupting over his arms as the chilly air touched his skin. Despite the cold, the ache in his groin had grown almost unbearable, and he quickly stepped out of his shoes and socks before pushing both his trousers and boxers down his legs, sighing with relief as his painfully stiff erection burst free of its confines.

Rebecca could only gasp, her big doe eyes shamelessly drinking in the sight of his masculinity before a hungry smile turned her lips. Feeling the heat of her gaze lingering upon him, Richard couldn't resist smirking before moving to join her on the black sheets. Relishing the image of her spread out beneath him, his eyes fixed on his last obstacle. Reaching out, he hooked his fingers under the hem of her panties, now visibly damp and glistening with dew, and dragged the sodden garment down her legs, leaving her completely exposed to his ravenous gaze.

Visibly trembling, Rebecca opened her legs, inviting him to continue. His mouth watering at the sight of her sex, he tossed

the garment aside before leaning forward, drawn by the heady
scent of her arousal, to hover above her folds.

"Mr Martin?" Her breath was shaky with need and
impatience, as she watched him. "What are you do-ohhh!" The
words fell into a long moan as his mouth descended upon her.

Plunged into a world of sensory delights, he thrust his
tongue into her molten depths, stroking her plush inner-walls.
She had a spiced, tangy flavour, and he was immediately
addicted.

"Mmm…that feels so good…Mr Martin…" gasped Rebecca,
her sweet voice breathless with pleasure as his tongue
explored her channel. Savouring the taste of her, Richard held
nothing back and ate her greedily. His tongue lapped and
twirled, drawing a maze of intricate patterns across her inner
walls before suddenly withdrawing between his jaws, only to
plunge deeper into her centre.

Her hips jumped against him and he glanced up to see her
head rolling back, her eyes closed and mouth open in a long
moan. Grinning inwardly at the look of pleasure etched upon
her features, he slid her legs over his shoulders before seizing
her buttocks, supporting her weight easily, and drawing her
closer while swirling his tongue around the deepest part of
her, making her buck and cry with pleasure.

"Ohhhhhhhh!!!" she moaned before seizing white knuckled
handfuls of the sheets, her hips rolling wantonly against his
mouth, demanding more.

"Mmm…you're delicious," he murmured against her flesh,
rolling his tongue to the rhythm of her body and feeling his
cock jump as her sounds of pleasure sent a pulse of electrified
excitement coursing through his nerves. Absorbing everything
he was doing to her, Rebecca could only writhe and moan as
her senses were overloaded and he could feel the mounting
tension within her as she approached her heavenly summit.

Far from finished with her, however, Richard withdrew his
tongue from her heat and drew it gently up her folds to
teasingly circle her clitoris before closing his mouth over the

beauty's swollen bud, a grin crossing his thin lips at her sudden cry of rapture.

"Ohhh-shit-yesss!" she shrieked, her big brown eyes dark with lust, widening to the size of saucers as his lips wrapped around the tiny bud and drew it into the heat of his mouth, suckling it. When his tongue flicked it, slender fingers tangled in his hair, dragging him closer as her hips bucked wildly against his orifice. "Ugh-right there…don't stop-ahhh-yes, yes, yes, YES!"

He focused all his attention on that small bundle of nerves, delighting in her cries of ecstasy while skilfully swirling his tongue over and around, switching randomly between sharp licks and teasing rolls again and again; keeping her purposefully on edge as the sweet oblivion welled up within her. Clearly unprepared for the rush of sensations, Rebecca could do little more than gasp and pant and cry out in delight, her fingers tugging urgently at his hair whilst her hips bucked and rolled beneath his sinfully wicked motions.

And then, suddenly, the truth of his situation caught up to him.

Ohhh God…*what the hell am I doing!* Richard thought, yet all the while unable to resist admiring the way her body danced as his tongue expertly jabbed at her clit, his firm grip holding her in check even as she strained for more. This wasn't him. Richard Martin never cheated; he was a loyal husband who loved his wife. He didn't do things like this, he couldn't, it wasn't right…

Desperately, he tried to conjure up a vision of Alice but the image of her seemed to linger just out of memory, dancing before his gaze within a haze of smoke and mist before a sharp, agonising pain shot along the length of his erection, reminding him of his own pressing need. Beaten, his body acted on its own accord and he caught the bundle of nerves between his teeth while humming a low rumbling *"Mmm…"*

"Ohhh right there…right there-oh God-ughhh I'm cumming…oh God-oh God-ohhh goooohhhhhhhh!!!" Rebecca cried, losing all control, deliriously thrashing her head and arching off the sheets; her whole body trembling with the force of the climax ripping through her. Unchecked, Richard worked her down from the heights before gently lowering her onto the bed, her eyes falling shut as she basked in the wondrous aftermath. This was his chance. It wasn't too late. All he had to do was get dressed and leave, now.

Yet his brain was fogged, and his limbs wouldn't move. He was standing on the bank of the *Rubicon*. Should he cross its depths, there would be no turning back, he would be lost, adrift in purgatory, and everything he loved would be at stake, forfeit. If Alice were to learn of it, their marriage would be over, his son would grow up to despise him, friends and family would shun him like a stray dog. And yet, could he live with himself if he didn't, knowing he'd come this far only to turn away, and always wondering what it would have been like?

But then the decision was taken out of his hands. Flushed and panting, Rebecca's eyes fluttered open, and she looked up at him dreamily. "Come on, come on…don't stop now. Ohhh God, I'm so hot. Please fuck me, Mr Martin! I need you to fuck me…"

How could he resist?

Alea iacta est.

Crawling up the length of her body, covering her slender frame as he rose above her and settled between her splayed legs. He didn't worry about a condom; he knew Rebecca had been on the pill since her sixteenth birthday. Alice had taken her to the hospital to get a prescription. Seeing the lust burning in those innocent doe eyes, the last of his resistance melted away, and he plunged into her molten core.

"Ohhh," Rebecca moaned at the sudden invasion, her eyes widening and head rolling back into the mess of tangled sheets as he entered her, burrowing inside bit-by-bit, filling her completely.

"Ughhh…" Richard groaned once he was completely embedded within her liquid heat, almost losing himself in the feeling of inner walls stretching and wrapping around his engorged flesh. The urge to move was so overwhelming that it took every bit of his willpower to remain still, relishing the feel of her tight embrace as he drew in deep ragged breaths and waited for her to adjust to his size. He'd known she wasn't a virgin for some time; but she was still so tight and though he was far from huge, he must have been considerably larger than what she was accustomed to. The realisation sent a delightful thrill down his spine, and his cock twitched.

"Ahhh…" cried the girl, her inner muscles tensing around him so tightly that he was afraid he'd hurt her and began to withdraw. "No! Don't stop. Do it again…."

His cock throbbed dangerously at her words and the slick snugness of her walls made him pant as he began to rock his hips. He moved in small rowing motions, delighting in the friction between their bodies. Arching beneath him as he rolled his hips, Rebecca seized his buttocks with both hands, her fingernails digging into his flesh before dragging trails of fire up his lower back as her legs wrapped around his flanks, crossing at the ankles, and urging him to go deeper while rocking urgently against his gentle motions.

"Ooohhhh God! Give it to me Mr Martin…I want it…I want it…ahhhhh-yes-yesss" Her words fell into an endless stream of moans and gasps as he drew back until just the bulbous head remained encased within her, before thrusting back into her hard and fast. She jumped at his intrusion, her delicate insides rippling and convulsing around his hard length, trying to draw him deeper. Enjoying the feel of her squirming beneath him, he repeated the motion, again and again, building a steady rhythm that had him delving deeper with every thrust. He'd meant to be slow and gentle, to take it easy on her, but she had proved his undoing in that first delicious instant.

He felt maddened, bewitched, and so utterly out of control. Lust burned hot and molten through his veins, and just the sight of her writhing beneath him, wantonly begging for more, was nearly too much for him to bear. Suddenly there was nothing gentle in his motions, just a desperate, unyielding need.

"Ughhh…so-so tight," he growled; his voice choked with pleasure as he thrust back inside her plush passage, filling her completely, the feeling of her inner walls squeezing his returning flesh almost pitching him over the edge and he knew he wouldn't last much longer. It had been over a month since he and Alice last had sex, and the torment of the night's games had left his cock so sensitised he thought it might burst at any moment. *But not yet. Not yet!*

"Ohhh fuck…your dick feels so good…oh-oh-ohhh…don't stop…don't stop!" cried Rebecca, eagerly meeting every one of his downward strokes with an upward roll of her hips, her nails clawing madly at his back each time his pelvis grazed her clit. He was certain she was leaving marks, but at this point, it was hard to be concerned about anything, even of discovery by his loving wife, who was waiting for him in the flat below them.

"Mmm…So is this what you want, Rebecca?" Fighting to ignore the rush of pleasure creeping up his spine as he plunged into the deepest parts of the beauty, Richard held nothing back, hastening his thrusts until the bed beneath them seemed to be rocking to their wild rhythm. The sound of it all was music to his ears; the squeaking of bedsprings, the wet slapping of flesh on flesh and, of course, Rebecca's overwhelmed moans.

"Yes, yes…it was always you…I've always wanted you, Mr Martin…Oh God! Feels so good, fuck me harder…HARDER!" A cry of rapturous delight tore from her lips as his hips snapped in deep, long strokes that made her spine curl and her breasts bounce. Like him, she was nearing her peak. He could feel the balls of her feet beating against his arse, urging him to push her over that summit she so desperately yearned to reach.

Somewhere, buried deep in the depths of his subconscious, a part of him dreaded that inevitable conclusion, perhaps still hoping that this was all some wonderful, but monstrous nightmare and that his failure would banish this all away, like a foul odour on a great gust of wind. He might even have felt guilty for using the girl so thoughtlessly, had she not been writhing wantonly beneath him, meeting him thrust for thrust and begging for more. But he had come too far to stop now.

Feeling his release building, his sanity hanging by a thread; he reared back, his hands coming up to seize the swells of her buttocks, hoisting her off the sheets and pulling her firmly against him as he continued to thrust into her wildly. Inhaling sharply at this new angle, Rebecca's head rolled back in a voiceless cry and her hands fell away to brace against at the wall, searching desperately for some kind of purchase while doing her best to match his furious rhythm.

"Ah…ahhh-oh my God-oh my God-oh my God…I can't take it… it's too much…too big!" she shrieked, her fingers clawing at the walls and eyes wide with pure ecstasy. "Oh yes…yesssss…don't stop…I'm all yours Mr Martin…I've wanted your hard cock inside me for so long…you can fuck me whenever you want to…just don't stop…don't stop!"

The room was thick with the musky scent of sex. Grunting as he surged inside her, Richard savoured the sight of her pleasure-drunk features as his hands, roughly kneading her tight young arse like dough, guided her motions in time with his own. Spurred on by her heated encouragements, and the wondrous feeling of her molten channel writhing around his sensitised organ, he slammed into her mercilessly. His back was afire and he could feel beads of sweat rolling down his brow as he thrust hard and fast between her silky thighs, working tirelessly to push them both off their approaching peaks, the tingling sensation down in the base of his spine warning him of his impending oblivion.

"Ohhhh God…I can feel it…I'm going to cum…. fuck me, fuck meeeeee!" Rebecca cried, racing towards another climax and sobbing with pleasure while thrashing her head from side to side. "Ohhh-yes-yes…I'm cummingaahhhhhhh!" her voice dissolved into a shrill cry of pleasure, and her inner walls erupted, convulsing around his thick length in a wash of molten warmth as she rode the orgasm, quivering and bucking against him uncontrollably.

Richard groaned in primitive delight, teetering on the brink, watching avidly as she came undone before the feelings the girl was stirring finally proved too much and a thunderous roar burst from his jaws. Slamming into her one last time, he felt something deep inside his abdomen contract and pulse, and then there was only the fire coursing through his veins as he released his essence into her warmth.

Exhausted beyond measure, they collapsed together in a heap on the bed.

Breathing hard and trembling with miniature aftershocks, Richard had just enough sense left to roll off the beauty, withdrawing his softening arousal from her still vivacious channel. Whimpering at the feeling of emptiness, Rebecca curled into his flank, the feeling of her nestling against him, drawing a low moan from the exhausted man as all notion of time slipped away. For several long moments, he was content to just bask in the glow of a much-needed release. Sleep's warm embrace dragging him down to that peaceful abyss…

He jerked at the sensation of falling, shattering the spell and leaving him cold, naked, and very much awake.

I need a shower. It was a strange thought. He knew he should have felt guilty, afraid, and perhaps even sick to his stomach, but oddly, a sense of calm detachment seemed to have settled over him and all he could really think about was how clammy his skin felt as the sheen of sweat covering him began to dry. He felt movement against his arm and glanced over to see Rebecca sleeping peacefully beside him, with an arm draped over his front and her head resting peacefully on his shoulder. She was smiling contentedly.

Chapter Five

"I have to go." He had tried to say it softly, so as to avoid disturbing her entirely, but his throat was dry and what came out was a raspy parody of a voice. Her body quivered in surprise at the sound and her eyes fluttered open, glassy with unshed tears.

"But…but can't you stay with me tonight?"

"You know I can't." In truth, he would have liked nothing better than to stay with her, but he knew Alice would be growing worried and it wouldn't be long before she came looking for him. The thought of her finding them like this sent the first true shiver of fear down his spine, and with the idea of her barging through the door, dressed like Rambo and armed with enough firepower to orbit Schwarzenegger in mind, he gently pushed her aside and sat up. Rising to his feet, he quickly set about collecting the garments that were scattered across the floor. Yet his mind was only half on the task, and as a result, he had done up more than half of his shirt's buttons before realising two of them were in the wrong hole. Even so, he couldn't keep from cringing when the cloth touched his back. The skin there felt painfully raw and inflamed; he'd need to be careful Alice didn't see the marks for a couple of days.

Finally dressed, though appearing curiously dishevelled, he straightened up and was about to leave when he heard the rustle of bedsheets.

"Please…Richard, promise me this wasn't just a one-night stand," Rebecca called out and despite his better judgement, he glanced back and his heart nearly broke at the vision of her sitting there, desperately trying to hide her nakedness by clutching the soiled sheets to her chest, her ivory skin almost glowing and big doe eyes sparkling pleadingly. Even after such a thorough fucking, she was no less a vision of innocence and purity, the sweetest of temptations.

"We'll see," he said, trying to keep his voice flat and features stern, hiding the sudden stab of emotion in his chest. He left without a backwards glance, shutting the bedroom door firmly behind him, doing his best to ignore Rebecca's tearful sobs.

Chapter Six

His back burned and the spray cut clean to the bone as fat wet snakes slithered down his arms and legs, so cold they burned.

Eyes hooded and vacant, Richard watched the run-off collect around the shower drain, swirling around and around. The blood was almost washed away, leaving only long accusing fingers of dark crimson streaking across the porcelain.

Time had lost all meaning. Seconds and hours bled together until…

"Goddamnit!"

He wanted to scream. To shout. To bellow like a bear in a cage, being dragged through the streets for the amusement of a medieval mob, roaring and bawling in a show of futile outrage at the hard, inescapable reality. Yet the pitiful grunt was all he dared with Alexander in the next room, liable to stir at the smallest sound, and Alice sleeping peacefully just across the hall. So instead, he took it out on the shower wall the way an angry child would beat a pillow.

Red-hot knives stabbed between his knuckles and up his arm in a blast of near-crippling agony as he hit the wall hard enough for bone to crack against the porcelain. Regardless, he ground his knuckles into the tile, relishing the agony it induced, needing it and not knowing what else to do.

Then the moment was gone, and Richard was left shivering in the cold, hot tears stinging his eyes. "Wh-what the fuck have I done?" The question rang hollow, even to his ears.

What had he done? He'd fucked his babysitter, a girl almost young enough to be his daughter. He'd cheated on his wife. And, what was worse, he'd loved every fucking second of it. Then he'd fled.

He could still hear Rebecca crying in her room.

Her sobs had chased him out of the Blaire's flat like a pack of hounds snapping at his heels and it had been all he could do to make it back to the flat without breaking his neck. Alice had already gone to bed when he came bursting through the door. Deep down, a more rational part of him was relieved he didn't have to explain to his instinctively suspicious wife why he was getting in so late, or the fact he smelt like sex and his shirt was misbuttoned, but in that moment, all he could think about was a shower. He'd barely spared a moment to look into their bedroom to check on her before jumping into the bath and cranking the water temperature as low as it would go.

Goddammit! What the fuck had he done! Why had he even gone to fix the computer in the first place? It wasn't a vital job. Rebecca might have been in a state, but it could have waited until morning. So, why the fuck had he gone to the fix the bloody computer, when he'd known, he'd just known it was a bad idea.

Alarm bells had gone off the moment Alice had suggested the girl fancied him. He would have pressed her for more, but then she kissed him, and his world had dissolved to just the feeling of her luscious body pressing into his.

It had been much the same the night they first met, when she'd cornered him in The Burning Book's storeroom. He'd been getting a fresh crate of beer when he'd noticed her leaning against the door. He hadn't noticed her slipping in after him, and the sight of the tiny brunet, all curves and smiles in a black wrap-around dress that could only have been painted on, standing there with her hand on her hip almost had him jumping out of his skin.

Only the Lord alone knew how he managed not to drop the bottles in each hand.

Her smile had only grown more sinful when he'd told her she was in a staff-only area. Then, with a cock of her head and a pouting moan, she'd been on him and he'd promptly forgotten all of his fears of getting caught.

Richard would have stayed. He would have, but then Alice's remarks about Rebecca rung in his ears. Suddenly, he couldn't get the girl out of his head and he'd felt so ashamed that he just needed to get away.

The irony of it all did not escape him.

Self-loathing twisting his guts, he opened and closed his fist, working the feeling back into the stiff digits. They all moved. That was good, nothing broken, but they hurt pretty bad and the throbbing in the knuckles was enough to make him wince with each flex. Then again, that was good too. He deserved the pain.

Christ, I need a drink.

The thought came from out of nowhere but had a restorative effect that had Richard thumbing the shower panel. Pulling the curtain back before the deluge had ceased, he stepped out of the bath, grabbed a towel off the rail and, heedless of the water still running down his legs, made straight for the kitchen.

The oven's display showed it was just after two in the morning.

Out of habit, he made to fill the kettle, but then at the last minute opened the top cabinet. The British Empire might have been built on tea, but this called for something stronger. And he needed to get royally shit faced. Rummaging through the various jars, bottles, and tins, he retrieved the mostly full Bushmills they kept for when Alice's parents came to visit, before grabbing a glass from the draining board.

Pouring himself a measure, Richard threw his head back and downed the whiskey. It burned all the way down, but the liquor brought the warmth back, lessening the sickening knot rooted in his gut, so he savoured it all the same, relishing the hard flavour and distinctive aroma that curled up his nose-

"C-C-Christ," he bit out, coughing so violently each breath rasped like sandpaper, and his hand shook as he filled the glass again. This time making it a double, he stowed the bottle, and its now notably emptied contents, back into the cupboard before exiting the kitchen, drink in hand.

The living room had lost all its warmth as Richard half-sat, half-collapsed onto the sofa. Bathed in the soft light of the standing lamp they kept on a timer to dissuade thieves from getting ambitious, inky blackness pooled along the edges of the walls. Long shadows stretched across the floor like the bars of a cell. His cell.

Wary of another coughing fit that might rouse his wife, he only nursed the drink, sipping the dark amber liquid while staring over the rim of the glass at the dark outside the window.

What have I done?

Hardly a frequent or heavy drinker, the Bushmills made his eyes heavy and his head feel light as the alcohol took effect. The question haunted him, ringing through his ears while flashbacks of the last hour played out before his eyes.

His cock stiffened at the memory of Rebecca standing in the doorway in nothing but that robe. The way her slender curves rigged in his lap. The taste of her on his lips. Her breathy pleading as he tongued her clit. The feeling of her tight little cunt exploding around him...

He hated himself for what he'd done. He'd cheated on Alice, broken his vows to her and risked their marriage. He'd used Rebecca, fucked her like a bitch in heat. Then, worse still, discarded her so callously even though he knew, well suspected, she had feelings for him.

God in fucking hell, he was a beast.

A part of him still couldn't believe it. Here in the safety of his home, on his sofa with a glass of whiskey, the night felt like a bad dream. A God damn fucking nightmare. Only he'd woken to it. The night was like a dream he could only half remember, slipping out of his grasp like pale wisps of morning mist curling around his fingers whenever he tried to focus on one moment. All except for those moments. They were sharp and clear and played before his eyes whenever he'd closed them.

What the fuck was wrong with him? He and Alice were finally getting their lives back to a sense of normality… How was he going to look her in the eye again, knowing that he'd… Christ, what would she say? What would she do? He'd ruined everything. And just when it had all seemed to be going so well. In layman's terms-

"I'm fucked." He toasted the declaration by downing the rest of his Bushmills. "Oh God. *Al*, I'm sor-"

The timer on the lamp's plug clicked over, cutting the power.

Darkness consumed him

Chapter Seven

There was comfort in sleep. The fool and coward's comfort. The comfort of hiding in the dark and fooling himself it had all been a dream.

Caught between sleeping and waking, Richard stared up at the ceiling. Autumn morning half-light crept through the curtains over the bed, turning their bedroom dark and grey. He didn't hear the cars speeding down Stroud Road, trying to beat the early morning rush hour, or the occasional gurgles coming through the baby monitor. Nor see the furniture taking shape in the gloom. He didn't want to wake up.

He wanted to sleep and dream and pretend. Better that than face reality and the consequences of what he'd done. Having to see his wife every day, holding her in his arms, making love to her, looking into her eyes, seeing the love there, and knowing, just knowing, he'd betrayed her.

Yes, he didn't want to wake, but the warm body wriggling beside him made it inevitable…

He blinked when a hand brushed up his side. Long, delicate fingers, feeling up his ribs and across his stomach. Then there was only softness and warmth. And a faint hint of cinnamon.

A sideways glance showed Alice sleeping next to him on a bed of her mahogany tresses. She must have rolled onto his side sometime in the night and, half covered by the quilt, was curling into him, head resting on his shoulder. She looked so peaceful. Content. Utterly oblivious to everything that had taken place through the night.

Her peace tore at him. Yet he was captivated and watched her sleep regardless, her delicate beauty enrapturing him the way the radiance of the moon enslaves a wolf.

He had to tell her, but how? A part of him wanted to confess now and have done with it. To wait would only make things harder, more complicated.

Excuses flitted through his mind. He was drunk. He'd been desperate. It hadn't meant anything. It was the usual lineup of dirt-bag husband excuses. Though he made sure to steer WELL clear of anything even hinting Alice bore some responsibility. That would not go down well.

Once, he even contemplated suggesting Rebecca had instigated it all. That got chucked out as quickly as it came. No matter what, he needed to keep the girl out of this.

As fond as she was of their babysitter, Richard knew his wife well enough to know she did not share her toys. And if that confrontation with Scarlet last night had just been Alice marking her territory...

Then, he had a pretty good idea of what she would do to him.

That thought made the idea of letting her sleep in a little longer, all the more tempting.

"Alice..." he mumbled. She'd think it odd if he didn't wake her. It would make her suspicious…

Alice mumbled something unintelligible in answer. Still more or less asleep, she shifted closer to nuzzle the hollow of his neck.

Richard stiffened at the contact, a shiver of pleasure rippling up his spine.

Her very closeness was an aphrodisiac. The feeling of her pressed against him, long willowy legs brushing over his calf, full breasts crushed against his side through her cropped sleeping sweater. And her mouth. God, that wicked mouth, brushing so softly over his skin, a mere tease of contact, igniting and sending tingling sensations surging through his skin down to the base of his spine.

Suddenly awake, alert, and very aware of that tale-tell stirring between his legs, Richard blinked, then glanced down to see blue-green eyes looking up at him.

For the longest moment, Alice only watched him, lips pursed and eyes bright with a look that had his cock suddenly harder than steel. Then, slowly, she pivoted, propping her head up enough to rest her chin on his ribs. "When did you get in?"

"Late." The vision of her had the words sticking to the back of his throat. "Did you wait long?"

She moaned a low throaty affirmative, placing a soft kiss just above his nipple while, in a tease of friction, one deliciously long leg slid across to straddle his thigh, making Richard all the more aware of the feeling of her body on his. And the dampness pushing against his leg. She was soaked. The silky heat of her arousal burned through her panties as she stretched out, caging him beneath her, as she walked soft butterfly kisses up his torso.

"I couldn't sleep," Alice purred, her words low and throaty without a trace of sleep. She bit down on his earlobe and tugged, fingers teasing down the flat of his stomach to his boxers. "I just kept thinking about you pushing me up against the fridge, grinding this big, hard cock into my pussy." Long fingers closed around him through the cotton of his underwear, holding, squeezing, then rubbing. "It got me so hot. In the end, I needed Antonio…"

Richard had to bite back a moan. Antonio was Alice's name for the B.O.B her friend Samantha had bought them as a gag gift for their 5-year anniversary. The image of his wife stretched out on their bed, her luscious body arching in throes of pleasure as she worked the toy between her legs, turned his cock to steel within her grasp. Until he recalled just what he had been doing while she had been putting on such an exquisite display and the knot of guilt that lodged inside his gut threatened to chase his erection away.

Alice's mouth claimed his, her tongue sweeping in with lush licks that sent tingles shivering up his spine and brought him back to full mast.

She took his mouth hungrily, her lips moving over his, full and soft and completely at odds with the hot demand that seemed at once to make his head spin while keeping his attention fixed solely on her. And all the while, she was stroking him. Slowly, her tiny hand unable to encompass his girth, but pumping him from root to tip in long, knowing motions, had him instinctively rocking into her, grinding his groin against her palm.

God, how did she always know? Know just how to touch him, how to play his body like a fiddle?

It was maddening. He needed to touch her, but no sooner had his fingers swept through the lush fall of silky locks to tease over her spine than she pulled back.

"I-it got me so horny," she panted, trailing hot little kisses down the line of his jaw. "Knowing you could barge in at any moment and catch me playing with Antonio. I wanted you to watch, to see what you did to me, see how wet I got thinking about your big dick," she spoke slowly, every low throaty syllable an intoxicating seduction. "I was right here, riding my B.O.B, waiting for you to come and see what a naughty wife you have. But you never came. Then I remembered you were up there with Rebecca. Is that why you left me all alone?" Her mouth was everywhere, kissing every bit of skin she could reach as she shuffled slowly back...

Her tongue dragged over his nipple, down the plane of his chest to the elastic of his shorts, only to pull away. "A-Alice..."

His wife rose slowly to sit straight backed between his legs, throwing the covers off, and pushing the lush fall of her hair back behind her ears, the pink of her tongue sliding across those full lips as her eyes found his. Then, "Was she a bad girl for you?"

Oh fuck!

"What?" Ice rushed down his spine and it was all Richard could do to keep the panic from his voice. Fuck, she knew. How could he have been so stupid? Of course, Alice knew. How could she not? Now he was-

"Was she a bad girl?" Alice said again, her voice seeming to grow even more playful as she leaned down to where his erection was visibly straining against the confines of his shorts, the slick tip pushing up from beneath the elastic to leave a slick and shiny trail around his belly button. "Was she still wearing that sexy outfit she had on last night? That cute little pink top and those faded jeans."

Warm air rushed over his crown as those full luscious lips wrapped around him through his underwear and slid up to bite the waistband and tug it back to reveal the fullness of his desire. "Or had she changed into something different, something special, for your eyes only? Stockings? High heels. Maybe a pink babydoll-mmm…" She licked him. The point of her tongue slid slowly up the centre of his column in a long drag from base to tip. "Did you like seeing her like that? Flaunting her body for you in a naughty nighty, her ass and legs on full display, those lush tits peeking out, begging to be sucked. And what about her pussy, that tight, juicy little pussy? Did she taste good?"

Mouth dry and desire shivering through him, Richard couldn't stop the words, "So-so goo-oohh!"

Lips stretched wide and checks hollowed, Alice took the head into her mouth and sucked him greedily. She took her time, going neither fast nor slow, but with all the determination of a woman who loved giving head and wasn't afraid to let the world know it.

In a dark corner of his brain, Richard knew he should be disgusted with himself. Alice thought they were playing. To her, this was just a game to spice up the mood. She had no way of knowing he had been balls deep inside their neighbour's daughter last night. And to top it all off, instead of confessing his sin, he was letting her give him one hell of a blow job. But he couldn't resist. It had been so long since he'd felt those luscious lips wrapped around his dick. And her eyes…

Fuck, Alice's eyes were incredible. Deep and stormy, they seemed to shift between grey and blue depending on her mood, and he could stare into them for an eternity and never look away. There were times she had brought him to the brink of cumming with just a look.

It was at once too intense, yet not enough, and Richard had to fist the sheets against the urge to grab, claw, and drive her mouth all the way down on his cock. The lush heat of her mouth glided along his shaft, never taking more than an inch or two in. And so slow. Damnit, how can she be so slow…

"A-Alice…"

She pulled off just as slowly, her eyes burning into his all the way. "Mmm-did you make her your new little cock whore? I bet she was just begging for this big dick." She fluttered her tongue over the slit, making his whole cock tingle and his butt clench. Then she was licking him, that little pink tongue sliding up and down his length. "Did you make her beg for your cock?"

He couldn't think or focus on anything but the feel of her tongue. Then she was taking him back into the delicious heat of her mouth, her head bobbing up and down, the delicious suction of those full lips sliding along his shaft, drawing him deeper. It was too much.

"Yes."

Alice moaned her approval, her eyes bright and burning into his as she pulled off. With one small hand still stroking him, she crawled on all fours up the length of his body, slowly, with her body low and back just that bit arched so he could feel the weight of her breasts dragging up his belly, soft and warm through her thin cotton cardigan, before she reared, like Aphrodite rising from her pool to straddle his waist.

"Oh, you're so bad," she purred, and gave him one final stroke before bringing her fingers up to her mouth and sucked them clean with a low moan. "Mmm… I can taste her on your cock. Did she drop to her knees and suck your big, yummy, married dick first? Or did you just bend her over and fuck her brains out?"

Jesus, her games were going to kill him. "N-neither, Ioh…"

The words trailed away in a low moan as she rolled her hips, sliding his cock along her folds through her soaked panties, showing him how wet she'd gotten. Then, with her right hand, she hooked two fingers beneath the garment and pulled it back, exposing her pussy to his gaze.

"Mmm… yeah baby, what did you do?" Alice purred, taking his cock in her left hand and coating his crown in her cream before pressing it hard against her clit with a slow roll-

She stilled, that sweet little mouth dropping in a voiceless gasp as Richard's hands seized her hips and held her fast as he began working his thick crest into her moist heat. "This."

He'd had enough.

Breath seething, Richard could barely contain himself as he pulled her to him. Even after all their years together, and the birth of their son, she was still so deliciously snug, and he could feel her plush walls stretch as he filled her inch by inch until she'd sheathed to the hilt. The perfect fit for his cock.

"Oh… Oh god! Baby wa-wait…" Alice gasped, her eyes unfocused. Reaching back, she grasped his knees to brace herself. "Not so… you're too… too-oh god!"

Breathless, Richard could only nod, her slight movement altering his angle of penetration. It wasn't much. Just enough to send a rush of sensation up his spine as her slick, velvety walls wrapped around his cock, pulsing and sucking him in as deep as he could go.

The prior night was gone and done. Now it was only them and he bit, chewed, and clawed against the instinctive urge to throw his wife on the bed and just take her. It had been weeks since the last time they'd gone a few rounds. She'd need time, time to adjust, time to get used to the feeling of being filled with him. So instead Richard just watched her, drinking in the sight of Alice straddling him, her head tipped back, the bounty of lush mahogany tresses cascading down to the small of her back, the plunging neckline of her cardigan revealing a feast of golden skin as her breasts strained against the cotton, imprisoned from his view by a few struggling buttons.

He wanted to see more. He wanted to see her.

"Mmm… you feel amazing, so tight," he purred, reaching up to tug the button from its fastening, bearing her full and luscious cleavage. "And such beautiful tits."

"Yeah, better than hers?" Alice panted, her back curling in offering as he sat up and took the peak of a single dusky nipple into his mouth.

"Much."

He teased her mercilessly, raining soft kisses down across her breasts, his wily tongue lashing down and around, refusing to pay her nipple any attention. Her skin was growing hot and he could feel her shake in his arms, pleading for more. Yet she held on until he sucked the stiff peak into his mouth, his hands crushing her to him and grinding her down on his cock with just the right amount of force to make her creamy walls pulse around him.

"Liar."

Low and breathy, the heat in her words sent a shiver straight down his spine, moments before long fingers fisted in hair and dragged his head back. Dark and lustful, Alice's eyes burned hungrily into his as she lowered her full lips to his, her lush tongue claiming him in a possessive dance that both thrilled and terrified him. This wasn't part of her game. She wanted him to know he was hers. Her husband. Her lover. He was her man, no matter what, and he'd better not forget it.

She rolled her hips, breaking the kiss and rising until only half of him remained inside her.

"Mmm… Mr Martin," a soft, girlish voice purred. His heart leaping into his throat, Richard's eyes shot up to meet

Rebecca's big doe eyes, his wife's sharp, angular face now soft and long. Then, she dropped back down, her lush heat clenching down, like a second mouth sucking him in…
Bolting upright, Richard just managed to brace himself on the armrests of his chair as it righted itself and almost pitched him headfirst into his desk. What the-

Reality caught up with him. He wasn't at home. He was at work in his office.

Sweating, heart pounding and his cock straining against his trousers, he collapsed back into the treacherous piece of furniture. Cupping his hands over his head and dragging his fingers down his face, he did his best to bite down on a sarcastic laugh. "Thank God. Just a dream-"

"Yo Dick, you feeling alright mate?"

Chapter Eight

It never ceased to amaze Richard how, even when dressed to meet Holmes & Raine's business dress code, Mark McClaine always had the look of a second-hand car salesman. It was his perpetual grin. With that boot polish-black hair and moustache, it made him look like John Challis's Boycie in Only Fools and Horses, just without the sincerity.

Perched in the open door with his arms crossed, he was grinning at Richard like the cat that had got the cream. "Not looking too good there, Dick. Everything okay at home?"

"Yeah, I'm fine mate." Richard forced a smile. "Just, just got a lot on my mind, that's all."

Mark gave a dry laugh. Then, still grinning, he straightened and strolled over to his desk, the closest to the door, and dropped into his chair. He spun it around to face Richard in the adjoining cubicle. "I bet you do."

Richard did his best to ignore him. Him, and the chill that shivered down his spine. It wouldn't do any good. McClaine was like a Jack Russell with an old sock whenever he got the sense he was getting under someone's skin. And that was all he had, a scent, an inkling. Just a hunch. He didn't, couldn't know.

He was waiting for him to bite. Richard could see the mirth dancing in his eyes and knew it would be a mistake. So instead, he turned back to his computer. The screen was asleep, but a quick nudge of the mouse brought it alive. Prompted by a security box, he entered his password then watched the various excel spreadsheets pop back up. He bit back a groan. Would it have been too much to ask for a computer virus, or maybe just a good old power cut?

The Prometheus Account.

It had been due well over a week ago, and Scarlet had been on at him to get it done and on her desk by the end of the day.

He'd been working on it all morning, but with everything that had happened, his head just wasn't in the right place. And all the while, Mark had watched him, grinning that inane, shit-eating grin. Just the prospect of a long afternoon of it all over again had him blindly reaching out for his mug of tea. It was cold as ice, but he didn't care.

McClaine cocked a brow. "Ya know that tea's been sitting there all morning, right?"

"Mhm…" Richard murmured, chugging it down, not even tasting it as the memory of Rebecca purring his name in that hot wanton tone burned his ears.

Mr Martin…

"I flushed my pen out in it while you were in the land of nod."

"Mhh-" Eyes widening as the words and the acrid ink flavour registered, Richard pivoted and retched, spitting out the vile mixture into the waste bin beside the desk. "You… asshole!" Coughing, it took everything he had not to hurl the mug at McClaine. What little of his curse made it through the spluttering, however, was lost in the other man's laughing.

"Hey! Why aren't the pair of you out for lunch? Trying to bugger each other over the desk or something?"

Wiping his mouth with the back of his hand, Richard shot a withering sideways glance at Dave Sing. "Or something."

A third generation English-Nepalese, from the generation who had turned their back on the ancestral beliefs and completely assimilated to western culture, Dave Sing was also tall and thin. Handsome, with almond skin and copper eyes, but jet black that hair that he kept short and spiked. He'd joined the firm shortly after Richard, a fresh-faced graduate from Coventry University. Young and ambitious- Richard liked him well enough. An asset to the team, but in dire need of seasoning.

His own lunch in hand, the office's third resident settled in his own seat and was about to take a bite of a generous beef burger when he got his first close-up look at Richard. The burger dropped into its wrapper. "Geez Rich, you look awful."

"Yeah-"

"Yeah, well, what do you expect?" McClaine cut in, just managing to get control of his guffaw. "Ben Dover here had a wild weekend after the do last week."

"What?" Richard rounded on him, his heart in his throat. No, he couldn't know about Rebecca. There was no way he could know, unless-

"Oh, come on, Dick, don't give us any of that old pony. That look your missus got when she saw old Walrus Face's daughter putting the moves on you. You can't honestly expect us to believe you didn't get a little bit. Alice damn near started fucking you right there in front of everyone."

"Fuck off," Richard warned, but inside he felt the knot his insides had wound loosen. Slightly.

McClaine shot Sing a sly look and added under his breath, as if to keep the man sitting just meters away from hearing, "Pity she didn't. What I wouldn't do to see that fine ass bouncing-"

"*Mike!* I'm warning you," Richard growled. "Shut your fucking hole or the next thing out of your mouth will be your teeth." He emphasised the threat by pushing back from the desk and rising to his feet, the rancour contorting his features into a look of such maleficence it had both Sing and McClaine backing away.

McClaine raised both hands in supplication, his face turning pale. "Woah, Dick, woah. I'm just busting your balls.

Okay. Okay? I-I I'm sorry. Jeez… just relax. Relax." He was on his feet and backed round the desk.

Richard watched him go, letting him put a bit more space between them before dropping back into his chair.

All the tension seeming to evaporate from the room at once, and McClaine let go of a deep sigh. "We cool? God, my heart's beating so fast I think you were about to give me a coronary."

"Well, you do deserve it from time to time." Richard kept the bitterness from his tone. McClaine was the sort who needed a slap now and then, and he'd enjoyed the opportunity. No matter what, he loved his wife too much to let that sort of slander pass unchastised, but it wasn't worth settling at work. She'd be the first to tell him that. A man has to do what a man has to do, and the first thing a man had to do was to care for his family. Everything else, including giving mouthy gits a smack in the gob, came later.

"Ouch! That hurt. No, seriously mate, what's with you today? You've been bumbling around here like a zombie high off its head."

"Well, can you blame him?" Sing looked up, his burger already much reduced. "You said it yourself. Scarlet has it pretty wet for him. And you've heard the stories."

"Yeah, but come on, you don't believe all that shit, do you? What would she have to gain?"

"What do you mean, what would she have to gain?" Sing looked incredulous; his speech momentarily dissolved into the singsong accent of the Hindu.

"Why would Scarlet want to sleep with Tommy Cox or that asshole Mike in legal? She's a bird. They don't spread their legs for their underlings. What could they do for her? I mean, she's the big boss's daughter. Why should she shag anyone in the firm? If she wants a promotion, or a pony, all she has to do is ask 'Daddy', and Walrus Face will give his little princess anything she wants."

"Please, that is such misogynistic bullshit. A woman can be every bit as abusive as a man. Haven't you read Disclosure?"

"I saw the film," McClaine cut in, and then his features twisted with a leer. "And I tell you, that Demi Moore can suck my cock any day…"

Richard was only half listening to them. He had heard the stories, too. And like McClaine, usually dismissed them as idle office gossip.

Whatever else she might be, Scarlet was undoubtedly a very beautiful woman, and beautiful women in positions of power and authority attracted rumours the way a dog drew fleas. Often as not, they were just stories spread by jealous colleagues or bitter subordinates left in her wake- and Scarlet wasn't short of those. Quite the reverse in fact, but she was also the daughter of the firm's MD, Derick Holmes. The consequence for any employee caught besmirching her good name would be unpleasant, but after their encounter on Friday, Richard was no longer entirely convinced all the stories were *just* stories, but he wasn't about to admit it.

There'd been a look in her eyes. A certain, predatory gleam...

"Okay, that's enough," Richard snapped. "Have either of you actually spoken to anyone who actually fucked her? Or heard a story that wasn't from a guy who spoke to a guy?"

McClaine's grin dropped. "No."

"Well no," Sing admitted, shoving the empty burger box into a desk drawer. "But Jasper Hawkins told me he once saw her going down on the girl from the mailroom." He looked vindicated.

Until McClaine asked, "Umm, Davey-boy, remind me, what happened to Jasper Hawkins?"

Sing shrugged. "Walrus Face kicked him to the curb."

"For?"

"Improper conduct."

Richard barked a triumphant laugh. "Ha! Exactly, telling tales about his daughter. See, he was talking out of his arse and got canned for it. So, with that cleared up, can we get off this subject? I don't fancy getting sued for libel." "Slander," Sing corrected.

"What?"

"Libel's written. You mean you don't fancy getting sued for slander."

Richard gave him the finger. "Oh, shut it Apu. I don't give a damn. If you have to be so pedantic, why don't you take a look at this," he scooted back, making room for the pair. Sing and McClaine exchanged a look, then pushed back from their own desks and walked around to his. "I told Scarlet I'd get this report over to her this morning, but the numbers don't add up. I don't know. Is there something I'm not seeing?"

"So?" McClaine asked, coming up to peer over Richard's shoulder. "You know the drill. If it doesn't add up, just attach an advisory."

Sing nodded in agreement. "That's company policy."

Hemmed in by the tight confines of the one-person cubicle, Richard felt the room growing noticeably stuffier. "I know, but something just doesn't feel right."

"Geez, Dick!" McClaine exclaimed, slapping a hand down on the desk. "Why are you making this so hard for yourself? You know the bitch has a major stick up her ass about this sort of thing. Just give her the report. It's not your job anymore-"

"Mr Martin?"

The semi that had been slowly diminishing surged to renewed life as Richard's heart leapt into his throat, his head snapping up. And then he was back there in that bedroom, naked, with *her* stretched out beneath him, his cock buried to the root in her lush, grasping heat. That sweet voice hot and panting in his ear.

"Ah… ahhh-oh my God-oh my God-oh my God… I can't take it… it's too much… too big!" she shrieked, her fingers clawing at

the walls and eyes wide with pure ecstasy. "Oh yes... yes... don't stop... I'm all yours Mr Martin... I've wanted your hard cock inside me for so long... you can fuck me whenever you want to... just don't stop... don't stop!"

Rebecca stood in the office doorway.

It was the first he'd seen of the girl since their tryst Friday night, and she looked amazing.

Her white button up blouse was smart and conservative, and while too short to reach her knees, that skirt would have to go a hell of a lot higher to offend any granny's delicate sense of decency, or workplace dress code. Yes, there was nothing overtly sexual in her attire, but the thought of what she hid underneath- those lush full tits, her tight athletic build, made it all sexy as hell. And she was gorgeous, too. Her dark chestnut hair had been tied into its customary side braid and there was a little dusting of blusher to her checks, but it was her lips that caught his eyes first. There was a glossiness to them that immediately made him ache to kiss her, taste her...

She must have come straight from work; it was the only time she wore make-up.

"Hi Rebecca." The words sounded feeble, but it was the best he could do on the spot. Though he'd known this moment would eventually come, he'd been so obsessed with what he'd tell Alice, he'd never actually thought about what to say to Rebecca. "What are you doing here?"

"Mrs Martin called. She thought you might be getting hungry." She beamed a sweet girlish smile and held up a plastic bag. "You forgot your lunch."

"Ah... Thanks... Rebecca," he nodded, feeling suddenly embarrassed. He'd been in such a fluster that morning he'd left his Tesco's pasta salad in the fridge and hadn't noticed until he'd been halfway to work. "Just plonk it down over on that cabinet other there. I'll get to it in a bit. How much do I owe you?"

She beamed, sweeping past him and around the desks. "Don't sweat it, it's on me."

"Really?" He pivoted in his chair to follow her. "You sure about that?"

"Yeah, it's nothing. I wanted to check out the Victorian Market anyway, so it's no big deal." Her smile seemed to broaden. "And I got a *big* bonus over the weekend."

A big bonus? Fuck, what did she mean? Richard felt cold fingers trail down his spine. Was she planning to blackmail him, to keep what happened a secret? He wouldn't have thought so. The girl generally had all the sly cunning of a Care Bear. Then again, she had told Alice, and who had secretly told him, that she'd been saving to move out and get away from her father.

Hush-money could go a long way there.

Or was she after something else?

Something more *physical.*

The prospect made the knot in Richard's gut tighten and he was torn between terror and being a little turned on. "That's cool. Well, thanks Rebecca. I owe you-" "Urh,

Mr Martin, could I have a word with you? Um..."

"Ah, well, now isn't really the best time. You caught us at a bit of a bad moment and-"

"Aw, don't be silly Dick, we can spare the girl a moment," McClaine's eyes glittered darkly as he gave the girl a slow, less than subtle once over.

Rebecca quickly twisted away from his scrutiny. "Er-no! No, I understand." Then she gave Richard a sideways glance, a small smile curling those lush pink lips. "If you want, you could just pop round later… If you have the time that-that is, that is, please, I don't want to put you out and my dad will be out so -"

"Ah… No, that's alright." Remembering her standing at the door in that little black *thing*, Richard swallowed. He couldn't be alone with her, not there. He was safe here. This was his work; she wouldn't try anything here. And more importantly, nor would he.

He glanced nervously at his co-workers. They were both grinning like a pair of mangy hyenas. "Mind giving us a minute, lads?"

"Sure." McClaine gave Sing a nudge. "Come on Apu, let us leave Dick Hefner here to tend to his little lady friend." However, he paused by the door after the smaller man had gone through and threw a sideways glance back at Richard. "Oh, and enjoy yourself Dick, you're more in need of a blow job than any other white man in history." *Bastard.*

Richard cursed and turned away, flipping him the VSign over his shoulder. It was an almost impotent retort, but it was the best he could do with Rebecca in such close proximity. He couldn't risk over reacting. He couldn't take the chance of giving his work mate cause to think something was going on.

So he kept his attention locked on his screen, even after the door shut and the laughter drowned out by the hum of computer drives. Yet his eyes had a mind of their own and every few moments he caught himself glancing over in her direction as Rebecca jumped up to perch her ripe little derriere on the edge of his desk, her pencil skirt riding up as she crossed her legs to flash him a hint of thigh.

Thighs that had been wrapped around him just days ago.

Growing ever more aware of the stiffness between his legs, while his guts twisted into knots, Richard swivelled around to face her, blindly tapping a few keys to minimise the spreadsheets. Not that he thought she would have any interest in them, but PPI was such a hot topic, better safe than sorry.

Forcing down a dry swallow, he smiled pleasantly at her. "So, what's so urgent?"

"Well… I wanted to… um it's just that… Well…" She looked away, a blush staining her cheeks a dusty pink. "I'm sorry. About what happened on Friday, I don't know what got into me…"

"I think I have some idea." He couldn't help a dry chuckle.

"I didn't mean like that," Rebecca laughed, the sound high and girlish, breaking the tension that had been building between them.

For a moment.

Then the dam broke, and she started to cry. Fat, glassy tears rolled down her checks in rivers. "I'm so sorry, Mr Martin. I didn't mean for it to happen. Please, please don't hate me. I- I couldn't..."

Her tears raked him. "Hey, hey, hey, come here." Richard opened his arms. She all but threw herself at him, burying her face into his neck and sobbing loudly as he hugged her back. "It's okay, sweetheart. It wasn't your fault. Everything just happened so fast..."

Not sure what else to do, he held her till the tears passed, and then he continued to hold her, rocking gently from side to side. It felt good to hold her like this. She felt good. Her hair was silky soft against his cheek. That lean athlete's build fitting against him so perfectly, warm and so very inviting. Those lush young breasts pushing against his chest through the material of her uniform, tipped by dusky nipples that just begged to be sucked.

"Mr Martin?" Rebecca voiced, her tone shaky and uncertain, and he was suddenly aware she was looking down. Down at where the bulge was pitching a tent in his trousers.

Oh shit...

Heat burned across his cheeks as her head tilted back up to his, those full lips curling into a sly feline smirk.

"H-how was the market?"

No sooner had the words left his mouth, he knew they were a mistake.

Only, he had no idea what else to say. The question was the first thing that came to mind that didn't also involve the words fuck, cunt, cock, tits or cum- in one insidious combination or another.

"Oh… It's amazing!" She positively beamed at the question, her big doe eyes lighting up with mischief. "There are so many stalls this year, and the costumes. It's just like something out of Dickens' times."

"That's… nice. Err Rebecca I have to-"

She carried on regardless. "They've even set up a snow machine over the ice rink…"

"Rebecca-"

"But it's broken and…"

"Rebecca… look… I… I don't think-"

"You should hurry up and eat your sandwich, Mr Martin, before it gets cold."

"Rebecca…" He really needed her to stop talking.

"Mmm… it's pulled pork. I had the hog roast sausage. I normally prefer chicken, but when I saw them on the spit, I couldn't resist. They were just so big and thick; I wasn't even sure I could get it in my mouth-"

He took her mouth, kissing her hard and hungrily, drinking in her lushness.

It was madness. Utter madness. But Richard couldn't take it. He had to have her again. Pulling her into his lap, his hands slid down the lines of her narrow waist to cup and squeeze her butt through her skirt, crushing her to him, making her moan and arch. Fuck, she tasted even better than he remembered. There was no trace of cherries now. Only the lushness of her soft pink lips, and she was all the sweeter for it.

Rebecca didn't waste a moment. Burying her hands in his hair, she sucked his tongue like a woman possessed and moaned a low purr that vibrated through him and made his trapped cock throb against its confines.

Yet it wasn't enough. Nowhere near enough. He wanted more. He wanted her, wanted to rip her shirt open and taste those plump tits. Wanted to bury his face between her legs and eat her hot, wet cunt. Wanted to bend her over his desk, go balls deep in that tempting little pussy and fuck her like the hot little bitch she was.

She moaned a pitiful protest when he left her mouth, but it quickly turned to small kittenish gasps as he nipped a fiery trail down the long slope of her neck. Then she was like putty in his hands. Her hands dropped down to push his jacket halfway down his arms, before working on his shirt buttons, fumbling a bit as he sucked the sweet spot where her neck and shoulder met.

"Oh… Mr Martin!" Rebecca moaned, her head rolling back, exposing more skin for him to kiss. He greedily obliged, dragging the flat of his tongue along the dips and hollows of her throat. Meanwhile, his hands ground her on the ridge of his cock, sliding under the hem of her skirt and up to the warmth beneath. Up along the smooth, silky-soft skin of her inner thigh. Fingers stretching, brushing over taught tendons and reaching for the heat of her lush wet-

A door slammed shut somewhere down the hall, and Richard's heart leaped into his throat. He froze, a moment of clarity rushing over him in an icy cascade.

Shit!

"Stop. Stop- shh!" Seizing Rebecca's arms, he pushed her away, quite literally holding her at an arm's length as he threw a sideways look towards the door.

It was still shut, but the window would have given anyone passing by a front-row seat of their own dirty little peep show.

He watched it, not daring to blink.

Ten seconds.

Thirty seconds.

One minute and still nothing.

He let out a breath. That was close. He didn't want to think what might have happened if someone had seen them. Even now, with their flushed faces and dishevelled condition, it wouldn't have taken Doctor-bleeding-Spock to work out what had been going on.

"Mr Martin?"

Rebecca's voice was so quiet and unsure, it was almost a stranger's voice. He twisted back to face her, and the look in her eyes raked his soul. She couldn't have looked more hurt if he had slapped her.

"Rebecca…" The words caught in his throat. He'd seriously fucked up. Again. "We can't do this."

"Why not?"

Richard felt like the lowest piece of shit that had ever walked the earth. "You know why. I'm married, and I love my wife."

"She doesn't have to know."

"That's not the point. Alice deserves better than that, and so do you." Unable to look her in the eyes, he shrugged his jacket back into place before fixing his buttons. "I don't want to use you like that, Rebecca."

"I don't care. You can use me however you want. I-"

The sudden shrill shriek of a phone ringing cut her off. His computer monitor burst into life, and Alice's face stared back at them.

Chapter Nine

"Get down," Richard snapped, not exactly pushing the girl away but urging her off of his lap and down under the desk with an insistence that brokered no argument from her. Then, heart pounding like a drum in his chest, he turned back to the screen.

The Skype video call was getting close to timing out.

Resisting the urge to glance down to the girl's hideaway, he accepted the video call, then forced a broad smile. "Hey Al."

His wife's avatar minimised, and Alice's smoky gaze met his.

"Not interrupting anything, am I, *Dick?*" Even wrapped around an insinuation, her husky tone made his dick hard all over again.

Or maybe it was just the sight of her all dressed up in her *'work wear'*. No doubt, the sight of Alice in that tan blazer, button up blouse, and white pencil skirt had fuelled more than a few teenage boys to lock themselves in the toilets for an extended break.

"Nah, just taking my break. How's work?"

"Boring," she pouted. "I seem to spend all day either marking half-term homework or giving out detentions… Errr, I hate November."

"Aww… don't worry, love, it'll soon be Christmas."

She rolled her eyes. "Ha… ha… ha… Don't remind me."

Alice loved her work. She loved being a teacher, but there were times when the job didn't love her. "Speaking of Christmas, you left your lunch at home, so I gave Rebecca a call and asked her to pop in with something special for you."

Her tone was playful, but the edge to her voice sent a shiver down his spine, and he found himself glancing down at the dark space under his desk.

"Yeah… she just left." He picked up his still wrapped sandwich and held it up for her to see.

A ghost of a smile curved the corner of her mouth and the tip of her tongue darted out across her plump upper lip. "Mmm… good, because I have a little surprise for you."

Momentarily lost in all the memories of just what that tongue and mouth could do, Richard could only swallow. "Oh…"

She leaned back in her big black chair and began working on the buttons of her blouse. "I admit I was rather miffed with you over the weekend for getting in so late the other night, but I think I know a way for you to make it up to me…"

Richard couldn't believe his eyes. "Jesus, Alice… are you mad?"

"Come on *Dick*, I don't have long till my next class… mmm… one of my students might come by at any minute…" As the last button came undone, the blouse fell open to tease him with a glimpse of her breasts, full and firm and absolutely luscious, before she pressed it closed. "Whoopsie…"

"Tease."

"Aww… remember how we used to do this whenever one of us was working late… come on baby…" She let one corner of the garment slide down to reveal her left breast before cupping it. "Mmm… you like these baby, God I wish you were here… I'm so horny… I just want to jerk your big dick off with my tits and watch you paint them with all your yummy cum…"

Richard had to force himself to breathe as he watched his wife raise her tit up to her mouth and swirl her tongue around the pebbled nipple. She knew how much he loved her tits. Knew just how to use them to drive him wild.

"A-Alice…"

"Do you want me to beg for it… want me to get down on my hands and knees… and beg to see your cock…" The blouse fell open completely as Alice pushed her breasts together, making them bounce and jiggle before rolling the dusky nipples between her fingers and thumbs. "Mmm… you're so bad. Do it, Dick, I want your cock." And

his cock definitely wanted her.

That throaty husk of hers had him as hard as steel.

Sensation rippled up and down his length as it fought to be free of its restraints. So insistent and demanding, his white knuckled grip on the armrests of his chair was all that kept him from ripping open his chinos and giving her the show she craved.

Then he felt something brush against his leg.

He froze.

He knew he shouldn't look, but his eyes had a will of their own. Drawn down like magnets to watch the slow seduction of a hand rising from under the desk. Slowly, step by step, walking up his leg bit by bit towards the bulge of his cock, getting closer and closer and…

"*Fuck*…" A ragged breath left him in a rush as soft digits curled around his imprisoned length and gave it a testing squeeze.

"That's it, grab it baby, tell me how big it is… so big and hard and full of cum…" Alice panted in her hot breathy tone, the fingers of her left hand roughly attending to her nipple, twisting and tugging in the way that always got her hot. "Just thinking about you sitting there, jerking your big dick for me… mmm… gets me so wet. Does it feel good, Dick?"

"Yeah… so fucking good…" Richard groaned, Rebecca's small hand fisting him through his trousers, pumping along his length from root to head, her movements slow but urgent. He tried to focus on the screen, on his wife, to blot out the sensations Rebecca was sending sizzling through him, but he was too finitely aware of her. Aware of her shuffling closer, her head of dark chocolate hair creeping out from beneath the table, her free hand creeping up his other leg. Moving higher and higher towards his zipper.

He needed to stop this. He needed to stop her, but when he tried, his body had a will of its own. Instead of pushing her away, his hands just undid the fastenings of his belt and trousers. Then Rebecca's hand was dragging him from the confines of his boxers, and it was too late.

"Suck it." The command was out before he knew what he was saying.

"Fuck yes, baby, I love sucking your cock…" Alice moaned on the screen, thinking the command was for her. "I really wish you were here. Your cock's so big and tasty. I could suck it all day, jerking you off with my tits until you paint my face with your cum. Or would you just bend me over and pound-pound me… pound me from behind…"

She was getting close; he could hear it in her voice. Richard could imagine her hand under the desk, fingers pushing under the silk of her panties to rub her clit. "Stick it in me Dick. I need it. I've been such a naughty schoolgirl, bend me over your desk and punish me… punish me with it… spank my ass with your cock and use my naughty little pussy… she's so nice and hot and wet for you… just begging to get your dick off- oh shit!"

Through the speakers, the school bell sounded faint and distant, but it hit Alice like ice.

In a flash, she was up and pulling herself together as the hall outside filled with the shouts and bangs of children running to their next class. "Sorry babe, gotta go, but we'll finish this later," she promised, before killing the Skype connection with a click of her mouse.

Richard hardly noticed.

Instead, his eyes never strayed from the vision of Rebecca's big doe eyes staring up at him from beneath her bangs as her pink lips wrapped around his cock. A picture of innocence and wickedness. Then she was taking him in. Those lush lips brushing over his glands and down his shaft. The wet heat of her mouth enveloped him, sucking him in all the way to the gate of her throat, before pulling back to mouth his sensitive crown.

"You've no idea how long I've wanted to do this, Mr Martin," she purred, teasing his underside with slow licks. "I'm sorry, I know it's wrong, but after Friday night, I just can't help myself…"

"It's okay Rebecca, that wasn't… it-it's not your fault."

Richard groaned, his head rolling back as the hand still holding him began pumping up and down.

"It's alright, Mr Martin. I know you're only saying that. It's all my fault. I'm such a naughty girl, going down on you while you're talking to your wife. Have I been bad, Mr Martin?"

"Yeah, so very bad."

"Do you like it Mr Martin?

"*Yes.*" The feeling was so intense that Richard's death grip almost snapped the arms clean off his chair.

"Are you going to punish me?"

"Oh yes, I'm going to put you over my knee alright, and if you don't make me cum quickly, I'll bend you over and fuck you across this desk until you can't walk straight."

"Oh, promises, promises…"

She took him back into her mouth. Her cheeks hollowed as she sucked hard, head bobbing up and down while fisting his root, making up whatever she lacked in experience with enthusiasm.

"Mmm… yes, yes, yes… just like that…" Richard groaned, almost as much for her benefit as for his, the words just tumbling out as he melted back into his chair. His hands lost themselves in the silky softness of her hair. He gathered up and pushed back a wing of dark chocolate that had fallen out of place, before fisting it as the flat of her tongue swirled around his crest once, twice, thri- *oh fuck!*

The sensation came upon him so quickly, he didn't have a chance to voice a warning before his hot cum fired into her greedy mouth. His orgasm ripped through him hard enough for black spots to dance before his eyes, but Rebecca accepted everything he had to give her.

She drank every drop. Swallowing greedily as it flowed, sucking when the tide ebbed. And all the while watching him, those big doe eyes bright with… what?

Satisfaction at having brought him to orgasm so easily?

Or excitement about future possibilities?

Only when she had finally milked him dry and his fingers slipped from her hair did she release his still firm erection and stand back up. Taking the napkin from the uneaten sandwich, she wiped her lovely rosy lips clean. Stepping around his chair, she lent down and pressed a soft kiss to his cheek.

"I better get back. See you later, Mr Martin."

"Rebecca wait-" Richard started, but her cute little derriere was already sashaying out the office, the door slamming shut behind her.

His fist hit the desk, hard enough to make the structure tremble. "Shit!"

You stupid bloody bastard, he cursed inwardly as guilt and shame raked him with claws of ice and fire, respawning the sicking knot deep in his guts. How the fuck could he have been so stupid to have let that happen, again?

A ping sounded from the computer, making Richard's heart leap into his throat. His head snapped up to see the icon for the unfinished report flash. The ping was a pre-programed reminder to warn the user whenever a file had been open and inactive for too long.

Richard contemplated it for a second. "Fuck it!"

Tapping a few keys, he deleted his notes, closed the document and forwarded it in an email to Scarlet's inbox.

They were right. It wasn't his job anymore. What the fuck did it matter, anyway?

Shoving himself into his trousers and refastening his belt, he grabbed his untouched sandwich and took a bite.

Only, he'd lost his appetite.

Chapter Ten

"We're heading off, Dick. Catch you later."

Richard looked up from his monitor just in time to glimpse McClaine and Sing trot out the office with backhanded waves, like schoolboys ditching detention. "You guys off already?"

"*Already?* Do me a favour, Dick, take a day off, will ya."

"Go see the girls at Spearmint Rhino. They do your sort of favours, mate, not me."

McClaine shot him a look that could curdle custard, then raised his hand, pulled back his cuff and pointed to his TAG Heuer watch face. "See this? It's past five. That's clocking off time in my book. You might be prepared to work yourself ragged, but I've got better things to do than kill myself for old Walrus Face and little miss Tight Ass. Some of us have a life, ya know, see ya."

"You live with your mother!" Resisting the urge to flip him the finger, Richard turned back to his desk, his eyes landing on a mountain of paperwork. Work he'd been putting off while obsessing over the Prometheus Account.

He checked his own wristwatch, a Seiko his old man had given him for his eighteenth birthday. Sure enough, it was five thirteen in the afternoon. He'd been at it for five hours, five bloody hours, and hadn't even made a dent.

Bugger.

Exhaling a long, suddenly exhausted breath, he reclined back in his seat and pushed a hand through his hair. He supposed he should follow their lead and go home. This work could wait a night, and Alice would be on her way home soon enough, after she'd picked up Alex from her parents and battled her way up the stretch of M5 that connected Bristol and Gloucester, through the last of the rush hour traffic. They'd have a nice family dinner before sitting down to… what? Talk about their day?

That's good darling. My day? It was ok. I struggled a bit with that report, but Rebecca gave me a blowjob when she popped by. So all in all…

The thought had a dry laugh billowing up his throat.

How could he look Alice in the eyes again? Hold their son again?

No, he couldn't. Not now, not after…

The computer emitted a small double ring and an email notification window popped up in the bottom righthand corner of the screen. It was from Scarlet, though the address attached read *Tight_Ass_Bitch*.

Officially, no one knew who had hacked her email to change the address. Whoever it was though, their joke had backfired. Far from being annoyed or embarrassed by the stunt, Scarlet practically adopted the title, and never missed an opportunity to live up to it.

True to her unofficial title, the message was brief and to the point.

Dick
Drop by my office on your way out.
We need to discuss Prometheus.
Scarlet

"… Shit," Richard cursed and looked mournfully back to the paperwork and the potential overtime it offered. "Well, that puts the kibosh on that plan."

He closed the mail with a click of his mouse.

Chapter Eleven

Alice Martin wasn't a woman to beat about the bush.

She knew what she wanted and when she saw it, she went for it.

It had been that way the night she first met her husband. It hadn't mattered that he was at work or that they hadn't formally met, or didn't even know each other's names. She'd seen him, she'd wanted him, so she took him.

If she wanted something, the technicalities just didn't matter.

So when she saw a particular garment hanging in the window of the Bristol high street's *Sweet Temptations* Boutique, and felt that all too familiar draw, it had only been a matter of time.

Now fresh from a shower, with her hair still damp and her latest purchase hanging from her shoulders, she couldn't help grinning as she admired her reflection in her vanity.

The cherry red spaghetti strap gown was pure mulberry silk with a black lace trim and clung to her body in all the right ways to emphasise her curves and mile-long legs. It was perfect. Richard wouldn't know what hit him.

Just the thought of modelling it for him when he came home, of lying stretched out across their bed waiting for him to find her and fuck her brains out, sent a delicious thrill sizzling through her. Beneath the silk, her poor neglected pussy clenched, and her clit, still stiff and begging to be played with, throbbed, reminding her of how close she'd come during that session she'd orchestrated for him during her break.

Damn her and her blasted ideas. This wasn't how it was supposed to be. That call was only supposed to be a warmup *for him*. A tease to get *him* worked up and hard and oh so desperate to take her. Instead, it had backfired and left her feeling restless and on edge. She'd been unable to settle her mind on anything. In short, she was so fucking horny, it was all she could do not to fish out 'Antonio' from her bedside draw and start the party early.

Just the thought of the wand's intense vibrations rumbling against her pussy had her thighs rubbing together in a vain effort to settle the need burning inside her.

It would have felt so good too, but instead she forced herself into action and, taking the matching robe from the hook on the door, she turned and hurried out into the hall. There was too much left to do. She couldn't afford to indulge herself, yet.

Especially when, so far anyway, everything had been going according to plan.

Everything was arranged. She'd left work early to beat Richard home, dropping her last class of the day on a colleague who owed her a favour and missing the ever notorious M5 rush hour. Her parents had said they were fine looking after Alexander for a couple of nights so he was all taken care of, and she had sent everyone else they knew a polite, but firm, text message, warning they weren't to be disturbed.

Tonight was to be theirs.

A quiet candlelit evening just for them, to let go of all their woes, reacquaint themselves with each other's bodies, and give in to all their carnal desires.

It was just what they needed. What they both needed.

Though he said nothing about it, she knew Richard had been feeling stressed. It was all the usual stuff, really, just the little things. Under pressure at his new job. Worried about money. The stresses of moving to a new city and starting a family. Fairly mundane, but her husband had always insisted on dealing with it all by himself, and it was taking a toll on him.

She wanted to help ease his burden, to take them back to how they used to be, even if it was only for one brief night.

And there was always that other thing.

That one little thing a small part of her was so insecure about.

Alice wasn't usually the jealous type, but where Richard was concerned, she was possessive. She was possessive as hell, and it had not escaped her notice that other women were taking an interest in her husband. Of course, he had always been a good-looking man, but age, it seemed, agreed with him. The cute puppy she'd cornered in the stockroom had grown up into a fox that any red-blooded woman would have to be blind not to notice. And when they did, she had to resist the urge to go up to them and claw their eyes out.

Normally, she had the urge under control. However, Scarlet's undisguised flirtations at the party had been the last straw.

Richard was hers. Her lover. The father of her baby. Her soul mate, and it was time she reaffirmed their bond.

Just imagining all the ways she could have her way with him, could brand him, mark him as hers, had her lip twisting devilishly as she slipped into the kitchen to rummage through the fridge. She could get the ice cream out now, so that it melted a bit first. Or maybe it would be better to start with the wet celery, as they still had the flying helmet from that Halloween party the year before they moved and she could always use the egg whisk on his-

A frantic shriek sounded from somewhere on the floor above.

Chapter Twelve

The door was sleek pine with a bronze plaque embossed with the legend, *S. Holmes, Accounts Supervisor*. Being the boss's daughter certainly had its perks.

Richard knocked once, then pushed on through without waiting for an answer.

Seated at the immense leather-topped oak desk that dwarfed her and the rest of the office, Scarlet was working on her computer. Behind her, floor to ceiling windows boasted a picturesque landscape of the river below.

To a stranger, she might have looked oblivious, blind to the goings on around her, her focus dominated by her work, but Richard knew better. Scarlet was anything but oblivious. She was the sort of woman who woke up intending to conquer the world. Who missed nothing.

Without waiting for an invitation, he crossed the wood panelled floor, bypassing the plush leather sofa to take the simple leather and teak chair opposite her side of the desk.

She didn't look up, nod, or do anything to acknowledge his presence.

Nor would she. Not yet. Not until she was ready.

It was her game, a power play to remind the minion just who was the boss.

Well, at least she didn't make him pass her tea or pick pens off of the floor.

The office had been the department's briefing room before her appointment. Her predecessor had made do with the windowless coat cupboard three doors down. It was simple and functional, but large enough to impress. And beige. Very beige. Beige walls. Beige rugs. Beige leather…

Beige. Safe and soothing, and not at all Scarlet Holmes.

She was as bloody crimson as her namesake. And then a dash extra.

All heat and passion and searing raw emotion. And beauty.

Scarlet flaunted flawless skin, tanned to a soft peach hue, that complimented the waves of spun gold that tumbled down to her shoulders. She wore a tight white dress that showed off plenty of leg and had a deep plunging neckline to emphasise her figure. There wasn't a man alive who could deny Scarlet was *very* lovely.

The matter wasn't up for discussion. It was a fact.

And only skin deep.

Beneath the fragile beauty, she was as hard and sharp as steel. A lioness disguised in a little bunny's fur.

He ignored the urge to check his watch. That subtle hint would only prolong the game, though. Scarlet would see to that, sure enough. So instead, he amused himself by watching the goings on outside the tall windows behind her desk that overlooked the line of narrow boats and yachts moored along the Sharpness Canal.

The view was wasted on Scarlet.

When she turned to him, the bunny beamed up at him. "Hey Dick."

"Hi Scarlet," Richard smiled back, inwardly steeling himself. If she wanted to play her games, he'd play. "How was your day?"

It was a poor effort, but the best he could do on the fly. It got the job done.

"Oh, the usual, same shit, different day. You headin' home for the day?"

"Yeah soon, just had a couple of things I wanted to finish up first."

She ignored the prompt and just kept smiling up at him.

Sod it, she could have this round. "So, you wanted to see me?"

Her eyes were bright, and they laughed at him behind her glasses. She didn't need them. The lenses were from a cheap pair of reading glasses she'd got in a Pound shop, but the frames were designer and worth more than he made in a month. "Yes, we need to discuss Prometheus."

"Oh? How come?"

"Don't play coy with me, Dick." Despite her smile, behind the cheap plastic lenses, her eyes flared with blue fire. Behind the bunny, the lion was baring its fangs, a warning before the charge. "I told you I wanted you to make the Prometheus Account your top priority, yes?"

"Yes."

"Yes? That was a month ago. The report should have taken you a few days, max. And now you send me this?" She pulled a manilla folder out of a drawer and laid it open on the desk. A quick glance confirmed it was the paperwork he'd sent her earlier. "So, what's the game?"

"Game?"

"You could have knocked this up in a few hours. You have been, all afternoon. So, either you had a hunch, then lost your nerve, or you were slacking off to make me look bad. Which is it?" Closing the folder, she slid it aside, then leaned forward to face him, fingers tipped by perfectly manicured nails painted speckled gold, steepled under her chin.

"Scarlett I…"

"Do you have a problem working under me, Dick?"

"No."

"Then you had a hunch?"

"It was a stupid idea, not worth mentioning."

"You thought it was important enough to risk the contract."

Reaching into his pocket, he pulled out the flash drive with all his research into Prometheus and laid it on the desk. He'd forgotten about it amongst everything else that had gone on in the last couple of days and had only thought of it after receiving her email. He'd brought it along just in case. "It's nothing."

"Why don't you let me be the judge of that." She took the flash drive and plugged it into her desktop. With a few clicks of her mouse, all the documents were arranged on her monitor. Spreadsheets. Invoices. Tax returns. Everything he could find on Prometheus, but would it be enough?

A tight knot of tension wound around and around his guts like a python's coils. Financial reports. Richard watched her work. Those fierce blue eyes skimmed over the screen behind her glasses, moving from one article to the next while she caught her rose-pink lower lip between a perfect set of pearly whites.

He hated to admit it, but her look was sexy as hell.

She swivelled slowly back around in her chair to face him; her stare piercing. Not quite a lioness, but definitely not a flopsy bunny either. "All this shows is Prometheus recorded substantial profits. Hardy conclusive, *Dick*."

A low shiver coursed down his spine to tingle in his crotch as his cock stirred at the way she said his growingly official nickname. The accusation behind it made him feel like he was getting a telling off from the hot teacher all the boys fantasised about.

"Since the early 90s, Prometheus has consistently recorded growing profits. Yes, however, if you look more closely, you'll see the bulk of their earnings came from work throughout Ukraine, Estonia, Georgia, Kazakhstan, and the Baltic states. Nations recovering from the Soviet Union. Plenty of cheap labour, but a brassic economy. Prometheus's books took a slight hit in the Global recession but remained firmly in the black until 2012, when they expanded their operations into the Middle East. Work in areas of Turkey and Syria achieved record profits, despite the numerous conflicts raging in the region." He paused, trying to think how to put the next part.

"Go on..."

He took a breath, steeling his nerves for the plunge. "I think Prometheus has connections with Russian organised crime and is a front for criminal activity, including money laundering, drug trafficking and smuggling."

And there it was, the complete ruin of his career. And all packed up neatly in one sentence. Who says experience counts for nothing!

For the longest moment, Scarlet let the silence drag on. Her expression impassive, unreadable, neither bunny nor lion, but her eyes, once such a vibrant blue, were suddenly steel. "I see." Her tone was as cold and sharp as ice. "Those are very serious accusations, Dick. Ones we're required by law to report to the proper authorities and would almost certainly result in us losing the client, even if you're wrong. Can you prove this?"

"No," he confessed, then added hastily. "But there are too many anomalies for it all to be just coincidence."

"What anomalies?"

"The company was founded in the early 90s and received heavy outside funding, primarily from a now disbanded Russian-led consortium, at the same time Russian gangsters started moving west out of Moscow. They do business all over Europe but are especially affluent in areas of high Russian criminal activity and interest."

Scarlet nodded. "And their 2012 expansion?"

"The date they began expanding was just a month after the Russian President's second inauguration. It's not exactly a secret he uses the crime bosses as off the book enforcers, and the countries Prometheus has expanded to have seen heavy Russian influence since."

"They're war zones, Dick," she laughed without mirth, shaking her head. "Builders and developers often receive government contracts to repair and rebuild sites damaged in conflict."

"Yes, but usually after the war is won," Richard cut in. "I've heard of prudent planning, but if I'm wrong, whoever picked these deals must have one hell of a crystal ball. You should take him to the Cheltenham races next year. With this guy's luck, you'll make a fortune betting on the gee-gees."

She ignored the joke, instead turning back to look over the documents on her screen. "Well, the money laundering is self-explanatory. Dirty money finances the projects on the books, then returns as profits, but what about this trafficking and smuggling nonsense?"

What? Was she actually buying this story? He couldn't believe it; he'd half expected her to tear up his contract right there, even for suggesting it.

"They ship out their own equipment instead of hiring or purchasing on-site. A JCB is a pretty big bit of kit. Lots of places to hide something you don't want found, if you know how."

"But you can't prove it. Legally."

"No." His throat was so tight, he had to force the word out. "After tax is accounted for, their profits are all funnelled into an account in a private Depository Bank in Zurich. I can't track it from there without going through a long and costly legal battle."

"So…" she rounded on him, her voice as cold and sharp as steel. "Let me get this straight, because I'm a little confused. You're given a high value contract, told to make them your top priority, but instead of doing your job and having the report on my desk like you're supposed to, you dig into their business records and concoct some cock and bull theory about the Russian Mafia. And just to put the icing on the cake, you have no proof? Nothing to back it up. Is that about the sum of it?"

"More or less."

She sighed and shook her head.

That was it. She'd just fired her broadside and hit dead centre. He was sunk. He might as well go back and clear out his desk. Save the trip in tomorrow and have a lie in-

"Why did you keep digging? Why not just hand it in when you were supposed to after hitting a dead end?"

Richard had to work hard to keep his confusion from showing.

Why had he kept digging? Force of habit? Professional curiosity? His last job had done checks all the time, and he'd never let it go on for so long. There had just been something. Something not right. Something he couldn't put his finger on. Just something. Just…

"Just a hunch."

"A hunch?" She leaned back in her chair. "Well Dick, I don't know what to say, except…" Her full red lips spread into a wide smile, with just the hint of a white lion's fang. "Congratulations."

Chapter Thirteen

What the?

Alice's eyes widen at the sound, so high with pain and fear, like an animal caught in a trap. Forgetting her train of thought, her eyes darted up to the ceiling. It sounded like it had come from the Blaire's flat, but that could have been a trick of the building. The tower block's walls were paper thin and often as not, she could hear several things going on at once from any number of directions that sounded like they were coming from somewhere else. Just the other night she'd been treated to overhearing one couple's marathon sex session that had clearly sounded like it was coming from that very flat upstairs, but couldn't. After all, Richard had been up there, helping Rebecca with her computer.

A pity, if he hadn't been upstairs, it would have made quite the mood starter…

Another scream went out, louder this time and much more distinctive.

Rebecca. Alice's heart leapt into her throat.

"You worthless bitch!" a gruff voice half slurred, half barked, followed by the crash of something heavy smashing into glass, shattering it. "Stay still!"

Alice didn't wait for him to get his eye in.

Wheeling on her heel, she made straight for her front door, hurriedly tying the sash of her robe as she went. Another scream, louder, echoing as footsteps ran down the building's stairwell. Then suddenly they were on the landing, running, growing louder by the second as Alice ran to the door.

No sooner had she wrenched it open than Rebecca barrelled into her.

Just managing to catch herself, Alice pulled the girl to her, her arms going around her in a protective hug. "Hey, hey Rebecca, honey, what's happened? What's going on?"

"He's coming, please… I didn't touch… don't let him…" Sobbing, she clung to the older woman, her big doe eyes pleading, so wide they were almost round. The poor thing was terrified out of her mind.

The sight tore at Alice's heart and she pulled her closer, doing her best to sooth her with quiet words. "Shh… honey, it's okay, I won't, nothing's going to happen to you, I promise."

She almost couldn't believe this was the same girl she knew. Rebecca was always so upbeat and bubbly. Of course, she'd known there were some problems in the home. Even a blind man could have seen was nervous around her father and that he could be hard on her, too hard sometimes, but this…

The thought lit a fire in her mother's heart that threatened to burn them both to cinders. That the brute could do this to his own daughter. Drive such a sweet girl to such a fit of terror, sickened her to her very core. What parent, no, what kind of fucking beast could do such a thing?

Struggling to keep her tone soothing, Alice slowly steered Rebecca inside. "Come on, let's get you inside and I'll-"

"Come back here you little bitch!" the other voice bellowed from above amidst a thunder of footsteps. Then he was there on the bend on the stairs, Derik Blaire, red faced with murder and madness scorching his wild eyes. "Where is it, I want it, you fucking whore," he seethed, half lumbering down the last few steps like a hippopotamus, not even seeming to notice Alice. "You hear me? You're a whore. Just a fucking whore, like that bitch mother of yours, now give it to me!"

Rebecca stiffened at her father's call, her knuckles going white like bone as she clung on with a death grip. However Alice hardly noticed as she turned to look at the man. With a gaze as cool as ice, she gently pried herself free. Then, with a gently push, she urged the girl inside the flat. "Go inside," she instructed, her tone firm but just soft enough so that Derik wouldn't overhear. "Lock the door. I'll knock and call for you when it's safe to come out."

"No, please… don't leave me, don't let him-" Rebecca's eyes were glassy with tears and visibly pleaded for Alice not to leave her as she tried to cling to her arm. It was the same look she saw in the eyes of many kids on their first day of school, when their parents left them at the gates for the first time.

"I won't. Go on, I'll take care of this. You go put a brew on." It tore at Alice's heart, but she pushed her inside regardless and pulled the door shut with a firm slam.

She felt like a bitch for it but it was the only way. She couldn't deal with the problem at hand if she was concerned for the girl.

"What the fuck you think you're doing, bitch? Get the fuck out of my way!" he slurred angrily, staggering to a stop only a metre or so from Alice, swaying from one foot to the other. As if only just seeing her for the first time, he grinned in a way that made her feel dirty just for him looking at her.

"Alright *John*, I don't know what you're on tonight, but I think you need to go back upstairs and sleep it off." Alice wouldn't be cowed. He may have towered over her, but she was well accustomed to dealing with people bigger than her. She held his gaze with steely determination, doing her best to ignore the fact that the only thing protecting her modesty was a silk robe that showed off way too much leg and did nothing to hide the swell of her bosom.

"Don't you tell me what to do, you little cow," he slurred, sneering down at her. "I've had it with all you posh tossers… talking down to me… treating me like shit… That whore in there… took my shit… and now she's going to give it back or I'm gonna beat her ass black and blue then throw it out on the street." The thick stink of booze was coming off him in waves. He'd definitely had more than a skinful.

"No," Alice said firmly. "You're not going anywhere near her in that state. So just go back upstairs before I-"

"You'll what?" Derik Blaire barked, his mouth spreading into a mocking grin that could have curdled milk as he stepped forward, closing the gap. "What are you gonna do? Don't give me all that shit… Your man's not here to protect you. What you going to do to me, you little bitch? How are you going to stop me from taking whatever I want from your fat arse…" The threats were almost as ugly as he was. With that squat face crowned by a brush of chestnut-grey hair and a body like a barrel that had been sat on by something heavy one too many times, he gave the faint impression of being the love child of Bruce Willis and Ray Winstone. Only without the charisma, good looks, or height.

He was taller than her though. And that must have made him feel cocky because he loomed over her. Enough that she knew he'd be able to see straight down the valley of her cleavage soon enough. One of his hands slowly reached out to touch.

"You know, I'm sick and tired of you and limp dick treating me like I'm shit. Don't know why a cunt like you puts up with him. Look at those fat tits and ass… come on bitch, let me have a feel… mmm… too good for him… maybe it's time I show you how a real man treats his bitc-"

His words died with a sickening wet crunch.

Just before his fingers could touch the slope of her right breast, Alice rammed the heel of her palm up into his nose. Blood arced, and he wheeled away, howling in agony.

"Don't touch me," she growled. The very idea of this *thing* laying a hand on her provoked a fresh surge of fiery rage

inside her. How fucking dare he, this… *beast* think he could
touch her, even lay a single, filthy fucking finger on her.

Derik Blaire gave no sign of having heard her,
however.

"Bitch… you broke my nose," he spat out, glaring at
her with both hands clamped up to the ruin of his nose. Blood
was oozing out from between his fingers.

"Yeah, I did," Alice shot back, and slowly she sunk
down into the ready stance her instructors had ingrained into
her, ready to spring to the attack. It felt awkward to assume the
position again, but once upon a time, the position had been as
natural to her as any. "Try to touch me again, and next time I'll
break your hand and shove it so far down your throat, you'll
be scratching your balls."

His eyes widened, perhaps surprised by her threat,
then narrowed dangerously as hate and anger burned through
whatever was left of his common sense.

"Scratch this." He lunged, cranking his fist back and
swinging it up and around. It was a decent effort. If it landed,
it might very well have taken her head off, but he was nowhere
near fast enough. Pissed as a skunk as he was, the attack was
pitifully obvious and Alice danced away, ducking down under
his arm then sidestepping as his momentum carried him by.
Whatever it lacked in subtlety, the robe made up for in
freedom of movement, if nothing else.

Derik wheeled around after her, faster than anyone
could have expected from a man so deep in his cups, bellowing
his fury like a barbarian. His second swing was smaller, but
the distance between them was so slight, she couldn't dodge
him this time. Nor had she meant to. Instead, she closed the
gap. Stepping in and driving her left forearm up into the hook
of his arm, stopping it dead, as she folded her right arm and
swung it up, clubbing his broken nose with her elbow.

The sudden explosion of pain obviously seared across
the man's brain as his head jarred back and as his knees gave

way. He went down hard, collapsing on his back to lie in a heap, conscious but dazed and soon to be in a lot of pain.

Alice turned away, walked back to her flat door, raised a hand to knock, and the door open. Rebecca stood behind it, her eyes wide but her look of terror now replaced by a mix of puzzlement and disbelief. Clearly, she had been watching everything through the peephole.

"How…" she started but seemed to think better of it halfway through and instead went with. "I mean, he was, and you're so- I mean a…"

"My dad was in the SAS," Alice said, like that should have explained it all, stepping inside and shutting the door on the sight of Derik Blaire lying there on the landing, broken and bruised, like some beached walrus. "When the boys at school started teasing me, he had the PT instructors give me some private coaching, then had me doing drills with the lads at *The Lines* over the weekends. They even let me run the selection march across the Brecon Beacons over summer holidays, and no boy ever pulled my pigtails again."

That wasn't strictly true. There had been a few who had tried to make fun of 'the little girl', but they hadn't been laughing for long. A throat punch could be one hell of a punch line, especially when delivered by a girl half your size.

The memory made Alice's mouth curl, then she took in the sight of Rebecca's pale and haggard face and it fell away. "Come on, honey, let's go get you cleaned up."

Chapter Fourteen

Richard blinked, almost at a loss for words. Almost.

Congratulations? For what? Dropping a bollock? Making a complete ass of himself? "What?"

Scarlet's head titled, her eyes dancing and gleeful, both bunny and lioness. "Congratulations. You passed the test."

"Test? What test?" he demanded, incredulous.

"For the position of Financial Analyst," she said simply. "You applied for the position before being assigned to this department."

"Yeah, I remember." How
could he not?

It had been one of the few jobs he'd actually wanted. Similar seniority to his old role, but with a better salary and abundant career opportunities.

Or so the ad in the job centre had led him to believe.

What they'd offered was a polite brush off, followed by a role that was a major move down, with less pay, more hours and with every opportunity he could ever have hoped for, to kiss ass and get his ass kicked. However, with little Alex on the way, what choice had he had? It wasn't like he was getting headhunted by the Bank of England, after all.

"But that was over a year ago." he added, only just able to keep the bite from his tone.

Scarlet nodded, leaning back in her chair. The bunny had taken flight now. She was all lioness here, a queen in the heart of her territory, mistress of all she surveyed, and those hot, ice-blue eyes watched him keenly over her steepled fingers. "As you are aware, the role requires certain aptitudes. Qualities that are difficult to assess on a CV and in an interview. So, potential applicants are allocated a minor role in the company, then in due course, we allocate them a manufactured account to evaluate their performance."

"Hence Prometheus," Richard nodded, comprehension blooming. "Who seduced Zeus with plates of bones wrapped in fats to give offal covered beef to humanity."

"Then stole fire, and was punished by being chained to a rock for the great eagle to feast upon his liver each morning," Scarlet added.

"Very symbolic. So, if the candidate lacks the predisposition for the role, they're fed to the eagles?"

"More or less," she purred with a subtle tilt of her head that made Richard wonder if she wasn't entirely joking. "But, congratulations Dick, you've passed the test. Though I have to say, you were taking your sweet time about it. I was about ready to chuck your ass to the curb on general principle. Rather ironic, really. If you hadn't, you certainly would have been after I read what you sent me earlier. How long did all this take you?"

"About a day and a half," he shrugged, feeling very warm in his suit. It all made so much sense and was now so obvious. God, how could he have been so stupid? Russian organised crime. He must have lost his mind.

"Extraordinary. That's half as long as the last guy who passed the test." Shifting back in her chair and crossing her legs, revealing a lot of her soft, golden thigh, Scarlet brought a hand up to toy with a lock of her hair, studying him with renewed interest. "I must say, though, yours is certainly the most unique report yet. And all from the financial data you were provided and a bit of digging. Just extraordinary. You certainly have a vivid imagination for an accountant, Dick. You've been reading too much Andy McNab. Still, I might just have to commission you to write a novel." The corner of her mouth curled in the ghost of a smile and the tip of her pink tongue swept over her plump, juicy, pink lips. "A seedy little erotic thriller. Perhaps about a businessman caught cheating on his wife."

She let the suggestion hang there, but held his gaze just long enough for Richard's blood to turn to ice in his veins.

Shit.

Was it just a coincidence? Or did Scarlet know something? No, that was crazy. How could she? He was being silly. She couldn't know anything about him and Rebecca, unless- the sound he'd heard outside the office door. Someone moving around behind the door… Had it been Scarlet? Fuck. "So… I'm getting promoted?" *Smooth, very smooth, asshole.*

Whatever Scarlet had been expecting, that wasn't it.

She laughed.

She actually laughed. A soft, kittenish, and unmistakably feminine sound, as fair to the ears as she was lovely to behold. It was the first time Richard had ever heard it and despite his rather precarious situation; it surprised him to find the sweet melody suited her and made her appear more delicate.

He almost forgot what a bitch she could be.

Almost.

"Not quite," she chuckled. "Consider it more of a lateral move. You'll remain in my department, but within a role more suited to your talents. Get a nice little pay raise, your own private office three doors down the hall. Just what you need, a little *privacy…*"

"Is that a prerequisite for the position?" Richard asked, his throat growing tighter.

She giggled softly. "In your case, Dick, I think it's indispensable."

She was baiting him, daring him to ask the question. Both manoeuvring and mocking him. Just another game. Fuck, fuck, fuck!

"If you say so," he said simply, sidestepping her trap by the skin of his teeth. *Great, now all I've got to do is get the hell out of Dodge.*

He just needed an excuse.

Just one polite reason to-

Scarlet's lips twisted wryly. "Very good Dick, but as much as I'd like to sit here engaging in a bit of witty repartee with you, I don't have the time and you don't have the wit, so why don't we just cut through the bullshit." She removed her glasses and placed them on the desk before turning her computer monitor around for him to see.

Oh shit…

A video file was open on the screen, paused for the moment, but Richard recognised it as the feed from a security camera, a camera from his office. The camera that just so happened to be looking down at his cubicle. Where he was sitting… with Rebecca in his lap.

How could he have forgotten about the damn cameras?

Scarlet clicked her tongue, the lioness's merciless blue eyes fixed on him. "Now Dick, I don't care what my staff get up to on their lunch. Frankly, if you're off the clock, I don't give a fuck… so long as it takes place off company property."

She clicked her mouse, and the feed started replaying the scene. There was no sound. The audio was redirected to a pair of buds in the jack, but then again, he didn't need it. Every moment was still seared in his memory. Him and Rebecca making out in his chair. The call from Alice. Rebecca hiding. His wife stripping on the screen while the girl sucked him off… Richard hated to admit it, but even under her scrutiny, the memory of it was making him hard.

"Off the record, I have to say, I'm impressed. I thought the pair of you were just a boring, straight-laced, middle-class couple. The sort that argues twice a week and fucks once every leap year. I certainly never would have guessed Alice had it in her. I mean, I always suspected she had a bit of a wild streak in her. All these stuck-up bitches do, but to actually Skype her man at work to have phone sex! Bravo. And as for you…" She shut down the media player and twisted the monitor back around to face her, her eyes bright and mocking. "Well, look at the cock on you. And while a hot bit of young ass blows you under the desk, as well. Never knew you had it in you, either. I thought that only happened in bad porn."

With a shudder of self-loathing at his treacherous loins, Richard met Scarlet's gaze. "And I never guessed you were such a voyeur. What do you do, sit around here watching us all day?"

"No, not unless I have due cause to check the feeds. And when I spotted your little friend going into one of my departments, then strutting by my office door with that 'cat that got the canary grin' on her face nearly half an hour later… Well, it wouldn't be very professional of me to just turn a blind eye. Who knew what she was getting up to, or rather, who was getting into her…" she chuckled mockingly. "You should thank me, Dick. If someone in security had seen this. Well, who knows how far it could have gone…" She let the point hang there to let his imagination do the rest.

"Is that what happened to you? Did one guard catch you having a bonk and run off to tell Daddy?" The words were out before he could stop himself.

"Excuse me?"

Shit, now he'd done it.

He gritted his teeth against another outburst and tried to look contrite. "Never mind, I-"

"No, go on, *Dick*," she said, raising a hand to stop him, her voice suddenly very still and deadly serious. "So just what are they all saying about me? I'm the office slut? A hot fuck in the closet, or a quick suck in the bog type of girl? Or is it the old chestnut, daddy issues? Sleeping with all of Daddy's little minions because old Walrus Face wouldn't buy her a pony for her tenth birthday?"

"No one said anything about a pony," he admitted, resisting the urge to look away as a chill crept up his spine and he had the unmistakable feeling of shrinking into his chair.

"Then you've missed some of the more lurid variations," she continued. "No Dick, I've never been caught on camera. I'm not a slut, *Dick.* I just like sex and I'm not afraid to show it. Or enjoy it."

Richard wondered for a moment if he should ask, but she spoke with such resolve, he couldn't help himself. "And the stories about you with Tommy Cox, and Mike from Legal."

She shrugged. "They're true. I found them attractive and thought they would be a decent lay. So, I offered, and they took me up on it. They were under no obligations."

Richard was aghast. "They lost their jobs and their wives divorced them because of your affairs. Doesn't that bother you?"

"No!" Scarlet held up a dismissive hand. "Their wives divorced them because they found out their husbands were getting some on the side and didn't like it. And I sacked them because they thought banging the boss's daughter whenever she needed to take the edge off gave them the right to talk shit about the company. Clearly, they were wrong. If their wives had sucked their dicks once in a while, maybe they would've gone home to them instead of meeting me in the Travel Lodge. So, what do I have to feel guilty about Dick? I'm not married and I'm not lying to my spouse to bang a hot bit of ass." Her smile dropped, and her expression was suddenly as cold and hard as a diamond. "It's rather hypocritical, don't you think, questioning my morals when you're the one getting a little lip service from your bit on the side?"

She had it right, of course. And whatever else his faults might have been, Richard wasn't so great a fool as to try lying to himself.

What right did he have to criticize her?

They may have both been indiscreet, but she was single and a free agent.

He, on the other hand, was a married man.

"Yes. You're right, I'm sorry, and it won't happen again," he capitulated and finally looked down at his feet, running a hand through his hair. Scarlet nodded, accepting his apologies, but it wasn't enough. He felt the need to say more, to explain himself, or perhaps just get it all out in the open. "This all started Friday night, after we got home from the party, and I let myself get carried away in the moment. I made a mistake and now- "

"Why?"

"What?" The question was so unexpected, he rounded on her without thinking.

Yet Scarlet merely looked back, nonplussed. Then, as if he hadn't spoken at all, she calmly pulled open one of her drawers and pulled out a Tupperware tub and a small packet of chocolate dip. "Do you mind? I had lunch but seem to have missed dessert, courtesy of your little show."

He nodded, but without waiting for his response, Scarlet had already stood up and was walking around the desk to sit on the edge directly in front of his chair. She crossed her legs. "So, why was it a mistake?"

"You have got to be joking," he stammered, all too aware of their closeness as the floral scent of her perfume fogged his senses.

"Am I laughing?" she asked, undoing the container's fastenings before carefully balancing the lid on her knee like a plate, then tipping a variable punnet of fat red strawberries out onto it. "If I were joking, Dick, you would be in stitches. Now, this girl-"

"Rebecca," he cut in, perhaps a little too forcefully, but he didn't care. He didn't want her referring to Rebecca in that way. Like she was insignificant.

Scarlet shot him a withering, almost pitying look as she ripped the lid off of her dip. "Okay, *Rebecca*. You've known her a while?"

Richard nodded. "Yeah, she lives in our building.

She's our babysitter."

She exaggerated rolling her eyes, then plucked up one strawberry and plunged it in the dip. "I never would have guessed, still I suppose a cliché is a cliché for a reason. Okay, so you've known her a while. And she comes from a troubled home?"

"Y-you could say that," he trailed off for a second as he watched her bring the fruit up to her lips, her tongue sliding out to taste the chocolate. He forced himself to look away, his eyes quickly fixing on a point out the window. There wasn't anywhere else he could look. Her perch on the desk caused the already tiny skirt to rise higher while placing the swells of her breasts just at his eye level…

"Abuse?"

"Something like that. Her old man isn't much cop with men, but he can be a hard one with women."

"You sound like you don't like him." She bit down on the berry and moaned a low sound of pleasure that seemed to thrum down his spine, all the way to the base of his cock.

"We've had words." Actually, Richard had caught the little bastard threatening to beat his daughter black and blue after he'd had a few too many, and she'd come home late. So he had explained, from one father to another, that that wasn't any way to treat his daughter.

The guy had gotten the message, at least for a while. However, the sounds from their flat had been growing more and more volatile recently. No doubt he would have to reiterate that little lesson before long.

She popped the rest of the strawberry into her mouth, her tongue skimming out to lick up the single roll of sweetness that was creeping down her chin. "And I suppose her mum just sits there and lets him bully her around?"

"No, her mother buggered off and left her alone with the short-arse, went to live with a boyfriend in Leeds or Bradford or somewhere up North. Rebecca hasn't seen or spoken to her in years."

She pondered that for a moment, before picking up another strawberry and nibbling it thoughtfully. "No other family?"

"None," he swallowed, his mouth and throat growing dry as the office seemed to grow hotter by the second.

"Then I don't see the problem," she declared, then slowly took the whole berry into her mouth. "She seems smart enough, enough not to think you'll leave your wife for her. She's just confused, as most girls her age are. I dare say you're the strongest male role model she's ever had and can't quite work out how she feels about you. Give her a few weeks to work it out, and she'll meet some boy her own age. But if you tell her it was all a mistake, you'll probably just do more harm than good for the poor girl."

"And what about Alice?"

"Do you love her?" She forewent the fruit entirely this time and dipped her finger into the dip.

"Of course I do, but-"

"Would you leave her for this girl or try to lead either of them on?" Scarlet put her chocolate-covered finger into her mouth and sucked it clean with a long slow draw that had Richard's fists clenching in his lap.

"Never," he rasped, his gaze focusing on those pouting pink lips, and for the briefest moment, he wondered what that lush mouth would look like wrapped around his dick.

She shrugged. "Then? What about her? Sex isn't a luxury, Dick. It's a necessity. The body needs it like it needs food and water. If you're not getting any at home, then you need to look for it elsewhere. If having a little on the side gets the urge out of your system, just enjoy the adventure while it lasts."

"Spoken like a woman who's never been married."

Scarlet smirked triumphantly and gestured at him with another plump strawberry. "And who never wants to. Humans aren't monogamous by nature, so why should I be?

Just because society demands it? I'm a girl with needs who doesn't like to be tied down, and matrimony is one big leash, Dick, especially when there are so many men out there I haven't tried yet."

She dunked half the berry into the dip. "Besides, what good would telling her do? Cheaters say being honest is the right thing to do, but all they really want is to make themselves feel better about fucking up. She'll be happier not knowing."

"It's still wrong."

"How so? Is it wrong to grab a bite on the way home even though your wife is cooking dinner? No. You're hungry, so you eat. Why should sex be any different?" Her eyes then sparkled with mischief as she nibbled along the chocolate. "If it bothers you so much, just grow a pair and tell her. Or try for a three-way?"

"Now I know you're joking."

"Why not? It would certainly solve all your problems," she teased, stretching out one long graceful leg, the toe of her high-heel shoe, white to match her dress, brushing along his thigh and down his leg. "And it's certainly not adultery if your wife's banging her, too."

"Except Alice would cut my balls off and wear them as earrings," he breathed, forcing himself to look into her eyes, refusing to look down, all too aware of the unobstructed view she was offering him. Sharon Stone couldn't have done it better herself.

Holding his gaze, she leant forward until they were almost nose to nose. "I don't know. From what I saw, she's definitely full of surprises. It's always the up-tight ones that you've got to watch."

"Drop it Scarlet," he warned, gritting his teeth, his dick hard and tight and impossible to ignore.

"Am I right, Dick? I am, aren't I? Yeah, I bet she turns into a little nympho the moment her hair comes down." She dropped the plate of strawberries on the desk and reached out to finger his tie.

"Scarlet… I'm warning you." His throat was tight around the words as his heart pounded in his ears. Shit, he needed to get out of here. She was too close, he couldn't think, couldn't breathe, her damn perfume was fogging his head.

Damnit, why did she have to smell so good…

"Mmm… you know you're cute when you're flustered." She closed the gap, sliding off the desk and onto his lap so the crotch of her dress pressed against his cock through his trousers. "Come on, Dick, don't be greedy. She'll love going down on your little babysitter while you fuck her like a bitch in hea-"

Her taunt died in a surprised gasp as he seized a fistful of her blonde hair.

Chapter Fifteen

"Shut up."

"Dick!" Scarlet hissed. "W-what're you doing?"

"I said, shut your fucking mouth." His voice was low and deathly calm, a cocktail of anger and lust pulsing through him like nitro-glycerine. Richard lurched to his feet, towering over her…

Except Scarlet wasn't a woman to be dominated.

She was a fighter.

She'd fought every day of her life. Against her brothers, against peers who thought her beneath them, against subordinates and superiors alike who thought of her as an entitled and a spoiled brat. It was why she had fought so hard to graduate top of her class at Cambridge. Why she had taken this entry-level role in her father's company and would work her way to the very top, rather than just let him marry her off.

She wouldn't be cowed or humbled or let any man take advantage of her.

The moment her feet touched the ground, she pivoted, twisting free of his grip, her arm sweeping out, nails hooked to claw his face. She attacked with all the swiftness and ferocity of a cornered cat.

However, Richard was faster, twisting out of her reach, grabbing her wrist and dragging it around behind her back, forcing her down across the desk. Before she could fully comprehend what just happened, he was leaning over her, caging her there, pinned against the desk, his body deliciously hard beneath his suit.

"Scream, and I'll gag you," he warned, fettering both her wrists in one hand while the other tugged at his tie, loosening the noose.

"You wouldn't dare." Scarlett shot him an angry look over her shoulder, even as the raw emotion in his voice made her knees weak. No man, or woman for that matter, had ever been this way with her. She'd never known getting dominated could be such a turn on.

Who'd of ever guessed he had it in him?

Richard stared her down, his gaze fixed on that pretty little mouth of hers, her luscious lips just the right size and shape for sucking cock. He was sorely tempted to gag her anyway on principle alone, but he had a better idea.

He was sick of all her bullshit, her teasing, her constant shots at Alice. He might have fucked up, possibly ruined his marriage, his life, and be about to fuck up his career a whole lot more, but that didn't give her the right to belittle his wife. This time, she'd gone too far.

It was time to teach the *Tight Ass Bitch* a lesson.

"Wouldn't I?" A dark grin pulled at the corner of his mouth as he pulled the tie over his head and looped it round Scarlet's wrists in a simple slip knot. "You've been a very bad girl, Scarlet. Do you know what I do with bad girls?" He drew back to stand over her, one hand braced against the small of her back, holding her and her wrists down, the other pushing up her skirt, bearing the lush curves of her naked derriere.

"What?" she gasped, shaking, heat and embarrassment crackling through her, making it impossible for her to stay still.

"This." His hand swept down, slapping her right cheek with a loud crack. "I give them a spanking."

Scarlet couldn't help giving a little gasp. It didn't hurt, not really, but the hot sting made her clit pulse within its hood and she twisted against her bonds, trying to give the little bud some much-needed attention. "*Dick*... I'm your boss-ah!"

He smacked her ass again, the left cheek this time, and *harder*.

"No, Scarlet," he growled, trying to ignore the way her lovely derriere, now marred by a pair of red handprints, was wriggling against the bulge of his cock. Damnit, had she noticed? This would all be for nought if she knew she was affecting him too. He reinforced the assertion with another slap that actually made her jump. "You're a bad girl. Say it."

"No." Scarlet shook her head, but when the blow came, the delicious slap of skin meeting skin and the explosion of heat was too much. She bit her lip to hold the moan at bay, but there was no stopping the slickness between her thighs. "Say it." *Slap!* "I-I…" *Slap!* "Say it!" *Slap!*

"I'm a bad girl!" she moaned, the words flowing from her as thick and sweet as honeyed cream. God, why did it have to feel so good?

Richard raised his hand, then held it there. "Again."

"Mmm… I'm a bad, bad girl!" Biting her lower lip, Scarlet chanced a glance back, her eyes pleading, but for what? Mercy, or perhaps another smack.

His hand dropped to brush over her buttocks. She instinctively flinched away from his touch but relaxed when his fingers began kneading her backside, massaging away the heat. "You admit you've been bad?"

"Yes… very… mmm… bad…" Scarlet purred, pushing back against his hand as he made larger and larger circles. She was so turned on, so wet. What was he doing to her? Why was he making her so horny?

"Teasing me. Trying to seduce me. Belittling my wife." His hand slid down between her legs, fingers reaching, feeling, sliding along her wetness, pushing through her grasping heat.

"*Yes!*" Scarlet gasped, her whole world shrinking down to the feeling of his finger filling her, stroking her delicate inner tissues, swirling and stirring her into wild delirium. Greedy for more, she wriggled and circled against his swirling digit, spreading her legs wider, opening for him.

"That's it, you bad girl, and who's the boss now?"

She swallowed, her body clenching around the digit, the tension building inside her. "You are."

"Again," he growled, curling his finger to brush over that patch of rough tissue under her clit while thrumming the bundle of nerves with the pad of his thumb.

Scarlet gasped, her eyes widening as a fog settled over her thoughts. Sensation rippled outward from wherever he touched, only threatening to crash over her, driving her to the brink. Just not over it. It was the sweetest torture, the cruellest ecstasy.

No one had ever done this to her before, made her feel so vulnerable. It was delicious. "You… You're the boss… *Richard!*"

He couldn't remember the last time she'd used his Christian name. And the way she said it, so pleading and desperate, had his lips twisting in a dark grin before he leant down over her to lick the shell of her ear. "Good girl." He withdrew his finger.

Panic flaring inside her, she twisted right and left, trying to grab his hand, but the tie held strong. "No! Don't stop…!" She yelped as he swatted her arse again, the sting dissolving into delicious throbbing pleasure.

"Are you talking back to me? Bad girl," He growled, his tone low and primal, all but tearing at his belted trousers to liberate his cock. Taking himself in hand, he rubbed the crown along her slick, greedy cleft, the tip sliding through her swollen folds to graze her little bundle of nerves, making her shudder and gasp.

"No… please… Sir… mmm… don't stop… feels so good… I…" Panting, her pussy hot and throbbing, begging, no *demanding* more, Scarlet pressed back, circling her hips, desperate to feel him slide inside her, filling her, pounding her.

It did no good. He had her pinned to her desk, caged by his body, hands bound, completely at his mercy, and it only made her burn hotter.

"What? What do you want, Scarlet?"

"Please…" she heard herself beg. Her throat tightened around the word as she turned to look back over her shoulder at *him*.

This couldn't be the man she knew.

Her subordinate, dependable Richard Martin. The quiet, mild-mannered guy who never gave her a second look. That guy was fun to tease and torment, but did nothing for her, despite his thick dark hair, chiselled bone structure and broad build.

This man, who was now almost nose to nose with her, was different. Everything about him excited her. The way he looked at her, handled her, and just completely dominated her.

God, this couldn't be happening. Who was this man? What was he doing to her? She didn't do things like this, never at work, and she was never submissive in sex. She needed control. Her lovers were quiet and submissive, little more than tools for her pleasure, dildos with a pulse. They couldn't make her beg.

Yet this man had. And fuck, why did it feel so good?

"Louder," Richard pressed, enjoying the moment, relishing the turnaround, the power. He loved hearing her like this. So desperate and needy. All her poise and professionalism stripped away to leave just the raging wanton.

She licked her lips, her eyes smouldering, dark with desire. Needing to move, to take some control, she curled her hips, desperate to stroke her clit against his crest and ease the throbbing ache pulsing there. "Please!"

"Please what?" he asked, the deep growl of his tone sending hot shivers through her core as, bending his knees, he lined himself up, the broad tapered head of his cock nestling between her folds. Just one push and he would be buried inside her.

Scarlet couldn't bear it.

"Fuck me… please, fuck me-oh!" Scarlet gasped, her eyes widening and mouth falling open in a long moan as his hips snapped forward, driving in deep. The delicious shock of his cock sliding home rushed over her, making her head spin.

Too deep. Oh God, he's huge. How the hell does Alice ever ride this beast?

"Yeah, is this what you want, Scarlet?" he rasped in a low and sultry voice that just screamed sex. His hands dropped to her hips, fingers squeezing hard enough for her to feel the bite, both dragging her back and tilting her at just the right angle to take him. Not so much holding her as using her body to fuck her back onto his cock.

"Oh yes… oh yes… yes Sir!" she panted, her insides clenching, squeezing all around him, pleasure rippling out to her fingers and toes as she felt herself open to him, inch by sinfully thick, hard inch of him. Fuck, she'd never dreamed someone could fill her so completely. "Oh fuck… oh my God… yes… make me take it. I've been such a horrible boss, I need to be punished… mmm… punish that pussy with your big fucking dick!"

Richard was more than happy to oblige. "Don't worry, you're going to get everything you deserve."

Fuck, what the hell was wrong with him? He didn't dominate his lovers, didn't degrade or overpower them. This wasn't him. He'd never been like this with Alice, hadn't been like it with Rebecca… but he liked it.

"Just look at you, you bad girl. Getting fucked across your desk with your hands tied behind your back. Your snug little cunt milking my cock. You're just bloody loving this, aren't you?"

It was time to teach his boss's daughter a lesson.

She had been asking for this, well now it was time she learned to be careful what she wished for.

"Yes! Yes, I love it!" Scarlet moaned, writhing in his arms as his hips curled against her derriere. There was a momentary feeling of emptiness as he pulled back before his hands snapped her back to meet his hard thrust, making her feel every hard inch of his godly cock driving her up onto her tiptoes.

The feeling was so intense. She felt so stretched. So full.

It made her whole core pulse and tingle, and clench around him, but it was too late. He was already sliding out, almost all the way, then driving into her again, and again, until he was pounding into her greedy sex. "I'm a bad little whore… bad fucking whore… pound that pussy… it's yours- oh- oh God, yes, yes!

The orgasm came out of nowhere, rushing over her, leaving her a limp, shaking mess. He fucked her through it, drawing out her pleasure and driving her down into the desk so that her heavy breasts and stiff aching peaks dragged across the wood through her silky blouse. His body bore down on her, pinning her there so all she could do was struggle against the silk binding her wrists in a desperate need to grab something. the desk, him, anything that might give her a little leverage.

She shouldn't have liked it, but she did.

She never would have thought she could enjoy sex restrained, but this feeling of being under his control, powerless, at his mercy.

It was dark, primitive and so wild.

He knew just how to treat her.

He was splitting her open. Using her like a bitch in heat, and it was such a turn on.

She couldn't bear it. She needed to grab something, anything…

"Yeah, that's it, cum for me, you bad girl, cum all over my cock… mmm… spread that ass for me, show me your pretty little hole," Richard growled, drinking in the sight of Scarlet's bound hands grabbing her smooth alabaster cheeks, those perfectly manicured nails biting into the soft skin, spreading them wide to show him the tight rosebud nestled within.

The vision sent a hot shiver of lust down his spine, and he couldn't resist brushing it with his thumb, circling the sphincter, pushing in ever so slightly.

Scarlet could only gasp at the feeling against her pucker, the sensation causing her sex to clench around him. "Yes Sir… please, punish me, I need it… I… I…"

"As you wish."

He growled and Scarlet could have screamed as he pulled out.

Then his arms were around her and she came up and away from the desk. Then, as if she were as light as a feather, he hoisted her to her feet and walked her around the desk to the window.

"Put your hands on the glass," Richard instructed, the tie coming undone with a quick tug.

"What?" she asked, looking out the window, down across the canal, and the bustling hive of activity that was Gloucester Docks, where the whole of the city seemed to be wandering amongst bright colourful stalls.

He couldn't be serious. All it would take was just one person looking up and-

"Do it," he urged, slapping her ass again, the crack as sharp as a bullwhip and the sting enough to overwhelm caution.

She did as he commanded, bending forward slightly and pressing both hands against the window, the glass misting with her breath. "Good, now stay right where you are."

"What!" she snapped, her heart pounding in her breast. "Are you mad? The market's down there… someone might see, *Sir*."

"And I bet that gets you wet," he retorted, crouching down and nudging her thighs further apart so the musky scent of her sex fogged his thoughts. "Mmm… your cunt's all pink and slick and begging me to keep fucking her."

"No, Dick, please, that's… not fair. I don't- oh!"

He pushed a finger along her swollen folds, through her slick cream and into her lush depths, all the way to the knuckle. "Your dripping, you bad girl. Say it."

"No, please…" she panted, biting her lip to keep from moaning at the tingling shooting through her core. However, there was no resisting the choked sob as the digit twisted and curled, feeling and rubbing all of her most sensitive places at once. Nor could Scarlet stop herself from pushing back against him, her sex clenching. "Mmm… No! Wait, not here, there are so many people down there, what if someone looks up, they could see- "

"So what?" Removing his finger, he reached out and took her last few strawberries from the desk, crushing them to a juicy pulp in his hand. "Let them look, go on, let them see you for the little slut you are. Let the *whole damn city* see you for who you really are," he said, before putting his hand on her inner thigh.

"Stop… You can't… I'll scream…" Scarlet gasped, shaking as her clit pulsed at the feeling of his hand and the illicitness of the strawberry juice sliding over her skin, spreading it up her leg and over her butt. Then, it wasn't just his hands.

"Go ahead, scream all you want, that'll just make everyone look, won't it?" Richard said, following the sticky trail with his tongue, greedily licking up both the sweetness of the fruit and the salty flavour of her desire. "Maybe even someone in the office will hear and come running. Wouldn't that be something? Is that what you want, Scarlet? To prove all those dirty gossips, right?"

"No," Scarlet choked out, shaking, the throbbing of her core growing ever stronger as the slick glide of his tongue swept up her inner thigh.

"Then shut the fuck up before I gag that pretty mouth of yours," Richard barked, before pivoting and covering her swollen clit with the lush heat of his mouth.

Scarlet couldn't stand it.

His words were so dirty and crude, raw with lust. No one had ever spoken to like that.

It was such a fucking turn on.

She couldn't bear it. Just keeping her hands on the glass was torture in itself. She wanted to grab him, fist his hair, sit on his face, squeeze her tits, rub her clit, something, anything to-

"Oh… Oh my God… oh fuck-yes!" She gasped and moaned, squeezing her eyes shut against the feeling of sensory overload as he sucked hard and greedily on her little bud before lashing it with his tongue.

"You want to get caught, don't you? Yeah, I know you do. Your pussy's so juicy. Just the thought of it has your greedy little cunt all soaked. Don't pretend you don't like it. You're dripping for it…"

"No… *Dick!*… that's not- don't say things like that! Mmm… I can't help it… you're making me… oh no, no, please, if you do that… I'll…"

She was shaking, the waves of sensation crashing over her so violently her legs were in danger of giving way from under her as her fingers clawed the window for something, anything, to hold on to.

However, Richard showed no mercy.

"You'll what? Go on Scarlet, tell me," he pressed, swirling his tongue around the bundle of nerves, his hands fastening to her quivering hips, dragging them closer…

"I'll- oh fuck… oh my God… I'll… I'll…" She was mindless with the raw need to cum. And so close, when his tongue suddenly abandoned her clit to drag along her folds, the world shattered around her. "Oh God, yes, yes, fuck yes, I'm cumming, I'm cumming, I'm cumming, fuck, fuck…"

Richard tongued her through the climax, not stopping even as her hips trembled in his arms. For what he had in mind, he wanted her good and relaxed. "Yeah, that's it, go on Scarlet, cum for me, let the whole damn city see you cum!"

She bowed her head to press her forehead against the window as the waves crashed over her, the glass deliciously cold against her flushed skin. "No… please… why are you doing this to me, please, I can't take it- oh fuck, yes, yes!"

"Mmm… beg all you want, Scarlet, this is the mouth that doesn't lie." Deaf to her pleas, he buried his face in her cleft, devouring her with long deep licks, his tongue swirling while the rough of his jaw scrapped oh so deliciously along her inner thighs. "You love it. Say it."

Scarlet shook her head, but the words stuck in her throat. She was shaking, powerless against the urge to grind back onto his tongue as her clit pulsed and throbbed, pleading for just that little bit of attention to send her soaring to the starry heavens. "No! Please don't make me- oh fuck, oh fuck, okay, okay, yes, I love it, I love it! Use me, abuse me… please, please, please, I'm your naughty little fuck toy… oh God… that's your pussy, that's your pussy…"

His cock jumped at her wanton tone, but Richard pushed on regardless.

Not yet. She wasn't ready yet. Just a little more…

"So now you don't want me to stop?" he asked with a mock teasing tone, pulling back just enough to drag the flat of his tongue along her folds, from clit to base, then back again in longer and longer glides.

A shudder wracked Scarlet at the suggestion. Or perhaps it was another orgasm. "No, no, don't stop, don't stop, please, put your dick back in me, fuck me against the glass for the whole world to see, make me cum all over your big hard cock."

"No," he rasped, his tone low and primal as he worked his tongue higher, hands spreading her cheeks. "I'm not done with you yet."

"What-oh!" Scarlet gasped as warmth washed over her pucker, sending shivers racing up her spine and throwing fresh fuel on the already raging lusts. Then his tongue slid up to circle her virgin hole, teasing it with gently prods and flicks.

No one had ever done anything like this to her before. It felt strange, dirty and wrong, but so exciting. "Wait! No... no, not there, please- oh fuck!"

She panted, her back curling at the feeling of his tongue pushing through her tight ring of muscle. Then her mind went blank, consumed by the sensation of wet heat sliding in and out.

"Wow Scarlet, I've barely started rimming you and you're already drenching the floor. Who would have ever guessed you were such an anal whore, and in front of the whole city, you bad girl." He swatted her arse just hard enough for the pain to heighten the pleasure. "Just look at you, you're loving this, aren't you?"

"Yes! Yes, I'm a bad girl, your bad little slut, punish my little hole, I deserve to be punished... I deserve it... I... I-"

"Have the tastiest ass," Richard growled, leaning over her, his body caging her against the glass as powerful fingers fisted in her hair and dragged her head round. Then he took her mouth in a bruising kiss, his sinful tongue encircling hers, brushing and stroking and fogging her thoughts with his strong, heady flavour.

No, not his flavour, hers. He was forcing her to taste herself.

The revelation made her core clench at the very moment he slid inside her.

"Mmm... I could fuck your cunt all day, you bad girl," Richard groaned, his dick painfully hard and the temptation to give himself over to the feeling of her lush walls milking him was almost irresistible. Almost. Instead, he rolled his hips, stirring her grasping sheath before pulling out, his shaft slick and glistening with her cream.

Scarlet shuddered at the loss and made a pouting sound that dissolved into a low moan as he leant down to nibble the shell of her ear, hands dropping to her naked ass, spreading her cheeks for his cock to glide up, the broad crest parting her folds.

She was shaking, so on edge, her whole body was almost humming with carnal need. One little push would be all it took to push her over the edge-

"But now…" he whispered in her ear, pausing only to bite down and tug on her lobe. "I want to find out how tight your ass really is."

She stilled at the dark promise in his voice, eyes widening as the crown touched her pucker.

"Wait, you don't mean? Oh no…" she gasped, shaking her head.

"Oh yes, your ass is mine," he growled, rearing back to drink in the vision of her stretched out before him. Flushed and panting, her blonde hair had become a passionate mess and that once immaculate white business dress was rumpled the way that only a good, hard fucking could do, its skirt scrunched up around her hips to show off the full curves of her luscious, strawberry smeared butt.

It was a complete contrast from the woman he knew and filled him with a savage, primitive pride. He slid forward, pressing his slick tip against the ring of muscle. Soft and pliant from the multiple orgasms, her body opened before him.

"Oh fuck! Oh, fuck!" Scarlet gasped, her eyes going wide at the sudden burning sensation, the feeling of something hard, thick, and slick splitting her open. Instinctively, she tried to clench down, to force him back, but that only seemed to speed his invasion on, so the broad crest slid through.

"That's it Scarlet, let me in… mmm you really are a tight arsed bitch all right, but don't worry, not for much longer," Richard promised, curling his hips in small circles, trying to resist the feeling of her body wrapping around his crown, sucking him in. He needed to loosen her up first, or else this would hurt.

Scarlet could only groan. Somewhere, deep down and far away, a little voice was screaming for her to give herself over to him, to let it come, but she couldn't. She just… couldn't. He was too big. Too thick.

She'd never felt this full, so stretched. So…

She threw a look back over her shoulder at him, her blue eyes large and pleading. "S-sir, I…"

Their eyes met and she couldn't keep her gasp at bay at the wild look burning in his eyes, the warring emotions battling just beneath the surface. It was the most savage look she'd ever seen, the reflection of the beast that lurked in the heart of every man as he was visibly torn between restraint, and the instinctive desire to fuck, to rut and claim her as his bitch.

His grip on her tightened, the fingers biting into her hips, holding her still as he took a step forward, pressing her to the glass while his dick kept working back and forth, slick with their mixed juices, sending heat rushing through her.

"No, Scarlet, look straight ahead."

She obeyed, too far gone now to turn back.

Overhead, the sky had turned a deep lilac, slashed with shades of pink and orange that danced across the waters of the canal as the sun slipped away behind the horizon. Below, the fair was still in full swing and growing busier as people finished their work and came to browse amongst the stalls. Anyone could look up and see them.

Someone already was.

Her reflection stared back at her from the window, but with the face of a stranger, with flushed skin and a hooded gaze, framed by a dishevelled mess of spun gold.

Bent at the waist, she looked shameless, like a whore just begging to be fucked.

The sight was so erotic, she couldn't bear it and tried squeezing her eyes shut against the image, but it lingered, burned into her mind.

"No, watch Scarlet, I want you to see," Richard bit out, his voice low and so dark with lust that she couldn't resist. Her eyes locked to his in the glass, and his hips snapped forward, driving his cock into her heat.

"Oh!" she gasped, fighting the urge to close her eyes against the sudden rush of hot sensations. "Oh fuck… oh fuck… You're… you're in my ass… there's a dick in my… oh God, this feels so…." She could feel herself opening to take him all the way, her forbidden little hole stretching to fit him, and only him.

Richard pulled back slowly, letting half of his length slide out, then drove back in, drawing another ragged sound from Scarlet. It was a deliciously snug fit, with her inner walls wrapping around him like a fist in a warm velvet glove, squeezing him tight, trying to milk the cum right out of him with every stroke.

"Yeah… you like it, don't you?" His voice was thick and gruff, more beast than man. With each push and slide, his hands dragged her into the saddle of his hips, inch by hard throbbing inch until he was balls deep.

"Yes!" she gasped, surrendering to the sinfully wicked sensations rippling out from her ass, making her clit throb and nipples ache. "Oh my fucking God… this feeling, it's so… so intense, I- I love it…. don't stop, don't stop…"

"Don't worry, you bad girl, I won't stop…" he promised, his eyes drifting down to watch his dick sliding in and out of her forbidden little hole. "Yeah, that's it, mmm… goddamn, you're taking it up the ass like a proper little whore now."

"Oh God, yes… yes Sir, I'm your whore, please, fuck me, harder, make me feel every inch of that big cock pounding my tight little virgin ass." Not caring if they were discovered, she pushed against the window to meet each thrust, grinding herself back onto his cock.

"And whose ass is this, my little whore?" The words came unbidden.

"It's yours, all yours. I'm your good little anal whore. Split me open on your dick, make me take it. I love your cock in all my holes!"

"All of them? Even this tight little virgin ass?" he grunted, the slap of flesh meeting flesh rising around them, his movements growing more urgent with the feeling of his release building.

She bowed her head, pressing her brow to the window, the glass deliciously cool against her flushed skin. "Yes! All of them! I love taking it up the ass for you. I'm your naughty little office whore, that's just another hole for you, only you- oh fuck, oh fuck, Sir, please!"

"Please what?"

He was close, so fucking close. Not sure how much longer he could last, he pushed one hand down beneath the folds of her skirt, into the bounty of lush, wet heat. He was close, but so was she. He could feel it and rubbed her clit while fucking her with a single-minded need to make her cum just once more.

"Punish me. Sir, please punish me, I deserve it! Punish me, punish all of my holes every day." Scarlet couldn't breathe, couldn't think, she could only feel. Feel the heat and fullness moving through her ass, the waves crashing over her as rough fingers strummed her throbbing clit and turned her legs to jelly. "My ass is yours, all yours whenever you want… fuck, I'm gonna cum, oh fuck, oh fuck, I'm gonna cum on your cock, oh my fuckin… yes, yes, make me cum on your fucking cock! Fuck that ass, it's yours, all fucking yours, oh fuck, oh fuck, I'm cumming, I'm fucking cumming! I'm-oh!"

Her orgasm exploded through her, unlike any release that had come before, sending her soaring. Then she started to shake as the aftershocks claimed her, and Richard couldn't resist the feeling of her ripple around his thick, swollen cock.

"Yeah, that's it you naughty whore, cum for me, cum for me in front of the whole goddamn city- ah shit, I'm cumming too!"

He moaned, burying his cock in her one last time as he came, hard. Hard enough for small black spots to dance before his eyes.

Amidst the fog of her climax, Scarlet felt his release like a flood of heat deep inside her. It was the first time a man had ever come inside her, and she liked it.

He'd stained her, branded her with a mark that could never be erased.

It made her feel dirty, deliciously dirty.

She wanted more.

Chapter Sixteen

Richard's phone was dead when Alice tried to call him, probably because he'd been called into a last-minute meeting. Probably that bitch, Scarlet, trying to get her revenge. If so, there was no telling how long it would go on for, so she just fired off a quick text, explaining what had happened, in the briefest possible terms.

There was no need to go into details, no point worrying him.

Once the tick appeared alongside the message on the screen, showing the text had been delivered, she put it down on the side. With no further use for the device, she picked up her freshly brewed mug of tea and headed to the bathroom.

She walked in without knocking.

Inside, the air was hot and humid. The windows were fogged and condensation rolled down the tiled walls in rivulets as Rebecca sat in a bath of hot water, hugging her knees to her chest. She didn't look up as Alice sat down on the side of the tub, but she had got a little colour back.

Alice offered her the mug. "Here you go, honey. Have a sip of this,".

Rebecca, however, just kept her head down and stared blankly into nothingness. Or perhaps she was just too fascinated by the last few soap suds floating across the water's surface to notice.

Alice carried on regardless.

"Not thirsty?" She set the cup down on the floor, then softly started stroking the girl's thick waves of dark chocolate hair. "That's okay. Take as long as you need. You're safe, I promise…"

She had such beautiful hair, so thick and silky smooth. She should stop wearing it in that silly side braid. It suited her down, in a beautiful unbound wash that would probably go all the way down to her butt. And what a butt it wa-

No, stop it! Alice chastised herself. There was a time and a place for such thoughts, and this sure as hell wasn't the time. Though she could have thought of worse places than a hot bath and with that in mind, she decided there were better ways to comfort the lass, as well as keep her hands busy.

Rebecca instinctively stiffened as the older woman pulled her into a hug, but Alice did not pull back. Instead, she tried to draw her against her even tighter, rocking softly from side to side, desperate to give the girl all the feelings of closeness and security she knew she needed.

She softened slightly after a moment, then completely as inside, the walls began to crumble.

When she finally spoke, her voice was a whisper. "Really?"

Alice's heart soared, yet she kept her voice even and neutral to not spook the girl. "Really what, honey?"

"Safe?" Her voice was a little stronger with that one syllable, the hope behind it almost tangible, but there was a tremble there too, as if she hung on a knife's edge, about to fall through the ice at any moment. "You said I'm safe… did you mean it? Really?"

The desperate hope in that one question raked Alice and she could feel the tears burning at the corners of her eyes. God, what had that monster done to her? "Yes, of course I did, honey," she promised, "I promise. You'll always be safe with us."

The words sounded hollow to her own ears and woefully inadequate, but Rebecca must have heard the sincerity in them because, slowly, she tilted her head up. Her big doe eyes glistening as they met the older woman's. "Thank you."

It was all she could muster before the last of her walls came down. Her tears flowed freely as she threw her arms around the older woman and buried her head into the crook of Alice's neck, shaking with the sobs. Alice hugged her through it, doing her best to comfort her even as her face grew wet with her own silent sobs for the girl's plight.

"It's okay, I promise, it's all going to be alright," she soothed, lying as much as hoping, not really knowing what else to say. How could anything ever be alright again? Domestic abuse was an ugly thing, destroying even more lives than it took, and the effects could haunt the victims for years after. How was she ever going to live a 'normal' life?

Alice didn't have any answers, so she did her best to just comfort the girl as all her grief and fear came pouring out of her. Then, as quickly as it had hit, the storm passed.

"I'm sorry, oh god, acting like that, I'm so embarrassed…" Rebecca said when the tears ceased, her reddening eyes downcast and uncertain as she pulled away and slid back into the bathwater. Full as it was, the soapy water came up to the tops of her breasts.

"Honey, it's okay," Alice said gently, retrieving the mug from the floor and handing it to her. "Do you want to talk about it?"

Rebecca didn't respond. The question hung in the air between them. Alice waited patently. She didn't want to push Rebecca too far, but she also wanted to give her the chance to speak before the memories took root inside her, like a rot.

Slowly, Rebecca took a long swig of the tea, stealing herself. It would have been half cold, but it was better than nothing.

"*He* thought I'd stolen something." Rebecca spoke softly, but the venom with which she spat the word emphasised it more than if she had screamed it out. "Turns out he'd known all along I was saving up to move out. So, when he couldn't find something on his desk, he realised I'd had someone round…" Alice felt a lump forming in her throat, remembering how she had half encouraged Richard to go help the girl. "I told him I didn't know anything about it, but he didn't believe me, just started shouting things. He'd already had a lot to drink by the time I got home. Normally he stops after he's screamed himself out a bit, but this time he just kept getting worse, then when he started throwing things, I just panicked and ran."

"Oh, honey…" There were so many other things Alice wanted to say, to tell her, to reassure her things could get better, but when Rebecca began sobbing again, they all caught in her throat. Instead, she just pulled her back into another close hug.

Rebecca carried on regardless, the words pouring out of her in the rush of fresh emotion. "He never used to be like this. When I was little, he was always so kind and would play with me and take me out for drives or trips to the park, and then the pool or the cinema. But after mum left… oh god, what am I going to do now? I can't go back home, but all my stuff is up there, and I haven't got nearly enough saved to find a place of my own yet… so I… but how can I…"

Alice didn't have an answer. She didn't have any answers. How could she? The girl's world had just been turned upside down and inside out, then given her a prompt kick in the teeth for her trouble. It fucking sucked, but answers for things so large took time to be worked out. So, once again, she just held her, hugged her close, and let her get everything out. All the while enjoying the feeling of the girl's warm body pressed so close against her own through the robe.

She was sure Richard had thought she was joking, or just playing a game when she'd remarked on how beautiful the girl was. He wasn't completely wrong, but she wouldn't deny either that she had more than once admired the girl's long legs

in those tight little jeans she always wore and wondered what
it would feel like to have them wrapped around her head as
she feasted on her sweet little pussy.

Such fantasies were her naughty little secret, and she'd
never been ashamed of them, but she wasn't about to let them
ruin her marriage either. It wasn't that she was in the closet, or
that she'd ever officially claimed to be bisexual, but then, she'd
never said she was straight, ether. Straight, Bi, Gay, they were
all labels, and Alice hated labels. Why should she define
herself, or for that matter, what made other people think they
could brand her like a cow on the block?

She was just her. Alice Martin. Mother, wife and
teacher, that was all and in that order. Everything else was no
one else's business.

Then again, she'd never told him that when they'd first
hooked up, she'd been involved in an unofficial, on again off
again fling with her roommate Samantha. Nor that it had
continued after they'd started going steady, and that it had
only stopped when they'd got married. Even then, while they
had both moved on and settled down into actual relationships,
occasionally, whenever she or Sam had felt the itch, they
would arrange a girl's night to relive old times.

Richard had never asked much about the nights, so
she'd never lied to him about it.

It was foolish and reckless, she knew, and after, on the
drive home, she always promised herself it would be the last.
She loved her husband, but there was just something about sex
with another woman that she craved as well. She just couldn't
help it.

It was so thrilling, feeling the graceful softness of
another woman's body on hers, the way they shuddered and
writhed in the throes of ecstasy beneath her, and their sweet
moans as they soared over the edge…

Not to mention their instinctive skill for knowing just
how and when to touch. The old man's adage was very apt
and true. Only a woman knew what women wanted…

"You can stay with us," she said without thinking. An idea spurred as much by the heat rising off the bath and the lush floral scent of the girl's hair fogging her thoughts, as the devious ideas haunting her fantasies. "Stay as long as you need."

It was a stupid idea, and Alice could have kicked herself for saying it. The flat was too small, there wasn't room for them all. Where would she stay? There were only two bedrooms, and only one bed... where would she sleep, in bed with her and Richard- *no no... don't go there, don't go there.*

But it was too late. Her mind was already swimming with thoughts and ideas...

Naughty, dirty thoughts and ideas that sent a tingle of delicious shivers straight down to her core, making her pussy slick and clit throb once more.

"What?" Rebecca gasped, stilling for a moment, her eyes going wide as she looked up slowly from Alice's shoulder. For the briefest moment, she looked terrified, yet no sooner had their gazes met than she looked down, her lower lip trembling. "Oh, um... thank you, Miss Martin... for everything, you've been so kind, and I... but I can't stay here, I don't deserve it... I... I..."

Her words came out in a rush, and the self-loathing in them set a fire in Alice's soul.

Raising a hand to Rebecca's chin, she tilted the girl's head so she couldn't look away. Her big doe eyes were round and questioning, desperate for comfort and reassurance. "Oh no, no, no... don't say that. You've done nothing wrong." Breathless, Alice could feel her heart racing as she slowly dipped her head down. "None of this is your fault."

Rebecca shook her head, to overcome by the moment to notice. "No, it's not him. I've done something... something horrible. I'm a terrible person and I don't deserve-"

Alice's mouth silenced any further objections.

Chapter Seventeen

For the longest moment, Richard just watched Scarlet, the beast in him wanting to savour its victory, burning the sight of her stretched out beneath him into his memory.

Then the moment passed, and it plunged him face first into cold reality.

Oh fuck…

Scarlet looked back at him over her shoulder, her full lips half curling with that damn mocking smirk. "Mmm… was I a good little whore for you, Dick?"

"Knock it off, this… this was a mistake." He stepped back and quickly shoved himself into his trousers.

She cooed and wiggled her ass, her rosebud agape and weeping pearl tears. "*Aww…* what's the matter *Dick*, the bitch going to throw a fit if you're late?" Her eyes flashed, daring him to bite.

"Fuck you," he snapped, resisting the sudden urge to put her over his knee, his nose wrinkling as his fingers fumbled with his belt buckle.

She straightened up and turned to face him, but made no effort to straighten the skirt still hitched about her hips. "We already played that game, remember?"

She lightly teased the petals of her sex with a finger before bringing the shiny digit to her lips.

"Yeah, well, maybe I'd rather forget." He wheeled around and walked around the desk, refusing to watch, and doing his best to ignore the still obvious stiffness straining against his trouser leg.

No, he wouldn't be tempted again.

However, Scarlet would not be dismissed so easily. Coming up behind him from the desk's other side, she slid her hands around his waist to finger his shirt buttons while rising up on her tiptoes to nip his ear. "Aww… don't be like that, lover. Come on, why don't you let me take care of that for you? You don't really want to go back to Alice smelling like sex, do you? There's a private washroom and shower in Daddy's office. I could wash your back for you and-"

"Forget it Scarlet!" Richard snapped. Angry and tired of her games, he brushed her hands away and rounded on her, so they were almost nose to nose. "This never happened, got it."

Scarlet held her ground, however, her playfulness gone, melted away to reveal an expression as cool and hard as ice. All except her eyes. They burned hot and fierce. "Don't kid yourself, Dick, that was the fuck of the century, and you know it. How long has it been since Alice fucked you like that? You think your little shop girl can?" Her smile spread wide, as cruel and sharp as a knife. "You're going to want it again." She was right. About everything.

He wanted her. How could he not? He was only a man of flesh and blood, while she was the boss's daughter.

A young woman with a future as bright as her past was murky, a beautiful girl who played men the way a croupier dealt cards.

She was intelligent, sexy, and a damn great fuck.

She was Scarlet Holmes, his rock bottom, and he'd hit it hard, in more ways than one.

Now it was time to pick himself back up again.

So he turned his back on her and walked to the office door. Pulling it open, he didn't bother to look back. "Goodnight Scarlet."

At his back, still where she had stood, he could practically hear Scarlet seething when she hissed at his back. "I always get what I want, *Dick*."

It was the first time he had ever heard her composure crack.

He knew he should keep walking, to just let it slide, but sometimes he just couldn't help himself. "Then why don't you go up to your dad's office and fuck him instead?"

"Suck my clit you son of a- "

He pulled the door shut on her rebuff, and something smacked against the door. Something heavy.

Well, there goes my lateral move…

Chapter Eighteen

It was an accident. She hadn't meant to kiss her, but when the moment came, Alice just couldn't help herself. She crushed her mouth to Rebecca's soft pink lips, all the pent-up lust and desire that had been building up inside her, crashing over the banks and sweeping her away.

Perhaps shocked by the act, Rebecca didn't respond or pull away. Just made an adorable whimper in the back of her throat as Alice's lips slid over hers. Acutely aware of the gorgeous body against hers, so firm and tight but also soft in all the right places, Alice pressed on. Sliding her arms around her waist, she crushed her to her, making Rebecca gasp before thrusting her tongue into her mouth to feast on the sweetness within.

Deep down, a small voice warned that she should slow down. That she might scare the girl off if she was too forward too fast, but she couldn't help it. She wanted this little minx, wanted her in every way she could have her, and the fire raging down in her centre only drove her on. She kissed her hungrily, needing nothing else in that moment so much as to possess her, consume her, devour her completely. Her tongue curling round and round in the soft little brushes and slides that always made Alice's knees weak, until all the tension flowed from her young conquest in a low purring moan.

Then she was kissing her back, sucking on her tongue with a greedy hunger, those soft lips working up and down like she was sucking a cock. The very idea of it made Alice's skin tingle and pussy throb, and she couldn't help her own little moan when Rebecca grabbed her. One hand fisting her hair while the other clawed at her ass through the silk, almost dragging her into the tub. It was a deliciously aggressive act that she would never have guessed would explode from her doe-eyed babysitter, and one that pushed all her hot buttons. She knew what she wanted, and with girls she always enjoyed being the top, but it wasn't fun unless they played too…

Not to be outdone, however, she reciprocated, pulling the girl up and out of the bath. Water ran off her in a shower of rivulets and miniature waterfalls, splashing across the floor, but Alice hardly noticed or cared. She turned and backed her up against the bathroom wall, pushing one thigh between those long legs, pinning her there.

Rebecca gasped at the unexpected contact, her back curling in sweet surprise. Greedily swallowing the sounds, Alice slowly rocked and ground her thigh against the girl's bare pussy, delighting in the feeling of her slick heat. When she couldn't take it anymore, Rebecca broke away, a long sultry moan pouring from the circle of her lips as the friction drove her wild.

"Mmm… I love the way you taste… so sweet and naughty… so sexy…" Alice purred, leaning up to tease Rebecca's ear with her tongue as Rebecca's hips continued circling against her thigh. Her pussy was drenched. "Mmmm… I can't wait to eat your pretty little pussy."

"Oh god… Mrs… Mrs Martin… wait… We shouldn't…" With her breathing ragged, the girl couldn't get the words out but rolled her head back, offering more skin.

"No, I want you." Dipping her head, Alice attacked the graceful slope of her throat with hot, fiery nips before soothing the tender flesh with her tongue. "I want you to cum for me. Right here. Right now."

"But what about… Mr Martin…" Rebecca got out, all the while trying to drag her ravisher closer. Her nails bit into her skin through her robe as she answered each grind with one of her own in a desperate plea for more. Her question fell off into another wanton moan when Alice sucked her pulse spot.

She wanted it. Alice knew it. She could see it written in her eyes, dark with lust. Had felt the truth of it in the heat and hunger of her kiss. Yes, she wanted this, but there was something else, something holding her back. Fear perhaps. Fear of the consequences, of what it could mean.

It didn't matter. By the time she was done, she'd have forgotten them all.

"I doubt he'd mind," she said, pressing her thigh a little harder against the girl's pussy and the little bundle of nerves hidden within. "Coming home to find his wife eating out their babysitter..." Her own heart was racing with the idea. Just picturing Richard walking in and finding them like this got her so hot, one of her hands came up to cup Rebecca's breast. It felt amazing. So soft but also full and firm and as incredible as she'd imagined, it filled her hand completely. The peaked nipple poked into her palm, begging for attention. "Do you think he'd join us right away, or sit back and watch?"

"Mrs… Martin… Please… I-I…." Alice's clit throbbed with each hitch in Rebecca's voice whenever she rolled her palm over the stiff peak. The sound was so delicious, she wanted nothing more than to fuck a few more out of her.

Reluctantly, Alice abandoned her prize to raise the hand up to Rebecca's check. Cupping her jaw, she gently angled her face so she was looking her in the eye, wanting her to see the truth in her words. "He doesn't know I like girls, too. Won't he be *surprised*. He might want to watch, but I think he'd rather join us. We talked about this just the other morning, after he helped you after you babysat for us."

"You did? But I thought you would be ma-" The girl's eyes widened and there was a tremor in her voice that had nothing to do with the leg pressing against her cleft. A hint of something Alice couldn't bear right now. So she silenced her with a kiss, sealing her mouth over Rebecca's and sliding her tongue in to chase the demons away with slow, luxurious licks.

"It got him so hard, thinking about your perfect tits and this cute little butt…" she growled huskily, sliding her other hand downward. Fingers outstretched and feeling their way along the smooth flesh, teasing along the swells of her buttocks to the lush heat beneath. "Oh, he became a beast, telling me all the things he would do to you… then I suggested sharing you…"

"Please… Mrs Martin… I… we- Oh!" Rebecca buried her face in the crook of the woman's neck, low moans flowing from her thick and sweet as honey. Almost of their own volition, her knees slid apart as the digits brushed along her slick folds.

"That's it, open up for me honey, yes, let me in, good girl… mmm… you're so wet." Sliding one finger through folds into the slick heat, she grinned inwardly at the feeling of Rebecca's walls clenched around her digit, begging for more. "He fucked me so hard and deep, telling me how good this sweet little pussy tasted… how much he loved the feel of it wrapped around his cock, milking out every drop of his cum…" The memory of his cock pummelling her poor pussy with a mad beastly intensity that left her aching and unable to walk straight for most of the day sent a hot shiver tingling through her.

"You… Oh god… You mean you don't… don't mind?" Rebecca's mouth pressed so close to Alice's ear she could feel her desperation shivering through her skin.

It gave her such a sense of conquest. Knowing she'd done this to her. Reduced her to this luscious little wanton. But it wasn't enough. She wanted to take her all the way. To take this little good girl to bed and draw out the sex kitten that lurked beneath the surface.

"Mmm… would you like that, honey? Is that what you want? To feel my husband go balls deep in this tight little pussy and give you the fucking of your life?" she asked, easing her finger out then back in, adding a second finger as she did.

"Oh!" the girl gasped, the feeling of crashing over her and carrying her away. "Yes… please… please… I… I… oh god, yes, please, I… I… want… it, I want it…"

"Mmmm… your so fucking wet." Alice didn't let up. Sliding her fingers in and out, she felt and teased every part of the slick, delicate tissues she could reach, trying to touch as much of Rebecca as possible. "Are you going to cum? You're going to get this pussy nice and creamy for my husband's cock. Yeah, that's it baby, say it…"

"Oh god, yes! Yes! Please Mrs Martin, I want it, I - oh fuck, oh fuck, fuck, fuck…" She was close. Growing more frantic, she arched up onto tiptoes and curled one long leg over Alice's. Granting her thrusting fingers deeper access as she circled her hips into each plunge.

Fuck, she was so sexy. Alice couldn't wait to have her spread out beneath her in her marital bed, watching her arch and scream and cum over and over as she did such wicked things to her. "Say you want it as I make you cum all over my fingers."

Curling her stroking fingers, she reached out to that spot of roughened flesh beneath her clit. One touch was enough to have Rebecca's back curling as she threw her head back with a shuddered moan of surrender. "Fuck, yes! Please, I want to fuck your husband again, Mrs Martin!"

"Good gir-" Alice froze, her sense of conquest suddenly forgotten as she realised what the girl had just said. "Wait, what?"

However, Rebecca didn't hear the question, or the dangerous lowness to her seducer's voice. Her every focus was on the fingers buried inside her, and the fact they had stopped. Breathing hard and ragged breaths, she shook her head, almost mad with her closeness, mindless with that desperate clawing need to cum. "No! No, please, don't stop, I want his cock

again, Mrs Martin, please, please, let me fuck your husband again… please, please, plea-"
"What!"

Chapter Nineteen

Her fury was cold and sharp, cutting through the spell of the moment like a knife.

"W-hat?" Rebecca blinked, confused, her voice shaky as she was rudely dragged back from the brink and thrown into icy reality by the sense of Alice's fingers leaving her.

Alice just glared at her, her eyes so cold they almost blazed. Yet, for all her palpable fury, when she spoke, her voice was even. "What do you mean 'fuck him again'?"

"You mean you didn't…" she began, shaking her head, as if not understanding the question. "But… but you said… he told you and you talked about-"

Alice rolled her eyes. "We role-played my overhearing him fuck you that night, and-" As she said it, the wheels in her head suddenly turned and a piece fell into place. Realisation dawned, sending a cold wash cascading down her back to leave her legs feeling shaky. Her heart raced, beating a thunderous tempo in her ears. "Oh god, that was you! Wasn't it? Both of you." Her voice flared, going from icy cool to a raging inferno. "He fucked you that night, didn't he?"

Rebecca was shaking, her eyes wet and glassy. "Yes, but Mrs Martin, please I didn't, it just… happened, I never meant… I'm so sorry…" she sobbed, her words a desperate plea. But a plea for what? For her to understand? To forgive? Maybe both, or perhaps something else…

Alice searched the girl's face. Again, that small part of her spoke up. She wanted to believe her. There was no lie in her eyes. That was true. Only fear and worry. They were almost like the eyes of one of her pupils, when she'd caught them doing something they knew was wrong, and awaited the inevitable punishment. But just like those brats, there was no regret. She didn't regret having sex with her husband. In fact, she had probably been planning to do *him* again.

How fucking dare she!

She let out a sigh, jealousy enveloping her like the coils of a monstrous python. "No. No you're not. Not yet."

Rebecca's eyes went wide. She opened her mouth to say something, her pretty little mouth with lips swollen from the kiss, but all that came out was a squeak of surprise as Alice grabbed her arm. In no mood to hear whatever she had to say, she just spun on her heel and dragged her out the door, across the hall, and through the door to the master bedroom. Kicking the door shut behind them, she threw the girl to the bed, where she landed with a bounce. Then she just lay there, unmoving in a dishevelled, beautiful heap upon the bed, with her dark hair spread out beneath her, her eyes downcast, and puffy lips quivering.

The sight stoked the embers still smouldering in her core, and Alice slowly licked her lips, thirsty for another taste of the girl. She just looked so divine, like a feast spread out for her to devour.

"Mrs Martin…" Rebecca whispered, her voice shaky as Alice mounted the bed, planting both hands on either side of her shoulders, caging her with her body. "What're you-"

"Shut up," Alice commanded, the order firm despite the softness of her voice as she leant down, brushing the tip of her nose over the girl's. "Open that pretty little mouth without permission again, and I might just gag you up. Understand?"

Rebecca nodded, her eyes so big and wide as she bobbed her head up and down.

"Good, now stay right where you are…" Alice purred, dipping her head to slide her mouth over the girl's in a ghost of a kiss before sweeping her tongue across her soft pink lips. Immediately they parted in an instinctual plea for more as, despite the warning, she arched up to deepen the kiss.

Alice was faster, however. Greedy to taste more, she pivoted, dragging her tongue down the column of her throat before peppering hot, opened-mouthed kisses over the tops of her breasts. "Mmm… such beautiful tits…"

"Ah… Mrs Martin…" Rebecca panted, rolling her head from side to side as Alice's tongue circled her nipple in a tease at the things she had in store for her.

"You like that? Want more?" Alice purred, keeping her voice low so each syllable would tingle through the tender flesh.

God, it would have been so easy to go down on her right there. To throw caution to the wind and do everything she'd thought about doing to this little tease. To live out all her dirty, little, private fantasies. All it would have needed was just that one little push.

"Yes… yes… I want it… want more…" The words came out in a hot mess as Alice took the pebbled flesh between her lips and sucked. "But why… I mean… oh fuck… you don't seem very… or shouldn't you be more… mmm… mad at me?"

"Oh honey, I'm not mad. I'm furious," Alice promised, her eyes bright with a predatory gleam as she watched her twist and writhe under her sensuous assault. There was nothing sexier than watching a lover come undone. "How dare he keep you from me." She pulled away with a slow draw, lingering just long enough to graze her teeth along her assaulted nipple. Rebecca hissed with the light sting of pain, but Alice soothed it with a swirl of her tongue before switching to its twin. "Mmm… Just look at you. So sexy. You're perfect… my husband's perfect little toy." It was impossible to keep the edge from her voice at that. Just the idea gnawed at her like a dog with a bone, fuelling the blaze in her core. "Well, not anymore. You're my toy tonight."

"Yes… please… do whatever you want to me," Rebecca entreated, her voice rising in a sensuous moan as Alice worshipped that nipple the way she had the first. She couldn't help herself. The girl was just so sweet and lush, a feast spread out to be devoured. Nothing, not even the dirtiest and kinkiest of all her wildest fantasies, could compare to reality. Eager to begin, she pressed a hand between Rebecca's thighs, cupping her mound and sliding two fingers into her drenched heat.

"Oh, your pussy's so wet for me, you dirty girl," Alice said, abandoning her breasts to take her mouth, swallowing the long moan that flowed as sweet as honey as she swirled her digits through her cream. Once they were liberally coated, she pulled back and raised them up so they could both see they were slick and shiny. "I'm going to make you my obedient little fuck toy, but first, I want to see if your pussy's as sweet as your perfect tits."

Eyes locked with Rebecca's, she gave her forefinger a slow seductive lick before putting it in her mouth and sucking it clean, moaning at the musky flavour. "Mmm… you're delicious," she purred, then offered the other finger to the girl. "Wanna taste?"

For a moment, she looked like she might try to refuse, but when Alice pressed the glistening tip of her finger to her lips, they opened obediently. Her tongue slid out to swirl around the digit, licking up the juices coating it before taking it into her mouth, sucking greedily.

"Yeah… that's it, suck it clean, taste your sweet little pussy," Alice ordered. The sight and sounds of the minx's mouth sucking her own slickness from her fingers getting her wetter by the second.

Had she sucked Richard's cock this way? Strangely, the thought didn't inflame her ire, but made the throbbing of her clit so intense, it took most of her willpower to resist the urge to rub it right there and then. So hot and greedy, she was probably a good little cock sucker.

When Rebecca released her finger, sucked clean, Alice smirked down at her. "So, did you like your first taste of pussy?"

With her body almost quivering with need, the girl nodded but looked away from the older woman's knowing gaze.

"Do you want more?" Alice pressed, bending down to trail her tongue down that long neck before pulling back to blow softly over her nipples, stiff and begging for more attention.

Rebecca nodded again, biting her lip as shame and lust tinted her face an adorable pink.

"I can't hear you," Teasing, she dropped her hand to the girl's trembling inner thigh, close enough to feel the heat radiating from her cunt, the skin deliciously smooth and soft. Slowly, she reached a finger out to circle her clit.

"Yes!" Rebecca gasped, so mad with the need for release, the words came spilling out in a hot rush. "More… please… fuck me, Mrs Martin!"

Alice was happy to oblige.

"Mmmm… good girl…" she praised, sliding down her body and laying hot, open-mouthed kisses down her midriff and navel as she went. "You're so sexy… so perfect… my perfect little fuck toy…" With that final claim, she buried her face between Rebecca's legs, dragging her tongue along her folds from the base up to the clit.

"Oh! Oh fuck… Mrs- Mrs Martin…." Rebecca gasped, her head rolling back and body curling up into Alice's mouth as she licked up and down with long, lazy strokes. The flat of her tongue spreading her folds while the tip dipped in to slide through her tender tissues.

All the while she watched, peering up at the girl from between the V-junction of her legs, delighted in the sight of her arching under her mouth, writhing, head thrashing and eyes squeezed tight against the pleasure while her breasts rose and fell with ragged breaths.

"Does that feel good?" she asked, sliding up to circle her clit.

"Yes! Oh god, feels so good!" the girl choked out, completely overwhelmed and white knuckling the tangled bedspread in an effort to grind her hips against her tormentor's tongue.

It was one of the sexiest sights Alice had ever seen.

"You like me licking your pretty little pussy?" "Yes!" she gasped, shaking with her need.

"Good," Alice purred, giving the girl's clit a sensuous kiss. The musky scent of her flowing desire curled up her nose, as addictive and intoxicating as spiced wine.

"Now whose pussy is this?" To emphasise her question, she plunged her tongue between her folds, licking every part of the slick honeypot she could reach. Heady cream poured past her lips as her tongue probed, twisted, and flicked.

"Oh fuck! It's yours! That's your pussy, Mrs Martin!" Fuck, it sounded so hot when she called her name like that.

"That's right. My husband was only renting it when he fucked it, but you belong to me now," she growled, pushing the girl's legs back towards her chest, opening her completely. Then, curling her arms around her thighs, she dragged her cunt to her mouth.

"Yes… Yes… it belongs to you… oh fuck!" The moans left her in a rush as Alice focused all her attention on her clit.

"Yes, that's it, your such a good girl, such a good little fuck toy… Mmm… you're so wet and taste so good… does my good little fuck toy want me to make her cum?" she asked, shaking her head from side to side so her tongue wouldn't lose contact with the little bundle of nerves.

"Oh fuck! Yes!" she gasped, her tone rising higher and higher while the muscles of her thighs tensed in Alice's hands, her restraining hold just managing to keep her pinned beneath her mouth. "Please… please, Mrs Martin… lick me… fuck me… I want to cum… I want to cum for you…"

"Then do it, you dirty girl, cum for me… cum in my mouth like the dirty girl you are," she ordered, before taking her clit between her lips, her cheeks hollowing as she sucked, hard.

"Oh-oh my god…" Rebecca sobbed, her spine curling at the delicious suction as her hands grabbed for Alice's head, fisting her hair. "Oh fuck… there… right there…. Fuck! Yes! Yes! Ye…" Her words trailed away as her orgasm hit, crashing over her like a tsunami. It didn't matter. Alice took everything she had to give, sucking her through the rolling waves as her hips curled and undulated, fucking her mouth in all the ways that made her own neglected pussy throb.

Especially when combined with the sheer eroticism of watching this beautiful creature cum. Of knowing she'd been the one to reduce her to such a state of base pleasure.

When the storm finally passed, Rebecca tumbled back down to earth and collapsed into the sheets in a quaking mess with a heaving bosom, glazed eyes and flushed checks of a woman well fucked. With a last cleaning lick, Alice disentangled herself. Shrugging off the hand that had been tugging at her hair, she crawled up her body to press an opened mouth kiss to her lips to feed her the last of her own sweetness. Even in her haze, the girl drank it greedily, sucking at the slickness from her tongue with a soft purring moan.

"So, how was it?" she asked, a knowing smirk pulling at the side of her lips as she pulled away.

Rebecca exhaled, her breathing ragged as she tried to gather her wits. "Amazing, Mrs Martin…" She pushed a hand through her bangs, brushing back the tangled tumbles of her hair that had stuck to her misted brow. "Oh god… my clit's still pounding, I can't feel my pussy…"

"Aw? You poor thing. Well, guess that means I eat pussy better than my husband then." Alice teased, rearing back to sit on her haunches. Hey eyes sliding down, the vision of the girl spread out beneath her, spent and ravaged and so beautifully fuckable.

"Well... I don't know if I'd go quite that far." Her eyes glanced away, her blush deepening, if that was at all possible.

The mock challenge sent a thrill straight to Alice's core that made her drenched cunt pulse.

"Oh really, you little minx? I guess that's it then, isn't it? I was going to go easy on you, but now I have to remind you of your place." She undid the belt of her robe and gave a shrug so it pooled around her feet, leaving her just in the gown. It took all her restraint not to rip that over her head, too. The cool night air felt delicious against her overheated skin.

Rebecca's mouth fell open. "Wow... Mrs Martin, you're beautiful."

"Mmm... flattery won't save you now, honey." She teased, another spike of pleasure searing out from her clit at the hungry look in the girl's eyes. It was nothing short of burning desire. "And what about my tits?"

"Your tits?" The words were tentative but she couldn't help staring as Alice leant forward just enough to emphasise the tops of her breasts, shown off perfectly by the deep cut of the silk and lace.

"Yes. Do you like them too?" she asked silkily, lowering a hand to cradle the back of the girl's head, raising her up. "Do you want to taste them? Suck on them?"

Rebecca's tongue licked across her bottom lip. "Yes. They're amazing, but I don't-"

Her words were smothered to silence when Alice pressed her face into her breasts. For all her outward nervousness, Rebecca didn't hesitate and applied lip service to every bit of skin she could reach, peppering the tops of her breasts with fervent kisses.

"Mmm... good girl, that feels... So good... yeah, worship my tits," Alice panted. It was a delicious sensation. The feeling of the mouth on her skin merging with the desperate heat burning inside her and sending tongues of tingling fire flicking over her skin, driving her wild. Fisting the girl's silky hair, she pressed her face hard to her breast, dragging her where she wanted with one hand while pushing the gown's spaghetti straps down with the other, freeing her breasts.

Rebecca didn't miss a beat and dragged her tongue over the dusky nipple, making Alice gasp and arch. Her head fell back with a pleading whimper for more as the girl's hands came up to cup and squeeze her cleavage, sending waves of ecstasy down to her core. Meanwhile, Rebecca's tongue rolled around and around her nipple, winding her up tighter and tighter, before switching to curl and flick over the other.

"Oh fuck, that's it… mmm… yes, suck my tits, show me what a good little fuck toy you are!" Alice moaned in a shuddering breath, the sight of that pink tongue sweeping over her breast working her into a frenzy. Her breasts, though always sensitive, suddenly seemed to be intensely so. The feeling was divine yet woefully inadequate and made her feel ready to burst. Then soft lips closed over her right nipple in a hard suck, and something inside her snapped. Unable to wait anymore, she dragged Rebecca's mouth from her breast and pushed her back down on the bed. She landed with a cute little gasp that was quickly silenced when Alice climbed up her body and sat on her face.

Later, the despicable part of her brain that deals with second thoughts and regret will try to convince her that this was a bad idea. That Rebecca was a girl-sex virgin and she should have found a better way of coaxing her through going down on a woman than just shoving her cunt on her face.

But at that moment, Alice didn't care.

She was desperate, near mindless with the need to cum, and the first stroke of her lover's velvety tongue was like a burst of white hot firecrackers behind her eyes.

"Oh fuck, yeah, that's it, lick my pussy… Yes! Yes!" she moaned, throwing her hands out against the nearest wall to steady herself. Her back bowed with the sensations radiating from her core as Rebecca's tongue went to work, sliding through her folds with long lapping licks that turned her legs to jelly. Turned on as she was, she knew she wouldn't last long.

Rebecca was a quick learner. While her first lick had been a shallow test, nervous and unimaginative, they quickly turned long and smooth. Then her hands were around her hips, hands grabbing and squeezing her ass, drawing Alice's cunt to her mouth as her tongue plunged deep, drinking her in like she was parched and dying of thirst.

No doubt about it, the girl was a natural pussy eater.

"Oh god honey, you've no idea how long I've wanted to see you like this…" Alice moaned. Just seeing her beneath her, those wide eyes staring up at her from between her thighs as she ate her was stoking the fire in her belly, her nerves from her clit to her nipples were on fire, the heat radiating out to her fingers and toes. "Mmm… your pretty little face between my legs… licking my cunt like the dirty girl you are… such a dirty… dirty gi- oh fuck, oh fuck!"

Whether on purpose or by chance, Rebecca had found her clit, and the feeling of her lapping at the bundle of nerves drove Alice wild. It all felt so fucking good. The tight tingling of her nipples. The throbbing knot at her centre. All The things she was doing with her mouth, that made it feel like her lips and tongue were everywhere, licking, kissing and sucking her all at once. It all came together, and she was about to burst.

"Yes! Yes… Oh god… that's it… suck my clit… make me cum on your face- oh fuck, oh fuck, oh fuck, oh fuck!"

Doubling over, she clawed at the wall for whatever purchase she could find as her hips curled and rocked, grinding her sex into the girl's mouth, riding her face as her release exploded through her. Rolling curtains of an aurora blazed across her eyes as her orgasm crashed over her in great white-capped waves, washing her away from her body into a sea of bliss.

She wasn't sure how long she floated there, but when she finally opened her eyes, never having actually realised she'd shut them, Richard was standing over her.

Chapter Twenty

When he arrived home, the flat was dark and quiet.

It was only a short walk from the Docks, but he'd taken a detour to the 24-hour gym in the Gloucester Quay's, for a quick shower. Free membership was one perk of working for Holmes & Raine, and Scarlet had been right. He certainly didn't want to go home reeking of sex.

Freshly washed but still none the wiser as to what he was about to say or do, he'd practically dragged his feet all the way home. By the time he arrived at the tower block, the sun had long since gone down. Alice's car was in its usual parking spot, but a quick glance at the dark living room confirmed there was no sign of her inside. Nor Alexander.

He checked his phone to see if she'd tried to message him, but the screen stayed blank. The battery had died.

"Shit," he cursed quietly, the discovery winding his guts into a tighter string of knots. He'd been so out of it recently; he couldn't even remember when he'd last charged the phone. God only knew when the thing had died on him.

Had something happened to her? What if she or little Alex had had to be rushed to hospital? What if...

What if something hadn't happened...

What if she'd got worried because he was so late and tried to call him? What if, when he hadn't answered, she'd decided to check on him?

Just the prospect sent a cold shiver down his spine.

Had she seen them in the window? He'd been half expecting to get his collar felt the moment he'd left the building. Anyone could have seen and reported them to the police. Or perhaps he just missed her when he left the building and she'd run into Scarlet.

He had to know. He needed to speak to her. Maybe there was still time to – *what the fuck!*

He flipped on the living room light, about to plug the phone into the charging outlet there, when he heard it. A moan. Low and husky and *very* familiar.

Then the sound of wood

creaking. Bed springs squeaking

Someone calling.

Calling her name.

Then he was running through the room and down the hall to *their* bedroom door. A hard kick sent it swinging inward, and he stopped dead, his eyes widening at the sight of the bodies tangled together on the bed.

Alice… and Rebecca!

Chapter Twenty-One

Taking in the sight that greeted him on the bed, *their* bed, Richard didn't know what to say.

It was a new experience for him.

Good or bad, he usually could always be relied upon to spit out some sort of asinine observation. Of course, it wasn't every day you walked in on your wife riding another woman's face to what could only be described as an earthshattering orgasm.

Especially when it happened to just be their babysitter's face she was riding.

The same babysitter who'd been under his desk sucking his cock that very morning.

Ironic, considering they didn't even like sharing cutlery at dinner.

"Well, when you said you had a surprise for me, I wasn't expecting this." He forced himself to speak, the words catching in his throat, as thick and sticky as toffee as the sight of them tore at him. Tore and slashed with icy talons set aflame. The blaze scorched the surface to black blisters while the icy edge cut deeper than bone. It left him numb to the world but merged with the guilt of his own misdeeds to plague his conscience. "You've surpassed yourself this time."

His voice's flat tone and that detached look shimmering in his dark eyes quickly hit Alice in a cold cascade that twisted her stomach into knots of dread. She had never seen her husband look so… She couldn't put a name to it. It was neither anger nor sadness, but something in between. Something that seemed to hone the sharp lines and smooth planes of his broad, handsome face, somehow making him even more devastatingly attractive. Lost, no, forlorn, that was it. She had never seen him look as forlorn as he did just then.

It tore at her heart to see him so wounded, and it hung a weight of guilt and regret about her neck. Whatever her reasons had been, she'd never wanted to hurt him.

However much Rebecca's confession had stung her, the betrayal was only an idea, while he was seeing her with his own eyes. Just the idea of being in his shoes, of walking in without warning to find him going balls deep in the girl's tight little cunt, was enough to make her feel sick.

He was taking it in his stride though and, for all her wanting to comfort her husband and tell him how much she loved him, she saw his challenge. Saw it and accepted it, refusing to falter under his cool glare, but met it head on. Her eyes were hard and challenging even as she gave him her best sexy, faux-innocent pout. "Surprise, *Dick*," she purred sweetly, bending a hand down to stroke Rebecca's hair. "Someone let slip about how you helped her the other night, and well, I decided she needed a little lesson in manners."

And not to fuck with other people's husbands.

"Really?" If he hadn't just walked in on it, it would have been almost impossible to tell she'd just come down from a hard orgasm. Her voice was just as sensuously throaty as he'd ever heard it. His eyes glanced down to where the top of the girl's head was peeking out from between his wife's thighs. She'd stopped what she was doing when he'd spoken, and her doe eyes stared up at him, wide and unsure. "Funny sort of lesson."

"You know me," Alice shrugged, pushing the locks of her dark hair that had tumbled across her face back into place. It was an offhand remark, but he didn't miss the hidden meaning behind the words.

Oh yes, he knew her. Alice was a vixen. Beautiful, strong willed, determined. A woman who knew what she wanted. She also loved her games and could be a right ball breaker.

Hell hath no fury, as they say, and Alice was definitely not a woman to scorn.

"Umm... Mr Martin, I'm er..." Rebecca spoke up, her voice shaky.

"Oh, I think you can call him by his name now, dear. I'd say we're all well past the formality stage." Alice cut in, only half teasing as she touched a hand to her hair and, without breaking eye contact with her husband, directed the girl's mouth back to her pussy. "And I didn't give you permission to stop."

They were going to continue with him still there, standing over them. It was like she'd slapped his face.

"Well, would you like me to leave so you can finish your lesson?" Richard asked, trying desperately to keep his voice easy despite the storm of tension gathering around them.

If she sent him away now, then it would be over. Them. Their marriage. Their family. Everything.

Alice held his gaze for a moment, considering. Time seemed to hold its breath, then a current suddenly ran through her and her head fell back with a long moan. "Go? Oh no, no, no, you silly boy, I'm only... only just getting started. Now it's time for you to get your lesson." With her hips gyrating, curling and grinding into Rebecca's mouth as the girl resumed tonguing her clit. She pointed towards the chair that sat in the room's corner. "Go. Si-sit over there- oh fuck, Mmm... I want you to watch. Watch your little slut make me cum again." And without a word, Richard did exactly that.

It was odd. A part of him knew he should be and indeed was fucking furious. Furious at Rebecca. At Alice. At them both for what they'd done and what they were doing. However, there was another part, a much larger part, the part that had been winding itself up in guilt-ridden knots, that felt almost… relieved. He'd fucked up, he'd cheated, but now so had she.

People liked to say two wrongs don't make a right… and in an ideal world, they wouldn't, but the world wasn't a perfect place. Morally corrupt or not, revenge felt good.

So if this was what his wife wanted to do, to make herself feel better about the situation, who was he to stand in her way?

And after his own misadventures that day, with both Scarlet and Rebecca, it was a much more merciful punishment than he deserved.

Alice could have cried for joy at that moment.

She'd been so afraid. So terrified he might walk out of the room, and her life with it. The relief she felt, watching him drop into the armchair, mingled with the feel of the slick tongue fluttering over her oversensitive clit, almost made her cum again. No matter what, she loved her husband, and always would. She wasn't ready to lose him, but that didn't mean she wouldn't punish him when he'd been so naughty.

And he'd been a very naughty boy.

"Oh fuck! Yeah… that's it, slut, just like… oh fuck, oh fuck!" she moaned, the words leaving her in a rush, her hips curling, fucking Rebecca's hot little mouth as that wicked tongue fucked her. The knowledge that Richard was watching her do this turned her on more than she would have imagined. The throbbing in her clit and the waves of pleasure rushing through felt so much more intense this time round. It all felt so good. So good, her eyes instinctively closed against the sensation, but when she opened them again, it was to see her husband watching her from the chair.

And as their eyes met, it took everything Richard had to stay where he was.

Punishment be damned. His wife was trying to kill him, he was sure of it.

His cock definitely agreed. Despite its vigorous workout with Scarlet, the sight of his wife riding Rebecca's face had roused the organ to new life. It strained against its confines, forming a bulge in his crotch that ached for attention. Called out to be touched. Practically begged to be unleashed and plunged balls deep into either of their sweet creamy cunts.

It was a call impossible to ignore, and he'd almost had the button of his trousers undone when Alice noticed.

"No, *Dick*, oh fuck! No, don't you dare…" she warned in a sweet song of pleasure as, all her lingering inhibitions gone, Rebecca ate her eagerly. The pink of the girl's tongue was just visible between her thighs, sliding through Alice's folds before she switched to sucking at her clit. "Oh! Oh my god… This… this is a punishment, remember. Keep your hands at your side, and just watch. Watch your little toy eating your wife? She's all mine now. You can't touch her till I say, is that clear? Just sit there and watch me cum all over this little slut's face."

Oh yes, they were both definitely trying to kill him.

"Fuck… your such a tease," he groaned, stunned and barely able to believe his eyes, or his restraint. His mouth watered as he watched and remembered the succulent taste of his wife's creamy pussy and longed to be the one between her thighs, feasting on her cunt.

This was Alice he was watching, after all. His wife. His reserved but not at all repressed, little firecracker of a wife, riding the face of their babysitter and obviously loving it. How had he never known she was into girls? Fuck, just the thought of it drove him wild. Now his cock was so hard, it was really starting to hurt. The solid weight of it pushed against his trousers, so insistent it might very well rip through the fabric.

"Oh no, Dick… this isn't teasing. This is just the beginning- oh God, yes, yes, just like that, you naughty girl. Oh God, just like that, that's perfect, that's- oh God, oh fuck, don't stop, I want to cum all over that pretty fucking face- oh shit! Yes! I'm cumming, I'm cumming!" She threw her head back, her eyes closed against the orgasm that seized her, thrashing and bucking with the waves of sensation sweeping through her while her features were consumed by that tranquil, almost far away look Richard knew all too well.

The orgasm seemed to go on and on in one long continuous wave, but was actually a series of smaller intense ones that crashed over just as the last was fading away. When it all became too much and her body crumpled, collapsing to the sheets on her hands and knees, her hips bucking against the girl's mouth. Yet with the girl's arms coiled around her thighs, even then she couldn't escape and she had to push the girl's mouth away.

It was the sexiest thing Richard had ever seen.

As outwardly sensual as his wife was, she looked almost angelic when she came. Watching her cum had always been one of his favourite parts of their sexlife. Yet watching her do so for someone else was like seeing it for the first time, and it was just as exciting.

"Mmmm… you greedy girl" Alice purred, blinking through the black spots fogging her vision and crawling back around to kneel beside Rebecca.

"I'm sorry, but Mrs Martin, your pussy tastes so good," Rebecca explained with a smile that was sweet and innocent despite the wetness that glistened on and around her lips.

Alice made a face of mock astonishment. "Oh, you naughty girl, I'm going to have to punish you for that." Lowering her head, she pressed her lips to Rebecca's in a slow kiss, deep and sensual, drinking her in with lush licks while reaching down her body to the heat pulsing between her legs.

"Mmm… please do."

"I bet you can't wait for it, can you?" Alice softly stroked a finger through her swollen folds before pushing it inside, all the way to the knuckle. Rebecca gasped at the stimulation, her body squeezing Alice's digit tightly.

Alice loved her responsiveness. "Want me to use this pussy again, you dirty girl? Such a tight, naughty little pussy. How did my husband ever fit his big dick in there?"

"I can take a lot more than you think." Rebecca got out. She was trying to sound confident, but Alice could feel the tension amassing inside her, betraying her closeness.

"Well, I guess we better see about that," she teased, withdrawing her finger and coolly looking across the room to where Richard sat.

"Come here, *Dick*."

Chapter Twenty-Two

The low purr of his wife's summons sent a delicious shiver of pleasure rippling straight down to Richard's cock. Dutifully, he pushed up from the chair and, doing his best to ignore his aching cock, walked to the bed, his legs unsure if they were stiff or shaky. Rebecca and Alice watched his every move, their eyes dark and hungry, their lush bodies entwined and ready to pounce like a pair of tigresses watching a clueless monkey walk into their trap.

"That's it..." Alice cooed, trailing a finger through Rebecca's folds, coating the digit in her cream, then raising it up to her mouth to suck it clean with a moan. "Mmm... you've been such a naughty boy, *Dick*. Keeping this tasty little pussy all to yourself. So now you're going to do the right thing and show me everything you two did behind my back."

"Everything?" He asked, his mouth dry as his thoughts swam with the idea of what she was proposing.

"Everything..." The slow curl of Alice's lips was pure wickedness. "I want to see you eat her creamy cunt... go balls deep and fuck her until she screams." Then she turned to Rebecca and, touching her glistening fingers to her chin, guided her to look her way. Holding her eyes, she purred, "and watch you wrap that sexy mouth around his big dick and suck him dry."

Rebecca blinked at the command. Scared and uncertain, she looked like she might refuse before all the desire that had gathered within her won out and she nodded.

"Good girl," Alice breathed, pressing a soft, almost chaste kiss to her mouth, but Richard didn't miss her lips parting ever so slightly. His wife moaned, a sound that doubled the ache in his imprisoned cock as she licked the last taste of herself from those soft lips. Rebecca moaned, her mouth opening under that gentle coaxing to suck greedily at the older woman's tongue as she took her hand and placed it on the bulge of his cock along his trouser leg. Together, they rubbed with fingers entwined, palms twisting and stroking up and down through the coarse material until someone snagged the clasp of his fly tail. They dragged it down while the other dealt with the button.

When it popped free and the vice around his cock eased, Richard couldn't help a sigh. It promptly became a groan, however, the moment his wife dragged the elastic of his boxers back and lodged them a little less than gently beneath his balls. Yet that sting was nothing compared to the feeling of long graceful fingers wrapping around him.

"Mmm… now put your mouth on his big cock…" Alice purred, pulling back just enough to watch, and angled the hard length of Richard's dick downward until the head, dark and swollen, hovered just over Rebecca's mouth.

The girl didn't hesitate. Leaning forward, she took his offered cock into her mouth. Her eyes peering up at him from beneath sex tussled hair as her lush pink lips slid over his crown. The lush heat of her mouth engulfing him in a single smooth glide, cheeks hollowing as she sucked.

Fuck.

It didn't matter that he'd cum twice already. If she carried on like this, he wouldn't last long.

"That's it… mmm… get it nice and wet," Alice teased, biting her lips as she watched Rebecca take him in as deep as she could before pulling back, leaving it wet and shiny. When just the wide crest remained, she reversed track, her hands coming up to brace against his thighs, giving her purchase to push her mouth back down, attacking his cock like she'd been starved of it, making up for whatever she lacked in skill with eagerness.

It was something Alice never thought she'd see. Something she never thought she'd want to. A taboo act of betrayal that she should have found repulsive, but instead was pushing all her hot buttons and made her tingling pussy throb.

Alice couldn't understand it. She was a proactive woman, not a voyeur. She didn't stand on side-lines. Where was the fun in just watching other people have sex? The very idea sounded no different from watching porn, without the deniability. Yet as she released her hold on Richard's cock to let Rebecca have her way with him, she wanted to watch.

This was so much more than pornography. Porn was manufactured, soulless, devoid of life and all the things that made sex so fun, little more than bodies going through the motions. Compared to that, this was art. Pure erotic art in the making, all induced to inflame the senses. The sounds of Rebecca's mouth as it slid along his cock, the way her eyes peered up at him with a knowing yet scared and pleading fashion. The way Richard's breathing changed as his hands fisted against the feeling it invoked in him, even as his body started circling, feeding her more of his cock. Even the heady scent of sex rolling from them to fog her brain had her panting. It was pure carnality. A drug she was powerless to resist.

"Suck it, yeah, that's it you dirty little slut, you like it don't you, you love sucking my husband's dick," she pressed, cupping her free hand over the deep throbbing between her legs, fingers massaging the knot of her clit. Not as roughly as she usually liked, but just enough to stoke the storm burning inside her.

Rebecca's eyes flickered back to Alice, almost sparkling with mischief as she pulled her mouth off their lover's cock. "Yes, but it's just so big. Can you show me how to suck it, Mrs Martin?"

"Oh, fuck..." Richard moaned, head spinning as something almost gave way inside him. It couldn't be helped.

The vision of her kneeling there in all her naked beauty, a picture of angelic innocence with his cock still wet from her mouth, rising over her face as she said that. Well, it was almost enough to make him cum right there.

"Oh, you want to watch me?" His wife cooed back, all mock sweetness but for the sultry, wicked look that she fixed him with as she did. A look that always spelled trouble. Hot, sexy, fucking trouble.

Rebecca nodded, raising one hand to follow the line of veins that roped his cock. "Yes, please, teach me how to suck your husband's cock, Mrs Martin, please." *Fuck.*

Yep, no doubt about it. They were genuinely trying to kill him.

"Alright, you dirty girl," Alice purred, slinking over gracefully to press a feather soft kiss to the girl's lips before gripping his cock. "Mmm… first, go slow and tease him. Just focus on the head, worship it with your mouth and tongue…" To demonstrate, she did just that, bending down to circle her tongue around the flared crest before wrapping her lips around it and sucking greedily. Already so hard and thick, the heated flesh pulsed with each little flutter of her tongue, his desire flowing over her taste buds and straight down to the slick heat throbbing at her core.

"Oh fuck… A-Alice, no… wait… not so…" he moaned, his hands fisting against the urge to grab her hair, the tip of his cock suddenly tingling like it was about to burst.

Alice ignored his entreaty.

"Then lick his dick like it's the biggest, juiciest fucking lollypop you've ever seen." Releasing his tip to turn her head from side to side, dragging her tongue down his cock's flanks and underside to the root, never once losing contact. "Don't forget his balls… take them into your mouth and lick them all over- mmm," she moaned, her hum reverberating around his balls as she opened wide to lodge one against the roof of her mouth, her tongue stroking the underside, sent waves of lust crashing over him. Holding his gaze, she suckled one then the other, cradling them with her tongue and rolling them over and over before releasing both to lick back up his length. "When he's all nice and wet, worship him with your mouth, sucking like you want to get every drop of his cum…"

"Ah fuck…" Richard groaned, almost beyond speech as he watched his wife suck him deep into her mouth. The feeling of warmth flowing over his cock to draw him into a font of liquid heat almost made his knees give way and he couldn't help grabbing at her head, needing more.

"No Dick, no touching," she snarled, slapping his hands away before grabbing him with both hands and swallowing him. With her lips stretched tight around his girth and cheeks hollowed, she slid her mouth up and down, smooth and steady, taking him as deep as she could on every swing. Forgetting everything else. Her every thought and focus was consumed with the taste of his flesh on her tongue. The feeling of his cock moving through her lips and swelling in her mouth. The tortured ecstasy on his face as he watched her and the feel of his body, taut and straining against itself in the race to orgasm.

These were the moments she lived for. To have so much power over one so big and strong, to drive them crazy with lust, it was more than any mere aphrodisiac. It was enough to make her fucking cum.

"Mrs Martin?" The softly spoken question brought her back to reality with a hot spike that went straight to her clit. She glanced up to see Rebecca watching in awe. Her once innocent doe eyes were dark with lust and her lush mouth opened and closed in quick, panting moans as one hand clutched at her breast, roughly tugging and twisting the nipple. The other was nestled between her legs and was working savagely at her clit.

Guess she likes to watch too.

A fresh rush of heat surged down to her core at the thought of the girl masturbating to a show of her sucking off her husband.

Pulling off, Alice smirked up at Rebecca and slowly licked the taste of her husband from her lips. "Mmm… such a big, yummy cock. He's easily big enough for two mouths. It needs two mouths…" She angled his cock towards her. "Come here."

It was an order that could not be disobeyed. Clearly knowing just what was expected, Rebecca swooped down and dragged the flat of her tongue up his shaft. From where Alice still gripped, up to the tip and the older woman's waiting mouth.

"Oh… Jesus… fuck…" Richard bit out, his words a tangled garble of grunts and moans as their mouths came together around him in an opened mouth kiss.

Already fighting his own building orgasm, he knew he should look away. Should close his eyes or cover them or… something. Anything. Anything to block out the sight of their tongues duelling around his tip, licking and lashing in that erotic battle for dominance that made his heart pound, but he couldn't.

The sight of them together, his wife and mistress, working together to drive him out of his mind. It was just so taboo, so erotic, so fucking hot, that he couldn't bear to look away.

Seeing the tormented ecstasy on her husband's face, Alice took pity on him and pushed his cock up into Rebecca's mouth.

"That's it, good girl, now suck my husband's dick like I showed you…" she instructed, releasing her grip on his cock so she could slide her tongue down the side, tracing the veins that bulged along its length. All the while watching as the girl picked up right where she'd left off, mouthing and sucking at his crown like she was trying to suck every drop of cum out of his balls. "Yes, just like that… I love watching you suck his cock, go on, show us what a good little cock sucker you are…" Her encouragement drew a ragged sound from her husband, and she glanced up to see he was still watching them. His eyes locked to the sight of the girl's mouth wrapped around over his cock. "Does that feel good, Dick? Haven't I made her into such a good little cock whore for you?"

"Yes… oh fuck, so good" he growled out, his voice harsh and guttural and despite herself, Alice felt that knot of jealously in her heart winding tighter.

It was the first time she had ever heard her man sound so desperate. So wild and untamed, and despite herself, that small little voice inside didn't like it. Didn't like that it was this girl's mouth bringing it out of him instead of hers. In all their time together, no matter all the little tricks and games she'd played, she'd never been able to break his reserve. She could arouse the animal in him, but it was still a chained beast all the same.

Alice wanted to be the one to do this to him, to arouse such passion, to break his chains and take him over the edge.

And there was only one way she was going to do that.

She didn't give Rebecca any warning. Drawing back, she raised a hand up to the back of Rebecca's head and pushed down firmly, forcing the girl's mouth down onto Richard's cock. She didn't resist, absorbed in the moment, she went with it, swallowing through the initial shock to take him all the way to the root as Alice came up, curled her free arm around his neck and crushed their mouths together in a hungry kiss.

And she knew, in that moment, for him, it was her mouth around his cock, deep throating him.

It was too much.

The intensity of his wife's kiss, along with the feeling of her soft, sensuous body pressed up against his as the lush heat wrapped around his cock sucked it in all the way, finally drove Richard over the edge. His hands fisted in the waves of soft hair, holding Rebecca right where she was as his hips circled up into her mouth, the instinctive urge to thrust and fuck too powerful to deny. Near molten heat surged up through his shaft, but Alice swallowed the incoherent sounds that flowed from him as thick and hot as the cum he was pumping down Rebecca's throat. She swallowed it all greedily, moaning with a sweet purr of satisfaction that coursed straight down to the base of his spine, adding to the waves of ecstasy.

Then the storm passed and it was as if every muscle in his body had turned to jelly. With spots dancing before his eyes, he stumbled, almost losing his balance as his knees gave with that sent him tumbling into the bed's warm embrace. Darkness clawed at the corners of his eyes and with his heart still pounding like a drum, sleep didn't exactly sound like a bad idea.

Alice, however, had no intention of letting him off so easily.

"Oh Dick…" she murmured, throwing one lushly smooth leg across to straddle him. A small smile playing across her lips as she gazed down at him, dark eyes burning with predatory hunger.

"Wow… it's still so hard." Rebecca voiced as she rolled over and almost straight into his cock, still hard and not showing any signing of shrinking. She let out a long admiring breath and the feel of it wafting across his over sensitive glans made him gasp.

She looked up at Alice. Those big doe eyes, once so sweet and innocent, burned with the same dark, lustful fire that met them. Her tongue slowly swept across her lips. "Thank you for sharing your husband's cock with me, Mrs Martin."

The sweet, almost innocent way the girl said the dirty words, like it was for giving her an extra cookie, sent a fresh shiver of arousal through her. "She's such a good girl, isn't she, Dick? So sexy and polite, and such a good little cock sucker…" In truth, Alice couldn't help being rather impressed. Good as she was, Richard was just too big for her to swallow whole, but Rebecca had taken to it like a natural. And she looked so sexy with her husband's cock in her mouth.

"Yes, so good," Richard groaned, his voice low and tortured as memories of Rebecca's mouth gliding along his cock swam before his mind's eye. Recollections that caused his dick to twitch eagerly.

Fucking treacherous bastard!

Alice cooed a sympathetic sound that did not meet the wicked glint in her eyes. "Now you stay right there, honey, there's something you need to see..." she told Rebecca while turning back to the view of her husband stretched out beneath her. The sight of his hard body still covered by his shirt and trousers, though they were open around his most impressive of attributes, made her arch a brow.

Those would have to go. It was time to reaffirm her claim.

"I can't wait to watch you fuck her." She leaned down to nip and lick at his jaw and neck, running her hands down his chest through his shirt, fingering the buttons open as they went. "I know I said I wanted to watch you eat her tasty little pussy next, Dick, but watching her suck your cock got me so hot, I just can't wait. Dick, I need to get fucked, and I want her to watch it. I want her to see us and know that you're mine." When the last button came loose and the shirt fell open above his already splayed trousers to reveal his taut abdomen and well-defined lines she loved to lick. Not exactly a six-pack, but age, with the help of a good diet and a healthy workout routine, had been kind to her husband.

She rolled her hips, stroking her creamy sex with his length. "You're mine, Richard."

"Yes," he hissed, his jaw tight as her fingers curled around him. Her touch was warm, her hand small but strong, and skilful squeezing returned him to full hardness with a groan. "Yours, and you're mine."

The promise in those words sent a rush of relief flooding through her. The dedication that no one would ever come between them, so familiar yet suddenly so new and important, was as true now as the day he'd first promised her. She could see it in his eyes, the look of savage devotion blazing within them as he watched her notch his wide crest against her cleft, coating it in her flowing cream. More acute than ever before. A fierce promise just for her that made her heart flutter, and core throb with an ache to feel him deep inside her.

"I love you-ohh!" The words left her in a rush, her stormy eyes widening with the feeling of his cock pushing inside her as she let her body drop.

Fuck, she never tired of that burn. The feeling of being stretched, filled, split in half.

"Oh Fuck… no… wait…" Richard groaned, hands grabbing for the lush fullness of her bum, trying to stop her as her inner tissues wrapped around him, squeezing and sucking greedily, trying to draw him deeper. His cock, despite all the day's prior orgasms having leached away much of his sense of feeling, was still over sensitive from the one Rebecca's mouth had sucked from him.

However, his wife was in no mood to listen.

Needing to have him, all of him, inside her, Alice pressed on regardless. Her hands moving to his shoulders, pushing against his restraining hold, nails biting into his flesh as inch after delicious inch filled her pussy, still so sensitive and tender from the night's bounty of orgasms.

"Alice…" he bit out through gritted teeth, his words threaded with pained ecstasy, and shutting his eyes against the delicious sensation. His every sense and reason focusing on their union as lush, velvety warmth enveloped him to the hilt, squeezing like a fist.

"No! Don't… don't you dare close your eyes." She breathed through the sensations, needing to see. Nothing thrilled her like watching him, seeing him so on edge. Looking into his eyes, feeling his cock throb and swell inside her, and letting him see what he was doing to her in turn, the wildfire about to consume her as he reached places so deep inside.

The intimacy was so searingly intense, it was as if they were the only two people in existence. Only when he obeyed and their eyes locked did she move.

She started slowly, with small rolls of her hips.

She always needed to start off slow. No matter how turned on or wet she got, he was just so big, and her body loved it.

"Oh! Oh God… oh fuck, yes, Dick, fuck!" Alice panted, almost losing herself in the feeling of his cock invading her. Reaching so deep inside. Touching all the places she'd never known existed before him. She could feel her inner tissues clenching around his thick cock, refusing to let him go as she circled her hips, making her feel every delicious inch of him.

"Oh fuck, Alice, shit, you feel so good. Ride me baby, ride my fucking dick…" he panted, his breathing almost ragged from the feeling of her cunt tightening around him. Her slick inner walls fluttered with a frenzy as Richard let her have her way with him, wanting nothing so much as to watch her, his wife, ride him to her climax.

The sight of his wife above him, riding him. The thick waves of her silky dark main bouncing in a wild, sexy mess. Her skin flushed from pleasure and shiny with misted perspiration he longed to lick. Her eyes blazing down at him, fierce and hungry. She looked so wild and beautiful. A goddess of sex and beauty, riding him triumphantly, glorious and all conquering.

"That's right, that's how you like it, right Dick?" She panted, her orgasm building fast and strong with each circle of her hips and the grind of her clit against the flat of his groin. Then, leaning down, flattening her bare breasts against his chest so her stiff nipples dragged over his flesh in a tease of friction, she attacked his neck with hungry sucking kisses, drinking in the salt of his skin. "Mmm… Isn't your wife's tight little pussy just the best?"

"Yes, fuck, the best, always the best- oh fuck!" he groaned, teeth gritted and arching his head back. Giving her greedy mouth free rein to lick across his skin, even as it all became too much. He needed to have her, his wife.

He needed to fuck her as much as she did him. Suddenly, his body was moving, churning up into her sultry rhythm. Drawing back as she rose, then thrusting up to meet her as she came back down, meeting her with wet slapping thrusts that had them both curling in ecstasy.

"Oh! Oh my god… oh fuck… yes, that's it, pound that pussy, pound your wife's naughty little pussy…"Alice moaned, her breath hot and ragged on his skin. Her blood boiling with lust, and burning from the urge to fuck, she bit and licked across his shoulder and neck. Up to suck on his earlobe before claiming his mouth to drive her tongue into his warmth, mimicking the motions of his cock thrusting up into the clinging silken warmth as his hands brought her crashing down to meet him.

Fuck, he was so strong when he got like this, so powerful and wild. She loved it. The feeling of every inch of his masculinity piercing her, filling her to the brim. His white knuckled grip on her hips, almost painful but so good, both steadying her and raising her up, then slamming her down. Driving her wild as they went faster and faster until she was almost bouncing on him, clawing at his body, her nails dragging trails of fire across his flesh as each plunge and thrust found all the sweet spots and sent her soaring to new heights.

Overwhelmed, she reared back, her spine curling in a song of pleasure as her release swept over her like a tidal wave. The sensations hit fast and hard, sweeping her into the starry abyss.

"Yeah, cum for me, babe…" he groaned, mesmerised by the vision of her riding him over the edge, the feel of her cunt wrapping around him, refusing to let go even as he kept up his assault with the instinctual drive to join her in release. To come together, but, fuck, it wasn't enough. His cock was rock hard, but even the sight of his wife's perfect tits bouncing with the feeling of her lush pussy clamping down and sucking him deep wasn't enough to take him over the edge. Nowhere near enough.

"Oh god! Fuck! Yes, yes, give me all that dick…. I need it… I love it… I… I…"Alice moaned out, riding her release hard. Her whole body shivering as he fucked her through the waves crashing over her, and streams of stars blasting across her vision. It was one of the most intense orgasms of her life, a carnal nuclear blast, and it would have been so easy for her to give in and let the feelings carry her away. But she couldn't. She wouldn't. Richard hadn't cum yet. She needed to make him cum. Needed to claim his last release and wash all this away.

And that was when she glimpsed Rebecca perched across from them on the other side of their wide queen-size bed. Her eyes wide with their deceptive innocence, even as one hand kneaded a breast, fingers tugging and twisting the nipple, while the other rubbed herself between her legs, circling over her clit.

Their eyes met amidst the orgasmic haze and Alice knew it was time to kick things up a gear. "I want to see you sit on his face, my little slut."

Richard almost couldn't believe his own ears. Fuck, had Alice really just say that?

Just the thought of his wife telling another woman to sit on his face sent a hot thrill down to the base of his spine that at any other time could have made him cum. Then Rebecca was kneeling over him and the question was suddenly academic as she gazed down at him, biting her lower lip. Her eyes uncertain behind the dark fog of lust.

It reminded him of how she had looked spread out beneath him that night in her room, scared but eager. Innocent yet naughty, his sweet temptation. He gave a nod, and releasing his grip on Alice, giving her the freedom to ride his cock, raised his hands up to cup Rebecca's buttocks, steadying her as she swung one lusciously long leg across his shoulders. Then, facing his wife, she slowly lowered her pussy down towards his mouth, flooding his senses with the thick heady musk of her arousal.

"Oh! Oh fuck… Mr Martin!" Rebecca moaned, throwing her head back in a long moan as Richard's lips enveloped her, his checks hollowing as he sucked hard on her clit. Her flavour flowed over his tongue, rich and thick as honey, and just as sweet as he remembered.

"Yeah, you like that, my little slut?" Alice asked, entranced by the sight of his jaw working, his tongue working with the fluttering licks she knew so well. Fuck, when had she become such a voyeur? Just watching him tease the small pearl of the girl's clit got her own bundle of nerves throbbing. Her walls flexing around him, the aftershocks of her previous release still tingling through her as she remembered the feeling of that very tongue dancing across her clit, so it was almost like she was getting fucked and licked all at once.

Just the thought of it almost made her lose her mind. Needing more, she ground and rolled her hips into his, angling her hips just right so his broad crest rubbed against a sweet spot. "Mmm… feels so good, doesn't it? Sitting on my husband's face? His mouth eating your pussy while I ride him…"

"Yes, oh fuck, so… good… oh yes! Right there, right there!" It was only half an answer, clearly too distracted by the lashing of Richard's tongue, but Alice didn't care. She was just so beautiful like that, caught up in the throes of passion. So wild and passionate, a complete contrast to usual bookish innocence. It made her ache to taste her again and cupping the girl's face in her hands, she pulled her in to claim her mouth in a kiss. Thrusting her tongue into her sweetness to feast on her sweetness, drinking her in the way her husband was doing to her cunt.

Denied any sort of visual but hearing and picturing everything, it was all Richard could do to ignore the way his wife slid along his dick, bearing down on him like a silken glove. Rather, he focused all his attention on making Rebecca cum. Greedy to taste her orgasm, he curled his arms around her hips, digging his fingers into her buttocks and crushing her against his mouth and sucking at her clit.

"Oh god!" Rebecca gasped, dragging her mouth from Alice's and throwing her head back.

Needing more, Alice shifted, leaning in to suckle on the girl's neck as she rocked her hips, her next orgasm building hard and fast. "He's got such a good mouth, but his cock's even better…" she purred in her ear, catching the lobe between her teeth and biting playfully. "Such a big fucking dick, so hard and thick, feels so good…"

"Yes. Yes. Yes!" The words were out in such a rush, whether they were in agreement or a vocalisation of her pleasure, it was hard to tell.

Regardless, the result was the same.

"Do you want to feel it, feel his big cock stretch out your tight little hole… fucking you so deep… making you take every fucking inch…" Alice pressed, trailing kisses down the girl's neck.

"Oh god, please…" Rebecca whimpered, arching up into the other woman's touch, clawing Richard's chest for any sort of purchase.

Richard felt how the dirty talk was affecting not just Rebecca, but Alice too, making him groan into the girl's folds as his wife's clamped down on him, her walls squeezing him tight. His body answered without his volition, bucking and screwing his cock up into her luscious pussy.

"Please what, my little slut?" Alice asked, teetering right on the edge but wanting to watch Rebecca cum one more time. Heat rushed over her with the feeling of his cock moving inside her as she watched that sweet face contort so beautifully with pleasure. She bent down and caught a lush nipple between her lips. Sucking once before swirling her tongue around and around, then switching to the other. "Do you want me to let my husband fuck you? Go on, tell me how badly you want to feel his big cock filling up your tight little cu-"

"Yes! Oh fuck, please, please Mrs Martin, please can I fuck your husband… ohhh god… mmm… I can't wait, I need to feel his dick inside me. Please, let me fuck it, I want to fuck your husband's cock, I need it, I… I… oh fuck!"

Richard felt Rebecca's release break as he swirled his tongue around her inner walls, her thighs snapping closed around his head, squeezing so tight he could barely breathe amidst the smooth, warm flesh as she bucked and ground against his tongue. Regardless, he licked her through it, greedily drinking her in, lapping up every drop of her cream, the taste of her gilding his cock to steel.

Alice felt it too, the sudden surge of his arousal swelling inside her as Rebecca's body trembled and shook against hers. And she watched, avidly, needing to see that look in those big eyes one more time. See the pleasure, the releases, the freedom, the complete carnal abandon all billowing together in a perfect storm within those innocent doe eyes.

See it, remember it, and know that *they* had done this to her.

Just the thought of it shattered her mind into shards that cascaded across the heavens with each fresh pulse of white hot pleasure. Consumed by sheer sensation, she claimed Rebecca's lips in a desperate kiss, hugging her close as their bodies quaked together, clinging to her for dear life until the storm passed. Then the world moved, and they were crashing back down to earth, landing with a soft bounce upon the bed.

Richard didn't hesitate. Almost mindless with the need to fuck, to cum, to bury his cock inside them both and brand them both with his seed. One quick twist was all it took to send both of them tumbling off him to the covers. Then he was up, shrugging out of his shirt and kicking off his trousers, before rolling up onto his knees.

Rebecca's soft round bum wiggled enticingly as he came up behind her and, grabbing her waist with both hands, he rolled her over onto her hands and knees and dragged her back towards him. Still slick with his wife's cream, his cock plunged in deep, going all the way to the root with his first thrust.

"Oh my… Oh fuck! Yes, yes!" Rebecca gasped, looking back over her shoulder at him. Her eyes hot and lusty, calling out to him with a lustful passion in an unabashed plea for him to take her, dominate her, fuck her.

With a low growl, he began to move. Pulling back almost enough to slip free, before driving back home so his abdomen slapped against her checks with a wet smack as she pushed back.

"That's a good girl, mmm… take that big dick… that's it, take it, let him in…" Alice purred, her lip caught provocatively between her teeth and eyes smouldering as she watched them rut. Drinking in the sight of him, so big and strong, using her like a little bitch in heat and dominating her so completely as he drove in with a reckless abandon, like she was nothing but a hole to be used for his pleasure. And Rebecca was clearly loving it, her eyes almost rolling in ecstasy. Not that Alice could blame her, knowing how good it felt to have that cock filling her up. That he felt even bigger from behind and could reach even deeper. "Let your little pussy take it. That's a good girl, such a good little slut. Let him have you. Tell him how good it feels… how big and deep my husband's dick is…"

Stretched out as she was, she lay alongside them with her head propped on one hand and one leg bent at an angle for them to glimpse the fingers of the other reaching down between her legs.

Just like that, Richard was right on the edge.

The vision of his wife spreading her legs open further, revealing the slick and swollen state of her well fucked pussy as her fingers circled her clit, almost pushing him almost past his limit. While this wasn't the first time he'd seen her masturbate, he knew he would never tire of watching her. She was such a sexual woman, unceasingly sensual and a complete agent provocateur. He dared the universe to create a more awe-inspiring sight than that of Alice pleasuring herself.

"So-so big… so deep… Oh my god… oh my god…
right there, holy shit, Mr Martin, you feel so fucking good!"
Rebecca gasped, mewling like a kitten as her hips rocked,
greedy for more, her back curling as she pushed back,
straining to take him deeper. The waves of untamed hair
spilling down over her shoulders and across the bed as she
bowed with the pleasure of it. Head down and arse raised,
accepting his cock and the pounding it was giving, her moans
muffled a bit by the sheets as she buried her head in them,
even biting down against high sobs. Hands fisting and twisting
and knotting the sheets as he fucked her. Harder.
Faster. Needing to feel her cum just one more time.

"Naughty girl, you really wanted my cock, didn't
you?" he husked, his voice low and guttural, thick with a
primal edge, the beast in him taking over. "Fuck… such a snug
little cunt…" he groaned, loving the view of his cock sliding
through her folds, smooth as silk, then reappear slick with her
cream. The pretty pink of her pussy stretched wide and her
butt rippled with each meeting while his balls swung up to
slap her clit.

"Yes, yes, fuck, please, please make me cum, make
cum all over your- oh shit, fuck, fuck!" Her pleas were raw and
desperate, rising high to the heavens and merging with the
echoing *slap, slap, slap* of their meeting bodies. With each draw
and thrust, fresh proof of her arousal rolled down his thighs.

"That's it, it feels so good having all of his big dick
inside you, doesn't it?" Alice coaxed, her eyes lingering on the
sight of Rebecca's breasts, full and firm, swaying with the
movements of her body. Her fingers quickened, as if she was
trying to match their pace, the tense, throbbing heat in her core
spreading outward, spiralling through to her fingers and
swollen nipples. "Yeah, I know how good it feels, but you
mustn't be selfish…" And just to prove her point, she lent up
to catch the nipple of one swaying breast between her swollen
ruby lips, sucking gently before spinning away and
shimmying around until she was sat up with both legs on

either side of Rebecca's head "Now, are you going to be a good little slut and eat my pussy while you get fucked by my husb- oh!"

From his angle, Richard could just glimpse over her shoulder to see Rebecca pressing her face between his wife's legs. Though he couldn't quite see what she was doing, the wet sounds of her tongue were more than enough for his imagination to fill in the blanks.

Alice had no such obstacles.

With her heart thumping as the sexual energy sizzled through her blood, she couldn't bear to look away. Even as her head rolled back into the sex rumpled sheets, she was hooked. Captivated by the image of Rebecca's face between her legs, those beautiful eyes staring up at her from beneath a wing of dark hair while that tongue fluttered over her folds.

It was such an erotic view, one that put her right on the edge as she rimmed her hole, drinking her in. "Oh… Oh fuck… Oh my god… yes that's it, right there… oh fuck… look at you… eating my pussy… you're so sexy… so perfect… so fucking go- oh god, oh god, oh god…" Fireworks burst behind her eyes when the girl's mouth suddenly reacquainted itself with her clit. "Yeah, that's it, that's the spot, yes, good girl, you love that yummy pussy, don't you?"

"Oh fuck, yes, Miss Martin… fuck, I love it… so-so good, more… please… give me more…" She whimpered back, her answer smothered against her folds, but thick with desire and rising high as Richard filled her with his cock, pounding her and deep. Yet her eyes always stared up at her, gaze fixed upon her face and lips shiny with her cream as she sucked and licked.

It was all too much, but nowhere near enough, and each little pull of suction had her fisting Rebecca's silky hair and forcing her mouth harder against her cunt. "Fine Slut, you'll have more." Alice panted, her body burning. Her core was hot and throbbing and unbearably slick from the feeling of that tongue swirling around her clit. "Yes, eat that pussy, my little slut, eat my pussy and make me cum all over that pretty face."

The pleasure in her voice was a plea Richard knew all to all too well, a desperate instinctual sound, wild and primal. A sound only he had reduced her to.

He couldn't stand it.

With a growl, he started sliding Rebecca back and forth, fucking her cunt onto his cock in time to meet his pounding thrusts. Driving into her harder, deeper, until his broad crest was banging against the gates of her core. Even then, he couldn't get deep enough, the primal beast in him needing to both claim and punish this little minx.

Alice felt the change in him. Felt it in the sudden jarring thrusts that had Rebecca's mouth and tongue grinding over her pussy, and the moans that reverberated around her clit shot through her like white hot electricity, nearly making her cum every time he went balls deep. Then hands were grabbing onto her and crushing her sex to Rebecca's mouth as the suction around her bundle of nerves grew stronger and more desperate, like the girl was trying to suck in air through her pussy.

"Yes! That's it… yeah, so fucking good… yes…" she moaned, her eyes flickering up to his, recognising the look that burned back at her. Saw how good he felt, how close he was. She loved it. She loved watching him lose it and tilting her head back, she fixed him with a look that was pure wickedness. "Fuck her, Dick!" One hand clutching at her breasts, fingers twisting and tugging at the coral tips to ease the ache inside. The other fisted the waves of Rebecca's hair and pressed her face hard to her pussy as the girl's cheeks hollowed with a suction that had her bucking up off the bed. "Fuck her and make her cum! Make her cum all over your cock!"

"Oh fuck, Alice… don't… stop talking like that…" Richard barked, his breath seething through gritted teeth at the feeling of Rebecca's inner tissues squeezing him. Growing tighter with his wife's every word, tight and hot and wonderfully snug, trying to hold him in, refusing to let go. It felt good, too fucking good.

Alice's eyes flash at his outburst, her heart thumping and rolling and twisting a peaked nipple close to the point of sweet agony. "Oh, does my little slut like it when I talk dirty?" "Oh yeah, she loves it…" And as he said it, punctuating each word with the slap of flesh on flesh, Rebecca moaned helplessly, her body shaking with the orgasm ripping through her.

However, Alice ignored him, her eyes fixed upon the eyes peering up at her from between her legs.

"You like getting fucked like the little bitch in heat you are, don't you?" She pressed, tightening and twisting her hold on her hair while her hips rocked and ground against her tongue, straining up into the lush heat. Her core was tight and throbbing and eager to cum again. "Look at you, eating my pussy while getting fucked. That's my husband's dick inside you, filling up your pussy, my little slut. Yes, suck my clit while you take his big cock. That's right, make me cum on your face while you take my husband's big fucking cock…" "Do you like watching your husband fuck me, Mrs Martin?" Rebecca asked, raising her head slightly to ever so softly tongue her bundle of nerves with soft flicks. Yet beneath her pleasure flushed face, her eyes were pleading and desperate, needing to hear it. As if deep down, she still harboured doubts.

"Oh sweetie… I love it, watching you take my husband's cock while eating my pussy is so fucking sexy- oh fuck… oh fuck!." Alice's whole body bucked, an orgasm crashing over her when Rebecca's mouth enveloped her, that wicked little tongue thrusting deep to swirl inside her. It was like she was trying to find and lick all her sweet spots at once, sending fresh waves rippling through her, pushing her release on and on, until black dots were dancing before her eyes.

She couldn't bear it. It was too much. She was too sensitive, and with a last gasp, she pushed her head away.

"Enough…"

Richard watched his wife succumb to her orgasm with his own not far behind. The sight of it almost pushed him over the edge, yet he wanted more and stubbornly tried to hold it at bay. His eyes rolling back up to the ceiling, trying to focus on something, anything, to distract him. Distract him from the feeling of Rebecca's lush walls, milking him with greedy pulses. From the sight of his wife writhing in such sweet oblivion, and his cock sliding through the swells of the girl's butt, disappearing inside her sweet cunt.

Seeming to know his mind, Alice, with the spots fading but her body still tingling, lurched up to kiss his mouth. "And you Dick…" she husked, kissing like she owned him. Needing him to know he was here, and she was his. Her hands rubbing their way up the tense muscles of his arms and shoulders to fist the rough brush of his hair, crushing his mouth to hers. "Did you enjoy watching our little slut eat me while you fuck her?" A deep, guttural growl rose in him to answer her, sending shivers of desire rushing up her spine. His control slipping, his hips snapped with harder, faster strokes that literally fucked Rebecca down into the bed beneath them. "Doesn't her naughty twenty-year-old cunt feel good wrapped around your big, hard cock?"

"Yes, fuck, shit, so fucking good…!" He groaned, shaking with the tensions threatening to overwhelm him. The heat of her words tingling down his spine to stir the telltale throbbing down in the base of his spine. "Ahh Shit! Fuck… I'm going to cum!"

"No, net yet Dick." She ordered, pulling back just far enough to flick the tip of her tongue teasingly over his nose, but the purpose burning in her eyes steeled him to obey and linger in that hellish purgatory. "Turn her over. Let's finish her together."

Near mad with his need to cum, Richard didn't question her. Without losing his rhythm, he tensed his grip and rolled Rebecca over onto her back. Rebecca squeaked at the sudden twist, but before she asked, Alice threw a leg over her body and leaned down, their bodies fitting together like puzzle pieces sliding into place, her eyes glued to where his cock was gliding through her folds.

"Mmm… that's it baby… Your dick looks so good going in and out of her pussy." Her mouth watering at the sight of the wetness that was coating his cock with each thrust, she leant in and swept her tongue through Rebecca's folds.

Richard couldn't believe his eyes. "Oh, fuck… Alice…"

She didn't answer. Relishing the heady taste of their mixed juices, she twisted her head ever so slightly to slide between their grinding bodies, licking ravenously, greedy for every drop. Unceasing even as beneath her, Rebecca wrapped her arms around her thighs and bent up to attack her clit, sucking with equal hunger. Swollen and so sensitive from too many orgasms so close together, the sudden rush of sensation was so intense, it was almost too much. But she fought on, suddenly needing both her lover and her husband to be there with her.

Richard already was, and certain he might lose his mind at any moment, he went with her. Blindly reaching down to grasp the back of Rebecca's legs, he pushed them back to frame Alice's shoulders, opening her fully and tilting her hips up towards her devouring tongue. The vision of his wife's head between Rebecca's legs, licking her clit as he fucked her, driving him wild. Past the point of no return, he pounded into the girl's lush grasping heat with his last reserves, going so rough, the bed shook, the headboard banging against the wall in a call that screamed hot, passionate sex to any that cared to be listening. He didn't care. He didn't care if the entire building, or everyone in the whole damn city knew what they were doing. All that mattered was them. He and Alice, together till the dawn, and whatever wonders lay beyond as they walked together, side by side and hand in hand, into this new chapter of their lives.

"That's it Dick, hold her legs back like that… mmm… so sexy… such a sexy little pussy… I love watching you fuck her… yeah… fuck that pussy…" Alice moaned, grinding down onto that wonderful mouth. The high rising moans that poured from her every time she watched Richard's cock driving into the root, reverberating around her clit and through her, out across her nerves, until she felt like a string too tightly plucked and about to snap. Her pussy was hot and throbbing, burning with need. She could sense it in Rebecca too, and met her husband's gaze, needing to see, to watch him go over that edge again. Her eyes were hot and daring him to deny her as she rolled Rebecca's clit with her tongue. "She's such a good little slut for us… yes… Now baby… fill her sweet little pussy up, Dick. I want to lick all your cum out of her… cum for me."

It was a command he was powerless to resist.

"Fuck, fuck, fuck!" he grunted as he pounded into the girl for the final time, burying himself to the root, white hot fire burning out from the base of spine. Stars raced across his eyes with each pulse of heat that shot through him and for a moment, it felt like he was caught in a vortex, having his soul sucked out of his body in the most powerful orgasm of his life. Every sensation was so intense, it was agony.

An exquisitely sweet agony, made all the more potent by Alice watching him.

Alice loved watching Richard cum. Hearing the ragged sounds as he dragged in breaths. Seeing the pleasure twisting and contorting his usually so calm expression, the wild look in his eyes. Feeling that shudder course through him as he flooded her cunt. There was nothing sexier than seeing her man climax, and knowing it was because of her. Even now, he was cumming, flooding Rebecca's pussy with his seed for her.

She couldn't bear it. Her own climax hit like a storm as Rebecca's orgasmic moans bombarded her clit. Fuelled by its passion, she pushed him back just in time for his cock to slide free and release the last spurt of his cum across her breasts.

Before she took him into her mouth, lips stretching across his crown, cheeks hollowing.

"Oh shi… Alice!"

Moaning at the taste of pussy on his flesh, she sucked hard and didn't release his shrinking length until she'd cleaned it of every drop. Yet that wasn't enough to quench her thirst and even before Richard had tumbled back onto the bed, she'd buried her face back down between Rebecca's legs. Caught up in the trailing after glow of so many powerful orgasms much too close together, she could only tremble and moan as Alice lapped at the mingled juices, thrusting her tongue deep.

Only when she'd scooped up as much of her husband's cum as she could reach did she pull away and, turning around, crawled shakily up the girl's body. With the taste of them still on her tongue, she took her face in her hands and softly kissed her trembling lips, feeding her their mingled juices before cupping her cum-splashed breasts and raising them up for the girl clean.

"Good girl." She praised once the job was done, before pulling her close as she let herself finally give into the softness of the bed and the warm soft body beside her. Then the darkness at the edge of her vision consumed her.

Epilogue

"Where's Alex? I'm guessing you didn't do all this
with him just down the hall." Richard mused, staring up at the
darkened ceiling above. He hadn't needed to look to know
Alice was awake. He just sensed it.

She was snuggled against his right side with an arm
draped across his chest. On his left, Rebecca was still asleep,
with her arms locked securely around his arm and her head on
his shoulder. He didn't bother to wonder how they'd ended up
like that. From being spiralled casually around the bed to
snuggled together beneath the sheets with their heads just
managing to fit together all on one pillow. In the grand scheme
of things, that seemed rather inconsequentially irrelevant at
this point.

His wife didn't look at him, nor even open her eyes as
she snuggled closer, her head resting on the place between his
shoulder and pectoral, the softness of her breasts pressed
against his ribs. "Hmm… No, he's with my parents. I dropped
him there this morning before work and said I'd pick him up
on my way home in a couple of days."

"Thank god for that." He grinned, chuckling to
himself. "Otherwise, by the time he hits puberty, we'd be
spending all our money on shrinks."

That made the corner of Alice's mouth curl wryly as
her fingers drew circles across her. "Well, don't count it out

just yet. Poor boy, who knows what nightmares he might have after a couple of days staying with my parents… But mum's been nagging for some time with him, so I thought why not take advantage and have a little *quality time*."

It was impossible to miss her sultry purr, and the salacious meaning of it sent a hot shiver down his spine, reawakening his cock, though it complained bitterly at the sums. "oh, so um… how did this…" He glanced down at Rebecca, whose face was a mask of innocence and serenity, betraying none of the deeds she'd performed that day that were at such a stark contrast to anything anyone would call innocent.

Though she couldn't see with her eyes still closed, she understood his meaning. "Her dad thought she'd stolen something of his and got rough with her again."

He stiffened at her words, but the tension in him seemed to disturb the girl on his arm as she shifted suddenly. So he forced himself to relax.

"That bastard," He bit out.

There was so much fire and barely restrained venom in his voice that Alice opened her eyes. "Relax, I took care of it," she purred, leaning in to press soft kisses to his throat as the hand on his chest slid down the line of his abdomen.

"Yeah… how bad?" he asked, swallowing as he felt her hand working lowering, and his body responding to it. Her slow sucking kisses quickly smothering one fire with another. The tempting wench…

Edging higher, she took the lobe of his ear between her teeth and bit hard enough to make him hiss. "Mmm… let's just say he'll think twice before attacking a woman half his size again."

"He what!" He jerked back suddenly, his head snapping round to fix her with a look that was almost murderous. "Fucking hell, that's it! I'll kill him."

He meant it too. Alice could see the fury in his eyes, the murder. While Richard would never intentionally hurt her, she'd always known he could and would kill for her. Would do whatever it took to protect her and their son. She loved him for it, and at times it was a major turn on to see and feel him cut loose and go all alpha male.

But it wasn't helping now.

"No, you won't. It's done. I handled it, so forget it," she said, moving her hand back to his heaving chest, urging him back down to the bed. Besides them, Rebecca stirred, rolling away from them. That movement seemed to help ease his storm, and he nodded for her to continue. "Anyway, we came in. I ran her a bath. Then we got talking and…"

"Things came out," he offered quickly, voice heavy and eyes dropping low.

Shame twisted his guts into tight knots.

"Yeah, you could say that," she shrugged, trying to look nonchalant about it, but even as she said the words, she had to look away, unable to meet his eyes.

She still felt it still, that hurt, the sting of betrayal, his betrayal.

That he could have hurt her so cut him deeper than any blade. "I'm sorry, I don't know what came over me… it just sort of-"

She nodded. "*Happened*. Yeah, I know." The coolness in her tone could have cut glass.

"But now you're okay with… everything." It was a stupid as fuck question to ask and he knew it as soon as he said it, but he needed to know. Needed to know if she could move past this.

"Well, I wouldn't exactly say I'm over the moon about you fucking our babysitter behind my back…" She let the words hang there for a moment, and time seemed to hold its breath before she met his eyes once again. "But then again, I'm not exactly in any position to judge, am I? We weren't exactly playing truth or dare and having a pillow fight when you burst in, now, we're we?"

And just like that, all the tension had suddenly vanished as she smiled up at him.

Despite himself, Richard couldn't help but grin back at her. "No, I guess not."

She nodded. "So, it's agreed then. Next time, we discuss things first, then we fuck them."

Her husky promise turned his cock to stone. "Next time?"

"Well, you enjoyed tonight, didn't you?" she asked, climbing atop his waist so the stiff, and still a little sore, head of his cock was notched against her folds. "No one said it has to stop. Where's the fun in having a bi-sexual wife if you can't experiment a bit?"

"Bi, huh? When did that start?" he arched his brow as his hands brushed down her spine to cup her buttocks, loving the feel of their firmness filling his hands. His wife really had the greatest ass, and though they'd never discussed doing anal, he couldn't help wondering if she'd be interested.

"It's new…" she purred, giving a slow roll of her hips that coated him in her quickening cream and teased her clit. "Something I'm thinking about trying. Care to help?"

"Sure, where's the harm in a bit of *experimentation…*" His hands squeezed her arse suggestively, grinding her harder against his shaft, one finger reaching out, wetting itself in her juices then teasing across her puckered anus, pressing just hard enough to make her gasp.

"Oh! You naughty boy! I'll remember you said that…" she teased while pushing back just enough to feel herself opening beneath the tip, but just the tip. "Maybe we should bring a boy to bed next time. I could suck all his cum out while you fuck me. Wouldn't that be fun?"

"Cheeky," he groaned and, pulling back, gave her ass a swat that had her gasping with a mix of surprise and pleasure. "I think I better give you a spanking for that one."

Alice's eyes lit up at the prospect. "Oh, please do-"

"Ummm… Mr & Mrs Martin?" A small voice cut in.

Stilling, they turned to see Rebecca staring back at them from her side of the pillow.

Alice smiled and reached out to stroke her check. "I think you can call us Richard and Alice now, honey."

However, the girl edged away from the touch, her big doe eyes glassy and lip quivering. "Sorry, it's just… Well, I'm sorry I've caused you both so much trouble. You've both been so kind to me, and I... well… Maybe I should go…" With crystal tears rolling down her cheeks, she threw back the sheets and jumped off the bed, the pale skin of her naked body almost seeming to glow in the low light.

Quick as a snake, Richard's hand shot to catch her arm and pulled the sobbing girl back down to the bed. "Hey, hey… shhh… it's alright…. You've never been any trouble for us."

"Yeah, it's all alright," soothed Alice, wrapping her arms around the girl and pulling her into a hug. "You're safe with us, besides I said you could stay with us while you figure out what you want to do, and so stay with us you shall."

Slowly, Rebecca raised her head to look at the couple, her eyes uncertain, as if she was too afraid to believe them. "Really… you don't mind… even after I…"

"Fucked my husband?" Alice shot her husband a sideways look, her tongue sweeping across her lips. "No, I rather enjoyed watching it, if I'm honest." Bending down, she kissed her tears away. "I don't mind sharing him with you, though I'm not sure I'm ready to share you with him yet. Maybe you should convince me…" She kissed her deeply, licking into her mouth, mimicking the same motions she'd used on her pussy until the girl softened and moaned beneath her. "The night is still young, and I think it's time I introduce you to a very special friend of mine." She rolled away, onto the other side of the bed, and opened her bedside table drawer. Seeing what she wanted, she grabbed it and rolled back to face the pair with a grin that was pure wickedness.

In her hand, she grasped a XL magic wand rechargeable vibrator.

"This is Antonio."

Her First Time Daddy

Chapter

ONE

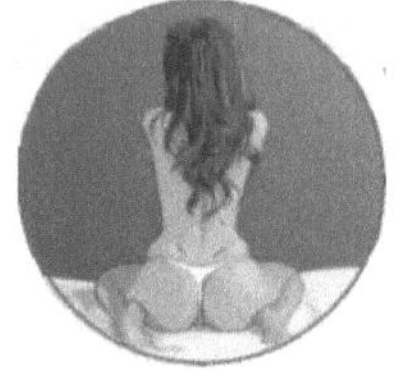

Amanda Burton sighed happily as she pulled her sleek Jaguar XK convertible into her driveway. Nothing beat a drive with the top down after a long day showing potential buyers all around the west country to look at houses. Even the inevitable paperwork that followed was remedied by a sunset drive. Now all she needed was a glass of wine or two, a long soak in a hot tub, and she'd kick off the weekend with a few rounds of much-needed sex with her husband.

The air was heavy with a perfume of wildflowers and far to the west, the sun had slipped behind the rolling green horizon, turning from blue to a deep lavender before the oncoming wall of night. Killing the engine, she stepped out of the vehicle. Not bothering to put the XK's roof back up or collect her briefcase from the boot, she walked up the path to her home whilst fishing in her pocket for her keys.

The door slid inwards as she brought her key up to the lock.

Strange. Stepping back, Amanda looked up. All the lights were off. A quick glance around confirmed hers was the only car in the drive. She shrugged it off. *The girls must have forgotten to lock up on their way out.* It certainly wouldn't be the first time her daughter, Camila, or one of her friends had left the door ajar. Amanda was just glad they'd moved down to Ashcott when they did. God only knows what might have happened if they still lived at the old house in Hereford.

Say what you want about remote villages in the middle of nowhere. They certainly had a much lower crime rate than cities and towns. And the commute had its perks. Shutting the door firmly and securely behind her, Amanda shrugged off her jacket.

She froze, ears pricked and searching. She could hear something, faint and indistinct, like a voice lost in the wind.

Her curiosity piqued, Amanda looked around, trying to figure out its origin, half expecting to find Camila on the phone to one of her friends. *Upstairs. It's coming from upstairs.*

Stealthily as a jackrabbit, Amanda ascended the wooden stairs and made her way along the landing, the sound growing louder with every step. She stopped outside her daughter's room. Grabbing the handle to open the door, she suddenly had an idea and instead sunk to her knees before placing one hand against the side of the door. She brushed a stray lock of her dishevelled hair away from her ear.

Not so very long ago, Amanda would probably have just barged right in all guns blazing, but recently Camila had been growing increasingly secretive and prickly where her room and personal space were concerned. She wouldn't take kindly to someone, specifically her mother, bursting in unannounced. Amanda had a very good idea what was going on.

Barely a month ago, Camila had found herself her first real boyfriend.

She listened intently, her ear pressed against the wood, for any sound coming from within the room that might explain her daughter's absence. From her own experiences as a hormone-driven teenager, she fully expected to hear the hurried whispers and scattered moans that always indicated a passionate nookie session. However, she couldn't hear much of anything except for a very faint sobbing.

Finally, curiosity and parental concern got the better of her. Lightly pressing her palm against the wood, she silently forced the door open a crack.

Camila's room was one of the smallest in the house and was lightly lit by the low glow of her bedside lamp, casting it in a comfortable light that revealed its surprisingly neat and tidy furnishings. Taking a second to let her eyes adapt to the low light, Amanda immediately looked to the large queen-size that was situated at the back of the rectangular room. She was surprised to find not her daughter, but Camila's friend, Tracey, curled in a weeping ball.

Amanda threw open the door and hurried across the room to the sobbing girl and pulled her close. Without hesitation or a word of protest, the girl accepted the hug and cried into her blouse.

"Tracey… What's wrong, honey?" she asked gently, running her hand through her waves of golden hair, trying to soothe the distressed eighteen-year-old.

Tracey Fox never cried. In all the years Amanda had known her, she'd watched her grow and flourish. For as long as she had been Camila's BFF, she had never cried. Even as a girl, despite her wide eyes and deceptive, doll-like innocence, she had looked at life with the tenacity of a bulldog. What could have happened to turn her into such a wreck? And where was-

"C-Camila…" Amidst the sobs, the girl's voice sounded choked and almost inaudible, but Amanda heard the name all the same. It was like a cold wash down her spine. She didn't push her, however, but continued trying to soothe her with soft words.

When her sobs finally began to subside, Tracey looked up at her with a stranger's face and a look in her eye that made the older woman want to cry out in horror. Gone was the rosycheeked, bright-eyed girl. Now, she was only a shadow, a ghost of her former self, pale with puffy eyes that still freely leaked tears. Amanda felt her throat tighten and a pain stab her chest. Without thinking, she put both arms around the girl and held her close.

"W-we were watching T.V. Jeremy …" Tracey seemed to be on the verge of fresh tears at the mention of Camila's boyfriend and Amanda felt a sudden surge of wrath towards the boy who now dominated so much of her daughter's life. "He came round. He'd been drinking and…"

"Go on, honey, don't worry, you can tell me. What happened?"

"He pulled Camila into his lap and started making remarks about us here all alone. She didn't say anything. Then he said something, suggested we play together. I thought he was out of his mind, but she only laughed and said, said it could be fun."

"She did what!"

"I said no, but Jeremy, he wouldn't listen. He started grabbing his… himself through his jeans, stroking it so we could see… Camila. She was tugging on my arm, trying to get me to come closer. I-I told them I wasn't interested, so they both got angry. They ca-called me a prude and started joking about how I was still a virgin. Finally, Jeremy… called me a frigid…cock teasing bitch!"

"No!"

Tracey nodded, tears flowing freely once again. "He said I wasn't worth the effort of getting hard for, then said they were leaving and Camila…she… she…."

"Shh- shh, it's okay sweetheart, it's okay." The dam was well and truly broken now, so Amanda did what she could to soothe the girl once more through the babble of unintelligible sobs. Amanda couldn't believe what she was hearing. Of course, she'd known that both Camila and Tracey, despite both being beautiful, curvy young women, had had trouble with boys growing up.

Neither she nor Mark liked Jeremy very much. There was an arrogance behind his movie-star good looks and smouldering eyes and a swagger that just didn't sit right with Amanda.

Her husband, however, had a much more eloquent way of putting it. *The boy's a cock.*

A threesome, really! How could he even suggest such a thing in her bloody house? To think her own daughter could turn on her friend for that little shit, of all people. Amanda made a note to personally cut his cock off and feed it to him if he ever came near Camila again.

"What's wrong with me?" The question came out of the blue and at first Amanda wasn't sure Tracey had said anything.

"It's okay honey, it's okay. There's nothing wrong-"

"Then why?" she snapped, her body rigid. "It's just sex. Everyone does it! So why, why did the thought of him touching me-"

"You're not ready, that's all it is."

"But I am ready. I want to. But I just…can't." The word came out as a sigh and all the aggression and tension in her body seemed to leave her with her confession.

"Trust me, when you meet the right one, and you're both ready, you will. And it'll be worth the wait."

Slowly, Tracey looked up to meet Amanda's gaze. "Was that the way it was for you?"

"Yes."

"Was it Mr Burton?"

"Yes." Amanda couldn't help but smile, remembering how it had felt to be young and caught up in the spell of first love. And then, noticing the way Tracey appeared to be hanging on her every word, she had an idea. "Is there someone?"

"Well… yes- no, no, I shouldn't be telling you- I- I have to go!" Cheeks tinged pink with embarrassment, Tracey wheeled, but Amanda seized her arm before she could make it off the bed.

"Hey! Wait a second. Come on, you can tell me..."

"No, it's embarrassing."

"Is he good-looking?"

"Yes."

"Is he a boy at Strode?"

"No."

"Oh...Do I know him? Does he live nearby?"

"Y-yes."

"Close?"

"Very." Tracey was looking at the floor and seemed to be studying the plain, simple carpet with all the scrutiny of a master architect as her cheeks burned crimson and she twisted the bedspread with white knuckles.

Was she afraid? What did Tracey have to be afraid of? She'd gushed over boys with her before. One of the perks of being a *cool* parent was that your daughter's friends came to you for advice. Tracey had been Camila's best friend since they started secondary school, so she already knew the types of boys she was attracted to-

Then the penny dropped. "Ah. I see."

Tracey stiffened, and she had to force herself to meet Amanda's eyes. She looked like a deer caught in the headlights. "I'm so sorry, I never meant-"

"It's fine sweetie. I understand." She had caught Tracey sneaking peeks before, but she had always dismissed it. With his tall, broad build, thick waves of sandy blonde hair, cobalt eyes, and a biostructure that would make a stone mason weep with envy, it came as no surprise to Amanda that her husband caught considerable amounts of attention from the women around him. Why should this hormone-wracked teen be any different? He was a very good-looking man. What redblooded woman wouldn't enjoy the odd bit of voyeur pleasure? It was half the reason Amanda, though not prone to jealousy, enjoyed taking every opportunity to flaunt herself on his arm whenever they went out. *Marking her territory*, as he would put it. She forced a reassuring smile. "And you don't have to worry about a thing…"

"What do you mean?"

Amanda put a comforting hand on her shoulder. "Tell me honey, have you ever heard of *The Lifestyle*?"

"Y-you mean swinging?"

She nodded an affirmative. "That's one word for it, yes."

Tracey nervously licked her lips, the pink of her tongue darting out across her soft peach-coloured mouth as she tried to find the words. "So…you're? I mean, you and Mr Burton are…have?"

"Swung?" Amanda offered, bringing an adorable tinge of pink to the girl's otherwise flawless, milky, pale skin. "Yes, well, we've never been, what you'd call practising, but some old friends of ours in Hereford were. They've always been very open about it, but were careful to make sure it never became an issue. They understood not everyone agreed with their lifestyle choice. Well, over drinks one night we got to talking. A little too much wine, the odd touch here, a flirtatious remark there. One thing just sort of lead to another. It never became a regular thing, but we'd go around now and again. They introduced us to other practising couples they thought would be a good fit for us. Some worked. Others, not so much. These days, though, we only really partake in the occasional long weekend *retreats*."

"But what about Camila?" Tracey cut in. "She's okay with you two doing this? I can't believe it. I'm her best friend and she never said anything about you two being into any of this to me."

"Because she doesn't know. No one around here does. It's none of their business."

"But you want me to-"

"Sweetie, I don't want you to do anything. I understand this is a lot to take in and if talking about it makes you uncomfortable, then forget it. We're not talking about joining a cult. You don't have to do anything you don't want to, and if you want to stop, you only have to say. It won't make any difference to how we feel about you."

"But if I-" Tracey cut in, her voice panicked as if she was suddenly afraid the offer might be withdrawn at any minute. "I am. If I'm okay with… with everything, you'd be willing to, to let me, to let me and Mr Burton…"

"Why not? It's nothing we haven't done before." Amanda gave the girl's shoulder a reassuring squeeze and leaned down to press a soft kiss to her lips. "And besides, a girl's first time should be special, with someone who knows what he's doing. And Mark is very, very *good*."

"But what if he doesn't? He might not want to-"

"What if he doesn't want to be your first, or doesn't want to fuck the brains out of a hot little eighteen-year-old?" Her full rosy lips arched into an unmistakably feline smirk. "Leave that to me."

Chapter TWO

"You want me to do what!" Mark thundered, all but spraying his tea across the living room wall.

"Now don't overreact. All I said was I want you to go upstairs and have sex with our daughter's best friend," Amanda countered, remaining perfectly calm and collected even as tingles raced down to the pit of her stomach.

"Overreact?" Lost for words and battling to keep calm, Mark took off his glasses and began to clean the lenses with the hem of his shirt, fruitlessly rubbing at an invisible smudge. "Okay, let me see if I've got this straight. You come home from work to find Tracey crying upstairs after having some sort of fight with Cam about her still being a virgin, and you come away from that thinking that the best thing we can do to help is me fucking her?" Sliding his glasses back onto the bridge of his nose, he shot his wife a scrutinising stare. "Did I miss anything?" His question dripped sarcasm.

Amanda frowned. "I'm serious, Mark."

"You are, aren't you?" Mark groaned, slumping all the way back into his chair and rubbing the bridge of his nose. "Fuck me."

"Later dear. And please, watch your language," Amanda countered, sitting down beside him on the leather sofa. A half amused, half reassuring smile tugging at the corner of her mouth.

He sighed and put a hand on her thigh, giving her a reassuring squeeze through the fabric of her pencil skirt. "Hun, you know I would do anything for Tracey. She's practically one of the family. I just think taking her virginity is asking a little much." That was putting it mildly. The whole idea was crazy, yet he'd seen that look in her eyes before and knew she was convinced and set on this path. A blunt approach wouldn't work here. For now, he needed to be diplomatic to make her see sense.

As if she could read his thoughts, however, Amanda slid down off the sofa.

"Amanda?" he warned, his eyes drinking in the sight of her crawling provocatively between his legs and a delicate hand reaching out to tug on the fly of his trousers. "Stop. Are you crazy? Tracey's just up- oh!"

Looking up at him, Amanda smiled and pulled his awakening cock from his trousers. "Oh, I don't remember that bothering you at the Christmas party last year." Then, holding his legs open with her elbows, she teased his tip with flicks of her tongue, before licking long trails down his shaft, moving from the tip to the base and vice versa.

"Tha-that's because you-you-oh fuck." The protest died in a long moan as lush lips enveloped him, sucking him into the damp cavity of her mouth, her tongue pressing against his velvet flesh and teeth scraping over the glands.

"Now back to the subject of Tracey," Amanda pronounced around him, the vibrations of each syllable shivering down his shaft, making his fingers bite a whiteknuckled grip into the leather. It was a sudden rush of pleasure to his system and all Mark could do to vocalize his pleasure was to release a series of long, low grunts and moans.

He fought his immediate desires however and managed to gasp, "Let's not, not now."

"Okay dear, let's not *talk*," and Amanda promptly pulled back from his rigid arousal and wiped the corner of her mouth. "Not now…"

It never ceased to amaze Amanda how Mark, whose mind had been clouded by lust mere seconds ago, could become so alert so suddenly- a point that was very well proven by the way he so quickly lifted himself up to look at her as he exclaimed "No! No…it's alright dear. We can talk…we can talk about anything you want to. "

Men, so easy. All a girl needs to know is which button to press.

"So…are you ready to hear me out?" she asked, before mouthing his crown, sweeping her tongue around and around, resuming her oral assault full force. Mark tried to respond, but all that came out was another long moan. Instead, he just nodded vigorously.

Inwardly grinning like a Cheshire cat that just caught a big fat canary, Amanda closed one hand around his shaft and began softly jacking him, just to make sure she had his complete attention. "Dear, do you recall how difficult it was for me to feel comfortable with you, you know… *intimately,* when we started dating?"

With Mark's nod, Amanda pressed on.

"Well, Tracey is in that same place, now more than ever. She's confused and scared and feels like everyone around her is pressuring her to take that next step. She needs someone she feels comfortable around, who knows what's he's doing, to take her by the hand and show her how wonderful sex can be."

It was a dual assault. Her attentions igniting a fire in his veins. Her words conjuring up visions of Tracey spread out beneath him, her supple body full and bountiful, writhing and arching in sweet ecstasy. Excited to the point of delirium, he could only shake his head and splutter a protest.
"No…ah…what about- oh God… Ca-Camila?"

Amanda's fingers flexed, tightening almost to the point of pain. "What about her?"

"Tracey's her best friend, I…can't…it's wrong!" he managed to muster between moans, his wife's hand steadily picking up speed, pumping him, driving him insane. Mark knew that if he didn't hold on, the pleasure his wife was creating would push him over the edge.

"It's none of her business. Cam and that asshole started all this by proposing that they have some sort of twisted threesome." She was making progress and now all she needed to do was give him that final push. "Besides, this is nothing we haven't done before."

Mark seized a fist full of her hair, tugging and twisting, but when he spoke, his voice was perfectly calm. "I thought we agreed never to talk about that."

"I know, but I miss it, baby. I miss watching you fuck. Watching you use and take what you want and turn those women into babbling sex-crazed wantons. It gets me so… hot." She consumed as much as she could, sliding her mouth down his shaft in a tight seal, taking half of him in one go, then hollowing her cheeks as she pulled back. "Don't you want to feel those soft lips…wrapped around your hard cock…" Wet slurps punctured each of her impassioned expletives as she repeated the long pull, her head bobbing faster and faster. The imagery she was conjuring made her clit throb and liquid heat pooled in her belly. "Feel her tight little pussy quivering, clenching…as you watch our daughter's best friend's big tits bouncing as she rides your dick-"

"I'll do it…" He had her on her back before she knew it. He used his grip on her hair to pull her off him and to her feet before launching her across the sofa. She bounced with the first contact, but then he was on her, devouring the lips that only moments before had been wrapped around his cock. "Later."

With one hand cupping her bottom, the other was kneading her breast through her shirt. He began the delicate and most practised art of toying with her body, working her into a frenzy that had weak whimpers flowing from her very soul. The urge to surrender to his hunger was as intoxicating as honey wine, sweet and so delicious. It took all the power she possessed to wake herself from the pleasurable haze and to gather her wits.

Amanda quickly did the only thing she could think of.

She reached down and fisted the *root* of his desire.

"Bad Boy."

This was crazy.

Mark hesitated on the landing, just outside Camila's door, the weight of what he was about to do resting around his neck like the hangman's noose. *What the fuck are you doing?*

He carried on regardless, slowly turning the handle to his errant daughter's room and opening the wooden door. He could do this. Amanda was right. This wasn't the first time they had indulged in The Lifestyle. That point did little to distract him from his nerves, however. Experienced or not, it wasn't every day that one's own wife commissions you to fuck your daughter's best friend, and a virgin, of all things. It was a daunting prospect and one that carried with it all the pressures of the first time you have sex. And even though he knew he should relax, the thought made him feel like a virgin all over again.

He was just trying to quell the feeling when he heard the soft, alluring moans from within, turning his still hard cock to steel in his trousers.

The room was lit only by the dim glow of the bedside lamp, the soft illumination creating a sensual atmosphere. Tracey was stretched out across the queen size, one hand fondling her breasts through her top, slender fingers pinching a hardened nipple. The other was hidden from his view, having slid beneath the waistband of her jeans all the way to the wrist. He could just make out the outline of her knuckles moving beneath the crotch, coaxing those sexy little sounds.

"Please Mr Burton, take me. I want to feel you in me…"

Dark cloudy eyes opened wide as they wandered from the tantalizing dance of her fingers, up over her alluring bosom, to finally settle on her angelic face, shrouded in strands of dirty gold. With her cheeks flushed and eyes half-lidded, she had the look of a siren basking on the rocks, luring ships of desperate sailors to their demise and ruin on the rocks. But what a way to go…

"Mr Burton," Tracey moaned, pinching her clit viciously between her thumb and forefinger, then sliding another one of her long fingers deep within her creamy slit. "Oh God…Mr Burton…You're so big, Oh God…Mr Burton…Oh, Mr Burton…Oh…Ooh…Mr Burton! I'm cumming! I'm cumming! I'm…" The mini-orgasm hit her in waves and Tracey's voice died away, lost on the tide as she climaxed on her hand, tiny ripples washing over her with increasing intensity, then ebbing away just as quickly.

Panting, she brought her fingers up to her lips, each digit shiny with her desire, and began licking them clean.

Tracey couldn't explain it, couldn't understand what had come over her. She had been so nervous.

She couldn't believe it was going to happen and was so afraid it might all turn out to be a dream, that at any moment she might wake up to cold reality. Finally, the one person she had been craving for years was going to be hers. After so long, all her dreams were about to come true and she would lose her v-card, and to Mr Burton, her best friend's father.

The idea was so deliciously forbidden that a tide of heat had washed over her. Her mind had flooded with images of Camila's dad on the beach. The family had taken her and a few of Camila's other friends with them to Weston-SuperMare in the summer holidays. His large muscular body stripped bare and swimming shorts that teased the outline of his hard cock whenever they were wet.

Before really registering what she was doing, her hand had undone the fastenings of her jeans. Her thumb lightly brushed against her clit and a low moan slipped past her lips as warmth spread through her. She began playing with her clit, rolling it between her fingers before moaning louder as she tentatively slipped a finger inside her entrance. Lost in the moment, her world melted away like chocolate, and Tracey gave herself over to the pleasure.

There was a creaking sound and Tracey's eyes immediately snapped into focus to discover Mark standing in the doorway, leaning leisurely against the timber frame, arms crossed, watching her with the eyes of a hungry wolf.

"Mr Burton!" she exclaimed. Embarrassed, she tried to cover herself with the quilt.

Mark only smirked, staying silent except for the rustling of his clothes as he closed the door behind him before walking across the room and sitting down beside her on the bed. Tracey couldn't move or speak as she watched him with a held breath that made her head spin; something had changed in Mr Burton. And she liked it.

It turned her on to think she could evoke such a change in this Adonis, and without even giving it much thought, she lunged at him. Pressing her soft lips to his in a rough kiss, her tongue licked across his lips, begging for admittance. His strong arms wrapped around her trim waist, lowering her onto the bed's soft embrace. When he opened, their tongues met in a fierce battle for dominance that made her toes curl and skin tingle.

The heated duelling of their tongues went on until their need for oxygen grew too great. Her thoughts foggy and panting hard, Tracey couldn't help flashing a toothy smile as she drank in Mark's equally dishevelled and aroused condition. Skin flushed and hair dishevelled. He had never looked so yummy.

Taking her devious little smile as a challenge, Mark flashed her that same grin, then seized her wrists and pinned her hands above her head. He straddled her hips, careful not to put too much weight on her, before leaning down and covering her soft lips with his own. However, instead of the passion and ferocity like the last, this kiss was soft and tender, and he gently nibbled her top lip before tending to her lower with a soft suck that made her arch beneath him.

Never once did he make any move to deepen the kiss. Instead, he stocked her ardour with a gentle intimacy that was left to burn in the fires of her arousal.

"Oh! Oh please… Mr Burton!" Tracey tried to break free, needing more than this, desperate to at long last, fulfil all her wild fantasies. Though gentle, his hold was as firm as iron fetters around her wrists. She lacked the strength to overpower this man, so there she remained, firmly locked in his strong embrace while his lips teased her, sending her spiralling into hot, needy delirium.

Only when he had judged her thoroughly worked up did Mr Burton reclaim her mouth, his large hands brushing down her arms and spine to curl around her waist, crushing her against his hard warmth.

Whimpering under his savage intensity, Tracey clung to her friend's father as though her life depended on it, her fingers losing themselves in the softness of his hair as his tongue delved deep within her mouth. She could feel his hands running over her body, his every touch searing through her clothes, heat pooling in her centre. She sighed in delight when he cupped her buttocks and gave it a firm squeeze.

Needing more, she slid her leg up to his thigh and over his hip, opening herself up to him and giving her better leverage. However, she couldn't contain herself when the immensity of his arousal pushed against her covered womanhood. She broke away to loosen a long sweet gasp, her eyes nearly rolling, her head thrown back. It was too much, too good.

"Mmm-Mr Burton!"

Delighting in her responsiveness, Mark trailed openmouthed kisses along her jaw and down the slope of her neck to her collarbone, occasionally stopping to nip the sensitive skin and then soothe it with his tongue. All the while, he gently stroked her abdomen, his fingers creeping up under her top, exploring the soft bounty beneath until he came to her breasts. With the pad of his thumb, he outlined the boundaries of her cleavage, every so often teasing the peak of a pebbled nipple. Smiling as he felt her arch into him, he licked his lips. *Time to kick things up a notch.*

All it took was a moment. A sudden jerk, the shriek of tearing fabric. He tore her top down the middle.

Surprised, Tracey squeaked as she was left bare to his gaze. Mark silenced any further protest with a kiss. There could be no resisting him now.

Pulling back, Mark almost licked his lips. *God... she's just gorgeous.* Tracey's breasts were full and firm but just large enough to fit in the palm of his hand, her flawless milky complexion accentuating her rosy nipples.

Taking his weight on his arm, Mark let his fingers wander over Tracey's curves, his hand closing over her breast, stroking and kneading it with a touch that made the girl gasp for breath every time he brushed her swollen peaks. His cock twitched at her eagerness, reminding him she was not the only one in need of relief. Suddenly very aware of the awkward stiffness amassing at the base of his still-imprisoned cock- which happened to be growing more uncomfortable by the second- he bent down and took a pebbled bud between his lips, fiercely nipping her before soothing the sting with licks and sucks.

Moaning in agonised pleasure, Tracey lifted her hips and started rubbing against the man above her, all her selfdoubt and nervousness forgotten. She didn't care anymore. All she wanted was this beast inside her, to feel him filling her, stretching her so completely she'd be ruined for other men. But still he continued to take his time, sucking first her right breast, then her left, before laying a trail of soft butterfly kisses down to her abdomen as he settled between her legs.

She all but screamed as a mini orgasm crashed over her when one large finger rubbed down the centre seam of her jeans, tracing along her swollen folds. "Please… Mr Burton?"

"Please what, Tracey?" Mark teased, sliding the offending finger up and down the garment's crotch a few times before fingering the fastenings. "What do you want, sweetheart?"

"Do it?"

"Do. What?" He drew out each word with sultry emphasis before undoing the buttons. Catching the zipper between his teeth, he dragged it down, opening her up to his gaze.

"Stick your cock in me!" Tracey all but screamed it, hot, embarrassed, needy tears burning the corners of her eyes. But she didn't care. She needed this. Had needed it for so long. She didn't want to wait anymore. She wanted him. "Fuck me!"

"Good girl." Mark removed her jeans and panties with a practised ease, tugging them both down and off her long willowy legs before casting them aside. Then he was once more hovering over her. Tracey had never felt so small and vulnerable, compounded by her own nakedness while he was still fully clothed. As much as she needed to feel him inside her, she wanted to ogle and worship his flesh, to see him in all his virile male glory-

Stars burst before her eyes as two fingers slipped inside her. Her whole body seemed to ripple around the very new and unexpected presence inside her. The teen's hips lifted from the bed to press his fingers deeper inside her hot channel. She moaned wantonly when they curled, rubbing a spot that made her thrash in ecstasy. But then his thumb began lavishing attention upon her clit, flicking and circling the way his tongue had teased her nipple, and it all quickly became too much. He seemed to know exactly where to touch her, what she wanted before she did, and the tightness, the knot in her centre, warned she would spill over the brink at any moment.

Only she didn't. Just when she was on the edge, an orgasm surging up to swallow her, he pulled his hand back.

"No!" Eyes widening, her whole body arched to follow him, and she threw a pleading hand out to try and drag him back between her legs, but it did no good. Grinning like the devil, Mr Burton brought his fingers up to her eyes, coated with juices, her juices, before licking them clean. *He's…tasting me.* The idea was as erotic as the show of his tongue slithering out to lap at each of his fingers in turn, and she suddenly longed to take those fingers into her mouth and suck them clean herself.

With her thoughts foggy and so close to release, she made no move to resist as the warmth of his breath washed across her abdomen, tickling her sex, before his tongue parted her folds and slid into her core, sending tendrils of pleasure through every nerve in Tracey's body.

"Mr Burton…Ah…Ah!" Tracey gasped, seizing fistfuls of his ebony mane, her hips rolling into his mouth when his teeth gently scraped her clit. "Oh God…urmph…" She could feel his tongue swirling around inside her, stroking and lashing her velvety inner walls as her nectar flowed into his open mouth. Yet it was the way he was staring up at her from between her legs, his eyes dark and burning, that she found the most carnal, pushing her closer and closer to her desired peak. And when he suddenly switched tact to suckling her small bundle of nerves with a low rumbling, something finally broke. "Uh-uh-uh-uh-oh…God! Ah-Ah-Ah…Cumming! I'm cumming!"

Then her vision turned white and melted away.

Chapter

FOUR

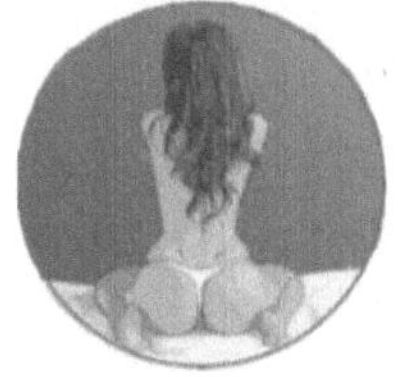

"Mmm… that was fantastic, sweetheart. You were amazing."

The words dragged her from a post-orgasm haze more effectively than a bucket of ice water. Blinking through the fog, Tracey awoke to find Amanda Burton standing over her. Her hair was down, a fall of soft and silky raven curls that tumbled more than halfway down her back. She'd changed out of her work clothes into a little silk robe that was tied at the waist and stopped much higher than her knees. It did nothing to hide her matching black stockings.

"Mrs Burton? What are you-"

"Shhh…" Amanda put a silencing finger to the girl's lips. "Just relax, the best is still to come."

Tracey obeyed and didn't utter a word, only gave a nervous nod, her heart fluttering at the prospect of what she had in store for her.

Amanda's smile broadened. "Good girl." Then she turned from her to face the base of the bed where her husband stood, shirtless, in all his male glory. Stepping in close, so he towered over her, she brought the hand that had silenced their newest toy up to brush a feather softly along one bicep. She gave him a long look over, from toe to head, and then back down to linger on a point of immense interest. "Was it good for you too?"

Catching her hand in his, he brought it up to his mouth and kissed each of her fingers. "I was just having a little fun, love."

The kiss came hard and fast. His lips claiming her mouth with a singular passion, drawing her in deep, while his free arm hooked around her waist and spun her so that as he sat down on the edge of the bed, she landed in his lap.

She knew she shouldn't, that this night was for Tracey, but when her husband's tongue found her own, Amanda couldn't resist kissing back, wanting to absorb the sweetest sensations that only he could stir inside her with just the faintest touch. Drawing her in close, Mark hooked a finger through her robe, tugging the belt loose before slipping a hand through the folds to cup one of her breasts.

She gasped when he twisted her nipple, just hard enough for her to relish the cocktail of pleasure and pain, and then pushed him away. "No!"

He arched a brow. "Tease."

Breathing hard, Amanda had to resist the urge to kiss that cocky grin from his ridiculously handsome face. "Later, dear… this is for Tracey, remember."

At the mention of her name, Tracey could only nod her agreement, her eyes wide and mouth dry. She had seen other people kiss before, of course, but there had been something so raw and primitive between the Burtons. It was hot. She wanted more and watched on, unabashed, as Mrs Burton got to her feet and let her robe fall to the floor.

The sight of the older woman's naked bounty brought a tinge of pink to the girl's cheeks as she struggled to decide where to look. She also couldn't help feeling somewhat inadequate by comparison. Amanda's breasts were larger, her body better defined, with a full sexy arse and long smooth legs that gave her a feline grace as she prowled up the bed on all fours. A stalking panther ready to pounce.

"Now let's get your lesson underway," Amanda teased in a breathy, sensual tone that sent tingles down Tracey's spine, before leaning in.

"Mrs Burton…" The kiss took Tracey completely off guard. It wasn't the chaste, almost motherly kiss she had grown accustomed to. No, this was hot and hungry, as the older woman practically devoured her with such demand that it would not be denied. It was such a strange feeling, but very pleasant and a little bit naughty. Tracey had never entertained thoughts about kissing another woman before, not even for experimentation purposes, but if this is what it was always like, she liked it. And with the sexual energy coursing through the room, she voluntarily succumbed to the older woman's wiles.

The kiss ended as quickly as it began, and Tracey's eyes fluttered open to find the Burton's sitting around her. "Okay Tracey, this is how it's going to work," Amanda instructed in a very matter-of-fact tone, as though they were discussing something as every-day as the weather. Taking the teen's hand, she guided her off the bed so that her husband could lie down. "Mark and I are going to walk you through this every step of the way."

Tracey swallowed and nodded, her heart thumping loudly. She couldn't remember ever being so nervous.

"Just stay calm and play it by ear. Everything will come naturally, sweetheart," Amanda whispered soothingly, remembering all too well her own unease during hers and Mark's first night together. The thought brought a glint to her eye, a secret smile tugging at the corner of her lips. "I promise you're gonna love it."

Tracey nodded again, but the words did little to soothe the uneasy tightness in her lower belly, and she suddenly longed for the floor to open beneath her. So, Mrs Burton gave her a gentle push, and the matter was decided.

Half stumbling and half falling, she fell onto the bed to be swept up in Mark's arms and pulled atop a wall of hard male. She could feel his terribly aroused erection straining beneath her naked bottom. It felt enormous, much too big to ever fit inside her. Far from being a turn-off, however, the idea and the feel of the splendid specimen of masculinity beneath quickly rekindled her earlier fires. She wiggled her hips so his bulge nestled its way along her pelvis to the throbbing heat at the apex of her thighs. Swept up in the warmth of her arousal, she dipped her head to kiss her best friend's dad.

Matching her hunger, she felt him demanding entrance to her mouth. Not giving herself a chance to hesitate or second guess, she parted her lips and met his tongue greedily with her own. He tasted different, his masculine flavour spiced ever so slightly by a subtle heady essence. Her essence, she realised excitedly. She could taste herself. Excited by this discovery, she sucked his tongue greedily, growing almost drunk with ecstasy from their combined flavours, before suddenly pulling back and nipping a fiery trail down the exposed flesh of his neck.

Mark shuddered when she found the sensitive spot that joined his neck and shoulder and lashed it with her tongue, remembering how he had worked her body to that feverish pitch and knowing she was getting payback. It took every bit of willpower he possessed to keep his hands on the mattress and resist the urge to just throw the little minx to the bed and take her. *Payback's a bitch.*

In control or not, however, he couldn't stop himself from bucking against the tempting wench. Tracey suddenly moaned as his hardened cock rubbed up against her clit through his trousers.

"*Attagirl,*" Amanda purred, coming to stand around beside them, where she could see them both clearly. "Do whatever feels natural. Have fun with him, but remember, this is a marathon, not a race. So just take your time and learn what he likes." And just to prove her point, she took his earlobe between her lips and sucked.

"Oh!" Tracey gasped, her eyes widening at the feeling of Mark's body jumping beneath her and the weight of his cock grinding deliciously into her tender folds. Oh God, how she wanted to feel *that* inside her, stretching her to the point where even the slightest movement would make her see stars, to ride him into the sweet oblivion of *la petite mort*.

Amanda winked and licked her lips. "Understand?"

Nodding frantically, Tracey shifted to place her hands just below his collarbone and slid carefully off his lap to crouch between his legs. Careful to maintain as much skin to skin contact as possible, she laid a trail of licks and kisses down his hardened chest. A lifelong sportsman with a particular fondness for rugby, his body was littered with scars and she took special care to delicately lick each and every one before biting down on his flat nipples. As her mouth went lower, her fingers slid lightly down his arms to the waistline of his trousers. After popping open the last button, Tracey threw a hesitant glance at Amanda, who only nodded in encouragement.

"That's it, just take it slow. He's a big boy, but that just gives you more of him to play with." Seizing her hand by the wrist, she forced the girl to take the bull by the single, very large horn.

He was so thick that her fingers wouldn't meet as they closed around his velvet skin, just beneath his ridge. She could feel him pulsing within her grasp when she pressed her thumb on his sensitive tip. The spongy head was already slick and shiny with precum, and her thumb slid easily round and round his slit before, with Mrs Burton's guiding touch, giving him a wary stroke that drew a soft moan from his lips.

"Oh fuck..." he panted, his head momentarily falling back into the pillow and a fine sheen slowly forming across his upper body.

Her confidence growing, Tracey repeated the move, only a little longer this time, going from base to tip. She could feel him throbbing in her palm, his head swelling with each stroke, silently pleading for her. His thick, musky scent made her mouth water. Turning her eyes up to meet his once more, she leaned in and took him into her mouth, her lips sliding over his crest.

"Easy, not so fast," Mrs Barton warned, putting a restraining hand on her shoulder. But it did no good.

It was a delicious sensation, holding the head of his cock with her lips. Mark's flavour spilt over her tastebuds like thick syrup, fogging her brain. Remembering some of the more *interesting* clips she had found online that Cam had lent her, she slid both of her hands down to his taut, muscular thighs and began slowly bobbing her head. However, despite her enthusiasm, she quickly realised that she couldn't support his enormous cock without the aid of her hands. Moving one from his knee, she placed it at the base of his length and tried to take more of him, but her jaw began to ache before she got even half of him in.

And despite herself, she started to worry she wasn't doing it right. In the movies, there was never any doubt that the guy getting blown loved it, but while it was obvious from his light grunts and moans that Mr Burton was enjoying her attempts at a blow job, he just didn't seem to be enjoying it enough. She forced herself to try and take him all in.

"Tracey, no!"

A cough hit her like a tidal wave the moment the blunt tip smacked into the back of her throat. Then she couldn't breathe. It was too much, too big. Hot tears burned her eyes as her throat constricted, closing her airways so completely that panic ran like ice through her veins. The sensation was so overwhelming that she almost leapt off the bed, coughing violently, wheezing to catch her breath.

Amanda was already beside her, a hand rubbing circles over her back to calm her while she whispered soothing words. Like Tracey was a horse on the verge of bolting. "It's okay, sweetheart. That was just a bit too fast. It's okay…okay." But it wasn't okay, not in the least.

Swallowing back tears of shame and embarrassment, Tracey forced herself to speak. "Mrs Burton… I think… I think I need a little help?"

Amanda needed no explanation. In truth, she had been pleasantly surprised at how quickly Tracey had gone on her own. She had the general idea. Experience would fill in the blanks. All she needed was guidance and a bit of *refining*.

"Okay, now, watch closely," she instructed, shifting to kneel between her husband's legs. "You have the right idea, but there's no need to rush. Men like to be teased and worked up. The longer you keep him going, the stronger his orgasm will be." Demonstrating her point, Amanda bent down and began lightly kissing and licking his tip until Mark felt as if he was going to burst.

"Amanda…oh God…so good!" he gasped, his head rolling back in sheer pleasure as he felt her tongue dance across his velvety head before wrapping him in its warmth as ever so slowly, she began taking his cock into her mouth. There, Mark found he was incapable of words and his eyes visibly rolled back into his skull. The feeling of her tongue wrapped around him, massaging him into a delirium too great for him to stand. Struggling against the pleasure, he managed to moan, "Amanda… more…more" before losing himself again as he felt his dick hit the back of her mouth.

Smiling inwardly at his desperate plea, Amanda slowly pulled away and flashed a sultry smile at Tracey. "Care to join me?"

Nodding, not trusting herself to speak, Tracey moved in beside the older woman. Together, they eyed his erect cock with obvious desire and began licking and sucking his member together. Mark, shocked by the sudden feeling of two mouths sliding over his sensitised flesh, was unsure of what to do with his hands. Grabbing fresh fistfuls of the bedsheets, he had to fight the urge to watch them as strands of curly gold and silky raven hair tickled his stomach and inner thighs.

Together, they feasted on him.

Tracey eagerly followed the older woman's example, licking his shaft from the base to just below his tip, while Amanda busied herself with his balls, gently sucking one into her mouth. Slathering it with her tongue, she then released it, moving on to the other. She repeated this again and again until Tracey switched to kissing his tip, slowly taking him back into her mouth. His cock was so sensitive from being repeatedly brought to the brink that Mark could feel even the slightest attention to his arousal. The feeling of teeth lightly scraping over his crown was almost more than he could stand. He so badly wanted to look at them, to watch Tracey's head bob up and down, his stiff member disappearing and reappearing through her luscious pink lips while his wife all but swallowed his testicles. Instead, his eyes were shut tight and his head was pressed back into the pillow.

He couldn't remember it ever being this good.

Swinging had never been his thing. When some of Amanda's friends had told her about *the lifestyle*, she had been enthralled with the idea. Mark had just assumed it was because all her friends were doing it, but he hadn't jumped at the thought of sleeping around. Amanda had known this almost as soon as she'd suggested it, but he had gone along with it just to make her happy. Much to his relief, his wife seemed far more interested in watching him shagging other women than welcoming other men between her legs. He never denied that he didn't mind being watched, but the sex had been lacking all the same. It had always felt more mechanical than passionate and he'd never really been into it, just going through the motions. It had been nothing like this.

"Oh fuck! Mmm -yeah just like- oh shit, I'm going to cum!" he cried, his tone guttural, as the pleasure grew so intense he was pushed over the brink.

Tracey heard the desperation in his tone. She knew what was about to happen and it filled her with such a feeling of pride and conquest to know that she had done this to him. She wasn't ready to swallow, though. That was a step too far out of her comfort zone.

"Don't you dare," Amanda hissed, a wild glint flashing in her eyes as she seized a fistful of the girl's hair, forcing her down and his cock to slide all the way into her mouth. "Come on, swallow every drop."

Eyes widening in panic, Tracey tried to resist, but it was already too late. She swallowed instinctively as the first shot of Mr Burton's cum hit the back of her throat, filling her mouth with his thick, salty cream. Oblivious in his release, Mark's hips rolled as he rode his climax.

"That's it baby, isn't she such a good little cocksucker?" Amanda urged her husband on, the throbbing in her clit growing stronger as she felt the resistance ebb out of Tracey. "Yeah, give her all your cum."

"So…so good," Mark panted, dark spots dancing before his eyes. Fuck, he hadn't cum that hard in years.

Chapter FIVE

Totally into it, Tracey licked Mark's cock clean with ravenous hunger, like she was licking melting ice cream on a hot summer day. It wasn't a particularly sweet or pleasant flavour, but there was something about its saltiness that grew on her as she drank every drop he had to give.

"Good girl," Amanda praised, letting the girl up while assessing her husband. Reeling from the force of his delayed release, Mark lay breathless on the bed, but he was still half hard and ready to go again. Capable, she decided, but nowhere near ready for what she had in mind.

Amanda turned and kissed Tracey full and hard and with all the raw sexual energy that the night had left sizzling through her core. She tasted as sweet as ever, like strawberries and cream, seasoned with Mark's saltiness. The memory that her mouth had been wrapped around her husband's cock just a moment ago excited her all the more.

Taken by surprise, the girl was motionless at first, then the older woman's tongue found hers and reality caught up. She squeaked in surprise, her body stiffening, but Amanda pulled her in close. She abandoned Tracey's lips in favour of capturing a pink nipple with her tongue. Already madly aroused, Tracey arched and tossed her head back in a cascade of gold, moaning long and low as they tumbled back into the bed's embrace.

"Mmm… Such beautiful tits," Amanda purred, sucking and tonguing the ripe bud. Tracey's fervour grew.

"No-oh! Don't say that, it's embarisi-oh there, right there!"

"Yeah, you like that? Want more?"

"Yes… oh God, oh God!" The whole world seemed to burst with light, heat, and pleasure as Mrs Burton's finger slid into her, curling up to tease her g-spot while the pad of her thumb manipulated her clit. "...Feels so good… please, more, I want more!"

"Don't worry, sweetheart," Amanda cooed, glancing across the bed to Mark. He was transfixed, his cock rapidly returning to full mast. She grinned inwardly. "I'll give you more." And she pulled away.

Tracey felt close, and her eyes snapped open. She immediately made to grab Mrs Burton's retreating hand, desperate to bring those fingers back. She'd fuck herself on them if that was what it took for her to get off. Amanda just batted her hand away and settled herself between the girl's thighs.

"Be patient sweetie, I promise you're going to love this." With a seductive smile, she pulled the girl's right leg over her left, while hooking her own over hers. "And I think you can call me Amanda now."

"Mrs Bur- Amanda, what are you-?" The question died as their pussies kissed.

It was an odd sensation, all friction and heat, but one that elected moans from them both. So she might tease her husband just that little bit longer. Amanda rocked their bodies together, the position just right for their clits to grind together.

"Oh fuck!" Tracey moaned, arching her back and crying out in ecstasy, the pleasure hitting her like the waves of a tempest, crashing over her fast and hard. "Yes…fuck me…fuck me…oh God…yes!"

"Uh… Fuck…. alright sweetheart…" Amanda groaned, delighting in the hot shivers rippling through her, the circles of her hips growing more forceful. "I'll fuck you…uh…now…cum for me…oh!"

Tracey couldn't stand it. It was too intense, too hot. Her body felt like fire, tongues of white flame spreading out from her wet and throbbing cunt. She was so close.

But it wouldn't come. She could practically feel herself dangling on the edge. "I can't!" she whimpered.

"Oh baby, yes you can." Amanda pressed, rising to close the gap between them and attack the hollow of the girl's neck with licks and nips while grinding their clits together. "Let it all out so Mark can see. He's watching. Let my husband see that pretty face of yours as I make you cum. Then he's going to take your precious virginity and make you cum on his big, yummy cock. Go on, cum! Cum! Cum!"

Mr Burton. She knew she shouldn't look, but Tracey couldn't help herself. Mr Burton was watching, and it made her belly flutter. He was wreathed in shadow and light, dark and deliciously dangerous, his eyes burning brightly as he watched her with a predatory hunger, his cock standing tall. He wasn't touching himself and that excited her. *All this for me.*

"Mr Burton, I-I…Oh fuck, fuck! I'm cumming! I'm cumming!"

"Attagir- Oh shit! Yes! Yes, right there, oh! Yes! I'm cumming too!" Amanda followed almost immediately, pushed over the brink and into oblivion.

Relaxing into their simultaneous releases, the two women slipped into a serene afterglow.

Tracey felt like she was floating in a warm bath and just staying awake became a chore as her eyes grew heavy and all the cares of the world seemed to float away. If this was a dream, then she hoped she would never wake up.

Through half-lidded eyes, she watched Amanda slowly rise to her knees on shaky legs and manoeuvre around to sit beside her husband and whisper something in his ear. He nodded, and then she was gone. Mark was looming over her.

He scooped her up as if she weighed nothing and placed her gently down at the head of the bed. She felt the mattress sink under his weight as he crawled up the length of her body.

"There's no going back after this, Tracey." His voice was gruff, but when he cupped her chin, his touch was gentle. "Are you sure this is what you want?"

Even now, he was still concerned for her, but the thought of him stopping had her arms snaking up around his neck. She arched, opening her gates. "Mmm… I've never been so sure." She husked, rolling the heat of her moist arousal along his cock. "Mr Burton, please, *fuck me.*"

He nodded, easing forward. Tracey's head rolled back onto her shoulders, her lips parting and her eyes falling shut as his broad crest slid slowly inside-

A bolt of pain ran up Tracey's spine as she felt the excruciating pop of her virginity.

"It…It…hurts…" she whimpered, fighting back tears and digging her nails into his back so hard that trickles of blood ran down his skin.

"Relax…sweetheart," Mark mouthed into her hair, fisting the sheets against the urge to fuck her as her inner walls bore down on him. He needed to wait, to let her adjust, but fuck, she was tight. "The pain will pass. It's better this way, just like ripping off a plaster. Now you just need to relax."

Tracey could only nod and cling to him, dragging in deep breaths as the pain began to fade. The pain turned into pleasure and Tracey felt herself floating away.

Torn between torturous pleasure and exquisite agony, Mark could only grit his teeth against the desire to cum right then and there. "God, your pussy feels so good."

His words were anaesthesia. Tracey wanted more of him, wanted to feel him move inside of her, pounding her, fucking her to insanity, the heat of his seed filling her to the brim...

She couldn't stand it. Moving her hips, she began to grind against the base of his shaft, making them both moan and draw in a shuddering breath.

The thrill she got from their union was breath-taking. Tracey eagerly tried to take more, but Mark's hands trailed down to cup her bum, his powerful grip holding her still.

"Mr… Mr Burton…please…I want…" she moaned, her body's need for him growing almost frenzied as he rolled his hips. He was being gentle, lightly touching her, teasing. No, this wasn't what she wanted.

"What do you want, sweetheart? Go on, tell me…"

"Fuck me," she growled, legs crossing over his buttocks. "Now!"

He smiled, then thrust down as she moved to meet him, forcing her to take another two inches of him.

"Mr…Burton…" Tracey gasped, all defiance melting away as he withdrew almost completely from her depths. She felt infected with an empty feeling as he pulled back before finally thrusting home. "Oh…oh God! I'm gonna burst! Yes, Yes! Don't stop, don't ever stop... I want more. Make me scream!"

"Don't worry sweetheart, you're about to get the fuck of your life." Her pussy was slick and tight, her inner muscles clenching around him. He pulled away before returning fast and hard, slamming into her, every inch of him filling her.

"Oh, fuck…Fuck me, fuck me!"

"Yeah? You like that, Tracey?" he teased, thrusting into her harder, faster. "You like getting fucked by your best friend's dad?"

"Yes…Yes… your cock feels so good, like it's splitting me in half!" she moaned, every thrust hitting deeper than the last. "Oh my God! Don't stop! Don't Stop…"

Mark complied. Holding nothing back, he ravaged her sweet young body with wild abandon, working his cock inside her tight folds with urgency. She was beautiful, her naked body dancing to his rhythm.

A high-pitched cry escaped her lips as Mark thrust deep, grazing her g-spot. She cried out in a frenzied passion, her nails raking his skin. Tracey was losing control.

Mark could feel both of their releases drawing close and was trying his best to keep his under control. Tracey needed to cum first. He reached down to where their bodies were joined and began playing with her sensitive clit, rubbing it gently with the pad of his thumb.

The tidal wave of her orgasm crashed over her with colossal force, sending her senses into overdrive. She convulsed and contracted around his throbbing cock, her cream coating his stiff shaft as he pounded her straight through one orgasm and into a second. He let out a low grunt of pleasure as he erupted inside her.

They stayed like that for a few minutes, basking in the afterglow of their respective orgasms, before he wrapped his arms around her and drew her close as he rolled onto his back.

Amanda sat down beside them on the bed. "Havin' fun?"

Tracey giggled girlishly while Mark shot his wife a half-smile. "You could say that."

"Good." Amanda matched his smile, then bent to whisper in Tracey's ear. "Now that you're a woman, sweetheart, how about celebrating with your first threesome?"

"Really?" Surprised, Tracey weakly tried to sit up, but her jelly arms wobbled so dangerously, she could only manage a slight tilt of her chin. "But I don't…I mean…what…"

"Just move over sweetie, there's nothing to it," Amanda assured before climbing over the pair and sitting against the headboard. She opened her legs, revealing her glistening folds and, with a kinky smile playing across her lips, beckoned the girl closer with her finger.

Mark could only watch dry-mouthed as Tracey climbed off him and crawled between his wife's thighs. Amanda then motioned for him to join them. Smiling to himself, he rose and slid into place behind Tracey.

Placing her head next to Amanda's slick sex, Tracey buried her face into Amanda's heat, remembering how Mark had devoured her own.

"Yeah… Oh God Tracey… Oh… yeah… just like that…." Amanda moaned, rolling her hips and grinding her pussy into the girl's face. At the same time, Mark grabbed Tracey's waist and lined himself up to enter her. Looking up, the couple's eyes met, and he gave her a wicked smirk before he teasingly slid the tip of his cock up her still tingling and oversensitive pussy, to her ass.

"Mmm…decisions, decisions…" he pondered.

Smiling back, Amanda reached forward with both hands. She grabbed and spread Tracey's cheeks, opening the girl up to her lover. "Here dear, fuck her virgin ass."

Tracey looked up, her eyes glazed with uncertainty. "But Mrs Bur- Amanda, doesn't it…? Isn't that supposed to hurt?" she asked.

"Don't worry, honey," Amanda said, smiling down at her. "Mark's very good at anal. It'll sting at first, but I'm going to make sure you enjoy every second." She twisted them around and positioned herself underneath her.

Smirking as he watched his wife devour their lover, Mark moved back into position behind them. Holding Tracey's hips still, he pressed the tip of his cock into her rear entrance.

"Whatever you do Tracey, don't tense." He warned before moving forward, pressing home. The admittance to her rear made Tracey's whole-body arch in simultaneous pain and ecstasy as Amanda greedily tongued her clit.

Allowing her a few moments to get accustomed to the sensation, Mark began to slowly work his length back and forth, sliding that little bit deeper inside her as he did. "Shit… so tight, so… tight…"

Unfortunately, this was a new sensation that even Amanda's incredible oral skills couldn't disguise. Tracey was forced to squeeze her eyes shut as sharp stabs of pain ripped through her petite body. However, long fingers quickly replaced that pain with pleasure as they began squeezing the nub of her clit, testing it like a ripe grape while she tongued her folds. Tracey reciprocated.

"Oh, Mr Burton…" Tracey moaned, her head starting to spin. "Please… it feels… good… so good. More… I want more. Please!" Then she buried her face between Amanda's thighs, locking her lips around her clit, sucking wantonly.

"I knew she'd love taking it up her butt- oh! Yes, suck it, sweetheart, that's it, mmm," Amanda managed between moans. "Give it to her baby, fuck her, fill her tiny ass with your big dick!"

Hearing the pair's demands, Mark began to vigorously fuck the teen, slamming his flesh into her, filling her little butt with his cock with every thrust. Tracey moaned with delight as his hard cock filled her arse over and over, making her small body rock and sway to his undeniable rhythm.

The room was quickly filled with the trio's moans, their cries of pleasure working to drive each other to their own peak. It wasn't long before Tracey felt another earth-shattering climax brewing from the couple's affections.

Her body over-burdened by the taste of Amanda and the feel of Mark. Tracey's core tingled, and her body throbbed as Mark drove into her harder and faster, pushing her over the edge.

"Uh…oh God! Mrs-Mrs Burton! …I'm…I'm cumming!" Tracey groaned around Amanda's clit, pushing her to her own climax.

Mark's head lolled back as a series of low, guttural moans escaped his mouth. It was too much. He thrust into Tracey as deep as he could before releasing a howl as he came, filling her tight bowels with his hot seed in the rush of another powerful orgasm. The sensation consumed her in an instant and Tracey's world went black.

Coming down from their high, the lovers relaxed in each other's company, riding the remnant waves of their orgasms. It took some time for Amanda and Mark to realise that Tracey had passed out after her third orgasm.

"Thank you, baby," Amanda murmured, snuggling into her husband, enjoying the heat he gave off as she listened to the deep rumble of his heartbeat. "Oh…What for, my love?"

With a knowing smile, she leant up and kissed her cheek. "For doing this, for Tracey. I know it couldn't have been easy for you."

"It was nothing honey." He grinned and kissed her forehead. "Anytime."

Under my BFF's *Daddy*

Chapter One

"Oh, bugger it!" David Street cursed, using his laptop's touchpad to highlight the paragraph he'd just written, and then deleting it with a tap of the key, collapsing back into his desk chair. He couldn't believe it. After working on it all morning, he was actually two paragraphs *behind* where he'd started.

He glowered at the screen, the cursor mocking his ineptitude with its constant blinking on the blank Word document.

A lot was made of the blank page. It was often said to taunt writers, to intimidate them with the immense space to fill. He never saw it that way, however. To him, the page wasn't a weight tugging him down. It was a challenge to overcome, fresh clay to be moulded however he saw fit.

No, the page wasn't the problem.

It was the pressure. The drive to outdo himself. To make this chapter better than the last. For the book to be new and exciting in a world where the well of creativity had run dry.

And time was running out.

His agent had been on the phone only that morning to tell him the publishers were getting impatient. That he had missed his deadline, and they wanted to see something by the end of the week or they would insist on the return of his advance.

"Bloody ingrates," he scoffed, leaning so far back in his chair until he was in real danger of falling on his arse. "You make them millions one day and they're kissing your ass. But one little bit of block the next, and it's *'hasta la vista, baby'*." He emphasised the Schwarzenegger impression by shooting a finger pistol at the ceiling before a scream, then a splash, had him on his feet and looking out the office's window.

Below, his daughter, Stacey, lay out on one of two inflatable beds drifting along the surface of the villa's large pool, sunning herself while her friend Cassandra swam lengths.

The girls spent most of the week like that. Enjoying the hot summer days and the awe-inspiring views over the Bay of Gibraltar.

David had taken a moment to enjoy them too, though his view had been one quite different. His gaze followed the figure in the water, his eyes locking onto the sheer ivory white bikini as she power-stroked through the crystal blue water from one edge to the other. Without stopping, she dived under, rolled and kicked away from the wall to repeat the lap.

She did this five times before swerving and swimming towards the edge closest to the villa, where they'd left their towels.

It was a scene straight out of David's own dirty little movie. Time almost seemed to hold its breath as Cassandra pulled herself up easily out of the water, throwing back her bountiful mane of raven hair. Rivulets sparkled in the sun and cascaded down her long neck, full breasts and flat belly. Then she was up on her feet and towelling her hair, her head turning up towards the house. Finding him.

Their eyes met and David knew instinctively that she knew he had been watching her.

He'd been caught, but the idea only sent a hot shiver tingling up his spine as he dragged his eyes away. Feeling a little hot, he decided he needed to take a break.

And maybe have a little fun in the sun himself...

Chapter Two

"Ah… this is the life!" Stacey sighed, stretched out across her inflatable.

Cassandra didn't answer, just led back on her float and kicked gently away from the edge, sending her float drifting lazily back across the surface of the pool. Overhead, the sky was as blue as she had ever seen it. Stretched out below at the base of the western slope of the rock that dominated the eastern side, the slender crescent shaped town of Gibraltar seemed quiet and sleepy. Beyond that, the still azure waters of the bay stretched out as far as the eye could see towards the black lines of the distant Spanish coast.

It was paradise. Their very own little slice of heaven. Cut away from the rest of the world the way Gibraltar itself was separated from the rest of mainland Europe.

So then why couldn't she bring herself to enjoy it?

'I'm sorry, Cass, but you're just too boring for me,'

Nathan's voice answered, ringing through her memory, thick with all the self-assured arrogance she had once found so exciting.

Now it only made her skin crawl.

It shouldn't have mattered. They'd only gone out a couple of times. Hell, they hadn't even slept together yet. Not that he hadn't been trying, of course.

It shouldn't have mattered to her what he thought. But it did.

It mattered. She hated that it did, but it did matter to her.

It mattered because she'd always been *that* girl. The plain Jane that played everything safe, with her routine and comfort zones. Unadventurous. Unspontaneous. Boring.

"Hey Cassy, are you listening?" Stacey asked, loud enough to snap Cassandra out of her daze.

"Huh? What? Oh, sorry Stace…"

Pushing her sunglasses up into her sleek and tidy blonde bob, Stacey rolled over to fix Cassandra with a look. Concern shadowed her pale blue eyes. "Are you okay?"

"What?" Cassandra forced a smile that she knew wouldn't reach her eyes. "Course I am… why… why wouldn't I be?"

"How about because you've done nothing but mope since we got here." She was right, of course. "Geez, girl, I told you the guy was bad news."

"N-no… it's just… err… Stace… do you think I'm boring?" Cassandra blurted out.

"What? No! Did he tell you that?" Stacey demanded, bolting up so fast the inflatable wobbled dangerously.

"Pretty much… he just wanted to make it clear. It was definitely me, not him."

"How *thoughtful*," Stacey sneered, then her expression softened as she reached over to touch her friend's shoulder. "Cass… you like what makes you feel comfortable, that's all.

There is nothing wrong with that. It doesn't make you boring, just you. And if that fucker can't accept it, then that's on him. You are a great catch. So what if you're not that adventurous. With a bod like yours, any guy would be drooling to go out with you. You just need to show it off now and then."

"What with my fat ass and belly?" Stacey rolled her eyes. "I still can't believe you made me buy this thing. I wear more in the shower."

"What? It looks great on you. You've got all the right curves for a bikini, and your tits look great in it. All you need now is a sexy little skirt to show off your legs and maybe a…" Cassandra's stomach dropped as her friend's eyes lit up with an all too familiar look. Oh no, she wasn't thinking… "I know, why don't we go across the border and hit the town for a girl's night? Do a little shopping in Puerto Banus. Have a few drinks. Find a couple of hot Spanish boys. You know what they say, the best way to get over a bad break up is getting under a hot lay..."

"Eww... no!" Cassandra laughed in mock disgust. Why was she not surprised. Shopping, drinks and sex- Stacey's holy trinity. Though not exclusively in that order.

"Aww… Okay, what about just shopping and drinks then? Come on, Cass, it's only an hour away. We can be there and back again before it even gets late. And you got all those euros for spending money… and it's the off-season, so the sales are on. Just imagine the bargains!"

"Yeah, thanks, but I think I'll pass. My girls and I are staying right here. But you go."

Stacey slumped back on her inflatable with a sigh. "Na, it's ok, I don't want to leave you all alone with Dad."

"Don't be silly, this is your break too, you go, have some fun, your dad barely comes out of his cave any way right? It'll be just like I have my own private little getaway." Even as she said it, Cassandra couldn't help a glance back towards the house, her eyes moving towards Mr Street's office window, disappointed but not surprised to find it empty.

However, Stacey was already halfway across the pool to the ledge and didn't bother to reign in her excitement as she called back, "Kay, if you're sure!"

Then she was up and out and almost skipping across the villa's back porch, before vanishing through into the kitchen without so much as a backwards wave.

Cassandra watched her go with the smallest of smiles. God bless Stacey. She always knew just what to say.

Not.

She always had the right of it, but translation got muddled in transit, somewhere between her brain and her mouth. But her heart was in the right place.

It was her idea to come out here. No sooner had Casandra told her flatmate and old childhood friend what had happened with Nathan, she was on the phone to their boss getting them both some time off. Stacey never left anything to chance and knew Cassandra well enough to know she would likely try weaselling out of what she had planned by simply saying she couldn't get the time off. Only as an afterthought had she then called her dad to ask if they could use his villa in Gibraltar for the week, with an extra helping of the daddy's little princess routine just to make sure.

She needn't have bothered. Mr. Street had always been cool like that, even before his divorce. Firm but laid back, and a big strong softie with a softer spot just for his daughter and her friends.

Or it might have had something to do with the fact he'd already been out here and wouldn't have to worry about his nice tidy villa getting trashed by a pair of boozed up party girls.

Not that he'd have had much to worry about on her account. Stacey might have been the good-time girl, but being the boring little introvert that she was, Cassandra rarely ever went out to party. And she never, ever got pissed.

I'm sorry, Cass, but you're just too boring for me.

No! Inwardly screaming defiance, she rolled off the inflatable and plugged down through the pool's crystal waters. After the warmth of the Mediterranean sun, the depths raked her like shards of ice as she kicked angrily for the bottom, then rolled and torpedoed from the tiles for the surface, breaching up to grab a breath before breast stroking for the edge. Nathan's words constantly echoed in her ears, taunting her.

No, that wasn't who she was. Stacey was right. She'd prove that arrogant son of a bitch wrong. She could step out of her comfort zone. She could do the unexpected.

She could… She would… Oh, who the fuck was she kidding?

Hauling herself out of the frigid waters, she made straight for the lounger where she'd laid out her towel, lying back and wrapping it around her like a cocoon. It was hopeless. If she didn't even have the balls to go out on an impromptu shopping trip with her best friend, how the hell was she ever going to break out of her slump?

What could she do to break the cycle?

Who-

"Room for one more?"

Chapter Three

The familiar, low rasp sent a hot rush sizzling down her spine and tingling out to her fingertips.

Oh god, that voice!

Her heart suddenly fluttered like a robin red-breast in a cage and Cassandra's breath caught in her throat as she twisted round and saw *him* walking out of the house.

David Street, Stacey's dad. A god among mortal men.

A feast to behold, he was tall with long limbs, dressed in tan shorts, sandals and a plain white short-sleeved shirt that stretched tight over broad musculature. Beneath those thick waves of raven black hair, his face was like a chiselled slab of white marble, hard and brutal with a sharp nose, wide jaw rough with the morning's growth, and full lips she had so longed to feel pressed against her skin.

And his eyes were the stormiest shade of grey she had ever seen, and so intense, they seemed to crash over the banks of her own and wash her away.

"Oh, hey Mr Street." Cassandra forced herself to smile, but couldn't drag her gaze from the vision of him coming to stand over her with a colourful drink in hand. It didn't help that he'd left the top three buttons of his shirt open, teasing her with a glimpse of the treasure beneath. "Sure, help yourself."

Oh if only I could… David mused, drinking in the bounty stretched out before him, before stepping around her lounger and instead settling down on the next. "Thanks, how's the sun?" he asked before sipping his drink.

"Hot and bright. Just another beautiful day in paradise," she said, forcing a broad smile and trying to remember she was meant to be on holiday. She was supposed to be enjoying herself, not a bag of nerves just because her friend's dad was sitting next to her. Sitting next to her while she was dressed in nothing but this damn micro bikini!

Then he chuckled, a deep warbling rumble that rose up from within his throat to crash over Cassandra as he turned to look at her. "You say that now, but give it a couple more months and you'll be pinning for some good old English weather."

She could feel his eyes moving over her body, devouring her from head to toe, and the heat of his gaze made her skin flush and tingle.

"If you say so…." She licked her lips nervously, her mouth suddenly dry. "How's your book coming along?"

Realising he was staring, David quickly dragged his eyes back out across the bay. Past the menagerie of brightly coloured sail ships, an immense cargo tanker was cutting through the dark turquoise waters towards the Spanish port. He focused on it, trying to ignore the stirring between his legs. It didn't help.

"Oh… you know, it's coming along, about as well as British Rail. I've got the nucleus of a plot, but it's missing…

something. I don't know. It's there, right in front of me, but I just can't see through the block."

"The dreaded block huh, is there anything I can do?"

Oh, he could think of a few ways.

Every author had their ways of dealing with writer's block. It was just an unpleasant fact of life in his trade, like taxes, the government, or Amazon's ever shifting policies. Making a big deal about them wasn't going to make any difference, you just had to be practical and deal with it. Sex had always been a great help for him when trying to get over the wall.

Fuck, how long had it been since he'd last gotten laid? Three months? Four, at least. Not since his divorce. Too long. Much too long if just looking at Cassandra in that sexy little thing was getting him hard.

He'd need to do something about that once the girls had gone home.

But first, he needed to make it through the next few days without making a fool of himself.

He coughed, trying to drag his attention back to the tanker, the coast, a bird, anything but the flawless curves of the beauty beside him! Dammit, just being so close to her was a fucking turn on. "No, not unless you can slow down time, get the publisher's off my back or know a trick for breaking down the wall."

She hummed for a moment, as if actually mulling it over. "Afraid I'm fresh out of ideas, though I might know a guy with an undead dragon that could deal with that wall of yours."

"Thanks, but I already have an ex-wife," he joked, and they both chuckled. It was official. Ex-wife jokes were funny no matter the situation. "So, where's my daughter scampered off to?"

"Shopping, where else?" Willing herself not to look at him, Cassandra forced a chuckle, the same one she used whenever customers told the same bad joke she'd heard a hundred times before. "The sales are on in Puerto Banus and she's been dying for a chance to splurge."

She could do this. It was just Mr Street.

The man she had known almost as long as she could remember.

Who had indulged her girlish princess fantasies when she was eight and had jokingly promised to marry her when she was all grown up.

That used to take her and Stacey to dance class every Saturday.

Her best friend's recently divorced and sexy as hell dad, who she'd spent years fantasising about.

David couldn't help another chuckle of his own. His daughter was nothing if not consistent. "Ah yes, as you said, where else." He took another sip of his cocktail, a crystal drop of condensation rolling down the glass to touch his lips as the sun beat down on them, the air growing hotter by the moment. Or maybe it was the alcohol.

Considering the already almost half empty glass before deciding he'd had enough for now, he laid it down gently in a shady spot before rounding on her. "So she just left you here all alone?"

The concern in his tone was so disarming, Casandra met his gaze without thinking and touched his shoulder with a placating hand. The contact sent a thrill racing through her fingertips. "It's okay, I don't really feel like hitting the town now and anyway, I'm not alone. You're here with me." The words were out before she could stop them, and the confession made her cheeks burn. Yet she didn't look away.

Yes, she was all alone with her bestie's daddy at his Gibraltar Villa.

Out in the wilds, miles from anywhere or anyone who could hear her scream – or beg as his sexy mouth did such wicked things between her... Dammit!

Why did he always make her feel this way?

Then Stacey's words echoed in her ears. The best way to get over a man is under one…

"You poor girl," David cooed playfully. "Trapped on the Rock with just this decrepit old man for company."

She couldn't resist the bait. "Aww… you're not so old, and the silver fox look is a classic for a reason."

"Cheeky minx!" he snapped in mock outrage, but couldn't keep the corner of his mouth from curling. "You're not too old to go over my knee, you know, young lady."

She shrieked girlishly, playing along in her best upperclass voice and squealed, "Oh no, don't spank me, please, Mr
Street!"

The mock innocence of the words sent a thrill racing down to the base of David's spine, igniting thoughts of her bending over to bear the swells of her luscious derriere for his judgement, trembling slightly as she awaited the sting of his hand striking her flawless skin.

Just the thought of it stirred his desire to a rod of iron.

"No, really," he forced out, crossing his legs, inwardly cursing and trying in vain to coax the beast back into its cage. "What are you doing here with me? Why didn't what's-hisname come along, ugh… you know, that guy with the funny hair…"

"Nathan."

Just saying his name brought the taste of ash to her mouth. No, she didn't want to think about him, not here, not with Mr Street, when she'd just been starting to forget him. But the dam had cracked, and no sooner had the words left her lips, her eyes had burned with hot, salty tears as all her buried emotions suddenly boiled to the surface. "He dumped me."

"Oh God, Cass, I'm… I'm so sorry." David didn't know what else to say. What else was there to say?

He'd never met the boy, but Stacey had told him about Cassandra's new boyfriend once or twice and there had been a few pictures of the two together on Facebook.

He had rather reminded him of Justin Bieber.

He just had one of those faces he couldn't help wanting to slap.

Somehow, however, he got the feeling voicing that thought wouldn't help very much.

He'd never really been a great one for dealing with emotions. It was one reason his ex-wife had listed as grounds for divorce. Siting him as a cold, unreachable iceberg of a man who had sucked all the joy and happiness from her life. She had even gone so far as to use it to justify her rampant extramarital nymphomania, saying it was just a way of seeking the warmth of human comfort. The honourable judge Blackwood had been sympathetic but expressed the suggestion that if that were the case, he would have thought one lover would have been enough, rather than five. For his part, David had just said he was one of the old school and as such, an ardent follower of the philosophy *actions speak louder than words*.

With the dedication and spirit of all true believers, heedless of his body's treacherous desire, he wrapped an arm around her and drew her close.

She was shaking as all the unsaid hurt and emotion that had welled up inside her suddenly burst its banks. "He said I was dull and boring and passionless and couldn't-" Her words dissolved into thick wet sobs as the tears came and she just buried her face into the crook of his neck.

David couldn't bear it.

"Then he's a fool," he promised, crushing her to him. "You're a wonderful person, Cass. You deserve better than that and you should be with someone who knows how special you are, who knows how lucky he is to have you."

She didn't respond, just kept sobbing, so he held her close and waited for the storm to pass. Yet his *little brain* couldn't help but notice how well she fit in his arms, the sunwarmed softness of her skin, and the way the heavy weight of her full breasts were squashed against his chest.

No, dammit, don't think like that, you dirty old sod!

He chided himself, but when he took a breath to clear his brain, he only inhaled the sweet fragrance of her hair, still with hints of her wild berry scented shampoo.

Then it was suddenly over. She was still, her breathing deep and even as she looked up at him from beneath her dark bangs, the last wet tear sparkling down her cheeks in the sunlight. "Thanks, Mr Street… er, Stacey told me the same thing."

"Well, she's rarely wrong." He forced a reassuring grin.

She blushed and looked away, out towards the coast, unable to meet his eyes, while resisting the urge to snuggle closer. Cassandra revelled in their closeness, the feel of his arms enveloping her, holding her close and tight.

She never wanted the moment to end. "I'm sorry… I don't know what came over me." She made to pull away…

Except David wouldn't let her go. "It's okay, we all need to let go sometimes," he soothed gently, cupping her chin and gently turning her to face him, before gently brushing the tear away with his thumb. "Break-ups can be tough."

They were so close, Cassandra felt like she was getting drunk on him. His scent, his warmth, his very presence was enveloping her, intoxicating her. All it would take was one little push, and she would finally know if those lips tasted as good as she'd imagined.

"Was that how it was for you? With your divorce?" The words were out before she could stop them, and when his hand dropped away, she would have done anything to take them back. "I'm sorry, I shouldn't have… forget I said anything. It's none of my business."

Again he held her fast, refusing to let her pull away, denying her any chance of escape.

"No, no, it's fine," he urged, sighing and running a hand through his hair. "My marriage was over years ago. It just took me a while to figure it out. Then I just didn't want it to, so I threw myself into my work to avoid it, but it was only a matter of time. After that, well, I just didn't really care anymore."

She couldn't help herself. There was an edge to his voice she'd never heard before. It sounded darkly dangerous, and very sexy. "So it doesn't bother you at all?"

"It did, at first," he growled. "When I found out, but not because of what she'd done. Only that she'd done it behind my back, rather than just come out and tell me she wanted a divorce."

"Did she say anything after?"

"No, what was there to say?" he said simply, before reaching down for his cocktail and bringing it up to his mouth. Cassandra's mouth dried as he swallowed the colourful contents of the glass, his head arching back and the muscles of his neck rising and falling while the first drops of perspiration rolled down his skin.

Cassandra's nails bit into her palms. They were close enough for her to lean in and lick up the drops.

"Do you blame yourself for… what happened?"

"No." He shrugged, then laughed. He actually laughed, a deep rich sound that rolled over her like dark chocolate. "We just married too young, settled down too soon, then grew apart. Becky wanted one thing, and I wanted another."

Their eyes met, and the contact sent a fresh wave of heat and awareness ebbing through her. Instinctively, she looked away. "So… what are you drinking? "

"This?" He raised the near empty glass, almost as if he was toasting her. "It's a Tequila Sunset."

Cassandra arched a brow. "Isn't it a bit early?"

"I won't tell if you don't," David shrugged, his eyes bright with mischief. "And hey, when in Spain…"

"But isn't Tequila Mexican?"

"Smart ass," he grinned ruefully. "Actually, the indigenous Mexican Indians brewed a fermented liquor from the same plant. What we know as Tequila was concocted by the Conquistadors after their brandy ran out, making Tequila actually Spanish and Spain's only indisputable, worthwhile contribution to western civilisation. Just the thing for out here in the tropics. All the kick, but none of the mess."

He raised the glass to finish it, but at the sight of the drink swirling within the glass, Cassandra couldn't resist. "Could I try? Just a sip."

"My dear girl, there's nothing but a sip left."

"Please Mr Street, I left my water in the kitchen and it's so warm out here…" she asked sweetly, batting her eyelashes.

Tempting minx

David cursed inwardly, his cock twitching at her little act. Dammit, the thing would start hurting if he didn't get out of here. Forcing his smile to stay in place, he shifted ever so slightly to pass her the glass. "Help yourself." And

that was when she saw it.

It was only a momentary glance as she reached to take the offered drink, but it was enough. Enough for her to note the bulge straining against his thigh through the fabric of his shorts, thick and huge. Enough to send a shiver racing through her and to have her grabbing the offered cocktail, downing it in one go.

God, had she done that to him?

Then their eyes met again, over the rim of the empty glass, and the warmth of the spirit raced down to burn between her legs. It made her brave, ready to take a leap.

Still holding his gaze, she lowered the glass back to the ground, before slowly sliding her tongue across her lips, collecting the last of the fruit-laced bravery there. Then, moaning a throaty purr, she asked, "Mr Street, would you mind putting some sunscreen on my back for me?

Chapter Four

David's blood ran cold at the question.

"I don't know if that's such a good idea, Cass. "

Yes, that was it. Cass was the name he always used when he was playing the role of the adult. That was what he needed now, to be an adult, to set boundaries. To get the hell out of here and back to his office before he did something really stupid.

However, Cassandra glimpsed his other head twitching against its prison.

"Aww, how come?" she cooed, all innocence and sweetness, scooping up and offering him her bottle of factor 40, silently praying her nerve held. "Please, Mr Street. You don't want me to get burned now, do you?"

David stared at the bottle like it was a coiled viper, poised to strike. This was his last chance. He needed to go. Just get up and go back inside. He could do it. Just get up and go. He had to, before…

Taking it from her, he rose up and walked around her lounger to stand over her before popping the cap. "Roll over."

The command was clipped and said with such primal authority, it sent a fresh shiver of excitement tingling through Cassandra. She obeyed immediately. Rolling onto her front, she pulled the wash of her raven hair aside before starting on the fastenings of her top.

"I think that's going too far."

"But I'll have tan lines, Mr Street," she implored, barely able to keep still for the thought of his hands on her bare skin. Just managing to finger the knot loose despite the knots in her tummy, she added sweetly, "I know you'll be a gentleman and not look."

"Of course not," he bit out, squeezing a generous amount of the sunscreen onto his palm before smearing a long line across her shoulder blades. It wasn't cold. Not after a morning sitting out under the Mediterranean sun, but she shivered and squirmed all the same as his hand circled around and around, teasing down her long neck and across her shoulders, massaging it in.

He worked until he had applied it all and then kept going. Her skin was just so warm, so butter soft. He couldn't get enough.

And nor could Cassandra.

"Mmm… that feels so nice Mr Street… mmm… lower," she panted, burying her face in the lounger to keep him from spying the blush heating her face. God, what was she doing? This was Mr Street, her best friend's dad.

This was insane, but she didn't care.

She'd been dreaming of this moment. This intimacy with him.

Cassandra had craved the feeling of his hands sliding over her skin, the sensations those big, powerful hands would send sizzling straight down to her throbbing centre.

If this was her one moment with him, then she intended to make it count and enjoy every second.

David was happy to indulge her and applied a fresh squeeze of lotion.

Guided by her soft, kittenish moans, he worked his way down the delicate curve of her back, his thumb playing along her spine like the strings of a violin while his fingers danced along her ribs. Accidentally, one finger brushed along the side of her milky white breast and she sucked in a breath that made his cock tighten and twitch.

Fuck, this was bad. He needed to get out of here, away, back to the safety of his office. A place he could look but not touch. Never touch! This was Cassandra, for Christ's sake. His daughter's best friend. Her fucking flatmate!

Needing to put some much-needed distance between them, he manoeuvred to the base of the lounger, dragging his hands around the contours of her upturned derriere and down her gloriously long legs. He tried to focus, to clear his thoughts, but the distance only made it easier for him to devour the vision of her stretched out before him. His eyes immediately locked onto the small triangle of white material between her legs. Still slightly damp from her earlier swim, her folds were clearly visible against the fabric, the nub of her clit swollen and pleading for attention, betraying her arousal.

This was affecting her just as much as it was him.

And that revelation made it impossible for him to pull away.

He worked his way back up from her ankle and along her calf. Stroking and brushing, his touch as light and teasing as a feather, the premise of applying the lotion forgotten, making her writhe and moan. Then, as his fingers brushed over her inner thighs, she raised her hips and subtly parted her legs just that bit wider, opening herself to him.

It was all the permission he needed.

Cassandra couldn't stand it. His hands were working her into a frenzy, making her skin tingle wherever he touched. She had to grab the edges of the lounger to battle against the urge to slip a hand beneath her suit and soothe the fire throbbing between her legs.

Was this really happening?

Was she really letting him do this?

Him! Mr Street, her best friend's daddy, was touching her! No, not just touching her, massaging her, seducing her with his every touch. How long had she dreamed of this moment, of his hands on her skin, sliding up her legs, finger tips pressing higher and higher and-

She bit down on a surprised squeak as something brushed across her folds.

David slowly brushed his thumb along her folds, tracing them through the swimsuit, feeling the heat and wetness burning there. Somewhere deep, deep down, the moral man he'd been was desperately trying to drag his hand away. Screaming that this was wrong, that they needed to stop, but he couldn't resist. All her sexy little moans were driving him crazy.

Cassandra didn't object, nor did she move at all. She lay still beneath him, trembling as goose flesh rose across her legs, her breath coming hot and ragged as he stoked the liquid heat throbbing in her core.

This wasn't the sweet and innocent girl he'd known and watched playing with dolls, pretending to be a Disney princess. That child was gone. She was a woman now. A lush and beautiful creature, with all a woman's primitive hungers and needs.

She needed him.

And he was happy to oblige, gently pressing down, rubbing the pad of his thumb around her, feeling the heat burn. His fingers traced along the line of her thong, teasing around the fabric. His fingers caressed along her inner thighs before pushing beneath her suit into lush heat, making her gasp and roll her hips against him, inclining back and opening herself completely to his invading digits.

He leaned down and whispered in her ear. "This is a *very* bad idea."

"No!" she sobbed in protest, squeezing her eyes shut against the rush of tingling pleasure as his finger curled to stroke the spot. "Please, I've wanted this for so long, Mr Street-oh!" Her breath caught when his thumb strummed her covered clit, making her writhe beneath him. "I-I-I won't tell anyone… please, I'll be… such a good girl for you… I'll never tell a soul… please…"

"Good, because even if I wanted to, I can't stop now," he promised, withdrawing the finger from her heat and offering it to her, teasing the pad across her soft pink lips. Obediently Cassandra opened and her pink tongue flicked out, tentatively tasting the cream coating the digit. She drew him in and her cheeks hollowed as she sucked it clean.

It was such an erotic display. If he were a younger man, he might have succumbed to his lust right there.

Age had its compensations.

Instead, he dipped his head and laid a feather soft kiss on her nape. It was a surprisingly intimate gesture given their current position, and she gasped a soft breathy moan as he did it again, and again, trailing kisses down her back. Slowly. So slowly. Slow enough to make her wriggle beneath him as the heated tension inside her wound in ever tighter knots with each flutter of his tongue. And as he kissed down the soft curve of her lower back, his fingers hooked under the strings of her bikini bottoms and dragged them down her legs.

The heady perfume of her desire greeted him, invading his senses, making his mouth water. With his cock straining against its bonds, growing evermore uncomfortable by the second, he pulled back to admire his handiwork. "You're so beautiful."

It was the first time anyone had ever said that to her. Cassandra felt her skin burn with a heat that had nothing to do with the desire throbbing inside her. "No, please don't stare at me like that…"

"But I want to," he growled, raising one hand to caress her derriere, marvelling at the silky softness of her skin. God, she was just so perfect. Her ex must have been mad to even consider breaking up with her.

Shifting his hands ever so slightly, cupping the perfect handfuls of her cheeks, he spread them just enough to reveal the crinkled flesh of her rosebud and the slick, swollen folds below. "Mmm… you're so wet, you naughty girl."

"Oh god, no please, this is so embarrassing, I can't help-oh!" Her voice left her in a gasp when the tip of his tongue swirled around her pucker, sweeping and flitting and driving her wild. "No… please… not there… that's so… dirty…"

"Yeah, and you like it, don't you?" He switched tact, his hands drawing her to him while tonguing her tight little rosebud.

"Yes!" she sobbed, her back arching even as the world melted down to just the illicit feeling of his slick tongue driving through her sphincter to feast on her little asshole.

God, she couldn't believe she was letting him do this. And she couldn't believe how good it felt. Though no virgin, Cassandra had never let any past lover play with her butt. She'd just never been able to see how anyone could draw pleasure from doing such things, but with Mr Street, it all just clicked. There was nothing she wouldn't do for him, and her body knew it, relished it.

Her body demanded it.

"Yeah, good girl…" he purred against her pucker, smirking inwardly as it made her shiver, working his tongue in and out against the clutch of her hole. "What do you want?"

"W-what? Oh… oh god… please… I-I-wait!" Panic flaring at the feeling of his tongue leaving her, she threw a look back over her shoulder to see him smirking back at her. "Don't… don't stop… please…"

With eyes dark and gleaming with a savage hunger, he seductively licked the taste of her from his lips. "Mmm… you've got such a tasty ass Cassandra, I could eat it for days…"

"No, don't say that…" She'd never heard Mr Street talk like that before. She liked it. His crude words sent sensations tingling through her, hardening her nipples to tight points that ached to be sucked, before he rushed downwards once more.

"Then tell me what you want," he purred, bending down to touch his lips to her hole in a soft butterfly kiss. Then, slowly kneading the lush curves of her derriere, spreading them wide, he gave the flesh between a long languorous lick. "Go on, you dirty girl, give yourself over to your desires. Tell me the things you think about while playing with your pretty pink pussy. What naughty fantasies bring you to that hot, sticky end…"

"I can't… please… it's embarrassing." She couldn't keep from panting now. Her heart pounded harder as he repeated the slow lick again and again. Each one a little longer than the last and she couldn't resist wriggling her hips back at him as the tip of his wicked tongue neared the font of her heat throbbing between her legs. A deliciously naughty jolt zipped straight through her centre.

She didn't know how much longer she'd last if he kept this up. Why did it have to feel so good?

And then…

"If you say so…" The husky rasp of his voice tingled against her inner thighs, making her shudder and whimper. Then he dragged his tongue down her sex, through her swollen folds to flutter over her clit. Sweeping and swirling, stirring her lower belly into a wet, throbbing blaze.

Cassandra couldn't stand it.

"Oh… oh god… no… please… don't make me say it… I… I…" Back bowing, she squeezed her eyes shut against the storm, but it wasn't enough. She was shaking, her climax building.

"Tell me, Cassandra."

That voice. The way it commanded her name, ordering her to obey. She was powerless to resist as he thrust his tongue deep inside her creamy centre, pushing her over the edge and licking her through her release. Each sweep of his tongue prolonged the waves crashing over her, pushing her higher and higher, until the words flew from her in a gasp… "Fuck me, Mr Street!"

Chapter Five

"Good girl," David praised, savouring this view of her, bent over, quaking, mouth open yet eyes squeezed tightly shut against the orgasm that still surged through her. It was such a surreal image. This innocent girl he'd watch grow up dissolved into a wanton little sex kitten, beautiful and innocent yet primitive, desperate, and so fucking sexy.

He wanted to ingrain it into his memory forever and guided one of her legs up and over as he did, rolling her onto her back.

Cassandra went willingly, panting, basking in the sweet afterglow. Her eyes opened, searching, pleading. "Please... Mr Street... fuck me, please..."

"Shhh... Cass," he'd reverted to that familiar easy tone she knew so well, and said the words so softly, for a moment, she dared hope this sweet torture was about to end, and all her fantasises were about to come true.

"I love watching you cum." He swooped down, tasting her with a long lick along her sex.

"Oh god!" Cassandra gasped, her back arching at the toe-curling contact.

She couldn't stand it. He was driving her insane. She wanted to twist and writhe away from that oh so sinfully wicked mouth. To grab her tits, pinch her nipples, finger her clit. To bury her hands in his hair and force his mouth just where she needed it.

Yet she couldn't. Her ecstatic body wasn't listening to her anymore.

"Mmm… Yeah, you like that, Cass? Want more?" he purred, dragging the flat of his tongue back up through her folds to circle her little nub. "You've got the sweetest little pussy, so warm and slick. I can't wait to feel you wrapped around my cock, squeezing me like a tight little fist as I make you cum. Do you want me to make you cum? Would you like that? Want me to make you feel good and this tight little pussy purr?" He dipped his head to cover her clit with his mouth, his checks hollowing as he sucked, igniting sparks behind her eyes.

It was too much. Struck by the sheer eroticism of seeing the man's head between her legs, feeling him devouring her with his wicked, sinfully dirty mouth, she was like a ship caught in a tempest. Her fingers clutched the lounger's cushion in a deathly grip.

"Yes! Please, Mr street… oh fuck… oh my god… oh yes… yes, eat my pussy, it's all yours… oh fuck. I'm cumming, I'm cumming!"

He growled, loving this side of her. It was a side of her he had never known. Should have never known. A side of her that was as forbidden to him as the infamous fruit was to Adam. And like all forbidden fruit, she was all the sweeter for it. He loved this view of her luscious body arching from between her smooth thighs, the sight of her flushed with passion, wild with desire, the sounds of her pleasure, the feeling of her shuddering around him.

Yet it couldn't slake his thirst for her, his hunger for more. He wanted more. He wanted all of her, completely and absolutely, to spoil her for any other man, to make her his. "Fuck, you cum so easily. Yeah, do it again, Cass, cum for me."

"Yes! Yes! Oh god, oh Jesus… that feels so good… Mr… Mr street, you're- oh fuck!"

"Yeah, what do you want, Cass?" he pressed, as he lapped at her making sure she could feel every syllable beat through her tasty little sex as his greedy tongue pushed through her spasming tissues to drink from the very centre of her erogenous being.

His cock tightened dangerously, desperate for attention and jealous of his tongue.

It was all he could do not to go balls deep in her luscious pussy right then and there.

"Fuck me," she moaned, squirming and writhing as her body dissolved. God, Nathan had never done this to her, never made her feel this way. It was like his tongue had a mind of its own and knew just where to touch her, what to do to drive her wild. It was too much, too good…

"Louder." There was a delicious, almost devilish edge to his words now, and she knew he was enjoying toying with her.

"Fuck me!" The words left her in a shriek, her head rolling as he worked her into a storm, her body shaking with the tension of her building release as she suddenly tittered on the brink. "I want you to fuck me, Mr Street! Use me any way you want. That's your pussy. Bury your big dick in me. Make me your whore. I'll be a good little fuck toy for you. I'll… I'll… oh god… oh fuck I'm gonna cum… I'm gonna- oh god, don't stop, don't… stop… oh… god…" Then her release exploded through the hot, throbbing knot at her core, the waves surging over her, sending her reeling, soaring like no orgasm that had come before it, shaking her to her foundations, leaving her basking in a sea of stars.

Only when she had finally stopped shaking did David abandon his newfound treasure, but not before attending to her fully bared jewel with a soft, almost chaste kiss. She arched and gasped excitedly, her clit still too tender and sensitive from such a powerful climax for any more direct stimulation just yet.

And the knowledge that it was he who had brought this little sultry vixen so much pleasure and had pushed her over the shattering brink with just his mouth, filled him with such a primitive pride, he just couldn't help himself.

Coming back down to earth, blinking through the black spots dancing before her eyes, Cassandra was treated to the view of David standing before her with his trousers open, fisting his imperious cock.

It was a scene straight out of her dirtiest dreams. Yet they were only fantasies. Pale shadows of the reality of the Adonis standing before her. Over her. Almost close enough for her to taste his salty musk. All she would have to do was lean up and open her mouth…

"See something you like, baby?" he purred, watching her with dark, hungry eyes. He watched her as he stroked the full length of his cock with slow pumps that made the thick crest swell and glisten beneath the warm Mediterranean sun.

It was the most erotic thing she'd ever seen and made her still tingling pussy throb needily.

Her mouth suddenly dry, she could only nod. Her eyes reverted to the view of his thick cock, which now seemed so much bigger than she'd expected.

A hell of a lot bigger than Nathan's, that was for sure.

Her heart racing, she slowly raised her legs, bracing the flat of her feet on the sunbed, baring herself to those hungry eyes, inviting him to finish what he'd started.

He accepted immediately, covering her body with his and crushing his mouth to hers, kissing her hungrily. His wicked tongue slipped between her lips to tangle with hers, the very same tongue that just moments before had been devouring her.

She moaned at such a dirty thought and greedily sucked his tongue, her hips arching up, curling against the weight of his desire, desperate to get it where she wanted it. Where she needed him. The head of his cock, hot and slick with pre-cum, slipped and slid between their bodies and left a slick trail down her belly to...

David pulled away, dragging his mouth from hers with a low growl.

"You're so beautiful, Cass..." he growled, breathless, his voice hot and hungry, eyes holding hers as his crown pressed against her slick folds. "If you want to stop-"

Shaking her head, Cassandra didn't give him a chance to finish. Stop? Like hell, she'd been waiting all her life to have him like this. No way was she about to stop now. Wrapping her legs around his waist and arching her hips, she urged him on, digging her heels into his backside so...

"Oh... fuck!" she gasped, her heart thundering in her ears as the world shrank down to the feeling of *him* inside her, his broad crest pressing through her sex, stretching her to her limit, filling her inch by delicious inch.

Oh god, it was too much! He was too much, too thick, too hard, too... big!

No, not big, huge, hung like a fucking stallion!

David could only groan a low, choked sound at the feeling of sliding into her warmth, her plush heat wrapping around him, sucking him in. It was the sweetest torture. Just watching her sexy little mouth open with that first sweet shock of penetration, her eyes widening, losing focus, rolling back before snapping forward in the rush of wild, untamed pleasure.

Fuck, it was a miracle he hadn't cum already.

He knew he needed to be patient, to wait and let her adjust, but the urge, the need to take her, to rut, to fuck, to claim this little sex kitten as his own, was inexorable.

"M-Mr Street… Please…" Cassandra wasn't entirely sure what she was pleading for.

The words left her in a rush as he rolled his hips, pulling out a little before driving back in.

Her back bowed up and off the sunbed at the feeling of being stretched so deliciously and stuffed to her limits. And not just in the physical sense. This feeling, the connection between them, the way he was watching her, it was all so intense. Way too intense. She'd never felt anything like it. Desperate to burn the feeling of him inside her to memory, she clenched around him.

"Oh fuck," David hissed, squeezing his eyes shut against the sudden rush that nearly pushed him over the edge. "Don't do that…"

"Mmm… sorry," she panted, provocatively biting her lip. She wasn't sorry, god she loved the way his cock was twitching inside her, thickening and hardening all the more.

"Oh, you naughty girl, so that's the way you want to play it, huh?"

It happened so fast she could barely react, her pleasure drunk brain only really registering the way his cock surged inside her as the flair of his hips spread her thighs wide, opening her up in the very best of ways while those powerful hands raised her legs, guiding them up over his shoulders.

"Is this what you want?" he asked, staring down at her, gently, rocking his hips to emphasise his meaning as his hands ran down her legs to seize her waist. His hold was gentle, but firm, powerful, unescapable, and kept her pinned against his abdomen at just the right angle for her to see where their bodies joined.

"Yes…" she gasped, trying to meet his teasing roll with one of her own, but was restrained by the hold he had on her.

"Does it feel good?"

"Yes…" She could feel tears welling up in the corners of her eyes as each time he circled his hips, the flat of his abdomen ground over her clit. Growing desperate, maddened by the subtle tease of friction, she twisted and writhed, needing to break free, her hands tearing at the lounger's cushion for any sort of leverage.

"You want more?"

"Oh… god… please, Mr… Street… you're… I… I'm…" Oh god, why was he being so cruel? She was so hot, hotter for it than she had ever been. Couldn't he see that? See how badly she wanted him?

"That's it, Cas, let it go, tell me what you want…" His voice was soft and low, but the predatory gleam in his eyes was pure deviance. He pulled back until just the tip remained inside her, leaving her feeling cold and empty.

Yet the sight of his cock, rising from her depths, wet and shiny with her cream, was unquestionably the sexiest thing she had ever seen.

"Yes, I want more! More! Fuck me more! Bury that big dick in me. Pound my tight little pussy, that's your pussy, give it to me… give it to me- oh my god, oh my god, oh my go-oh!" Her pleas dissolved in a long moan as he drove back into her, going balls deep within her slick, eager walls in one smooth drive.

"That's right, Cas, you're mine now, mine. These beautiful tits. This tight little cunt. All mine." He punctuated each claim with another curl of his hips, withdrawing and thrusting, emphasising his claims, determined to make sure she would never forget.

And she quickly lost herself in the feeling of his thick cock stretching her, filling her like nothing she had ever imagined.

"Yes. Yes! Yours, all yours! Oh god, hold me down, make me take it, make me watch your big fucking cock pound my little pussy, oh fuck, feels so good," Cassandra moaned, her head rolling and her back bowing up off the lounger, offering her body up to him, letting him use her as he wanted, however he wanted.

And David couldn't get enough of her.

Sex had never been like this with his ex. To her, for all her extramarital activities, the Kama Sutra was a menu in an Indian takeaway. She'd been greedy and demanding, selfish in the quest for her own release.

Cassandra was as different as different could be and he wanted to show her how special she was, make her feel as treasured as she deserved.

Already close, he knew he couldn't last long, so rather than holding back, he gave her everything. Draw and thrust, draw and thrust, over and over again as he pounded her slick folds, going deeper with every stroke, making sure she could feel every inch of him. The wet slap of their body's meeting rang out with the squeaks and groans of the lounger beneath them.

Cassandra only moaned her approval, letting him take her, letting him take what he wanted as she moved with him, her ardour burning just as fiercely. Rocking beneath him, her tight sex clenching, squeezing him as he drove into her hard and fast, dominating her completely and sending her spiralling towards another climax.

God, if he kept this up much longer, she had no doubt she would be deliciously sore by the morning, and walking funny for days.

God, "Oh god… oh god… oh-oh M-Mr Street… Yeah… yeah… yeah… oh my god… oh- fuck! Fuck, that's so fucking good!" She couldn't stand it. It felt like the place where they were connected was melting away in a sparkling electric storm that tingled out to every nerve in her body. "Oh, fuck… oh… oh… oh my god, oh fuck, don't stop, give me that dick, use my little pussy, give me all your fucking cock, I want it, I wa- oh- Oh fuck, I'm cumming, I'm cumming all over your cock…"

She was being too loud. They were out in the open, their modesty shielded only by the small wall that encircled the property. Anyone walking by would hear them. However, Cassandra didn't give a damn. The almost nirvana-like high she was cresting left little care in her. Nothing could pull her from the incredible sensations sweeping through her like wildfire, shoving her to the point of madness.

"That's it, Cass, cum for me, cum all over my dick as I fuck your brains out!" he growled, his jaw clenched tight, fighting to hold back his inevitable climax. His taut muscles flexed deliciously beneath his skin as he loomed over her, stretching out, his hands moving up from her waist to cage her beneath him as he drove into her, fucking her through her orgasm. Sweat glistened like oil across his brow and chest. His impossibly hard cock seemed to swell inside her.

And knowing that she could do this to him, push him to the brink of his sanity, drove Cassandra wild.

"Oh my god, please, feels too good, use me however you want, that's your pussy, I just want to be your little fuck toy, I just… I just, oh god, I can't take it, it's too good. It's too good!" Her voice died away as, trembling, shaking, she was hurled from her peak to tumble through time and space, lost in the stormy throes of the orgasm of her life.

"Yes, that's it, cum, cum… cum- oh fuck!" he gasped, squeezing his eyes shut and throwing his head back in a great bare-toothed growl as her sex bore down, wrapping around and milking his cock to the point he couldn't hold back any longer. However, before he could pull out, her legs crossed, wrapping around him and locking at the ankles, drawing him in, needing to be closer.

"No… don't… leave it in… I want to feel you cum inside me Mr Street, give it to me, fill me up with all your cum!" Then her hands were in his hair and their lips crashed together as he unleased rope after rope of creamy heat deep inside her.

They clung together until the tremors passed before disentangling from each other's embrace enough to roll, so Cassandra lay astride him on the sunbed with David still inside her. Panting hard with aftershocks still zinging through her, she buried her face in the crock of his shoulder, inhaling deeply, savouring the cocktail of their mixed scents upon an air of salt and sex. Cassandra relished the feel of his powerful arms enveloping her, holding her close, his cock softening and the warmth of his seed throbbing inside her. It just felt so right, so perfect, that she wanted nothing so much as to stay like this forever.

Despite herself, she couldn't help a small chuckle.

Looking down, David arched a brow. "Something funny?"

"No, I was just thinking," she mused, trailing one hand through the curls of his dark dusting of chest hair. "When Stacey told me the best way to get over Nathan was a quick hookup, I don't think this is quite what she had in mind."

"No, I bet not." He gave a bark of laughter. "But I think I prefer our way."

"Hmm…" she agreed. Spotting a stray drop of perspiration rolling down his neck, she quickly swept it up with a sweep of her tongue, following it up all the way to his ear. "But you know what?"

"What?" His mouth twisted in that devastating smirk. Deep inside her, his still semi-hard cock reawakened, stiffening, and lengthening like a serpentine phoenix rising from the ashes.

She pulled back to meet his eyes, biting her lip. "I'm not entirely sure I'm over him just yet. Maybe I need to take another plunge under my besties' sexy daddy. What do you think?"

Thinking back to his office and his unfinished manuscript and the looming deadline, David couldn't help but grin back. "Always do what the doctor orders…" Then he kissed her and pulled her back down onto the lounger.

He had till the end of the week to finish the book.
Plenty of time.

Daddy's Naughty Gift

Chapter ONE

Josh Winchester had never thought his life would be like this.

Growing up, he had just been a simple lad with simple dreams. Finish school. Get a job. Marry his dream girl and have the two point five children. Live happily ever after like they always did on the telly.

Becoming a DotCom millionaire- back when such things had been possible- fresh out of college, and following it through to the list of top fifty billionaires certainly wasn't part of the plan.

But when life gives you lemons, why settle for lemonade? Make a fucking cheesecake.

However, that cheesecake had become something of a tart these days.

Drained from the evening's exertion, Josh hardly noticed the *bing* of his penthouse's private elevator as the doors slid apart to reveal an opulence that had long since lost its sparkle.

Marble floors and gold inlay sounded nice, but when it all came down to it, the only difference between that and the stick-on gear you bought down at the DIY store, besides the price tag, was the prior just meant something else to polish.

He could afford the expense, but the prices the local cleaning companies charged to come out and do a property in Knightsbridge were highway robbery with violence and buggery.

With an exhausted sigh, he stepped out of the elevator and made straight for his bedroom down the hall, shrugging off his jacket and tugging his tie loose as he went.

It had been the usual hullabaloo that it always was on Christmas Eve. He'd been representing his organisation, *Firewall,* at a charity ball for the rich and famous, pretending not to know all the funds raised would actually get carved up amongst the host and organisers to pay for the spread and décor.

Strange as it might seem, he'd used to enjoy the yearly shindigs. The pomp and glamour masked behind a veil of festivity and good will to all men, and an opportunity to press flesh with the stars without them begging for funding for whatever vanity project they were fronting.

That was while his wife was alive. His angel. His Sonja.

The uncontested love of his life. And his greatest regret.

Without her on his arm, the charade just wasn't worth the effort.

Pulling at his dickie bow, desperate to loosen its noose around his neck, he pulled open his bedroom door, and suddenly stopped dead, his eyes wide in disbelief.

Chapter TWO

Compared to the wealth and opulence of the rest of the penthouse, Josh's bedroom was little more than a cell. A quiet, almost humble abode with only the most plain and functional of furnishings. A simple double bed flanked by side-tables, a wardrobe against one wall, and a chest of draws on the other. Simple, practical and minimalist, just like its owner.

A Black Country boy born and bred, Josh had never been entirely comfortable with the trappings of wealth. It was just too big and too much. He liked things small and poky, like his parent's place on the council estate where they'd grown up. So when they'd stumbled across a place with what the estate agent had described as a glorified coat closet round the back, he'd made an offer there and then. While Sonja had busied herself turning the rest of their home into a palace fit to house any denizen of high society, he'd been erecting his man cave. It was a quiet little piece of Birmingham, the only place he could really call his own. His Sanctuary.

And someone had violated it.

Lying in the middle of the room was perhaps the biggest sack he had ever seen. A cavernous cloth bag with a red and white fur trim worthy of old Saint Nick himself, and all his reindeer pulling that damn sleigh too.

What was it doing there, in his bedroom?

"What the?" Josh mused slowly, arching a brow, before treading in and circling the sack, giving it a slow walk around. What on earth could it be, and how could it have gotten in. His secretary, Reina, might have dropped it round if something had arrived at the office while he was away, but she always let him know when she did. But it was well past office hours, and she never trespassed into his private rooms. Noticing a card attached to the silk ribbon that tied it, he reached out to read it, but the contact caused whatever was inside to move.

"Christ!" Cursing, Josh lurched backward, as if expecting a cobra to rear up before him. However, when nothing happened, the bag stilled as whatever was inside settled. He took a breath. Waited for a moment. Then, when still nothing happened, he slowly reached out and poked the sack again.

It wriggled, and then there was a noise, soft and excited, like… giggling.

Curiosity getting the better of him, he undid the ribbon and opened the sack-

"Surprise!" An excited voice cheered and Josh felt the air being punched from his lungs as a red and black blur burst from the sac and hit him in the chest, sending him tumbling back to the floor. Grunting as his back hit the ground, he found his head suddenly buried in a mass of wavy black hair rich with the scent of forest fruits and a pair of sapphire blue eyes staring back at him, bright with mischief.

"Erica?"

"Merry Christmas *Daddy*." His stepdaughter beamed before swooping down and crushing her lips to his in a lush, hungry kiss.

Chapter THREE

She tastes like… strawberries, Josh realised as Erica's mouth moved against his, sucking hungrily at his lips before her lush little tongue found his own and coaxed it into a dance that made his cock hard within its prison.

Stroking. Teasing. Swirling. Drinking him in as her hands fisted in his hair, drawing him close so he could feel how soft and small she felt against him. How warm and inviting.

Yet for all that, he couldn't help but wonder if this was how her mother had tasted.

He supposed it was. They had always been so alike. Near identical in fact, except for the obvious age difference, and even that had been less and less noticeable near the end. That same bright smile and playful expression. Those same full lips and little nose that would twitch adorably whenever she laughed and sneezed. The same soft, wavy dark hair that tumbled down to the flair of their dancer's hips and long legs.

So alike, he could have almost believed it was her mother kissing him.

Yet she had never kissed him, and it was that thought that gave him the strength to pull away.

"Erica! What are you doing?" he demanded, his breathing hot and heavy as he glared down at her, eyes dark with lust. "And just what are you wearing?"

His surprise was well warranted.

Though no one would ever call Erica's wardrobe *conservative*, she'd surpassed herself this time. Hell, it was unquestionably one of the sexiest things Josh had ever seen. A piece of crimson cloth trimmed with snowy white fur that hugged her body like a second skin. Hung off her shoulders, it both accentuated the slope of her neck while boasting a deep plunging neckline that left nothing to the imagination and went perfectly with the thigh-high flounced skirt that, even from that angle, teased a glimpse of her derrière.

"Aww… don't you like it?" she pouted, the corner of her plump pink lips curling with a naughty half-smile. Her big innocent eyes widened and stared up at him with a look that was both innocent and sexy as fuck. "It's your Christmas present."

"My Christmas present, huh?" Josh said slowly, and couldn't resist giving her another long once over. Coupled with the black belt and gold buckle, sleek white hold ups, black knee-high boots, she had assembled the perfect Sexy Santa Dress.

And it certainly lived up to its name. Even the innocent fluffy red and white santa hat complemented the get up. The only thing missing was the blow up reindeer for her to straddle and cheer *Ho! Ho! Ho!*

Dragging his eyes away, looking up at the ceiling, then down at the floor, anywhere that wasn't in her general direction. "Well, it's lovely, but I don't think that's quite my size."

She giggled, a sound as sultry and as sweet as whipped cream. "No, silly, this is just the wrapping. I'm your present."

"Well, colour me surprised," he answered warily, watching her slink closer, ever aware of her closeness and how hard it was getting to keep his hands off of her.

Curse his body and its needs. He really needed to get laid at some point soon. Celibacy was fucking with his head. "Especially when you're supposed to be staying with your friends down in the Riviera for Christmas break. And I've already wired you the airfare and spending money."

She giggled again and cocked her head, her grin positively Cheshire cattish as she tapped a finger to her chin. "Yeah, I know I told you that, but then how else would I ever scrimp and save enough money from my measly little allowance to pay for *this*." She ran both hands down the little sexy Santa dress, just to emphasise how obviously expensive the thing was. Or was it so he could see how well the silky material hugged her full breasts and flat belly.

Josh's mouth felt impossibly dry as he couldn't help but notice, not that he hadn't already. Damn, youth is good these days. "We'll call it money well spent. Now what are you doing in my bedroom?"

"Well, it's like I said Daddy, I'm your present. Tonight I'm all yours…" And with one last little step, she closed the gap.

"Erica, what are you talking about?"

"Don't be coy, Daddy," she purred, reaching up to finger his buttons. Her light touch was just enough for her fingers to ghost across the hard ridge of Josh's cut midriff, the eternal testimony to his personal trainer's perseverance, sending tingles beneath his skin before working their way up. "Mummy never did this for you, did she?" Her hands moved up to touch his face, her skin so soft against his shadowed jaw. "Married all those years, and she never so much as kissed you."

That was true enough.

Josh had known Sonja from way back when. All the way back to play school, in fact.

They'd stuck together through thick and thin, never more than a few steps apart. But while he had loved her from the very first, for her, he was never anything more than a friend. Her dearest friend, perhaps, the brother she never had, but never more than that. Josh had been so deep in the friend zone, he'd as good as had a map of it tattooed on his arse.

They'd remained close all the way through their school years, but after that, when he had gone off to Coventry Uni, Sonja had taken a gap year. To find herself, as she'd put it. Instead, she'd found herself up the duff, courtesy of some fucking jerk that had thought it might be fun to 'stealth' her, and then had fucked off to distant climbs as fast as his Birkenstocks could carry him when the *joke* backfired.

Unbeknownst to him, Sonja's family were Catholic and while she was not a believer herself, her respect for their beliefs meant she had never gone onto proper birth control.

Of course, two months later, her condition had started to show, and she'd faced the prospect of telling her parents that she was about to become an unmarried, single mother. The prospect had terrified her; so much so even the unthinkable option of a termination had quickly become the lesser of two evils.

That is, until Josh had proposed. The plan was simple enough. With his shares skyrocketing and a swiss bank account that would see him welcome at any Tory ball, they could hop onto his company's new jet, fly over to Vegas and get married. Then her family would never know the truth. She could claim the baby was his. And in Josh's young, naïve mind, he would finally have a shot with the girl of his dreams. After all, they were married and living as man and wife. Why wouldn't they be together.

Unfortunately, Sonja had never quite seen it that way.

No sooner had they moved in together than she'd made it obvious which rooms would be hers. And so their sham marriage became just that, a sham.

A show they put on for the world.

It just so happened he was also putting on a show for Sonja, too. Pretending to be happy with their arrangement when he was anything but.

He'd thought he'd had them all fooled.

Seems Erica knew him better than her mother had.

"She was so mean, but I'm gonna make it all better Daddy." Delicate fingers fisted in his hair, drawing him in close while she leant up on her tiptoes, her soft lips brushing softly against his. Her eyes drifted closed, and she promised, "Tonight, I'll be your reward. Your good, obedient little fucktoy stepdaughter, *Daddy*..."

Chapter FOUR

Daddy.

He hated it when she called him that. Hated the rush it gave him.

Hated the thrill it sent rushing down to the base of his spine.

Hated knowing she was just doing it to provoke him.

It might have been different if she'd called him that when she was little.

But she hadn't. She'd never called him it growing up.

Back then, he'd been Uncle Josh.

They'd never lied to her. She'd known the truth, even if she'd been too young to understand the reasons behind it. She'd known he wasn't her father. Just her mummy's friend who they lived with.

Who she could always trust and who would be there for her, no matter what.

And he'd always done his best to live up to that promise.

Even after Sonja had passed away, he'd strived to be there for her.

She'd been well into her teens by then and just called him Josh.

Sonja's loss had been hard on them both, but Erica had processed it well. She'd cried and wailed, rebelled, fought, stole, and even ran away. All the usual stages a child that had lost a parent went through. She'd grieved, and Josh had been there for her, weathering the storm until eventually she found the peace that she needed to carry on.

Then one day, not long after her sixteenth birthday, he'd come home from a long business trip and there she'd been waiting to greet him in the doorway. Before he could say a word, she'd thrown her arms around him and declared, "Daddy's back."

And there it was, the phrase that had shaped his life from then on.

In retrospect, he should have put a stop to it then, but he'd just handled her the same way he had her mother and just let it go.

Well, maybe it was time to change that.

"Tonight, I'll be your reward, your good, obedient little fuck toy stepdaughter, daddy..."

Josh knew he should refuse her. Tell her to put some clothes on and go to her room, but when she said it like that, how could he refuse?

Reaching out, he circled his arms around her waist and pulled her to him. In his arms, she felt deliciously small and delicate. Like fine china that might shatter if he was too rough with her.

She sighed, burying her face into the crook of his neck and inhaling deep, the delicate scent of his aftershave making her belly do somersaults, before lifting her chin slightly to look him in the eye. He met her stare; the desire reflected in those dark sapphire depths making his cock ache as, with his heart drumming in his chest, he dipped his head. She met him eagerly, rising onto the tips of her toes to press her mouth to his, arching up against him, needing to be as close as possible.

Josh knew it was a stupid thing to do.

No, a fucking ridiculous thing to do.

This was Erica, for Christ's sake.

Sonja's daughter.

Maybe all grown up, but still his stepdaughter.

Of course, he had never actually fucked her mother, which called into question the legality of their whole marriage. Which meant she was really nothing but a gorgeous young woman offering herself to him.

His best friend's daughter.

And as she pushed up against him, moaning the sexiest, kittenish sounds he'd ever heard, Josh could feel the heat of her skin burn through the Santa costume, and it drove him wild.

Wild enough for one of his hands to slide up her back, fingertips playing along the curve of her spine to tangle in her hair. She gasped at the sudden possessive ferocity and he pressed on, his tongue sliding in deep to feast on her sweetness, licking and swirling around. Drinking her in like a parched man's first cup of water, needing to savour every drop, her flavour as sweet to him as the rarest wine, his very own fountain of Ambrosia.

Lost in the taste of her, he didn't notice they were moving until he felt the base of the bed knock against the back of his legs and send them tumbling to the mattress. He landed on his back and Erica astride him.

Erica gasped at the sudden switch. Then, giggling playfully, she pulled back to look down at him stretched out across the bed beneath her. It was one of the sexiest things she had ever seen. The image of her stepfather in his ruffled shirtsleeves, his usually immaculate sandy hair tousled and that boyishly handsome face glazed with the desire she'd so longed to see burning for her. She'd never seen him look like this before, his expression so raw and primitive, almost bestial as his lust-darkened eyes seemed to burn hot and fierce.

It got her hot to see him looking so wild and dangerous, and she wanted to sear it into her memory. Taking a deep breath to calm herself, her heart fluttering like a robin redbreast in a cage at the thought of what was to come, she bent down and draped herself across him.

"You've no idea how long I've wanted this, *Daddy*," she purred in his ear, her low silky tone sending a fresh shiver down Josh's spine, making his cock swell and jerk within its prison as she kissed his nose, her hair tickling his cheek and making him groan softly at the tease of her touch.

The sound gave Erica such a thrill. For all her outward confidence, she hardly dared to believe this was real, that this was Josh, her Stepdad, beneath her, allowing her to touch him this way.

How long had she wanted it so?

It wasn't natural; she knew it. He'd been like a father to her.

Like, but never was.

Her father had never wanted her.

Josh was nothing like her father.

He was always there for her.

For no other reason than he loved her.

She would never meet another who could love her as Josh did. A love that was pure and selfless, totally and completely, and she wanted to make him happy. To give him that one thing he so dearly wanted.

And now could never have.

Chapter FIVE

Erica had never understood what was wrong with her mother.

How could she never have known how Josh felt about her?

He'd practically had it written all over his face whenever he'd looked at her.

Why had she never returned them?

He deserved so much more.

She wanted to give him that, be the wife he should have had.

She wanted to be his wife, his lover, the mother of his children, and the woman he deserved.

But first, she needed to prove she deserved him. She needed to prove she was worthy. And there was only one thing she could give to prove how much she loved him. So, she dropped a kiss on his jaw and swept her tongue along the ridge to tease the spot beneath his ear. Just the taste of him sent her desire into overdrive. Needing more, she kissed and nibbled his neck fervently, not even noticing when his hands came up and buried themselves in her hair.

"Oh God Erica," Josh moaned, his head rolling, exposing more flesh for her to attack oh, so sweetly, loving the feel of her luscious lips and her slick tongue on his skin.

Bolstered by his sounds of pleasure, Erica pressed on before her nerve gave out. Fingering the buttons of his shirt, she spread the cotton open and swept down to explore the planes of his body with her mouth, learning the slope of his shoulder, the chiseled muscles that made up his arms and stomach. Her teeth tugged gently at his flat nipples. Addicted to the taste of him, she quickly lost herself in his rich flavour and the sounds of his soft panting breath and wanton groans.

"Mmm… you like that, Daddy?" she purred, dipping her tongue into and around his belly button. Josh's hips jerked up at the contact, his erection brushing her breast as he arched and groaned, pressing his head into the pillow. Feeling the heat of his desire, Erica looked down and contemplated the impressive bulge straining against his trousers, growing more and more evident as she edged her way down between his legs.

"Mmm… so hard already?" With a trembling finger, she traced the outline of his cock through the fabric, marvelling at how big and hard it felt, even through his clothes.

"Minx…" Josh hissed through gritted teeth, fisting and twisting the sheets against the feeling that he was about to cum in his shorts on his first date. Fuck, what was she doing to him?

Though she delighted in the desperate, tightwire edge to his voice, Ericka took pity on him. Coyly licking her lips, she popped the button of his trousers before swallowing down the big knot of nerves in her throat as she tugged on his fly.

Only for it to jump beneath her fingers as her stepfather's fully engorged cock burst free of its prison to stand rampant before her eyes. Unbeknownst to her, whenever he had to get done up, Josh always went commando. The trousers were just way too confining. Not that she minded of course. Quite the contrary.

Erica could only stare wide-eyed at Josh's cock. Of course, she'd already seen her fair share of the male anatomy. She was a Manchester University student after all and as many of the male student body were as equally keen to show off their 'equipment' as the girls were to see it. However, she'd be willing to bet barely a fraction of all those young bucks would pack anything as big as the example standing before her.

At the very least, he was a good ten inches and as thick as her fucking wrist! Captivated, needing to touch, to feel him, this new part of him, she reached out and ran her fingers up his cock, from a base buried in a light nest of dark hair to the tip, hot and slick. Feeling his heated skin pulse under her touch, she wrapped her fingers around him, amazed at the incredible heat and the silken texture stretched over something so hard. She squeezed and watched in fascination as Josh's hips bucked, pearly drops flowing down his length. Leaning down, she lightly touched the tip of her tongue to the head of his cock, lapping up the pre-cum like a sex kitten in its saucer of milk. It tasted bitter sweet, but all her brain could register was that this was Josh's, and for her that made it as divine as Devonshire cream.

"Wa-wait, Erica you-you don't have to… oh fuck…" Josh groaned, his head rolling back onto his shoulders as her hand started to jerk his cock.

"Mmm… that's it Daddy, just relax and enjoy your present." Erica purred, blowing a soft breath across his sensitive flesh before swooping down to take his crown into her mouth.

"Oh, fuck…" Josh hissed at the feeling, his back curving at the sensation of being enveloped in the lush heat. When her cheeks hollowed as she sucked, it was all he could do to keep his hands off her. "Er-Erica… yeah, yeah, just like that, just… like… oh fuck!"

Erica couldn't get enough of listening to her stepfather's pleasure drunk groans and moans as she sucked him. It gave her such a thrill, such a sense of triumph, to know she had done this to him. It got her so fucking hot. She needed more and began bobbing her head, her mouth gliding up and down, each downstroke letting a little more of his length pass through her lips.

Helpless to do anything but lie there, Josh could only groan an indistinct sound somewhere between and a moan and a hiss. His flesh was so sensitive at that moment, he could feel every minimal movement of her tongue against his crest, and each time she inhaled, his cock swelled and pulsed until it felt ready to burst. That in turn only excited his stepdaughter further and by relaxing her throat, she took as much of his dick in as she could.

"Oh God, Erica… fuck!" At the feeling of her taking him into her throat, Josh's eyes rolled and this time he couldn't stop himself from burying his hand into her bounty of dark tresses. When she moaned from his forcefulness, the vibrations traveled along his aching cock and almost pushed him to the point of no return.

Erica sensed her stepfather's orgasm drawing near. In her mind, she imagined him releasing his seed all over her, painting her face and body with his essence to mark and brand her as his. However, for now she wanted to taste him and, keeping her lips wrapped around his length, she sucked hard.

"Oh fuck, Erica… w-wait… don't suck so ha-ohh!" The long groan was the only warning before his hips bucked beneath her and a rush of hot cum flooded forth and down her throat as she worked to swallow as much as she could.

Only when her mouth was almost overflowing did the flow finally slow to a few soft spurts of cream. Panting hard and skin shiny with perspiration, Josh slumped back onto the bed, black dots dancing before his eyes. Fuck, he couldn't remember the last time he'd come that hard.

Watching him with a self-satisfied smile tugging at her lips, Erica quickly swallowed the last of his release before pulling away. Despite having just had an orgasm, his cock remained tall and proud as she rose to her feet. "So Daddy, are you ready for the rest of your present now?"

Barely hearing her through the haze settling over his muddled brain, Josh forced his attention back down, just in time to watch her grab the fluffy hem of her Santa suit. Erica pulled it up to her midriff to reveal her long silky smooth legs, tight flat belly, and flared hips dressed with a white thong threaded with crimson silk.

"This is all yours tonight, Daddy…"

The sight made his mouth water. Then their eyes met, and she ever so slowly licked her lips as she hooked a finger beneath the front of her panties and tugged the garment to the side.

"Mmm… you've always been so good to me, well now I'm here to return the favour…" she purred, her hand sliding down between her legs. Erica's tongue snaked out to moisten her lips as her fingers made long, slow strokes through her folds to tease the needy pearl that stood swollen and erect, begging for attention. "Make love to me like your wife, or punish me as your little Christmas fuck toy. You can do whatever you want with me. I'm all yours, Daddy-"

"Erica!" Josh moved like a tiger, tearing away his shirt and pushing off his trousers in a single bound. Erica made a sound that was half a scream, half a laugh as he seized her and threw to the bed. Then he was on her, caging her with his hard body and dragging the Santa suit up and over her head, leaving her in nothing but the soaked panties.

God… she's gorgeous!

He gazed, drinking in the sight of her as if for the very first time. The tightness between his legs suggested his fully revived cock agreed.

He'd always known she was beautiful, but until this moment, he had never seen her for what she was. Never seen her for the woman she was.

Well, watching her suck him off then play with herself right there on his bed in front of him had certainly taken care of that. This wasn't just Sonja's daughter. This was a beautiful, wanton creature that wanted him.

And damn it, he wanted her too.

Chapter SIX

Erica stared up at him, her eyes wide and a little uncertain. This clearly wasn't part of her plan. "D-daddy?"

A growl rumbled in Josh's throat. That blasted name again. Well, it was time to put a stop to that. Bending down, he looked her dead in the eye. "My name is Josh."

She swallowed hard and nodded. "Josh."

"Good girl," he praised, his mouth brushing over hers in the merest ghost of a kiss before sweeping down to her neck.

"Josh..." she gasped, curling beneath him, crushing herself against his hard torso as he nipped and sucked a lightning trail all the way down to the hollow of her throat. "Josh," she moaned again when one hand cupped her right breast, his thumb brushing and teasing her pebbled nipple until she couldn't take any more. "Take me... please."

"No, not yet…" Josh growled, his tone low and hungry with desire, brokering no argument. Then he was sliding down the length of her young, nubile body, dragging his tongue down the valley of her breasts to her abdomen and scattering butterfly kisses around her belly button, before rearing back up to her breasts, stinging and soothing one then the other with quick nips and licks.

Erica was helpless against the sensual assault.

"Oh God, please, Josh, stop teasing me," she pleaded, squeezing her eyes shut against the storm he was stirring up inside her, but it did no good. The sensuous electricity that went zipping through her skin every time he tongued her nipple, making her tremble and writhe, was just too delicious.

She couldn't keep still.

Which was just how Josh wanted her, and delighting how responsive she was, he abandoned his prize to bend down, trap the hem of her sodden panties between his teeth, and dragged them down and off her legs.

The display sent a violent rush of desire through her before a sensuous moan flowed from her lips as she felt his tongue part her folds. "Josh… oh fuck!"

Through the fog of sensation that was descending over her, Erica's mind somehow registered that she could actually see him watching her from between her legs as he did such unspeakable things to her pussy, his eyes dark with carnal hunger burning in them as his mouth feasted on her, the very idea amplifying each stroke of his tongue as it swivelled through her creamy folds. Captivated by the sight, she couldn't look away, but the intensity was all too much for her body, and her legs wrapped around his head and back, at once trying to block the site from view while refusing to let him end his assault.

No sooner had she done so, however, his arms snaked their way around her thighs and wrenched them apart, away from his head, forcing her to watch him eat her pussy.

The idea of it alone was beyond erotic and instinctively her hands buried themselves in his hair, fisting and tugging as he feasted on her, tonguing her cunt with long deep licks, before switching targets and suckling at her clit with a low rumbling hum.

And just like that, her universe seemed to combust as the knot in her centre came undone in what she could only describe as the orgasm of the fucking century. Her sex clenched, her body arched, and squeezing her eyes shut against the storm as La petite mort swept her away.

With the musky scent of her cream pervading his senses and turning his cock to iron, Josh had never been more ready to fuck in his life. Yet, as small and tight as she was, he knew he needed to be patient. He needed her to be ready, or else he would hurt her. He'd never hurt her.

He'd waited for this for so long, he wouldn't ruin it now. Not now, not when she was finally his. And she was his. If only for this one night. She was his, his wife, his Sonja.

So it was only when he felt her come undone that he acted. Pulling free of her death grip and rising over her, took himself in hand and prepared to slide home.

Blurry eyed and still trembling from the force of her climax, the first thing Erica noticed was the blur of Josh's body looming over her. Then, piece by piece, he slid back into focus, and she realised he was smirking, obviously pleased with himself. Rightly so, in her opinion, the smug bastard had certainly paid her back, and she had to admit, the look suited him.

Then she felt something hot brush over her clit, sending tingles sizzling outward, and her eyes shifted downward to see him aimed for penetration. Despite herself, she couldn't help wondering if that thing was actually going to fit inside her.

He must have been able to sense her hesitation, however, because he paused, and that cocky grin faltered.

"Erica, if you want to sto-"

"No!" she gasped, fisting the bedspread, desperate and beyond caring about anything but feeling him sinking balls deep. "Do it! I need your cock… please… I'm ready… I've never been more ready… stick it in and fuck me with your big, perfect co-oh!"

One quick push was all it took for his broad crest to part her folds and press home. Erica's back curled at the feeling, her eyes going wide and her hips bucked up to meet his.

"Fuck… Erica…" Josh panted, trying to push down the urge to cum right then and there. Somewhere, deep down in the forgotten halls of his head, he knew he should wait, give her time to adjust before pressing on, but he wasn't sure he would last that long. He couldn't help himself. She was just so fucking slick and snug. He needed to feel her cunt wrapped around him.

And Erica was right there with him. She loved the feeling of him filling her, of being stretched and stuffed, of having him inside her. It was everything she'd imagined, and so much more. She wanted more. More of these feelings, this ecstasy. It was like a dream she never wanted to wake up from. She was sharing a level of intimacy with someone she never thought possible to reach. And she loved every fucking second of it.

"Oh God… Josh… yes… that's it… Mmm… feels so good…" she panted, her head rolling back as her body opened up and took everything he had to give. Yet just when she felt ready to burst, his hands were seizing the back of her knees and hiking them up onto his shoulders as he leaned over her. Then he started circling his hips, pulling out, then driving back home hard, setting off supernovas in her core. "Oh, fuck… Oh my God… So big… Oh fuck… Fuck… Fuck me… Fuck me…"

Josh loved hearing her say such dirty words. For him, there was nothing sexier than a posh bird talking dirty. And his little Erica was the poshest bird there was. A proper little London socialite, the cream of an expensive English education. Yet here she was. Spread out beneath him, naked and begging for it like a greedy little sex kitten.

"Mine," he growled, his voice deep and bestial with desire, dropping one hand down to thumb her clit.

"Yes!" she answered, looking him dead in the eye so he would see the truth in her words. That she was his, now and always. "Yours, all yours- Oh-oh my God, oh my God. I'm going to cum, I'm going to cum again…" Her words trailed away as she apexed, yet she refused to look away. He was close, too. So very close. She could see it in his eyes and was desperate to feel him, to feel them take that final step together.

She moaned, "cum for me, Josh! Fill me up with all your cum!"

And that was the final straw.

He took her mouth in a hot, hungry kiss, swallowing her needy moans as he crushed her to him. The *V* of his hips spread her open, his cock sinking all the way to the root on that final plunge before she felt the rush of heat flooding her centre, branding her as his and his alone.

They could have stayed like that forever. Bodies entwined. Mouths locked. Their souls and hearts joined as one. They might have, or it could only have been a few minutes. All they knew when they finally separated was that it 'twas the night before Christmas, and all through their penthouse, not a creature was stirring.

Still tingling with the aftershocks of such an intense orgasm, Erica snuggled into his side, draping an arm and leg across him, and slowly curled a lock of his chest hair around a finger. "Merry Christmas, *Daddy*."

"Minx," Josh snorted. But, rather than taking the bait, he threw an arm around her and drew her close. "You're not too old to go over my knee, you know."

"Oh… promises, promises," she teased, but lacked the energy to carry the game any further. So instead, they just laid there together, and if only for those few precious moments, all was right with the world.

The End

Her Bad Boy Protector

CHAPTER ONE

They should have been laying low, keeping a low profile, but there was little chance of anyone noticing them here. It was the sort of place that no one asked questions. The club was as underground as it was possible to get.

With the bright LED beams bouncing off the reflective disco ball, the walls seemed to shake as the rock music screamed out from the concealed sound system in a maelstrom of sound that had the patrons dancing with renewed life.

Encircled by Luke's strong arms, Sophie felt like she was floating on air and her body seemed to be moving of its own accord as she revelled in the sensation of being so close to this man.

It was stupid and reckless. He was her guard, her protector, the man her father had charged to keep her safe. If they were discovered, they could both be killed, but she couldn't help herself. She'd seduced him.

She'd seduced him because when she was with him, she wasn't just Mr Larry's daughter. She wasn't just an underworld princess or the daughter of the East Coast's most notorious gangster. With him, she was just Sophie.

With Luke, she felt alive. Alive and free of her gilded cage-

"Sophie." The warning in Luke's voice shattered the moment like the fall of a sledgehammer. Looking up, she realised that the music had stopped and none of the other people on the floor were dancing anymore.

"Luke... What's happening?" she asked, but Luke wasn't listening. Instead, a stern look had come over his face as he looked past her. Not accustomed to her lover ignoring her,

Sophie followed his eyes to the club's main entrance. There, flanked by a pair of goons, a man in his early forties, with neatly cropped salt and pepper hair, dressed in a tailored and very immaculate Armani suit and leather coat, was talking with the doorman.

Sophie recognised him immediately as her father's consigliere. The right hand of God.

"We've got company."

"Victor," she whispered, her deep cerulean eyes widening as panic flared inside her breast like cold fingers coiling around her heart. "What are we going to do?"

Luke didn't answer. One of the goons, a large man dressed in a navy blazer and matching chinos with a squashed face, stepped forward.

"All right, people!" he yelled, his deep voice sounding more like a growl than speech. "We're looking for two people. A man and a woman. We know who they are and that they're here, so stay out of our way. Don't try to play the hero and you won't get hurt."

"They are looking for us!" Sophie whispered, grabbing his hand and clinging to his arm with a death grip. "Luke, what are we going to do?"

Time and again, they'd discussed what she should do if they were discovered, but now the moment was here, she was lost.

Watching for a moment as both goons began to push through the dancers, Luke waited, a calculating look playing across his handsome features as his eyes poured over the scene. There were too many innocents for him to shoot a way out, but if they did not move, then it would just be a matter of time until they were caught. They had only one choice and subtly looking from side to side. A small smile graced his thin lips when he spotted a back door.

"Over there," he whispered, nodding to the door. "Move slowly and don't look back. Go now and I'll meet you outside."

Sophie didn't hesitate. Keeping her head down, she walked through and around the throng, taking care not to draw anyone's attention. Blessedly, her movement attracted little notice and she couldn't help breathing a sigh of relief as she felt the cold steel of the backway's handle beneath her fingertips. Pressing her palm gently against the leaver so it wouldn't make a sound, she pushed it open a crack and slipped silently through into the cold night air before pulling it closed.

The door opened out into an alcove for a flight of concrete steps up to the alley behind the club. Taking the flight at a run, a quick glance confirmed it to be empty. However, she didn't have time to get her bearings. No sooner had she emerged out next to the fire escape ladder than the door beside it suddenly burst open.

CHAPTER TWO

Spinning around, she had a moment's dread that Victor must have seen her and doubled round to cut off her escape, but instead, Luke emerged out with his Beretta M9 in hand. Pivoting, he shoulder-slammed the door shut and gave the escape lever a twist that ripped it off its hinges, jamming the mechanism.

"Quick, someone will have heard that. Up the stairs."

Sophie wanted to protest. The stairway was very similar to the ones in old action movies. It was so dilapidated and rusted, it looked like it hadn't been maintained since Hitchcock used it in North by Northwest.

One look from Luke, though, silenced her. They didn't have a choice. The main road would be out of the question, as Victor would have placed a guard or two at the building's entrance, just in case they tried to run. The alleyway was a lost cause as it ended with a wall which looked too high for either of them to climb. They'd have to chance it and find a place to hide upstairs, while the goon squad followed his distraction out here and searched the surrounding area. They could make their getaway later when the heat had died down.

They made it up to the first level without any interruptions, their every step making the old steel structure sway and tremble. Before Sophie could make a move towards the door, Luke shook his head and directed her to the second flight, making her curse under her breath. Yet when she felt Luke's arm on her shoulder, she forgot her inhibitions and let him shepherd her up the creaky stairwell. Still, they needed to get off these bloody stairs before they collapsed from underneath them. Luke seemed not to share her distress, however, and instead, he pressed her on like she was little more than a stubborn child.

Somehow, the structure held out and as they stepped onto the brickwork of a balcony; the pair breathed a sigh of relief. They had made it.

"Well, well, well... look at what I have found," chortled an all too familiar voice. Sophie pivoted around to find Victor standing on the railing, his own M9 trained on Luke's heart. "Now, be a good boy Luke, drop it."

Lips pursed so tight they formed a white line, Luke dropped the Beretta, so it landed on the grating with a cling, then nudged it over the side with his boot.

"That's a good little dog, and you princess," he turned the gun on Sophie. "Your escapades are getting more creative. What did you promise him?"

Tears burned the corner of Sophie's eyes. "Victor, please..."

"Was it your heart?" he grinned, his face contorting into a twisted look of sadistic glee, like a child pulling the wings off a fly. "Well, we all make mistakes. Your father has already forgiven you. In fact, he has a gift for you. He'll give you his hear-ahh!" Luke didn't blink, he just acted, lunging forward. He caught the older man's arm, raised it high, so the M9 pointed skyward. Then he hit him. It came in hard and fast, with all his power behind it. A storm of force that drove into Victor's belly with a meaty slap and sent him tumbling back and over the edge.

CHAPTER THREE

Not staying to hear the sickening splat, he quickly opened the fire door and ushered Sophie into the deserted corridor lined by rows of doors. Stepping in after her, he walked partway down the corridor and then tried a door.

The door slid open with no resistance and he held it open for Sophie before pulling it gently closed behind them. Unwilling to relax just yet, though, he pressed his ear against the door and listened for any sound of movement on the other side. Victor's death would undoubtedly attract the attention of his goons, but he doubted they would come up here. After all, what self-respecting couple on the run would hide inside the building they knew was being searched? Especially after killing the right hand of God.

Luke kept his ear pressed against the timber until he was sure that the coast was clear, but turning around, his breath caught in his throat.

They were in what must have been the club's penthouse suite. It was easily larger than any of the apartments and hotel rooms they had stayed in over the last few months and, without a doubt, far more luxurious. Pine furniture of various degrees decorated the spacious chamber and an immense, king-sized, four-poster bed took up almost the entire span of one wall.

Sophie stood in the centre of the room, the low light seeming to give her an eerie glow as she fixed him with a look that made his mouth run dry. There was a passion in her eyes, the likes of which he had never seen there before, and when she came to him, it was with all the grace and speed of a stalking tigress. Crossing the breadth between them in an instant, she jumped into his arms and crushed her lips to his in a searing embrace.

Momentarily forgetting about the soon to be vengeful goons, their lips parted, and tongues met, causing Sophie to moan as she felt the hungry passion explode within her breast. With a frenzied desire, her hands ran over every piece of Luke's back while his own sought her hips, crushing her to him as his rough palms groped the firm flesh of her buttocks through the fabric of her tiny maxi dress.

Locked together until the need for air grew undeniable, Sophie pulled back, playfully biting her lover's lower lip as she did. She wanted to go further, but Luke's confused look made her pause.

"Sophie?"

"You did it. We're free," she whispered, her mischievous hands slowly creeping down his body as she spoke before cupping his cock through his jeans. "Oh, I want you Luke. Mmm…watching you got me so hot!"

Tempted as he was, Luke couldn't draw his mind away from the goons hunting them, but then his lover's fingers began to work at the fastening, pushing the garment down his legs to pool around his ankles.

"Oh Luke, you bad boy. Already?" she whispered before a sultry smile played across her lips as she unhooked her legs from around his hips and slid silkily to the floor. Hard and impossibly large, Luke's erection stood rampant and unable to resist. She reached out to touch him.

Running her fingers along his flesh, she couldn't help but stare at it in wonderment as she slowly explored. His arousal felt like steel dressed in silk and it twitched every time she completed a stroke, drawing a moan from Luke, who was rapidly losing the will to resist her advances.

Tough guy that he was, he was trying his hardest not to groan, as it would show her she was doing something he really liked, but his body seemed determined to betray him. She had only just begun, yet he could already feel his legs quaking. He told himself not to look down, as he knew the image of her kneeling before him while she played with his straining cock would be the end of him. Just the thought of those silky blonde locks framing her face and sapphire eyes that made her seem as innocent as a kitten...

Only she was anything but innocent.

"Sophie... Oh God!" he gasped, unable to hold back a moan as she suddenly swirled her tongue around the head of his cock before she pursed her mouth into a tight 'O'. Gently, her hand travelled up and down his shaft as her mouth enclosed over the tip, overloading Luke's senses and turning him into a gibbering, pleasure drunk fool.

Watching her lover's head roll back as she continued to slowly slide his shaft into her mouth, Sophie felt a delicious sense of power overtake her. It was so exhilarating to think that she could have this much power over anyone so strong. Not wanting to squander it all in one go, she slowly ran her tongue along his length while letting her breath wash over his skin as she exhaled.

"Oh, oh, oh sweet Jesus..." he gasped as he felt a pool of pleasure mounting inside his loins. "So good, Sophie you're... so good..." He could feel her tongue swirl around him, its silky wetness massaging all his most sensitive spots as she took more and more into her mouth.

Sophie continued to stroke and touch him with her fingers, letting his moans guide her until she felt Luke's hands suddenly thread through her hair and begin forcibly guiding her to where he wanted. Although he was careful not to be too forceful, unless he risked accidentally hurting her, Sophie could still feel her throat tightening around the shaft as she struggled to accommodate the mass. This was by no means her first time attending to the large male's shaft, but so large was he that no matter how much practise she got, the girl knew she would never be able to accommodate his full girth. So, doing her best to relax her throat, she took as much of his dick in as she possibly could.

An inaudible groan left Luke's parted lips as he felt his love relaxing her throat, encasing the majority of his arousal in an oasis of intoxicating sensations. He badly wanted to push her head further down onto his cock, but the risk of hurting her was too great for him to chance it.

Sensing the pressure against her head lessening, Sophie began to pull away, allowing a fresh breath of air to fill her lungs as she very gently scraped her teeth along his organ before repeating the motion of taking him into her mouth once more. The act made her lover cry with delirious pleasure and glancing down, he found he couldn't stop himself from watching the blonde's head bobbing up and down on his shaft as she looked up at him with those deceiving, innocent blue eyes.

"Oh... God... Sophie... you're so... beautiful!" he gasped, unable to tear his eyes off the sight of her as he felt his release draw closer.

Delighted by his words, Sophie couldn't resist moaning and the vibrations which travelled through her throat reverberated all along his shaft, causing the enthralled male to moan in turn as his hips began to buck forward in a display of wild passion.

"Oh... oh... God... don't stop!"

Fortunately for him, Sophie had no intention of stopping. Seeing how close to the brink her lover was, she doubled her efforts, drawing a fresh tide of moans and groans from Luke as she pulled back and wrapped her tongue around the pulsing head before taking all of his cock into her mouth once more.

"Oh... Sophie... I'm... stop... cum... close..." he whispered, teeth clenched tightly as a fresh wash of pleasure hit his body like the stormy waves of the sea. How badly he wanted to watch her again, to see her head bob up and down on his shaft and witness his thick cock disappear and reappear from her luscious lips. Yet despite all his desires, he dared not look, for he knew it would be the end of him. In truth, he was far from sure of how he had made it this far. Her touch just felt so good that he thought even the tiniest of her graces might be enough to bring him to a steamy release.

His release was building, however, of that much he was certain. Like a pool of molten ecstasy, he could feel it slowly cooking him from within as it fought his every effort to suppress its rise. So stubborn was Luke that he was trying to hold it off for as long as possible. Intent on enjoying the sensations a little more, he snatched a quick breath and...

Without warning, a tremor suddenly ran through him as the last swirl of Sophie's tongue brought him flying over the peak and into the white abyss of *La petite mort*. With a long cry bellowing from his lips, his fingers convulsed in her hair as his hips pushed him deeper into her mouth and a tide of his seed poured down her awaiting throat.

Trying not to gag as the thick seed exploded into her mouth, the Underworld Princess swallowed as much of her lover's bitter-sweet cum as she could before letting his softening appendage slip from her lips as she felt his hands release their grip on her hair. With a seductive grace, she wiped the corners of her mouth before licking what remained of his seed from her fingers.

Coming back down to earth, Luke was about to say something, but the sight of Sophie seductively licking her fingers in a fashion which held a great amount of resemblance to the way she had been attending to his shaft, poked the fire in his loins back to life.

Noticing his revival, the blonde beauty looked up at him with a very pleased smile playing across her glistening lips.

"You enjoy that baby?" she asked, the satisfied look never leaving her even as she brushed a stray lock of her blond hair aside. Luke didn't answer her vocally. It was time for payback and without saying a word, he reached down and grasped her by the shoulders before hoisting her into his arms and carrying her over to the bed, bridal style.

Dropping her into the embrace of the soft mattress and feather duvets, Luke couldn't help taking a moment to admire the way Sophie's sexy form lay sprawled out before him.

"Luke?" Sophie asked as he covered her body with his. She was quickly silenced as he leaned down and lightly kissed her lips before crawling down the length of her body to the covered cleft between her legs. Poised over her like a watchful eagle, he let his hands trail up the toned skin of her thighs, pushing the material of her dress up as they went until the bright purple colouring of her obviously soaked thong was revealed to his eyes.

Sophie panted with lust and excitement, not quite sure whether she could truly believe her own eyes as she watched him deeply breathe in her scent before exhaling a heated breath over her most secretive spot. The sensation of it washing over her mound made her body shiver with delight. Using his teeth, he gripped the hem of her underwear and pulled it down her legs.

Feeling his mouth water at the sight of her clearly glistening cleft, Luke began to push her thighs further apart until her knees had to bend and her legs had opened to him like the shining gates of heaven as he hungrily pulled her to his waiting mouth.

With the utmost care, he stuck his tongue out and expertly ran it over her moistened entrance, making Sophie abruptly still as he was careful not to enter her just yet. Her breath began coming in great gasps as he greedily lapped up all the thick fluid which she produced and teased her by making no sign that he ever intended to move on. *Paybacks a bitch, Princess.*

"Luke!" she finally cried, the desperate anticipation of what was to come burning inside her core like a furnace, its incredible heat threatening to consume her soul. "Stop teasing me, you basta... Oh!" Her words melted into a long moan as she felt her lover press his slick muscle into her core.

However, Luke wasn't about to abandon his efforts just yet and he only probed inside of her, gently running his tongue along the edges of her inner depths whilst gathering up her cream, relishing her heady flavour.

Streams of pleasure coursed through Sophie's veins as her lover's gentile ministrations took the edge off her desires, but they were far from able to satisfy the white-hot need throbbing at her centre. In no time at all, she was rolling her hips against his mouth to signal that she wanted more. His grip on her body was tight, however, and he refrained from allowing her too much control as he continued to tease her core with his devilish tongue.

"Luke..." she whined, growing slightly breathless as the wanton heat in her abdomen grew almost unbearable and forced her to fight all the harder against his hold. "Please!"

The sound of her desperation made Luke inwardly snigger and, for a moment, he considered giving her what she so badly desired, but he couldn't resist teasing her a little more first.

"Please what, Princess? What do you want?" Luke could barely contain his glee as he mumbled the words against her hot flesh, drawing a high moan which almost sounded like a shriek from Sophie.

Unwilling to speak, she tried again to press her hips against his wondrous mouth, but lacked the strength to match his deathly tight hold. Instead, a defiant passion flared up in her eyes as she breathlessly leaned forward to see that he was now looking up at her from between her legs.

"Eat me!" she finally said in a voice that matched the defiance in her eyes. "I want you to eat me. You big meanie."

"As my Princess wishes," he purred, smirking at her angry admission as he slid his tongue between her folds and over her clit, making the girl cry out as his tongue hungrily lashed the bundle of nerves.

Feeling his attentions shoot through her nerves, Sophie released a scream of ecstasy as she spread her legs wider, silently begging him for more. He took the bud into his mouth and began sucking on it hard.

"Luke… oh yes… fuck… there… right there!" she moaned. Her hips rolling in time to the motions of his mouth, her hand slid onto the back of his head and sought some kind of purchase amongst his raven mane. His lips were now gently tugging at her sensitive clit as his teeth lightly gnawed the bud, causing her moans to turn to white-hot screams. He was so good. It was maddening, and she rocked, cried, and arched in all the ways that made Luke mad with lust.

The sight of her succulent body arching up beneath him made Luke's cock throb as he lost himself in her sweet scent, the taste of her which flowed across his tongue, and the sounds which rang in his ears. The entire experience of pleasing Sophie with his mouth was so intoxicating that Luke thought he might grow drunk on it. However, the growing ache of his renewed and very prominent cock was becoming so undeniable that he knew he could not continue like this for much longer and so he released her clit and turned his attention lower.

"No! Don't stop! Oh God, Luke don't sto… oh my God!"

Words failed Sophie as she suddenly felt her bodyguard's tongue leave her clit and plunge deep into her centre. Her entire body seemed to go rigid as he licked her with unerring accuracy, his devilish tongue flicking, swirling, and driving her into a frenzy as it delved deep into her core. She couldn't think. The burning pleasure and the heat of her desire blinded her to the world and as his tongue moved in and out of her, she could feel the tight knot of an orgasm collecting inside her. It wouldn't be long now…

Watching her reaction with immense interest, Luke continued to drive his tongue deep inside Sophie, not stopping even as he felt her thighs start to contract around his face as the waves of her pleasure mounted. Writhing beneath him, she

desperately ground her hips into his face as she made such
lovely noises.

"Oh God, Luke!" the beauty cried, arching her back off
the bed so far that she should have feared her back would
break, and squeezing her thighs so tight that her lover had to
pull them apart. His tongue was just so relentless. It was like
she was just some toy he chose to play with and the burning
look of desire that she could see play across his eyes made her
all the hotter. "Oh… I'm going to- Oh-oh… fuck! Oh fuck, fuck,
fuck!"

With a wicked smile, Luke watched as his love's head
tossed. The pleasure of his mouth on her sex had already made
her lush milky skin flushed, and the sharp blades of her nails
cut intricate webs through the bed's sheets. Her legs shook
from the pleasure that crashed through her.

"Luke!" Sophie came with enough force to break every
bone in her body, bucking off the bed as the knot at her centre
ignited and went supernova.

Feeling her climax hit as her inner muscles tightened
around his tongue, Luke rode out the storm with her, holding
her tightly to his mouth as he drank every drop of her fluids.

Her climax began to subside after a few moments, but
the experience of it left Sophie feeling drained and very
satisfied. Its burning heat radiated through her with an
unquenchable passion, but even that was not enough to
quench her lust. The flames of her desires were quickly
rekindled when she saw Luke begin to stand, revealing to her
gaze the true extent of his want for her as his cock stood so
proudly. The nature of it was impossible, yet somehow, he
seemed even larger now than he had before.

With an excited hush overtaking them, Luke climbed
onto the bed. But before he could even get into position, Sophie
suddenly threw her palms against him. Pushing against his
broad chest with all her strength, she flashed him a sly smile
that spoke volumes. He lay back without argument, ready to
embrace her with all his being as she straddled his waist, her

gaze locked to his as she slowly began to lower herself onto him.

Sensing the hot sheath of her core slowly taking him in, Luke couldn't help but groan and it took all of his selfcontrol to fight the urge to buck and ram himself inside of her. No matter how many times they fucked, somehow, she always seemed to remain so deliciously tight and just the feeling of her snug heat surrounding him was almost enough to make him cum right then and there.

Taking her time as she slowly lowered herself onto the brunt of his erection, Sophie couldn't help but moan low as she savoured the feeling of him filling her like no other man ever could. Already she felt stuffed to capacity. She knew every part of his male biology would be demanding for him to take her now, claim her, and fuck her to heaven and back. But she also knew he would be fighting those desires tooth and nail, so she was free to take her time...

"Mmm… so big!" she purred, keeping her eyes locked on his as she rolled her hips, working more and more of him inside.

"Fuck! Sophie!" he groaned out, as the feel of her tight heat grew ever more around him, causing his breath to come in short gasps as she tested the limits of his self-control to the last tether. Unwilling to risk causing her pain, though, he willed himself to stay in check and refused to move, even as he felt her squirm above him. Only the tautness of his muscles and the long, seething breaths he dragged in through clenched teeth revealed the fever that raged inside of him.

Minutes passed like the span of a lifetime and finally, after what seemed like an eternity in purgatory, Luke was finally able to let out a sigh as he felt his love settle herself onto the base of his shaft. He had not dared to move an eyelash during the ordeal, but now his desire was mounting, and his eyes were growing dark, making it a struggle for him to focus as the veins in his neck bulged due to the strain of his defiance.

Sophie wanted to scream as the burning sensation of him stretching and filling her body crashed into her. Disoriented and shaken to her very core, she basked in the sensation of him filling her with a look of utter ecstasy on her face. It seemed that no matter how many times they enjoyed such wonderful trysts, she would never be able to adjust to his size.

Far below them, the booming sound of the club had resumed and echoed up, signalling the goons had moved on in their search. But neither Luke nor Sophie could have a care for such trifling things. Lost in the raging tempest of sensations, they were trapped in the violent swells of a vast ocean and unable to move as the waves of their passions crashed into them without mercy. However, once the throbbing of her clit had woken Sophie from her trance-like state of bliss, she couldn't hold back and rolled her hips into his.

The action made Luke's hands fist in the sheets, her teasing motion adding fuel to the fire that raged inside him, forcing his breath to be drawn even more shallow as he lent up and tried to work more of his shaft inside of her. However, noticing his attempt to take back control, Sophie smacked his chest hard enough to make him hiss and still, before continuing to grind their hips together in small circles. Despite the burning need that had set her hollowed loins on fire, she was not yet ready to surrender control just yet. To know that she could be the master of one so strong was a sensation so wonderful and made her feel so… powerful.

For the first time in her life, she was in control of her destiny.

However, she grew tired of the tepid pleasure that rolling her hips brought her, and so she laid her hands flat against his taut stomach muscles for support. She felt a shiver run through him at her touch, then raised herself up until he nearly slid out of her, and then plunged back down in one stroke.

"Oh... God... Sophie," Luke gasped, fighting to stay in control as he felt the abrupt plunge into paradise. He was unable to restrain a long moan as he felt her slick walls massaging his burning column into climax. "Oh, fuck... so tight!"

His words caused a smirk to spread across the blonde's pleasure-etched face and she began to raise her arse once more, repeating the action at a treacherous pace.

He thwarted her plans, however, when on her third drop, Luke found he couldn't resist any longer and surprised her by bending his knees, allowing her to slide a little deeper onto his shaft. The sudden jolt it sent along her nerves had her throwing her head back and a long moan echoing from her gaping lips as her hands pawed all over his torso as she tried to catch her breath. But in those precious seconds, Luke had gained the upper hand, and he emphasised that point by placing his hands on her hips and lifting her before impaling her again on his thick cock.

She screamed out at the feeling of him filling her, all defiance melting away into pleasure as her instincts took over and she began to ride him like she had not a care in the world.

"Oh, God! Y-You feel so good baby!" she moaned, her hands leaving their spot on his stomach to slide up her body and roughly fondle her breasts through the fabric of her dress as she lost herself. "Oh, God… Oh Jesus… Oh fuck! Luke… yes!"

Watching his lover's display through half-closed eyes, Luke wanted to chuckle, but the sudden echo of a creaking floorboard brought the cold realisation of their present situation crashing down on top of him like a cold rain.

"You're being too loud Princess… *mmm*… the whole damn city is gonna hear us," he whispered. As much as he enjoyed the sounds of her moans, he couldn't take the risk of any lingering goons getting wind of where they were and barging in. Yet despite his words, he couldn't resist increasing the speed of his motions.

"But… you're… so… big! Oh… God, yes!" Sophie cried, her eyes shutting tight as she felt him increase the tempo of his thrusts, making her body bounce on his with a wild abandon that filled the room with the sounds of their bodies slapping.

Irked by her lack of concern, Luke wanted to reprimand her further, but all he could muster was a long moan as he felt the way her impossibly tight pussy was massaging every centimetre of his cock as it slid up and down him with more vigour. Soon, even his reservations about moaning aloud had dissipated and lost in the fog of pleasure. He couldn't remember why they had hidden up in the suite in the first place. Freed from those shackles, he was now more than happy to encourage the wanton girl as he hungrily watched her fondle her breasts.

"Oh yes," she moaned, arching her breasts into her grasp as the pleasure seemed to double every time he was fully encased within her. "Oh, yes… yes… baby… let me ride you… let me fuck you. You're so hard… so big… uh…. harder baby… fuck me harder! Make me cum!"

"Oh… that's it Sophie! Ride me Princess," he groaned, matching his pleasure-enthralled lover thrust for thrust, timing his motions to catch her on the downstroke. "Yeah, you like my dick inside you don't you Princess?" A small, knowing smile played across his lips as he watched her roughly grope herself. Oh, how he ached to be the one touching her, but instead he had to enjoy the show, watching intently as they succumbed to her palms like clay while she bounced upon him, bringing them both closer to a much-needed release.

"Oh yeah, it's so hard! So fucking hard! Uhhhh!" she cried, yet despite the clenching of her inner muscles, her lover's thrusts never faltered, and she continued to bounce up and down on him with a fervid passion. "Fuck my pussy… oh yes… baby, please fuck me harder! Harder! Oh, God!"

Lost in depths of their passion, neither noticed that the bed's wooden headboard was now slamming loudly against the wall, its thick timber frame proving to be no match for the power of the lovers coupling as the Underworld Princess bounced her lover's immense column with all her might. Like a blazing inferno, she could feel the pressure building in her abdomen, signalling her coming climax even as she desperately tried to hold off the massing pleasure. However, it was like trying to block a river with only a hand full of stones and she was helpless to prevent herself from becoming swept up in its current.

"Ugh! Fuck you feel so good Princess!" Luke groaned, his hips lifting off the bed to meet her on the way down with an upwards stroke of his own. His brain was overloaded as his every sense tried desperately to process the scene that was playing out before his eyes. Not only was he breathing in the potent cocktail of her scent mixed with the tangy aroma of sex, but the sight of his beautiful Princess riding his cock like she was Annie Oakley almost finished him. "Are you gonna cum, baby?"

"Oh yes! Fuck! Oh, God! Oh God! Oh! Oh! Oh fuck! Ohhhhhh!" she cried, her teeth clenching as fresh tides of ecstasy crashed into her body. She couldn't think. The feeling of having him inside her alone made her delirious, and the fast pace he had set was enough to make her lose her mind. Her orgasm was building. All it took was one last thrust, and then a blinding light exploded behind her eyelids.

It came upon her so fast and hard, she hadn't been prepared for its onslaught. Lost in the pleasure, her head snapped back and her nails bit into the skin of her breasts as quaking tremors ripped through her like a hail of lightning bolts.

"Yes! Yes! Ohhh! Oh fuck me! Ohhh! Yes! I'm cumming! Oh fuck! I'm cumming!"

Hearing her slurred cries, Luke couldn't help but groan in delight as he felt her inner walls contract around his manhood in a wash of her cream. It felt like she was trying to milk his shaft dry, and the pleasure it stirred within him as he thrust to the hilt was incomprehensible. Yet despite all his strength, Luke could only muster the power to resist her for two more quick thrusts before following her over the peak. With a deep shout, he filled the room with the sounds of his surrender and a river of his seed exploded into her waiting cavern.

Starved of energy, the couple lacked even the strength to speak and fell together on the bed without a word said. Enveloping the girl in his arms, Luke pulled her close and pressed a tender kiss to her forehead.

"Happy Valentine's day, Princess Sophie."

The End...

Paying off Her Stepbrotehr's Bullies

CHAPTER ONE

The shower stall was thick with steam, the hum of the motor reverberating through the walls as fat beads of condensation ran down the natural brown stone tiles and fogged glass door. Tipping her head back into the spray and sweeping the sodden, honey-coloured tresses from her eyes, Mina Carring uttered a low, throaty moan as the scalding water pelted her naked body, washing the stresses of the day away.

She longed for moments like these. After a long day posing for cameras and listening to photographers and directors screaming at each other like toddlers contesting for their favourite toy, there was nothing more relaxing than a scalding-hot shower.

And it really hadn't been her day.

Even from the outset, nothing had seemed to go to plan. It all started with her sleeping through her alarm and oversleeping by more than half an hour. Then the coffee maker had died mid-brew, forcing her to start the day without her vital morning fix. Later, matters were only made worse by the combination of morning rush hour and a minor accident that had left her stranded in a long, snaking queue of traffic down Route 405, more than an hour after she was supposed to meet with her agent for a late breakfast. Finally, there was that debacle of a photo-shoot.

While few, *knowledgeable* individuals would describe the life of a model and actress as easy, that one shoot had just about taken the biscuit. It should have been so simple, so easy. Just one shoot, little more than a day's work, modelling a new fashion line for a new European branded clothing store that would be opening on Montana Avenue sometime in the summer.

There had just been one problem. The French photographer commissioned for the shoot considered himself a born-again Guy Bourdin, but seemed only to bear a striking resemblance to a toad, and had insisted on having the natural lighting and mood of every shot to be exact to his vision. Yet there were not enough hours in the day or positions of the sun, and in the end, an afternoon's shoot had to be spread over three days. Today had been the last and was an easy two hours posing on a rock rising out of the surf and walking across the deserted stretch of beach. However, it seemed Pierre the Toad had woken up on the wrong side of his fishpond and before she had even had a chance to change, he was screaming that 'this was wrong' or 'that was out of place'.

In the end, chewing her bottom lip was all she could do to stop herself from telling him just where he could stick his precious vision.

Despite the heat of the shower, Mina shuddered at the memory. She'd so desperately wanted to leave, to quit and go on with her day the way she'd been planning to for some weeks. She wanted to go out to Griffith Observatory with Mark and their parents for lunch before taking them on an expensive shopping trip down La Brea Avenue. After all, it wasn't every day her little stepbrother turned 21. Yet the restrictions in her contract forced her to finish the job, regardless of her prior engagements or that slimy, selfaggrandising toad's attitude problems.

Now it was up to her to make it up to Mark.

Reluctantly, she hit the button to shut off the water before throwing open the glass door. Wet and dripping, but feeling fully refreshed, she let the little rivulets of water run off her before stepping out from beneath the dripping shower head and onto the fluffy white bath mat that encircled the stall. Courtesy of the shower, her spacious ensuite was warm and misty, but a single open window hinted at the tiniest chill. Her skin prickled at the delicious contrast as she took a towel off the heated rail and patted herself down. Vigorously towelling her hair with one hand, she opened the door to her connecting master bedroom and sauntered inside.

Spacious and airy, she'd had its walls painted a passionate shade of crimson shortly after purchasing the property and furnished it with fittings of deep oak, making the room feel more intimate. Shafts of deep red light filtered through the gaps in the drawn curtains to flood the room with a natural illumination as the sun sank beneath the distant horizon. However, it was the south-facing windows and outer balcony, offering splendid views overlooking Beverly Hills, that made this her favourite room in the house.

She had already selected her clothes for tonight from the walk-in-wardrobe and had neatly laid them out across the queen-size bed's black Egyptian cotton sheets. Forgoing underwear, she dropped the towel unceremoniously onto the floor and tugged her black slim jeans up her long, willowy legs and over her buttocks. She deftly fastened the buttons, then pulled a powder-blue, long-sleeved, babydoll-style top over her head. Though not tight or revealing, the thin fabric moulded to her still damp skin to leave nothing to the imagination. It made her feel naughty, and the thought of Mark seeing her like this ignited a warm tingling feeling in the pit of her stomach.

No! Stop it. That's not why you're going to see him.

When fully dressed, she crossed the bedroom in several quick strides to her dressing table, where arrayed around the oval vanity mirror, was a variety of jewellery boxes, perfumes, brushes, creams and other beauty utensils. Her likeness glowered back from within the glass.

Mina tried to picture the person who had been looking back at her five years before, and then the little nine year-old girl she'd been fifteen years ago. So much had changed. She felt older, drawn, and tired with the weight of a lifetime's mistakes forever bearing down on her.

Yet still so much was the same.

The same wavy golden hair, angular features, and sparkling azure eyes that had won her that first audition peered back at her. She had been a meek, quiet child back then and her father had thought the experience might help her come out of her shell. He'd had to drag her to that audition kicking and screaming, after a director saw her perform the role of the Pied Piper in her school play and suggested she audition for a role in his new movie, *Eternity's Wisps*. The film had been a low-budget B-movie, a science-fiction collage of *Star Wars* and *Star Trek* with just the smouldering, gritty hint of *Sin City* thrown in. It was the ill-born brainchild of a writer long past his best trying to rekindle the forgotten glory of the '80s space-race movies, and had held all the prospects for success as a thriller starring Robert Pattinson.

Considering her reflection, she took a shiny black comb inlaid with lapis in hand and began brushing the tangles from her hair until it framed her face and fell down past her shoulders in a wash of sun-kissed curls.

Had her mother looked like her when she was her age?

Mina often pondered the question, even though she knew she would never have the answer. She had not known her mother. She had been too young to remember when she had vanished into the night without a word. Her father never spoke of her, no matter how much she had pestered him. Out of respect for him, Mina had never searched for her, never hired a private investigator or reached out in any way, despite numerous offers from several prime time talk shows.

There were no photos of her in the house, no traces or details online. It was almost as if she'd vanished off the face of the earth and all Mina had left was a name.

Angela Willis.

The name brought her no comfort or rush of recognition however, but instilled only the deepest sense of sadness that threatened to overwhelm her in a surge of suppressed emotion whenever she thought of it. She had questions, so many questions. Was her mother alive? Where was she? Why did she do it? Did Mina mean so little to her? Was it something she'd done? The list went on and on. She had forgotten how many times she'd asked herself those poignant questions and bore that inevitable, terrible weight of doubt and self-loathing. Yet, as much as she longed to know the truth, Mina had never wanted to hear the answers. Some things were better left unknown. And as much as people claimed it would set you free, the truth could be a far more bitter pill to swallow than ignorance.

Utterly engrossed in her thoughts and her grooming, she didn't notice the figure coming up behind her, just out of sight of the mirror, and almost jumped out of her skin in fright when a pair of strong arms suddenly coiled around her waist and drew her backward. Without thinking, she made to lash out with the comb and break free of her captor, but then went limp, the makeshift shiv slipping from nerveless fingers as thin lips teased the sensitive place on the back of her neck, just behind her left ear. Her knees went weak and a low moan escaped her.

Only two men knew about that little spot.

"You look beautiful tonight," Jason whispered against her throat, sending delicious shivers down her spine as his fingers slipped beneath the waistline of her top to glide across her flat stomach. A tingling sensation zipped down to her centre. Damn him, how did he always know just how to touch her?

"Mmm…thanks, but I really need to go-oh…I'm already running late and Mark's party is-oh, god…" Words failed her as he began laying fiery little nips and kisses along the curve of her neck before ravenously gnawing on the sensitised tendons. She noted that he hadn't shaved today and her toes curled at the feeling of his stubble-roughened chin as it brushed against her softer skin.

Jason William Scott Stoker had been her boyfriend for the better part of three years. They'd met while filming *The*

Devil's Messenger. He had been her co-star and character's love interest, and they had instantly hit it off, their chemistry as sizzling off-screen as it was on. Though she couldn't explain it, there was just something about his geeky sense of humour and Newcastle accent that she found enthralling. Seized by the passion of the moment, she swivelled in his arms to catch his lips in a hungry kiss while she tangled her fingers in his dark mop of frizzy hair.

The embrace was instantly hot and heavy. Taking the offensive, Mina eagerly curled a long leg around his thigh while she traced her tongue across his lips, demanding entry. Groaning a low sound, he acquiesced, his hands moving down the curve of her spine to paw her derrière through the tight denim. Though tall and lanky, he was uncommonly strong and she couldn't help but utter her own low moan as he drew her closer, allowing her to feel the weight of his desire pressing against her, stoking the fire that suddenly burned inside her. Then their tongues met in a fierce dance, their teeth gnashing violently as they battled for dominance, manoeuvring blindly back towards the bed.

Almost knocking her heel on the bed's heavy oaken frame, she trailed her fingers down his neck to press against his upper torso before she pivoted, breaking the embrace to send him tumbling to the bed. He had a handsome face, rugged with a defined jaw, an easy smile, and emerald-green eyes that could make her go weak in the knees with just one look.

Smirking at his stupefied expression, she bent over his prone figure, her hair spilling over her shoulders to glide lightly over his cheeks, and kissed him again, but it was only a chaste, teasing touch, a ghost of her former passion, and she drew back before it could develop into something more. Confused, Jason's eyes narrowed and he shot her an incredulous look as she rose to her feet, but she met the stare with only an apologetic smile.

"Sorry, tiger, but I'm already late." She pivoted on her heel and went back to the dresser. The mauled reflection that greeted her had her lips pressed together in a tight line. Nearly tutting in disgust at the sight of the red blotches on her neck and swollen lips, Mina shook out the dishevelled, and quite unrepairable ruin of her hair before tussling it with her fingers, trying to bring some order to the chaos.

"Do you want me to come with you?"

Her eyes darted to his reflection in the mirror. He was now propped up on the bed by his elbows, his eyes bright as he watched her with an almost lazy smile.

"No, its fine." Casting a look across the cabinet, she selected one of her foundations and began applying it to the red marks. "This will just be a quick visit. Dad and Alexis are having dinner at Le Cœur de la Mer so Mark is having some friends from university round. I'll just drop his gifts off, say sorry for missing him earlier and wish him a happy birthday. Then I'll be on my way home."

Jason's eyebrow quirked at her. "All that, just for a quick visit?"

Men!

Placing the cosmetic back on the dresser with a roll of her eyes, she then selected her favourite lipstick from the selection. "A girl has to look her best."

"You're always at your best. If only you'd let yourself see it."

There was a depth of emotion in his voice Mina rarely heard there. It made her feel uneasy, as though the heavy knot in her gut was rising to block her throat. Her fingers trembled as she applied the lipstick and she tried to swallow, to force it down.

Don't say it- "I love you."

She stilled, his words striking her like the crack of a bullwhip. Ice ran through her veins as their eyes met in the mirror and she saw the desperate pleading within them.

Please, not again.

At the end of her silent appeal, her mind ran to the two small, velvet-lined boxes he hid in the bottom draw of his bedside table beneath his socks. She knew he'd kept them. Had he bought another? God, she hoped not, since the thought of rejecting him again weighed like a stone in her heart. Why couldn't he understand she wasn't that kind of woman?

Jason frowned at her silence, then pushed away from the bed to sit straight-backed with a resigned sigh. "Can't you say it. Just once?"

I wish I could

But she wouldn't lie to him. Forcibly swallowing the lump in her throat, Mina closed the lipstick and placed it back amongst the others before wheeling around and giving him her best reassuring smile. It did not quite reach her eyes however. Almost cool, they held his imploring look as she walked towards the bed, her feet seeming to glide over the soft carpet without a sound. Then, she bent forward and rested both hands on the footboard, until his eyes were level with her breasts. She drew in a breath, just enough to lift the swells of her bosom and emphasize the way the very thin fabric stretched over her cleavage.

She wanted to love him, she really did. He was a good man, fun and dependable and deserving of someone much better than her. But her heart was a fickle bitch, devoting itself to a lover, opting to never truly open up. She'd seen where that road led and what came of giving herself to someone completely.

Despite himself, Jason's eyes flickered downward at the movement and lingered there, the shape of his manhood rising sharp and strong against his jeans, tenting the otherwise slack denim. Mina smirked, her plush tongue darting out suggestively over her rosy lips. "Hold that thought for me, lover boy." Jason's eyes darted back up, but she was already backing away. "Wait up for me and I promise, when I get home, we can pick up where we left off."

She felt cold steel against her fingertips as her hand blindly closed around the door handle. "Until then, here's a little preview…" As her left hand pulled the door open, her right grabbed the hem of her top and dragged it up, flashing him a provocative view of her cleavage.

Then she was gone.

Her heart thundered with excitement as she bolted before the door had even closed behind her, a broad smile on her lips as she envisioned Jason chasing her through the house before having his way with her against the door. Pushing her top back into place, she almost ran down the house's spiralling staircase into the airy foyer. Slipping on a designer pair of brown leather boots and the matching jacket, she grabbed her keys off the oak side table and the plastic shopping bag beside it containing Mark's presents, before opening the ebony front door and stepping out into the cool evening air.

The sky was a dwindling tapestry of pink and orange beneath a sinking sea of violet, the sun long hidden behind the western horizon. Los Angeles was nothing but a ghostly silhouette, the city a prisoner in the twilight purgatory that divided night from day.

Bathed in the golden glow of the hanging iron lamp, she walked past the four huge columns of pale alabaster stone that supported the upper balcony, and down the porch's three wide steps. In her wake, the heavy door slid shut with a booming bang.

Parked in the centre of the ringed pebble and coral driveway, and polished to a high shine, was her sleek, black, Luxury Ride Lexus RX 350. Clicking the key to unlock the vehicle before pocketing the fob, she clambered into the driver's seat, carefully placing the shopping bag in the passenger seat's foot-space. She dragged the door shut behind her, strapped on her seat belt, took off the handbrake, and pressed the ignition. The engine bellowed to life, emitting a deep rumble that had the seat vibrating deliciously beneath her. Mina slipped the shifter into drive and put her foot to the accelerator, sending the SUZ roaring forward. Pressed back into her seat by the sudden motion, she drove around the doughnut-shaped driveway, passed through the high-arched, black iron gate that marked the end of her 1.2 acre estate as it swung open automatically at her approach, and without looking, turned sharply onto the winding street beyond.

CHAPTER TWO

Turning off at the lights, leaving Benedict Canyon Drive and the majority of the traffic in her rear-view mirror, she sped down the long Sherman Oaks Boulevard. The road teemed with clusters of convenience stores and a dozen or so minor residential streets, each lined with modest two-storey homes that branched off on either side. Counting each junction off, she swerved down the eighth to find the street chock-ablock with parked cars. Though her father's house was more than halfway down the stretch, the sheer number of cars parked along it forced her to pull over beside the dark silhouette of a broken streetlight standing on the curve of the cul-de-sac that ended the road.

Overhead, the sky was black, night's cloak having fully descended. There was no moon, but stars twinkled merrily overhead, dotted here and there, shining brightly against the all-consuming blackness in their ageless tapestries across the celestial sphere.

Turning off the ignition, she undid her seat belt, opened the door, and clambered out into the night, a shiver running down her spine as her hair began to flutter in the wind. Despite it being mid-October, there was an unseasonable bite in the night air and she drew her jacket close before retrieving Mark's presents from the passenger side. Reaching into her jacket pocket and locking the SUV with a click of the fob, Mina started down the left-hand sidewalk, past nine near-identical, modest yet homely properties, and up the paved driveway.

Even from the bottom of the street, her father's house was easy to spot. Parked across the sloping garden were half a dozen cars and a colourful banner draped from the roof, proclaiming 'Happy Birthday Mark' in red and gold glitter, but only half visible amidst the low glow of nearby street lights. Party music boomed from the open windows and door. As she walked up the drive, a group of young men were loitering on the doorstep, smoking and conversing amongst themselves in hushed tones.

Spotting her approach, the one that stood farthest back, leaning against the doorframe beneath the porch light with a cigarette dangling from his lips, gave a slight nod. The excessive amount of gel in his flaming red hair caused it to glisten like amber at the movement. All at once, the group fell silent and wheeled about to confront her. By their sheepish expressions, she could tell they were up to no good but she chose not to say anything. When they realised she was not a cop, the group begrudgingly shifted a step to let her pass.

Curls of pale smoke weaved around her as she stepped onto the porch, and the air was heavy with a sickly sweet aroma that had her stomach churning with the first breath.

Marijuana!

Taking care not to look any of them in the eye, Mina carried on without a second's pause. She could feel the heat of their lecherous leers on her as she passed, following her every step and giving her an all-encompassing once-over before finally settling upon her backside. They watched her with all the subtlety of a pack of starving hyenas studying a zebra herd, sending a shiver that had nothing to do with the cold crawling up her spine.

Just as she was about to cross the house's threshold, one of them muttered something she couldn't hear that had the rest sniggering. Pausing mid-stride, Mina had a momentary impulse to wheel about and ask them if they'd like to take a picture, but then she put it from her mind. They weren't worth the breath.

Inside, she found a scene straight out of *American Pie*. Music was blaring from an iPod boom dock speaker system that had been set up on the living room coffee table. Across the narrow foyer, she could see an aluminium beer keg in the kitchen amidst a buffet-style bonanza of party foods on disposable plates. And there were people everywhere either commingling in gangs of three or five, or gyrating mindlessly against one another to whatever musical abomination happened to be playing over the hi-fi.

The only thing missing is Seann William Scott shouting profanity.

As she surveyed the scene, Mina could hardly contain her look of amazement. While she'd known Mark had been given run of the house for the party, their parents having gone out for dinner and a show before spending the night in a hotel, she'd certainly never expected something so very, well, unMark.

She just hoped they didn't destroy the house. It had not been easy getting her father to agree to the idea…

She should have known better than to let the conversation turn to the matter of money, let alone direct it there. But when they had drifted to the inevitable topic of Mark's 21st birthday in two weeks, he'd said her stepbrother would be home from university that weekend and had asked

to have the house for a party. Mina was so excited she couldn't
help herself. Mark had never been very social. While his
friends had been playing in the park and going round each
other's houses after school, he'd spent hours playing Diablo
and Crash Bandicoot.

In all the years they'd lived together, he'd never had
more than a handful of friends round so there was no danger
of the party getting out of hand, however her father had still
been reluctant. She, on the other hand, made no effort to hide
her enthusiasm. Without thinking, she'd offered to make
arrangements for him and her stepmother to have dinner at
her favourite seafood restaurant and then spend the night in a
top hotel on La Cienega Boulevard.

"No, Mina."

"But Daddy."

"Absolutely not," he snapped, his voice dangerously
level as he watched her from behind the rim of his tea cup. His
deep green eyes that had beamed at the sight of her only an
hour before, were suddenly cold and impassive, an unmovable
expression she knew all too well. "I've told you before, I pay
my own way."

Mina just wanted to squint, leer, and stick her tongue
out. For a moment she considered telling him his way couldn't
cover so much as a starter at Le Cœur de la Mer, but then
thought better of it.

As Sid James said, 'We're not called John Bull for nothing.'

They were in the Denny's on Tiverton Avenue, seated
at their usual booth in the far corner opposite the row of
windows looking out at the tinted windows and clay brown
bricks of the Palomino Restaurant and Bar across the road,
having their usual brunch. It was unusually quiet for ten
o'clock on a Sunday morning, with only a few groups of two
and three at a handful of tables and one young blond waitress
serving the floor. There were times Mina would have been
glad of the solitude. She missed spending quality time with her
father, sitting back on the sofa and discussing their day while

watching his old *Only Fools and Horses* videos like they had
when she was little. At this moment, she would have been glad
of the distraction, or any distraction for that matter.

"Hiya, is everything okay? Can I get you anything
else?" the waitress asked, pausing at their table with a tray of
dirties in each hand, her notepad tucked in her uniform
trousers' back pocket. Barely more than sixteen, with a head of
fire-kissed curls hastily dragged back into a bun and an uneasy
but friendly smile, she paid Mina little notice and the actress
could have kissed her for her timing.

"No. We're fine, thank you," James Carring said, his
eyes softening as he lowered the cup to the table and smiled
amiably at the girl. "Could we have our cheque please?"

"Certainly, sir, I'll be right ba…" The words died on
her lips as she turned to carry on to the door leading through
to the kitchen and her eyes fell on the older blonde. Sparkling
blue pools widened in recognition. "Oh, my God! You're Mina
Car…well of course you are…I mean I just didn't…I'm such a
fan an…I just loved…and um…well, could I, that is, if you
don't mind, may I…" She seemed on the verge of a
breakdown. In her excitement, her hands were shaking so
violently it was a miracle both trays didn't go clattering to the
floor. Then a sudden calm fell over her and she took a deep
breath before asking "can I have your autograph?"

Mina felt her cheeks growing hot and she had the
sudden impulse to bury her face behind one of the standing
menus on the table, or look out the window at the Palomino to
watch the slow train of people walking the sidewalk. Or
anywhere but at the waitress watching her expectantly and
who looked like she might burst into tears at any moment.
However, also very much aware of the eyes suddenly
swivelling in their direction, with more than a few threatening
camera phones, Mina chose not to humiliate the teen further.
Her lips curled in a reassuring smile. "Sure."

James Carring smiled bemusedly, his brow quirking with ill-disguised amusement, the way all parents did when they knew their children were embarrassed.

"Really!" the girl beamed, then her cheeks reddened and she looked away sheepishly. "Oh, my God. I'm so embarrassed, I can't believe I just said that, but thank you. Thank you. Let me just get your bill and I'll be right back." With that, the waitress whirled around in a pirouette worthy of the Bolshoi, all but ran past several diners signalling for service, and through to the kitchen without dropping so much as a spoon.

Mina watched the younger woman disappear behind the swinging door with her mouth open. Half expecting to see her come bustling back in at any moment, she turned back to find her father had already taken his wallet from his coat pocket and was fingering through several twenties. She was about to tell him she'd cover it as he had paid last time, but he seemed to know her mind and shot her an imperious look that held her tongue.

Easing back into the red padding of her seat with a defeated sigh, she turned her eyes down to her unfinished chicken salad. She prodded one of the apple slices with her fork, the flesh all but saturated with dressing. He never changed. Why did he always have to be so English? Not only did he always insist on paying, but he doggedly refused to accept her help, even when he knew he couldn't afford it.

"Well," she began after a moment, steeling herself for a second assault. "How about this? I know the maître d'. If you give him a ring and tell him you're my dad, he'll give you a discount."

James's finger paused and he looked up from the notes to fix his daughter with a sceptical eye. "A discount?"

"Yes, just a discount." She gave him her sweetest smile, apprehension winding her insides into a chain of tight knots under her father's scrutinising gaze. That very look had made her crumble often, made her feel like he was seeing through her masks to the little girl she'd once been.

For an instant, Mina thought her father might press her, to try and ferret out a lie. But he gave only a small nod, then drew forty dollars from his wallet and placed it down on the table. "Okay."

"Okay?"

He nodded again and Mina couldn't help the trace of a smile that curled at the corner of her lips as she dragged her handbag from where she'd pinned it between the table and her foot and began rummaging inside for her phone. It wasn't a complete lie. Grey if not white. She was on first-name terms with the maître d' and he would let him have a table for two at a knocked down price, but only because Mina would be calling later today to explain the situation and arrange to have the lion's share of the bill diverted to her account.

Her father watched her impassively as she copied the number from her phone onto a napkin. From his unmovable expression, it was hard to say whether or not he believed her, but he knew well enough his wife wanted Mark to enjoy his 21st and James Carring would do almost anything to see his wife smile. He took the napkin from her when she handed it across the table, glanced at it and then tucked it into his pocket along with the wallet.

"You're still very fond of the boy, aren't you?" he asked without looking at her.

Mina gave a small shrug. "He's my little brother." There was little point in denying it. Their parents had known how close she and Mark had become while growing up together. Though if they'd had any notion of how far that relationship had gone, she doubted they'd be quite so complacent. "What kind of sister would I be if I weren't?"

"Yes."

Across the diner, the waitress burst through the door to the kitchen, punched a few details into the computer at the pay station, and was then weaving a path back to their booth, bill in hand. James smiled at the look on the girl's face, the way she tried to appear professional but couldn't quite hide her excitement, then shot his daughter a sideways glance and added, "But he's only your stepbrother."

With her ears ringing from the raucous bombardment, Mina slipped into the mass of writhing hormones and weaved through the crowd. It had been several years since she last visited the house, but she found it had hardly changed and remained much the way she remembered it. The house had the same mocha carpet and pale beige walls adorned with hanging family photos. The same sturdy box-television sat in the living room, and cabinets sat opposite the grey four-seater settee, presently a makeshift bed for an amorous young couple engrossed in a heated game of tonsil-hockey. Her father's faded chocolate leather Barcalounger in the far corner, beside his antique and securely locked liquor cabinet, was forgotten and almost completely buried beneath a mound of coats. Yet there was no sign of her stepbrother.

Depositing the bag amongst the other gifts encircling the television, only half pleased to see it was by far the largest, she turned on her heel and decided to check the kitchen. Mina tried to ignore the heads twisting in her direction as she edged around the improvised dance floor, pressing a path through the revellers, eyes peeled for any glimpse of Mark. Yet, as she weaved between the tight press of bodies, Mina couldn't help but curiously eye their peculiar array of body art, hairstyles, and tattered ill-fitting attire. Was this what the 'kids' were into these days? At only 24, was she already so old? Then again, were they really so strange? When she was in school, she could recall baggy clothes, raiding shopping centres armed with spray paint, losing her virginity in the back seat of a 1969 Dodge Charger, and even occasionally snorting coke in clubs. But the phases that had come and gone as quickly as David Beckham's haircuts. Was this merely how the modern youth rebelled against authority?

When she found Mark, would he still be that geeky, awkward teenager, or resemble the ill-fated love child of a central African tribesman and a '70s punk rocker…

She passed between the already ajar French doors to the large adjoining dining room, where a large group sat playing rounds of billiards, with their clothes as the stakes. Moving through to the kitchen, Mina muttered a curse under her breath.

Small but also practical, the kitchen had wide windows that looked out across the back garden, now swallowed in inky blackness. Fragments of light danced off the dull aluminium appliances, and the kitchen was as much a bustling hive of activity as it ever was. In the far corner, a tall, broad-shouldered man with rich black hair was talking to a beauty of a girl with a bob-cut of dirty-blond hair and whose high, bountiful bosom stretched the front of her tiny cotton sweater almost to ruin. By the windows, a trio of beersplattered frat boys had made a game of juggling disposable cups and drinking a beer whenever they dropped one. There was a gaggle of girls gossiping and giggling, herds of boys posturing and showboating- yet still no sign of Mark.

A glint of gold caught her eye and a broad smile spread across her lips. Hung pride of place upon the inner wall in the sterling silver frame with swirling gold inlaid runes along the edges that she'd bought them for their last anniversary, was a photo from her father's wedding day. It showed him standing on Descanso Beach, with pale white sand underfoot and the Catalina Casino sitting just above the sea's calm blue waters in the background. He was resplendent in his tailored three-piece wedding suit and the top hat that hid his salt and pepper hair, and stood with a protective arm around his new bride, Alexis. She and Mark were there too. Mark, the nervous six-year-old best man, half hidden behind the groom's legs, she the beaming flower girl at the head of the party, clutching a bouquet of white roses and clad in a gorgeous ivory satin gown that was an almost exact miniature duplicate of the bride's wedding dress.

Had it really been fifteen years ago? It was almost inconceivable, yet the last decade had just seemed to fly by so fast. She had developed the habit of losing track of time. She could remember that day so vividly, however. Mark had been nervous, so nervous that when the moment came for him to pass the rings, his hand had been shaking so violently he had dropped them in the middle of the aisle. Alexis was the very definition of a blushing bride, graceful, demure, and utterly beyond all reproach even as she *blindly* tossed the bouquet in such a way that only Mina could have caught it. And her father…Mina had never seen him so happy. All throughout the day he had beamed with joy and just the sight of his new bride coming down the aisle had lifted years from his weathered face, banishing the spectre that had loomed over his shoulders for so many years.

The spectre was of course her mother. A ghost of a memory that had chased him from his home on the outskirts of the town of Bodmin, Cornwall, and hounded him across the Atlantic. For eight long years, Mina had watched her father flounder in a sea of depression, her young heart tortured by the clawing feeling of utter helplessness from knowing there was nothing she could do to help or, worse still, that she was the cause. He never said it. He loved her, adored her and lavished her with all the affection a father owes to his child. Yet she had seen it nonetheless. She had seen it in his eyes, in those pools of emerald green in the rare, unguarded moments when his walls came down and he did not see his daughter. When there was no love, emotion, or feeling in his gaze, only a question. Why? For she was the living reminder of the woman he had loved and lost, the shadow of the woman who had torn out his heart…

A deep rumble from her stomach shattered her contemplations. Suddenly very aware she hadn't had any dinner, Mina shot a curious glance towards the food spread across the kitchen's long rectangular island counter. It was the typical party selection- BBQ chicken wings, cocktail sausages, crisps, nachos and, around the large aluminium keg, a ring of pizza boxes that glistened with cheese and toppings. The sight enticed another complaining rumble from her stomach.

Unable to resist, Mina walked over and helped herself to a large slice of pepperoni pizza, her mouth watering with the first breath of its heady aroma. Taking a large bite, she moaned appreciatively as the forbidden morsel flooded her senses with flavours, and she turned around to find a ravenhaired Adonis towering over her.

"Hey, you're Mina, right?" Though noticeably quieter in the kitchen than the living room, he still had to raise his voice to be heard over the roar of the music. "Mina Carring, Mark's stepsister?" At her perplexed nod of affirmation, he grinned, revealing two perfect rows of pearly whites. "Remember me?"

Taken aback, Mina took a reflexive step back before giving him a once over while chewing the delicious mouthful of bread, spiced meat, and melted cheese. While she couldn't place where they might have come across each other before, upon closer inspection, there was something familiar about him. It wasn't his face, though he was certainly comely, in a smouldering, clean-shaven, square-jawed, Hugh Jackman and Luke Evans sort of way. It was his eyes- she had seen them before. They were blue, flecked with spots of gold, and seemed to gleam with a mischievousness that she was sure had stolen a fair few hearts. Yes, she knew those eyes from somewhere.

Over his shoulder, she glimpsed the blonde standing with her arms crossed, looking very put out and glaring at Mina with undisguised hostility.

A name formed on the tip of her tongue, just out of reach…

His grin never faltered. "It's Daniel. Daniel Cornwell. You used to babysit me and Mark every Saturday."

His words struck her like a lightning bolt and Mina had to resist the impulse to spit her mouthful of pizza across the floor. Forcibly, she swallowed the mouthful.

"What! No, you can't be. Not little Danny." She was almost certain her jaw must have dropped and her eyes glanced towards one of Mark's old school year photos that hung on the kitchen wall, studying the dark-haired sprite standing next to Mark who had tormented her mercilessly every weekend. He may have grown taller, but there was no mistaking that impish grin. "Jesus Christ, you grew up."

Daniel's eyes twinkled mischievously. "Yeah… well, I haven't needed a babysitter for quite a while now."

"So I see…" she almost purred, unable to resist noticing how his plain black polo-top stretched across his chiselled torso. Feeling suddenly warm, she tossed the partially devoured pizza slice back into its box before grabbing one of the nearby bottles of mineral water, unscrewing the lid and taking a long swig, washing the last of the dry bread down. The water was refreshingly chilled, however it did little to ease the warmth that spread through her abdomen. "So who's your friend?" she asked after taking a second drink.

Daniel's eyebrow arched, giving her a swarthy but quizzical look that would have had Roger Moore green with envy. Suddenly unable to muster the words, her throat as coarse and dry as sandpaper, she nodded towards the door leading through to the foyer before taking another drink from the water bottle. He followed her gaze just in time to watch the beauty he'd been speaking with moments before slink out of the kitchen.

"Ooh, that's Monica. We were friends in school and were just catching up," he remarked in an innocent, offhanded tone that did not match the glint in his eyes.

"Yeah, if you say so…" Mina teased, her lips curling knowingly as she recalled how his eyes had been glued to the girl's generous cleavage. Seemingly unaffected by her departure however, he never so much as blinked an eye when his would-be conquest grabbed another reveller's arm in the hallway and proceeded to drag the stunned youth into the living room. "Well, she seems… *special.*"

Daniel turned to face her, and Mina felt her stomach tighten as his blue eyes looked into hers. Suddenly all traces of the boy she'd known so long ago were gone and instead, a man stood before her, wild and untamed with a fierce intensity in his gaze. For a moment, he was silent, but his eyes held her captive. He reached out to touch her cheek, his fingers rough against her softer skin. When he spoke, his voice was low and deep. "I'd forgotten just how beautiful you are."

The kitchen felt very warm. Her heart quickened and she opened her mouth to speak, but the words stuck in her throat and her voice trembled beneath his gaze. His head began to dip forward, closing the gap between them. He had a very nice mouth, Mina decided, perfectly shaped. Drawn to his lips, she edged forward, her eyes growing heavy as she inhaled his strong, masculine scent. He smelled of salt and sand.

A loud splash shattered the moment, followed by roars of laughter and a slurred curse. Mina's heart jumped into her throat and her head snapped round. One of the jugglers, a ruby-faced youth with short sandy hair and a squat build, had mistaken his drink for one of the empties, hurling it into the air only for it to turn end over end, spilling the amber contents upon his head. Drenched from head to toe, with his clothes clinging to him and beer running down his face in rivulets, he performed an exaggerated bow as the sight had his friends doubling over in fits of laughter.

"Oi!" Daniel barked, his voice bristling with such naked anger that all three went stiff as he moved past Mina with his white-knuckled fists clenched at his sides. The kitchen fell silent, the music playing in the living room fading into the background. At once, all eyes turned on Daniel. The floor and walls seemed to tremble beneath the heavy thump of each slow, purposeful stride.

His height dwarfed everyone around him and when he finally came to stand over the three, Mina's stomach tightened. She couldn't tell if it was with arousal or fear, or both.

"This is not a fucking frat party," he growled. His voice was low and he pronounced each word with deadly emphasis. "Now, I'm going to say this only once. If you want to clown around, then fuck off because I'll ram these cups down your throats if I see you pulling this kind of shit again." Coming to a stop barely a stride from them, he glared down at them, towering over the tallest by more than a foot. "Do I make myself clear?"

Only one, the drunkard dripping with beer and wearing a bemused grin, dared meet his gaze. He swayed slightly, shifted his weight between his feet, opened his mouth to speak, then lost his nerve as Daniel arched a brow. His hard eyes bore into the drunk kid's droopy sockets, and the youth turned his eyes down to the floor. All three nodded meekly.

He dismissed them with a curt sideways nod, sending all three bolting for the dining room, stumbling and tripping over each other in their haste to escape. Mina could barely keep her grin at bay as she watched them go. The ruby faced juggler fell flat on his face in the doorway and Mina glimpsed Daniel's hard expression suddenly blossom into a broad smile. The sight had her heart fluttering in her breast, like a bird soaring to the heavens.

Oh God, what am I doing? Her stomach wound into knots. *This is crazy! He's Mark's friend for fuck's sake!* The thought had her cheeks burning bright crimson. Forcing her attention back to the now, she found Daniel standing over her. Yet she saw only the mischievous-eyed boy. *Hmm… Interesting. Where did that come from?*

"W-well, that was… impressive." Her voice was shaky, her lips tingling with the ghost of the kiss that almost was. "So, what are you doing with yourself now? Do you have a girlfriend or… something?" she stammered, desperate to distract herself from the smouldering fire burning through her centre, the words flowing from her without much thought. Realising what she'd asked, Mina's cheeks burned all the fiercer and she took another draught from the almost empty bottle, hoping to drown in its clear depths.

Daniel's grin broadened, the muscles beneath his skin stretching the left corner of his mouth almost all the way back to his ear. Then the golden flecks in his eyes glinted, and he took the bottle from her hand, tipped his head back, and began to drink. Her breath caught in her throat as she watched, eyes wide and mouth hanging ajar, entranced by the subtle motions of his stubble-roughened throat, his jugular rising and falling each time he swallowed, draining the bottle.

Hopelessly entranced, it was only by pure chance she glimpsed him watching her through the clear plastic out of the corner of her eye. Like a deer in the headlights, Mina stood rigid, her feet rooted to the floor. She should have been embarrassed, ashamed of being caught staring at him so brazenly. Yet the look in his eyes, so full of mischief and zealous confidence, sent a tingling rush surging through her centre.

Get a grip, girl! You can do this.

She held his gaze regardless, forcing herself to don the calm, stoic mask she displayed during auditions, determined not to betray any hint of the effect he was having on her.

Screwing the lid onto the empty water bottle, Daniel tossed it over his shoulder into the half-full rubbish bin. A single drop of water rolled down his chin, but he brushed it away casually with the pad of his thumb. The gesture left a slick trail across his jaw that Mina longed to taste.

"It's girlfriends," he confirmed, his smirk never faltering. "And no. No, I'm not seeing anyone at the moment." His eyes peered down at her keenly, as if gauging her reaction, before he added, "Work doesn't really leave much time for relationships."

Despite herself, Mina couldn't help but raise a slender eyebrow. "Oh? And just what manner of nefarious employment is that, then, young Daniel?" she asked. Her lips curled in a small, playful smile. "The last time I saw you, you were going to become the next Batman. You would even run around the house wearing your mother's tights on your head for a cowl and cape. Did your dream come true? Is that it? Do you wander the dark city streets at night, fighting crime in a desperate quest to redeem yourself for how you tortured me as a child?"

"Not quite." Though he had the good grace to appear embarrassed, her remark left only a small, temporary dent in his cool composure. "Actually, I'm in the army."

"You're kidding!" There was no need for her to feign surprise. It was as genuine as her disbelief. Mina's eyes narrowed suspiciously and she watched him closely. Yet his expression was as genuine as any she had ever seen, those gold-speckled eyes gazing into hers, intense, never wavering. If he was playing her false, then he was a better actor than most of the A-listers in Hollywood. Nevertheless, Mina wasn't convinced. Deciding to play his game, she remarked, "Well, congratulations. And you just so happen to be out on parole for my little brother's party. How very *convenient*."

"Well, not exactly." He gave her an innocent look that did not show in his eyes. "I wasn't due any leave until June, but when I got Mark's message about this birthday bash, I had a word with the base's *XO* who owed me a favour, and voilà, here I stand." He spread his powerful arms, emphasising his presence.

"Hmmm…" It was only sheer force of will that kept her withering look at bay, his game quickly wearing Mina's patience. Yet he'd spoken easily, the words rolling off his silver tongue dripping with honey. *No lie!* "So the brass owes you favours?"

He dropped his hands back down to his sides and shrugged. "Sort of. His son went AWOL last year. After twenty days, I received a tip and found him in the penthouse of Hamburg's Kempinski Hotel with two hookers and a rather shaken goat. He was stoned out of his mind." He chuckled at the memory. "After confining him to the barracks, I had a private word with the Lieutenant Colonel. We made a deal. I agreed to report his son had voluntarily surrendered himself to me, and overlook his certain *indiscretions*, in exchange for him owing me a favour or two. I scratch his back, he scratches mine, as they say."

"A tip told you where to find an *XO's* son?" she repeated slowly, her brow knitting with confusion, the mask hiding her beginning to crack. Something didn't feel right. No, it couldn't be true. He was lying, he had always been lying. But what if…

"Yeah. I'm in the MPs," he said, then added sourly, "It was a stupid decision, really. Crooked Nazi bastard could have had me arrested and on a charge of conduct unbecoming, dereliction of duty, and whatever other jumped-up charge he could make stick at any time. But I wagered he cared more about his career and the damage I could do to his prospects for promotion if word about his son's little misadventure were to slip. After all, top-class hotels have such excellent security records these days." However, Mina was no longer listening.

"The M… Ps…" Her throat was suddenly dry and there was a noticeable tremor in her voice as the words stuck there, the pit of her stomach plummeting. "You're really serious, aren't you? You're not joking."

His grumbling forgotten, Daniel gave her a half-smile. "Afraid so. Hmm… not quite what you expected?" She nodded meekly, unable to look him in the eye. "Well, I can't say I ever envisioned myself as Captain America either. The shield's a little cumbersome, but at least I don't have to wear tights."

Mina missed the joke. All at once, the world seemed to slip away into a roar of white noise at his words, and the inescapable implications coiled around them, hitting her like an icy wall of water, crashing over her head and down her spine to drive the bottom from the pit of her stomach. *It can't be… it just can't be…* At a loss, she could only stare up at him in incomprehension, watching him talk but hearing nothing. It couldn't be true. No, she just didn't want it to be true.

Daniel Cornwell had been Mark's best friend since preschool. Yet despite their friendship, they were as different as gold and onyx. Mark was wiry, pale, and utterly beyond reproach while Danny was broad, dark, sly, and as prone to mischief as a chimpanzee, a damn sprite who had taken every opportunity to tease and torment her. Any time Mark had gotten into trouble it was always a sure thing that little Danny Cornwell would be at the root of it. It was difficult to imagine the routine, duty, and order of a soldier's life appealing to that boy, never mind the Bow Street Runners. However, here he stood, and though her every instinct warned it was just another dirty trick he'd concocted to torment her, she believed him.

It was only when she felt the thrill of his gaze on her, raking over her naked skin through her clothes, that she realised he'd stopped talking. He loomed over her, his handsome face marred by a concerned expression that had his sexy lips pressed together in a tight frown, those mischievous gold-flecked eyes watching her with a note of concern.

Shit! Cursing inwardly, her cheeks grew hot under his gaze and she glanced away, avoiding meeting his eyes long enough to brush a wing of spun gold that had fallen out of place back behind her ear. "So… the military police huh…?" she forced herself to say. The words sounded strange to her, as though she were speaking another language for the first time, yet, whatever the tongue, the notion was no less ridiculous.

"I know. It's crazy, right?" Daniel said, visibly relaxing and giving a small shrug of his very broad shoulders. "But I guess you could say I was inspired. I read a lot of the Jack Reacher novels in school."

"And you're enjoying it?" she asked awkwardly, unsure of what else to say, so giving voice to the first thought that occurred to her. "I-I mean you're only this young once. Are you sure this is what you want to do with your life?"

"Jeez, relax, *mum*," he laughed, rolling his eyes in a mocking gesture. "It's not a career choice. I just want to do my bit, see the world, and score whatever points I can for myself along the way."

In the living room a raucous cheer rose from the revellers as the music switched to a more popular song Mina still didn't know. Daniel, meanwhile, appeared not to notice and instead developed a thoughtful look. "Though I suppose it could be something of a family trade now. Dad joined up when he was my age and Gramps was in the first wave on Omaha Beach. They enjoyed their time serving Uncle Sam, so when I dropped out of school, I thought why not? It beats flipping burgers at McDonald's. So I signed my life away. Next thing I know, I'm out of boot and being shipped off to Germany."

Mina couldn't help but giggle playfully. He might very well be the sprite of memory, but in one thing he had not changed. He had a knack for making her laugh. "Well, I don't know about Jack Reacher. Your life sounds more like the makings of a John Grisham novel. Blackmail, corruption- you should become an agent. Mine's considering taking on a partner if you want me to put in a word for you."

"I'll keep that in mind." When he smiled, it was like the sun was breaking across the horizon and Mina felt her heart flutter against its cage as a bird would beat its wings.

What is he doing to me?

"So what about you? I hear you're seeing that Jason Stoker from *Insurrection*," he remarked, referring to the box office flop Jason had starred in. It had been released worldwide in December but had also been widely condemned. "Are things… good between the two of you?" Was that concern she heard, or mocking?

"Yeah, we're fine," she said with an offhanded twist to her lips. "We just moved in together last August, but how do you know about that? I don't recall adding you on Facebook." Mina's eyes narrowed suspiciously.

While she was hardly discreet, she never talked to the media about her personal life, publicly or off the record. As far as she was concerned, there was an invisible line dividing her career and her private life, and she never crossed it. Her Facebook account was one of the few places she posted intimate details, but to a contacts list consisting of around thirty of her closest friends and family. Unlike her Twitter profile, where she had over five hundred thousand followers, used solely to prank fellow celebrities. Orlando Bloom still hadn't forgiven her for a little Photoshop experiment she'd pulled just before the premiere of *Pirates of the Caribbean 5*, and Justin Bieber had tried to get a restraining order against her IP address.

"Are you stalking me?" It was only half a joke. *He is a soldier, after all, and an MP besides. Who knows what strings he can pull?*

Daniel chuckled. "You got me. I hack into your webcam every night to watch you get done-up in Kate Beckinsale's leather bodysuit and whip your little piggy." His guffaw fell silent when he caught sight of the warning in her eyes. "No. I read a few articles in *Dirt Roundup* that had some paparazzi snapshots of the two of you walking hand-in-hand along the Santa Monica Pier before going to dinner at Cavatina. You know he's gay, right?"

"What! Jason's not-"

"So this is the sister we've all heard so much about," a sly voice announced from across the kitchen. Her outburst died on her lips and Mina wheeled towards the source of the interruption to find four young men arrayed in a thin line, blocking the door leading through to the foyer. They all grinned wickedly and a shiver crept down her spine as she realised they all had their eyes on her. The one on the far left took an extra step forward to stand centre stage. Recognising his flaming hair, Mina realised these were the boys whom she'd encountered standing on the doorstep. "Well?" he asked. "Come on, Daniel, where are your manners? Introduce us."

His easy smile finally faltered and Daniel's lips pursed into a thin line as his eyes darted nervously towards her. But before she could ask what was wrong, he stepped into the space dividing her from them and swept out a hand towards the speaker.

"Mina, this is Sean." Despite his broad grin and runner's build, Mina couldn't help but think that his beady eyes, flaming red hair and flat, stubby nose gave Sean the face of a ferret. Oblivious to her thoughts, Daniel was already gesturing to the remaining members of the group. "Eric," he said, pointing towards a round-faced, pockmarked boy with listless brown hair, skin the colour of curdled milk, and dull green eyes, who stood at least a foot shorter than the rest. "Charlie," who was a lean-figured male who appeared older than his years due to shoulder-length silver-blond hair, a stubble-roughened chin, and clever grey irises. "And this imposing brute is Victor." Victor was the most striking of the lot. A broad, heavily muscled bruiser who dwarfed anyone in his shadow, who must have spent five hours a day in the gym and shaved his head twice a week to have his pate as smooth as marble.

Together they made an imposing, yet comical band of misfits. "They were in Mark's and my homeroom in high school." Daniel then waved his hand back towards her. "*Gentleman*," he sullenly muttered the word like a cobra spitting venom. "This is Mark's stepsister, Mina Carring."

Forcing a friendly smile, Mina raised an open-palmed hand in greeting. "Hi." None of them made any move to respond and instead, they just watched her, their eyes gleaming with predatory hunger. Her smile faded and the hand fell back to her side. "I'm not staying long, I just dropped by to wish Mark a happy birthday."

Thin, gaunt-faced Charlie sniggered and gestured back over his shoulder towards the stairs in the foyer. "You just missed him," he said. "He went up to his room about fifteen minutes ago. Had a little accident with his beer."

"Thanks." Nodding, Mina twisted back to Daniel and gave him a small smile. "Well, it was good to see you again, Danny." He looked like he was about to say something, but she interceded him by leaning up on tiptoes and kissed him softly on the cheek. Then, spinning on her heel, she darted between Victor and Eric, and walked briskly down the hall. She narrowly avoided barrelling into a startled boy carrying two cups of beer in each hand as she bolted up the sweeping stairs, taking the shallow steps three at a time.

What was all that about? she wondered, thinking back to the encounter in the kitchen and the change that had come over Daniel. A shudder crept down her spine. She couldn't explain it, but upon seeing him standing on the porch, she'd taken an instant disliking to Sean.

It's his eyes.

When he looked at her, they sat in their sockets like bergs floating on the ocean- cold and blue and only hinting at a danger lurking beneath the surface. And there was something else, a sort of madness that had nothing to do with the effects of the drugs. Did Daniel have some sort of history with Sean and those three other clowns? If so, then it was a sure thing that Mark had an equal share in it. So what were they doing here?

Despite the hive of activity and commotion below, the house's second floor landing was utterly deserted. Turning left at the top of the stairs, the soft carpet underfoot and the deep thunder of the party below muffling her steps, she swept down the dim, narrow passage, passing the door of her old room on her left and two others on her right. Stopping outside Mark's door, the last on the left, she raised a hand to kno-

What was that?

The sound was small, barely more than a whisper, yet it struck a chord that had Mina suddenly still as stone. There it was again, the whisper of a voice, too faint to understand but recognisable all the same.

He can't be.

Dropping her hand to her side, Mina sank to her knees and pressed her ear against the door, straining to hear over the ruckus going on downstairs.

A puckish smirk turned the corner of her full rosy lips.

He is!

CHAPTER THREE

Grasping the handle, she tried the lever and found the door unlocked. Mina said a silent prayer for someone to have finally fixed the old squeak and gave it a gentle nudge. Without a sound, the door slid inward and edging slightly forward, Mina peered through the crack.

Oh my!

The room was dark and dim. What light there was came off the small lamp on the bedside table, a soft golden luminance that enhanced the gloom and made the furniture appear surreal and shapeless amongst the shadows. Mark was half sitting, half lying upon his bed with his back propped against the woven metalwork headboard, naked and vigorously stroking his stiff length.

Mina licked her lips, her heartbeat rising to a thunderous storm within her breast as her greedy azure eyes devoured the voyeur's feast laid before her, memorising every detail. University life had certainly seemed to agree with him. Where once he'd been boyishly spindly, he'd grown limber with long, well-defined legs and a firm abdomen just hinting to the rippling muscles beneath his milky skin. Her knees began to quake and tremble.

By the look of him he had just come from the shower. His hair was still damp and half plastered to his face while drops of moisture glistened across his torso, rolling down his skin and sparkling like diamonds when they caught the light. Entranced by the slow roll of liquid, her eyes were drawn to a single fat drop that slithered down the flat of his abdomen until it vanished within a nestle of dark curls. Her gaze settled on his hard length and she had to bite her lip to rein in her low, wanton moan.

Only the head remained permanently in view, a swollen, purple-grey bell shining with a thick sheen of precum and pulsing so vividly it was a wonder it hadn't already burst beneath his attention. Oblivious to his audience, Mark's hand slid up and down the shaft, his motions swift, purposeful, and very well practised. His breathing was low and urgent, coming in short pants punctuated by the occasional low groan, like a great snorting beast preparing to charge. With each stroke, his fingers flexed around the length of his shaft, tightening and loosening, simulating the muscular convulsions of his fantasy lover, causing fresh droplets of glistening syrup to form on the tip.

He must be in a hurry, she realised breathlessly, *probably hoping to finish and be back at the party before anyone realises he's gone.*

Drinking in the sight of his hand pumping up and down in that urgent rhythm, Mina's mouth began to water. Accustomed as she was to the sight of male nakedness, there was something so erotic, so deliciously taboo about spying on him, watching him indulge in this most private of moments. At the apex of each stroke, a spike pulsed through her centre. She was suddenly very aware of the liquid heat that exploded through her centre and of the dampness seeping through the crotch of her jeans.

She needed to go, a part of her suddenly urged. Now was not the time for these games. It was too dangerous. There were too many people, and should one of them venture up the stairs and discover her... The consequences didn't bear thinking about. Besides, they'd agreed these dalliances had to stop. They had both agreed. Yet the risk, that thrill of seeing how far they could push the boundaries and the ever-present danger of discovery that loomed over them, had always made their games so much more exciting. *I need to…*

A haze was amassing, shrouding her thoughts, making it difficult to think as desire's liquid heat ran molten through her veins, fanning the smouldering embers in her core until they erupted in a raging inferno.

I need to…

The thought danced in and out of her comprehension but was quickly little more than a distant memory lying just beyond her grasp.

I need…

Her plush inner walls responded to his motions, clenching around a phantom cock in time with his strokes while her clit swelled with arousal, its need for contact growing almost unbearable.

I need…

Bit by bit, her hand began to slip beneath her jeans…

"Oh- ffuck… Mina!"

Mina froze as her heart leapt into her throat at the familiar call. Reality returned in an icy wash that cascaded down her spine. Dragging her eyes from his shaft, she hauled her eyes up to where she expected to meet his startled gaze, only he wasn't looking towards her. In fact, he hadn't noticed her at all. His narrow face was leaner, almost gaunt, but also older, yet with the same soft features and floppy mop of hair that almost masked half his face. Hidden beneath the wispy strands of dark chestnut, his chocolate eyes never wavered from a small glossy rectangle of photo paper Mina hadn't noticed before, cradled in his left hand, the quickening rise and fall of his stomach obscuring it from her view.

"Mina… ugh fuck… so tight…" he grunted, in a voice little more than a whisper. "So tight… I love it!"

It was at the wrong angle for her to make out clearly. However, possessed by a sudden insurmountable curiosity that had a mass of moths fluttering through her insides, she squinted and tilted her head from side to side, trying in vain to get a better view. As if he sensed her silent plea, the hand grasping the photo tilted ever so slightly towards her. Mina's eyes widened. The photo was of her.

The little weasel was jerking off to a picture of her! The realisation sent a hot tremor down her spine that got her long legs quaking, the teasers of a mini-orgasm echoing out from her centre. Well, she'd have to put a stop to that.

Clambering to her feet, Mina quickly composed herself. Feeling the same nervous thrill she always experienced on the first day of filming, she took a calming breath and glanced back over her shoulder to check that the hall was still clear of spectators, before she slipped into character and gave the door a nudge. It swung inward to emit a satisfying crack against the wall. Stepping inside and flicking on the light switch, the actress proclaimed, "Well… well… well… what have we here?"

Bright, brilliant luminance flooded the room, banishing the shadows. Thrown into sharp contrast, Mark's room appeared just as she'd remembered it from her last visit. Glossy skinned maxi-posters bedecked every wall. An Ikea corner desk, stashed away in the near corner, was strewn with rings of hard-backed textbooks arranged around her stepbrother's prized Alienware laptop. The sofa he'd inherited from his grandmother sat opposite an entertainment centre about ready to collapse beneath the treasure trove of devices burdening its many tiered shelves.

Only his overnight bag, lying half-open on the floor, gave any indication Mark was only home for a few days. Clothes, damp with something that looked suspiciously like beer, were scattered around the holdall. *A little accident indeed,* she thought coldly, remembering Charlie's snigger.

But just what sort of accident?

Bolting upright, torn so rudely from the arms of his fantasy, Mark immediately seized one of the pillows to cover himself. He looked like a rabbit caught in a trap. Upon seeing it was Mina who'd discovered him, however, he visibly relaxed, but couldn't meet her gaze as his normally pale complexion turned a vivid shade of pink. "Mina… what are you… no… how did you… I… I swear… this… this isn't what it looks like…"

How original.

"Oh? Is it not?" she asked coyly, cocking her head to the side and fixing him with a pondering stare. There was a soft *thump* as the door slid closed behind her under its own momentum. "You know, I'd expected something less cliché. Though I have to admit, I'd also thought you would know that, if you must sneak off in the middle of your own party to give yourself a treat, lock the bloody door!"

Never taking her eyes off him, Mina reached back and turned the locking mechanism, the bolt slamming into place with a reassuring *click*. Then, with all the predatory grace of a lioness stalking a mouse, she advanced towards the bed with deliberate slowness.

A bright splash of colour stained his cheeks as Mark looked down at his floor where his towel, still sodden from his shower, lay discarded and Mina had to resist the urge to giggle. He was so cute when he was embarrassed.

Coming to stand over him, she snatched the photo from his grasp. "What's this?"

"It's nothing!" His head flew up and he tried to grab it back but the motion proved too difficult while still pressing the pillow to his person and instead, almost toppled to the floor. Smirking, his stepsister sidestepped his desperate lunge and raised the snapshot into the light.

It was indeed a photo of her, taken two years before when she'd treated Mark to a week's holiday in Cyprus. It showed her reclining back on a deserted stretch of sandy beach in nothing but a white, close-fitting swimsuit, her skin glowing gold in the late afternoon sun and head tilted away from the camera towards the horizon. He'd probably kept it hidden away in his underwear draw, and stumbled upon it.

"Well, at least this means you're no longer stealing my panties," she said matter-of-factly, causing Mark's face to burn such a shade of red she wondered if he was about to cry with sheer embarrassment. Deciding to take pity on him, she casually threw the photo over her shoulder.

"Now, little brother." She shrugged off her jacket and let it fall around her feet before carefully stepping out of her boots. "Do you remember what I said the last time I walked in on you?" Slowly, ever so slowly, Mark looked up from his feet to meet her gaze, his eyes wide and questioning, and there was something else. Hope. There was hope there, but also uncertainty, as though he didn't dare believe what was happening for fear that it was all too good to be true. Mina understood his hesitancy. After all, they had both agreed never again, but damn it, she didn't care. She wanted him. Wanted him as she had never wanted any man before.

Holding his gaze, Mina slowly sat beside him on the edge of the bed. As she reached out to place a delicate hand upon his knee, she could barely rein in her victorious grin. The touch was light, gentle, almost cautious, but even so, Mark's back went as stiff as a board. Hard muscles rippled beneath warm skin, tensing at her touch. She pretended not to notice the way his eyes glanced downwards to watch her hand as though it were a venomous insect and she innocently tilted her head.

Keeping her movements soft and slow, so *tortuously* slow, she slid the offending hand higher. His flesh was hot against her fingers, the muscles beneath harder than she had expected. As she moved higher up his thigh, she could feel the tension amassing. A playful smile pulled at the corner of her lips.

"But what about…" His jaw was tight and what was left of his voice in that choked squeak gave out when her hand paused just below the pillow. Still endeavouring to resist her however, his hand began to shake, his knuckles turning bonewhite as he pressed the pillow firmly to his groin. Her smile grew ever more coy and she raised her palm and swept her fingertips over his skin, drawing swirling feather-light patterns over the skin of his inner-thigh, just skirting the boundary of the pillow.

"If you want me to make you cum…"

She pivoted, swinging a long, perfectly toned leg across his waist, straddling him, barring escape and bringing them nose to nose. Leaning to the side, she ever so softly brushed her lips over his in the barest hint of a kiss, inwardly smirking as she felt him subtly shift to try and meet her, before mimicking the motions of the hand upon his thigh with the tip of her nose, sketching an intricate weaving web across his flushed cheek. She could feel his breath quicken, growing short and frayed, the warmth of each washing over her neck and sending tingling sensations shooting down her spine to the wet heat pulsing between her thighs. When her lips came within a hair's breadth of his ear, she whispered in a voice threaded with promise.

"…just ask."

The look in his eyes when she drew back made her feel like a cat toying with a mouse, glorying in the sweet ambrosia of holding such power over another living creature, just before it pounced.

"Mina…" Mark gulped, his tongue darting out to moisten his lips. "We shouldn…"

Welding her full lips to his and thrusting her tongue into the warm cavern beyond, Mina silenced him with a hungry open-mouthed kiss. She didn't want to hear what they should or shouldn't do. She only wanted him and abandoning her teasing ministrations upon his thigh, Mina snatched the pillow from his grasp and cast it aside before she fisted her hand in his hair, the strands of dark chocolate softer than sable. Her free hand rose to cradle his jaw, the roughness of his skin rasping her palm and arousing her all the more as she swept her tongue in long circuits around his mouth and over his teeth, coaxing his own to dance.

Mark groaned an indeterminable sound, the deep resonance reverberating through his throat to tingle over her lips. Accepting the embrace, his arms encircled her narrow waist to paw wantonly at her full rump as he tried desperately to draw her closer whilst she cradled his head in her palms. He yielded without a struggle, their tongues thrusting, twisting, swirling around and around in a passionate dance before a low moan rumbled through her. Mina felt his renewed erection prod her thigh through her jeans. Feeling her core grow moist at the touch, she snaked her hand down his neck, her nails scraping over his flat nipples and down his torso before moving lower, the warm flesh of his stomach trembling beneath her fingers as she reached between their bodies. Coiling her digits around the base of his manhood while rubbing her palm across the glistening tip, she gave him a testing stroke. His hips bucked into her hand and he broke their burning embrace to drag in a ragged breath.

"Mmm… such a naughty boy…" she purred, slightly breathless from the kiss but smirking playfully nonetheless as she leaned back, settling herself above him. Within her grasp, his shaft was like a column of steel wrapped in molten silk and though he was well within average parameters, in her small hand he felt huge. She could feel him throb with excitement as blood surged through the bulging veins. Mina gave it a shake before stroking along his length from base to heap, stretching the velvety skin tight before completing each stroke with a firm squeeze just beneath the swollen lip of his corona that made the bulbous head swell. "Getting this hard from thinking about your stepsister. So do you want big sis to make you cum?"

"Yes…" he hissed through gritted teeth, his eyes wide and breath shallow as her talented hand continued it's ministrations, his hips jumping in sheer delight as she pressed the pad of her thumb upon the sensitised head.

Mina smirked wickedly, enjoying his look of desperation before releasing his shaft. With his relief nearing, Mark made a furious sound of protest but she paid it no mind as she got to her feet, turned around to face the foot of the bed and then sat back down. Kneeling over his waist, she then shuffled back until she was literally crouching over the length of his body with her head just above his abdomen and presenting him with her denim-clad buttocks.

Placing her hands on his inner thighs, she massaged the supple muscles with her palms and cast her gaze down to see his rampant erection standing proudly to attention, jutting over his chiselled thighs. Ropy veins bulged along the distended trunk and the mushroom-shaped crown glistened with precum. Up this close, it seemed bigger than she remembered and the musky scent of his arousal made her mouth water as she dipped her head and brought her lips close enough for the warmth of her breath to wash over his sturdy length.

"Ah…" he gasped and she could feel him tremble with pleasure, his engorged shaft twitching in excitement. Encouraged by his display, she reached out with her tongue and used the tip to skilfully scribble her signature across the organ's glans before she dragged it up to the weeping point, dousing her taste buds in his flavour. Relishing the familiar salty tang of male excitement, she flicked her tongue over the slick summit before she almost wrapped it around the bulbous head, slowly taking him into the damp cavern of her mouth. Closing her lips over the head, she began to earnestly suck the slick rubbery flesh while her tongue continued to swirl around and around, down to the sensitised ridges along its rim, making him shudder with pleasure.

With every sweeping crease and wanton suckle, his flesh pulsed within her grasp and she half heard him groan something incomprehensible, his voice low and laboured as her tongue danced. She noticed the tension that gathered in his thighs as he resisted the urge to buck, so she decided to take pity on him and slowly took him deeper. Her pouting lips stretched and formed a tight seal around his shaft as she leisurely leant forward, enveloping all but the last inch of him in her mouth. It was a necessary evil to avoid her persistent gag reflex. Even so, he filled her tiny orifice completely and she was forced to breathe through her nose as she held him in her mouth.

"Oh… fuck… fuck… Mina!" gasped Mark, his breath catching in his throat as she eagerly began to suckle the length of his arousal, drawing back and rising up at a tortuously slow pace until she held just the bulbous crown between her pearly whites. The salty taste of his arousal flooded her senses and she repeated the motion, dipping down while gently scraping her teeth along his engorged length before she rose up again, all the while sucking vigorously. The sounds of his pleasure sent hot shivers rushing all the way down her spine to spark deliciously within her molten sheath.

She had always loved performing oral sex. She had relished the power it gave her and the control she could wield over another person with just the tiniest motion of her mouth and tongue. It was so empowering and utterly addictive, but for all her bravado there was something she wanted even more.

She could feel the need burning deep within her, a fire that seemed to originate within her clit and rage outward along her nerves to keep her ever on edge. Mina fidgeted restlessly as slick rivulets of her dew rolled down her thighs, and she knew she needed her own release, so she suddenly ceased her attention. Pulling her mouth off his now glistening shaft, she flashed a look back over her shoulder at him, a sly smirk pulling at her lips as she saw his eyes squeeze tightly shut and a pleasurable grimace contort his handsome features. His hands had a white-knuckled death grip on the sheets and she could hear his breathing come in short, ragged gasps.

Perfect.

"Hey squirt, instead of just lying there, gibbering like a codfish, why don't you put that mouth to proper use and eat me? Sucking your dick is making me so wet…"

Unscrewing his eyes, he stared at her incredulously as she wiggled her butt provocatively, clearly not daring to believe what she had suggested, before nodding excitedly, reaching up and fumbling with the button of her jeans. For a moment he was all thumbs, but then managed to release the fastening and, hooking his fingers under the waistband, dragged the denim down.

She shivered as the cool air touched her most sensitive spots, contrasting so deliciously with the heat of her desire, before the warmth of Mark's breath was suddenly washing over her folds. His hands seized the full globes of her buttocks and dragged her down to his waiting jaws, his tongue slithering out to lap along her core. Parting but never entering her folds, he teased her with three long, gentle licks before finally thrusting into her depths. Her skin prickled with goose flesh and a low, sensuous moan echoed from her lips as she felt the thick muscle, slick from a manic lust, writhe inside her, spiralling, thrashing her quivering walls and feasting upon her syrupy dew. He devoured her with such a ravenous frenzy that she could not help but tighten her grip on his thighs and roll her hips against his tongue.

"Mmm… you naughty boy… oh… yes you dirty, naughty boy…" she moaned, as Mark's tongue orally fucked her. Although the pleasure this treat provided wasn't spectacular, he was doing so much better than the last time. Mina knew he must have been practising. Strangely, the thought of him doing this to some other girl filled her with a momentary surge of anger. A sudden, and very delightful, swirl of his tongue quickly buried her thoughts and lavished her folds with attention, avoiding any contact with her sensitised clitoris. He began to withdraw and then thrust back into her tight passage, greedily lapping up her flowing nectar. She felt a surge of emotion and such a rush of pleasure that it seemed to set every nerve in her body ablaze.

Exhaling hot panting breaths but determined not to be outdone, Mina wasted no time getting back to work on him.

Taking him in her mouth once again, she swirled her tongue around his crown, synchronizing her motions with his assault as she resumed bobbing back and forth, sliding her lips along his hard length, continuing to use her teeth to apply a gentle pressure. It was difficult work for his wicked tongue was stirring up a storm within her and it took all of her concentration to push the feeling of him writhing within her to the back of her mind, ignoring it as she would that itch you could never quite scratch.

Vaguely she heard him drag in a ragged breath and she could feel his muscles flex excitedly beneath her palms. He suddenly started to buck and roll beneath her, forcing his rampant arousal a little deeper down her throat as he moved to meet her descent. Anticipating the kick of her gag reflex, fear blossomed in her heart and she panicked, trying desperately to withdraw and breathe only to feel a sudden scorching bolt of white-hot ecstasy rip through her, stilling her as Mark's devious techniques altered.

With supreme confidence unsuitable for a man caught masturbating to a picture of his step sister, he began to worship the core of her erogenous being with swift licks and prods. Frozen in a wash of tiny climactic aftershocks, her world shrank to just the sensation of his tongue circling her engorged clit, her every sense focused entirely on the fiery kisses that flamed her entire being. In such a delirious state as this, the sensation seemed to last for an eternity, but was then shattered as a barrage of fireworks burst behind her eyes as his lips closed on her sensitised nub.

Fire ran through her veins and her body jumped with the mini-teasers of an orgasm, yet his fingers held her firm against him as he pressed the tip of his nose inside her while fiercely suckling the tiny bud. Pulse after pulse of insidious bliss surged along her nerves, throwing her into such a state of delirium that she couldn't hold back a wanton chorus of delight, her voice reverberating through his shaft in such a way that she felt him shudder in pleasure and growl around her bud. The sensations were so divine that her back arched on its own accord, yanking her suddenly clear of his cock and she moaned her pleasure without thought or care, heedless of anyone who might overhear them at that very moment. "Oh… right there. Right… ugh… yes, suck that clit. Ugh holy fuck! Oh- my- God- oh- my- God…"

Her heart was thundering in her ears as her vision dissolved into a collage of vivid colours, and she forced herself to recover and resume working on him. Barely able to think through the storm of pleasure clouding her mind, she was determined not to be out done. She focused all of her attention on bobbing up and down on his cock while massaging the glans across the domed head with her tongue. Relishing the bittersweet flavour that spilled across her taste buds, she began to earnestly suck the organ, earning a low, pleasureinduced hum from Mark that had her body backing into him and rocking against his ravenous lips.

It wouldn't be long now. She could feel her muscles clench and there was an unmistakable tightness building in her lower abdomen that could only foretell a much-needed climax. Judging by the way his shaft was pulsing between her lips, she knew Mark must have been close too, but despite her best efforts, she was certain she would reach that glorious peak before him. Deciding it was time to break out the heavy calibres and try something unconventional, she edged her right palm along his thigh to cup the weight of his balls in her hand. Mina gently kneaded the velvety sack while raising her left up to her lips, coating the digits in copious amounts of saliva. When sufficiently lubricated, she reached down and trailed the glistening point of her index finger's nail along the soft skin of his perineum to his anus. Noticing how his cock seemed to grow harder and thicker between her lips, she grinned inwardly before she pressed against the puckered sphincter. Mark's body jumped at the forbidden contact before going suddenly still as she slid the well-lubricated finger through the two tight rings of muscle into his anal channel. Going just past her second knuckle, she then curled the digit and began exploring the dry, spongy walls until she felt the bumpy mound of his prostate.

"Ahh… Mina!" Mark gasped as she pressed down on the gland. His anal channel clenched tightly around her finger and he spilled his molten seed into her mouth. Thrilled by his salty essence, she suckled greedily, swallowing every drop of his release as he writhed beneath her in a fit of euphoria. Mark accidentally scraped the chiseled edge of his incisors across her clit as he threw his head back and arched off the bed. A sudden volatile cocktail of pleasure and pain flared through her at the contact, pitching her over the edge. Indescribable sensations of pleasure surged through her, originating from the lightning raging within her clitoris and pulsing deliciously through her every nerve until her mind was consumed by her release. At its crescendo, everything became too much. Her eyes squeezed shut, and she could feel herself shake violently as all notions of time and space slipped away. She hung there in limbo, poised between consciousness and oblivion, suspended in a heavenly sea of euphoria before plummeting back down to earth to ride the current of aftershocks.

Her skin tingled as she came slowly down from her high. Blinking past the fog of delirium, she felt Mark relax beneath her and quickly swallowed the last of his seed before withdrawing her finger from his tight anus. Releasing his balls and easing her mouth off his still-hard length, she reared back and sat straight-backed astride his torso. Her legs wobbled dangerously, barely able to support her weight, and she almost jumped out of her skin when Mark's tongue resumed licking her, making slow, languishing sweeps along her folds, scooping up her dew like drops off a slowly melting ice-lolly.

Extremely sensitive after such an intense climax, she couldn't help but exhale hot wanton pants as each gentle crease made her sensitised clit throb with need. She forced her body to move. Rising up, if somewhat unsteadily, she stepped out of her jeans and kicked them across the room before she threw a leg over his torso, pivoted, and came around to face him. Seeing the confusion in his expression, she flashed him a coy smile before crouching over his eager erection.

"Mmmm… that was fun but now just sit back and enjoy the rest of your present Squirt, because big sis is about to rock your world," she said before brushing a long strand of her rich blond hair that had fallen astray back behind her ear. Holding herself above his stiff manhood and balancing on the balls of her feet, she placed her left palm flat upon his abdomen to steady herself and reached down between them with her right. Wrapping her fingers around his arousal to position him, she lowered herself until she felt his rounded head slip between her folds. Compared to the heat boiling within her, Mark's shaft felt positively chilled and she shivered with pleasure as he pressed against her opening. She rolled her hips, sliding the sensitive tip along her hidden valley to brush the nub of her clitoris, sending a jolt of sensations surging along her nerves.

Biting her lower lip in pleasure, she rocked back and forth, caressing him with her velvety furrow and coating the mushroom-shaped crown with her hot nectar, all the while smirking as she watched him squirm beneath her, her every motion eliciting a desperate sound in response. Yet like a good boy, he followed her instructions and made no effort to interfere or hasten her, leaving Mina free to tease him until the fiery passion raging within her core grew too great to resist. Eager to continue and almost trembling with pent-up passion, she rocked forward…

"Oh!" she moaned, her head rolling back in utter delight as she felt the first delicious shock of penetration surge through her when the bulbous head of her stepbrother's cock drove through the tight ring of muscle into her channel. Her breath caught at the sudden wash of pleasure that radiated through her lower body and she released her grip on him. She placed her palm on his abdomen before leaning back, mewing as her inner walls stretched to accommodate him, moulding around inch after wondrous inch until he was sheathed to the hilt within her.

She held herself there, savouring the sensation of having him inside her. While he certainly wasn't the biggest she'd ever had, the feeling was very pleasurable and just the thought that it was her stepbrother's cock buried inside her sent a naughty thrill tingling down her spine to her fingertips. Impaled as she was, she could feel her plush walls pulse deliciously in time with her heartbeat, convulsing around him in such a way that her whole centre began to throb with desire. Suddenly unsure of how long she could hold herself in check, her head dropped down to admire the image of Mark splayed beneath her. Though he had not moved once, he clutched the sheets in a white-knuckled hold once more and his lips were pulled tight in a grimace as his restraint was strained to its limit.

As their eyes locked, she gave him a reassuring wink before gently biting her lower lip as she resumed rolling her pelvis in tight little circles, massaging his engorged length with her velvety walls. Though her motions were slow and gentle, she was a well-practised dominator and the pleasure it gave her was enough to throw her senses into overdrive, feeding her need and making her skin prickle with electricity. Rocking back and forth, she ground their hips together, her muscles contracting around him at the delicious friction between their bodies and sending pulses of white-hot pleasure surging up her spine.

"Aah! God! Mina…" panted Mark, his breathing laboured and pupils constricting to pinpoints under the strain of keeping still. "Feels so-so… good, I have to…"

"Mmm… like that, baby? Want big sister to ride you harder?" Mina asked, barely able to keep her composure as the fires raged within her core, rising with each roll of her hips. Bit by bit, she could feel her pleasure building, and carried by the surge of sensations, she began to pick up the pace, pushing up with her feet until she had just the rounded head inside her depths, leaving her feeling almost empty, before slamming back down. As she settled upon him, the tempting heat caused Mark to groan a low, desperate sound and his hands seized her full buttocks as his knees bent on their own volition.

They moaned in unison as the new angle pushed his shaft deeper inside her, but Mina never lingered and continued moving along his length. Keeping her eyes fixed to Mark's lust-darkened orbs, relishing the sight of him contorting in such pleasurable agony, she slid up and down, working his rigid cock in and out of her tight pussy. With each deep plunge, soft moans fled her lips and her pace quickened, until the bedsprings were creaking with her movements as she bounced upon him.

Beneath her, Mark was panting through clenched teeth, uttering low moans every time he was fully encased inside her, his fingers groping and kneading the tight mounds of her buttocks, his trimmed nails digging in just hard enough for her to feel the sting and know he was leaving small halfmoon marks.

"Ooh… like that, baby? Mmm- you like watching your sister bounce on your cock, don't you? Yeah, I know you do. It feels so fucking good…" she purred, the sensation of his cock stretching and rubbing against her inner walls as she gyrated upon him, sending hot shivers rushing up her spine. With her every move she could feel that familiar pressure mounting inside her, a low burning pleasure amassing at the base of her spine, and she struggled to keep her motions fluid. Yet her body needed more, and on the next downward plunge, her hips rolled subtly to rub her G-spot along his length.

The sudden jolt had her hands pawing the flat plane of her sibling's stomach and her mouth fell open in a long moan. Sensing her muscles tense around him, drawing him deeper into her depths, she couldn't help but tilt her hips so that every stroke would brush that sweet spot.

"Ahh… ahh… God! It's… it's so hot… ugh… so… hot!" Mina moaned, her core dissolving into a pit of molten wildfire and sending a rush of warmth coursing through her veins. Swept along on the furious tide of her orgasm, she could no longer hold herself back and began bounding up and down with renewed vigour. It was getting harder for her to breathe, her lungs squashed by the constricting hold of her top, the cotton growing tighter by the second. No! It was too tight! So hot! She needed to breathe. Her back arching, she raked her hands down Mark's flat abdomen and up her thighs to where the hem of her top clung to her midriff. Seizing the garment in both hands, she dragged it up her body, breaking eye contact for the first time as she pulled it up and over her head in one effortless motion before carelessly flinging it off the bed to the floor, leaving her utterly naked. Mark's gaze immediately fixed on her cleavage.

Typical.

The air felt chilled and her skin prickled under his hungry gaze. The feeling of cool air wafting over her fevered flesh served only to make the fires burn fiercer. She brought both her hands up to cup her perky breasts, expertly kneading the pliant flesh while rolling her already pebbled nipples between her thumb and forefingers. She was so sensitive at that moment that even the lightest touch was electric, and she arched wantonly into her own touch, trying to receive more of the pleasure shooting through her body.

The sight of her shamelessly groping her breasts while riding him however, proved too much for Mark and he instinctively bucked up to meet her downward motion.

"Ah!" she gasped, tossing her head back in sheer ecstasy as his sudden forcefulness drove him deeper, her walls stretching and rippling around him, sparks of pleasure igniting behind her eyes. Caught off guard, her legs gave way and she had to throw her arms out as she doubled over in rapture. Bracing her palms against his shoulders, nails biting into his skin, she tried to gather enough breath to scold him for his disobedience but he was well past caring and with a primal grunt, began thrusting upward into her liquid heat.

"Ugh! Mina… your pussy's so small, so tight… I love it!" he gasped, his eyes alive with feral lust, driving into her with desperate, almost mindless strokes. The sound of Mark's voice saying such dirty things gave her a naughty thrill, and he was being so rough with each thrust she could feel the fire in her loins spread as her channel pulsed, sending bolts of whitehot desire travelling along her nerves. Forgetting her objections, Mina gave herself up to his powerful thrusts.

Moving with him, matching him thrust for deep, penetrating thrust, she rocked and rolled her hips, bouncing vigorously upon his shaft, filling the space between them with the wet slaps of flesh meeting flesh as her nectar ran down her thighs. Delighting in her exuberance, Mark rocked and thrashed and groaned beneath her, his forceful lunges delving ever deeper into her plush depths as her eager hips gyrated, riding him with increasing fervour.

"Oh… you bad boy… ah… ah- yes… you like your stepsister bouncing up and down on your dick? Mmm… want me to fuck you harder- oh… God… your dick feels so go… oh… God!" she moaned, damp strands of her rich golden hair spilling over her shoulder as she rose and fell upon him, her mind consumed by his hard length filling her, then retreating, only to fill her again.

Releasing her grip on his shoulders as white-capped waves crashed over her at his every thrust, she stretched her hands out across the rumpled sheets to seize the headboard, using it for leverage to roll her hips against his with greater urgency. Hovering over the curve of his neck, panting hot, wanton breaths as the inferno raging in her core burned with fresh intensity, signifying her building climax, she bent down to take his earlobe between her teeth, flattening her breasts against his torso. Her pebbled nipples dragged against his torso, her body on fire. She suckled on the fleshy nub of his ear before laying a fiery trail of licks and kisses down the side of his throat to nibble along the ridge of his collarbone.

Utterly fixated upon the feelings amassing inside her, she was barely aware of the bed trembling beneath their passion or the repeating *thump* of the headboard striking the wall. Neither did either of them notice the dot of crimson glowing at the base of the bedroom door.

Gnawing wantonly on his collarbone, alternating between sharp nips and soothing licks, her sounds of pleasure muffled against his shoulder as the smouldering sensations burning through her dominated her senses. She felt the fire building inside her again, preparing to erupt. God! She was close, so very close. Yet it was not enough, nowhere near enough, and unable to stand the torture a moment longer, she pushed away from the headboard. Rearing back, both hands coming round to grip his upraised knees, she tossed her head back and cried out in sheer euphoria.

"Oh, God! Mark… your dick feels so good… oh, baby-yes…" she gasped, her pert breasts bouncing in time to the rocking of her hips and tight buttocks smacking against his thighs with a lewd, wet *slap*. Using her grip on his knees to help speed her movements, she focused all her energies on reaching her peak, meeting his every thrust with a plummeting descent and grinding her pelvis against his in tight circles. Every time their bodies joined, her clit banged against his pelvic bone, igniting a lightning storm within the bundle of nerves that propelled along her spine to every fibre of her body, pushing her closer and closer to the edge of sweet oblivion. "Ugh… fuck, yes! Give it to me… I want it. Harder, oh fuck, oh fuck, fuck, fuck, fuck…"

"Ah… shit- Mina… I can-can't take it… your-your pussy is so-so… I'm going to cum!" moaned Mark, his eyes hooded and glazed, his pale skin flushed and glistening with a sheen of perspiration, and his face a mask of absolute ecstasy, contorting his features. He was bucking beneath her, his cock swelling inside and jerking excitedly as her inner walls convulsed around him, his grip on her buttocks tightening to the point of agony, both steadying her and urging her to go faster, harder.

"Yes-yes… cum inside me… grind that cock into me… fill me up- oh, my God!" Mina was frantic, rising and falling, rotating her pelvis down onto his bucking shaft's upward thrusts, riding him with such feverish abandon that her body shook as she raced towards her release. "Make my pussy cum- oh fuck- make that pussy cum again- oh God, oh God, oh God." She was so close, her clit was pulsing and she could feel a tongue of flame lash her depths, the tight knot of fire within her core rippling and quaking, sending renewed shivers of delight to prickle her skin.

Mark seemed to know just what she needed. As she writhed above him, one of his hands released its grip on her and slithered down her mound to where they were joined, and two of his fingers closed over her swollen clitoris, rolling it back and forth between the digits as though he were testing a grape. The simple touch was like a strike from a bolt of lightning. Already on sensory overload, this fresh assault pitched Mina over the edge and the plateau came upon her so abruptly she only had time to impale herself upon him, trying to take his rigid length as deep as possible, before the ball of fire erupted inside her.

It began somewhere deep inside her, a spark, a burst of white-hot fire rippling outward, coursing through her, crashing against her until it had completely overwhelmed her senses. On their own volition, her hands released their grip on his knees and rose up to tangle in her hair, her lips parting in a voiceless scream of ecstasy. The world slipped from focus as vibrant streams of aurora glazed her vision. She could feel herself shaking in throes of pleasure, every nerve in her body suddenly electrified, her muscles convulsing in a flood of liquid pleasure. Swept up in the turbulent passion of her climax, she dimly heard Mark gasp and moan, his voice low and echoing as if she were hearing him from far away, before he shuddered beneath her and a rush of molten heat flooded her depths.

When the tremors finally subsided, every muscle in her body went limp and Mina tumbled into her lover's embrace, panting long, ragged breaths as an afterglow settled over her like a warm blanket, and mini-aftershocks coursed along her nervous system. Resting her weary head just beneath his chin, she ignored the unfatigued part of her brain that insisted she should hurry this along and instead settled into a comfortable embrace, his arms encircling her narrow waist and drawing her against him as she nestled upon him, listening to his heart's erratic beating slowly settling into a rhythmic march.

She'd forgotten how much she enjoyed these moments. No words were needed. It was just the closeness, the intimacy of being with someone who knew her better than she knew herself. With Mark, there were no illusions, no promises, and she didn't have to play a character from a script or meet the public's impossible expectations. She only had to be herself, if only for these brief moments, and he would accept her for better or worse, never judging her, only loving her as only he could.

Afterglow made her eyes heavy. Snuggling into the crook of his arm, listening to the deep thumps of his steadying heartbeat, she felt the years slowly lifting until she was once again the girl crying in her room, lost and broken. It had been prom night, but she'd come home after her date had dumped her before the eyes of their entire school year. Finding the house empty, Mina had sealed herself away and wept till her eyes were red and sore and then there had been a knock on her door.

"Go away" she'd tried to yell through a fit of sobs, but her voice was little more than a croaky whisper. Mark hadn't listened and had come in. Again she demanded him to leave her alone, but he wouldn't, he'd just stood in the doorway, watching her, taking in the sight of her curled up on her bed, dress dishevelled and her makeup smeared and tear-streaked. When she finished, her little stepbrother crossed the room and swept her into his arms. Still crying, she tried to pull away and then lashed out, kicking and scratching as if she were fighting for her life before beating her hands on his chest. He never let her go. Three years younger, but already bigger and stronger, he held her close until the storm passed and she went still.

They'd remained like that for the longest time. Mina didn't say a word, only basked in the comfort of his embrace. When she did finally stir, she found him already watching her, his brown eyes big and round and glassy with fear. She'd never seen him so afraid and when their eyes met, she did the unthinkable. She kissed him. It was their first true kiss, but the first of many. In his arms, she felt free in a way she'd never thought possible. They'd tumbled together onto the bed, their lips and fingers avidly exploring this new territory. He'd set a fire in her soul and suddenly the world around them had ceased to exist. They made love well into the early hours, their hunger for each other apparently unquenchable. Though a confessed virgin, he'd played her body with an intuitive familiarity, each time building her up to new heights of pleasure before bringing her crashing down, over and over and over again, until dawn's pink and gold light had bathed their spent bodies at the peak of a final release…

Mark suddenly shifted beneath her, shattering her reverie, his softening shaft slipping from her, causing her to groan in displeasure as the feeling of emptiness that followed shattered the spell that had fallen over her, dragging her back to cold reality. She found him already watching her, his perpetually unruly hair a sweat-sodden mop of chestnut strands, falling over his eyes and a goofy smile turning the corners of his lips.

He was just so cute. The sight brought butterflies to her stomach and she leant up, pressing a gentle, almost chaste, kiss to his lips before drawing back and returning the smile.

"So squirt, did you enjoy your birthday present?"

Mark's smile broadened, his eyes sparkling with emotion beneath the strands of his hair. The tip of his tongue swept across his lips, moistening them, and he brought his hand up to cup her chin, the pads of his fingertips gently brushing over the soft skin. "This was fant-"

"Well, isn't this something?"

CHAPTER FOUR

The voice was like the crack of a bullwhip. Eyes widening, Mina whirled around toward the source, her heart leaping into her throat and a cascade of icy terror rushed over her. Standing there was none other than *little* Daniel Cornwell. His eyes were downcast and he wore a sheepish look that didn't suit his growth spurt. Fanning out on his flanks were Sean, Eric, Charlie and Victor, their lecherous stares quickly reminding her of her nudity. Her skin burned with embarrassment, so she seized a fistful of the duvet and, with a great tug, heaved the blankets up from beneath them to her chest, covering her breasts and lower body.

Oh, God, this can't be happening. How much did they see? What are we going to… no, wait, maybe they've only just arrived. Maybe we can bluff our way through this.

The door behind the boys was closed but the sounds of the party going on downstairs was as raucous as she remembered, suggesting her and Mark's absence had not been seriously noted.

"I don't know about you guys, but I'd say this party just keeps on getting better and better," sniggered Sean, his eyes gleaming with dark amusement and never once leaving the spot where her breasts had been on display just moments before.

"Hey… what the fuck, Sean! Get outta here!" Mark growled, making no effort to cover his nudity as he shot daggers at the group. Then he turned to Daniel, who shrunk slightly before his boyhood friend's betrayal. "Danny?"

"I'm sorry, man, I couldn't stop them…" Daniel, at least, had the good grace to look ashamed before giving a sideways glance towards Victor who, standing just to his left and easily the biggest of the group, must have outweighed him by more than five stone of pure muscle. Nonetheless, Mina somehow doubted the sincerity of his apology and refused to look at him. He had always been at the root of trouble.

"No, I think we'll stay," Sean declared, ignoring Daniel's hurried excuse and stepping past the pair of taller men, his toothy grin never wavering. "That was a fine show you two put on, but personally I think it deserves an encore."

What? His words sent an icy chill down her spine as dread festered in her heart. Could he possibly be suggesting what she thought he was? Were they mad? Yet when she cast her eyes over his followers, she could plainly see they were all thinking along the same lines. Did they know something she didn't? What could possibly make these brats think she'd agree to such a thing?

"What are you talking about?" snarled Mark, his voice low and deadly as he rounded back on Sean. There were only a few strides of width separating them, and Mina couldn't help but note the way Mark's fingers were twitching, as if he wanted nothing better than to strangle the weasel. It was then she noticed the gadget in Sean's hand.

"I'm talking about this." Without once taking his eyes off Mina, he raised his smartphone up for both her and Mark to see the video playing across the face. It was of poor resolution, courtesy of the extended zoom used while recording, and the sound of the party below had distorted the sound. She supposed she should have been thankful for those small mercies, but the picture was not so grainy that she could not easily recognise the rutting bodies upon the bed, seen from a dozen different angles, nor fail to identify her own pleasureetched expression as she vigorously rode the male body beneath her. "Imagine if this went viral. Maybe I should upload it to YouTube right now? I wonder how long it would be before the media found it. Ten minutes? Five? I can just read the headlines now. *Sex Tape Released of Child Star Mina Carring Fucking Her Stepbrother.*"

Feeling suddenly numb as realisation dawned, she cast a quick glance back to his entourage to see that the trio all had their phones out, and were displaying similar recordings. "I think it's fair to say your career would be ruined. Oh, and you have a boyfriend, don't you? I wonder what he'll think of this? And your parents…"

He shrugged suggestively, and all four smiled those knowing smirks they'd worn when she saw them in the kitchen. On the outskirts of the group, Daniel's gaze darkened and he looked away. And suddenly the penny dropped.

Realisation dawned, crashing over her like a wall of icy water and leaving her feeling sick. She'd been set up. They'd known. Somehow, they had known the truth behind Mark's absence and told her where to find him so she'd walk in on him in the act, then followed her up to witness the aftermath that unfolded. No doubt they'd been hoping she would scream and shout and make a scene that would have brought the entire party crashing in, humiliating Mark on his birthday. Only it hadn't played out as expected. No, instead she'd not only played into their hands, but landed right in their pockets.

But how in God's name had they gotten in when she'd locked the door… unless.

Her eyes darted to Daniel, and it fell into place. Of course, little Danny Cornwell. A securely locked door had been no barrier to him when he was ten. Why should time, bestselling thrillers, and a military training to invade someone's privacy have done anything to deter or dissuade him?

"Why… you… son of a bitch! Give me that!" Mark roared, leaping to his feet with fists balled, about to lunge for the fiery-haired youth. Sean hastily fell back a step, clutching the device to his chest and fingers coming alive on the touchscreen. Mina seized Mark's wrist, stopping him dead. "No, Mark," she said, her voice flat and betraying no emotion as she held him back before staring fixedly at her blackmailer. "What do you want?"

His smile broadened and Sean lowered the phone. "Hmmm… I knew you'd see things our way. What do we want? Why, we want what he had.."

"No," she growled, trying to mask her nervousness with the same cool mask of confidence she often portrayed on set. "I'll pay you whatever you want, but I'm not going to fuck you!"

"You'll do what we want. So long as we have this, we own your ass," Sean barked, his beady eyes narrowing in anger. Yet Mina held firm, her heart hammering against her chest as she tried to judge how far she could go. If they pressed her, she knew she'd have to give in, but then if they carried through with their threat, they'd get nothing. They'd have to bargain. Fortunately, Sean seemed to be thinking the same thing. "Ugh… fine! No fucking. Give us a blow job, then."

"And if I give you one, then you'll delete the videos?" she asked, her stomach roiling at the thought but managing to spit out the words. Sean nodded in confirmation. "Very well." Mark whirled to confront her, his eyes disbelieving. "B-but Mina…"

"But what, Mark?" she snapped, rounding on him with more rancour than she intended. "What are you going to do? Beat them up and destroy their phones, hoping you can get them all in the seconds it will take for just one to upload it to YouTube?" Shrinking before the anger in her tone, Mark opened his mouth to protest, letting it hang there for a moment as he tried to find the words, then closed it in defeat. As he sat back down on the bed, she turned back to Sean. "Just a blow job?"

"Just blow jobs," he reiterated, his smile returning and eyes twinkling with malicious excitement.

Mina nodded, her eyes boring into his with a chilly disdain, unable to look at her stepbrother for fear of what she'd see reflected in his eyes. They were bluffing. They just had to be. They must know the legal ramifications she could bring down on their heads if that video was released. At the very least it was an invasion of privacy, to say nothing of the professional and emotional damage. Yet if she called it, and they did indeed upload the video, did she dare sue and make it public record? In the court of public opinion, filing a suit was as good as announcing the video's authenticity, but to do nothing and hope the storm would blow over could be even worse. People would speculate why. And if she tried to claim the video was faked, how long would it take some pasty little techno-servant hiding in his parents' basement watching blurry Sailor Moon re-runs to download a copy and prove it was genuine?

Mina shuddered at the thought.

No, she couldn't let that video come out. If it did, the media fallout that would follow would devastate their parents, and Mark's life would be ruined, just when he was starting to come out of his shell. She might have grown out of touch with the fashions of the modern youth, but the hunt remained constant. That age-old instinct to pick out and torment an outcast. The video would paint an irresistible target on his back and render him a laughingstock for the rest of his days, and there would be nothing she could do to help him. Though they were not true blood siblings, the story would have paparazzi sniffing around and following her every move, waiting for that perfect scandal shot like hungry dogs awaiting the steak to fall from their master's plate. If just one snapped a shot of them together, it would be splashed across every trashy supermarket rag, naming them a 'real-life Cersei and Jaime Lannister.' She would never be able to see him again, never see her family again. In the end, she would have ripped her family apart, hurt everyone who ever loved her, and left nothing but a trail of pain and wreckage in her wake. She would become that which she had always dreaded. Her Mother.

CHAPTER FIVE

"I'll do it."

Defeated, she rose up to stand upon the bed and released her grip on the sheet, a disgusted shiver running down her spine as she felt the heat of their gaze following its descent over the swells of her bosom and down the flat plane of her stomach to finally rest at the apex of her thighs. Despite his reservations, at the sight of her standing completely bare before them, even Danny could no longer hide his interest and the picture of them all ogling her nakedness so brazenly made her stomach turn.

Why don't you take a picture? It'll last longer!

Biting back the sarcastic retort, she stepped out of the pool of bedding and, stepping down from the bed, walked to the centre of the room. At her movement, Sean, Eric, Charlie and Victor seemed to awaken from their stupor and began hurriedly shedding their garments. Daniel, however, made no such move to disrobe. Despite her cool demeanour, Mina couldn't help a sense of trepidation as she watched them.

Could she really go through with this? Sex with Mark was one thing. They were more than lovers, more than siblings. He was her confidant and secret-keeper. They shared a bond that went beyond love and blood. This, however, was something else. This was blackmail, and only a judge's order away from prostitution. Could she live with herself, knowing she'd sold herself to them. What if it ever came out? She'd forever be labelled a whore. The news would destroy her father, and humiliate Jason. Her heart thundering, hot tears began to burn her eyes. She wanted to scream, to beg and plead for them not to do this, that she would pay whatever they wanted. Then she caught the icy gleam of madness in Sean's eyes, the sneer twisting his face as he kicked off his trousers, and knew it would do no good. Forcing the tears back, she took a deep, nerve steadying breath and said "Mark… please, don't look. I don't want you to see me like this."

Sinking to her knees, the carpet oddly coarse against her bare skin, she watched the naked foursome converge on her, their fully engorged arousals bobbing proudly between their legs with their movements as they fanned out, towering over her and half encircling her in a crescent ring. Despite her revulsion, Mina couldn't resist letting her eyes trail over their forms, giving them each a once-over. Sean was closest. Neither fat nor thin, he was covered with a thin pelt of shaggy ginger curls and a nest of freckles across his abdomen. Victor stood beside him on her left, huge and broad with Herculean muscles like chiselled marble and without a trace of hair to blemish his bronzed flesh. Farthest on the right, Charlie was sword-thin with smooth, milky skin and a gold ring hanging from his right nipple. Hanging back on the left flank, stout and shaped like badly kneaded dough, Eric was by far the most comic of the group and was looking questioningly around at the others, as if waiting for instructions.

Desperate to get this over with as quickly as possible, she shuffled forward and opened her mouth. Her heart hammering against her ribs, she glanced up at Sean, saw his toothy grin and firm nod, before dipping forward. He was about average length, but his erection bent sharply upward just beneath the head and she could feel the tip of his mushroom-shaped organ scraping along the roof of her mouth as she took him into her damp cavern. Inhaling the thick musky scent of his arousal, she used the point of her tongue to lightly trace the sensitive ridges on the organ's underside while closing her lips around the place where the shaft curved and suckled lazily.

However, when he tried to grab her head, Mina slapped his hand away and pulled off. He arched a quizzical brow at her, but she held his gaze with a look of steadfast defiance. "Just a blow job. No touching."

"Oh," Sean's face softened, his eyebrow lowering, then his features hardened in a look of livid fury. He struck her with an open palm across her cheek that produced a sound like the crack of a bullwhip. "Now listen slut. I'm in charge here. Not you. Not your little fuck toy over there, or that pussy Daniel. Me!" Spittle rained from his lips as he spat the word out like a child throwing a tantrum. "So I'll touch whatever the fuck I want and if you dare say no to me again, we'll upload the videos. Got it?"

Refusing to look away, Mina touched a hand to where he'd hit her. The skin was hot against her fingers. The blow had stung, however there was little pain. It wouldn't leave a mark.

But did she dare push him further? She wasn't worried about the recordings. He couldn't upload them now. If he did, he'd lose his only leverage to get what he wanted, and he knew it. He'd threaten and shout and try to strong-arm her to his will, but it would be all bluff until he was sure she wouldn't give in. No, the videos on their phones were the least of her worries for the moment.

She cast a sidelong look at Mark upon the bed. He sat hunched over, muscles tense and fists balled amongst the sheets, ready to spring. His lips were pulled back in a deadly grimace. She could take whatever they threw at her, but he looked ready to snap at any moment. She nodded.

Sean smirked, his beady eyes glittering venomously. With the same hand that had struck her, he roughly cupped her chin and forced her eyes back to him, fingers digging into her cheeks. The touch made Mina's skin crawl yet she forced herself not to pull away and the ginger nodded too. "Good, now get back to work."

Mark shifted, and for a terrible instant, Mina was terrified he would throw himself at her abuser, but he stayed on the bed.

Loath to give this slimy weasel any pleasure, she stared up at him and forced herself to imagine her Jason standing over her, envisioning his shaggy chocolate curls and firm jaw, his broad build and crooked grin, and his deep, piercing gaze…

"Oh yeah, that's more like it… mmm- that's it, suck it, slut," moaned Sean, his head falling back in sweet euphoria as she began eagerly suckling his organ. Though the fantasy wasn't much of a distraction, it was nonetheless enough to ignite a lustful fire inside her, the flames licking that cold and empty cavern deep inside her. It fed off her every thought and grew into an all-consuming blaze that threatened to envelop her at any moment. Swept up in its roaring tide, she went to work on him, focusing all her energies on stimulating his organ's sensitised head, sucking voraciously while swirling her silky tongue around and around the slick, rubbery flesh.

As her attentions grew more impassioned, the weaselfaced Sean's breathing became laboured and his hips began to rock against her, urgently fucking her mouth's damp cavern. Adjusting to match his erratic rhythm, Mina quickened her pace, twisting her torso this way and that with such energy her perky breasts jiggled, her head rising and falling with his undulating hips, the furnace of her core growing slick with a flood of liquid desire as she imagined the familiar mask of pleasure settling over Jason's features.

Barely aware of the others arranged around her, her hands rose on their own invitation to grasp both Charlie and Eric's swollen members. As her fingers closed around them, the boys released a pair of low groans and she could feel their hard lengths writhing in her grasp. They had the feel of steel shafts wrapped in heated silk. Slurping and sucking intently

on Sean's cock, being as loud and crude as possible, she began
to pump her hands in perfect rhythm with the bob of her head,
making all three thrust and churn into her pleasurable
embrace.

"Oh, fuck… almost there, yeah… I knew you'd be a
first-class cock sucker. I bet you love it, don't you… oh shit!
Your mouth's so hot, I can't wait to fill it up with my cum,"
growled Sean, his voice hitched and the jerk of his hips
growing more sporadic as a pressure gathered in the base of
his spine. Mina could feel his orgasm building too. She could
taste the salty flavour of his pre-cum spill across her tongue as
his arousal swelled and throbbed between her lips.

The realisation was enough to break her fantasy.
Sensing his desperate need to reach his peak, she felt the
irresistible urge to be naughty and pulled back, pausing only
to flick the weeping tip with the point of her tongue before
leaving him completely. As the heat of her mouth left him,
Sean visibly stiffened and turned his gaze down on her. Eyes
lived and jaw clenched tight, he uttered a protesting gasp and
tried to drag her back but she ducked beneath his clumsy grab.

Payback's a bitch, you little ferret-faced fucker!

Grinning inwardly, she rounded on the imposing giant
standing just to her left, nearly poking her eye out as his
engorged manhood jutted towards her. Despite Victor's bruiser
build, his cock stood about 14 centimetres and appeared the
same width as two of her slender fingers, it's bulbous crown a
deep red, pulsing dangerously in testament to his arousal.

Ohhh… compensating for something are we, big boy?

Barely able to contain her amusement, and more than a
little relieved to find his size was not exactly proportionate,
Mina shifted her attention from his loins and trailed a
contemplating eye up his marble-like front to take in his look
of intense concentration. Holding his gaze while her hands
continued to work their magic upon his fellows, she bent
down, her lips parting, the moist heat of her breath spilling
across Victor's throbbing head.

"Ugh… I'm going to cum!" gasped Victor. It was the first time she had heard the brute speak, his voice high and uncommonly squeaky for someone of his size. Before she could absorb the hilarity of his quirks or the gravity of his statement, his engorged shaft stilled, swelled, and expelled a long rope of his creamy seed that splattered across the roof of her mouth. Surprised by his abrupt release, Mina could only stare in wide-eyed disbelief as two more bursts filled her mouth before she closed her lips and, with a shiver of disgust, swallowed the bitter fluid. Both Eric and Charlie uttered a mix of mocking laughs and pleasure-thick groans at the brute's premature climax as her hands glided along the full length of their shafts, the velvety skin slick and writhing beneath her touch, but Victor was immune to their disdain. Panting in exhaustion, his eyes closed and muscles slack, he swayed slightly before taking an unsteady step back and toppled to his arse with a force that made the floor tremble in his wake.

Sean promptly stepped over the downed behemoth, his eyes ablaze with primal hunger. Without warning, his hand seized the back of Mina's head, his fingers twisting through her hair in a grip she was powerless to resist as he dragged her forward. Overbalanced and hissing in pain, she tried to protest but before she could utter a word, the head of his cock passed between her parted lips. Eyes widening, she lurched back in sudden panic yet couldn't break his hold as he continued to apply pressure, forcing her to take him in, her lips stretching around his shaft. When her tongue brushed against his frenulum, the ginger-haired man uttered a low moan and his hips jerked, thrusting home into her warmth, causing the rubbery tip to bang against the back of her throat, triggering the terrible, jarring kick of her gag reflex. Feeling her eyes water, Mina instinctively tried to pull away, but Sean held her firm, his eyes glaring down into hers with a manic intensity as he loomed over her, daring her to make him stop.

Unable to breathe, she desperately tried to swallow his engorged organ to grab a breath, but only succeeded in making a wet, throaty gargle as her muscles drew it into her pharynx, choking her. Openly crying as his hand forcefully pressed on the back of her head, she felt his bulbous crown burrow deeper and deeper. It felt coarse, like a rolled-up sheet of sandpaper, and much larger than she remembered. Icy panic crashed over her, yet Sean was merciless and pressed on until he was fully encased within her throat, her lips nestled around his hilt and his balls banging against her chin.

Mina's jaw began to throb painfully, her head spinning from lack of oxygen. Desperate to hold on to reality, her hands stilled their movements and squeezed Eric and Charlie so tightly both boys grunted before spilling themselves into her grasp. A heavy fog of dizziness descended over her mind. Black spots danced before her eyes as her vision slipped in and out of focus and her heart thundered in her ears. Starved of oxygen and on the brink of unconsciousness, she was dimly aware of a sharp pain across her scalp as Sean's dexterous fingers fisted in her silky hair. Then he moaned something incoherent at the feel of her throat convulsing around his swollen length, released a roar of pleasure and unleashed a wash of liquid heat down her throat.

He held her there, forcing her to take in every drop off his release until his orgasm had passed and his nerveless digits released their hold. Sensing the pressure lift, she used the last of her energy to pull back, her chest heaving as his shrinking cock was removed from her airway. She dragged in great lungfuls of life-giving oxygen, only to suddenly wretch and cough violently. Doubling over as the fit inflamed her already raw pharynx, Mina had a momentary glimpse of the trio exchanging glazed looks, their manhoods shrivelled and semispent, before a bitter aftertaste flooded her senses and she was almost overwhelmed by the urge to vomit.

Gritting her teeth to hold off the rising tide of sickness, she brought her hands up to cover her mouth only to find her fingers doused in thick, creamy semen. Her stomach roiled as she inhaled the musky scent of the boys' climax, yet she forced herself to swallow the salty aftertaste before reaching out and picking up one of the discarded garments. Using it like a handkerchief, she towelled her hands until every last drop of their combined essence had been scrubbed from her skin. Using a clean area of the garment, Mina dabbed away her few remaining tears and wiped away any excess saliva that had spilt down her chin. Finally satisfied she was clean, but all too aware of her pressing need to take another shower before returning home, she discarded the article of clothing and turned her gaze up to see Sean, Eric and Charlie still standing over her but with their heads all turned towards the same direction and all wearing identical, knowing grins. Following their gaze back across the room, she felt her stomach plunge at the sight of Danny still standing by the door.

One more to go.

CHAPTER SIX

"So how bout it, Danny? Are you man enough to play with the big boys, or would you rather try your luck with Mark instead? You two always did make a cute couple," sneered Sean, his followers chuckling in agreement. They were like hyenas baiting a lion.

Daniel just stood there, his jaw tight and fists clenched. His eyes darted from one face to the next, perhaps gauging their resolve, before looking past her to where she knew Mark was watching. He held that look for a long moment, his expression shifting slightly as he and Mark exchanged a silent conversation, then his attention shifted to her and what she saw there made her stomach do cartwheels before it plummeted down a black, bottomless pit. Want. Pure, unadulterated, naked, burning, lust.

"Er… fuck you, Sean!" he growled. He then reached down, seized the hem of his black polo-top and dragged it up, revealing the hard, chiselled muscles beneath before pulling it over his head and carelessly discarding it to join the many other articles of clothing that littered the floor. Easily more Jason Statham than Arnold Schwarzenegger, Daniel's body was broad but also wiry, his pale skin stretched tight across sculpted muscles defined into works of art. The sight ignited a spark of desire inside her core and her insides lurched as he reached for the button of his dark navy jeans, a prominent bulge straining against the denim.

Crossing the room in four long strides and shouldering past his tormentors, Daniel took up a position before her, looming over her like the god Ares. Without taking his eyes off her, his fingers smoothly released the fastening of his jeans so that his engorged arousal sprang free of its confines as he pushed the garment down his thighs and knees to let them pool around his feet. Danny was left standing before her in all his Herculean glory.

Oh wow, so big. He certainly has grown up.

The dull ache in her jaw returned as she marvelled at his size, estimating him to be an easy nine inches at least. Mina gulped nervously and looked up at him with wide eyes, imploring him not to make her do this. Yet he was unmoved, his normally pale and impish blue eyes dark and smouldering with desire as he drank in the sight of her naked body kneeling before him. Crestfallen, but nonetheless determined not to let him see her sweat, she rose back up to her knees and, refusing to meet his gaze, obediently parted her lips.

"No."

Mina stilled, more out of surprise than obedience, not daring to believe her own ears but hoping against hope her prayers had been answered and she would not be forced to endure this last, humiliating disgrace. Yet the feeling of his powerful hand coming to rest comfortingly on her shoulder made her heart leap all the same and slowly, cautiously, she tipped her head back. She only caught a glimpse of his bright, toothy grin before his hand suddenly pushed her backward. Caught off guard, she gasped in surprise and twisted with his hand to tumble to the ground in a heap on her front with her backside raised in the air, her landing blessedly cushioned by the carpet beneath.

"Danny? Wha-?" Her voice failed her as, looking back over her shoulder, stray strands of her golden hair falling over her eyes, she glimpsed him step out of his pooled jeans and sink to his knees behind her, his erection jutting out before him.

The sight sent an icy cascade down her back and, realising his intention, she wheeled in desperate flight and began to crawl away only to have his hands snap out and seize her narrow waist in a vice-like grip that held her firm. Her heart pounded in renewed panic as she began to claw at the carpet, desperate to get away. Yet, against Daniel's awesome strength, she may as well have been wearing knitted mittens and he effortlessly dragged her back. "No! No! Let go of me! We had a deal. I said I'd only give you a blow job, nothing more. You can't do this!" she pleaded, yet despite her protests she couldn't help a low sigh when his tapered tip brushed against her still engorged clitoris.

Her stomach tightening into tight knots, she cast a desperate look around the room, hoping against hope that perhaps Sean or one of his followers might step in to stop this but, to her horror, they were all making themselves comfortable on the sofa, wearing wide grins and hooting encouragement. Even Mark was as quiet as a mouse and couldn't meet her gaze as his renewed erection stood to attention between his thighs. For all his objections, he seemed to have quite enjoyed the show.

Treacherous little shit!

"Yes, well, I never agreed to that deal," Daniel growled, his voice thick and guttural with primal passion as a toothy grin transformed his handsome features into a predatory mask. "Besides, I've waited too long to have you like this to just let this chance pass me by!" He snapped his hips forward.

"No!" she cried, but her protests dissolved into a pleasured moan as she felt her swollen folds part beneath his blunt tip, the rounded head pushing effortlessly through the tight ring of muscle into the cavern beyond. Mouth ajar and eyes widening, Mina wanted to scream, yet, unable to speak through the feeling of him entering her, she could only whimper and gasp. Danny drove on regardless however, his fingers tightening to a near bruising intensity, drawing her back as he edged forward, pushing deeper into her snug warmth.

No! Stop! You're going to rip my pussy apart!

He was so big. It felt as if he were splitting her in two and she could feel the shaft's every vein and ridge rub against her inner walls as he pierced her core, stretching the plush, yielding flesh and tight ring of muscle to its limit as she struggled to accommodate his impressive girth. Deep down she knew she should not be enjoying this, that it was wrong, that he was as good as raping her, but her body was betraying her and she could feel herself growing wet with desire. Torn between burning agony and exquisite ecstasy, repulsion and delight, she clutched the carpet in white-knuckled fists and took everything he had to give, her back curling at the feeling of sheer fullness, until he was fully sheathed within her tight embrace, his hard pelvis nestled against the full curves of her upturned buttocks.

"Oh wow… th-this is great," Daniel grunted, his arousal nestled so deep within her he was very nearly at the mouth of her womb. Then, without giving her time to adjust, he began to pull out, leaving a cold and terrible emptiness in his wake. Exhaling a relieved sigh, Mina used the momentary reprieve to catch her breath, yet despite her best efforts to appear unaffected, her walls clung to him, attempting to draw him back. When only the bulbous crown was lodged within the gates of her dew-slickened womanhood, she couldn't help dread the impending loss. Just before he slipped from her snug embrace, he drove back inside her hard and fast, making the beauty gasp involuntarily in a delicious cocktail of pain and pleasure as his heavy shaft plunged deeper, the sensation overbalancing her senses and setting off a burst of starlight behind her eyes. Yet it was only the beginning. Taking her gasp as a signal to continue, Daniel began to snap his hips back and forth, establishing a fast, feral rhythm, his strokes deep and hard and growing more wild with his every re-entry until he was savagely pounding her up-thrust womanhood with primeval ardour. "So-so tight… it- it's even better than I imagined."

"You- you mean you've imagined this? You've thought about fucking me before?" gasped Mina, breathless, overwhelmed, and utterly lost in the sensation of his big, hard cock pillaging her depths, yet all the while trying desperately to keep her senses. With his every thrust, a surge of raw sensation crashed over her as he created such sweet friction inside her, the pain of his initial entry long forgotten, making her head spin and body throb with white-hot pleasure.

Daniel grunted in affirmation, driving into her so forcefully she couldn't restrain the small groans of pleasure that escaped her lips. "W-when I was younger. I couldn't help it… you're just so gorgeous! I-I'd get so hard every time I saw you, and I lost count of how many times I masturbated while thinking about you. Sometimes, when I was spending the night round, I would even pretend to be asleep and when I heard you go for a shower, would sneak out, force the bathroom door open a crack, and spy on you…"

The beauty moaned at his confession. "Oh- fuck… you were always such a bad boy. Did watching me make your big dick hard? Did you enjoy seeing me all wet and soapy? Did it get you hot, being a dirty peeping Tom, imagining what my body felt like, what I'd do to you if I caught you?" Mina couldn't believe what she was saying. The very idea that Daniel had been spying on her made her clitoris throb. It was still hard for her to believe this was really happening. She was actually being fucked by her stepbrother's best friend and, deep down, she was allowing it to happen.

God, this is crazy, what am I doing? Why am I not stopping him?

It would be so easy, all it would take was one word from her, a scream, a shout, just one little command and he would cease the maddening assault that was making her blood simmer.

Yet it feels so good!

She was shaking, her mind reeling, revelling in the speed and forcefulness of his deep, pummelling strokes, the feeling of his thick cock rocking within her, fucking her, stretching her, filling her like none ever had before, making her feel like an innocent virgin, and powerless to silence the moans spilling from her in hot, lustful pants. Every time he drove into her, she could feel him rub against her inner walls, and as he pulled out, the swollen ridge of his corona dragged against their tight embrace, sending fiery bursts of pleasure surging up her spine. She'd had several lovers over the course of her life, but this was the first time one had ever used her like this. Never before had she been fucked so forcefully, so deeply, so purposefully. It felt like she was going to burst in the most wondrous way and as her knees began to grow hot, she anticipated having some very difficult-to-explain rug burns in the morning.

"Yeah, and whenever I caught you mas-masturbating with the shower head… Oh fuck…" Daniel's voice trailed off for a moment, as if he were trying to relive the treasured memory, and his fierce pace wavered slightly as he tried to breathe, speak, and moan all at once. "It got me so fucking horny. I couldn't help reaching into my boxers and imagine I was fucking you against the glass."

Mina couldn't stand it any longer.

Oh God… Mark, forgive me but I can't take any more.

"Then… mmm… what are you waiting for…fuck me! Fuck me with that big cock… I want it!" she begged, surrendering to the fiery storm of pleasure raging inside her core.

Biting her lower lip in sinful ecstasy, she shot him a wanton look back over her shoulder and watched his handsome features grow tight with pleasure as her hands pushed against the carpet to meet his strokes, her full buttocks meeting his hard abdomen with a wet *slap*. Rocking to the rhythm of his thrusts, drawing herself forward as he withdrew only to slam backward to take him as deep as possible on reentry, she fucked him back with equal vigour, a low moan rising in the back of her throat as she felt his length tunnel deeper into her warmth. He felt so big. It was a wonder her body could take all of him in.

"Mmm… your cock's so big and hard! Oh-yes- pull me back on that dick…make me take it, I want it, I want it!" she heard herself pleading, the words spilling from her in a lustful tide as liquid pleasure pulsed through her veins. Mina rocked urgently against Daniel's thrusts, bouncing and grinding her shapely rear upon his driving cock while she tossed her head from side to side in maddening delirium. She could feel herself tighten as she approached her third climax of the evening, an infernal storm of molten sensations gathering deep within her with each stroke.

It would not be long now. Already she was approaching the summit, hanging on the brink of that sweet abyss as his magnificent cock stretched her almost to the point of breaking. Yet it was not enough. Needing more, she released her right hand's death grip and blindly reached beneath her. Cupping his swinging testicles in her palm, she could just hear his ragged breaths and low groans every time he drove into her as she groped the velvety sack, her index finger gently prodding his rocking perineum, his low, guttural sounds of pleasure driving her wild until she couldn't stand it any longer. Relinquishing her grip on him, her searching fingers slid up to nestle between her gyrating thighs and attack her swollen clit, urgently seeking the release her body so desperately craved.

"Mm- mmmm- oh God! Oh fuck! Oh!" she gasped, her cries arching in sensual delight, her movements becoming almost frantic as she expertly manipulated the bundle of nerves. Rolling her fingers counter clockwise, her legs began to tremble and shake as hot pulses surged through her nervous system, heightening the sensation of his thick cock filling her. "Ohh… oh! I can't take it… it's too good… don't stop. Fuck me! Fuck me! I'm cumming! I'm cumming!" Then her orgasm hit her.

It began with a slight tremor in her lower abdomen that spiralled along her nerves to her nipples, radiating throughout her body in intense waves as the burning heat within her erupted. Overwhelmed, flashes of colour ignited behind her eyelids and her head snapped back, a voiceless cry spilling from her parted lips as every muscle in her body shook and the hand that had been vigorously rubbing her clit abandoned its ministrations to rise up and fist in her silken locks. She felt like she was burning in a fire of pure sexual passion and she vaguely registered Daniel's strained groan as she writhed around him, yet he never let up and continued pounding her with deep lunging strokes, fucking her through one release and into another.

"Holy… fuck, fuck, fuck, fuck! Oh God. Oh… Oh, fucking God I can't stop cumming!" wailed Mina, thrashing uncontrollably as an even stronger climax suddenly overtook her, plunging the euphoric beauty into the fires of sensory oblivion.

So- so hot, oh God! It's too fucking incredible! I can't stand it!

Moaning and gasping with every breath, her only thought was to escape this sex god's clutches before he killed her and she desperately tried to stand, only her legs were shaking uncontrollably as wave after white-capped wave crashed over her and they could not support her.

Taking advantage of her helplessness, Daniel drew back and then plunged into her to the hilt, fully sheathing himself within her before going still as his hands relaxed their hold on her hips and slid down her quaking legs to seize her ankles. With a predatory growl, he jerked them back, causing his lover to gasp in alarm as he bent the limbs back until her feet were pressing against her buttocks, spreading her open, before clambering to his feet and adjusting his grip to hook his fingers over her hips while pressing his wrists against her heels to pin them in place.

Upside-down and hanging near vertical from his arms, Mina couldn't help mewing uncontrollably as Daniel resumed wildly fucking her upraised sex, his powerful hands easily supporting her suspended hindquarters. He was like a machine, never wavering, driving into her heat with long, deep strokes and as he established a merciless rhythm, the bedroom seemed to come alive with the whoops and cheers of their audience. Strangely, the sounds of their applause did little to impede her burning desire. Consumed by the primitive pleasure of being dominated, the beauty had forgotten that she and Daniel were far from alone in the room, but now the idea that her tormentors, not to mention Mark, were watching her in this shameful position, being fucked by this young stud with a big cock, made her clit and pussy throb.

"Oh fuck! You-you dirty bastard, you're going to make me cum again! Oh my God… oh… oh… oh yes" she hissed, "take that pussy… make me take all that dick… I love it… I love it!" In this position, she was completely open and vulnerable to her lover's every desire. Pure carnal heat spread through her abdomen, signalling that her next climax was already building. Mina desperately tried to match his pace, but he was thrusting into her so forcefully it drove all thoughts from her mind, leaving her basking in a hazy fog. She could feel his arousal's mushroom-shaped head penetrate her depths, stretching her plush core as his hips continued to snap back and forth, filling her completely with each hard stroke. Mina struggled not to scream as each lunging thrust jolted her body, hitting her sweet spot every time, sending hot surges of near orgasmic sensation rushing through her.

"Fuck! Yeah… is this what you want? You want my big cock fucking your tiny pussy? Then cum, cum, cum…" grunted Daniel, his tone guttural and breathing laboured. He must have been close, for Mina could sense the pressure gathering within him behind his motions, but he was stubbornly trying to hold it at bay while doubling his efforts, fucking her with the single-mindedness of a rutting beast, seemingly determined to ensure she reached her peak first. For Mina, it was all too much.

Delighting in the sensation of him slam into her scorching depths, the enraptured actress could do little more than mew, gasp, and moan, wide-eyed as her arms gave way beneath the onslaught. Supported only by his tight grip, his increasing vigour fed the fires spreading through her core and sent her spiralling towards completion. Crumpling into the carpet's soft embrace with arms outstretched, her succulent rump held up only by Danny's powerful hands, she buried her face into the floor to muffle her cries while her pebbled nipples temptingly rubbed against the textile. Her toes curled and her spine arched as he hammered away at her unforgivingly, driving her down into the carpet. His thick length surged harder and deeper into her tight sheath, sending intense surges of pleasure crashing over her and driving her closer and closer to the brink. A Herculean thrust penetrated all the way to her cervix and the cocktail of agony and ecstasy pushed her over the edge.

She began to shiver, the orgasm sweeping through her like a tsunami as the burning ball deep in her core erupted and great quaking tremors of release rippled outward to tingle in the tips of her fingers and pebbled nipples. Consumed by its irrepressible storm, her senses exploded as streams of light and colour danced behind her eyes once more. Rolling her head back, eyes wide and lips parted in a silent scream, she desperately clawed the carpet, seeking some sort of purchase against her spiral, before she lost herself, her nerves afire with carnal energy.

"Ah! Ah I'm cumming! Ah, oh my God… ah, ah- I'm cumming… cumming… cummming…" Regaining her voice, Mina suddenly knew she was screaming but no longer cared who heard her and gleefully gave voice to her pleasure, certain her cries could be heard amidst the blaring party below. It was

as if her world was being swallowed by the unquenchable fire
raging between her thighs. So intense were the feelings
coursing through her and eyes rolling, she rocked, shook, and
thrashed, euphoria smashing against her.

His stamina was truly amazing. Even as she quaked,
erratic convulsions gripping his thick, thrusting cock, he was
keeping up a constant pace, driving into her relentlessly,
pushing her pleasure on and on until his every thrust was
bringing her to orgasm.

Oh… God, when did I become so orgasmic?

"Ugh… I'm going to cum!" The words came
shuddering from Danny in a low growl, cutting through her
cries as her writhing walls rippled and clenched around him,
trying to hold him deep inside her, her nectar dousing his
swollen shaft before flowing freely down her abdomen. At his
words and desperate tone, Mina felt another climax pulse
through her and threw a look back over her shoulder, greedily
admiring the sight of his pale skin glistening with a sheen of
sweat, eyes shut and brow furrowed with concentration. His
square jaw was tight and his muscles bulged as he struggled to
hold back his release. Yet, even when racing towards his own
fiery oblivion, he didn't pause, but switched to curling his hips
against her upraised buttocks, urgently grinding his manhood
into her sensitised pussy as his grip tightened, nails biting
almost painfully into the silken flesh of her inner-thighs.

"Oh, oh fuck… mmmm you dirty boy, please… cum
for me, cum in my mouth," she purred, her lips curling with a
seductive smirk as she drank in the sight of her lover through
glazed eyes, suddenly overwhelmed by the need to taste him.
"Oh yes. I want it, let me suck you, I want to taste my pussy on
your big fucking cock as I suck you dry…"

Grunting with pleasure, Daniel gave a quick nod of
affirmation before cautiously edging back, withdrawing from
her quivering folds and carefully lowered her lower half to the
floor. Her befuddled mind barely registered the tingling
numbness in her knees as his weight left her, Mina shakily

pushed up from the carpet and pivoted around to find him looming over her, his rigid manhood, flushed deep crimson and roped from root to head with swollen veins, almost poked her eye out as it urgently awaited her attentions.

Licking her lips at the sight, her heart pounded excitedly with the thought of drinking his thick, creamy seed. She cocked her head and traced her eyes up his torso, considering the splendour of his lightly-toned abs and his pectorals that gleamed with a light sheen of sweat, to meet his lust-fogged orbs.

"Mmm… cum for me, baby," Mina purred, holding his gaze while she flashed him a sultry smirk, swooping down and hungrily taking just the pulsing head between her lips.

Closing her lips around the silky skin just beneath his corona, she suckled fiercely, practically raping him with her mouth, moaning at the heady cocktail of their combined flavours, as well as from the way her sex was convulsing to the echoing memory of his presence inside her, making her feel like he was still fucking her.

"Oh… fuck!" Daniel groaned in a tone low and strained, his head rolling back at the heavenly feeling of her mouth enveloping him. His hands came up to hold the sides of her head, his fingers lacing through the damp, silken strands of her hair.

Though not forcing her to take him any deeper, he had a firm hold on her to keep her in place. Mina watched him intently through sly eyes, smirking inwardly at the display of pleasure she had drawn from him, Mina curled her tongue around his sensitised tip, swirling it around and around. As her mouth worked her wonders, she brought her hands up, gently cupping the weight of his velvety sack in one while the other wrapped around his shaft, barely able to close her fingers around him, stroking the base in time with the motions of her tongue as she licked, sucked, and moaned.

"Ugh… Mi-Mina.. I'm… I'm…" Daniel gasped, knees quaking and his voice hoarse and urgent. Feeling his fingers tense in her hair, signalling his imminent release, Mina refused to relent and sucked enthusiastically, watching him squeeze his eyes shut before he emitted a low groan. A stream of thick, creamy seed erupted into her waiting orifice, splashing the back of her throat. Moaning happily, she greedily swallowed every drop as three more bursts of the salty elixir flooded her mouth. Though she had never really been a fan of swallowing, mostly out of fear of her pesky gag reflex, there was something about the taste of him that she found so addictive and it was only when she had drunk down all of his cum and his erection was beginning to soften did she release his shaft.

"Mmm… delicious," she purred, licking all traces of his release from her lips and watching the tension flood from her lover as he opened his eyes and blink repeatedly through a surge of dizziness as his senses returned. Yet before he could say anything in response, a hand suddenly seized Mina's shoulder and snatched her back, casting her to the floor. Landing on her back, she shook off her initial shock and looked up to find Sean kneeling over her, his crooked erection standing rampant between knobbly legs covered in a pelt of wiry ginger curls, the curved head swollen and glistening with pre-cum.

"Hmm- my turn!" he said, a snide sneer playing across his weasel face. Panting with desire and still trembling with the aftershocks of so many simultaneous orgasms, she watched through hazy eyes as he spread her legs apart and shuffled forward, moving into position, and in her pleasuredrunk state she never thought to protest. With a single hard thrust, he plunged into the pulsing liquid heat of her canal.

Though he was easily the smallest of her lovers, in all regards, Mina couldn't help but gasp with delight at her own violation as she felt her well-sodden womanhood take him in to his base, responding to his presence by tightening around the turgid shaft, and delectable pleasure surged through her one more.

Emitting a low groan at the sensation of her plush walls caressing his engorged flesh, Sean didn't waste a moment and, bracing his arms just above her shoulders, looming over her like a lecherous fiend of myth, began to grind into her, his hips rocking as he drew back before lunging forward like a barbarian, fucking her.

His pace was uneven but fast and rough, and he employed a rhythm of erratic stabbing thrusts meant only to heighten his own pleasure, a self-serving kind often learnt from frequent masturbation and watching too much porn, that had his features twisting. Mewing at the intoxicating sensation of the shaft's hooked head rubbing against the roof of her sheath, stimulating the sweet spot beneath her clitoris, Mina didn't resist and wound her arms around his neck as her lithe form arched, hugging his thighs with her knees, mild but undeniable pleasure spiralling through her core.

"Oh yeah! You like it, don't you, whore," Sean growled breathlessly, his misshapen manhood punching into her warm silken depths and balls slapping against her arse, the primitive pace growing more erratic as his pleasure built and perspiration dotted his skin. "Fuck… your pussy's so wet, you fucking slut. You want our silence? Then buy it. Buy it. Fuck that dick, take it all the way in your wet greedy cunt! I bet this is the best fuck of your life, go on, scream how great this is, how my big dick is the best you've ever had!"

Trying to tune out the sound of Sean's voice, Mina wanted to deny his bombastic accusation, yet her body was nonetheless responding to his mocking, trying to draw what pleasure she could from the fucking by raising her hips to meet his crude lunges. He barely filled the chilly void Daniel's absence had left inside her, but her head rolled back and little moans flowed from her parted lips while her nails hooked into this loathsome male's shoulders, making him hiss with pain.

No, she had to stop. This wasn't who she was. She didn't want this. She didn't do things like this, didn't enjoy things like this. This was so very wrong. It made her feel dirty and bad and… hot.

With his head dipped, his thin lips claimed hers, forcing her mouth open and muffling her moans as his slimy tongue thrust across her tongue. She could taste the sour cocktail of alcohol and dehydration on his breath, yet despite her revulsion, she kissed back with equal gusto, tongues battling and teeth gnashing. Keeping up his brutal assault on her delicate womanhood, Sean held the lip lock until her oxygen-starved lungs began to burn. As he finally drew back, she snatched a quick breath before leaning up, catching his lower lip between her teeth and gnawing it savagely. Yelping in alarm, Sean's hips suddenly bucked beneath, grinding deliciously against her bundle of nerves and making her gasp with delight as sparks of sweet pleasure burst behind her eyes.

Using her momentary distraction to escape, the fieryhaired delinquent moved downward, nipping a trail of fire down her milky flesh to the perky mounds of her breasts, the moist heat of his breath causing her skin to rise with goose bumps. He captured a coral pink nipple between his teeth and gnawed it like a piece of gristle. Feeling the sting of sharpedged incisors tug her sensitised nub, her skin crawled but her desire grew and Mina began to squirm and writhe against his crude thrusts in search of greater pleasure. The rough treatment was enough to keep her on edge, making her nipples ache and her abused pussy yearn for attention, yet it remained far from adequate, keeping her only on the brink.

As he worked to get himself off, Sean didn't notice the titanic figure come up behind him until a squeaky voice said, "Hey Sean, I want to fuck her too."

The announcement made the ginger go suddenly still. Slowly releasing her brutalised breast, his breathing rasping and his lust-fogged eyes narrowed, he shot a look back across his shoulder. Following his gaze, Mina found the imposing form of Victor standing over them, his hairless body stripped naked with a renewed erection barely visible between marblechiselled thighs. Even in her deranged state, the sight was almost comical.

"Wait your turn, *quick draw*," hissed Sean, a snide sneer twisting his lips as he laid another hard thrust into Mina to show his disdain.

"But I want to fuck her now!" Even in such an unnaturally high and squeaky voice, the unspoken threat was as clear and as deadly as a bare length of cold, naked steel and made all the clearer by the golem's terrible look of determination. Sean's confidence evaporated beneath Victor's stern expression. His smile faltered and he glanced nervously between the lustful beauty lying beneath him and the muscular goon.

Mina was his prize. Sean had wanted her the very moment she had slinked past them in the doorway without a backwards glance, like they were beneath her. Well, now she was beneath him. He'd stolen her, made her get on her knees, and beg for his cock like the whore she was. Why should he share his toy with this thick headed brute?

But then, Victor was the only thing protecting him from Daniel and Mark's terrible vengeance.

He was torn. Caught between a not so metaphorical rock and this soft lush place, but no more willing to give up his prize than he was willing to risk pissing off Victor and getting his ass kicked by her lovers-

His smirk returned, flashing a glimpse of predatory teeth and Mina felt her stomach roil with a forbidding sense of dread as his eyes settled upon her.

"Very well…" With a sudden burst of strength, Sean lurched sideways, rolling them over, causing her to gasp with alarm as her body was dragged with him and their positions switched. Finding herself sitting upright, she could only look dazedly between the pair, her world spinning until she felt hands curl around her hips and cool fingers hook between her buttocks, spreading her open and sending a foreign shiver racing up her spine. "Fuck her here."

And the reality of her situation came crashing down as a cold wash cascading down her back.

"What! You're- you're joking, right? No! No you can't! I don't want- I've never- no!" she cried, trying to break free by thrashing violently and pushing away from Sean's body, but the male's grip was too strong and her current position meant her every motion caused the cock inside her to lurch. Her sensitised clitoris ground against his pelvis, sending reluctant pleasure shooting along her nervous system, weakening her resolve. Heart thundering, she threw a desperate look back over her shoulder at Victor, hoping against hope the brute might be repulsed by the suggestion of fucking her arse, but to her dismay his face seemed to light up at the prospect.

"Really? Cool!" In his jubilation, his voice sounded more like a giant mouse's squeak than a voice, and in any other circumstance Mina would have found it a comical spectacle, but her thoughts were too consumed with dread. With bated breath, she watched the titan sinking to his knees behind her. Then unable to watch anymore, she looked away, starring doggedly ahead, refusing to look at either of them. Just the thought of seeing Sean's cocky weasel smirk and pale eyes gleam victoriously was more than she could stand.

Hands seized her waist, huge and as rough as sandpaper against her softer skin, holding her steady as an immense bulk bore down on her from behind, pressing her farther down upon the shaft spearing her pussy. Then she felt it, the blunt, moistened tip of the brute's cock, clumsily prodding the cleft of her buttocks. Three times he missed, and she couldn't help but gasp as each jab bumped against her tailbone or her tender unaccustomed skin. When he hit his mark, she sensed a terrible pressure push against her anus, the tight little ring of muscle tightening on reflex, trying to keep the invading mass out. Regardless, Victor pushed on, forcing his cock's tapered head through her sphincter into the dry heat of her virgin arse.

Eyes watering and palms braced against Sean's chest, her nails bit into his flesh and her breath hissed through clenched teeth. Mina wanted to scream as she felt her body open, stretching to accommodate the hard length. Sharp, stinging pain burned outwards from her abused hole as the giant drove into her without mercy. She knew she needed to relax or the pain would only grow worse, but her muscles had tensed involuntarily and even Victor's diminutive shaft felt suddenly huge.

"Ohh- fuck- yeah… she likes it, Victor. When you put your dick in her ass, this slut's pussy got so tight I almost fucking blew a load. I- fuck- bet she can't wait to get double barrelled…" moaned Sean, biding his time and remaining still beneath her, basking in the feeling of her inner walls clench around him as Victor forced her toned derriere to take him all in.

"It's fucking incredible!" squeaked Victor, squeezing his eyes shut as he buried the last inch of his dick in her rectum, almost losing himself in her rear passage's exquisite tightness. Saved only by the lingering desensitisation brought about by his last orgasm, he didn't waste a moment and slowly dragged his length halfway out before driving back in, working his hips back and forth, sawing in and out of her bum, growling and panting like a wild beast.

Pinned between the two hard bodies, Mina had no choice but to weather the storm as unadulterated shame burned a hole in her soul and foreign, but not entirely unfamiliar, sensations savaged her body. Her arse was blazing yet no matter how much she wanted to ease the burning agony, to reach back and stop the burly bruiser, her body wouldn't respond to her commands. Her tense muscles froze, and no words would form, so she was forced to endure the unweathering barrage. Then slowly, with fatigue and exhaustion beginning to take their heavy toll, her tired muscles began to relax and the fiery torment ravaging her anus melted away to leave a feeling of numbness before blooming into a feeling of deep tingling pleasure. It was far from jaw-dropping, but she could sense the pressure moving through her and, to her eternal disgust and self-loathing, she began to pant with elation at the sensation of each stroke getting faster and harder as Victor's entrances became easier, until the brute was fucking her full force.

Then, sensing the change stirring within her, with a gay whoop, Sean began to move beneath her, his hips bucking and his crooked cock stabbing her depths, sending a shiver of abject pleasure rippling through her. Her body responded instinctively, a flurry of gasps and short moans escaping her throat at the feeling of their hard lengths driving into her, sending her soaring into a sexual haze.

N-no… this can't be happening!

"What a dirty fucking slut. You like it, don't you? Both your holes are twitching. I bet you just love taking two cocks at once like some back-alley whore. Yeah, that's right… take them… take them, you horny fucking slut!" grunted Sean, emphasising each guttural slur with a sharp upwards thrust that rubbed along the slick roof of her grasping sheath and sent mini shocks pulsing through her core.

"Fu-fuck you… you bastards… no… no… not so hard!" she muttered, gnawing her bottom lip between her teeth to keep from uttering any further hints of desire as the pair began to fuck her in unison, her body rocking as they used both her nether holes for their pleasures. It was random and chaotic, with both men competing in a race to reach their gratification first, without a thought for a rhythm or coordination. One instant, they would drive into her as one, making her skin feel suddenly too tight and heart thunder, then Victor would draw out suddenly whilst Sean was still languishing in her muggy embrace and they would slide in and out of her successively, speeds varying until once again they would slam into her at once. It was dark and primitive and with none of the fluidity she needed to ride to release, just a barbaric hunger that constantly pummelled her fragile being, repeatedly dragging her towards a wretched peak only to suddenly cast her down.

Mina had never felt so ashamed. To know this was happening, and worse, that she was allowing it to happen, betraying everyone she held dear, made her feel like such a slut. Desperate to distract herself from the perverted reality of her situation, she glimpsed movement out of the corner of her eye and pivoted to see a naked Daniel moving around the mass of bodies to sit beside the equally naked Mark on the bed. They sat straight-backed, rigged and tense, a difficult silence hanging over them, their eyes darting around the room, not looking at each other but careful to avoid any glance towards the spectacle taking place before them in the centre of the room. Daniel took a breath, opened his mouth as if to speak, held it there, then shut it again, the do or die- first into the breach- momentum dying away as the weight of the night's events suddenly bore down on them.

It was finally Mark who broke the stalemate. Though their exchange appeared heated, in her current state Mina hadn't a hope of hearing what was being said over the barrage of grunts and moans filling her ears. She could only hope their friendship survived this ordeal.

A slender body moved round from her opposite side to stand in front of her, blocking her view of Mark and Daniel and presenting her with a very erect, cut penis. Confronted by the sudden vision of masculinity staring her in the eye, she glanced up, drinking in the gracefully willow frame and pale ivory skin, to find Charlie's stubble-roughened face gazing placidly back down at her. Though he didn't say a word, his meaning was plain. Knowing what he wanted, she saw little point in resisting. Opening her lips, she bent forward, taking his neglected phallus, its glistening crown, and its velvety length into her mouth. At the feeling of her soft lips as they wrapped around his sensitive manhood, Charlie gasped in sweet wonderment and his hands came up to fist in her dishevelled mass of yellow tresses. She began sucking him off while Sean and Victor continued pummelling her mercilessly from behind and below.

"Hey! Wait… guys… that's not fair! I don't want her hand again. I've already had a hand job! Now I want to fuck her too!" bawled Eric in a whining, childish tone, causing Mina to glance to her right where she could just make him out, standing on the edge of her vision, small and round and unashamedly stroking his renewed erection as he watched the scene unfold with unshed tears shining in his eyes. He made a pathetic spectacle, like a spoilt, fully-grown toddler crying for another bag of sweets.

"Ugh… Don't be su-such a baby, Eric… Does it look like she has another hole for you to fuck? And I'm not about to share this tight pussy-fuck! Her pussy's getting so wet, oh… yeah, that's it! Squeeze my dick dry, slut- so shut up and just enjoy whatever you get," snapped Sean, panting with pleasure as he drove into her at an ever more erratic pace, drawing closer and closer to his second release of the night. "You-you're so pathetic, you should consider yourself the luckiest motherfucker on earth we even let you join in."

"But Sean…"

"It's alright Sean," interrupted Victor. "You remember that girl I dated last year, Miranda? She had a thing for anal and would often stick her dildo up my arse while we were fucking, sometimes she would even fuck me with a strap-on she kept under her bed, so if the fat little piggy's really that desperate he can-"

The veil lifted in the blink of an eye and Eric looked suddenly appalled by the suggestion. "What! Fuck no! I'm not gay, Victor, you faggot!"

"Fuck you, Eric! You're only gay if you're attracted to men and want to suck cock," snapped the brute, his absurdly high voice rising even higher in his fury, and his skin, stretched tight over rippling muscles, flushed to the colour of a baby tomato. "An ass is just another hole to fuck, and as I'm the one who'll be getting fucked, ether come over here and stick your dick in me, or just go jerk off. I don't really care which."

Cowed by the naked fury in the larger man's voice, Eric looked down at his feet and shuffled awkwardly from foot to foot before moving around outside of Mina's line of sight. She shifted to follow but Charlie's grip on her hair held her steady and so, desperate to distract herself from the storm ravaging her lower body, she gave up and focused all her attention on worshiping his cock. Sucking furiously and bobbing her head, she slid back along his length before swooping down, taking him deeper on every swing until his fleshy cap banged against the back of her throat. She could only moan at the musky flavour spilling over her tongue, her throat relaxed and the agony of her gag reflex remaining a distant memory. Groaning, Charlie quickly began to roll his hips with her motions, trying to receive more of the wondrous sensation as his iron-hold in her hair forced her to take him deeper and faster. And for a brief time the trick seemed to work. Focused as she was on the job-in-mouth, she felt detached, almost disembodied, from the foreign forces moving within her.

Then something new off-balanced her. First, she felt Victor shudder and release a long, low breath that tickled the hairs along the back of her neck. Then he doubled over, burying his face in the crook of her shoulder as the cock in her arse seemed to become even harder, and she knew Eric had taken him up on his offer.

It was awkward, at first, but after a moment the pair fell into rhythm and Mina could feel the doughy male's thrusts into the brute's tight cheeks as a drumming echo that rippled through the layers of muscle to reverberate through her anus as Victor drove into her at the same instant. In the back of her mind, Mina couldn't help but envision the scene unfolding behind her. Victor, so huge and powerful, with bronzed skin stretched tight over bulging muscles and glistening with perspiration, doubled over with his features locked in a mask of pleasure as Eric, red-faced and panting, drove into his arse. Despite his objections, he was taking to the anal dalliance like a natural, eagerly venting his frustration out on the larger male's arsehole and fucking him with ill-disguised delight, his fleshy body jiggling with each fresh plunge. The thought sent a kinky thrill straight down to her core.

Oh… God no! Wh-why is this turning me on?

Sucking with a mad fury, she worked the cock in her mouth with all the fever of a professional as Charlie clutched at her head with both hands and began to buck and thrust into her moist orifice, trying to distract herself once more from the liquid desire surging through her veins, igniting an all-toofamiliar fire in her core. Yet it did no good. The room was heavy with the scent of sex. Every breath flooded her lungs with the musky aroma of sweaty man-flesh, causing a fog to fall over her thoughts as her ears rang with the repeated slapping of flesh on flesh and the deep throaty sobs and moans of pleasure.

Her clit, swollen and in desperate need of proper attention, was throbbing. Her nipples were painfully tight, aching for devotion, and before she realised what she was doing, one of her hands relinquished their perch on Sean's torso to creep up her toned abdomen and cup the swell of her left breast, kneading it the way only she knew how while twisting the pebbled nipple between her thumb and forefinger. Just that simple touch was enough to send tingling feelings surging down to her neglected clit and she couldn't resist moaning around the dick in her mouth. Unaccustomed to being so helpless, she longed to grab them as her hips began to roll and push against the shafts hammering her twitching holes, riding them and pivoting in just the right angle to quicken the heat amassing slowly within her while the press of bodies kept her restrained, bound like a rag doll.

No-no I can't cum from this… not like this…

Then, just as the fires began to creep from her core, fingers of molten passion, the vision of her masturbating became too much for her oppressors and she suddenly felt Sean stiffen beneath her.

"Oh yeah! Here I fucking cum!" he roared, his hips bucking off the carpet in two last upward thrusts before his length suddenly swelled and erupted within her, unleashing thick streams of his molten seed deep into her grasping sheath.

Mina wanted to protest, to shout that she wasn't ready, but sensing the heat blossoming deep within her, mixing with the cum already deposited in her womb, she knew it was already too late. Making a quick mental note to call her GP first thing in the morning, she then felt a sudden, kinky thrill as she realised, for the third time in less than an hour, a man had climaxed inside her- and she liked it.

Good, I really have become a slut.

The thought sent a shudder of desire thundering through her body and the way her muscles tightened and convulsed around his cock, coupled with the feeling of Eric repeatedly hammering his prostate, pushed Victor over the edge. Shaking, his back curled and his shaven head fell back against the smaller male's shoulder. He exhaled a strangled squeak and drove into her arse to the hilt, his cock twitching, firing a thick tide deep into her brutalised bowels at the exact moment Eric succumbed to his own bliss and filled the burly giant's tight arse with cum.

Her muscles tensed, hungrily milking the shafts buried inside her, and Mina could tell her legs were on the verge of giving way as the hot fluids slashed against her inner walls, dicks pulsing. Nonetheless, by the way he throbbed against her tongue, and the increasingly desperate speed with which he was fucking her mouth, she could tell Charlie wasn't far behind his companions. With her vocalisations still reverberating down his length, the beauty, determined to finish him quickly, breathed in a deep breath through her nostrils then exhaled, sending a rush of warm air spilling across the organ, tickling the tip and caressing the sensitised glans.

"Ar-oh!" gasped Charlie in a choked splutter as, surprised and overwhelmed, he gave one last wild thrust all the way into her muggy orifice. His fingers tightened to a white-knuckled grip on the roots of her hair, forcing her to hold him in as his cock swelled and pulsed, shooting thick streams of salty cum down her throat. The sudden jet made Mina cough and splutter but, recovering quickly, she swallowed and drank down every drop, moaning happily, until his orgasm subsided.

And with that, the deed was done and Mina Carring, budding actress and glamour model, had experienced her first gangbang.

CHAPTER SEVEN

Overwhelmed by the sheer force of the three simultaneous blasts, the foursome collapsed together in a huddle of sweaty bodies and tangled limbs. Panting hard as the afterglows burned through them, it was a full two minutes before any of them could muster the will to move, and then it was only to shakily stagger to their feet, withdrawing their softening shafts from her body and leaving the beauty huddled in a ball on the bedroom floor.

"Wo-wow… that… that was bloody brilliant…" panted Sean, his chest heaving and face suddenly as red as the hair covering his body, as he stumbled almost drunkenly about trying to pull his trousers over his legs. His companions each made similar remarks and comments of agreement, yet Mina was in no state to take note and only half watched them out of the corner of one eye while hugging her knees to her chin, trying to ignore the dull fire burning down between her thighs.

"Grr… there! You've got what you wanted!" Mark growled angrily, the low and deadly tone of his voice causing Mina to twist dazedly around to discover her stepbrother seething on his bed, his naked body almost shaking with inexpressible anger as he clutched the rumpled sheets with a bone-white grip. Beside him, Daniel sat poised, thin lips drawn tight and his handsome face overshadowed by a stern, emotionless mask, concealing his emotions. His muscles were tensed, a low tremor only just visible as it ran through him. He was prepared to spring at the slightest provocation. "Now destroy those fucking videos!"

Pulling his last article of clothing over his head, Sean appeared unmoved by the veiled threat and smirked broadly before reaching into his jean pocket and retrieved his phone. Unlocking the screen, he flicked through a few options before his eyes suddenly widened in a look of mock surprise that sent a surge of dread rushing down to the pit of Mina's stomach. "Oh, I'm so sorry, we deleted those recordings ages ago. While you were watching Danny there fucking your sister, as it happens." His grin broadened and he turned the smartphone around to show them its empty gallery. "Didn't I mention it? Well, no harm done." He shrugged his shoulders offhandedly before turning his eyes down towards Mina, the cruel amusement reflected back at her making his irises gleam like quicksilver. "And after watching how wantonly she begged for both your cocks, we knew a slut like her wouldn't refuse us... if given the right incentive."

His words cut so deeply, Mina suddenly felt as if she'd been pitched through a sheet of thick ice and was plunging through the black frigid waters of a bottomless sea of self-loathing, the weight of her own disgust crushing down on her.

"You bastards!" Mark roared, but before either he or Daniel could rise, the group retreated, throwing open the bedroom door and slipping out in an instant, flooding the room with the sounds from the party stilling raging below, the inhabitants somehow gleefully oblivious to the activities having taken place above their heads. And as the door closed in her abusers' wake, muffling the uproar once more, Mina had never felt so desolate, so hopeless, so... lost. *Am I a slut?*

The question rang hollow in her ears, a mocking whisper, taunting her as, in the back of her consciousness, she became aware of a warm, thick substance leaking from her pussy and rolling down her thighs.

Am I a slut?

She was not innocent, nor delusional enough to try to think of herself as one. She enjoyed sex. Even in her early teens, she had considered herself a sexual creature and had taken every opportunity to explore her sexuality. Yet never had she experienced anything like she had tonight, nor endured such a barrage of conflicting, thrilling sensations.

Am I a fucking slut?

She could say she'd had no choice, that she was doing it to save her career, or that it had been the only way she could protect Mark and save her family. Yet she could not lie to herself, and deep down she'd known, and she'd always know, that she'd liked it. She'd wanted it all. Everything, from the moment she'd stepped into the room to catch her stepbrother masturbating, and even getting gangbanged had played to her darker fantasies.

It was all so strange, so dirty. Although the merest thought of Sean and his cronies pawing at her body like ravenous hyenas devouring a baby antelope alive, made her skin crawl. The feeling of holding them all inside her, of being stretched and brutalised and dominated completely, was all at once so intense and yet woefully inadequate she had been brought to the brink of insanity. Even now, when the storm had passed, she could still feel the itch buzzing in her core, the liquid heat pulsing between her thighs, and she longed to suffer that maddening intensity once more, if only their clumsy stabbing had begun and released that slow burning ember deep inside her…

The soft, rhythmic thumping of feet walking across the floor broke her thoughts. Twisting towards the source of the commotion, the reverberations travelled through the carpet to echo in her ears, and she was slightly taken aback to discover Daniel and Mark standing over her, one broad and gloriously muscular, the other lean and spindly, both naked and hard as steel.

Oh, my God!

CHAPTER EIGHT

Her heart hammered excitedly as butterflies fluttered in her stomach, and she opened her suddenly dry mouth to question them. Before she could utter a word, Daniel bent down, hooked both of his strong hands beneath her armpits and hoisted her up off the floor. Squealing in alarm, she instinctively threw her arms around his neck and held on for dear life as Danny crushed her to his muscular torso and trailed his hands down to grip her firm buttocks. Tipping her head back, she felt a hot thrill surge down her back at the look of hunger burning in his gaze an instant before his lips claimed her mouth in a demanding kiss of equal, raging passion.

Sensing his rampant arousal pressing against her swollen folds demanding entry, she could only moan into their embrace, teeth gnashing and tongues dancing, as he lowered her onto his shaft, a deep, lustful moan spilling from her lips at the feeling of the swollen crown splitting her folds and filling her depths. Still wet with desire, her body remembered his size and adjusted to his presence as she enveloped his hard cock inch by inch until he was fully sheathed within her snug embrace. Yet he did not linger and no sooner had he fully lowered her onto his shaft, he resumed fucking her, withdrawing almost all the way out before driving back in with a sudden upwards surge, raising a hard pounding rhythm, his hips rising and falling in hard, fast strokes while powerful hands supported her weight with ease.

Her back curled at the feeling of him passing in and out of her slit, driving into her over and over again with hard thrusts. The beauty tore her lips from his and tossed her head back, eyes bulging and mouth open, hollering a ragged cry at the repeated feeling of fullness reaching deep inside her, stretching her to capacity. Wrapping her long legs around his waist and crossing them over his tight, gyrating buttocks, pushing him even deeper into her warmth, she used the hold as leverage to rock upon his thick shaft as her core erupted with a fiery pleasure that emanated to the tips of her fingers and toes.

Sensing the fire-wreathed pressure gathering in her abdomen, marking the resurrection of her building climax rising like a phoenix from the ashes, Mina was certain no other lover had ever penetrated- no- had ever fucked her so deeply as this Adonis. Moving with him and meeting her lover plunge for maddening plunge, Mina could only moan and pant and scream with wild abandon. Carried by sheer burning desire, she rode him with all the feverish bravo of a cowgirl breaking a wild stallion and hungrily rammed herself down onto his hard shaft, her inner walls coaxed into grasping convulsions around the hard length every time he was fully embedded within her. "Oh wow- fuck… oh… yes… yes… fuck me! Fuck me!"

"Fuck… ugh, God! Your cunt's so small… so wet… yeah ride my dick, baby!" Grunting at the feeling of her innermost recesses tightening around his hard flesh, his nails bit into her succulent rump. Daniel heaved her up, raising her almost all the way off his shaft only to bring her crashing down as he thrust upward. They both shuddered and gasped ragged breaths as he forced her to take him deeper.

Delighting in the sudden shock of him splitting her open, Mina lost all self-control. Leaning back, her arms drawing tight and spine bowing, supported only by his powerful hands, she surrendered to his will as he began to drive into her with fresh vigour, this new angle giving him the perfect leverage with which to fuck her. Greedily consuming her offering like some great lustful beast of ancient mythos, Daniel brought her up and down in a fierce crashing tide of raw hunger and desire, his hips rocking and grinding against her pelvis with such intensity, as though intending to ruin her for any other lover to come after.

"Oh… oh… oh God! Your cock is so big… so deep… oh I can barely take it… Oh- fuck! Fuck! Fuck… so huge…incredible! Ah …Yes… yes… YES!" His cock felt like a solid rod of titanium tightly wrapped in living silk, and was ripping her in half, reaching deep inside her, so very deep inside her he could barely fit. She was so wet, her nectar was rolling down her thighs in rivulets as his huge shaft moved in and out of her with ease, eliciting a wet, echoing, slapping resonance, and he was able to put himself as deep inside her as her body could take him and it felt so incredible. Eyes wide and mouth frozen agape, nearly screaming with each Herculean thrust, she could barely breathe through the inferno that overwhelmed her senses, pulsing through her veins with each quickening heartbeat as he sent her rushing towards her peak.

Seeming to sense that she was drawing close, he kept up his assault unchecked, fucking her in perfect time as he hoisted her up and down, his hard, steady strokes unaffected either by fatigue or by the pressure surely gathering in his loins, mounting bit by bit with each demonic thrust, building towards his inevitable creamy completion.

"Oh my God… Oh my God… It's too big… all the way- oh- in my stomach… but- omigod- so good… like you're splitting me in two… so good. Oh God, don't stop! Don't stop! Harder… fuck me harder… bounce me up and down on your dick… make me take it… give my tight pussy every fucking inch of your big oh- oh- oh!" Caught in the throes of ecstasy, she clawed his back, her perky breasts bounced with his rhythm, and his hands lifted and lowered her, controlling her like Sean and his henchmen had, as though she were nothing but a rag doll, but this was better.

The *la petite mort* almost upon her, she gazed up at him in utter rapture, held captive by the darkening storm of lust glazing his in fierce blue eyes, the intensity of his gaze drawing her into the very depths of his soul and she greedily sought to etch every part of his expression into her memory. The way his jaw tensed every time their bodies joined. It was the most erotic sight she had ever seen and proved to be just the catalyst she needed to finally push her over the edge. "Oh my God… oh… this is sooo… fucking good… oh shit! You're going to make me cum again… ah- ah- ah- ah- yes- yes- yes… you're going to make me cum… oh fuck yes! You're going to- omigod- omigod- I'm cumming, I'm cumming!"

It took all of a few moments, from start to summit, for him to bring her to climax. The dam broke. A pulse ripped through her body. Fiery pleasure blossomed in her abdomen, coursing through her veins in white-hot rivers of wildfire as she began to tremble uncontrollably, tossing her head from side to side, fireworks bursting behind both eyes, and lips spreading in a wide, toothy smile as the full force of the powerful orgasm washed over her.

In her delirium, she didn't notice Daniel's sideways glance, his subtle nod, or the shadowy form moving behind her as he continued pounding her. He hammered her relentlessly through the release, heightening her pleasure, sending her spiralling towards another even as her walls clamped down upon his throbbing shaft, holding him tight with all her might, and smothering him with her sticky nectar.

God, his stamina is amazi- Ow! What the fuck?

Seizing the moment, Mark had come upon her from behind. Taking advantage of his stepsister's distraction, he moved without making a sound, his long, dexterous fingers hooking over her hips to steady her as he manoeuvred into position. Lost in a fog of pleasure, her senses dulled by the powerful orgasm still raging through her, Mina sensed rather than felt the presence at her back and the swollen shaft rising between her already partially spread buttocks.

Mina's eyes widened, her limbs shaking all the more violently as her climax refused to subside, only seemed to grow all the stronger at the realisation of what was about to happen. The model and actress threw her head around but could only glimpse Mark out of the corner of her eye so looked up to find Daniel looking back at her knowingly. With a mischievous grin playing at the corner of his thin lips, he plunged into her warmth, her head spinning at the feeling of him stretching and filling her sensitised sheath, before tightening his grip on her to still her gyrating hips, holding her tightly against him as the head of her stepbrother's cock began to press against her anus.

After being broken-in by the stoic, squeaky Victor, her sphincter did not resist. Through the fog of fire and pulsing bliss, she felt an awesome pressure of hot, rubbery flesh forcing its way through the tight gateway of her flawless arse, popping easily past the ring of muscle and pressing her into Daniel. It hurt, but not as before. There was no pain, no burning agony, only a momentary numbness followed by an uncomfortable strained tightness, like she was already being stretched to her limit with only the head inside her. However, Mark was not done and continued to push his advantage, gently rocking back and forth on the balls of his feet, working centimetre after centimetre of his cock deep into the tight grip of her seamen-slickened bowels.

Whimpering softly, barely able to breathe through the intensity of the long length slowly filling her, goosebumps erupted all over her body and Mina curled forward to bite down, hard, upon Daniel's shoulder, tasting a splash of copper against the salt of his skin as her inner walls clenched involuntarily around him. His jaw tight, chiselled muscles bulging with the strain of remaining still, he groaned as her teeth grated painfully on bone while her plush sheath convulsed in vice-like contractions around his hard shaft. Then finally, with one last push, Mark had completely buried his whole cock in her luscious derrière and the turbulent concoction of pleasure mixing with the feeling of sheer, unparalleled fullness brought her to orgasm, right in the midst of her last.

They remained like that for a moment and in all her life, Mina had never felt so full. Pinned and suspended, sandwiched between her two young lovers, impaled upon their hard cocks, pressed fast against their hard bodies, their skin deliciously cool against the primal heat radiating from her core, it was as if every fibre of her being was stretched to accommodate these two studs. Visibly shaking as the force of the combined orgasms crashed over her, her pulse thundering in her ears and her vision dancing with white dots before her rolling eyes, she felt as if she were floating, and the last coherent part of her brain realised she was in real danger of losing consciousness. The embrace was so erotic however, that she couldn't have cared less and yearned for more as she began tingling from head to toe.

Two… two cocks feels so good!

"Oh -wow… fuck! Even after getting fucked by Victor, your asshole is still so tight, but don't worry Mina. I'll take care of that," she heard Mark promise through the haze that fogged her thoughts, just as her orgasms began to ebb. He sounded far away, yet his mouth was so close to her ear that she could feel his breath on the back of her neck, and she recognised that sinful, mischievous tone she knew all too well.

Then, without further ado, she felt him draw back, causing her entire body to shudder as her arse tensed, sucking at his shaft and trying to hold him in. He carried on regardless, his motions slow and purposeful, gradually dragging half his length from her bowel's embrace before pushing back in a little more firmly, then repeating the process, siring a rhythm that quickly had her eyes squeezed shut from sensory overload.

Clinging to Daniel as if her life depended upon it, as though he were her very anchor to reality, a pained whimper escaped Mina, the slight sting of her muscles stretching to accommodate so much pressure, until her arse began to relax, giving way to such a deep sense of pleasure. No doubt able to feel her body opening up to him, Mark held nothing back, withdrawing until only the bulbous crown remained inside her tight bowels and then slamming back in, making his stepsister's eyes pop open in surprise.

"Ah! Oh- yes!" she moaned into Daniel's shoulder, her heart pounding and nails biting deep half-moons into the hard muscles of his back as she felt the solid heat of Mark's dick sawing in and out of her arse. The sensation was so intense and wildly exciting that she thought she would combust, and she could feel her body shake, the pounding pressure, coupled with her awesome feeling of fullness and the huge cock that pulsed and throbbed deep within her, flooding her consciousness with the rawest sense of pleasure.

Yet before she could begin to comprehend the physicality of her lust, Daniel broke his fast and resumed rolling his hips, churning and grinding into her warmth, and the feeling of them both suddenly moving inside her had her throw her head back, a voiceless cry billowing from her rosy lips as every nerve in her clitoris went supernova.

Working together, the pair forged a relentless rhythm with one driving in while the other withdrew, thrusting- drawing- thrusting- drawing…

"Oh- my- God, oh- my- God, oh- my- holy… fuck!" Eyes wide and mewing breathlessly, Mina felt like she was about to combust from the delicious friction of both cocks moving inside her, rubbing against the thin membrane that divided them, making her pussy run wet with dew.

It was torture. It was ecstasy, as absolute as it was unbearable. Losing herself in the feeling of being so full, so stretched, of arms encompassing her and hot flesh rubbing against her skin, Mina constantly needed to remind herself to breathe as her sense of awareness leapt between the huge cock stretching her sex, the deep sense of fullness radiating through her arse and the needy throbbing of her clit. Overwhelmed, her body began to add its own motions, twisting, wriggling, and riding the hard shafts, her muscles convulsing as the inner walls of her pussy and rectum grew swollen and oversensitive, dissolving into writhing spirals.

"Fuck… your pussy's getting tighter," Danny growled, the deep resonance of his voice sending hot shivers down her spine. It was then she noticed his handsome face tilted towards her, his jaw tight and those piercing blue eyes dark with lust, watching her with a smouldering intensity that had her stomach winding into tight knots. "And that expression is so sexy. Do you really love taking two cocks at once so much?" He was emphasising each word with a hard thrust, his pelvic bone teasing her clit. "Why don't you tell us which you like best, Mina? What's better, my dick in your pussy or your brother's in that tight little asshole?"

"Urgh… I ca-can't decide… they both feel so good! Oh Fuck- oh fuck- oh fuck… I'm so- so full- oh fuck- fuck!" Deep down, she knew the question should have repulsed her, yet his words were so coarse and dirty, it only excited her further. "Oh, boys… oh, boys… oh- oh you're such bad, dirty boys… oh- my- God… I love it… fuck me harder… yes… yes…"

She was a vision of passion, rocking and bouncing and grinding between them, perky breasts jiggling, her features contorted with unearthly pleasure, and urging them on amidst ragged breaths. Her orgasm built like a great black storm upon the horizon.

This wasn't like it had been with Sean and his little friends. That had been so different, so violent and primitive, with them using her as a piece of meat, a tool for their own gratification. None of it could have prepared her for this, carnal instinct coursing through her veins. The intensity, the friction, the fullness, the sheer… feeling of it all, nothing was as it should be. She was just so sensitive, every feeling felt amplified and enhanced, pushing her towards the highest pinnacle of pleasure as heat- glorious, orgasmic fire- reached out from her core, spreading through every fibre of her being to consume her. Body and soul. Goddamn, it was too good.

"Oh fuck, Mina… your ass is amazing!" Mark groaned into her ear. His breath washed over the back of her neck and sent hot shivers down her spine. "It's so tight and slippery and- fuck- squeezing my dick so tightly… ugh… God, this is the greatest birthday present ever!"

Somewhere in the dark forgotten recesses of her brain, Mina registered Danny growling something in response, but she couldn't make sense of his words through the sudden fog of pleasure blanketing her thoughts. A sparkle caught her eye, a twinkle of starlight falling though the heavens. Peering through the haze, she discerned a bead of sweat trickling down his neck, leaving a glistening trail down his stretched skin. Entranced, she leant forward to scoop up the bead of perspiration before dragging her tongue back up his slick skin, delighting in the salty flavour. A low growl emanated from Daniel, before she took the lobe of his ear between her teeth. She suckled it wantonly, her every thought focused on teasing the fleshy nub until an anonymous hand suddenly slapped her stretched backside and the shock of the sting had her release the lobe in a surprised gasp, her head rolling back onto Mark's shoulder. Not missing a beat, her stepbrother claimed her mouth in a hungry kiss, his silky tongue sweeping past her bruised and swollen lips to pillage hers, while another set of lips suddenly enveloped her right breast, sucking greedily and sending electricity zipping through her bosom.

Relishing their touch, her back curled, arching into Daniel's mouth as his tongue circled her pebbled nipple, offering herself to him while slipping one of her hands from his shoulder and dragging her manicured nails down his broad torso before coiling the limb back around Mark's neck. Drunk on the hot, tingling sensations that were coursing through her body, she kissed him back with equal hunger, teeth gnashing and tongues duelling, nearly devouring him with her need. Her senses were ablaze and her whole world suddenly shrank down to just the feeling of the fierce fires raging in her core, the silky tongue circling and lashing her oversensitive bud, and the shafts sliding back and forth, impaling her, pounding her, fucking her. Oh, God, she was so close, she felt like she was about to burst. This wasn't sex. She was sex. *She* was sex embodied and personified, from the molten fires raging in her core to the desperate need pulsing through her clit and the tingling in her fingertips. She was Aphrodite. She was Isis. She was Venus. She was the goddess and the moon and the stars above.

Yes! I'm a slut, and God save me, I love it! I fucking love it! I-I…

"Urgh…" Mina gasped, dragging her mouth from Mark's, before she threw her head back and a desperate, primitive sound burst from her lips as the sudden epiphany sent the tight knot of fiery tension at her centre supernova.

In that moment, time seemed to hold its breath and she had a sudden inexplicable sense of rising before the calm abruptly descended upon her. Frozen in a state of limbo, with all perceptions of time forgotten, her heartbeat roaring in her ears and her body vibrating with a subtle, inexpressible tension, she hung upon that precipice for what seemed an eternity before finally plummeting back down to earth, her climax surging over her with raging intensity. Eyes rolling, muscles clenching, she desperately tried to give voice to her pleasure, but the words stuck in her throat and all that escaped was a strangled gasp before she began to tremble and writhe uncontrollably in her lovers' arms, the waves of pleasure ripping through her, sweeping her away on a tide of euphoria.

Daniel and Mark weren't done with her, however, and beneath the storm of fire and ecstasy Mina could feel them quickening inside her, their synchronised rhythm coming undone as her inner walls convulsed around them, becoming rougher, wilder and more erratic, then falling apart completely.

Mark was the first to break.

"Oh fuck, Mina, It's so hot watching you cu- fuck-fuck…" he grunted, the moist warmth of his breath spilling over the sensitive spot that joined her neck and shoulder in short, quick gasps. His mouth attacked the side of her neck, the wetness of his tongue swirling over her sweet spots in a way he knew drove her wild. He was close, the rational, almost dormant part of her mind warned, and true to her prediction, moments later his thrusts began hastening with the urgency of his nearing release.

Her stepbrother held nothing back, driving into her with a quick, furious tempo that made her arse feel electrified and had her rebounding against Daniel's motions in the perfect angle for his pelvis to continue rubbing against her throbbing clit, the repeating friction causing sunspots to flicker before her eyes.

Yet Daniel only groaned at the feeling of her muscles clenching around him, the low sound reverberating through her bosom while his tongue flittered over her painfully stiff nipple. His strokes were growing ever more intense and purposeful, making her feel every inch, ridge and, vein of the magnificent cock ramming into her, the mushroom-shaped head striking her deepest, sweetest spots with each plunge, birthing writhing tongues of white fire that surged through her pulsing core to the tips of her fingers and toes.

They were relentless, never slowing, their powerful hands squeezing the firm mounds of her arse with bruising intensity, supporting her and manipulating her, fucking her, pushing her on, dragging her orgasm out longer and longer and making her tingle from head to toe. They moved as one but at the same time with complete indifference to each other, together but also separate, one fucking her with wild abandon, the other playing her body with all the precision and skill of a London orchestra. Losing all control, she could do nought but cling to them for dear life, utterly at their mercy, their low moans filling her ears and the musky aroma of sex infesting every breath. The waves grew and lengthened, sweeping over her with greater and greater force until she could no longer tell where one ended and the next began.

"…Fucking dicks… oh yeah… give them to me… yes… yes- yes- ah- ah- ah!" The words burst from her in a ragged cry as she tried to snatch life-preserving breaths amidst a crescendo of sobbing cries, the world spinning around their tangled bodies. Even before the waves had passed, her body was mounting the crest of another climax, the fires sweeping through her… No, she had to stop, needed to catch her breath, she couldn't take it, it was too good, too…

Hot. I'm so… so hot… my pussy… my ass… they're melting… Oh God… no! It's too much… I'm going crazy… I'm going… I'm going…"

Unable to stay in sync, they rammed into her with unbridled vigour, their hips slapping wetly against her skin as her nectar ran down her thighs in rivulets, each powerful thrust driving her against the next, so deep she could almost feel their cocks meeting in her stomach. Then, seemingly by chance, they both slammed into her at once and that sudden sweet shock of incredible fullness cast her spirit from her body, from the mass of tangled flesh, through the roof, into the night sky above, soaring through the heavens until, finally, darkness enveloped her.

CHAPTER NINE

Somewhere a phone was ringing.

It sounded far away, yet too near for her to ignore, like a subtle voice in the wind, whispering to her through the thick morning fog and dragging her from the warm cocoon that enveloped her.

Half asleep and reluctant to lose the welcoming comfort of sleep's embrace, she rolled over and buried her face in her pillow, stubbornly trying to block out the interruption before groaning a low, mournful sound, surrendering to the inevitable. With her eyes still shut and the phone's shrill ringing echoing in her ears, though sounding distinctly closer now, she sat up, causing the duvet covering her to cascade down her front, revealing her creamy skin and pert breasts. Stretching her arms out above her head, her muscles stiff from her long slumber, she then rubbed the sleep from her eyes with the base of her palm before opening them enough to discern the first grey light of dawn filtering into the room, shrouding it in gloom. Blurry-eyed, she had to blink thrice before the world slipped into focus.

Mina didn't remember falling asleep. She felt exhausted, drained, and so very weary. Her eyes were heavy and her throat parched with a salty, bitter flavour souring the back of her mouth. Oddly, there was also a dull, but oddly satisfying soreness throbbing in her lower abdomen. What recollections she had were like the memories of a dream she had just awoken from but already forgotten, a dream of tangled, naked bodies writhing in passion.

She'd expected to awake in her bright cavernous bedroom, snuggled in her goose feather bed and luxurious Egyptian cotton duvet, but the weak morning light revealed a small cluttered chamber with poster-adorned pale grey-blue walls. The air was heavy with a stale musky odour and wherever she looked there was rumpled clothing scattered across the dark charcoal carpet.

Mark's bedroom!

Icy realisation dawned. Throwing off the sheets and scrambling out of bed, she bolted across the room, her long legs wobbling dangerously with every step, before diving for her jacket amidst the scattered garments. Fishing through the pockets, taunted by the repeating buzz of the vibrate alarm, she finally managed to withdraw the phone only to catch a momentary glimpse of Jason's photo on the caller ID before it died in her hand.

Cursing under her breath, she activated the screen. Sure enough, there were at least half a dozen missed calls from Jason, as well as twice that many texts and two, no doubt very scathing, audio messages. Releasing a heavy breath she hadn't realised she'd been holding, Mina had a sudden overwhelming urge to hurl the device to the floor and stomp on it.

Like all directors, Jason tended to overreact, though in this case she supposed his suspicions would not be entirely unjustified. No doubt there would be some very tricky questions to answer when she got home. And if the number of missed calls was any indication, it was going to take all of her skills to smooth this one over, and she certainly meant *all* of them.

Her head snapped up at the sound of rustling, eyes darting towards the source of the disturbance. Mark was asleep on the bed, rolling onto his side with one hand buried beneath a pillow while the other dragged a handful of the bedsheets to his chest, his narrow, boyishly handsome face covered by a stray wing of wispy, chocolate-coloured hair.

There was no sign of Daniel, though in the cold light of day, or rather early morning, she supposed that was probably a very good thing. In her current mood, she wasn't sure if she would have killed him, or pounced and taken him for another five rounds. The sight of him had a smile tugging at the corner of her lips. She loved Jason and she would miss him. They had had many good times together and the thought of losing him left a sickly feeling in the bottom of her gut. Yet if the day ever came when she had to choose, there would only ever be one winner. Yet that was by no means the sum of her troubles.

Daniel. Sean. Charlie. Eric. Victor. She had bought their silence and complacency with her body, and they had deleted their recordings as agreed. However, nothing could undo what they had seen. Mina's stomach tightened at the thought. Maybe, if she was inexplicably lucky, all four would hold their tongues, taking the secret to their graves, but that was a gamble of long odds. It would only take one slip to let the cat out of the bag.

No, she knew it was inevitable, whether slurred amidst a drunken rant or as an anonymous tip given pride of place on the cover of some gossiping celebrity trash magazine, the truth would come out. It was only a matter of time.

Her innards churned with a sudden sense of hopelessness, but Mina tried to put it to the back of her mind. She wished she knew what to do. There was nothing she wouldn't give, nothing she wouldn't do, to protect Mark. He was more than her stepbrother, more than a lover. He completed her, made her feel whole in a way no one else ever had, or could, and for him she knew she'd relive last night all over again without a moment's hesitation. However, when that awful day of reckoning arrived, could she protect him?

Tears began to burn the corners of her eyes. Quickly blinking the unshed moisture away, she cast a rueful look back at Mark, watching him sleep until a reluctant smile tugged at the corner of her lips. A storm was coming, but no matter what devastation it would unleash upon them, they would face it together, as they always did.

Grabbing what comfort she could from that thought, Mina quickly turned off the phone and slipped it back into her jacket. She would need it later, when she made that grovelling call to Jason, apologising for not coming home, insisting she'd merely lost track of time and spent the night kipping on her father's bed. But for now, all she wanted to do was have a shower.

Clambering awkwardly to her feet, she gathered up her clothes from the floor and folded and placed them neatly in a pile at the foot of the bed before tiptoeing across the room. Lingering by the door, she took one final look back, smiling fondly as she etched the image of Mark sleeping into her memory. Turning back, she grasped the handle, eased the door open a crack and slipped silently through, pulling it closed as she went without making a sound.

The hallway was inky black. Pressing her back against the door, the wood cool against her skin, Mina waited with bated breath, her ears peeled for the slightest sound, yet the house was as still and silent as the grave. When she was certain she was alone, she let the breath go in a heavy sigh. Turning on her heel, she hurried past the closed door of her father's empty room and past the framed family pictures she knew were hanging upon the walls, masked by darkness, their unseeing eyes watching her naked body pass with voyeur's delight. Her feet padded with every step, the carpet soft underfoot, and she moved quickly, silently, and with all the grace and elegance of a stalking tigress towards the far door, pausing only when she came to the mouth of the stairs.

Hugging the wall, she edged forward and peered around the bend, but the foyer below was vacant except for the crumpled Styrofoam cups, crisp packets, a pizza box, and a mass of other rubbish littering the faded carpet.

Damn punks, Dad will freak if he sees this mess!

Still reluctant to pass through the shafts of light blazing from the floor below for fear of being spotted by some hungover reveller just waking from a drunken slumber and stumbling into the foyer, she drew back. Taking a breath, gathering her courage, she raised her leg, and then the deed was done.

With the sun warm upon her skin, she sprang the gap into the cloak of darkness and ran the last few steps to the bathroom. Throwing open the door, she darted in without a backwards glance.

Long and narrow, with deep blue walls and white vinyl floor tiles, the bathroom was the smallest room in the house. With a tug of the pull switch, the thin chamber flooded with bright yellow luminescence that belied the weak light trickling through the frosted glass of the only window. Noting the already drawn shower curtain around the bath, she reached in, turned the shower temperature dial to full, pushed the power button and quickly withdrew the arm just before she heard the rush of water and the pitter-patter against the cloth. Whilst waiting for the water temperature to rise, she busied herself with taking a neatly folded towel from one of the shelves of the tall linen cabinet and hung it on the towel rail, taking care as she did not to glance at the mirror above the sink. She would not dare to look at her reflection, fearful of who, or what, she'd see staring back at her.

Pulling back the curtain, releasing a great billowing plume of steam, Mina clambered into the bath and stepped under the spray. Letting out a contented sigh as the scalding water cascaded down her naked body, slowly turning her creamy skin baby pink, she stood motionless beneath the pelting torrent with her head tipped back, letting it purge her, cleanse her and wash away all remnants of the night before and then carry her away. Completely engrossed in the shower, she didn't notice the dull creak of the bathroom door opening and closing.

A warm fog enveloped her. The heat was therapeutic and reached deep inside her, soothing the dull ache in her abdomen, the proof that last night had been anything but a dream. Feeling the stress flow from her body, she took a bottle of citrus-fresh shower gel from the caddy hanging off the fixtures, popped the cap and squeezed a generous portion of the lemon-scented substance onto her palm. Closing and replacing the bottle back on the shelf, she began washing her arms, purring with delight as she did at the silky sensuality of her hands moving across her skin, her heart suddenly pounding beneath her breast.

There was something so… sexual, about washing in the shower. Surrendering to impulse and letting her hands work their magic, they slid down her flanks, down her smooth thighs and drew perilously close to the folds of her womanhood before rising, gliding ever so lightly up the flat plane of her belly to cup her breasts, her nipples rising beneath her soapy palms. Her heart beating fast, she bit back a moan as she began to roll the pebbled buds between her thumbs and forefingers, sending a tingle surging down to her centre.

I am a slut.

There was a sudden damp rustle, and a frigid breeze brushed her skin. Her head whipped around to discover Mark standing over her. He was completely naked and an almost inaudible groan escaped her as she watched him step over the rim of the tub, her greedy eyes drinking in his tight buttocks and bobbing erection, before realising how she must have looked. She dropped her hands to her sides, her cheeks burning with a sudden nervous blush.

Mark pulled the curtain closed behind him with a gentle tug before turning to confront her, his eyes gleaming with dark, predatory hunger, the spray plastering his fringe to his forehead. She could feel his gaze upon her soapy breasts. Feeling suddenly embarrassed, she tried to say something but before she could fathom a word, he closed the gap between them and claimed her mouth in a deep, devouring kiss, his arms coiling about her waist and pulling her against him, his engorged arousal poking against her hip.

Here we go again.

The End.

Alpha Bitch

Chapter ONE

Danny Royce knew this was a bad idea. A terrible idea. The worst idea in a long sad history of bad ideas. He didn't have any choice. He was desperate.

He needed her help.

And it meant going back there… Lupus Latr.

A small quiet place built along the Avon to all the rest of the world, Lupus Latr looked much like any other little village across the south of England. A collection of traditional old houses and shops lined a warren of weaving roads that all led to the central hub of the community, a thatch-roofed pub with a wartime memorial on the doorstep.

Yet it had a secret. A secret the villagers had kept and protected since before the age of

Druids. When the old gods had ruled the land, the spirits walked the earth, and man and beast were as one.

Danny's stomach started to loop when he saw the signs for the historic little hamlet, but he wasn't sure if it was trepidation or anticipation. It was quite probably both.

It had been eight years since he'd left- or rather since his mother had packed their bags and spirited them away in the dead of night. It felt like he'd been running ever since.

But there came a time in everyone's life when they had to face their demons, and as he pulled his old Rover into the village's only car park, Danny knew his day had come.

Overhead, the sky was melting away from shades of pink and orange to a deep magenta.

On any other day, it would have been a beautiful night.

Welcome home Danny he mused, switching off the ignition and climbing out into evening air, fragrant with the scent of cut grass. Just the way he remembered. It was good to know it still smelt the same, if nothing else.

There'd been a time he knew every street and building. His father's family had been key members of the community since Roman times after all. His blood was as much a part of Lupus Latr as the stones and mortar. When he was small, he'd played in the fields, fished in the rivers, and hunted in the woods. As he grew, he attended the local schools and made a name for himself on the rugby grounds. Then eight years ago, on the eve of his eleventh birthday, she had arrived in town, and everything changed.

A point made clear by the commercialised front of his hometown.

"Fucking McDonalds," he pondered, passing by the building that, eight years before had been a little greengrocer shop but now sported the infamous neon 'M'. There was a Costa Coffee too, even a goddamn Dominos. The smell of the cooking meat made his stomach rumble, reminding him that he hadn't eaten anything since breakfast.

He'd left London in such a rush, even skipping out on all his afternoon lectures. Danny had been desperate to put as much distance between himself and that girl as possible. Before the urge took him again.

No, he needed to get this done.

He could still feel it, burning inside him. The heat. The awareness. The throbbing energy crackled through his skin, making it feel too tight for his body. The hunger. The raw, undeniable need.

Dormant for the moment but there all the same and growing stronger.

Danny couldn't understand it.

It had begun about a month ago, the morning he started attending ICL. It had started off like an itch he couldn't quite scratch, a tingle of sensation racing down his spine while he'd been moving through the halls to his first lecture. Then he'd heard footsteps behind him and glanced around just in time to see a girl running by. Suddenly his every sense was focused on her, and he couldn't stop himself from giving her a long, slow once over.

She was a cute little thing. Long raven hair that cascaded all the way down her back, half rim glasses that framed her angular face and sat high on her nose, a small mouth with peach-coloured lips, and sparkling blue eyes. Dressed in a conservative button up white blouse and slim-cut blue jeans that showed off long athletic legs he longed to feel wrapped around him, she was the walking embodiment of a smoking hot bookworm fantasy.

He'd managed to drag his eyes away just in time, but she must have sensed him watching her because no sooner had he done so, her head had snapped around to fix on him.

Her big blue eyes had narrowed suspiciously, but far from being intimidated, the challenging look had sent another tingle down his spine, stirring his beast.

Then, just like that she was gone, vanishing amongst the surrounding press of bodies as quickly as she had appeared, leaving just her heady scent in her wake. A scent clean and fresh with hints of vanilla and cinnamon. He inhaled it greedily, his mouth watering.

That had just been the beginning. As it turned out, not only was the girl- he soon learnt her name was Jackie Hunt- attending ICL, but she would also be attending all of his lectures. As she sat just two seats down from him, she was also just close enough for him to faintly catch her scent on each breath. It was close enough to make his heart race.

And it had only gotten worse, the urges growing stronger and harder to control.

He'd almost lost it that morning when she'd cornered him in a corridor, all fire and brimstone, demanding to know why he was constantly watching her. And it had been all he could do not to push her up against the lockers and silence her with a hungry kiss. He almost had when she'd stepped in close and started to prod him in his chest with her finger. The beast in him had taken over and closed the gap, his head dipping so they were almost nose to nose, lips just brushing-

If she had stood her ground, he didn't want to think what could have happened. Instead, she'd softened under him, rising up on her tiptoes to meet him, lips parting for him.

That momentary surrender however, had broken the spell.

He'd fled.

No apologies, no hurried explanation, just turned on his heel and bolted as fast as his legs could carry him. Which was probably for the best, because her furious shouts had hounded him all through the halls.

If Jackie had been anybody else, Danny might have hoped she'd forget about it. It was

Friday after all, and that meant she'd have a whole two days of free time to get it out of her mind, but Danny doubted Jackie Hunt had ever let herself forget about anything. She was possibly the most stubborn girl he had ever known, and he wouldn't put it past her to hack into the school database to steal his address and come round to his lodgings, just to kick his ass.

And if that happened, he didn't want to think about what might happen.

He needed to sort this out.

He needed help.

He needed to see…her.

Erza. The Werewolf Princess. His Alpha.

There'd be plenty of time to grab a burger on the way home if he survived that long.

Chapter TWO

Wolf's Run was not a trail you would find in any *A to Z* or guidebook, but every inhabitant of Lupus Latr knew it like the back of their hand.

It was a short walk up from the village centre, along the high street, then a sudden sharp turn at the Butcher's, up an alley, and along a cobbled path into the woods. That was the marker and the boundary, where the old world and the new meet went separate ways. Where the villagers could cast off their skins and embrace their true nature and run.

Even for all of the danger he knew would lie ahead, Danny walked easily through the trees. It felt good to be back on the run, to walk in the footsteps of his ancestors and breathe in the free air. The city was too cramped, too confined. There was nowhere to move and even the air was a poisonous smog. The confinement had made his skin crawl. It had hung around his neck and bound his limbs like iron fetters. Here he was free in the way nature had intended. The beast in him longed to be let loose, to be allowed to run and hunt as he had when he was a pup. To reclaim his kingdom.

However, he forced it down, knowing he needed to stay focused on the task at hand.

That wasn't why he was here. Those days were long gone, forgotten, given over to history and darkness along with all that was left of his kin.

Yet even as he walked along the ancient path beneath a canopy of oaks, chestnuts, and beeches, his eyes scanned the space between every trunk for the slightest hint of movement.

They were out there. Danny could feel them watching, waiting, preparing to launch their attack.

It didn't matter that his father had once been their Alpha. After he and his mother had fled, they would have been cast out, exiled. Where once he had been a prince, he was now an invader, and he was trespassing on sacred territory. He would have only one warning, one chance to plead his case for safe passage, before they would attack.

It was their way. The wolf's way.

Snap.

Danny froze, his ears pricked trying to pinpoint its direction, suddenly very aware of how dark it was getting. Night was creeping in as the hour drew on, and he still had two miles to go to Lacum Hall, the seat of Lupus Latr's ruling family.

His father's ancestral house.

His heart raced. He waited, silently counting down from twenty, fighting to keep calm. If he made a sudden move, or anything that could be considered aggressive, the attack would be immediate, and for the kill. There was no room for softness in this world nor mercy, only submission or death.

Only when he was certain no attack was- for the moment anyway- forthcoming, did he slowly raise his hands into the air and turn a full circle. "I'm alone, I didn't come to fight."

His voice rang out through the trees, but only silence answered.

"Hello," he pressed. "I know you're out there. This doesn't have to get unpleasant, all I want is to talk." Still there was no answer.

Danny slowly lowered his hands. They were out there. He could feel them watching him. Just out there in the dark, beyond the range of his human eyes. His beast could sense them lurking in the dark, waiting, watching, hunting.

With his guard still up, he turned and continued on down the trail. It was a dangerous move. Nothing was a more inviting target than fleeing prey, and his instincts were roaring at him to turn back. To stand his ground, force them out, and show he could not be herded like sheep but that was the beast talking. The Alpha's way. He had turned from that path long ago.

So he walked on slowly and carefully, ever aware of the occasional rustle of leaves and distant twigs snapping underfoot as he was followed along the trail. He walked until the trees opened up and he emerged out into a clearing. On the opposite side, just past the tops of the trees, Lacum Hall stood visual over all its domain, high atop the summit of Monkshood hill, bathed in the light of the autumn moon just as he'd remembered it from all those years ago.

Beneath it, the encircling wall of yew and oaks was a patchwork of shadows. Within it, darkness moved against darkness as a beast much like his own stepped out into the clearing.

Danny watched it move into the light. At a first glance, a casual observer could almost be forgiven for thinking it was a man. Almost. Against the dark, it walked upright into the illuminated space, but it was larger than any man had a right to be. Impossibly large. As it stepped out of the shadows, it was impossible to miss its unnaturally long limbs tipped by razor sharp talons, its broad body covered in thick fur, its canine head framed by pointed ears, and powerful jaws large enough to crush a man's head in one bite.

And for all that, he couldn't help but laugh. "Jake, is that you? Little Jake Evans, well didn't you get big."

The werewolf's only answer was a deep growl that rumbled up from its cavernous torso like thunder as it stalked out of the shadows, advancing on him.

Danny held his ground, then heard movement behind him, the sounds of branches cracking and something big stepping out in the open. Careful not to make any quick movements, he slowly glanced back. "Ah, Bill, was that you back there then? Well, can't say I'm surprised, you two always did stick together. Have you tried licking your own balls yet, or do you just do each other's?"

The second werewolf was the spitting image of the first, but where Jake's pelt was a dark chocolate colour, Bill's was a lighter tawny colour shot with gold. Together they advanced, penning him in and closing the trap.

"Okay, now look, guys, I just want to talk with Erza, we don't have to do this," offered Danny, still trying to keep his voice level and calm even as he looked from one werewolf to the next, watching his chances of escape shrink by the second.

Jake snapped his jaws in answer, wet and shiny with hunger while opposite him, Bill raked a yew with his claws, leaving great gouges through the bark. When he brandished them his way, the challenge was clear to see.

"Ok, maybe we do." Sighing, Danny shrugged off his coat. Looking down at his feet, he took a deep breath, and gave himself over to the fury that raged in his soul. He'd come this far, there could be no turning back now. "Alright, come on then you bastards. Come and have a go if you think you're hard enough!" His head snapped up and his eyes burned as bright and as fierce as the moon above. "Come on!" His challenge dissolved into a long bestial howl, their ancestral homage to the goddess of the hunt. The orbed maiden with white fire laden whom mortals called the moon.

It was time to remind these pups just who they were fucking with.

Chapter THREE

In the movies, the change is traumatic and terrifying. It's a devastating ordeal that rips the body apart as the beast breaks free of its bonds to unleash its terrible, unquenchable hunger upon the world. Then again, everyone knows the movies are full of shit.

In truth, for those that ran with the moon, the change was as natural as a bird taking to the wing. It had been many centuries since the goddess of the hunt had held her sway, but the turn came as easily as if she had been watching over them from up on high in those days of old.

The beast exploded out of him, tearing through skin and cloth alike in a rush of coarse black fur. His bones twisted and lengthened, muscles swelling with a storm of ageless bestial power. Then the wolf stood tall, its huge lupin head thrown back with the last haunting notes of homage, announcing its return to the heavens and all the inhabitants of *Lupus Latr*.

He didn't care. He wanted them to know. He wanted all of them to know, even *her*.

To the flanks, Bill and Jake straightened up, their bodies tense and cautious. They had the advantage of numbers, but Danny was older and had the blood of the once unbroken line of Alpha running through his veins. Their Alpha's. Only the worst kind of mongrel mutt would ever consider such a foe easy prey.

Danny sensed their agitation, and his wolf gloried in it. Let them fear him for they should all fear him. His time had come, it was time to reclaim his birthright and to take what had been stolen from him and his family. His home. His pack.

With a low groan, he bared his knife-like canines and slowly swept his gaze from one to the other, their eyes locking in challenge.

Who dies first?

They answered together, dropping down onto all fours and exploding into a run charging directly for him. Danny glanced from one to the other. Bill was the closer, but even by werewolf standards, he was huge. A great golden monster, all raw power and muscle. Yet he was not built for speed as he was already starting to lag behind while the smaller Jake was closing the gap.

Two foes. One chance.

Letting his instincts guide him, Danny pivoted to confront the smaller werewolf first, bracing himself to take the hit head-on. It would take all his bestial strength for a werewolf mid-charge could strike with enough force to floor an African bull elephant.

Yet just as the beast was bearing down on him, close enough to smell its rancid breath in the air, it veered away. Danny knew, even before he'd pivoted to glimpse the incoming blur of golden fur, that he'd been humbugged.

How could he have forgotten? Wolves were team hunters, after all, trained from pups to hunt and work together. One would lure the prey out, distract them with a faint, while the other would move into position and then pounce. It was the oldest trick in the book.

And the most predictable.

He twisted away from the oncoming rush of tawny gold fur and then spun to wrap his forepaws around its ribs and midriff. With one hard kick off from the ground, he tackled the other beast and sent them both tumbling down in a furious storm of snapping jaws and disembowelling claws.

As the larger, Bill hit the ground first. Landing with him, Danny didn't waste a moment. He used all his bestial weight to pin the bigger beast on his back and laid into him with a fierce barrage of punches, holding nothing back. He needed to even the odds quickly. Alpha blood or no, Wolves were pack animals. A lone wolf couldn't hope to stand against the pack, even if it was only a duo.

However, Bill was no pushover. He twisted wildly, desperately trying to buck his opponent off while his hind paws racked his thighs, tearing the already tattered remnants of his jeans to bloodied confetti strips. It was all Danny could do not to get thrown. Needing to steady himself, he dodged the snapping Wolfen jaws and grabbed the other werewolf's head just beneath its pointed ears. With a sharp tug, he dragged it up then smashed it back down onto the hard earth, and repeated it again, like a monkey opening a nut, until-

Agony seared up Danny's leg as powerful jaws chomped down on his ankle with bone crushing force, dragged him back and with a single twist, hurled him around into the solid trunk of a tree. He hit the bark with a loud crack, the force of it knocking the wind right out of him, and it was only through sheer willpower and adrenaline that he was able to get back up again.

Bill was back on his feet too. Stood up straight, he appeared to be shaky and wobbling a little on his hind legs, but his eyes had lost none of their fire. He wasn't down and out just yet.

Jake, meanwhile, was only just getting started.

This time his attack was no feint. He came in an explosion of hatred, barrelling into Danny like a bull at the charge and tackling him back into the tree trunk. It drove all the air from his lungs, but his beast was beyond such things and countered by driving his knee up into the other werewolf's balls. Jake expected it though and twisted to take it on the thigh, but the pivot opened up some much-needed space between them. Danny went straight for his opponent's head, using first a right then a left to drive him back before bringing them both together and down in a hammer blow across the beast's shoulder blades.

A human would have been laid out cold by that, but the other werewolf only grunted and quick as a viper, clamped its jaws down on his wrist. Rows of teeth sharper than steak knives sliced through muscle and flesh. In all the Animal Kingdom, there was no bite that could compare to a werewolf. Capable of biting through bone, timber, and even steel like butter, it made the great white shark look like a suckling lamb and even in his beast form, the pain was excruciating.

Danny howled a furious roar and twisted right and left, trying to pull away, the bite searing up his forearm like silver nitrate in his blood. Jake moved with him however, refusing to let go even as they both smashed into the tree, shaking his head and turning the meat of his arm to mangled mince. Then something enormous slammed into them from behind and arms coiled around him, half restraining, half tearing at him with murderous razors, drawing lines of fire across his torso and flanks.

Bill!

He twisted and struggled, trying to escape, to buck one werewolf off or throw the other against the tree, but every time one of them started to give, the other would press him back. So they surged back and forth, locked in a tight knot, until even his beast started to succumb. His limbs felt heavy, like lead weights trapped at his sides, and his head felt suddenly light, his vision swimming in and out of focus.

Then a stray gust of cool air blew across his face, and he smelt it. That scent. The scent that had haunted his dreams. Her scent!

Erza.

She was out there, watching them, watching him fight for his life. Watching him, his family, the last remaining wolf of the unbroken line of alphas in Europe die.

No! Just the idea of it set a new fire raging in his heart, flooding him with bestial rage. He was the son of an alpha, the last of an unbroken line of alphas, not some cow to be led to the slaughter. How dare she! He'd show her.

No, he'd show all of them.

And suddenly Bill's hold seemed to weaken. His arms, thick and corded with muscle beneath the shaggy golden pelt, gave way bit by bit as Danny pushed out with his elbows, opening up a gap. It was only a tiny thing, a slip of space scarcely large enough for a mouse to squeeze through, but it was enough. Enough for him to rip his arm free of the press of Wolfen bodies and smash his elbow back into the bridge of Bill's nose.

The werewolf howled in surprise and agony as the hit snapped his head back and sent him reeling. Seizing his chance, Danny jerked sideways, grabbing Jake by the throat and throwing his other arm back, the arm with his teeth still embedded in it.

A loud crack split the air as the werewolf's head smashed against the tree, hard enough that the bark splintered in a shower of twigs. His eyes rolled back. Jake's mouth opened in a long groan as he slumped to the ground. For a long moment, his lupin form just sat there, then the muscles began to twitch and writhe beneath the skin. Bones clicked back into place. The ears and muzzle shrank away, and the thick pelt fell away to reveal the frail unconscious human body beneath.

He looked just the way Danny remembered. Older sure, but still with the same wavy brown hair, sharp features, and small athletic build. With his head slumped back like that, he looked like he could have been taking a doze.

A quick glance back confirmed that Bill had reverted back to his natural state and was knocked out cold on his back with a very obviously broken nose that now looked more like a squashed pig's snout. The werewolf's regenerative capabilities would probably have him fixed up by the time he was on his feet, but he'd be feeling that for a while.

The thought had him hanging his head, all thoughts of victory tempered by the memories that these had been his friends, once. Damn it all, it wasn't supposed to be like this.

He'd only come here to talk, not-

"Well, you certainly haven't lost your touch, Danny," a voice from the past laughed.

Chapter FOUR

Danny's head snapped up, his eyes narrowing on the figure standing on the edge of the tree line. Tall but with a wiry athletic build. Sandy blonde hair tumbling messily down to his shoulders. A shit-don't-stink grin plastered across his narrow face.

Recognition flared deep inside my wolf. There was only ever one man in *Lupus Latr* with the gall to taunt a fully turned werewolf. Against what could only be considered his better judgment, Danny forced his beast back down into its cage and with it, his rich black pelt and Wolfen features dissolved away to reveal the man beneath.

With the tattered remnants of his shirt and jeans hanging off him, he nodded to the other man and asked "Shane…you up next?"

"What? Me? You mean after watching you take Pinky and Perky there apart like warm bread? You must be joking." He seemed genuinely amused by the notion, and if nothing else, he certainly hadn't come dressed for a fight. Werewolves fought in fur or leather, not Calvin Kline. "Nope, I'm just here to escort you up to the big house. Erza is expecting you." He raised a hand in the direction of *Lacum Hall*. "After you…"

Danny didn't argue. He'd already come this far, what would be the point? He just turned his eyes up to the summit of the hill, to where the ramparts of his childhood home reached up to stab the sky. To where he knew she was watching him and knew the time had come.

With a shrug he started to walk, going beneath an arch of interwoven branches and up along the ancient path of old moss-covered stones. "Erza knew I was coming? How?"

"Wish I knew. She rarely steps out of the house, never leaves the village, but she always seems to know everything that's going on everywhere. I've got no idea how she does it. Social media has nothing on Erza," Shane joked, falling into step beside him. "Anyway, she announced the other day you were coming home, and then this morning she told the three of us to come out here and greet you. Didn't say when of course, just to set up and wait." His eyes dropped down to Danny's side. "Are you going to be alright with that?"

Danny shot him a confused look. Seeing the other man's look of concern, he followed his gaze down to the twin rings of bite marks that circled his wrist. To an observer it would have looked like a savage wound, a latticework of torn and ragged flesh thickly encrusted with dry blood. However, it was a scratch compared to the damage Jake's jaws had dealt him and within the hour, it would be just another set of scars.

He shrugged it off. "Such hospitality."

"Don't give me that, Daniel," Shane snarled, his eyes suddenly blazing the furious gold of the wolf. "You know our ways. You know what happens to wolves that run out on their packs. You've got to prove yourself before we offer up a fatted calf but that doesn't mean we didn't miss you." And just like that, the storm passed, his features softened, and he was throwing a brotherly arm over Danny's shoulder. "Damn, it's good to see you mate. It just hasn't been the same around here without your family running the show. The whole village is excited. You remember Miss Babs, the baker's wife that used to assist at the school? She wanted to set a big welcome home sign over the village hall. Hang balloons up everywhere. She even went on about setting up some of those huge picnic tables in the square and getting everyone to bring something like they used to do at fairs in the Middle Ages. Ya know what I mean?"

Danny couldn't believe his ears. They missed him? Were pleased to hear he was returning. The idea left him feeling strangely relieved, like a weight had suddenly been lifted from his shoulders. He never would have thought the pack would welcome him back so readily after he'd abandoned it to Erza's fate.

Shane let out a long whistle. "Yep, we were all set to have a big welcome home party in the Slaughtered Lamb, for you, but then Erza forbade it. Said no one was to say a word to you until she'd spoken with you, well except for me of course. Though personally, I didn't figure on us sharing many words. Thought she had just sent me out here just to make sure Pinky and Perky over there didn't kill you. Still, it looks like the old wolf's blood is still burning strong." And then his expression was suddenly thoughtful. "Hey, have you heard anything about your brother?"

"Deckland?" The question surprised Danny, and he couldn't quite keep the excitement from his voice. "No, why? What happened?"

It had been years since he'd had word from his big brother.

"No idea, that's why I asked," Shane shrugged, letting the arm fall from Danny's shoulder. "He just up and vanished about the same time you did, after he lost the challenge. A few of us thought he might have sought sanctuary, but none of the other packs have seen a trace of him since. It's as if he just disappeared."

"I see," Danny sighed, his heart sinking. "Last I heard, he'd gone over to Canada, but he doesn't keep in touch. We haven't spoken in years."

Deckland, his big brother, their father's heir. It had always been assumed that he would take over the ruling of the pack when their father passed. It was the role he had been born for. His whole life had been spent training for the day he would assume the mantle of their ancestors. And unlike so many heirs to their father's throne, he was well suited to his birthright. Strong as their father but with their mother's calm manner and rational temperament, he would have been a good heir. Then that dark day came when their father's body was carried back from battle.

At such times, it was tradition for all the pack to gather around the fallen alpha's body and those who wished to succeed him could make their claims. Words were said, oaths were made, claims were voiced. Then the true test would begin.

Deckland had stood up first, sworn to defend the Village and its pack with his claws till his dying breath, and none of the pack had challenged him. None but her, an outsider who had just walked into the village that very morning with nothing but the clothes on her back and a name that no one knew, but tradition said all could challenge for the title of Alpha.

So the challenge had been issued and Deckland, for all his strength and training, had lost.

Erza had ruled *Lupus Latr* as the Alpha from that day, and no one had seen Deckland since he had escorted her to the private ground that had been used to decide such contests since the ancient days.

"Damnit," Shane growled under his breath, before musing to himself. "We could really use him right about now."

That got Danny's attention. "Yeah? Something going on I should know?"

"What? Ah, no, no, no, nothing like that," Shane laughed nervously, before continuing in his best offhand tone. "So, er what about your mum? Mother was hoping she'd be returning with you, and you know what-"

"She's dead," Danny cut him off, the words out before he could stop them.

Shane's eyes widened and he immediately bowed his head. "Oh…I'm, I'm sorry mate."

"It's fine, just one of those things." Danny forced himself to look straight ahead, resisting the burn of tears forming at the corners of his eyes. Yet he couldn't keep the hitch from his voice as the memories flooded his head. "It's been almost two years now. She just never really got over losing dad that way."

"Wolf's bane…" The eternal pinning and longing wail of a wolf who had lost its mate and was cursed to waste away to a piteous end. There was no worse end for a werewolf than the slow death of a broken heart.

Just the mention of the ailment sent a shiver through them both.

Danny nodded, one stray tear rolling down his cheek. "Yes. She fought it as long as she could but…well, you know."

"Yes, yes of course." Shane raised his gaze and looked up through the woodland canopy to the darkened celestial sky. He'd never really known the details of the mating of the last Alpha and his mate, but their stories were legends amongst the pack's elders. "May their spirits find each other in the great sky plains," he said, reciting the prayer of reuniting lovers with more reverence than Danny would have expected.

"Run far and free...until we meet again," Danny finished, before turning to Shane, his expression suddenly hard. "What does Erza want to see me for?"

"You came to talk, didn't you?" Shane shrugged, but his grin was absent still and the nonchalance didn't show in his eyes.

Danny grabbed his arm, stopping Shane in his tracks. "Yes, but that doesn't explain her wanting to see me." His hold was like iron around the other man's wrist, his tone matter of fact. "I'm a son of the last Alpha. With Deckland gone from our lands, I'm the greatest threat to her control of the pack. Other alphas would have me killed on sight. So why does she want to see me?"

Shane wouldn't meet his eyes. "I'm not supposed to-"

"Don't give me that shit. You know something," Danny snapped. "You just said Deckland would be useful right about now. Why? What the fuck is going on? Tell me or I'm gone. I came for answers. I won't be a pawn in a power game."

Torn by indecision, for a moment, Shane looked like he might protest further, then the war of his conflicting loyalties swung, and their eyes met. "Ah…alright, you'll find out soon enough anyway, but you can't tell *her* I told you. Alright?" He was more imploring than insisting.

Danny nodded. "Go on."

"Okay. Things are bad, mate. And not just for us, but everyone. All the packs, and even the rogues in the cities like you," he sighed. "It's Wyverns."

"Wyverns?" The question hung in the air for a moment, then Danny couldn't help a dry laugh. "Yeah, so what. When aren't they a problem? When haven't those sheep shagging thunder lizard shifters been out to devour anyone who didn't shit scales? They're just a fact of life, like fleas and humans."

"This is different," Shane growled, his eyes lacking any hint of humour. "Look, it wasn't just your dad who fell on Hengest's Hill. The old wolf sent a number of Wyvern chiefs to the dark skies that day, and that power vacuum has given rise to a new power across the border. A chieftain named Emyr has been conquering any clan that wouldn't join him. Last year he marched on the Brecon Beacons and old King Edmundwyfgit

Blood Wing bent the knee and surrendered the triple crown of wing and claw to the upstart. Now he rules over all the clans."

"How do you know this?" Danny asked slowly, disbelieving.

Wyverns were not like the other Paranormals. They didn't mix with humans, nor integrate into society. They existed in savage tribes across Wales, in a world that hadn't evolved since the dark ages. Shane was unlikely to have seen their movements on his Twitter feed.

Shane just shrugged again, shaking off Danny's arm. "Erza. She's been trying to warn the packs. Some have listened, mostly the older packs with strong ties to the village, but most send our messengers away with their tails between their legs."

"Well, tell them to try calling first next time." The witticism fell on deaf ears.

"This isn't a joke, Danny. They think it's a trap, a ploy to seize control of their packs. They don't trust her, the lone female Alpha that unseated Alfred Long Claw's eldest pup."

"Well, I can't say I blame them," Danny laughed again, his face twisted with disbelief. "I mean come off it and have a day off, this all sounds like a bad Ronnie's sketch. For fuck sake, if you'd turned up on my doorstep and told me that story, I'd tell you to lay off the strong cheese at night. Wyverns can't work together. Put four tribes of the buggers together at breakfast, half of them will be dead by lunch. Everyone knows that."

"Well, everyone is wrong. They're out there, an army of those winged fire breathing buggers, and if Erza's right, they're coming our way." His eyes were bright with the words, not the fierce bright fury of the wolf, but the fever of a true believer. Whatever lunacy had been going on here, it was obvious Shane believed every word of it. "The fight is coming mate, whether we like it or not, and we'll need all the packs united together. Mark my words, if we don't all stand together to meet them, the age of the wolf will be done." Then he turned on his heel and continued on along the path up the hill.

Danny watched him go.

Wyverns amassing, was it even possible?

Just the thought sent a shiver through him.

The wolf packs had been at war with the Wyverns since they first settled in Wales, long before even the Romans dared to settle on English shores. Raiding parties would cross the border to pillage and burn and occasionally a few of their clan chiefs would band together and attack a pack head on, but an army? A real army of monsters. It was as terrifying as it was ridiculous. There had never been anything of the like. Not one of their Kings could ever have hoped to muster such numbers.

But there had been no lie in Shane's eye. Had he seen it, witnessed it on the move? What could make him believe in the impossible with such certainty?

He double timed it to catch up. "Look, alright, say I believe you, John Snow, what does this all have to do with me? If Erza wants me to fight, she could have just asked on a picture postcard. What's with all the secrecy?"

"Honestly?" Shane's eyes softened. "I don't know mate, she keeps everything close to her chest, but whatever she asks, just, hear her out and give it some thought. This isn't the world we grew up in anymore."

Then, as if by magic, the veil of woodland suddenly parted, and he was the boy Danny remembered once again. "Ah well, here we are. Welcome home.

Chapter FIVE

As vast as it was ancient, the *Lacum Hall* was a bastion of Victorian gothic architecture that had the look of Bella Lugosi's weekend place.

Danny's eyes went wide as he stepped up to the monogrammed gate beneath a pair of huge stone wolves, rearing up and locked in mortal combat to form an arch. It looked much the same as he envisioned it, like a page torn right out of his memories, a physical link between his past and the present. Yet time had played her hand against his ancestral home. With each passing winter, the gardens had become overgrown, creeper ivy had crawled its way up the missionary and there was a thick pelt of dust covering the inside of the windows. It was as if the spirit of the hall had abandoned it with him and his mother, and the building had been withering away day by day ever since. His childhood home was still there, but it seemed diminished, a hollow husk robbed of its former majesty.

"Well, I'm off. See you in the lamb later, when you're done here. First rounds on me." Shane said, hanging back by the treeline.

Danny glanced back at him. "You're not coming in?"

Shane's eyes widened at the suggestion, and he looked up to the upper levels, as if expecting to discover Erza watching them. "You're kidding, right? Erza will have my hide on her wall, and my balls for chew toys if I step in there uninvited." He laughed, but the sound was half-hearted and not enough to convince anyone he was joking. He shook his head. "No. Thanks but no thanks, afraid you're on your own in there. Good luck, and remember, just hear her out before you answer."

"Yeah… sure, catch you later." Danny nodded, lingering there to watch the other man turn back and vanish into the trees back the way they'd come. And for a long moment, he was sorely tempted to follow, to forget this fool's errand and go back, but back where?

Home? Did he even have one really? Since his mother had died, it had been like he was simply going through the motions, never really settling, never marking *his* territory.

University? What was for him there, a life living a lie, pretending to be something he wasn't, and a girl who probably hated him that he couldn't go near for fear of just face fucking her on sight whenever she came too close.

What else was out there for him?

Where else could he be what he was?

What other pack would accept him?

The man in him balked at the idea of returning to the village, but his wolf longed to re-join its pack and carried his feet up the stone steps to the front door. With a deep breath, he raised a hand to knock, but a cool breath of wind whispered across the stone, gathering and scattering the leaves littering the porch as the heavy oak creaked inward. *Well, that's not creepy at all…*

"Erza?" Danny called out, pushing the door open all the way. "Hello?"

Only silence answered his call, so he stepped cautiously inside.

The entrance hall was much the same as he remembered. Huge and cavernous with walls both of unfinished stone and wood panelling with the same ancient oak furniture scattered around it. The same depictions of nature scenes decorating the walls. Even the same Persian style rug running up the length of the grand staircase to the levels above. All that was missing were the countless generations of his family's portraits that had adorned the wall before. Now they were gone, leaving nothing but the dark outlines that marked where each had hung.

Danny had expected this, yet to see it with his own eyes. All those generations of his family, removed and shoved into the attic, like they had never been. Despite himself, Danny's eyes instinctively moved to the nearest shadow. His parents' portrait had hung there. A fresco in vivid colour of the pair of them sitting on a sofa, with his brother standing at their father's side, and he sitting in his mother's arms.

They had had so much fun that morning, and Danny had often paused to stare up at it and remember the day as the years moved on. His mother had kept a copy too, framed and sitting on her side table in a corner of her little council flat, but it was only a pale imitation. Yet the comfort it had brought her had helped her resist the bane's inevitable end far longer than anyone would believe possible.

Now it was all he had left.

"So, low and behold, the Prodigal Son returns…"

$$Chapter\ SIX$$

A woman glared down at him from the top of the staircase. She was a striking beauty with a sharp chin and high cheekbones framed by a wild mane of tumbling raven hair that fell almost to her narrow waist. Garbed in a long dress of crimson that hugged her curves and enhanced the contrast of her ivory skin and ink black hair, she was just as tall and as fierce and beautiful as Danny remembered.

"Erza…" he breathed out. Danny then dropped down to one knee, head bowed. "Alpha of the Lupus Latr pack, I humbly beg your protection as I wander your lands. I swear by the celestial maiden that I shall do your pack no harm, nor seek to undermine your rule, lest my wolf be tamed, and the pelt ripped from me to adorn your hall."

It was the traditional oath a wandering wolf would swear to the resident pack Alpha when travelling through their lands, to show they meant no mischief.

And with a coy, almost mocking smile pulling at the corner of her mouth, Erza recited back, "And I grant you leave to run through my woods, hunt my prey, eat from my table and lay by my fire. Rise with your tail high, in the protection and friendship of Lupus Latr."

With each vow, she descended a step so that by the time she was done, and he could rise, they were almost eye to eye. Hers gave him a quick once over, taking his measure. Her smile twisted like barbed wire. "Though from the look of you, it might be too late. My guard dogs weren't too rough with you, I hope?"

Her question had Danny's eyes dropping down to take stock of his appearance. His shirt was a ruin of torn and goresplashed ribbons, his jeans split at the seams, and the remnants of his boots were reduced to aged sandals. "Maybe a little..." he mused to himself, before gold flecked chocolate clashed against icy blue as his gaze locked with Erza's for the first time. "But, not nearly as rough as I was on them."

She arched a perfectly curved eyebrow, then threw her head back in a throaty chuckle that rolled over Danny like silk. "Well, it's good to know that humans haven't softened you up too much." As she spoke, she descended down the last steps of the stairs and swept past him, passing just close enough for him to catch hints of her scent fragrant with pine and freshly cut grass, before throwing open the door of what had been his father's study. "I hope you weren't expecting a fatted calf. I can spare a robe for your shoulders, and shoes for your feet, but first, why don't you tell me what the hell you're doing here."

"Shane said you wanted to see me. He said there was something you wanted to talk to me about," Danny answered, following her through to the study.

It was like stepping through a door in time, back into his childhood when he would play on the floor in this room and play knights and wolves with his toys.

In his father's day, the study had been a reflection of his personality. A masculine space, all dark wood furniture and leather sofas. Tall bookcases had lined the walls, stuffed with row upon row of books, ancient, dusty tomes and frayed dog-eared paperbacks. There had been tables strewn with maps, display cases exhibiting every kind of weapon known to man or beast, a wealth of strange and colourful artefacts Danny could have never begun to comprehend. At the back of the room had been the desk, a great ancient piece of dark oak with decorative etchings of running wolves carved all around the top. His father's chair had sat behind it, an imposing leather-padded highchair with the back carved into the bust of a great snarling wolf's head and positioned just beneath the tall windows that looked across the village. His father's huge desktop computer was gone though and, in its place, sat a little compact laptop.

"And I do," Erza said, crossing the space to the drink's cabinet in the far corner. "But that's not what I asked. That's why you're here now. I want to know why you have come back, after all these years, to my pack. And spare me the bullshit story about getting homesick. We both know better."

"I wouldn't dream of it," he lied, just managing to slam his mouth shut on those very words. She was right of course. It would have been a lame line at best, at worst pathetically transparent. Once an exile, the wolf knew better than to return to its old pack if it valued its life. However, reluctant to meekly give away the one ace up his sleeve, he deflected the question. "Shane said you knew I was coming. Didn't your crystal ball tell you why?"

"Perhaps…" she purred, selecting a ruby decanter and pouring out two fingers into two glasses. Then, with a glass in each hand, she met him in the middle of the study.

With a smile that was every bit as feral as the she-wolf she was, she offered him the drink in her left hand. Her eyes were bright and dangerous with a look that made Danny feel like she was looking straight through him, daring him to refuse. "Or perhaps I just want to hear you say it."

He hesitated. Was it all a bluff? Or did she know? Know why he'd come home. Know how desperate he'd grown.

No, he couldn't take the chance. If she was telling the truth and she caught him in a lie, things could go south real quick. It wasn't worth the risk.

So he took the drink. It was a foolish thing to do. Other Alphas might have poisoned it. After all, maybe he had never arrived. Maybe he had died in the struggle or had a heart attack on the walk up the hill or got struck by a bolt of lightning. Who was to know? Only Shane knew he was here after all, and he would be easy to silence if it came to that. No one would challenge Erza over the fate of a rogue. But he had his doubts. If she wanted to kill him, poison wouldn't be quite her style.

Erza was the first female Alpha in recorded history.

The other packs looked down on her for that.

If she was going to kill him, she wouldn't do it in the dark.

Poisoned chalices and knives in the night wouldn't secure her rule.

She'd want every werewolf in England to hear of it and know she did it.

That she could do it.

She would do it.

She would need a show.

So he bit the proverbial silver bullet and drank it all in a single gulp. It was hot and smoky and burned like fire all the way down. "I need your help."

Her eyes flashed with something, a wild raw emotion that was both victory and fury all at once.

"Obviously, but what are-" The words caught in her throat as she took a step closer, then stopped dead in her tracks as she caught his scent, and the musky flavour beneath. That scent! Her nostrils flared, tasting the air and her heart suddenly raced as each breath sent waves of sensation coursing through her, igniting her core, making her breasts heavy and nipples peak beneath the soft weave of her dress. "How long?"

He stiffened. He'd never been this close to her before, and the sheer awareness of their proximity had him unsure of where to look. His cheeks started to burn under her inscrutable glare. As beautiful as she was treacherous, holding her stare for too long could be more dangerous than staring at her tits.

Of course, that didn't make the latter any less dangerous.

"Sorry? How long…What?"

"How long?" Erza repeated, breathless, suddenly feeling very hot as the fire started to smoulder in her core, growing stronger with every breath she took. Part of her wanted to run, jump away and get some much-needed distance between her and him. But that voice was weakening, growing distant and quiet beneath a fog, and instead another voice, as sweet and seductive as caramel whispered it was already too late.

She knew she needed to fight it, to resist, but at the same time, she couldn't help appreciating the sight of the young wolf before her. The way the torn and tattered remnants of his clothes hinted at a tight strong body. Not bulky, but corded and well defined with natural muscle, just the way she liked them. His face was still a little boyish, but the lines of the man he was were clear to see against his thick black hair that was just that bit too long, and his storm blue-grey eyes were as sharp as glass.

When she'd taken over the pack, she'd never given Danny much thought. He'd been just a snot-nosed boy of little consequence. His big brother had been her only concern then, the only thing standing in her way.

However, Dereck Royce was long gone now though, and this brat had grown into a hot young man, still wet with the blood and sweat of battle. A stud who'd started his first cycle without his pack to guide him, and an ally she desperately needed in the war to come.

The solution was obvious.

"Fine, sit!"

Chapter SEVEN

The order hit Danny like a crash of icy water to the face. "Pardon?"

It came as such a surprise. He was sure he had misheard.

"I said, sit fucking down!" Quick as a snake, she snatched the empty glass from his hand, placed both on the nearest table, then pushed him back down onto the nearest sofa.

"H-hey wha- wait a minute! Erza, what are you do-" Danny trailed off, his eyes going as wide as saucers as she pushed down the shoulders of the sleeves of her dress and let it slither down her body to pool around her feet.

Unashamedly naked, Erza just glared down at him. "What does it look like I'm doing boy? Just shut up and strip."

She wasn't in any mood for games.

Not now.

Not after what he'd done to her.

"What? You can't be-" His cheeks burned, and Danny looked away.

"Get out of your fucking clothes!" she snarled, putting her hands on her hips and kicking the garment on the floor away. "You're in heat."

"What!" In his surprise, his eyes snapped back up to her, but got lost partway and instead locked onto the rosy tips of her full teardrop-formed breasts. Though she was of relatively small stature, the werewolf Alpha was nonetheless full figured and beautiful, with long legs, a tight flat belly and a bountiful bosom that would more than fill each of his hands.

"What's the matter, cat got your tongue?" Erza growled, her eyes darkening with wild lust, raking over the sight of him stretched out before her until they landed on the tell-tale bulge forming in his trousers. The discovery sent a fresh rush of heat through her core. "You better enjoy the view while you can, boy. This is a one-time thing. Don't think I'm about to become your bitch."

Swallowing what little moisture was left in his mouth, Danny forced his eyes up to meet hers. "But I can't be, how's that possi- hey, stop!" He shouted in a sudden rush as she grabbed fistfuls of his trousers, half tugging, and half trying to rip them apart.

"You want my help? This is the only way," she snapped, even as he grabbed at her hands to force them away. Her heart pounded. The wet heat in her centre had begun to throb insistently. Damnit, now just being close to him was turning her on. "Damnit, do I have to do everything myself...Errr...fine!" Her eyes flashed lupin gold, and the space between them filled with the sound of tearing cloth.

Danny might have been a werewolf, the son of a long unbroken line of Alphas, but his trousers were merely humble cloth. No match for the raw power of a werewolf. With a twist of her wrist, the already shredded denim tore at their very fibres and exploded in a rain of confetti.

"Mmm...Well, aren't you just full of surprises," Erza purred, drinking in the sight of his arousal standing rampant, huge by any standard and easily as thick as her wrist. She licked her lips. "This is going to be fun."

Wild eyed, Danny could barely speak through the lump in his throat. "No, stop, you can't be serious- oh!" His words dissolved in a long moan as lush heat enveloped him.

Curling her fingers around his thick base, delighted in the knowledge that they couldn't meet in the middle, Erza greedily mouthed the head, fighting back a low moan as his thick musky flavour flooded her senses.

Though not the most obliging of women, Erza was no blushing virginal bride. Long before she had taken the mantle of Lupus Latr's Alpha, she could pride herself on being a very proficient lover- and cock sucker.

It was the only reason she had survived this long.

Her mother had been a slave of a Wyvern chieftain, a prize snatched from her pack by a raiding party that had gone back over the border before she could be rescued. If they had known she was pregnant, they would have probably just slain her there in the clearing where they had found her, but she had been a good slave, so the chieftain had allowed her to bear the child.

Born into servitude, Erza had quickly learned to use any and every weapon at her disposal. She had no disillusions. Sex was a weapon, and when she started to mature, her sex appeal was as deadly a weapon as her wolf, and if used correctly, could be much more *effective*.

For all his arrogance, the chieftain was no fool. He had always known there was a danger in keeping a werewolf as his pet and Erza knew if she grew too powerful, the bastard wouldn't hesitate to remove her from his service. So it had been up to her to find a way of making him overlook her ever increasing power. Fortunately for her, the old pervert also had a penchant for beautiful women, and when she'd offered herself to him, he'd been quick to accept.

It must have been such a thrill for the beast, to have her writhing and moaning beneath him, knowing she'd offered herself to him, and believing she had no idea how he'd killed her mother the year before.

Even now the memories of what she'd done for him, let him do to her, made her skin crawl. Yet it had been her who'd had the last laugh, because while she was his obedient little sex slave, he had kept her at his side, a prize for his clan to ogle and envy, and she had listened and learned. Learned the ways of her enemy, how they thought, their dark arts and powers. And when the time was right, she'd taken her revenge.

In the dawn, all the clan had found was his body tied to his bed, with her slave collar embedded in his throat and his disembodied cock in his mouth.

She'd never told anyone about her past.

It was her secret shame and her greatest strength.

And now it was time to show this young pup his place.

Just like she'd taught his brother, that day she had first arrived in the village.

"Erza, wait…stop…we really shouldn't… Don't dooh!" For all his awesome power, Danny had never felt so helpless. The sight of her lush lips flowing down his length, her cheeks hollowing as she sucked greedily, taking him in all the way to the gate of her throat in one slow plunge while those dark, predatory eyes stared up at him. Watching him. Daring him to interfere. It was too much.

Torn between sinful pleasure and exquisite agony, the urge to push her off or fist her hair and force her down, to take him to the root- he didn't know what to do. He couldn't stand it, nor could he look away.

So he just watched, his knuckles turning white as he fisted the sofa's plush leather against the pull of lush warmth.

"Mmm…does that feel good, boy, does your big cock like my wet little mouth?" Erza purred, pulling back to flutter her tongue over his tip, delighting in his shuddering gasp and the salty, musky goodness that coated his crown. By the moon, she loved having so much power over him, seeing the conflict in his eyes, of having him helpless beneath her, and knowing he could turn at any moment. She'd forgotten how much she enjoyed the feeling of wielding power over a warrior so much stronger than her. It was such an exquisite feeling, such a turn on, a delicious cocktail of danger and power.

She wanted more and dropped down to lavish attention on his sack.

"Fuck, Erza…" Danny groaned, his head rolling, the feeling almost too good for him to resist.

Her tongue drew a figure of eight over and around each ball, before she sucked one then the other into her mouth, rolling them with her tongue and relishing the rich flavour. Erza dragged her tongue back up the underside of his length, to greedily mouth his wide crest.

"Don't think I'm doing this to please you. This is just sex. You're giving off so many pheromones, you're triggering my heat cycle. So I'm going to take the edge off by fucking your brains out."

And with that, she was all business.

She went all out. Taking him back into her mouth with their eyes still locked, going fast and sloppy, bobbing her head up and down with the same furious intensity she would apply to any battle. He was so thick and deliciously hard, but also soft and warm, like steel wrapped in warm silk.

Yet it wasn't enough. Erza wanted more. Wanted to claim him. To suck him dry and mark him as hers. To push him to the very edge, to make him gasp and writhe and submit.

"Erza…please…" Danny groaned, gritting his teeth against the feeling of her mouth gliding along his arousal, of lush heat sucking him in with long, rhythmic pulls. His eyes pleaded with her to stop but his wolf begged her to continue as his body and mind warred within him.

God, no, fuck, she was going too fast, he couldn't…couldn't think…couldn't… couldn't… "Oh fuck…your mouth's so…f-fuck!"

"Yeah, that's it, you like it don't you…" Sensing the change in him, the werewolf Alpha smirked inwardly and pulled back, only to cup her breasts. "Mmm such a big, tasty cock." Pushing her cleavage together around his meat, she slowly started moving up and down.

Danny couldn't stand much more. The warmth and softness of her full tits surrounding him, the silky feeling of skin rubbing against slick skin, just watching his cock sliding up through the valley of her breasts was such a wild fucking turn on.

"God…Feels so good…oh fuck…don't…don't stop you fucking bitch…" he groaned as, with his head starting to spin, his hips instinctively lunged, fucking her tits with wild abandon.

"Oh, I won't stop until you've blown your load all over your Alpha's tits," Erza promised, relishing the feel of him between her breasts, huge and hard and scorching hot. So hot, the heat of his desire was brushing over her lips, thick with the musk of his arousal, making her lips tingle and clit throb. "Does it feel good squeezed between my tits? Come on, fuck them, boy, fuck your Alpha's tits, paint me in all your juicy cum. I want to taste, lick you all up, suck your balls dry then ride you till you can't remember your little human bitch's name!"

Though his need to cum was growing fiercer by the second, her gloat cut him like ice. "Wait, how do you know about Jackie?"

"Why else would you be so backed up?" she teased, dipping her head down to flutter her tongue across his tip. "When werewolves find a potentially acceptable mate, they go into a heat cycle. A real werewolf would have claimed her on site, fucked her for everyone to see. One ride on this big dick and the little bitch would probably beg for you to mark her."

"N-no, don't talk about her like that!"

Feeling his bestial energy spike, as well as the way his cock seemed to swell and thicken and pulse against her skin,

Erza pressed her advantage. "Aww, what's the matter boy, are you in love with her? Has the little human wench already made you her bitch? Well, don't worry, by the time I'm done with you, you'll have forgotten all about her."

Her head dipped and she took his crown into her mouth, her cheeks hollowing as she sucked long and hard.

It was all too much. The heat of her mouth. The silky softness of her breasts squeezing around him. The sight of her sucking him while she worked him between her cleavage, and all the while continuing to watch him, her predatory gaze fixed and unblinking, seeming to see through him. It was too much.

"No!" Danny half groaned, half choked, squeezing his eyes shut against the sudden rush as his release overcame him. Yet for all his protests, his wolf would not be denied and as he unleashed rope after rope of thick cream into her mouth, his fingers buried themselves in her raven tresses, holding her fast and firm, forcing her to take every drop.

However, Erza only relished his sudden forcefulness, and sucked greedily, milking him for every drop he had to give. Even after his release began to ebb and his fingers slipped from her hair, she kept up her assault, refusing to let him go soft on her.

When black spots started dancing before his eyes, Danny could only groan. "N-no…Erza…stop…no…no more…"

"Now, don't be like that," she pouted, pulling back to fix him with a look that would have almost been a reproach if she had not been so coyly licking her lips. "You should be honoured." Then she winked, and the look became pure predatory hunger as she rose up to straddle his waist. "I hope you're ready, because I'm about to give you the greatest fuck of your life!"

And before he could object, strong dextrous fingers coiled around his revived length, angling it upward as she sunk down. Then it was too late.

"Erza! Sto-!" Danny gasped, all objections leaving him in a long moan at the feeling of sliding into her lush heat, her warm silky walls wrapping around and sucking him in. "Mmm…too late for that…you're all mine now…" she purred, lowering herself down, fighting back a moan herself at the sensation of being filled inch by inch.

Fuck…he's huge.

It had been so long. She'd forgotten what it felt like to be completely full, stretched, stuffed with thick hard cock. How had she gone without it for so long? Why had she been denying herself this feeling, this sense of completion. It was intoxicating. She wanted, no, she needed more and circled her hips.

And Danny was powerless to stop her.

"Erza…. Wait…I…I…." he groaned through gritted teeth, gripping and twisting the leather against the delicious friction from her inner walls squeezing and sliding along his cock. Yet his eyes were fixed on where they were joined, captivated by the view of her folds sliding along his cock, rising and falling, leaving him wet and slick with her desire. It was the most erotic thing he'd ever seen.

"Yeah, that's it, boy, watch me take in your big cock," she husked, bending down to slowly lick up a fat bead of perspiration that was rolling down his neck. Pressing in close so he could feel her breasts press against his skin, she followed the salty trail with the point of her tongue up to his earlobe and whispered "You like that baby? Having your princess's pussy wrapped around your big dick?"

Beyond words, Danny shook his head, yet couldn't silence the little gasp that left him as she reared back. Not fooled, Erza grinned toothily down at him and wiggled her hips while dragging a hand down his chiselled torso, scraping the points of her nails over his flat nipple. "Yeah, you like it don't you, come on I know you do, let me hear you say it!"

The delicious cocktail of pleasure and pain was too much for Danny.

"Yes," he hissed, seizing her hips and dragging her back down, burying himself to the balls in her lush heat.

Erza gasped, throwing her head back, her eyes wide and back bowing with the sudden delicious shock of the deeper penetration, of feeling muscles getting stretched for the first time. Yet it only fuelled the blazing desire pulsing through her. "Oh fuck, fuck, that's it, this big fucking cock is all mine, oh God! So big and thick, mmm-yes, fuck me, fuck me!"

Bracing her hands on his taut abdominals, she rode him hard and fast, rolling her hips to push up and up until he was almost leaving her, then dropping back down.

Danny was right there with her, powerless against the feeling of her heat squeezing and sucking his cock, enslaved by his own raging lust. He couldn't help himself. Everything about this was wrong, but he just couldn't fight it anymore. His hips rocked against her, meeting her downward plunge with hard upward thrusts as his hands clawed at her luscious derriere. Needing to fill her lush cavern, to claim her and mark her as his and leave her in no doubt who she belonged to.

"Oh…fuck…oh my God, yes, so deep, mmm…yes…take that pussy, stuff it full with your big dick…" she panted, her words turning feverish as the pleasure spread out from the pulsing knot at her centre. It wouldn't be long now. God, it got her so hot, knowing she could do this to him, knowing she could make him lose control and take him to the very edge. Knowing she'd broken him. "Oh fuck…oh my fucking God, feels so good, so fucking deep, oh yes, oh fuck, oh my God, oh my God, so close, make me cum, make your Alpha cum!"

Drawn by her sounds of pleasure, his eyes moved up her body, taking her in, in all her majesty. Her skin sleek and glistening with a mist of perspiration as she rode him, full breasts bouncing, her mane of dark hair floating around her fierce, pleasure flushed face. She was beautiful. A goddess.

And for the moment, she was his.

It was too much.

"Er…Erza…wait…sto-oh fuck…somethings…I'm gonna cum!"

His declaration hit her like a lightning strike. "What! No, not yet! Don't cum inside me!" No, he couldn't cum, not inside her, not now. She was in heat. Her cycle had been triggered. The probability of the seed taking root now was as good as certain.

Yet it just felt so good, she couldn't stop.

"Can't stop!" He was too far gone, sucked in by the feel of her lush heat fluttering around swelling desire. His release ripped through him, overtook him, consumed him. And then there was only the beast.

"No! Oh God, no, stop, stop…I'll get- oh fuck, oh fuck, oh fuck!" Erza groaned, but it was already too late, he was so hot and hard inside her. Her hips wouldn't stop moving. Her pussy wouldn't stop clenching. The pleasure spiralling out from her centre, tingling along her nerves, and out to her nipples, fingers and toes, making her bear down on him, milking him to the brink. With a long howl, he crushed her to him, his fingers inescapable and biting into her glutes as scorching heat flooded her, pushing her over the edge into sensory oblivion.

Except Danny wasn't satisfied.

Taken by the current of desire that had overwhelmed them both, he twisted out from under her, throwing her down onto the sofa, then seizing her hips, flipped her onto her front. Still riding the waves of her orgasm, Erza was only half aware of this, until the sudden delicious burn of his broad crest sliding through her folds, going all the way to the root, had her head rolling in a long voiceless moan.

She wouldn't have thought it possible, but he felt even bigger from this angle. No, not bigger. Just fucking huge. However, before her pleasure frazzled brain could fully begin to comprehend the feeling, he was moving. Easing back then driving hard and fast with deep stabbing thrusts. Those big, powerful hands dragged her back against him, grinding her ass into the saddle of his hips, making her feel every inch of him until she felt ready to burst. Regardless, her greedy sex took everything he had to give, desperate for the next.

"Errr...fuck...so tight...so...tight..." he growled out, breathless, mindless. More beast than man.

"Oh God...oh fuck...so good...so deep...yes, pound that fucking pussy..." Erza could only claw at the leather, desperate for any purchase to push back against him, to match him, take back control, but it was useless. He was dominating her totally, driving into her with such wild abandon, the sofa rocked with him, vibrating, shaking with his violent rhythm. If they kept this up, the damn thing would probably tip over.

"Yeah, this what you want, Erza?" Danny growled, his eyes dark and fierce with primitive lust as all his instincts billowed to the surface. The urge to fuck, to dominate, to conquer this arrogant female, to claim her as his. And he forgot about his mother and brother, he forgot about his father's pack, he forgot about Jackie. For a few brief moments, he forgot about the world, and gave himself over to his wolf. He became the werewolf he was born to be.

"Yes!" she gasped, pushing back against him as much as she could, silently pleading for more. Unable to bear the shame of her words, her surrender, but refusing to let him stop. She was too far gone, too turned on. Damn it all, this couldn't be happening. It shouldn't be happening. She was Erza, Alpha of the Lupus Latr pack. No rogue puppy should have been able to top her. It was wrong, all so wrong, but then why did it feel so good?

"Fuck your little cunt's so wet and greedy, Erza," he grunted, driving his cock into her hard and deep, so deep. "You like it rough, don't you? To get fucked deep and hard? To take my cock like the dirty bitch you are?" No, what was happening to her?

It was just too much. The fullness, the delicious tease of friction over every nerve ending in places she'd never known existed. Her clit throbbed, aching for attention as his body tightened with every word out of his mouth.

And the way he said it, in that low, gravelly, bestial tone. It was like sex given voice.

"Yes, yes you little bastard, give it to me!" The words left her in a rush that she couldn't control, a fit of passion rising up with the sounds of their bodies as they met, slapping, crashing together, faster and faster. The sound of her submission only spurred him on to stir up her pussy to a blazing white-hot tempest. "I love that dick so much, fuck me harder, shove it in me, stuff it in my pussy…"

"No! Whose cunt is it, Erza?" He snapped, one hand burying itself in her hair, fisting and twisting, dragging her up onto all fours, and then back against him. So she could feel the heat of his skin on her back. Feel his heart pounding in his chest as his hips started to circle, driving her wild.

"Yours! Oh, fuck that's your pussy! It's yours…please…don't stop, don't stop!" Sounds she'd never known she could make escaped her every time he was fully sheathed inside her. Unable to move, unable to escape, she bore down on him, her every sense zeroing in on the feeling of him thickening within her, throbbing. "Yes! Oh fuck, oh fuck, it's yours! I'll be such a good little fuck toy for you, fuck me whenever you want, yes, stir up that little cunt, it's yours… make me cum again, make me cum all over your big dick!"

"That's right. You tried to dominate me, use me like some fucking toy, but you're my bitch now. This pussy is mine!" He growled through the feeling of her insides as they wrapped around him, squeezing him, sucking him further in. Danny loved the sounds that she made, her throaty guttural moans and high squeaks, the way she called his name as he bottomed out inside her. The sense of primitive conquest was delicious.

To know, he'd done this to her.

He'd done the impossible.

He'd made her feel this way.

He'd torn through her walls, stripped away her control, broken the icy armour she'd encased herself in for so long to reveal the sexual kitten within.

It was enough to push him over the edge.

And with black spots suddenly dancing before his eyes, he crushed her to him, forcing her to take him balls deep as he came.

"Oh fuck! Oh fuck! I can feel your…oh fuck!" Erza gasped out, the throbbing knot in her centre spiralled out of control, igniting in an explosion of white fire that radiated through her, around her, at the feeling of heat flooding her womb.

This was it, fuck, he'd cum inside her twice, she was pregnant for sure. She knew there would come a time when she would regret this moment, that she would curse her own stupidity for getting so carried away, but that was later. For now, there was nothing she wanted more. "Yes, that's it, give me all your cum, fill me up, breed me, breed- oh fuck, I'm cumming, I'm cumming! I- "

With a savage twist, he dragged her head round and his mouth descended on hers, silencing her cries with a hungry kiss. It was their first kiss and the intimacy of it shredded her, tore at her, shattered her into a thousand tiny pieces of starlight right there in his arms. Yet she craved more, needed more.

Their bodies tumbled together to the sofa. Drunk on the taste of her, Danny kissed Erza until her body stopped trembling. However, it was only when he felt her going limp in his arms did he finally pull back.

Embarrassed, he looked away, not sure what to say. "Er…sorry."

"*Idiot*" she snapped, panting, the aftershocks of the strongest orgasm of her life doing nothing to lessen her outrage as she twisted out of his arms and to her feet, just managing to catch herself before her knees gave way. At some point, the solid oak legs of the sofa had given way, but she neither cared nor really noticed as the sensation of him leaving her left her feeling cold and hollow. "Who said you could fucking kiss me?"

"Well, um…It just seemed like the thing to do…" Danny mumbled, feeling suddenly very warm as he resisted the urge to watch her. "Sorry. Didn't like it huh?"

"You apologise too much," she snarled, not daring to look at him as she pulled her dress back on, just in case he saw her blush. Oh, she'd liked it alright, but she'd be damned if she let him know it.

Well, this certainly hadn't gone according to plan.

She'd only wanted to talk to him, to convince him into giving her rule of the pack his patronage, something that might help her when dealing with the other pack, but this…

She touched a hand to her belly, where the warmth of his release still burned inside her, an inescapable reminder of what they'd just done, and the consequences.

This was so much better.

"Tell me Danny, did Shane tell you why I wanted to speak with you?"

"Sort of," he nodded, suddenly fascinated by the pattern of the tiled floor. "I don't believe a word of it, but he told me you thought Wyverns were amassing to invade England."

"That's right, but this isn't about what you believe. You'll see the truth with your own eyes soon enough. No, this is about just getting the word out." Turning on her heel, she sat down beside him on the sofa. "I need your help, Danny. I've tried to warn the other packs, but they won't speak with me. I'm a woman of no true birth. But they would listen to you."

She said it with such sincerity that Danny was almost tempted to believe her.

"So you want me to be your messenger boy?" He let out a dry laugh. "That'll never work. I am a rogue now, remember. A mutt. They're as likely to kill me as they are to consider a treaty with me."

"No Danny, I don't want you to be my messenger." She put a hand on his knee. "I want you to rejoin the pack, as it's Alpha male."

Danny's head snapped up, his eyes wide and disbelieving. "You can't be serious."

"I've never been more serious. Marry me, bind my name to yours, give my reign the legitimacy of your family name."

He brushed her hand from his knee and stood. "You're mad. I'm out of here."

"And where will you go? Back to your human bitch? You think your desires are stated?" She followed him to her feet, but barely rose as high as his shoulders as they stood side by side. "This was only the beginning. They're only going to grow stronger. You need to learn to control yourself. Do this for me though, and I'll teach you how to control your urges," she insisted. "You need me, and I need you, it's a fair bargain."

Her words followed him as he stormed naked out the study, and out of his childhood home, hounding him long into the night after the heavy door had slammed shut.

Chapter EIGHT

"That fucking bitch!" Danny growled, running. Running as if his life depended on it.

The change overtook him as he passed through the wolf gate. His own beast ripped through him to explode through the brush, not noticing as thorns and skeletal twigfingers snatched at his pelt and the flesh beneath. He no longer cared what lay ahead or where he was going. He didn't look back.

He just needed to get away from her, from his past, from this place and just run, and run and-

Fuck it all, how could he have been so stupid?

How could he have ever thought coming back would solve anything?

They were all mad. Mad and crazy and out of their fucking minds.

So fuck them. Fuck Erza. Fuck Shane. Fuck Bill and Jake and the damn fucking lot of them. Fuck them all!

So he ran, and kept running, until he found himself standing once more at the gates of the hall, with the great wolves looming over him. Danny bared his fangs, but neither sentinel accepted the challenge.

He wanted to go, to run far away, but he couldn't.

This was his home.

And they needed him.

He remembered Shane's words and the desperate pleading look in his eyes when he asked him to just listen to Erza. Well, he'd listened. Danny wanted so badly to deny her, but he couldn't deny his friend.

Now he had an answer.

He found her back in the study. She'd redressed and was sitting at his father's desk. Her laptop was open atop it, next to the noticeably half empty decanter.

"What are your terms?" In his lupin form, his voice was a low gravely baritone, more of a growl than words, and for several long moments, she almost appeared to have not heard him. Then, slowly she looked up from the screen.

Undaunted by the sight of his wolf standing in the doorway, she just fixed him with a cool, unreadable glare. "Our marriage? Exactly as I said. You'll re-join the pack, marrying me to assume the role of an alpha male. It'll become a show of unity. I will then be able to talk with the other packs and warn them of the enemy to the west. In return, I'll teach you to control your wolf."

"And your war?" he barked, his nostrils flaring. The room was still rank with the musky aroma of sex. Just the scent of it was enough to bring back visions of her spread out beneath him, her tight pussy milking his cock. She'd been a bitch in heat moaning for more, and the mere memory of it was enough to have his shaft stirring for another round.

"My war?" Pushing back away from the desk, she got up and walked around the desk. "The war is upon us, Daniel, whether you believe it or not. If, when the time comes, you don't want to fight, feel free to run and hide back in London." Danny's eyes narrowed on her. Her taunt rankled him, made his cock throb with a fresh desire to show her what her place should have been. He resisted the urge to bite and instead forced his wolf back into the box. His lupin form dissolved away to reveal the man beneath who stood unashamedly naked before her. "And what about Jackie?"

"Jackie?" She arched a neat and perfectly curled eyebrow. But then her gaze dropped down to where his cock stood rampant between his legs, tall and thick and ready to make her submit once more, and she slowly licked her lips. "Oh, you're little, human bitch. What about her? I'm talking about a political marriage, Danny, nothing more. Monogamy doesn't enter into this. If you want to take her as a beta-mate, that's fine, but make no mistake. Our son will inherit your father's pack. Understand?" She thrust a hand out to him.

He just glared at it for a moment, regarding it like a coiled viper, ready to lash out at any moment. Then, slowly, he reached out and took it. They shook hands, binding the agreement with something far more powerful than ink or blood.

The word and honour of their wolves.

"Welcome home, Danny," Erza smiled, her other hand reaching out to wrap around the base of his cock and stroke from root to head. "Or should that be, *Alpha.*"

Her *Dark* Savour

Chapter *One*

Lucian

It was time.

The last light of dusk was slipping into inky black and high overhead, through the canopy of clouds and pollution, the heavens have come alive with all the magnificence of the celestial sphere. Thousands of sights no human eye could ever see.

The hour of the wolf, the time of the vampire, had come. The time to hunt, to feed...

I inhaled the backstreet in a breath and a shiver slithered down my spine at the heavy perfume of things that didn't bear contemplating. Needless to say, it was rank. Human cities often carried a certain pungency about them, so much waste and body odour, pressed together in such tight quarters, left its mark. They had gotten used to the stink and given enough time, even a vampire could adjust. But that place...

Its particular ripeness was absolutely foul.

I pressed on regardless. Lured by that single overpowering aroma that clung to this place. Beneath the stink of shit. Blood. It leads me like a carrot dangling in front of a donkey, teasing my fangs, my mouth watering.

Sooner or later, the thirst always won. And I'd left it too long.

The way was dark but up above and all around, the city burned bright. False light. Humanity's instinctive terror of the dark and all that lurked within, cloaked by darkness, had driven them to harness the power of the sun and turn night into day. Edison's great folly. The old man had sought to create a warm light for all mankind, warmth and safety for every home. Instead, his invention had made them arrogant. Naive.

Humanity had grown careless, wrapped in their protective cocoon. So they'd forgotten the perils of the night, the hunters in the shadows and all the things that fed on them when the sun went down.

And had allowed darkness to creep back into their world.

I paused mid-stride. The trail swung off the beaten path and down the mouth of an alley a few meters ahead and I felt the instinctive thrill. I was getting close.

Men. Four of them. All in leather and denim. Huddled so close together that to any passers-by, they looked just like any other bunch of dudes out smoking, drinking, and whiling away a night on the town. But the smell was on them. Blood and fear. It was old, maybe weeks dry, but they were rank with it. And their eyes were all fixed on the mouth of the alley, waiting.

They'd do. A small smirk tugged irresistibly at the corner of my mouth. It would be so easy.

Though they gave no outward sign of noticing me, their hearts quickened as I walked into the open, the palpitations pulsing through their clothes. Then they all turned and the biggest of the group, a brute of a man with a face like a bulldog and a spider web tattoo etched across his shaved pate, stepped forward. "Hey man!"

Spinning around, I did my best to look surprised as he pushed himself forward and walked towards me. The others fell into step, spreading to his left and right. "H-hi, can I help you?" I said, my voice shaky.

"Yeah," *Spider Web's* stride quickened, moving in for the kill. "Gotta light?" His hand was in his jean's pocket. No doubt a ploy to make me think he was reaching for his cigarettes. Idiot. He had something there. Its outline was clearly defined against the denim, but it was too long and thin to be anything like a carton of smokes. A flick knife probably. Knife crimes had been on the rise over the last couple of years. Easier to conceal than a firearm, with a considerably lower criminal sentence for carrying one if caught.

They were out of the alley and encircling me, closing in. I pivoted right then left, making a show of trying to watch them all at once, of being afraid to have my back to even one of them. "E-excuse me?"

Just a few steps closer.

"Hey, he asked you a question," the one to my right asked, a lanky black, all smiles and teeth and-

My eyes narrowed on him. Something was wrong. He smelled wrong, like meat just starting to rot. Corruption. Disease.

I shifted my focus back to Spider Web. Dogs followed the alpha, the biggest and strongest of their pack. Bullies and cowards followed the same logic. He would give them orders. And the corruption was heaviest in him. And that could only mean one thing.

My hunger promptly dried up. I'm not the fussiest vampire, but I do have some standards. Feeding off of scum was all well and good, however, killers and rapists riddled with venereal diseases were about as appetising as mouldy bread.

Promptly dropping the farce, I turned on my heel and moved on.

"Hey! I asked if you 'ave a light!" Spider Web shouted, and I half expected him to come after me. "Fucker, I'm talking to you!"

The pair on my left barred my way. One dark, short, and squat with arms corded in muscle. The other tall and doughy with lank blonde hair. They looked a right comical sight with their arms crossed, standing the sort of straightbacked posture a bouncer might adopt to look tough barring a club door. They were more Del and Rodney Trotter than Ronnie and Reggie Kray and as I closed the distance, Del Boy made to grab my arm.

"Touch me, and I'll take your arm and beat you to death with it," I promised, my voice low and deadly serious, but loud enough for all the group to catch every word.

The Trotter brothers promptly stepped back.

"What are you doin', no- stop, fucker, come back here…" Impotent, Spider Web could do little more than hurl obscenities at my back, like a child whose mother had just taken his favourite toy away. Eventually, they're swallowed by the night, and I went on, all the more famished but with nothing to show for the experience.

Then I heard it. Low and far away, but unmistakable.

Unsure of what else I might find lurking amidst the warren of 'abandoned' warehouses, I followed it cautiously. At first, it was little more than a thrumming beat in the air, but it grew with every step, leading me down to an old, dilapidated structure sitting just on the river. With its windows bricked over, parts of the roof missing or stolen, and red brick walls well decorated with layers of graffiti, it would have almost certainly been condemned long ago. No doubt, whatever developer had secured the plot would be chomping at the bit to tear it down and turn it into an extension of the outlet megastore across the water. Demolition notices already adorned most of the surrounding buildings.

The booming music emanating from within indicated that it was not entirely deserted. Walking around the perimeter, I found the entrance to an old subterranean coal bunker near the edge of the water. A padlock dangled off one

rusted handle, unlocked and undoubtedly the entrance to
whatever party raged inside.

The door opened smoothly, despite the rust, onto a
gentle slope of the bunker's coal chute. Thick layers of black
coal dust lined the walls so I'm careful not to touch anything as
I edged down the slope. It's a tight fit, just barely wide enough
for me to shuffle through. In its day, this would have been
filled by river steamers or bargemen selling and shipping coal
up and down the water to power the warehouse's great
machines. With the passing of fossil fuels however, it had
obviously been converted into a dumping ground and squatter
site.

Rubbish bags. Shopping trolleys. Drugs and other such
paraphernalia. You name it, it had it.

The only door leading to and from the bunker was all
the easier to see by the slivers of light between it and the frame.

I knocked, and a doorman answered, slowly pulling it
open but barring my entry with his impressive bulk. More than
six feet of muscle, he had to outweigh me by more than five
stone, a mass that his black and white striped top struggled to
contain.

He sneered down at me. "Members only."

"So I see." I glanced at the nearest pile of rubbish bags.
"Discerning clientele?"

His sneer twisted. "Very."

"And if I want to become a member?"

"Not accepting new members." He seemed to be
having difficulty keeping the smugness from his voice. "But if
you give me thirty quid, I'll let you in with a guest pass."

"Ah, and if I happen to of left my wallet at home?"

"Then I'm afraid I'm going to have to ask you to leave,
sir. Where would you like to land."

"Oh, I don't think that will be necessary." It certainly
would have been fun watching this brute try to strong-arm me
out, but time was of the essence and that sort of struggle

would have drawn too much attention from the denizens within. Instead, I simply looked him in the eye.

It took all of a few seconds. All brawn and no brains, the doorman refused to look away, yet was no match in a battle of wills and visibly quelled, until all defiance had fled him. "Of course, sir." He conceded, shuffling back like a whipped dog with his tail between his legs "Welcome."

I walked past without sparing the weak-minded fool a second glance, into the warehouse's interior. It was massive, three stories tall with catwalks running along the second and third that had been converted into frames for the speakers and lighting. Amidst the gaggle of perilously thin bodies dancing around a performing DJ, a mass of dusty old crates and plywood lengths had been fitted together to serve as a makeshift bar. Old and well-used tables and chairs were haphazardly scattered around, the sort you might find at a cheap DIY store sale and were likely to collapse the moment you started to get comfortable.

The atmosphere practically buzzed with energy and sexual tension.

I circled the floor twice, weaving in and out amongst the bodies, taking the time to admire some of the choicer morsels as I went, their tight young bodies writhing to whatever beat pulsed through the sound system, adorned in as few garments as possible, hearts racing, blood pulsing. It had me practically salivating at the thought of plunging my fangs into their milky-

Then I forget all the rest, my eyes locked on a stark and desolate beauty, seated on the edge of the crowd.
Detached and alone in a sea of life.

The first glimpse of her had me at first doubting my own eyes. She certainly didn't have the look of someone you'd usually find frequenting a shithole like this.

Dressed in jeans and a red long-sleeved turtleneck, there was nothing showy or made up about her. The beauty was all her own. And she was beautiful, with soft, delicate features and diamond blue eyes framed by long flowing curls, dark and lustrous as ravens' wings. But there was more. Behind that girl next door exterior. An edge. A stiffness. A haunted tension that never should belong in one so young.

Hmm… interesting. Resisting the impulse to walk straight over to her, I detoured over to the bar and ordered a drink. All the while keeping one eye fixed on the girl at the table.

At its heart, the hunt was nothing more than a game. It could be played with subtlety or like a bull in a china shop. The latter was easier, but far less satisfying, or fun. And where would we be without a little fun now and then?

"That'll be a tenner, mate."

I glanced back. The bartender, a greasy guy with enough oil in his hair for it to shimmer and dance with colour beneath the laser lights, stood over me, an impatient look on his face and a clear drink in a dirty plastic cup waited on the bar.

I looked from him to the drink, then back to him. "It's half empty."

"Too bad, that's all we have." He makes no effort to hide the kegs and bottles stacked behind the bar. "Don't like it? Fine, piss off. But you still gotta pay."

"Really?"

"Yea, really-" I looked him in the eye and the words die in his throat. "Well, um… of course, I can set up a slate for you. Yes, I'll get a slate put in your name, Mr… oh it doesn't matter, I'll just put down my name, no problem…". He turned and scurried off out of my sight.

"Pathetic."

Not bothering to watch his retreat, I reached into my jacket and took the hip flask out of the inside pocket. Careful to ensure no one was watching, I unscrewed the lid and poured a measure of the crimson contents into the cup.

Shoving the flask back into its hideaway, I turned back to watch the girl, a small grin tugging at the corner of my mouth, revealing the hint of an ivory fang.

She was very, very lovely…

"Is this seat taken?"

She whirled around, eyes widening at the sight of me looming over her. I had to force back my toothy grin. She looked like a scared little rabbit. A rabbit with the most beautiful eyes I'd ever seen.

"Um, I suppose so." Her voice trembled but I'd already pulled the seat back and had made myself comfortable. She looked away quickly, her heart already racing, those big blue eyes flitting back and forth, desperate for something, anything to look at other than me. *Good, I'm already affecting her. This may just be easier than I thought. A few more little pushes and this delicate little rabbit will be all mine.*

And she would be mine.

"I'm Lucian," I said, taking a sip of my drink, just slow enough for her eyes to focus on my mouth.

I could practically feel her heart fluttering as her eyes lingered just that moment too long. Then she pulled herself together and hurriedly looked away. "Kate."

"Beautiful." I smiled. "Such a beautiful name for such a beautiful girl. But a beauty by any other name would be no less exquisite." I extended my hand.

Uncertain, her eyes moved from my hand to my face, back down to my hand, then back to the sea of bodies rippling around us.

"Would you prefer *come here often?*" I dropped my hand. "How about what's a nice girl like you doing in a dive like this?"

"Is that the best you've got?" She said it without looking, but the tension in her voice betrayed her. She was interested, and she was overcompensating to try and resist my *charms*.

"Oh, my dear girl, you have no idea." This was going to be easier than I thought. "You're not waiting for anyone, by any chance, are you? I'd hate to interrupt."

Her head whipped around; eyes suddenly bright. "What makes you think I'm-"

"Such beauty should never be unaccompanied," I smirked across my drink at her before making a show of looking past her. "And by the way you keep watching all these people, I'd say you're looking for someone."

Kate visibly relaxed. "What sharp little eyes you've got."

"I have my *talents*, just wait till you get to my teeth." She blushed and dropped her eyes to the table. "So," I pressed, "who's the lucky fellow?"

"It's just a friend."

"A friend?"

"Yes," She sipped her otherwise untouched drink. A Henry, judging by the strong smell of citrus. "She's been badgering me all week to come to this party and barely ten minutes after we get through the door, she disappears." She was lying.

She had a talent for deception for sure. Her story was simple and plausible, her delivery perfect. If I had been anyone else, she might very well have pulled the wool over my eyes. But she could not lie to me. I could tell, I could always tell.

Nevertheless, I played along. "Good friends are hard to come by. Would you care for some company till she gets back?"

"N-no, it's fine." She drained her drink. "I saw her going off with some guy a little while ago. No doubt she'll have him balls deep by now and will have completely forgotten about me. So, I'll be leaving soon."

"For home?"

"Yes."

"Is it far?"

"Far Enough."

"Do you drive?"

She scowled. "I don't think that's any of your business."

Her anger only inflamed my amusement and desire. There was some fire in my little rabbit after all. "The city's no safe place for a girl all alone. If you're not driving, I wouldn't dream of letting you walk home all alone. Anything could happen."

At my words, Kate sucked in a breath. Suddenly she was as white as a sheet.

"No, thank you. I'll be fine." She pushed back from the table, grabbing her clutch as she got to her feet. "Nice to meet you, Mr Lucian." Then she was gone into the crowd.

I watched her go, unable to resist admiring the way her jeans hugged the curves of her buttocks as she sashayed through the bodies. I couldn't wait to sink my fangs into that luscious derrière. "The pleasure, I'm sure, will be all mine."

CHAPTER *Two*

Kate

The body lay on the cold steel table for me to identify. A white sheet covered him, but it had been pulled back to below his chin, but just above the red smile cut from ear to ear.

The face was a ruin. Once so lean and handsome, the thing before me is black and blue and swollen with cuts and bruises. More a haunch of rotten and beaten meat than a man. And the blood, so much blood.

I couldn't bear to look. He was unrecognisable, yet I knew. I knew this was him. I knew this was David.

I knew this was my brother.

I forced myself not to run as unshed tears burned the corners of my eyes.

Anything can happen. Yea I suppose he was right about that. There were monsters out there, monsters who'd stolen the only person I had left.

I walked without thinking, letting my feet lead me wherever. Anywhere. I didn't care, I just needed to keep walking. Until…

Until what? They found me? I thought they'd find me in that shithole. They'd found David there, or at least that's what the police thought. Evidence had been lacking. Witnesses unwilling to come forward.

They didn't care. No one cared about one dead boy raped and butchered in a gutter.

But I cared.

He was my brother, and I wanted the bastards who did *that* to him.

But instead, I'd found him. Or rather he'd found me. Lucian.

Just the memory of him made my belly flutter.

There was something off about him, I just couldn't put my finger on it. He was just too suave, in that old fashioned, debonair, Jane Austen and Mr Darcy sort of way. From the moment he opened his mouth, he had just exuded charm. And that face, all sharp lines and smooth planes, he was a work of art carved from pristine white marble with black pearl eyes glinting out from beneath tumbles of thick jet-black hair just that bit too long it begged for a hand to run through it. He was the very embodiment of dark and dangero-

I froze, a cold cascade sloshing down my spine. *What was that?*

"Hey babe, you lost?" A man's voice, deep and guttural called from behind me, close. Very close.

Swallowing, I turned and found myself surrounded.

"A hot little dish like you must be pretty stupid to be walking around this neighbourhood all alone," the body that came with the voice was immense, a big thuggish brute with a spider's web tattooed on his bald head. "You a ho looking for work?" The others all gave him space as he stepped forward, like mangy dogs backing from the alpha. "Well, we don't pay for cunt, ho, ya hear me, we fuck it. Ya hear that boys, we fuck it till it's broke!"

They all began to snigger and lick their lips at that, and my hand dropped down to my clutch, its familiar weight giving me strength.

The black guy on my left stepped forward, grinning with a set of large pure white teeth. "Where's your pimp ho? Little bitches shouldn't wander the streets all alone. Anything could of happened..." He stepped in close, one hand brushing over my shoulders to scoop up my hair. He brought it up to his nose and sniffed, making me shiver with revulsion. "Good thing we found you."

"Yeah, anything coulda' happened." The giant grinned as the two to my right closed the gap. "Don't worry, you're safe now. This is our neighbourhood." I'd been snared like a mouse in a trap.

It was *them.* I knew it. I couldn't explain how, but I just knew.

"And nothing happens on your streets without your say so." My voice came out as cool as ice and I had to keep my fist clenched around my clutch to keep from shaking.

"Ya could say that yea."

"Did you, do it?" I knew this beast killed David, but I needed to hear it. Hear him say it, confess.

"Do wha?"

I saw red. How could he not know? The black guy was tall. Much taller than I. And the way he was trying to cover my back to keep me from running away left him completely open so that when I jammed my elbow back, it hit the one place it would do the most damage.

His grunt caught them all off guard. They'd expected me to run, to plead and beg. Never to attack. So they were too late to stop my hand as it slipped into my clutch.

They all stepped back when I pulled out the Browning Hi-Power Mark I.

It had been my father's old service pistol. He'd carried it through his national service. I'd found it buried amongst his things whilst I was clearing out their house after their funeral. I'd kept it along with a few other mementoes and forgotten all about it until tonight.

"Two months ago!" I snapped, raising the pistol so the business end pointed straight for the giant's torso. "A boy was murdered here! Did you, do it?"

"You talking crazy girl!" one of the men shouted, but I didn't look at him. My eyes were set on the giant. He looked too calm, like he didn't care, but his eyes. They burned with fury. I had drawn a gun on him and that enraged him. How dare I; this was his neighbourhood, his street, and I had the nerve to pull a piece. *Good, let the bastard squirm, he should know what it felt like.* He'd made David suffer in the worst possible ways. Well, I would make him pay. *For my brother.*

"What makes you think we had anything to do with it?" Another voice shouted. The black guy, I guessed. Good, none of his friends were coming to help him, he was alone, and he didn't like it.

"It happened here in *your* neighbourhood."

"Bitch, please! That was talk. Just talk. We had nothing to do with it."

"Yea, po-po would have been all over us."

"Bullshit!" I spat it out, all ice and fire. *They did it. I knew they did. They murdered my brother!*

"Yea, it's bullshit, sweetheart" the giant growled.

"You killed him?"

"Yea. Little cunt wouldn't shut his fucking mouth, so I opened his throat. Whatcha gonna do about it? Shoot me?"

"Yeah."

"Bitch, you ain't got the minerals." He laughed, a deep grizzled laugh that sent ice straight through my belly. "Go on then, blow me away in cold blood. They'll stick a mad ho like you in some dyke slam to eat fanny for twenty years. Bet

you'd like that, wouldn't you, all the pussy you can eat. They'll
be lining up to get a piece of you. So, go ahead if you're
serious, shoot me, shoot me, shoot-" I

pulled the trigger.

I had expected a bang, for the Browning to kick back as
they did in the movies. But all that came out was a click. A dull
metallic click no louder than a whisper, but at that moment it
bellowed like a clap of thunder.

Ice rushed through my veins. My eyes dropped to the
pistol, then back up to the giant and I tried again. And again.

Nothing.

He smiled, a cruel twisted thing, like barbed wire
wound into knots across his face. "Works better with the safety
off."

He grabbed the Browning, his immense paw
encompassing the barrel, and wrenched it out of my hand.

I didn't have time to scream. One moment I'd been
standing there, the next I'd been pressed up against a wall,
hard enough to drive the breath from my lungs, with one of
them driving his arms against my neck while the others pawed
at my clothes.

Panic and bile leapt into my throat. Gasping, fighting
for breath, I tried to push the arm away, but the giant thwarted
my efforts and pinned my arms above my head. He applied
just enough pressure for my joints to scream in protest, and for
a single heart-stopping moment, I thought he might break both
my arms.

No, this can't be happening. Hot angry tears burned my
eyes, yet I fought the pain that seared up my arms and lashed
out. My knee hit something soft, and one of them grunted and
cursed for his balls. I would have laughed, but I was too
swamped with the instinctive need to flee, to escape, to make
that desperate break for it.

The fight left me however when a titanic force
slammed into my stomach. I went limp, the pain enough that I

would have doubled over, but the restraining arm held me where I was.

"Hold still you little bitch." A voice hissed. "The more you resist, the worse this gets for you."

A roll of duct tape appeared, and a hand wound the binding round and round my wrists, to the point all circulation was cut off and my fingers began to tingle.

The giant stepped in to dominate my view, my father's Browning raised and pointed at my face. "Go on, look. Look down the barrel, you see the bullet?"

I could. The muzzle was black, much too dark to see down. But I could see the bullet well enough all the same. "Answer me, can you see it?" "Yes." And so much more.

I could smell the gun pounder, filling my nostrils in thick grey clouds, acrid and pungent against the night air. I heard the bang of the shot, saw my head snap back, my face a ruin. And red, so much red. Red smoke, red pulp and bone, a red cloud, and red blood everywhere.

"Good now open wide. I want you to suck it. Come on, suck it."

A part of me tried to be brave, screamed for me to tell them to go to hell and then shut my mouth tight. But the fear pulsed through me, making me shake, and hot tears rolled down my cheeks as, bit by bit, my mouth opened.

"Yeah, good girl. Your brother was an obedient bitch too. I fucked him bloody then handed him round to the rest of the boys, and when they were done, I cut his throat. If he hadn't been such a good little whore, I'd have cut his dick off and fed it to him. And if you try to run, I'll cut your tits off and-"

A deep growl rumbled through the night.

"What the fuck?" The giant lurched back and through the tears, I saw a dog coming towards us. A very big dog. All black and shaggy, like a Game of Thrones Direwolf, only not quite so cute and cuddly.

And I was almost positive it was looking at me. Then, it dipped its head, ears pricked, and fur raised, and growled another warning. It reverberated off the brick walls and shivered through flesh and bone.

"What's that?" one man asked, fear evident in his voice as he sized up the canine.

"Just a mutt," the giant shrugged, surveying the dog warily before turning his icy glare back to me. I shrunk under his gaze. "What, you'd pass up this fine piece of ass just because a mangy stray barks at ya a little."

"Well, that's a pretty big fucking stray, mate. Jesus, look at those teeth…"

The dog snapped a warning and the black guy turned and ran, tripping and stumbling over his own feet as he went.

"All right, that thing is starting to piss me off," Web turned to the two remaining men. "Del! Jake! Skin the fucker."

They both looked at each other, sharing a look like they were about to piss themselves there and then. Then they nodded and turned to the dog. I saw a flash of silver as they pulled flick knives from the depths of their coats.

I couldn't look, couldn't watch them butcher the poor creature. I could hear the dog growling and the men's footsteps echoing, then silence. No howls or moans of agony from the dog as it was murdered. No grunts and growls from the men as they got off on killing my canine defender. Just an eerie quiet.

The silence cut deeper than their knives ever could. And it was almost a relief when the two thuds, the unmistakable sound of bodies hitting the ground- Wait, *two* thuds?

I opened my eyes and could only stare at Del and Jake's dismembered bodies lying on the ground, pools of blood spreading out around them. But there was no dog.

Lucian stood over them, his pitiless eyes fixed on the giant.

And I don't know if I should laugh or scream.

"What the fuck?" The big man stuttered, his voice warbling in terror as he moved away from me, releasing his grip on my wrists. Visibly shaking, he turned my father's Browning on Lucian. "Bastard!"

My screams mingled with the crack of the shots as bloody mists burst from Lucian's back. The first should have killed him. It went clean through his heart. The second and third took him in the gut. Yet Lucian remained standing, taking each hit without so much as a grunt. Shot after shot, bullet by bullet.

"Jesus Christ, what the hell are you?" Eyes bright with panic, the giant stepped forward and cupped the pistol in both hands, raising it up for a finishing shot like they did in the movies.

It happened almost too quickly for the eye to see. One moment Lucian had been standing there, dark and pale and devastatingly intense and handsome. Out of reach and without a hope of dodging the shot. Then the Browning was arcing through the air, along with one of the hands that grasped it.

And Lucian stood over the giant.

CHAPTER *Three*

Lucian

Say what you like about undead fiends, no one can accuse me of not being a vampire of my word.

I didn't bother to pretend I was not enjoying myself. There was something so very satisfying in being the servant of justice.

Seizing the paretic piece of filth by the scruff of the neck, I heaved him up one handed. Big and brawny, he must have weighed more than 18 stone of pure muscle, but in my grasp, he was little more than a child. His remaining hand fumbled for his knife, but it was of little consequence. That butter knife would have served him no better than it had his dead friends.

"W-w-what are you?" he choked out the words.

The stain of blood was thick in the air, and I knew I should feed while there was still some life in his veins, but the thought of feeding on *that*. It was enough to turn the stomach.

"I'm hungry."

His eyes widening, Web screamed and the metallic scent teasing my fangs was suddenly cut by acid. He'd pissed himself.

One swipe was all it took. The screams died in a gurgle as I tore out his throat and dumped his carcass to the ground, to rot with the rest of the filth.

When the last of his life's blood had bled away, I turned to Kate, but she had slumped to the ground. Head back. Eyes glazed.

I felt a momentary spark of concern, however a quick check revealed that she had only fainted. Hardly surprising really, given what she had just witnessed. Shredding her bonds, I traced my thumb down her jawline and to her neck, fingering the pulse of her veins pumping hot blood just beneath the surface of her skin.

I mustn't leave her here. If the law found her there, they would likely try to pin all the deaths on her. *Girl slays three, possible self-defence*, made a much better story in the papers than *murdering vigilante on the loose, police baffled*. If she tried to tell them what she saw, they'd just stick her in a madhouse. And if she didn't, if by some miracle she got away, she'd probably end up there anyway.

She'd seen what lurked in the shadows, up close and in vivid gory detail. She might never get another night's sleep again.

Or she might not live to see the dawn.

"Ahhh little rabbit, you're proving to be a lot more trouble than I bargained for." Rising to my feet, I scooped Kate into my arms and thought of home. "Typical woman." Together our bodies slipped into mist.

CHAPTER *Four*

Kate

It was as if I was awakening from a dream.

Blinking through the blurriness, I found myself lying on an antique sofa in a large open room that was all leather, stone, and timber. High ceilings. Oil paintings and ancient tapestries upon the walls. Timber furnishings. It was as if someone had built a medieval fortress straight from the pages of history, and it all culminated in the lord's chair in the centre of the room. A high wingback. A leather cushioned throne.

Lucian sat in it like he was born to that chair, eased back with one leg crossed, drinking a tumbler of ruby red, a man completely at ease and in control of his surroundings. The master of all he surveyed.

Except he was no man.

He was watching me. He didn't show it, but I could feel his eyes on me, observing my every move the way a wolf eyed a deer.

Panic's cold fingers encircled my heart. *Oh God. Where am I?*

There were three doors in sight, but all were too far away. I'd never make it to one before he'd be upon me, and even if I could, I had no way of knowing which led out of this place. The only window was closed and opened out into blackness. *How high could we be? Almost certainly too high for me to survive the fall but would that matter if-*

"Ah!" I screamed and almost fell over the back of the sofa in fright as Lucian seemed to just materialise before my eyes, so close we were almost nose to nose. I'd never seen anyone move so fast. Hell, I hadn't even seen him moving so fast. It was as if he'd moved faster than light. But that was impossible, wasn't it?

He put a calming hand on my shoulder. His expression was impassive, but there was warmth in his eyes. It soothed my panic. "Shhh…You're safe. You fainted, I brought you here to rest until you recovered."

I had to fight to keep my fear from my voice. "And you couldn't take me to a hospital because-"

"They ask too many questions."

I swallowed. "What are you?" Each word was like a stone in my throat as my belly twisted in dread of the answer.

"I think you know."

"Say it," I pressed him. "Tell me!"

"A vampire."

And there it was. The answer I had been expecting, dreading, and craving.

It was ridiculous of course, and if I hadn't *seen* him, I'd have thought he was off his meds. But I had seen him, and I believed it. I believed him. I believed my eyes and what I'd seen.

"And you killed those men."

"Three of them, yes. The fourth ran, but he won't get far." He said it like it was something as every day as remarking on the weather.

"Good." I made no effort to keep the satisfaction from my voice.

He arched a brow. He might have taught the move to Roger Moore himself; it was as natural to him as a bird taking to the air. "Good?"

"They murdered my brother."

His lips pressed together and curled in one corner. "You're welcome."

"So, what now? Are you going to..." I trailed off, unsure of how to put the question into words.

"Feed on you?" He asked. "Yes."

I swallowed; my mouth suddenly dry. "You're going to kill me?"

He laughed at that. He threw his head back and laughed. It should have pissed me off, but despite myself, I was immediately enthralled to the sound. He laughed like my one question was the funniest thing he'd ever heard, and it was as far from the cackling horror movie stereotype as it was possible to be. It was full and deep and rolled over me like a warm hand brushing down my back, the fingers playing my spine.

I could have listened to that sound for the rest of my days, but his humour dried up as suddenly as it had come. "Why would I kill you?"

"But you said-"

"I'd feed on you, yes."

"That makes no sense," I said, and I felt my face screw up in confusion, my cheeks growing hot with embarrassment. I felt like a child in a difficult class, with a teacher who only spoke in riddles. "How can you feed on me and not kill me?"

"At any time, there is enough blood in a human body to quench my thirst more than five times over. I don't need to take your life to survive, just some of your blood."

"So, you've never..."

"Killed to feed?" Lucian said before slowly getting up from his chair and walking over to a stone minibar. "On occasion. But they deserved their fate, like our mutual friends tonight." From a selection of crystals, he picked the brandy decanter and refilled his tumbler with a deep ruby red. "Of course, there are some that make a habit of it, but that runs its own risks. The Vampire Council takes a dim view of drawing unnecessary attention to our kind."

"A vampire council? There's a council made up of vampires out there?"

"Yes, the elders. The oldest and strongest of us. They rule the vampire nation from its seat of power in London."

"Vampire Nation! How many of you are there?"

"Thousands."

"Thousands." I parroted; not quite sure I had heard him right.

"Yes, thousands." I could feel myself getting warm from the amusement in his tone, like he was humouring an inquisitive child, full of endless questions. "I dare say you've seen some, maybe even spoken to a few of my kind before. Once vampires had to be cunning to survive, but it is so easy to blend in now. We need only a set of fangs. And a little charm."

"But, what about sunlight? You'll die if you go out in broad daylight!"

"Just a myth." He sat down beside me on the sofa, and I didn't recoil. I don't know what it was about him, but he seemed to exert a pull that made me want to be closer to him the longer I spent in his company. It was strange, but also kind of nice. "Vampires are extremely sensitive to ultraviolet light. It will weaken us, even burn if one doesn't feed regularly. But fatal, no." He grimaced as he took his first drink from the glass. "Err, cloned blood has its uses, but it tastes like shit."

It was meant as a joke, I knew, a poor attempt at humour to ease the tension that had amassed between us, but I was beyond such things now.

"Can I see them- y-your fangs I mean, can I see them, please?" My voice faltered but I stayed firm, desperate for something, anything to focus my attention on.

If my request surprised him, Lucian gave no sign. He watched me over his tumbler for a moment, and I knew he was thinking the proposition over. That pissed me off. What, did he think I was a silly little girl who couldn't take it? If I could stand the thought of him drinking my blood, I could take this.

He must have come to the same conclusion because he eventually put the tumbler down on the coffee table, looked at me, grinned a wide grin, and – there they were.

They came down slowly, his canines lengthening, sharpening. I watched, entranced, my heart quickening until they were fully unsheathed, deadly sharp and pearly white. And I couldn't resist. Before he could draw them back, I reached out and brushed my thumb over the white. It was sharper than it looked, like running my finger down a steak knife, and I didn't even notice I'd been cut till I saw the blood.

It rolled down my finger in fat beads and left a thick red smear. The sight had my mouth running dry, but before I could pull my arm back, Lucian had seized my wrist. His grip was firm, his fingers like iron tentacles as they wrapped around me, holding me where I was as he kissed my cut. I shuddered in pleasure, his decadent mouth working its magic, stirring me to into a fervour as he sucked my thumb, his eyes burning into mine.

Panting, my voice trembling and heart pounding, I asked "H-how will you do it?"

"However you desire." He purred and released my finger. The cut had healed. "I'll bite you of course, but the rest is up to you." Slowly, delicately, he touched his thumb to my neck and stroked back and forth, his touch cool but stirring. "The carotid artery works well but any of the major blood vessels will suffice." He stroked that single digit down my arm, the pad of his thumb raising goosebumps wherever it touched. Then taking my wrist in hand, he brought it up to his lips. He kissed the skin and I bit back a gasp of pain at the sudden sting as a fang punctured deep and ruby blood welled around his lips.

This time I could actually feel him drinking me in, tasting every bit of me, but then something soft and silky brushed over the wound and sent a rush of tingles through my nerves straight down to the pit of my tummy. It made me hot, hot enough to push my thighs together, desperate to quench the needy ache massing there.

When he lifted his head, my skin was unblemished. "The ulnar artery is best for a quick snack, but I prefer the femoral artery. The food there is so much sweeter, and just the act of feeding there can give the strongest orgasms…"

Suddenly I was in his lap. I should have been outraged but I could only moan in sweet ecstasy as his mouth dropped down to my neck, kissing, licking, ravishing me with his vampiric hunger.

He was done talking, he had tasted my blood and now he wanted more. But I needed to ask him one last thing, so I forced the words out. "Mmm… will I – oh God- will I, will I turn?"

He didn't even bother to raise his mouth from me. "Only if you want to."

And then we were done talking. His mouth took mine with a hunger, stealing all logic and reason from my mind. His kiss was rougher than what I had expected, but when he tugged at my bottom lip with his teeth, I knew I would learn to like it. I felt hot and needy, and I yielded to him as he pulled me to him, his tongue coaxing my mouth open with lush creases across my bottom lip that had the embers of my desire blazing into a wildfire.

My tummy flipped excitedly as he stood up, his fingers biting deliciously into my rump as he supported my weight,

crushing me to him. My hands lost themselves in his hair as his tongue ravished my mouth, swirling round and
round my own in a dance that had my toes curling. Then we were moving…

No, not moving. Floating!

The feeling lasted for a moment. I caught only a glimpse of our surroundings, swirling by, pale and ethereal, as if we were enveloped in a cloud, passing through walls and rooms alike. Then I was on my back, on the largest bed I've ever seen, with Lucian poised above me. He looked so smug; like he had me just where he wanted.

I switched our positions with a hard shove. He didn't resist and as I pushed him over, I rolled with him, swinging a leg across his hips to straddle him.

"Now then, Mr Lucian. Just lie back. This won't hurt a bit."

He watched my movements and his smile turned positively amused. "Mmm… a little bit of pain isn't necessarily a bad thing..."

A shiver ran down my spine as I noted how his eyes glittered in the low light, their onyx depths a rich ruby black. Leaning down, I lightly kissed each of his eyelids in turn. "You have beautiful eyes." I sighed, grinning as I felt the way he shivered as my breath licked across his cool skin.

I kissed his nose, then his cheeks, then his chin, maintaining as much contact as possible. My hair brushed his bare neck and he groaned softly as it tickled him. I sighed again, hardly daring to believe that it was all real, that it was happening. It was all so sudden yet felt so right. He was a vampire, but he'd saved my life. He'd murdered to protect me. Our chemistry was undeniable, and I couldn't help that feeling, the feeling of being drawn to another person. Irresistibly, overwhelmingly, beguilingly, and seductively drawn, like a helpless moth to a sexy vampiric flame.

I dropped a kiss on his jaw before sweeping my tongue up the curve of it, lightly teasing the spot beneath his ear.

Slightly salty and sweet, the taste of him spread across my tongue and I shuddered. I needed more, so I began to kiss and nibble his neck. I barely noticed as his hands reached up and buried themselves in my hair.

With a fiery passion, I explored Lucian with my mouth. My tongue mapped the curve of his collarbone as my fingers urgently worked to divest him of his shirt. My lips trailed the slope of his shoulder and the hard contours of his chest. His wounds were gone, the gunshots he'd received healed and vanished. There were no scars, no blemishes. He was perfect, a block of ice, chiselled and sculpted and wrapped in skin. I licked along each ridge, using my teeth to tug gently at his flat nipples as I travelled his body.

I was lost in the taste and feel of him, in the sounds of his soft panting breaths and groans.

A gentle tug of my hair suddenly brought me back to reality and I lifted my head obediently to meet Lucian's glazed eyes.

"I watched Troy burn, heard Pompei's screams swallowed up, walked the plagued streets of London and battled werewolves and fairies and elves alike, but keep doing that, and that wicked little mouth of yours might just be what finishes me off for good." The vampire's voice was low and strained, and I couldn't help a smile of satisfaction as a feeling of immense pride filled me at the knowledge that I could elicit such a reaction.

"I won't let it kill you." My smile grew as I dragged my hands down his chest, letting my nails scrape over his delicious pale skin. He hissed a long, sharp sound that made a shiver run down my spine as my nail drew over his nipple.

Taken by an idea, I bent down and blew against the scratched area. The sound deepened and turned into a low groan. I continued to blow against his nipple until his eyes fluttered shut, then I dropped my mouth down and slid my tongue over his flesh. His eyes flew open, and he bucked up against me. Keeping our eyes locked together, I bit down and then pulled back to blow, making Lucian growl as he bucked his hips up against mine again. We both moaned as our bodies ground together.

Pulling back from his chest, I worked my way down the quivering flesh of his stomach to his abdomen, stopping only to gently kiss his navel before I dipped my tongue into his belly button. I felt brazen. His hips jerked at the contact and his erection brushed the full swell of my breasts as he dropped his head back against the pillow. Curious, I looked down and contemplated the very impressive bulge in his jeans for a moment. Admiring its already remarkable girth, I took a deep breath as I slid further down his legs.

"May I?" I asked in a teasingly girlish voice, fingering small patterns over his jeans, tracing his outline.

Beyond words, Lucian could only nod, so I sat between his legs. My fingers shook as I undid the button of his jeans, but I pushed on and tugged them down his muscular legs. He raised his hips to help me get them all the way off but couldn't help moaning in relief as his desire sprang free.

My eyes fixed on his arousal and my belly fluttered with nervous excitement while heat seared my veins. I couldn't resist licking my lips like the cat who'd found the canary. Though I had little in the way of prior experience to compare him to, I knew immediately that no normal would match the example standing rampant before my eyes. He was a very big boy.

Tilting my head to the side, I reached out and ran my fingers up his cock from its base, buried in a light nest of dark hair, to the mushroom-shaped tip.

CHAPTER *Five*

Lucian

Trying to relax, I closed my eyes against the vision of Kate between my legs as her fingers wrapped around the length of my cock. I groaned as my shaft pulsed in her grasp. Her thumb pressed on my sensitive tip, and she started to stroke, her palm gliding from base to head. I barely held onto coherent thought as she began to pick up the pace, my hips rolling to meet her hand-

My eyes shot open as I felt something warm and wet wrap around the head of my cock and I could only watch as Kate sucked me, her eyes big and cheeks hollowing. I had to fight against the almost overwhelming urge to buck up into her mouth, so I seized fistfuls of the bedsheets to stop my hands from fisting her mass of curls.

"Oh shit, mmm…Kate!" I moaned, and she gave me what I wanted, taking all of me into her sinful mouth. I was so hard at that moment, so aroused that just the feeling of her breath wafting over my cock was enough to push me to the edge as she drew back.

She took her time. It was obvious that this was all new to her, but she had the general idea and wasn't afraid to try new things. I could feel her teeth pressing in and drawing back, her tongue fluttering, stroking the underside. She altered speed, angle, depth, testing, trying to find the things that brought me closer to the brink. One of Kate's hands encircled the base, massaging the exposed skin of my shaft with her forefinger and her thumb as she continued bobbing her head. It became all too much. God, no woman had ever been able to drive me this mad.

Kate must have felt my release coming on. As much as I tried to suppress it, my body was shaking, and my cock was twitching. Wrapping her lips around my head, she sucked hard while jerking me vigorously.

"Oh God, Kate!" Her name left my lips in a gasp as I went over the edge, and I could feel my release exploding into her mouth in thick jets. She swallowed it greedily, sucking me dry and not missing a drop. I came harder than I could ever remember, and the force of it left black spots dancing before my eyes. And it left me thirsty, very thirsty.

That drink at the bar had taken the edge off, but the taste of her blood had almost undone me. Now, I needed to taste her again.

By the time the spots had passed, my little rabbit was perched above me. Her lips were pursed, her eyes hooded. She looked so very pleased with herself. She was also still fully dressed, while I had allowed her to divest me of all garments.

It was time to correct that.

"That was… well… most delightful." Before Kate could react, I had her on her back. She bounced when she landed on the bed, and I pushed her further into the mattress and her head sank into the pillows. Yes, this was where she belonged. Under me, in my bed, at my mercy. "Now, allow me to return the favour."

Her eyes widened at my low, sultry tone and I felt her heart flutter. She liked this side of me. Good. She was mine, to do with as I liked, and to worship for all time.

Kate wanted to say something, another witty comeback perhaps. She had quite a mouth on her, this one. But I kissed her before she could give the words voice. I kissed her hard and hungrily and our lips moved together in the way that would make her forget. It did the trick. No sooner did I claim her tongue than she melted beneath me, and her eyes drifted closed. Kate was not the only one enjoying the embrace and I had to struggle to keep my attention fixed on the task of undoing her jeans, rather than lose myself in the sensation of her tongue on mine as she explored the lines of my fangs…

She gasped and tore her mouth away when my finger slid through her slick folds, hooking up to rub the place behind her already swollen clit. "Luci-oh!"

"Mmm Kate, you're already dripping." I purred as I raised myself up to look into her eyes.

I held the look as my finger delved deeper, my thumb rubbing slow circles around the tiny bundle of nerves, purposely denying any contact there. Kate arched, her hips circling, silently pleading for more while pushing her jeans down those long willowy legs. I continued to deny her any such contact.

"Lu-Lucian, please!" She gasped, thrashing her head in the mad desperation of a person purposely being denied that one thing their body craved. And so, I took pity on her and pushed a second digit into her warmth while I bore my thumb down on her clit.

The sudden contact had her bucking, writhing, and shattering around my fingers and I watched as, for the first time in her young life, she was undone by another person. It filled me with a sense of primitive pride. I'd done this to her. I'd taken this beautiful creature and, simply with a touch, had reduced her to a mumbling scattered pool of desire and sex.

I was sure I had never seen anything more beautiful in all of my undead life.

This lovely creature had the smell of a virgin. Usually, this would have deterred me. There was no sport in feeding on virgins. They didn't have the experience to play the game, too easy to overwhelm and bend to my will. And, for all the weight that was put upon virtue, innocence made the blood bland. Lust, debauchery, and all the other sins of the flesh gave flavour, and I liked my food well spiced, flavoursome and aged just right.

But something had risen inside me, something primal that demanded more, demanded I make her completely lose herself and surrender to me. Make her mine.

Slowly, easing my fingers from her as the waves of her release ebbed away, I divested her of her jeans and boots in a single move. Free of their confines, her legs opened for me as I settled myself at her entrance. She moaned as my renewed erection bumped her clit and she didn't protest as I pulled her top over her head, revealing her lush milky white breasts topped by stiff rosy peaks.

Settling over her, I took her lips again, only this time the kiss was much more tender as I pushed forward. In the wash of such an intense orgasm, I knew Kate would be ready and relaxed, and I was confident she would barely feel the sting of her lost virtue.

She stiffened at my entry, the feeling taking her by surprise, but then her body opened to me and I began to rock against her as I worked myself deeper. She was tight. Orgasm or no, she was a virgin and I knew that I needed to work her slowly or else risk hurting her in ways no woman should suffer. Yet the need to take her clawed at me and the delicious feeling of her plush inner walls wrapped around me drove me on.

"That's it, take me in." I moaned and tried to fend off the desire to cum right then and there as I withdrew almost completely. I held there with just my tip inside her, letting the feeling of emptiness consume her, then I plunged back in.

"Luci-oh, oh God! Yes!" she moaned, whimpering as my rough fingers rolled over her throbbing clit. "Please… don't… don't stop… " She leant up and laid hot open-mouthed kisses along my neck.

I groaned and ground into her. "Go on baby, ask me to fuck you...and I will." I murmured into her ear, rocking into her depths, then withdrew again. "Kate… God, you feel so good… yea, beg me to fuck you… "

"F-F-Fuck me," she whispered desperately, her blush deepening. The words didn't come easy to her, but she rolled her hips against mine, coaxing me on, as her nails scraped down my back. "Please…fuck me Lucian… I want it… I want-" She suddenly screamed out my name at the feeling of me going balls deep, filling her to the brim, and all conscious thought melted away into a white-hot sea of pleasure. "Oh my god… Lucian! Oh, it feels good…It feels so good!" She cried, kissing me again as I repeated the move again and again, each thrust sending waves of pleasure crashing over her.

I groaned at the sensations radiating through her tight confines, every sense overloading as her irresistible scent filled my head and made my mouth water. I had never held out this long before feeding and my thirst was growing by the second. I was starving, yet I fought my very nature, for this girl.

Kate pushed against me and rolled us over so that her body straddled mine. Placing her hands on my shoulders and planting her feet securely on the bed, she started to ride me, moving up and down my cock without a shred of modesty.

"Oh! Oh! Ohhh!" Kate moaned as she crashed down on my cock, causing me to penetrate deeper.

She was growing more comfortable on top, her strides quickly becoming longer and harder, an upwards glide, then a crashing down slam. "Uh-uh-uh-oh…Lucian! Oh, fuck!" She gasped, working her body along my length with increasing vigour as her hands slid up her body to fondle her breasts. The gentleness was gone and the sex-crazed beast inside the young woman had emerged.

I leant up and I moved my hands to her back and ran my fingers along her spine while kissing along her collarbone. I could smell fresh, young blood rushing through her veins and it only served to drive me on. "Faster," I ordered, and the command was met with Kate's body sliding at a rapid pace against my own. She let out long, loud moans every time I was fully encased inside her. I nibbled on her jawline, following its curve to the other side of her neck and suddenly, unable to help myself, I bit down, causing her to gasp.

"Yes-yes-yes-oh Lucian!!" Kate cried. "I'm gonna cum! Oh fuck, I'm gonna cum again!"

"No Kate! Not till I'm ready, we're going to cum together, my little rabbit!"

For Kate, that seemed to be the final straw. "Oh God, Lucian, bite me!"

It was as if time held its breath. "What?"

"Please…" Kate was shaking, her eyes pleading. "Turn me. I want… I want to be…"

"No." My voice was level and firm, brokering no argument. Then I softened, my fingers stroking her spine. "You're too young. You have no idea what you'd be giving up. I can't."

"I don't care! I want to give it all up. I want to forget, I can't take it anymore. I see their face's, Lucian. David and my parents. Will I see them in my dreams every night if you turn me? Will I hear them calling-"

"You'll never forget. They'll never leave you, they'll become an eternal part of you. You'll carry them with you, through the ages till the end of time." My next words were like stones in my heart. "But the pain will go."

She nodded. "Then do it. Take my pain away. Anything is better than this… I can't… I won't…Please!"

"You'll be my thrall." I declared. "My servant. Bound to my will and do my bidding till the end of days. Is this what you want?"

"Yes!" She panted, so hot, needy, and desperate, I almost gave in. "There's nothing left for me here. A vampire, your thrall… slave, I don't care. I can't go back. Take me any way you want. I'm yours!"

"There is no going back," I warned. This was her last chance to back out. Her final chance to come to her senses.

"I know."

"Good." I kissed her hard before crushing her to me and laying her down on the bed. My fangs plunged deep into her throat at the same time as I ground myself back into her depths. Orgasmic screams filled the room as I drank from Kate, savouring every drop of her sweet nectar as I drained her to the point where she had not a single drop of blood left within. Feeling her go limp in my arms, I felt a sudden stinging sensation stab at my throat as I cut my veins with a sharpened talon. I leant over and spilt my own blood into the woman's waiting mouth. "Everything I am is yours, and all you are is mine. Blood of my blood, flesh of my flesh. Together forever…"

I completed the bonding.

She died in my arms and was reborn, awakening to the world a fledgeling vampire, my thrall, my companion, and would grow to become the great love of my eternal life. But that is a story for another time…

L.M. Mountford hopes you have enjoyed Give Us Bad Boys &
Billionaires.
Now please enjoy this preview from the sexy and thrilling intro to his
Rogue Warrior Trilogy.

Downtown Port Angeles looked rather like uptown, midtown, and every other residential part of the city. A varied collection of single and two-storey timber fronted cottages with paved driveways and big front gardens. The whole place had the feel of a quaint little suburbia where everyone and their dog knew your name and your business.

In other words, what I'd call hell.

Fortunately, I wasn't here to admire the view. I wanted answers, and according to Ned's scribble, Miss Porter lived at 13 King's Way. The name meant nothing to me but courtesy of my phone's Maps App, it didn't take long to navigate the warren and turn the Porsha off West 10 Street. For all the grandeur of its name, King's Way proved to be just another quiet little street ending in a cul-de-sac with about half a dozen single storey cottages around it.

Number 13 was the first on the left. A single storey cottage painted baby blue, with a wraparound porch, likewise painted cedar red, and a 2004 Ford Explorer Sport Trac 4x4 on the drive.

I parked the Porsche up behind the pickup, killed the engine, climbed out and marched up to the house, not caring if she was alone or if someone was in there with her. If I was lucky, maybe she had a boyfriend over and I could work out some of this frustration on his face.

Until then, her door would do. I knocked three times, banging my fist against the wood hard enough to make it rattle in the frame. Then I waited.

Damn her, I got her that fucking job back, so what was her problem? What was she playing at?

I knew I needed to breathe. I was pissed off and had to calm down, but I wasn't in the mood for all that crap right now.

"Coming!" Jane's voice called from inside.

Footsteps approached from the other side of the door. A chain rattled. Then the door opened and Jane Porter stood there in a pair of tight little white shorts and a blue and red checked shirt, her hair tumbling down her back in a wash of raven waves and smiling as she read something on her phone. "Mrs Wilde, I'm afraid this isn't really a great time, 'cause I just lost my job and I- you!" Her smile dropped when she looked up and saw me standing in her doorway.

Praise where praise is due, Miss Jane Porter was not slow to react. No sooner did she see me than she was slamming the door in my face. It's not exactly an original move, though. Nor was it the first time someone had tried it. I shouldered my way through before she could shut it all the way. She almost went with it, skidding backward, but I caught her wrist and twisted her round, driving her back against the wall. The door swung closed behind us as I slapped a palm over her mouth to keep her from screaming and stepped in close enough to pin her there, caging her with my body.

I expected her to fight. To lash out and squirm, or kick, bite and scratch at anything she could reach with all that fiery spirit she'd shown when Roy and his mates had surrounded her. Instead, she just stood there, with her arms hanging at her side and eyes as large as dinner plates.

"Scream, and I'll gag you, understand?" I warned, keeping my voice low and level but looking dead into her eyes so she knew I meant it.

She nodded slowly. Or, at least, gave as much of a nod as she could with half of her face in my hand and nowhere to move. Still, I had to give her points for effort.

"Good," I said, forcing a little smile to soften my expression as I eased my hand back a little. "You know, you should really check who's at the door before you open it."

"Please…" she whispered, her voice shaky, clearly too unnerved for levity. "What… what do you, I mean, what are you doing here?"

"Why did you quit your job?"

"What?" She blinked, as if that was the last thing she'd been expecting.

"You heard. Why did you quit your job at the bar? Last night you said you needed it, so I got it back for you. Now I hear you've quit, and I want to know why."

My question seemed to steady her, however, and she visibly hardened under my interrogation. "Because of you, you asshole!" she spat back, suddenly all fire and venom. "Because of what you did."

"Me? What did I do?" It was my turn to play dumb. Admittedly, it helped that I didn't have a clue what she was going on about.

"Don't bother. I saw Ned's face! You beat him to a bloody pulp!" She accused, beating her hands on my chest. "Who the fuck do you think you are? You can't just go around beating people to get what you want! And why? To get me my job back after you fucked it all up! Do you think I'd accept anything from you after what you've done?" *Oh fuck!*

That's what this was all about. The beating the Russians had given Ned. Of course she'd think that was my handiwork work, why wouldn't she? She hadn't known he'd had company when I arrived and sounds like she hadn't stuck around long enough to ask.

No wonder she's pissed off.

I backed away a step, giving her some space, raising my open-palmed hands in a universal show of innocence while trying to calm the fuck down. "Hey, hey, cool it, I didn't do that."

"Fuck off!"

"Really, Scout's honour, he was like that when I found him, and anyone at the bar will tell you I didn't do that to him."

She crossed her arms. "Oh yeah? How?"

"Because he looks too damn good." Probably not the best choice of words, but I couldn't help myself. Fine ass or not, her attitude was really grating on me.

Her eyes flashed dangerously, as cool and as sharp as ice. "Bullshit. Who else would do something like that?"

"Roy and his friends from yesterday, that's who," I snarled back through gritted teeth. "They came by to play a game of twenty questions with your boss, and they didn't like some of his answers. If I hadn't arrived when I did, chances are he'd be taking a trip into intensive care right about now, with you in the bed next to him, but don't worry, I took care of it. They're all sorted. If you don't believe me, go ask, then you'll see what it looks like when *I* give someone a slap."

She wasn't in a mood to accept my reassurances and pressed on relentlessly, stabbing a finger into my chest. "Nothing will ever be sorted so long as there are people like you in the world. Yeah, I know your sort. You walk around like you own the place. Like you can do and take whatever you want. Selling drugs and guns, turning honest people into junkies and whores desperate for their next fix! Men like you, *and Roy*, you're all the same. Animals! Nothing but dogs fighting over a bone, and you'll bite anyone that tries to stop you!"

Okay, this time she had gone too far.

This girl had been rude since the moment she first saw me. She'd accused me of beating up her boss- which I hadn't- and of getting her fired- okay, that I might have had a hand in, indirectly. Now she was calling me a dog and saying I was no better than Roy, a Russian thug that had threatened and abused her. A stinking, filthy Russian animal!

There was a time when she might have been almost right. The streets of New York City were dangerous places. No one lived on them and came out clean, and there were times I'd done things I wasn't proud of to survive. As a boy, the law of the jungle, that concrete Manhattan jungle, had ruled my life. Then, after Don DeCampo took me in, I had changed. Since the day Turk found me, I'd hurt men. I'd killed them and watched them die, but they were all a part of that dark criminal world, never real people. Never innocent. I'd never stolen from honest people, peddled drugs or made women whores.

And when he put that bullet in my head, I was reborn.

That bullet gave me a second chance, a new life.

A life out of that shadow world for good.

I didn't care what she'd seen me or anyone else do. That wasn't an excuse.

I wasn't a fucking animal.

It was time she learnt that.

Miss Jane Porter had been a very naughty girl.

And naughty girls get spanked.

"Is that so?" I didn't wait for an answer, just grabbed her arm and spun her around to push her against the wall. She gave a small squeak of surprise, then went silent as I cupped her nape. Then I was caging her again, and leaning down I said, "you know nothing about me."

"Yes, I do, you're… dangerous," she whispered, her voice shaky and eyes wide with animal panic.

"And you like it, don't you?" Catching her wrists, I raised them up over her head and pressed them hard to the wall. Securing them both with my left, I brought my right down.

"What? No! Of course no- Ahh!" She gasped as I gave her right cheek a smack that was a little less than gentle, but produced a very satisfying crack. "What the fuck?"

"It's not nice to lie." I left my hand there for a moment, enjoying the feel of her ass in my hands through the thin cotton of her shorts, so soft yet also firm and tight. Only when I was sure that the first sting had faded did I raise the hand again, only this time I brought it down on her left cheek.

This was an excerpt from:

Five years ago, I was the DeCampo Familia's most feared enforcer, then they killed me...

Now I'm in hiding, a dead man walking.

All I had to do was keep my head down, live a quiet, *normal* life. But normal is a hard thing for a man like me.

I might just have been able to manage it, if trouble hadn't come looking for me In the form of a feisty barmaid.

A vixen probably half my age, with long raven hair and a backside that promised all sorts of trouble.

Hot, sweaty, all night long sorts of trouble.

I should have stayed away, but I was hooked from the moment she sashayed through the doors of the bar.

And when a few of the patrons started getting rough with her, the old me was ready to give them a lesson in manners.

However, times have changed. I wasn't in New York anymore and getting into a bar fight with five guys for her honour wasn't the way to this girl's heart or into her pants. Good thing I'm stubborn, because while her attitude might be frosty, the chemistry between us is hot and I'm not about to let her get away.

So first things first, I need to learn her name.

And just hope my past doesn't catch up with me and kill me first...

L.M. Mountford's goal in life is to be unique, a character who stands out from the crowd that you just can't help remembering with a bemused chuckle.

A born and bred country boy from the southwest of England, he knew from an early age that he wanted to write and spent most of his time writing story ideas or playing Star Wars on his PlayStation.

Not much has changed over the years, though his stories have grown decidedly dirtier, and he swapped the Star Wars for Call of Duty.

Dubbed the Lord of Lust in 2019 and a firm believer that nothing sells like sex and violence, he loves writing about hard and gritty romantic thrillers, loaded with action men, sassy heroines, and a whole lot of dirty, sexy heat.

He also loves meeting and chatting with readers who love his work. You can connect with him on facebook, or subscribe to his newsletter for regular updates.